In the Mothers' Land

"An exciting, demanding, satisfying thought-experiment—serious science fiction doing what only science fiction can do." —*Ursula K. Le Guin*

"Fascinating, beautifully worked out—a real treasure, a meticulously created society." —*Marion Zimmer Bradley*

"Elisabeth Vonarburg is a formidable new writer, and *In the Mothers' Land* is sure to appeal to those who enjoy thoughtful science fiction dealing with the human heart and mind." —*Julian May*

"Marvelous . . . Vonarburg's work has a seriousness of purpose that much American science fiction, even some of the best, lacks; moral issues and intellectual debates are an important (and exciting) part of her novels. . . . *In the Mothers' Land* is another strand in the tapestry of feminist science fiction that includes such novels as Ursula K. Le Guin's *The Left Hand of Darkness,* Joanna Russ's *The Female Man,* Vonda N. McIntyre's *Dreamsnake,* Margaret Atwood's *The Handmaid's Tale,* and Eleanor Arnason's *A Woman of the Iron People.* . . . Elisabeth Vonarburg has embarked on an imaginative inquiry with intelligence and art. . . . She has succeeded in creating a memorable addition to the body of sociological science fiction." —*Pamela Sargent*

In the Mothers' Land

by
Elisabeth
Vonarburg
Translated
from the
French by
Jane Brierley

Bantam Books
New York · Toronto · London · Sydney · Auckland

*This edition contains the complete text
of the original hardcover edition.*
NOT ONE WORD HAS BEEN OMITTED.

IN THE MOTHERS' LAND

*A Bantam Spectra Book / published by arrangement with
Beach Holme Publishers Limited*

PUBLISHING HISTORY
*Beach Holme Publishers edition published 1992
Bantam edition / December 1992*

ISBN 0-553-29962-X

Published simultaneously in the United States and Canada

PRINTED IN THE UNITED STATES OF AMERICA

OPM   0 9 8 7 6 5 4 3 2 1

Dedication

To all my mothers, and especially the first

Special Thanks

Several parts of this novel have been written and rewritten while I had grants from the Canada Council or the Ministry of Cultural Affairs of Quebec, to whom I would like to express my gratitude. A grant-in-aid was also generously made available by the Canada Council for this English translation and for the Canadian editions.

I would further like to thank the friends who suffered through reading all those different versions: Daniel Sernine ten years ago, and Elisabeth Gille who very sensibly refused to publish two of them. In more recent years, Jean Pettigrew, Serge Mailloux, Jean-Claude Dunyach and Yves Meynard.

Last but not least, special thanks to my translator, Jane Brierley, and my friend, author Candas Jane Dorsey, without whom this story would certainly not be what it is, either in English or in French.

As for the rest, only I am guilty.

1

Bethely

479–487 A.G.

1

The other side of the sun. That's what Lisbeï used to call the moon when she was little. It amused the gardianas in the west garderie—the Garderie, as she thought of it then. Sometimes she must have seen the moon in the daytime sky, before the sun slipped behind the garden wall. "Elli's eyes bright, means a good night," the gardianas would say. In any case, whenever she thinks of the west garderie, the phrase *the other side of the sun* glides through her memory like the pale or russet moons of childhood floating upward in the evening sky, symbols of forbidden time and space for the little mostas, for this was bedtime, sleeptime in the white rows of the dormitory, in the dim, breath-filled silence.

Yet if Tula hadn't been there, Lisbeï would probably never have lain awake dreaming of other sides, for Tula came from the invisible space that must surely exist somewhere outside the garderie, beyond the circular garden wall.

Lisbeï's first real memory is of Tula suddenly appearing in the garderie playroom. She is alone in her corner—it's already a habit. Lisbeï must be five at the time, since the infante mostas leave the nurseries to join the older ones when they can walk. (Tula—yes, the adventurous Tula!—was in fact a very late walker, nearly three.) Lisbeï is five and alone in her corner. She prefers it this way.

Why, she doesn't yet know, not really. She simply feels uncomfortable when surrounded by too many mostas. Luckily, the nurseries had been organized into relatively small groups just before her birth, otherwise Lisbeï would have gone mad among those hundreds of babies, and later amid that throng of small childreen. This way she's had time to learn almost unconsciously how to protect herself so that the presence of others is now no more than a vague uneasiness. It's as though they're making too much noise even when silent—giving off too many strange odors, maybe, even when coming back from the bath, all damp, pink, and clean. Too much of something, anyway. Lisbeï knows it's nicer when she moves away.

By the same token, the other mostas have had time to get used to Lisbeï. They forget how ill at ease she made them feel, and begin to think *they're* the standoffish ones, even start to bar her from their games. The gardianas are accustomed to Lisbeï's ways. They tried to include her in the circle of mostas at first, but it was no use. In any case, she seems to get along on her own quite happily as long as no one comes and takes her toys (as Meralda and her gang have begun doing lately). Real learning sessions are still ahead of the mostas. At the moment they're busy reciting little rhymes from memory, learning to manipulate needle and thread, and making paper cutouts or clay models, so Lisbeï's attitude poses no real problem for the gardianas. At first she tried to explain. "What a lot of nonsense!" snapped old Tessa, to whom she recounted her strange perceptions. She didn't try again. The gardiana's incredulous disapproval had been so strong that Lisbeï realized she must be different from everyone else.

She's five years old and playing quietly by herself. Now she's used to it and even thinks *she* chose to be alone. Somehow, though, it's not like Rubio, Turri, and Garrec, also playing by themselves in another corner. For one thing, the gardianas call them "boys." Why or when this began Lisbeï can't remember. "Boys," say the gardianas, and the trio lift their heads as one. They're always together, do everything together, and that's why they're almost never spoken to individually. Or maybe it's the other way round: because they're always called "boys," they have a rather hazy idea of their individual identities—but Lisbeï is too young to understand this. Anyway, their solitary state isn't like Lisbeï's. She can't quite put her finger on the reason. If you asked her, she'd say other mostas don't like playing with the boys, and it's different because she's the one who doesn't want to play with the mostas. Lisbeï is also too young to realize that the gardianas' attitude is what sets the boys apart and that, like the other mostas, she instinctively imitates the gardianas. Why would she realize it, anyway? The gardianas themselves are unaware of treating the boys differently and would probably be very surprised if you pointed it out.

Cubes, rectangular blocks, balls, pyramids—Lisbeï is playing with blocks that fit into specially cut holes in a piece of wood, holes that are square, oblong, round, and triangular. Just one place for each, but Lisbeï takes a perverse pleasure in slipping the little cube easily into the big oblong hole, or balancing the two pyramids on their tips in the round holes. Each new gardiana tells her it's not the way, but leaves her alone when Lisbeï shows them she knows exactly how to do it. They walk off shaking their heads as she goes back to fitting the cubes into the oblong holes and the balls into the triangular ones. Apart from her desire for solitude, it's her only whim. She's a model mosta otherwise, and the gardianas are prepared to overlook this small lapse.

The door opens and a round, blue silhouette fills the space. The gardiana must be bringing other new mostas besides Tula, but Lisbeï can't picture them, although she can visualize the big mostas arguing afterward over who'll take care of each one. All she remembers is . . . what? The light, that's it. Tula seems to appear in a pool of sunlight. Later Lisbeï realized the impossibility of this: the light from the windows in the west garderie playroom never reached the door that way. But Tula's colors are so brilliant, she has such an air of . . . newness, like a marvelous living doll with her russet, almost red, halo of hair, her skin so white against the apple-green tunic, and her large, aquamarine eyes—but at the time Lisbeï doesn't know enough to use this word. They are just blue—no gray, no, blue-gray-green, sparkling and staring at Lisbeï. Tula's small hand lets go of the gardiana's tunic, and her little legs carry her unsteadily forward, right across the room to Lisbeï. The small pink mouth spreads in a moist smile. Lisbeï has unconsciously stepped forward and now hugs the little body against her own. It's warm, pungent, luminous, as with the other mostas but in exactly the opposite way. How can she explain it? Being with someone, feeling their presence inside or outside your own body like a sensation of heat, light, or smell. But with Tula it's right, she feels this is where she belongs and that the other belongs and knows it, too. And the soft flesh against her cheek feels like something remembered, she doesn't know what, but she has already felt the warm curve of flesh on her lips, the arms around her, somewhere, sometime, with the same enveloping light, the same warmth in which her inner and outer body changed places, the flash of delight, the resilient pressure on her face, and this mysterious flesh that melts into her, filling the hungry void. . . .

In fact, she isn't sure. She's remembered Tula's arrival so many times since then that it's become the memory of a memory remembered. Perhaps it happened quite differently. Which one of them recognized the other? Like a chick coming out of the egg, instinctively responding to its mother's image. But who had imprinted on the other? Tula, emerging from the nursery, on Lisbeï? Or Lisbeï, rising from that time before remembrance, on Tula?

She didn't think about this at the time, though. Nor, surely, would a five-year-old have reflected that Tula was a miraculous gift, the intersecting of another space, which opened a wedge in her closed garderie world.

The two gardianas, puzzled and speechless at first, quickly recovered themselves. "Very well, Lisbeï, you'll take care of Tula," they said, and that was how she and Tula learned each other's names. The other mostas were surprised and immediately jealous at this incomprehensible, mutual choosing. Lisbeï remembers Meralda's surreptitious pinching in the days that followed, and the scuffles and quarrels over nothing. She believes she remembers the odd feeling of triumph and anguish that filled her, the certitude that from now on it was she and Tula against all the others.

How did she reach the conclusion that in order to preserve this triumph and appease the anguish she must know everything about Tula? She did reach it, in any case. But one doesn't ask questions in the garderie. Lisbeï had learned, better and faster than any other mosta, to sense the currents of good will or reserve in the gardianas, and she submitted to the tacit law of this small world: *You don't ask the gardianas questions: you wait for them to do the asking.* Lisbeï didn't know it at the time, but for her, more clearly than the others, this unwritten rule hung in the air like the sustained note of a great diapason: *that which is, is good; that which is not doesn't matter for now; all questions will be answered.* Who knows? Lisbeï might have become a mosta like any other, then a dotta and an adult like any other. If it hadn't been for Tula.

The idea occurred to Lisbeï that if Tula had appeared in

this way, she could disappear, too. (Not a conscious idea, really, but a vague, persistent uneasiness.) Before, she'd *wanted* to be alone, but now she had no desire to return to her previous state. For the first time in her life she had something to lose.

For the second time, in fact. But she had no memory of her arrival in the west garderie nursery, of the two weeks spent hovering between life and death, with the wet nurses surprised, exasperated, worried, or sorrowfully resigned until her mother came to nurse her for several months—a thing unknown in Bethely. Lisbeï would not learn of this unorthodox episode from Selva. The Mother of Bethely preferred not to be reminded of it.

The West Tower garderie was the most recent of the three Bethely garderies. Unlike those attached to the South Tower or the East, which were big, square structures on the old model, the builders had tried something more daring in the way of architecture. It stood in its large, enclosed garden, a round building that looked rather like the snail-shell curl of the Bethely hobskoch. Lisbeï, to her delight, discovered this resemblance at about the age of six when she learned to draw a map of a building. The three inner coils of the spiral, almost equal in size, formed the top stories housing the great nurseries. The small mostas came from there: this was one of the minor certainties of the garderie that had satisfied Lisbeï until then, although she didn't remember coming from the nurseries herself. She knew there were other, still bigger mostas on the ground level—the largest coil in the spiral. The central staircase stopped there, and you could see a little of this level on the way out to the garden: a big, round hall opening onto corridors lined with blue and yellow mosaics and rows of doors, exactly like the second level. Nothing very exciting. You never saw the big mostas, the ones over six years old, any more than the littlest ones in the nurseries saw those over three. Each section was self-contained, with a refectory, a dormitory, an infirmary, showers, and rooms for work and play. Even the garden timetables were staggered to prevent all the mostas from appearing at the same time. (Despite the watchful gardianas, the garden wouldn't have survived the ravages of all those hundreds of childreen bursting with energy after being cooped up indoors.) Like all mostas of her age, Lisbeï knew vaguely she would one day join the big children on the ground level, but it was inert knowledge, floating unattached in her mind much as she herself had floated unquestioningly in the eternal present of the garderie. Before Tula.

The garderie, its levels either known or guessed, and its vast garden were the beginning of the world. That is to say, the garderie *was* the world during the first four or five years. The West Tower stood just far enough away to make it invisible from the garden, and the bottom two thirds of the east windows on the various levels were painted over. The idea that the world might continue beyond or after the garderie was slow to filter into the minds of the second-level mostas. Because the gardianas never talked of it. Because it was one of those questions you very soon learned not to ask. Because (as Lisbeï very well perceived, and as the other mostas may have dimly sensed) the gardianas didn't really believe in such a world. Neither Lisbeï nor the other little mostas could tell the difference between the gardianas' belief in an outside world and their doubts about the mostas' future in this world.

Didn't the mostas realize the gardianas came from the exterior and returned to it? No, not really. Of course the gardianas changed from time to time. But no one ever saw them enter or leave the garderie: there was no door in the garden wall. In the same way, no one ever witnessed the arrival of the babie mostas or the departure of the mostas who never came back. Lisbeï had been on the second level for over a year (although she had no real sense of time passing). She had been assigned to a group on coming to this level from the nursery. Since then, most of the oldest mostas in the group had disappeared. She knew (with that unconnected, useless kind of knowledge) they must now be on the ground level, since they hadn't gone to the infirmary.

Mostas going to the infirmary—this was another of the garderie's certitudes, a major certitude. It was such a frequent event that it had become part of the fabric of normal life in the garderie. You got sick. You went to the infirmary. Sometimes you came back. More often you didn't. "She's gone to Elli," the gardianas used to say—probably somewhere above the ceiling (but higher than the nurseries), because most of the gardianas raised their eyes when they said this. All the mostas, Lisbeï better than the others, could sense this was one of those things-that-simply-are, things that are good, somehow: the gardianas weren't sad—they accepted the fact. It was normal "to go to Elli," or "to be with Elli." *Elli is everything, everywhere, what you see and what you don't see,* the gardianas added in the slightly singsongy voice that Lisbeï later learned to recognize as a ready-made answer. The mostas' questions stopped there.

But Lisbeï couldn't stop there. Tula's existence required more explaining, her future presence demanded more assurances. Lisbeï had a baffled sense of movement at the edges of her world, a mysterious, dim coming and going, which she must explore in order to exorcise it. There was *before Tula* and *after Tula.* Some of the garderie's certitudes crumbled in the face of a new anxiety: where did you really come from, *before?* Where did you really go, *after?* As long as this double threat existed, Lisbeï had the strong feeling that she could lose Tula among the shadows lurking on either edge of her world.

She started asking questions, and the inevitable cycle began: the gardianas were at first disconcerted, then secretly exasperated; the other mostas, quick to catch the adults' reactions, became teasing and sometimes hostile. If she had adapted so well until now, it was because of her faculty for perceiving other people's emotions, although in a somewhat confused way (only Tula came through with vivid, resonant clarity). But this very faculty now became a source of disaffection. Before, when she sensed the gardianas' displeasure or embarrassment at her questions, she recognized the signals to say no more and forget it. Now these became signals to remember and return to the subject another time, but more deviously. So far the gardianas had been almost superhuman beings who had aroused a respectful adoration; but now they sorted themselves out gradually into those who were or were not willing to answer, the unfair repositories of a knowledge that must be dragged out of them. They became adversaries, a means to an end.

Of course she didn't think of it this way, not at the age of five (although later, when she was seven and left the garderie, yes). In all probability she would soon have encountered the defensive wall erected by the gardianas in a conspiracy of silence, had it not been for Mooreï and had Tula not fallen ill.

Mooreï, before being Mooreï, had been the gardiana-who-answers. She appeared out of nowhere one day, just like the other gardianas, and quickly became the one who most often looked after the dozen childreen in Lisbeï and Tula's group. She wore a red tunic and seemed much younger than the usual gardianas-in-blue. For Reds to visit this or any garderie was an event out of the ordinary. Mooreï was the first Red Lisbeï had ever seen. Perhaps this was why she noticed the age difference. Then suddenly, with an intuitive leap, Lisbeï wondered whether the gardianas were mostas who had become big.

Lisbeï lay on her bed, far from Tula. It was nap time, and the invisible tides of the dormitory had not yet swept the two of them into the same corner. She pretended to sleep, but in fact she was wide awake. Until now she had used the word "become" without a second thought. Now its meaning had changed, and it seemed the very essence of that mysterious movement which she had noticed since Tula's advent. You *became* big, bigger, and even bigger again! She had always thought you were little and then suddenly bigger, like the interminable quilts the gardiana Melanthë put together during sewing lessons. You cut up bits of fabric and sewed them together, one after another, and then you had a quilt. Size and age were separate states, and when you added them onto one another, they formed a quilt—that is, a mosta. But now she realized it didn't happen that way. The fabric and the cut-out pieces *changed while staying the same!* The fabric *became* the pieces that *became* the quilt, just as Tula had become a little mosta after being a babie mosta and . . . The fresh pleasure of the orderly regression stopped at this point. Did you *become* a babie? From what? What were you, before being a babie?

Mooreï, who at that point was merely the gardiana-in-red, showed no annoyance or surprise. "What do you think you could be?"

So unexpected was this remark that Lisbeï took a while to respond. Gardianas asked pretend questions. But this one seemed very serious, very attentive, as though she didn't really know the answer.

Before being a babie, being small, small . . . Had Tula been smaller? "Small, small, small?" said Lisbeï, holding her thumb and index finger a little apart.

The new-gardiana-in-red pressed Lisbeï's thumb and forefinger together. "Even smaller."

Couldn't you see her, then? And, with abrupt illumination, "She was with Elli?"

The gardiana smiled, surprised but pleased. Lisbeï could feel it. This was an invitation to go on, and Lisbeï ran through the links in the chain: Tula now, then smaller, then a babie in the nursery getting tinier and tinier as . . . as you *went back in time.* That was how you *became,* in *time!*

The gardiana nodded, still attentive. All right: in time. So in the time before, Tula had been with Elli—so tiny you couldn't see her, the way Elli is invisible but everywhere. But how did she come from Elli? There was nothing and all of a sudden there was something, someone, Tula?

The gardiana waited. Seeing Lisbeï silent and perplexed, she said, "It's like the apple and the seeds, Lisbeï."

There were apple trees in the garden that bore small fruit, tart and delicious, with a prettily symmetrical pink heart. But this was too brusque a change of subject. Lisbeï's eyes grew round. The gardiana waited before replying, and watched as the other childreen, who had been playing, started arguing about a hobskoch game. She heaved what seemed a private sigh. "Anyway, you'll soon be a big girl," she said, leaning toward Lisbeï. "Soon you'll learn how to grow plants. You take a seed from a plant, a tiny, tiny seed, and you put it in the ground. The earth nourishes it, and the seed gets bigger and bigger until it sticks up out of the earth and becomes a plant. . . . When the plant is big enough, it makes seeds too. You see, Lisbeï, the apple does the same thing with its seeds."

Lisbeï's eyes were as round as ever, but now it was with the surprised joy of understanding. It was almost like Tula's irruption into her existence, this sudden inner light. Seeds that make plants that make seeds. Tula had been an invisible little seed in Elli. Was Elli the earth, then?

"The earth, the sky, everything everywhere," said the marvelous gardiana-who-answers. It wasn't a ready-made response but a joyful assent. "But babies aren't exactly plants, Lisbeï. They don't grow in the earth."

Lisbeï could sense the gardiana waiting (a thing unheard of) for a fresh question. It came almost by itself, hardly a query. After all, there were only two kinds of people in Lisbeï's world: gardianas and mostas. "They grow in the gardianas?"

The gardiana broke into delighted laughter. (Oh how new, how nice it was, this sense of having really pleased someone!)

"Yes, Lisbeï, in the tummies of women. But all women aren't gardianas."

Women. A new word. Lisbeï glanced rather shyly at the gardiana's belly. The gardiana was . . . a women?

A *woman.* Yes, naturally, and so was Lisbeï.

"I can make babies grow? Tula could have grown in my tummy?"

The gardiana registered surprise, then amusement. No, not yet—Lisbeï was much too little. When she was bigger, yes. You had to be an apple tree before you could make apples, wasn't that right?

The gardiana-who-answers patted Lisbeï's cheek gently and went to calm the squabbling hobskoch players.

Indifferent to the puzzled, scandalized (and jealous) stares of Meralda and her gang, who had been watching this interchange from afar, Lisbeï ran to Tula. She had a new story to tell. Her enthusiasm was a little dampened by Tula's "why?" and "how?" How did the little seeds get into the women's tummies?

"Maybe they're already there, like the seeds in the apple." What a fascinating idea! Were there seeds inside the seeds inside the seeds? Four-year-old Tula couldn't see anything interesting in such abstract speculation, however. She was quite willing to concede that someone put seeds in the tummy. Elli, most likely. But how? Well, by the little button in the middle of the tummy (Lisbeï's imagination galloped forward with exhilarating freedom). Then how did the babies get out? A babie was a lot bigger than a seed. Well, maybe they cut the tummy open, like an apple, and—

Tula wrinkled her nose. No, it was a nasty idea. The babies must come out by the button—on this they agreed. That night when they were getting ready for bed, they examined their bellies. The button didn't really look as though it would open. Maybe it would change when they got big.

What a delightful game for Lisbeï to watch ideas fluttering through her head like colored butterflies, to be caught and put together to make a story—like a quilt—for Tula! But this story raised ever more difficult questions as it unfolded. Could the gardianas on the second level have made all the mostas? Even if they were big and could grow several babies at once, their tummies surely couldn't manage . . . Lisbeï giggled helplessly at the picture in her mind: a gardiana, as round as could be, floating away in the sky like a ball that wouldn't come down again!

On the other hand, if the gardianas grew babies like apples on a tree, there ought to be a lot more mostas in the garderie, even taking into account the unseen mostas on the ground level or in the three highest levels, the nurseries, where there were many more. And if the mostas became women, where would all these babie-makers stay? There wasn't room for them in the garderie, so where . . .

That night, as Lisbeï turned the question over and over, another docile butterfly folded its wings and let itself be caught. These babie-making women were *somewhere else*. They were *outside*. Like the garden was outside the garderie, and the garderie outside . . . whatever was on the other side of the wall. That's where the gardianas came from! And the new babies! Just like a before and an after, there was a here and a somewhere else. And in a way (the butterflies spun dizzyingly by), it was *the same thing!* When you became big, you moved not only in time, but in space. Yes of course: there was another space on the other side of the wall.

Here Lisbeï's imagination suddenly stalled. What was on the other side? There must be garderies and more garderies. . . . Her imagination moved forward again. Relieved and heavy-eyed, she let herself slide into an infinite succession of garderies, with their gardens and dormitories, and—who knew?—their other Lisbeïs and Tulas.

"No!" said Tula next day, sticking out her lower lip. "Just you and me, nobody else." But Lisbeï's game, "smaller-bigger," was an instant success. Tula is smaller than Lisbeï, who is smaller than Sita, who is smaller than the apple tree, which is bigger than the fountain, which . . . and so it went. Then there was "older-younger." They spent delightful hours putting together different chains that crisscrossed or interlinked, stretching in all directions as far as you cared to go. Tula was on the very-small-mosta chain, which was also the young-mosta-chain, which was also the dressed-in-green-chain. It was the same unceasing progression that took you from the outside to the nurseries, to the second level, to the ground level, to the—

To where? Where did you go after that? Lisbeï didn't really want to continue the chain in this direction. Outside, for her, was mainly the place people came from—gardianas, babies . . . and Tula, the miracle of Tula. To think people could *go* there was too close to the idea that Tula could disappear again to the unknown place whence she had come.

That morning Tula didn't want to get up. Lisbeï must have been nearly six years old—it's difficult to pinpoint events in the garderies, where there were no calendars or birthdays. Tula was too hot, Tula was tired. . . .

Tula was sick!

"Only a low fever," said Nereï, the gardiana. Nothing ominous, just that moment of silence, opaque, resigned. She gathered Tula in her arms and walked away. Lisbeï followed, furtively touching Tula's dangling hand. But it wasn't really Tula, that faint glimmer smothered in cotton depths, that dwindling resonance like the voice of someone falling into a dark, growling pit. Lisbeï burst into tears. The gardiana turned around with an exasperated sigh. "For goodness sake, Lisbeï, go to the refectory with the others. Don't be so silly."

Sick, Tula sick, Tula in the infirmary! Lisbeï caught up with the other mostas, trying superstitiously not to think the fatal thought: *Is she going to come back?* But of course she couldn't help thinking it, what with Meralda (a sly gleam in her eye) and the others saying, "Perhaps she's going back to Elli. Lucky Tula!"

Tula with Elli, invisible once more, everywhere, but unreachable? No, no! Elli didn't need Tula! Elli was everything, everywhere, Elli was always with Tula, just like Elli was always with everyone else, and Elli didn't need Tula. Elli had no *right* to take Tula back after giving her to Lisbeï, or else Elli was wicked, wicked!

The gardiana Tessa came up behind Lisbeï in a wave of righteous indignation. It was very, very bad to say such things. Lisbeï was selfish to want to keep Tula for herself (selfishness was a major sin in the garderie). "Elli knows what Elli is doing, and if Elli wants Tula back, it's because Elli knows how to love better than you, Lisbeï!"

Lisbeï picked at her breakfast without saying a word and left the refectory with the others, her heart heavy with guilt, yet filled with a sense of rebellion that refused to go away. No, Elli couldn't love Tula better, it wasn't true, it wasn't!

The rest of the day passed in a kind of fog. Lisbeï doesn't remember much. She must have gone about the usual business of the day: sewing, drawing, and carpentry, with long stretches in the garden and the refectory at noon, and then naptime, eyes wide open and dry in the shadowed dormitory. And Mooreï wasn't there, Mooreï who would surely have answered her questions! There was only Nereï and the other old Blue, Tessa, annoyed at seeing Lisbeï silent, clumsy, absentminded, the object of furtive glances from the other childreen —glances at first mocking, then perturbed, surprised, and worried. What's the matter with Lisbeï anyway? Tula has gone to the infirmary, but it's normal for mostas to get sick, isn't it? Isn't it? And the gardianas, exasperated at this threat to their small flock's blissful ignorance, had to invent new games and tell stories until nightfall to make the others forget about Lisbeï's incomprehensible behavior.

That night, for the first time in her life, Lisbeï broke the rules. It wasn't really deliberate. She couldn't sleep: there were needles in her bed, in her head. She felt like shouting, crying, literally jumping out of her skin. In the end she got up. Everyone was asleep. She slipped by the somnolent figures, her bare feet silent on the cool mosaic.

And nothing happened.

But it was forbidden to leave the dormitory at night except to go to the toilets. And that wasn't where she was going; she was heading for the exit door. Nothing happened. No scolding voice, no gardianas, no Elli, although Elli saw everything everywhere, all the time. Lisbeï found herself in the corridor. In the half light shed by the dimmed gasoles, everything was different, bigger, higher. All that empty, silent space, and Lisbeï completely alone in it. Strange, it didn't feel unpleasant. Rather the opposite, in fact. Then the pleasant strangeness of this discovery evaporated. She wasn't too sure where the infirmary might be, since she'd not yet been in that part of her floor (minor cuts and bruises were taken care of in the dormitory; the infirmary was for serious cases).

That morning Nereï had headed for the central hall with its staircase. Lisbeï did the same, skirting the dark stairwell, excited by the fleeting thought that, if she wanted, she could go down it as far as the unknown main floor. Then she halted, uncertain where to turn next. A light shone beneath a door in one of the corridors. Since she must do something, at least keep moving, she went toward the door. The frosted glass glowed greenly from the light within. Not a sound. What should she do? The impetus that had carried her out of the dormitory dissolved as garderie rules reasserted their hold.

Lisbeï stood in front of the lighted door. Perhaps it wasn't even the infirmary. She stood rooted to the spot, unable to walk away or go forward.

Suddenly there were shadows moving behind the glass, muffled voices, Lisbeï staring at the door handle about to turn, turning . . . and Mooreï's voice pulling her out of the nightmare.

"Lisbeï! What are you doing here?"

And right after came another sort of dream—or at least, once she found herself back in her cot, it *seemed* like a dream, a moment unrelated to anything else.

Another gardiana was with Mooreï, a stranger in blue. Lisbeï stammered something about Tula, and Mooreï said, "She's sleeping and mustn't be disturbed. She'll sleep for several days. We must wait, Lisbeï." Gray, that was what Lisbeï sensed in Mooreï: a dispirited fatigue. Terrified, she burst into tears, but the other gardiana knelt down and took hold of her bare arms . . . and what was it, this ripple of echoes, this spreading phosphorescence, this amazement dancing back and forth between the gardiana and Lisbeï? The gardiana's face must have been very close to hers, but she remembers nothing about it, just the murmuring glimmer and the flash of indignation in the midst of her stupor: what right had this gardiana to . . . it was only with Tula, the light, the resonance, the sharing!

The hands fell away, the echo faded; the hands returned, the echo grew. "She's in no pain, Lisbeï," said the unknown gardiana. "But she may not wake up. We must be brave, Lisbeï. It's the malady."

The Malady, Lisbeï understood. At first you were tired and feverish, as you were with other sicknesses, but then you went to sleep, a deep, deep sleep. If you woke up, you'd never be sick again, the stranger said. Lisbeï felt oddly tranquilized by the inner tumult she sensed in the gardiana. The violent emotions—sorrow, anger, but hope as well, so different from the assured, rather unimaginative placidity of all the other gardianas except for Mooreï—had the effect of focusing her attention on the gardiana's words. *If you woke up, you'd never be sick again.* But you might not wake up. She must be patient. Go back to the dormitory and wait. Mooreï would go with her.

"I can go back by myself," Lisbeï heard herself say.

And even more surprisingly, neither of the gardianas was angry.

"Run along, then," said Mooreï. "I'll tell you if Tula wakes up."

In the days (three, four?) that followed, the other mostas no longer paid any attention to Lisbeï, and the gardianas were reassured: Lisbeï was behaving herself again. They did not know that Lisbeï was waiting for Mooreï.

And Mooreï came. It was during break. Elli was raining, and the mostas were in the playroom instead of the garden. Meralda and the others were playing knucklebones rather listlessly. Lisbeï was in a corner with her slate, drawing a picture of a fountain with the water continually recirculating, coming back, *coming back*. Mooreï came into the room. Lisbeï had an overpowering impulse to rush over to her, coupled with an effort to suppress it that left her feeling weak. Mooreï walked around saying hello to the childreen and asking about their activities. Lisbeï, eyes on her slate, sensed rather than saw the red dress stop beside her.

"She's awake," murmured Mooreï.

The slate fell noiselessly on the thick, braided rug, but Mooreï had already moved away to sit with the other gardiana. She took some blue knitting out of a big basket and began to work. Singing as she knitted. An unfamiliar song. After a while she asked the room at large, "Do you know the song of Elli?" And no, of course the mostas didn't know it— what song? said Meralda, always quick to recognize a good-natured gardiana.

"The song Elli sings while drawing the thread."

What thread? Ah, that's a long story.

The mostas began to cluster around Mooreï. Lisbeï, who would have liked to run to the infirmary, finally joined the seated circle of childreen, overcome by curiosity. The gardianas often told stories, but—well, they were useful stories. Such as the-silly-mosta-and-the-little-matchstick. Or the-staircase-that-ate-mostas. Or the-mosta-that-had-to-knit-her-bed. They had never told stories about Elli.

"What thread," repeated Mooreï pensively. With a twist of the wrist she slipped the needles out of her knitting, unraveled the rows, and began rewinding the wool onto the ball. Then she took another ball—yellow, this time—and broke off bits of wool, knotting them to the unraveled blue thread at irregular intervals. The mostas gazed at her, spellbound with surprise and delight. "The thread Elli knits with, of course," said Mooreï, at last winding up the blue wool with its little yellow tags. "Elli created everything, as you know. One day, Elli decided that Elli was bored with being all alone, and so Elli took a bit of Elliself and began to unwind Elliself, like a ball of wool. And that's how Elli made the daylight and the night, earth and water for the plants, and . . ." (as she talked she unrolled the blue ball until she came to the first yellow knot) "and look! Elli created us—you, Meralda . . ." (a yellow knot), "and you, Tallie . . ." (another knot), "and Garrec and Lisbeï, Meï, Pia . . ."

Soon a pile of blue wool lay on Mooreï's lap. She picked up the ends, tied them together, and began to knit. A blue row appeared beneath the needles. "And at the same time as Elli unwinds Elliself to create everything, Elli draws Elli's own thread, like Aragna the Spinna. You know Aragna?"

"Yes, yes!" the mostas chorused. They knew the tireless Spinna, who was always being held up as an example—well, and so?

"Well, Elli knits the world at one end, and *at the same time* Elli unravels it at the other. As I'm not Elli, I can't do it so well, but it's a bit like this. Elli doesn't always knit the same thing, naturally. It would be too boring. Elli changes the color of the thread, or the kind of stitch or the number of stitches, and in this way Elli is always pleased with Elli's knitting because it's always new. Elli also likes to discover Elliself from time to time in Elli's creations as they appear, because you must remember Elli is knitting and unraveling Elliself."

The first yellow knot appeared on the needle, "There, Meralda, that's you; you've just been knitted by Elli. And you, Tallie, and Garrec, Lisbeï, Meï, Pia . . ."

The mostas had caught on and called out their names as the yellow knots entered the blue rows. Soon there was no more wool except the end tied to the beginning of the knitting on Mooreï's lap.

"Time to start over," said Mooreï, holding out the full needle to Meralda. Meralda giggled and pulled the needle. The nearest mostas began pulling on the thread to unravel the knitting.

"It's never ending, do you see? We constantly come from Elli and return to Elli. Some sooner, some later. Like Ricia, or Fenora . . ."

Who had gone to the infirmary and hadn't come back. Meralda added in a positive voice, "Like Tula."

And of course Lisbeï couldn't stop herself from crying

out, with furious joy, that Tula was cured and would soon come back from the infirmary!

The others turned to Mooreï, who bowed her head in assent.

"Anyhow," sniffed Meralda after a moment of thunderstruck silence, "Elli would have knitted her again."

"Yes indeed." Mooreï smiled. Tula would have found her place in Elli's love again, but her name wouldn't have been Tula, and she'd have looked different, because the kind of stitch often changes.

How do you know who comes back, then?

Mooreï smiled and ruffled Pia's hair. "Only Elli knows, Elli, who is the beginning and the end. Elli chooses the stitch. She knows who's coming back and who has to leave."

Why did little Meï have to ask, "Do you always go back to Elli when you leave?"

"No," said Mooreï. "When you're bigger—soon, when some of you turn six, like you, Meralda, or Tallie, or Rubio and Turri, and you, Lisbeï . . ." (the tone of her voice alerted Lisbeï) "you'll go downstairs and never come back. The little ones will stay. You won't see them anymore, and they won't see you anymore. In a way, for them it will be as though you'd gone to Elli."

They were going to be separated anyway? She and Tula? Because Lisbeï was going to become a big mosta and have to leave? Soon?

Mooreï's voice flowed on: the little ones would get big later on, and they'd go to downstairs as well. Lisbeï's painful fury abated a little. Tula wasn't that much younger. They wouldn't be separated for too long, would they? But she couldn't ask Mooreï in front of the other mostas.

Nor, at that moment, could she ask the true question: would there be other separations after the first time, as she grew bigger and Tula remained forever younger?

2

Antonë to Linta

Bethely, 12 Juna, 479 A.G.

As you see, my sweet, I have finally reached safe harbor (so to speak) in Bethely, where the only waves are the hills! I think I'll stay awhile, and you can write me here—your next letter, anyway. I hope it comes sooner than your last. Two whole months to cover six hundred klims is a lot, even taking into account the proverbial slowness of mail in the South-East. I rather think the Merici "forgot" the letter in a corner somewhere, because there's no forwarding address on the envelope. They weren't unhappy to see the back of me, I feel. I gave two or three of their fine, all-embracing certitudes too much of a shaking-up.

Bethely is a positive rest after two months in a Family of Juddites! Not that they're fanatic Progressistas here, mind you. I'd call them pragmatic Traditionalistas, somewhere between Believras and Progressistas. Oh dear—I'm getting caught up in the waltz of the labels, as you call it. The ways of Wardenberg are certainly hard to shake off.

I won't give you a guided tour of Bethely. The Capterie looks just like the descriptions in books. The engravings you sent me are somewhat out of date, particularly as they were done by someone who'd read Tonilù of Caranthe's trilogy once too often. The Towers aren't as dark or majestic, the fortifications disappeared long ago, and to put it in a nutshell, the Capterie doesn't appear to be forever brooding beneath a stormy sky. Of course I agree it's a historic place in many ways, but the people who live here don't think about it every minute of the day. Once a year, yes, during the Pilgrimage of Garde, and even then (from what I'm told) they seem to consider it more of a nuisance than a distinction. All the same, they don't spit on the trade pilgrims bring. On the contrary!

They welcomed me and listened to my explanations with

*polite friendliness. "They" means mainly Selva, the Capta
(twenty-two but looks younger), and her Memory, Mooreï (still a
Red at thirty-four: the renowned fertility of Bethely is no lie). I
haven't had much contact with the rest of the Family. They let
me look in the Archives quite readily, a pleasant change after
Merici. All the contents, including the Book of Lines, are open to
everyone in Bethely. Mind you, there aren't very many who
bother going to the Library. They're all too busy working somewhere else. If I dared (but I will), I'd say Bethely is a veritable
hive! Almost everything is done by hand. They've had hydraulic
power for nearly twenty years, but apparently it's only used in the
workshops. As in the rest of Litale, there is no electricity, although a river runs by the Capterie. The Harems made it into a
canal, which the Hives didn't go so far as to destroy, despite their
fanatic hatred of all Harem things. A question of religion, I
imagine—but given Bethely's rather cool attitude toward religious matters, it might just have been habit, so deep-rooted in
history as to be unshakable. Astonishing, isn't it? You'd think
that in Bethely, of all places, they'd be ferocious Believras.*

*The present Capta probably won't do much shaking up,
although she seems to take an interestingly nonchalant attitude
toward regional customs. For example, just a short time ago
Bethely switched to gasoles under her authority. They have shiny
new methane tanks and compressors, objects viewed by the oldest Family members with a certain amount of suspicion. She
asked me some intelligent questions when I outlined my research
project on the Malady. (Not in detail! Don't worry. I didn't utter
the fatal word!)*

*Well, I'm at it again. I guess I'll never learn. But you must be
getting used to it by now. The Malady rate here is 46 percent, but
the survival rate has risen to 9 percent! Enormous, don't you
think? If their Archives are to be trusted, there's a slow but steady
increase both in the Malady and in the survival rate. In any case,
it isn't an infection, because it's never contagious. And guess
what? Among survivors, the rate of post-Malady infections is
0.04 percent. It seems my theory is holding its own, doesn't it?*

*I'll try to preserve my "scientific objectivity." Still, you must
admit the figures, the statistics—well, you know what I mean. My
premise may have been subjective, but my intuition has had results, all the same. It's not my fault if I was traumatized by my
own Malady!*

But seriously.

Well, seriously, I fully realize I'm far from objective. You will admit, however, that I'm capable of assessing my personal interest in this research and including it in the equation. In any case, I don't want to be (or pretend to be) "objective." People in Bethely have a very "objective" way, for instance, of handling the problem of infant mortality. It's about the same as elsewhere in Litale, and I still find it . . . revolting. They've got more of the Hives in them than they'd probably care to admit. The childreen are brought up in the seclusion of garderies until they are seven, as in the strictest Juddite Families. Until then they're "mostas," nonpersons (they don't even know what "person" means until they get out of the garderies). Of course they have practically no education before the age of seven. "The less the mostas know, the less they have to lose if they must go back to Elli." Just think of the wasted potential!

Looking at it from another angle, though, I understand it: no emotional or intellectual investment in the childreen until their survival is sure. A logical, "rational" view. Of course it's all very well for me to object—I've never lost a childe.

But enough of that.

The curious thing, considering the relative proximity of the Great Badlands, is the low incidence of malformations. Here they haven't Wardenberg's narrow criteria about . borderline births. Some years ago they were still drawing the line at arms: you could live without legs in Bethely, but not without arms. The seriously handicapped live apart, on one of the Farms. They're nearly all sterilized, however. More waste. But I'll agree with the Juddites (and Wardenberg, although they make strange compagnas) that in extreme cases, given our present state of knowledge in genetics, prevention is preferable to having incurable individuals on our hands. As far as I'm concerned, however, the definition of "extreme" varies too much from one Province to another.

Bethely people aren't Juddites, when all is said and done, and the general atmosphere is rather pleasant. The childreen don't appear to be unhappy in the garderies, and they seem to integrate well into Family life, in spite of everything. They lead a fairly structured existence, but it's not overly rigid. Exceptions are sometimes allowed, and Bethely occasionally accommodates special cases. In fact, the Capta has led the way, as I mentioned earlier. Her firstborne couldn't adapt to the nursery at first. Naturally, mothers and babies are separated at birth. It doesn't cause problems, because the mothers (they usually say "genitrixes" here) have always been conditioned to expect it. The childreen

*readily adapt as well, and the nursing gardianas are fully compe-
tent. This babie, however, would have virtually starved herself to
death if Selva hadn't decided to see how things were coming
along—against all local tradition—and fed the babie from her
own breast for several months. You can imagine the Family's
comments. . . . Still, the childe has survived, and no one now
criticizes Selva. Not that anyone has followed her example—of
course not, Elli forbid! There's been no need to, anyway. They've
forgiven her this deviation from tradition. Anyhow, it sets a pre-
cedent.*

*I had found this incident noteworthy only for what it re-
vealed about Selva. But there was a surprise in store. When I
arrived last week, I met the childe in question. She's called Lisbeï, and her sister has been assigned to the same garderie. And
(take note) they're almost two years apart. Selva has decided to
space her pregnancies like ordinary Reds. The Family didn't say a
word. I imagine the personality of Mooreï, the Memory, has
something to do with it. She could have been a communicata—
she's a born conciliatrix and a Believra, on top of everything else;
no doubt she'd say the two went together.*

*But to get back to Lisbeï. She'll be six soon and hasn't had
the Malady. Normally, she shouldn't develop it now. (Although I
had it very late, and you too, didn't you? But that's still the
exception.) The younger one, Tula, had come down with it the
very morning of my arrival. I asked to see her, and Mooreï took
me to the infirmary the same evening. Lisbeï had escaped from
the dormitory in an attempt to see Tula—imagine! We surprised
her at the infirmary door. I was moved: although they aren't
aware of being sisters, the two must love one another very much.
I took her in my arms to comfort her. . . .*

*Do you remember the first time you and I touched each
other? It was like that. I went back to the younger one, Tula, right
away. I hadn't paid attention when touching her before, and the
fever had dimmed the sensation quite a bit. But there it was. Not
as strong as in the older childe, but* there. *She came out of the
coma four days later, and when I touched her then, it was much
clearer.*

*The older childe wasn't punished for her nocturnal expedi-
tion, by the way.*

*You will understand why I'm probably going to stay in
Bethely a little longer than planned. I haven't touched Selva—
there's been no opportunity. But I'm going to try. I want to find
out whether she's the source or whether the childreen's genitors*

are responsible. (Lisbeï is a Callenbasch, Tula a Belmont.) Don't worry: I'll be careful. No, I'm not getting caught up again in my theories of ten years ago. No more theorizing for me. I simply want to assemble the facts. I survived the Malady, so did you, the three from Lletrewyn, the two Angreseas, and this little Tula, and we all have this . . . faculty in varying degrees. Those are facts, aren't they? I'll admit dozens of others have survived the Malady (especially in Bethely over the last six years) without showing the slightest trace of this faculty. Still and all, just let me keep tracking down the facts, when there are any.

Time to stop: the Northern courria is about to leave. I hope you get this soon and that I'll hear from you quickly, too.

All my love,
Your Antonë

3

As Lisbeï had expected, the big mostas' ground level was the same as the one above. Different timetables, but the same rules—first and foremost being the unspoken taboo: don't ask about things unless the gardianas bring up the subject. (There was no Mooreï to help her now. Lisbeï wouldn't see her again until she emerged from the west garderie.) As on the level above, the newcomers were entrusted to older mostas for orientation. These tutresses took their role seriously, assuming an authoritarian stance from the start by only answering questions when they felt like it. There was no point nagging them, not even the ones Lisbeï recognized from the second level, like Sorel or Fendig-with-the-red-eyes-and-white-hair ("albino" was the proper word). Nevertheless, before several days had elapsed, Lisbeï had found a way to worm things out of Clara, the mosta in charge of her team. It was simple: don't appear to be asking questions; say things out loud as though talking to yourself. If you were wrong, Clara couldn't resist correcting you, rolling her eyes and pursing her lips exactly like Gardiana Marli. This tactic required Lisbeï to pass herself off as an idiot, but she soon realized people were more inclined to accept a witless Lisbeï than one who was too inquisitive.

Now that Tula was far away, now that their shared resonance no longer shielded Lisbeï against the garderie's troubling ambience, she sometimes longed to be accepted by the others. For a while she thought this would happen. There were enough mostas who hadn't known her before.

But Meralda and her gang had also come down from the second level. "Lisbeï is a little *strange,* you know," they began whispering.

Lisbeï could sense the inner withdrawal of the others and how they kept their distance. She knew she would find no friend on the ground floor. But when she felt too sad, she would think of the coming night, and her rancor would vanish.

She slipped silently through the shadowed dormitory, over the parquet and the now-familiar mosaics. She was still afraid, but it was a delicious feeling, because beyond the fear was Tula, waiting in the dark. They met under the stairway in a small storeroom where the shoe polish and brushes were kept. (For years the mere smell of polished leather filled Lisbeï with poignant nostalgia.) Near the end, since it was sumra and safer to go outside, they met in the garden. Lisbeï's real day began at this hour, when she relived it by recounting it to Tula.

Soon after Lisbeï's move to the ground level, the sun began to shine more often. This was *sprinna*. (A new word to describe something already familiar without changing it in any way. This was to be a characteristic phenomenon of Lisbeï's stay on the ground floor.) There'd been no name for seasons before. Why not? Clara revealed the answer in a condescending remark: the small mostas so often went to Elli before turning six that no one wanted to be bothered teaching them things they'd never use. Lisbeï felt like laughing when she thought of all the things she was teaching Tula before it was time—Tula, who had passed through the Malady and who wouldn't go to Elli now, not for a long while, anyway. It felt like a revenge of some kind, but against what or whom Lisbeï had no clear idea. Sometimes it was against Elli, but this made Lisbeï feel very uncomfortable, and she tried to think of other things. It was all too evident that Elli was more powerful and more dangerous to defy than all the gardianas put together.

A new element had entered Lisbeï's existence, for among

the big mostas' principal tasks was their introduction to the Word of Elli.

> *In the beginning was Elli*
> *Elli was before the beginning*
> *And the end will be Elli*

The beginning and the end, that was exactly what Mooreï had said, but how could there be something before the beginning of everything? Where had the seed of beginning been?

> *In the eternity of inchoate repose*
> *In the eternity of inchoate silence*
> *In the eternity*
> *Bodiless, voiceless, eyeless*
> *Elli was all and all was Elli*

The only part that made some sense was the fourth line, but the fifth hopelessly confused Lisbeï. With nothing, Elli was everything? (Marli nodded with disconcerting approval, although she quickly frowned. "Recite with the others, Lisbeï.")

> *Before the beginning was Elli;*
> *And Elli was the beginning*
> *For in the eternity of inchoate repose*
> *In the eternity of inchoate silence*
> *Elli was love, love was Elli*

Elli's love was so strong that in some mysterious way this love began to dance, and Elli created the dance *and therefore* repose—or so Lisbeï dimly understood. Then, because Elli wanted to express Elli's joy at this first creation, Elli created the word *and therefore* the silence. The gardiana's insistence on "and therefore" shed no light for Lisbeï. Anyway, what was the connection between this story and Mooreï's knitting? But the refrain ran on:

> *And in body and voice*
> *In eternity*
> *Elli was blind but all was Elli*

Why blind? Because without eyes Elli couldn't see Elliself. But was the all-powerfulness of Elli really that limited? Elli could simply have created a mirror.

"Exactly," said the gardiana tartly. But the next passage was even more puzzling. In dancing, Elli sees (creates?) a mirror image (where?) that Elli calls Ilshe, which Elli loses upon touching it and finally Elli decides to repeat Elliself (or unravel the thread, as Mooreï had explained?). Then:

> *Like the dance and the silence*
> *The word and the repose*
> *Elli looked at Elli saw Elli*
> *And from eternity was born the night*
> *And the day*
> *The word became the earth*
> *And the sky*
> *And the love of Elli created the woman*
> *And the man*

"What's thewoman-antheman?" asked Meralda, no doubt encouraged by the fact that the gardiana had been only mildly irritated by Lisbeï's comments.

"The woman, that's us," chipped in the intrepid Lisbeï, "the gardianas and the mostas."

The others looked at her, ready to ridicule this latest remark, but the gardiana frowned slightly and said yes, if Elli wanted it, childreen became *women*.

"And the antheman?" pursued Meralda, greatly daring.

"The man, a man," sighed the gardiana, enunciating carefully. "That's a boy when he grows up."

What? Boys weren't defective mostas?

On the second level there'd been the boys, the three-headed entity known as Rubio-Turri-Garrec. (Actually there'd been two others, although they very soon went to Elli, and Lisbeï could barely remember them.) But the boys *were* different from one another. For one thing they weren't the same age: only Rubio and Turri had come downstairs with Lisbeï and her group to join the big mostas. That was when their differences began to show. Redheaded Rubio was the bold one: "Me, I . . ." he'd say, and the gardianas called him "youyou" until he stopped. Blond Turri stammered, although it didn't stop him from wanting to talk as much as the other mostas. (Even after six years in the garderie! That showed a strong character. While they were still on the second level, Turri had proposed the game of seeing who could pee the farthest. The gardiana overheard him and was very angry: he'd never done it again.)

Still, as far as the gardianas were concerned, Rubio and Turri were still lumped together as "the boys," and the other mostas took their cue from this. The boys were always together, answered in unison when called, and now, more and more often, made common cause against the other mostas.

Lisbeï couldn't remember exactly when, but very early the other mostas began explaining to each other what boys were all about. Everyone knew they were called "boys," and that you said "he" instead of "she" when talking about one of them, because they were mostas who had somehow gone wrong, what with that little pipe sticking out. Of course no gardiana had ever said as much. No doubt they had always answered the inevitable first questions about boys with their imperturbable "that's-the-way-it-is." But the boys were mistakes—that was obvious, and so no one had ever bothered to find out for sure by asking a gardiana. After all, you couldn't play rough games with boys. The way the gardianas all sprang into action the first few times this happened made it abundantly clear: it was even worse than fighting among girls. Boys were only included in two games: Dungeon and Queenegarde. The gardianas who showed the little mostas how to play had never explained why; it had been that way since they themselves were childreen, so why would they question what was simply a fact of life? The gage to be delivered from the Dungeon, the trophy to be won by answering the Queene's riddles —it just had to be a boy, and that was that. What would you do if there were no boys? "There always are some," the gardiana had replied sadly, and her tone of voice convinced the small mostas that boys did indeed occupy an inferior status. In other games, boys usually ended up with the mostas whom no one wanted for the Choice, the ones who were never leaders in the ball circle . . . like Lisbeï before Tula came—although strange to say she found this an added reason for rather disliking boys. Anyway, there were so few of them that they hardly counted.

Why, though? If boys were mistakes, and if Elli had created everything, then why had Elli made mostas who weren't good for anything?

The question hadn't been put this way. "Why aren't there many boys?" Turri (or Rubio or Garrec) had asked one day.

"It's a punishment sent by Elli," answered the gardiana—probably old Tessa—not without a slight hesitation.

That worried them all: could they turn into boys if they weren't good?

"Of course not." Tessa pursed her lips, a sure sign she'd said all she was going to say. That was all the mostas needed, anyway: boys had done something bad and they'd been punished. Maybe they'd become normal when they got bigger, thought the mostas (especially the boys). Whether the little pipe was the fault or the punishment wasn't too clear, but it didn't matter, really. The boy question had been settled once and for all.

And now here was Marli saying something else! That the boys would keep on being mistakes and would grow into "men." Were they punished forever? Rubio and Turri were white as sheets; the others felt a twinge of pity.

"They aren't being punished—they haven't done anything!" exclaimed Marli, looking as though she wondered where in the world they'd got such a silly idea. But she quickly put on her sensible/knowledgeable face and explained that boys were part of Elli's creation, just like the other mostas, and Elli loved them as much as any of Elli's other creatures.

"But Gardiana Tessa said . . ."

"Surely not," interposed Marli firmly. "She must have said that the fact of there being so few boys was a punishment sent by Elli."

Wasn't it the same thing?

No, it wasn't at all the same thing. Everybody had been punished, and the boys weren't really the reason, but more the "agents" of this punishment. They were meant to have a little pipe, and it was neither a fault nor a punishment. That's how they were made and why they were called "boys," because they were different in this way even though everyone in the garderie was a "mosta."

Rubio and Turri were beaming. But Marli went on to recount a story that wiped the smiles away. In the beginning, Elli had created a big garden where an apple tree grew. There were as many boys as girls in the beginning. But the boys ate the apples before they were ripe, seeds and all, and Elli was very angry.

"Why?" asked Meralda. There was no holding her back that day.

"Because then the apples couldn't make other apples or apple trees," retorted Lisbeï, exasperated but unwise. Marli frowned.

"Who told you that?"

Lisbeï whispered Mooreï's name, feeling anxiety rise within, and perceived Marli's disapproving but resigned reaction. It seemed Mooreï shouldn't have told her. She knew Mooreï was different from the other gardianas!

"As a punishment," resumed Marli without further comment on the subject of Mooreï, much to Lisbeï's relief, "and also to give the other trees a chance, Elli decided to create far fewer boys than girls. But it's not the fault of today's boys." She stood up and clapped her hands. "All right, everybody. From the start now: *In the beginning was Elli . . .*"

That afternoon in the garden the childreen bubbled over with speculation. Meralda immediately pounced on Lisbeï. She'd caught Mooreï's name. Mooreï always paid smiling attention to Meralda, who was very fond of her. "What else did Mooreï tell you?"

Lisbeï couldn't avoid answering—in fact she had no desire to. For some reason that wasn't clear, Meralda's growing hold on the other mostas was beginning to rile her. When Lisbeï had repeated Mooreï's words, Meralda unerringly asked the crucial question.

"Who makes the boys, then?"

If women made babies in their tummies like apples made other apples with their seeds, and if boys were meant to have a little pipe, who made the boys? Girls had no pipes, and women probably didn't, either. The suggestion that girls might develop one when they grew older was brushed aside: who'd want such a ridiculous thing?

"M-maybe the m-men make boys?" suggested Turri in a soft stammer.

Everyone protested on principle, but the theory had an undeniably elegant symmetry: women made girls and men made boys. No one could answer the next question, however: what was the use of boys and men? Why did they have to be part of Elli's creation?

Lisbeï could have supplied an answer, but she kept it for Tula. The ordered progression of the Word was very captivating, accentuated as it was by the rhythm of the verses and the gardiana's singsongy recital. (Later the mostas would learn the real music of the Word and its celebration—the melody sung by Mooreï on the day when she knitted Elli for them.) *Like the dance / and the silence. The word / and the repose . . . The night / and the day, The earth / and the sky, The woman / and the man:* perhaps boys in Elli's creation were a kind of reflection of girls, to keep the symmetry. . . .

A lopsided symmetry. The real symmetry, the one Lisbeï had thought of right away when she imagined the mirror effect, was *Lisbeï / and Tula*—the continual circling of emotions that rebounded between them, the resonance, the shared light . . . (She hadn't told Tula about Antonë—she had really forgotten.)

Tula wrinkled her nose. "But we're not at all the same!" she cried, touching Lisbeï's curly black hair and brown skin, and placing Lisbeï's hand on her smooth, flaming red locks and milky whiteness. Lisbeï kissed her in response. How could she make Tula understand this certitude? The differences in their bodies didn't matter. What mattered was their identical light, *the* light.

Tula snuggled silently against her, warm and soft, and for a while Lisbeï stopped thinking while they caressed and rubbed against one another in the pleasuring they'd discovered a little while back. Then, peaceful once more, they watched the other side of the sun as it slipped through the clouds.

"Could I tell Garrec the bit about boys?" said Tula suddenly, speaking in a shy, small voice.

Lisbeï started, horrified at the thought.

"He's all alone here," said Tula quickly. "Now that the other boys have gone, nobody plays with him anymore. . . ."

Nor with me, revealed the unfinished sentence. But Lisbeï was adamant. What was Tula thinking of? No one, least of all a boy, must know what she learned from Lisbeï! Lisbeï had no right to teach Tula anything. She wasn't even supposed to *see* Tula!

Of course Tula gave in. But that night . . . that night was not entirely perfect.

They never spoke of it again. But there were so many other wonderful things to tell Tula! The Word of Elli, of course, but especially about learning to *read* and *write,* and *count.* The well-ordered series of numbers, the transformation of sounds into letters and syllables, words, and sentences, the progressions, permutations, and combinations were all so . . . logical, so satisfying, and at the same time this fresh knowledge opened up new spaces, spaces alive with the constant flow of ideas, spaces where Lisbeï could dream up endless stories. They seemed like living things that transformed themselves into something new almost without any help from her, and yet she was certainly the one writing the words and reading them. What extraordinary power!

When, for the first time, she drew the letters of her name on the slate (big capital letters, a little shaky on their feet), she also wrote TULA—quick, quick—rubbing it out hastily when Gardiana Faï walked down the rows to check their work.

Little by little the wave of speculation aroused by the first contact with the Word of Elli ebbed and vanished as they droned the verses day after day. It became the morning prayer, just another habit. The big mostas' other new habits were much more relevant, more absorbing.

Until the day when the gardiana Belinda fell ill right in the middle of the refectory.

She turned white and ran out of the room, but not fast enough. The mostas nearest the corridor could hear her vomiting. Another gardiana quieted the tumult of voices. Faï, the strict writing teacher and the oldest gardiana on the ground floor, walked into the corridor without undue haste, which reassured the mostas somewhat.

But Belinda disappeared. This worried Lisbeï more than the others. Belinda was a gardiana-in-red and young—a rare specimen in the garderie and therefore precious, since such gardianas usually answered questions more readily. Luckily her replacement was also a young-one-in-red. She had never worked in a garderie and was well-intentioned but awkward. What had happened to Belinda? The mostas wondered whether she, too, had gone to Elli.

"Of course not." The young gardiana laughed delightedly. "She's going to make a babie!"

Meralda said out loud what Lisbeï had thought to herself: "But her tummy isn't fat. . . ."

The gardiana smiled. It was too soon, just the beginning, she explained, unaware that the mostas hadn't the slightest idea of how babies came into the world.

"Do babies make you sick?" asked Meralda, scarcely trusting their good luck.

"Sometimes, to start with, when the seed isn't really settled in yet."

"But how do you begin making the babie?" inquired Meï, all innocence. Six-year-old Meï, pink and chubby-cheeked, resembled a babie herself.

The young gardiana stroked Meï's cheek. "Well, the mother mixes her seed with the male's seed in her tummy and—"

She must have seen Meï's eyes widen. A glance at the other mostas made her realize her blunder. She coughed and blushed, her embarrassment as clear to Lisbeï as to the others. "You'll soon learn all about it," she muttered. "Time for work, now. Faï is waiting."

Work! Faï, exasperated by the general inattention, cut short the writing lesson and sent them all out to work in the garden. *Mother, mother,* gabbled Lisbeï feverishly, indiscriminately ripping up good plants and changelines in her pea patch with quite unnecessary force. So *male* was the other name for man, to keep the balance. But what was the use of the male's seeds in the mother's tummy, since she was supposed to make girls? Anyway, how did they manage to mix all those seeds? Why mix them at all?

Meralda was bursting with answers. They got the seeds out of the males' tummies with a needle, just like they did for blood in the infirmary, and then they put the seed in the mother's tummy. . . .

"Couldn't she swallow it? " asked Meï, who hated needles.

Meralda was feeling generous in her hour of glory: "Or else she swallows it. Anyhow the seeds get mixed, and the mothers grow babies in their tummies. *All* babies," she emphasized, looking meaningfully at the boys.

Lisbeï managed to keep from asking how the women decided to have boys instead of girls. Or did Elli decide? After all, Elli had decided there would be fewer boys than girls.

The rest seemed content with Meralda's explanations—except for Turri and Rubio, clearly unappreciative of the idea that men, "males," couldn't make babies in *their* tummies.

"I know!" shouted Turri suddenly, breaking the others' smug silence. "I know how the seed gets in. That's what the pipe is for!"

The girls exchanged disdainful and amused grimaces. Just like Turri, always trying to find some good reason for that clumsy, dangling thing. There was no stopping him, however. He pressed on, ignoring the grimaces (and without stuttering, Lisbeï noticed). "Because it's hollow, it can go inside the male's tummy, suck up seeds, then come out again and put the seeds through the mother's belly button."

"It turns inside out!" cried Rubio, seeing the light. "Like a glove!" And he sucked in his cheeks loudly, his mouth puckering to a comical vertical slit.

"And when the boys get big, when they become males, it's always sucked in like that, like with girls but prettier, and it only comes out to give seeds."

And the girls couldn't get their own seeds this way because they had no pipe, he concluded with exasperating superiority. They made babies in their tummies because they had no choice.

Indignant and scandalized, the girls were speechless. Lisbeï, forgetting about being always on the sidelines, suddenly had an inspiration. She turned to the boys. "Show us!"

Turri, who didn't always distinguish between a good idea and reality, began to unbutton his pants. Rubio put a dignified halt to this proceeding. "When we are *big,* when we are *males,* then we can do it."

Lisbeï sniggered, and the others admiringly followed suit. "You'll never be able to do it. You're just a couple of flip-floppy gloves with no fingers!"

"Gloves with no fingers! Gloves with no fingers!" crowed the other mostas, instantly enchanted with the absurd aptness of the expression. They made as if to jump on the boys and tickle them (the only permissible violence). The boys fled. Turri tripped on his half-undone pants and broke his nose.

All the mostas, girls and boys, were punished with a week's forced labor in the gardens.

"You were pretty mean," said Tula that night.

Lisbeï was piqued by her obvious disapproval. After all, the boys asked for it by making up silly stories!

"You tell lots of stories, don't you?" retorted Tula.

Lisbeï stared, almost wounded. It wasn't the same!

"Why not?"

Lisbeï said nothing for a moment. Their difference of opinion and Tula's "why not" irritated her like a pumice stone grating inside her head. Of course they were different, stories by girls and stories by boys! There were more girls, in the first place, and they must surely know better than boys.

But Tula said no. Maybe she had a point. After all, when Tula wouldn't agree with Lisbeï or the other way around, who was right? Neither was "more" than the other. Tula simply saw the boys' story another way, that was all.

From the boys' side. How could Tula do such a thing! But Lisbeï's indignation faded before the memory of what she'd felt as she helped Turri up, crying and bloody-nosed. She'd perceived his distress and the fact that his tears came from something other than a broken nose. From the boys' angle, the girls had been mean. The boys had believed their own story—a much better version from their point of view.

But if every story had another side, how could you know who was right? Everyone couldn't be right at once, could they?

"Why not?" said Tula again, decidedly contrary that night. "When we say 'boys,' 'men,' or 'males,' the words are different, but we could still be talking about the same person at different ages. Even though we don't use the same words, everyone knows what we mean, don't they?"

Lisbeï found this rather vexing, but bowed to Tula's logic, although she decided to keep yet another story to herself. It had come to mind after the afternoon's incident: somewhere, probably outside the garderie, there was a woman's tummy, a *mother's* tummy, where she had grown. And another tummy where Tula had grown. And since they both had the light, perhaps they had grown *in the same tummy.* Never before had this occurred to her, but the knowledge that a baby was inside Belinda's tummy had suddenly given the idea substance. She even knew which tummy she would have liked to share with Tula. Mooreï's tummy.

4

Lisbeï/Journal

I can't remember when it began, Tula. Do you yourself remember when the separation started? Easy to say "when I left the garderie," but it seems to me now that it wouldn't have happened if we'd really been together then. You would have understood, guessed, known it wasn't my fault that I didn't tell you, and that I didn't leave you alone on purpose. At least you would have given me the benefit of the doubt. When I look back now, I feel it began earlier, when I was on the ground floor and you were upstairs. Yet we saw each other every night: I kept my promise. Perhaps it wasn't enough for you. What would you have liked? Should I have refused to go? But that was impossible, and we both knew it. Were you jealous? Jealous that I was learning things without you? I spent nights teaching you. And I always told you everything, I never kept anything for myself. Did you find me too enthusiastic? I enjoyed learning things, even away from you, was that it? But I learned them for you, thinking of you. They didn't exist for me until I'd told you about them. Everything was for you: writing, arithmetic, Elli, all the stories. I remember sometimes I had the impression you were a word written by me, changing and growing like plants in the garden, and I was so proud of you and of us! I almost understood that part of the Word where Elli creates the world at the same time as the words. In a way, that's what I did when I told you about my day. I was trying to find the best way of teaching you, or of telling you about things. Take the Word: I tried dozens of different versions before coming up with one you could understand. I explained it to myself in dozens of different ways to find a meaning you could accept.

Is that it? You would have liked me to let you learn for yourself? You didn't want to be my Word, my story, Tula?

I remember the night I showed you my circular magnifying glass. I had spent every free minute that day perfecting my twist of the wrist. I spun the glass on its edge. "Look!" I said. I thought you'd understand right away—it was so obvious to me. But all you saw was a circle of convex glass spinning on the floor. I explained that it was like Elli, like Elli's first dance. After inventing it, Elli dances so ardently that Elli becomes two—but in reality Elli dances with Elli's reflection in space. You looked at me sulkily, the way you did when something was beyond you. I spun the glass again. It looked like a twinkling sphere with the dull strip of the circumference trembling slightly somewhere in the middle and on the edge. I'd spent the day describing it to myself so I would understand it well enough to tell you. Of course Elli can't touch Ilshe without making Ilshe disappear, since this is an image of Elli, not a real person, a person who exists. That's why Elli decided to make real people, the first woman and the first man, who would in turn dance and populate the world.

As for you, you grabbed the glass as it was spinning and marveled at its properties, at being able to see the lines in your skin jump out at you. After that you asked me to show you how to spin the glass, and I thought you'd understood: to dance, run, turn, move so quickly that you see yourself as another, as a double! Like you and me, identical, together in the light but in two different bodies.

You shrugged, trying to spin the glass. "I'm not a boy," you said, but that wasn't what I meant at all! I was talking about us. Anyway, boys weren't important. Elli created the woman first and only afterward the man, because of the symmetry. Men weren't important, since Elli had decided to make fewer boys than girls. The story of the punishment because of the apples was a little awkward, though. If today's boys weren't to blame, why didn't Elli reestablish the initial symmetry of creation? The only answer I could come up with was that boys really weren't important, nor were men. While I was explaining all that, I lost track of what was left of my intuition about the magnifying glass. To tell you the truth, I can't really remember what it was now. I remember the flash of intuition the first time I spun the glass. Perhaps I'd already lost it when I began to share it. It was the memory, not the moment itself.

Not the moment itself. That's what you would have liked? To live the very moments, at the same time as I lived them? To live your own moments, not mine? Did you end up resenting me because you felt I was stealing something from you? But you were the one who asked, who insisted we meet every night and that I tell you everything! Don't you remember? You were the one who convinced me. "I'll go outside the dormitory," you said. Those were your words exactly. "I won't go to sleep and I'll go outside the dormitory." I was a bit scared, because I realized better than you what it involved. But you convinced me. I obeyed you then as always. I was always the one who did what you wanted—don't you realize that? I always did what you wanted and you punished me?

5

Lisbeï hadn't told Tula everything. She hadn't said she would have to leave the garderie one day, before Tula. She hadn't wanted to share the anguish. Much later, it occurred to her that Tula suspected as much and had waited for her to say something, that maybe her silence had been taken for an admission of future abandonment. As the days and nights slipped by on the ground floor, Lisbeï continually staved off the moment of telling Tula. Perhaps because she saw no explanation: there must surely be a world beyond the garden wall, but there was no gate. How did people get in or out? If she left the garderie, she could certainly get back the same way—or so she said to herself, but it was a hollow promise: the absence of a gate mesmerized her. She didn't even dare ask subtle questions about it, for fear the gardianas might give some irrevocable answer and it would be impossible to see Tula once she'd left. Only much later would she learn how mostas left the garderie.

One afternoon she felt weighed down with fatigue. During reading class she wanted to put her head down on her arms and fall asleep. Her own and the other mostas' voices seemed very far away as they read out the words on the big slate board. She wondered lazily if she were sick, but the weariness was so great that the thought didn't even frighten her. Maybe she'd stayed too long with Tula the night before and hadn't slept enough. It was so hot in reading class! Her body felt far away, too, and her fingers fumbled as she tried to undo the top buttons of her tunic. Slowly, she waved her slate to cool her face, aware of Faï's voice asking her something . . . the other mostas turning to look. She tried to answer, but nothing came. She was toppling into sleep, sinking into a cotton-wool silence where all was still.

Red. That's what she remembered later on. Red, every shade and tint, from deep scarlet to a translucent, shimmering white touched with pink. After a while the silence was replaced by an incredible sonority. How could she describe the sounds? More than anything they resembled the little irrigation streams that ran all night long between the plants in the garden, sometimes one drop at a time, sometimes cascading over the small rocks and bubbling up in eddies. But there was also a constant sizzling, at times like sparks, at others like the sound of oil sputtering in a red-hot skillet. Through it all came the sustained double beat of a drum, accompanied by the thwack of a door slamming back and forth in the wind. All these sounds combined to delineate a landscape, a space at once fluctuating and fixed, immense yet strangely circumscribed, where she could move but knew not how. She had no idea where she was, what she was: she was both here and elsewhere. . . .

When she awoke, it was to feel a hand on hers, to sense a faintly luminous presence. Could it be Tula? A voice said, "She's awake." Another voice said, "How can you tell? I don't see any difference." This voice was familiar, a name rose slowly from Lisbeï's torpid memory: Mooreï. And then the other voice answered, "I know, that's all."

Lisbeï made a gigantic effort and lifted her eyelids slightly. Through the lashes she could see a white splotch above a blue splotch, a face above a body, and farther away another splotch, red this time, a whole body. Mooreï. Lisbeï's eyes returned to the closer face: a smooth skin, deep black eyes beneath short golden-brown hair, a curved but unsmiling mouth. It was the glimmer of this stranger's light that smiled, as did her voice when at last she said, "Welcome to the land of the living, Lisbeï. You'll never be sick again."

This wasn't a total stranger. Lisbeï caught at a hazy memory: it was the blue gardiana in the infirmary, the night that Tula . . .

The name "Tula" drew her from her torpor, but the blue gardiana stopped her from sitting up. She had slept a long time, and now she must regain her strength before getting out of bed.

"A long time?" croaked Lisbeï. "How long?"

"Six days," said Mooreï. "A record."

Lisbeï didn't care. Six days, six nights, and Tula must have waited and waited! She fell back on the pillow in despair, only to ask when she could leave, weakly irritated to find her voice almost uncontrollable.

"You can leave in three or four days, when you've got your strength back," said Mooreï. There was a short pause. Mooreï, her tone different and curiously expectant, added, "And you're a big girl now, Lisbeï. You won't be going back to the garderie."

Lisbeï was too weak even to try to hide her horrified disbelief. The blue gardiana bent over her and murmured, "It's Tula, isn't it?" Impossible to deny it, not with the gardiana's hands clasped over hers, not with their interchanging lights.

"You see?" said the gardiana. She was speaking to Mooreï now, as though Lisbeï had replied to her question.

"But Tula couldn't know—" said Mooreï, amazed.

The blue gardiana turned to Lisbeï. "I'm going to see Tula now. I'm going to tell her you're awake."

In her voice, as in the faint murmur of her luminescence, Lisbeï heard something else, a promise, the assurance that the blue gardiana had guessed many things but would say nothing.

The blue gardiana was called Antonë and she was a Medicina. Twenty years old: she should have been a Red, but as she'd never been able to make babies, she was a Blue. She was a "peregrina," a Blue who went from Family to Family instead of staying at home. Lisbeï was a Green and a dotta. The mostas were Greens, too, but not dottas. It took Lisbeï some time to grasp the distinction. Normal Blues were usually over thirty-five, and they couldn't make babies because they had no more seeds. Only Reds could be "mothers," babie-makers. They were also called "genitrixes." Words, categories, hierarchies—the answers multiplied with dizzying speed on this side of the garderie wall. Most of the time Lisbeï couldn't tell which questions fitted with the answers people let drop in such a matter-of-fact way. The people thought they were explaining things, but mainly they revealed to Lisbeï the depth of her ignorance.

From now on the world was called Bethely. For the first few weeks, however, this new world was confined to the West Tower. There she learned the rules, the places where dottas were allowed to go and how they could get there. Lisbeï sighed with relief each evening as she found herself in her bed on level three of the West Tower. "24-E-3" stated the mysterious laundry mark on all the things that had been handed out to her. "Room Twenty-four, East Wing, Level Three," said someone carelessly, in answer to her question. There in the dark she could catch her breath and sort out her day by recounting to herself what she had learned, what she had understood, what she had not known before and must learn tomorrow or some other day. This ritual was somehow comforting. It was her way of being with the absent Tula, of talking to her, and she explained Bethely to herself in the words she would have used to explain it to Tula. "You see," she would say to the silence that she called Tula, "there is the Tower— the Towers, because there are three the same. Each is like . . . a big square cake, very tall, with layers of workshops and storerooms between layers of bedrooms. On top, like icing, is the roof with the big tanks of water heated by the sun." Down the middle of the cake, she'd say, a mouse has gnawed holes— a big, vertical hole for the "elevator" (reserved for heavy loads and wheelchairs, and strictly forbidden to the dottas). It would have to be a really big mouse, of course, to make a hole large enough for an elevator, or the hole containing the main stairs that corkscrewed around it. There were other holes all over the place, sometimes between only two or three levels. Some of them were just for ladders with well-waxed, narrow wooden treads. They made it possible to move around inside the Towers by a series of labyrinthine routes. (Later Lisbeï would explore them, her delighted curiosity tinged with anxiety.) The levels were divided into four segments by corridors, each ending in glass doors opening onto outside staircases— spirals or zigzags of delicately carved stone for the first three levels, then light wooden stairs that vibrated underfoot. Lisbeï ventured onto these very warily at first. Real cattewalks connected the Towers—South, East, and West—but these carefully maintained metal structures were for emergencies only, and strictly off-limits for dottas.

There were a lot of rules about how you moved around

inside the Towers. Fire drill, for example, took up a whole page in the precious little book given to the new dottas. It also contained simple maps of the Towers. Then there were the unwritten rules, the first being, as usual, not to ask too many questions.

Lisbeï's situation had been somewhat singular from the start. Not having left the garderie with Meralda and the rest, she'd missed the brief introductory ceremony and the orientation class that followed. Nevertheless, she'd been assigned to the customary "tutress," along with two unfamiliar Greens. You had to be old to be a tutress, twelve. Lisbeï's tutress was called Majda. She had short, reddish-blond pigtails, green eyes, and a wealth of freckles.

"I'm a real Bethely," said Majda, laughing but obviously pleased. This statement puzzled Lisbeï until she discovered Bethely wasn't just the Tower, the Towers, workshops, gardens, orchards, pastures, and fields, but also all the people who lived in the Towers (and on the "Farms" in the countryside). Bethely was the name of the "Family," the name of the "Line."

"So I'm not a real Bethely," muttered a disappointed, dark-haired Arië, another of the dottas entrusted to Majda.

"What about me?" queried the third Green, a shy, flaxen-haired childe named Lila, who limped because of a malformed leg.

Lisbeï said nothing, but thought painfully of Tula's red hair and flawless white skin.

"You're Bethelies, all the same," said Majda. "It depends on genes, and it's rather complicated. You'll learn all about it soon enough!" (This oft-repeated formula was a signal to stop asking questions.) Of course, Lila and Arië then turned to Lisbeï with her black hair and brown skin. They were puzzled. Was she a "ward"? One of those dottas whom Families exchanged? No, said the tutress, Lisbeï was a Bethely, too. Perhaps her mother resembled Majda's, or maybe Lisbeï looked like the male.

Majda knew her mother? She knew which tummy she'd grown in?

Lisbeï's way of putting it produced surprise and a little derision. Well naturally!—Majda's mother was called Maralie and worked in the blacksmith shop.

Majda imparted this information with a shrug, unaware that she had plunged Lisbeï into an abyss of uncertainty. It had been disturbing enough to find out that a childe needn't resemble her mother! What of the apple and the seeds story, in that case? Or the story Lisbeï loved to tell Tula, about the little mostas they would give each other when they were big enough to exchange seeds? And now to learn that a childe could take after a *male*? It simply didn't make sense.

For several days after this Lisbeï couldn't help looking at every Red she passed, whether in a corridor, on the stairs, or in the Tower's commonroom (as the refectories were called on this side of the wall). Which tummy had she grown in? Lisbeï sensed this was one of those unaskable questions, not because "she'd soon learn," but because it didn't matter. But how could it possibly *not* matter? Weren't beginnings always important? The first part of the Word was nothing but a long description of the First Beginning!

When, for at least the tenth time, Lisbeï nearly fell downstairs because she was eyeing a potential mother, an exasperated Majda asked what on earth was wrong with her. Lisbeï, still shaken by her close call, muttered that she was trying to see if she could find her mother. Lila and Arië began to chortle. Lisbeï tried to backtrack, smarting at their reaction. "The Instructions say we have to call all Reds and Blues 'mother,' so I . . ."

Majda sighed. "It's just a polite formality, Lisbeï." She looked very much the gardiana, condescending and resigned. "In a way, all the dottas within a Family are the childeen of all Reds and Blues. That's why they're called dottas. Not 'girl,' meaning a future woman, but 'dotta' meaning descended from a mother. That's also why we call the Capta of Bethely 'Mother.' " Lisbeï could sense the respectful capital *M*.

There was a capta more important than the captas of each level, above the kitchen captas or the garden captas. *The* Capta of all Bethely. She lived on the same floor as Majda and her three charges, and her name was Selva, but people always called her "Mother." If ever you did anything really bad, you had to appear before her, and it was very, very serious. How did she punish people? Majda laughed and replied that she'd never had to appear before the Mother, but (she lowered her voice and her three pupils instinctively drew closer) it was said that once Selva had sent someone away from Bethely, someone who'd got into a fight and hurt someone else, and she'd made her go and be with the *renegadas* in the *badlands*.

As usual, Majda gave no explanation for these terms.

They were but a few of the many enigmas tossed out each day, little pebbles strewn along paths that seemed to have neither beginning nor end. Sometimes Lisbeï despaired of ever knowing all the things she was supposed to know. At other times, after a day especially rich in revelations, she felt she simply had to listen, watch, and wait—three admonitions constantly echoed by the tutresses and, to Lisbeï's more subtle senses, by the cumulative ambience of the Tower. Sooner or later Majda would unwittingly let drop the answer to the only question Lisbeï could have coherently formulated, the one question she didn't dare ask: how did you get to the garderie? For she had seen a garderie from an upper level, its white and ochre spiral standing in the center of the great garden with the high, gateless wall. But was it really hers? Theirs? And how did you get in? Lisbeï had been carried out of the garderie in her sleep, once Antonë had pronounced her free of the Malady coma. She had woken up in the West Tower infirmary without the slightest idea of how she got there.

There was another gnawing uncertainty: what had Antonë told Tula? Did Tula know she'd left the garderie, or simply that she'd woken up after the Malady? What had Tula thought in either case, and above all what would she do, fearless Tula?

Still, Lisbeï couldn't be forever fretting about these questions. Life in this new world was too full, too busy, demanding minimum—no, maximum!—attention. Lisbeï's head was so brimming with all these things that there was hardly room for her own concerns. In retrospect, those first days in the West Tower seemed to be a perpetual whirl. Curiously enough, this sensation of vertigo began to dissipate the day Majda took the three dottas into the great central court. The weather was warm and sunny. They stood there, heads thrown back, looking up at the thirty-story Towers, so high, so high, their summits lost in the small clouds . . . they were going to fall, they were falling! Arië threw up—to Majda's great embarrassment, since other tutresses were on hand to witness the revolting scene. Lisbeï, in order to stave off her own dizziness, had thought about the garderie moon and how it had seemed to race through the clouds even though it wasn't really moving as fast as all that. . . .

And suddenly, just when her dizziness vanished, she realized she had a magic formula: "like the garderie." But of course! Outside was just like the garderie! A bigger courtyard, many more floors, many more people—lots and lots of people, all at once, all the time, everywhere, blue tunics, red tunics, green tunics, old people, young people, greeting each other or passing silently by, opening and closing doors, empty-handed or loaded down with all kinds of things, all seeming to know exactly where they were or where they were going or what they had to do. It was exactly like the garderie, only a bigger version, that was all, just as the ground floor had been bigger than upstairs, and upstairs bigger than the nursery. Lisbeï felt herself slipping momentarily into the familiar progression: it was bigger beyond the hills and green pastures surrounding the three Bethely Towers, and beyond that it was probably even bigger still. But this idea, even more than the dizzying illusion of falling Towers, brought on genuine nausea, and she quickly thought about something else.

Like the garderie. The magic formula stayed with her even when it wasn't particularly relevant. It became her touchstone, her refuge, her compass, an incantation she took with her everywhere, to the point where one day she forgot herself and said it out loud.

Majda stared in astonishment. How could the weavery be compared to the garderies?

Lisbeï, who had seen only one garderie from the West Tower, jumped on this bit of information. So there were several garderies?

Of course, one per Tower.

"How do you go there?" queried Lisbeï, throwing caution to the winds.

"You don't *go* there!"

Majda's scandalized attitude alerted Lisbeï, but she couldn't stop, not when she was so close! "All right then, how do you *come* from the garderies?"

"By the basements, of course!" Majda was now clearly disconcerted by Lisbeï's insistence. She added, "Dottas aren't allowed in the Tower basements."

Basements—of course! Forbidden. Not even shown on their maps. You went to the garderies by the *basements!* That was why the wall had no gate. Lisbeï hid her jubilation and accomplished the day's tasks in a fog of euphoria. Now it was just a matter of deciding *which* garderie. If Lisbeï had been brought to the West Tower after her Malady, then Tula must be in the West Tower garderie, mustn't she? Actually, the direction of the sun confirmed this surmise. With her destina-

tion clear, Lisbeï had only to find the route. As in the
garderie, most people in the Tower were asleep at night, even
though you could hear voices in the corridors after the big
clock in the South Tower had struck ten times. (Those muffled, regular vibrations were what she'd heard at night in the
garderie.) Arië, who shared room 24-E-3, was an especially
sound sleeper. You had to shake her to make her wake up in
the morning. And just like the Garderie, all you had to do was
stay awake in the dark, open a door, flit through the deserted
halls and stairways. . . .

   And here are Mooreï and Antonë coming back, very
tired and very late, from the infante infirmary in the west
garderie, where one more mosta won't see the sun rise,
Mooreï and Antonë climbing the stairs from the forbidden
basement, the stairs that Lisbeï is coming down on tiptoe.

6

Antonë to Linta

Bethely . . . when? Ellième? 480 at any rate.

My distant one,
At last a letter from you—a wonderful New Year's present. Its
worth to me is not in proportion to its size. Forgive this (mild)
reproach, my sweet, but you must admit your letters have been
rather scarce these past months. I know you must be very taken
up with the babie you're expecting. I hope you're not too tired,
though. You don't say much about how you're feeling. Of course
the Family comings and goings are interesting and amusing, but
I'd mostly like to know how things are with you.

   What about here? Well—lots of things. Selva is pregnant
again, following her miscarriage in Austa. ("Normal," so to
speak: a fetus without a brain.) And yes (in case you ask), I still
want to be present at the birth of this babie. The boy who came

*after Tula was stillborn. It's important for me to know if this new
childe will have the same characteristics as the first two. (Childe
or child, you never know, despite the statistics.) Don't worry, I'm
not going to wait around until she or he has the Malady! What it
all adds up to is another seven months here if all goes well with
this pregnancy.*

*It's in the outlying communities that things are really hap-
pening. I've finally gained access to the Termilli Archives. The
ever-convincing Mooreï interceded on my behalf. Now that I
know the neighboring Families a bit better, I realize just how
"Progressista" Bethely is by comparison. They've surely not kept
the upper hand over the die-hard Believras and antediluvian Juddites surrounding them, just because of Bethely's historical and
religious importance. Generations of Mothers must have been
able politicians as well. The previous Mother was Cemmelia,
Mooreï's older sister and the genitrix of Selva. Cemmelia was a
woman to reckon with, judging from what they still say in the
Towers, and fairly close in outlook to the most obdurate Juddites.
Selva's childhood and adolescence can't always have been a
bed of roses.*

*To go back to Termilli, however: all things being equal, I
had the same results as in Bethely. So far, nothing has turned up
to refute my basic premise. In fact, certain developments here in
Bethely seem to corroborate it. Do you remember Lisbeï, Selva's
firstborne? Well, she is now Selva's first living childe and will
probably be the next Mother. Like us, she had the Malady fairly
late. As far as I can tell, the intensity of her—well let's say
"faculty," although I'm getting very fed up with these euphemisms—increased afterward. Her younger sister's faculty also in-
tensified; she even knew Lisbeï was ill, although they were no
longer on the same level of the garderie and hadn't seen each
other for several months. Interesting, isn't it?*

*Selva continues to chip away at tradition, discreet but deter-
mined. She had Lisbeï taken from the garderie once she'd recovered from the Malady last Novemra, well before her seventh
birthday. Her reasoning, borrowed from me, was, "Now she'll
never be ill again." At least I've convinced her of that. According
to what Mooreï told me, this is in some way connected with
Tula's reaction to Lisbeï's Malady, and vice-versa. When Selva
heard about Lisbeï's escapade during Tula's Malady, she decided
to ignore it, although now she wants to separate them as soon as
possible. I've never mentioned the subject, either to Mooreï or
Selva. Nevertheless, I get the feeling Mooreï suspects something*

and that Selva knows *something. I'm not yet intimate enough
with Selva to bring the matter up. She's not the most approach-
able person in the world. . . .*

7

Lisbeï could have loved Selva if Selva had wanted to be loved.
But Selva had other things on her mind. For years now, she
had sacrificed much in order to be worthy of her position as
Capta of Bethely. She wasn't sure she could afford regrets.

Selva had already stretched the rules of tradition for her
firstborne. By designating Lisbeï as future Mother before the
childe had shown her fitness for this honor, Selva was again
flouting tradition. If she had dared, she would have begun
Lisbeï's instruction earlier. Seven was very late to start training as a Capta. But Bethely's garderie tradition was too
deep-rooted to be easily overturned: the little mostas, the "al-
most-people," were relegated to the closed world of the garderies (that was the etymology of the word in Old Frangleï:
"almost"). Only the dottas were real people, "daughters" (offspring, really, and not necessarily female) who had rounded
the fateful cape of the seventh year and survived the maladies
of early childehood—and possibly the Malady itself. They
alone had earned the right to join the adult world and know
their Lines. On the dotta's eighth birthday, the mark of each
Line was tattooed on her, one per shoulder. That was a more
humane system, wasn't it? For everybody. The mostas lived a
tranquil life in the limbo of the garderies, untroubled by fear
of death—a word that didn't exist for them—because the gardianas had no fear and never cried when a little mosta returned to Elli.

Nor did the genitrixes grieve for childreen they didn't
know. They hadn't nursed them and had held them in their
arms only once, for official recognition before formally handing them over to the wet nurses. After that they never saw
their own babies, although they nursed others. The geography
of the Capterie and the work program made it impossible. If a
Red wanted to look after childreen, she could ask to be as-

signed as a gardiana. She would simply work in a garderie where none of her childreen were lodged. Why run the risk of becoming fond of your childreen, of making each illness a wound, each death a tragedy? So many little mostas died. Each Red knew this very well: out of the eight or nine babies brought to term during the average sixteen years of fertility, three would survive, on average. The figures didn't lie. It was better to entrust children to the garderies and wait until they came out—or didn't. Later you might come across them, depending on the layout of the levels or the vagaries of people's work assignments (you didn't *look* for your childreen—it just wasn't done). Affection, if it occurred at this point, would not be the result of habit as in Progressista Families. It would be a mutual choice.

But this didn't apply to the Capta's children, of course. Not the first-living. The future Mother of Bethely was a special case.

Selva had wanted to love her own mother, but Cemmelia had not wished to be loved. Cemmelia had had other priorities. For many years Cemmelia had sacrificed much to be Capta of Bethely. She had been certain she could afford no regrets.

At first, after Antonë had taken her back to her room, Lisbeï had been terrified. Then she began to think about what had happened. Mooreï hadn't asked any questions. Was it a bad or a good sign? Mooreï hadn't seemed angry, though, just tired and very sad. Antonë hadn't questioned Lisbeï either; she had sat down on the stairs and explained why the garderies were garderies. Antonë seemed angry, but Lisbeï felt the anger wasn't really directed at her. Perhaps her transgression wasn't so serious, after all. The dottas were forbidden to enter the underground areas, but it had also been forbidden to wander around at night in the garderie. She hadn't been punished the first time she'd tried to find Tula.

Lisbeï had almost succeeded in comforting herself when, after breakfast, an unknown Blue came to get her. As they mounted the staircase, Lisbeï summoned up the courage to ask where they were going. The Blue glanced severely over her shoulder. "To see the Mother."

Lisbeï's heart kept beating. Lisbeï's legs kept moving, carrying her up the stairs. Lisbeï's brain, after an initial explosion of panic, suddenly became very calm, much to her surprise. The worst had happened. She was going to see the Mother. She was lost. What more could happen to her now? And without any conscious decision, her mind very calmly began to imagine the meeting with the terrible Capta of Bethely. It was almost involuntary: someone in her head had taken control and was making up stories or rather a variable story about what might happen. Of course it was an exorcism, but also (although she only realized it later and never forgot it) a kind of training, a preparation.

The possible stories came in series of variants. In one of the series, Lisbeï admitted to having a guilty curiosity about the underground levels. Sometimes Selva punished her severely, sometimes not. But Tula's name was never mentioned, nor the reason why Lisbeï had been heading for the basements. Mooreï and Antonë had said nothing.

In a second, more painful series, the Capta knew everything. Twist and turn as she might, the storyteller in Lisbeï's head couldn't imagine a happy ending. Invariably, Tula was taken from her, never to be seen again, or in such a distant future that it hardly mattered.

At this point the storyteller's imagination and Lisbeï's relative state of calm vanished beneath a wave of sharp despair, followed by pain, then anger. So the Capta had once sent someone into the Badlands? All right, Lisbeï would *escape* to the Badlands. And she'd come back and take Tula away!

Oh really? How? The storyteller persisted, undaunted. Was there a sardonic note in her voice? Lisbeï's anger doubled; it felt better to be angry, you didn't feel as much pain. How would she do all this? Well! Well . . . she didn't even know where the Badlands were. As Lisbeï found herself plunging into a morass of mingled fury and utter helplessness, the Capta's door opened, and a firm, clear voice told her to come in.

The office was a small, dark-paneled room at the entrance to the Library, on the fourth floor. Dim light filtered through a large window of thick glass. A table of polished wood that served as a desk stood beside the window, covered with neat piles of papers and notebooks. Empty chairs waited on either side. The only other pieces of furniture were a lectern and a small stool in the shadows at the far end of the room. A huge book rested on the lectern.

Lisbeï took it all in at a glance, at the same time that she sensed the presence of the Capta behind her, closing the door.

As she sensed the presence behind her, approaching her, walking around her.

As she sensed the presence.

The light, the warmth, the resonance!

But not as with Tula. No real echo in response.

The Capta of Bethely walked quickly over to her desk and sat down, arms folded. She was a Red, of course. She seemed quite young, younger than Mooreï, but not so young as Antonë (Lisbeï could compare ages, now). Two tight, thick braids of russet hair encircled her head. Wisps of short hair escaped to make a halo against the light of the window. Her eyes were fixed on Lisbeï—green eyes, or gray, or blue, that glinted in her white, white face.

Lisbeï, who had spent an hour rehearsing how she would lie to the Capta of Bethely, blurted out, "Are you Tula's mother?"

And hung her head, cheeks burning, feeling as though she were sinking through the floor.

Silence, then a sigh. Lisbeï looked up. The Capta of Bethely was still staring at her. "Yes," she said finally. She didn't seem angry. "I am Tula's mother."

She folded her hands on the gleaming surface of the desk and leaned toward Lisbeï a little. "You were born in Juna, Lisbeï. Do you know how old you are?"

Before Lisbeï could figure this out, the Capta answered for her. "We're in Ellième. You're not yet seven, Lisbeï, not nearly. You should still be in the garderie. I made an exception for you. Do you know why?"

Dazed, Lisbeï could only shake her head vaguely.

"Because you are the future Mother of Bethely. The future Mother of Bethely is a very important person. Did you know that? She's got to learn lots of things to become a good Capta. You're going to have a lot to learn. These things aren't learned in the garderies."

That wasn't how it should happen! Terrified and at the same time fascinated, Lisbeï grasped at one of the remarks she'd prepared. "Tula has had the Malady, too. She could come out of the garderie now. It's not her fault."

This last remark had been intended for later, but it had slipped out. Better finish it. "You mustn't punish her, it's not her fault. It was my idea."

"I know," said the Capta of Bethely. Of course she'd know. "But you mustn't think of Tula anymore. Tula isn't the future Mother of Bethely. She must be seven before coming out. That's how it is in Bethely. If we make too many exceptions, they aren't exceptions anymore, are they? In any case, you're big now, you're a dotta. You'll have lots of things to do besides thinking about Tula."

There was something so horribly final in the Mother's calm, in her lack of anger, in the leaden certitude darkening her light, that Lisbeï suddenly began to cry. She tried to stop, overwhelmed yet furious: she hadn't meant to cry, not like this, not now! But the tears had a will of their own, rising from Lisbeï's breast and tearing at her with great, painful sobs. Why had they given her Tula, then? They shouldn't have given her Tula!

She became aware that she'd shouted when the Mother spoke again, her voice tinged with impatience this time. "Listen to me, Lisbeï. I'm the Capta of Bethely and the mother of Tula, but I won't see her either until she comes out of the garderie. I must wait, like you. I am the Mother of Bethely, and when you are a Red, you'll be Mother of Bethely in my place. The Mother of Bethely is the mother of everyone in Bethely, not just a few. And she rules in Bethely only because she obeys the law like everyone else."

Why did you make an exception for me, then? Lisbeï would have liked to say it, but she said nothing. The Mother had risen and walked over to her, and now she was squatting on her heels in front of Lisbeï and taking her hands. And there it was again—the light and the warmth, and especially the resonance this time, yes, the echo, just time to feel the Mother's sorrow, an immense, many-faceted sorrow too complex and too deep to be understood by a little dotta who wasn't even seven years old. Her sorrow—her compassion.

And then the shrinking away (in horror?) the sudden burst of violence, like a door slamming. For a brief moment Lisbeï felt nothing at all, as though no one were there.

But the Capta was there. She dropped Lisbeï's hands, stood up, and folded her arms. She looked at a point somewhere above Lisbeï's head. Her aura had changed: no more emotions, only this cold, stiff barrier. Rejection.

The Capta of Bethely walked over to the lectern, imperiously signaling Lisbeï to follow. She rested a hand on the big book. "Every day at ten o'clock you will come here, Lisbeï.

You know how to read, don't you? We'll begin with the History of Bethely. Have you understood?"

Lisbeï nodded mutely.

"Sit down."

Lisbeï went and sat down in front of the desk.

The Capta opened the door and an old Blue entered, carrying a tray covered with strange objects. The Blue put the objects on the desk, one by one. There were little vials and things that looked like penholders, and white compresses. The old Blue told Lisbeï to undo her tunic and bare her shoulders.

Lisbeï obeyed.

"This won't hurt much," murmured the old Blue.

"Lisbeï of Bethely-Callenbasch, our daughter and our sister in Elli," said the Capta coldly, not looking at Lisbeï, "welcome to our midst."

When Lisbeï left the Capta's office, she bore the marks of her Lines: the blue triangle with wavy yellow lines denoting Bethely, and the two small black stars, one lower than the other, inside a red square, the mark of Callenbasch. The old Blue had lied or else she had forgotten: it hurt. But not a cry, not a moan had escaped Lisbeï. She had stared straight ahead the whole time. The Capta had stood in front of her throughout the tattooing, arms folded. Lisbeï stared at the Capta's belly, invisible beneath the folds of the long red dress. The belly where Tula had grown.

Much later she would realize that during this first meeting Selva had never said she was Lisbeï's mother as well.

Lisbeï could have loved Selva. For years, however, she would have to be content with confused and revolving feelings of respect, admiration, and hate.

The Book of Bethely was very big and thick. It was bound in tawny leather and bore the gilded stamp of Bethely on its cover and spine. The pages were stiff and had to be turned slowly, with care and reverence, releasing an odor that Lisbeï soon linked with History and with knowledge in general: the smell of leather, ink, paper, glue, and especially of the pictures with their protective sheets of thin, rustling onionskin. Every once in a while there were printed pages. There were very old drawings, some of them rather awkward, then engravings, and as you went farther into the Book, a different kind of picture—blurred and yellowed, a kind of thick board held between two glued pages with a rectangle cut out. Later they weren't so thick and the images were sharper, with contrasting ochers and sepias: *photographs* (a word Lisbeï had difficulty spelling for a long time). They were exact reproductions of History, a piece magically torn from space and time, or so she thought at first.

The first lesson lasted for a long time. Selva had taken Lisbeï in her arms to lift her onto the stool in front of the lectern (the light was there, but all too brief, distant, and forbidden). And Selva began turning the pages and telling Lisbeï the story of Bethely. All the drawings, engravings, and photographs showed the same thing: the Towers, hard to recognize at first, but as the pages turned, they were transformed into their familiar selves. The ruins that first surrounded them disappeared, and there were fields, trees growing, trails becoming paths, then roads. Triangular palisades with walkways and turrets rose up and were dismantled. The earth walls on which they had stood spread into a mound. New palisades arose, only to disappear in turn. Grass covered the old earthworks, and animals grazed there—brown dots for the wicows, golden yellow for the ovinas. Now it was the familiar round, flat-topped hill with roads snaking this way and that, beyond which gardens and orchards spread in concentric rings. The porticoes running around the base of each Tower were recent additions, not visible in the first photographs. By contrast, the three aerial walkways linking the three Towers were old, and had already been visible in the drawings.

One, ten, twenty pages: twenty, a hundred, a hundred and fifty years, translated Selva. Like a calendar, thought Lisbeï suddenly. The pages kept turning: here was the central court being renovated, the porticoes growing bit by bit around the Tower bases, the outside staircases proliferating like spidawebs . . . and now it looked like Bethely. This was 368 years ago, at the time of Alicia, first Capta of Bethely.

Selva could very well have begun Lisbeï's education in some other way, or have used some other book of History. But she knew what she was doing. Her mother before her had done it.

History, mused Lisbeï that night as she lay in bed telling herself about her day. History was like stories, and like stories it was *true,* only in a different way. Just as the Word of Elli explained why the world existed, why there was something instead of nothing, so History explained why now existed, and how yesterday became now. Until this point, Lisbeï had thought vaguely that she and Tula had their origin in the belly where they had grown. These bellies, these "wombs," these mothers, had grown in other mothers, other wombs, and so on in a series stretching back to Elli. She used to think only people had origins. But here were places and things with origins of their own, inextricably bound up with the origins of people. That was History, too, a sort of huge, invisible womb just like Elli's. Or rather, inside the First Womb that was Elli's. The Word and History made a whole, with History making the chain of links between the first woman created by Elli and this young Red, mother of Tula and Lisbeï, severe, unapproachable, and powerful, the Mother of Bethely.

It was Selva who opened the Book, who opened History for Lisbeï, Selva who gave her Bethely (and soon, step by step, all of Maerlande). And was it not Selva who had created Tula for her, who had given her Tula in spite of everything? It was as though the movement set in motion by Tula's appearance, all those shiftings, meetings, and followings, had led inevitably to this little dark-paneled room where Lisbeï, the future Mother of Bethely, had only to take her place in an order of things beyond her understanding, but which had awaited her from the beginning of time.

Everybody (starting with Selva) seemed so quietly confident that things were just as they should be. How could Lisbeï, far from Tula, resist the invisible and constant pressure of all those presences—Bethely, the Family, the world? It was so reassuring to know who you were, what you had to do, where you were going. Now Lisbeï went about the Tower with new confidence, feeling a kind of vague but enveloping affection for everything she saw. Sometimes, when she was by herself, she would trail a hand along the wainscoting on the corridor walls, scrutinizing the mosaics, fingering and sniffing the curtains. One day she'd be the Mother, one day she'd be Bethely. The corridors, the rooms, the great staircase, the little hidden stairs, all of them formed one big body that would be the image of her own: a living body, breathing rhythmically—the first wave of workas going out into the dawn at six o'clock, the last at nine; the coming and going of the three sittings of each meal; the exodus of the afternoon workas and the cross-currents at the end of the day, when the last afternoon teams flowed in past the outgoing teams of the evening; and finally, at ten at night, the lingering voices in the corridors as the great body of Bethely settled down before sleep. . . .

And if Lisbeï wasn't already asleep, she could sometimes think of Tula without too much pain. Since she was studying with the Mother and the Memory, she was allowed to have a big notebook for her homework. Each night she filled sheets torn from the notebook with tiny handwriting, making the precious paper last as long as possible. She wrote down the important events of the day. Sometimes she copied down the workas' timetables or drew a detailed map of each Tower, level by level. Bethely was like the little puzzle box that helped you learn letters and figures in the garderie: you pushed wooden squares around, mixing everything up until you got the squares in the proper order, left to right and top to bottom, A-B-C-D, 1-2-3-4, the Levels, the hours, the days. . . . Bethely was merely a bigger puzzle box, and you moved yourself from space to space. The empty space, the one that allowed you to move around, was the garderie. You filled the empty space with different squares until everything was in order and the empty space stopped after the *Z* or the zero. The space was a door—a door through which (because Lisbeï had earned this reward) Tula would one day come. And when she came, Lisbeï would give her the secret journal. She'd give her Bethely, and since she, Lisbeï, was Bethely, Tula would know *her* as well. Tula wouldn't be angry because Lisbeï hadn't tried to reach her in the garderie no matter what. Tula would understand.

Lisbeï had indeed thought about sending messages to Tula. But how? Who would carry them? She couldn't risk taking another dotta into her confidence. Would Mooreï or Antonë do it? Too dangerous. After all, she had to admit they'd given her away to Selva already. She didn't blame them too much, now that she understood how impossible it was to arrange secret meetings with Tula. They were two years apart. They couldn't have seen each other in secret for two whole years! They'd been lucky in the garderie. Five months had been too short for anyone to have suspected anything. To try getting to Tula from the Tower, though . . . sooner or later she'd be caught and that wouldn't help anyone, would it? No, Tula would surely understand. Anyway, this was the unspoken pact between Lisbeï and Selva, or at least what Lisbeï imagined it to be: she would give up Tula for the time being, and in exchange she would have Bethely with Tula, later.

She tried not to dwell too much on what Tula might be thinking or feeling. When the sadness, the sense of helplessness, became too much to bear, she tried to find comfort in the thought that one day she would work up the courage to ask Antonë to speak to Tula. The young Blue seemed more likely to help her than Mooreï. One day she'd ask her, once she'd proved her good faith so well to them all that the Mother couldn't blame her for wanting to console Tula a little. Later. Time was on her side. The tide that had brought her Tula and then separated them would surely bring her back again. Time in fact was like a big staircase, thought Lisbeï as she gradually dropped off to sleep, just like the now silent, great body of Bethely. A big, predictable staircase, going toward tomorrow and tomorrow and knowing exactly what tomorrow would be. One day soon (she checked off the squares on the tiny calendar she had surreptitiously made), Tula would be seven, and then she'd come and be with Lisbeï. They'd stay together, of course, because they were both daughters of the Mother of Bethely. And then one day they'd become Reds, and Lisbeï would be Mother of Bethely, and they'd make their babies together and never, never be parted.

8

Lisbeï/Journal

Bethely, 4 Fevra, 480 A.G.

It's like always-bigger boxes. Remember? Smaller-bigger? The smaller box goes inside the bigger box: the nursery, second level, and ground level go into the garderie, and the garderie into the garden, and both of them into Bethely. Bethely is the three Towers, but also the space around them. The family has Farms *farther away. That's our name for Offshoots. When a family has too many people, some are taken away to live in another place. That place is an Offshoot. The Towers plus all the Farms add up to the territory. It's very clear when you look at the map in the Book. So imagine yet another box: Bethely in the territory. And guess what? It keeps on going! The Family's territory is in a bigger place called "Litale." That's a* Province. *And Litale is in a bigger territory called* Maerlande. *Litale is full of other Families (but not in Towers) with other territories, and there are Families in other Provinces, too. All together they make Maerlande.*

The other Provinces are Escarra *in the South and* Bretanye *in the Northwest. Even farther to the North there's* Baltike. *And way in the East are the* Badlands. *No one's allowed to go there, because they make you get sick and die. But really bad people, renegadas, get sent there. The tattoos are taken off their shoulders—that is, they're covered up with a black tattoo, and they're sent to the Renegada Traverse. Look on the map I've drawn, and you'll see where it is. I've drawn the points of the compass for you (that's a cross showing North/South and West/East instead of up/down and left/right on maps). I copied it from the book—not the Book of Bethely, of course, but another one, the* geography *book. Geography is how you find where you are when you're traveling outside. It's really useful. But the Mother says we have to learn about History first, and that it's more important. (Traveling in time, you see.) Because the Maerlande on the map hasn't always been here. I mean, the map hasn't always looked the way it does now, and that's because of History, not geography.*

It's just more boxes. Think of it like that: Maerlande, then before Maerlande, then before-before. Before Maerlande there were the Hives. *Before-before the Hives, there were the* Harems. *There was something else before that, but it was a long, long time ago, and anyhow it wasn't at all good, worse even than the Harems and Hives, and there isn't much left, even less than the Harems, so we can't tell what it was really like. There aren't any pictures of it in the Book, anyway. And yet the Book goes back a long way. Wait—it's easier if I write it in numbers: 584 years. The Book itself isn't 584 years old. It would be all in tatters. But there are pictures and stories in it telling what it was like in Bethely 584 years ago, and since that time.*

The Hives. Well that's funny, because we still have hives in Bethely. But those are little houses for bees to live in. (I bet you didn't know bees had houses too! Neither did I.) The Hives, written like this with a big H, *were different. That was Bethely's name before it was a "Capterie." It was called "the Hive of Bethely." There weren't really any bees, but it worked like a hive,* with a Queene and a whole lot of workas (but they didn't work all the time). Now the Queene is called the Capta, and she isn't as wicked as the Hive Queenes because of the Carta. The Carta means the rules for all Bethely. There's a Carta for Maerlande, too.

Did you know the Queenegarde game comes from that? From the Queene, I mean. You see, in the time of the Hives, if you couldn't answer the riddles properly, they cut off your head. The Dungeon comes from the Hives as well. That's why you need boys to play. They used to fight *for* boys! Can you imagine? There weren't many boys then, either. The Mother and Mooreï say boys are very useful. Majda too. What for, I wonder? But that's something I'll learn about later. I'll tell you, of course.

The Hives were very, very bad. They were women, but they fought other women, they even killed them. (Kill means make someone die, go away and never come back. Like the infirmary. Except the infirmary doesn't kill you, only maladies and the Malady, as I told you. It's very sad, but that's the way things are, and we can't do anything about it.) Anyway, if the women were so bad, it was really the fault of the Harem Chiefs. They'd seen the Chiefs do bad things, and they just copied them. They didn't have Elli to guide them. They didn't really want Elli. It was a long, long time ago, and life was very hard, so all the people were hard as well.

That's why the Hive women killed a lot and—even worse—burned books! Then the Juddites rebelled, and Maerlande took the place of the Hives. It seems that many, many people died then, too, especially the bad ones in the Hives.

We don't know much about the Harems, as I told you. A lot of women were beaten by the "barbarian Chiefs." And just think: the Chiefs were men! (A Chief was sort of . . . like the Mother, the main Capta.) But men were different then. Like fierce beasts. The women were "slaves." That means they were like objects, that they worked all the time and had no right to do anything else. The Mother said this period is really hard to understand. I agree! Anyway, in the end the women got fed up, and they took the place of all the Chiefs in the Chefferies and started the Hives period. But there had been Garde at the end of the Harems to show the women how to make peace.

Garde is difficult to explain. I don't think she's like the Queenegarde. She's someone else, a real person. She got between the Harems and the Juddites who wanted to stop the Harems, and asked them to make peace. She was very brave and very good. They killed her—I mean the Harems killed her. But she came back. She hadn't died the first time and she came back. Wait—yes, she was dead the first time, but she came back anyway, and then she died again and came back. Twice. I know that sounds funny, she couldn't be dead and alive at the same time, but that's the way it was. It's a mystery, Mooreï said. Something that's really hard to understand. Like Elli, who is all and nothing, remember? It's kind of like that.

Anyway Garde came back and showed them how to make peace once again. But the Harems wouldn't believe she was the Daughter of Elli, you see. Not the real Daughter of Elli, not as old as that. We know it's true, though, because she died and came alive two times. And also because she brought us the Word. Garde is the one who taught us the Word, and we know it's the truth, because she came back after being dead. It's in the Book of Bethely because Garde was killed and resuscitated (that means she came back or was born two times) right here in Bethely. Some people say we can't be really sure about this, because her Compagnas have never been found. They were walled up in underground passages, but no passages have ever been discovered underneath Bethely. But that doesn't matter: Hallera clearly says that Garde was resuscitated two times in Bethely.

Who is Hallera? She's the only Compagna who wasn't walled up. She escaped and kept on talking about Garde during the time when the Hives were bad to Elli's disciplas. When the Hives ended, her daughter gave all her papers to the first Capta of Bethely, Alicia, and then people realized that Garde was truly the Daughter of Elli, and they really accepted the Word and everything. Bethely is the first Capterie. I mean, it was the first Capterie. Maerlande (that means the land of the Mothers) started right here. We even count our time starting with Garde. This year is 480 After Garde. We write it "A.G." Every year since the beginning of A.G. there has been the Pilgrimage of Garde. That's when a lot of people come here to think about Garde together and to pray. It's a lot of trouble for Bethely, but we've got to put up with it because Garde died and came back to life here two times. No one knows where she went afterward. I think she must have gone back to Elli.

9

Lisbeï/Journal

What would it have been like without you in the garderie? Ylene isn't like us, nor is Sanra. Everything would have been different.

    But I'm talking nonsense: it couldn't be different. The agreements with Belmont to take a Red from their Family as Selva's second Male had been signed before I was born. There would have been another one like you, in any case. (But what if she hadn't lived? Before Ylene and Sanra, all Selva's other babies died. No—I can imagine you nonexistent, Tula, but not dead.)

    I wrote an awful lot about the other sisters in my journal. I was . . . knocked for a loop, as they say. But curious as well. "You and me, nobody else." That's what you told me in the garderie. But there had been others, although they died. Others in Selva's womb, our womb. I remember as though it were yesterday the moment I learned this. It was hot, and I was in the bakery. We were making bread—do you remember the smell of yeast? I'd been kneading doughballs for at least two hours. Selva came into the bakery wearing a light tunic, something she hardly ever did. I noticed her large belly, and suddenly, as I listened to what the others were saying to her and what she was answering, I realized there was a babie growing in her womb. She tasted the dough, I remember, and laughed. She had pushed a wisp of hair off her forehead and left a bit of flour on her face. Someone wiped it off while talking to her. It must have been Torina, the oldest capta-cook. I don't suppose anyone else would have dared. Selva looked so young all at once. I remember thinking that she must once have been a dotta and a mosta like us: that was the first time the idea came into my head. Then she saw me and she put on her mask again. I stood there punching my doughballs fiercely, with Torina scolding, "Not so hard—at least leave some air for the bread to breathe!"

*Another childe, not just us in Selva's womb. I felt very
queer. As though I'd been betrayed, of course, but mostly it was
the thought that there might already be others in the garderies. Or
in the Towers. I knew who to ask—Antonë, as usual—but I
wasn't sure I wanted to. Finally the subject came up in conversation, but with Mooreï. "No, you haven't any other sisters yet." I
don't know whether I was relieved or disappointed. I noted down
the word "sister" in my journal, in any case. It's not a word often
used in Bethely. But we're only half sisters—like everyone else, in
fact. There are no real "sisters" in Bethely, since the only person
who can make them is the Mother, and Selva has chosen not to
have two consecutive children with the same Male. It was a
radical decision intended to resolve any future problem, or so I
suppose she believed. She hadn't counted on the light. (I'm still
using that word, after all this time! But I prefer it to any other. It's
as true a description, perhaps more profoundly so, as any of the
scientific labels used by Antonë or Kelys. It's the word I taught
you, our word for what united us in the days when you accepted
it. . . .)*

*I remember that when Antonë finally told me how babies
were made, I burst out laughing. She asked why. I was as much
surprised as indignant: Turri and Rubio hadn't been so far off the
mark, when you come right down to it. The mothers didn't make
babies all by themselves? How shocking! I was quite ready to
accept Selva as a third party between you and me, but this was
too much! At the same time I was pleased: I hadn't done badly
at understanding the Word of Elli. That story of the first woman
and the first man who populated the world had always been a
stumbling block for me. Men—these boys gone to seed—just
couldn't be that important. But now the fog began to lift. At least
my idea of symmetry had been right. "The woman / And the
man." Each one being a half of Elli, and each giving half of
herself in the form of seeds that danced together, that fused to
produce a whole person, another girl or another boy, who in
turn. . . . It was another kind of order, and I rather liked that.
And the main thing was that, even if the mothers didn't make the
childreen all by themselves, they were still the only ones who
could grow babies in their wombs! You didn't need a lot of males,
either, since only their seeds were important. Just a few males
could produce enough for Bethely in each Service period.*

*The Service—well, that was not so easy. I had a hard time
explaining it to you, and to myself as well. Antonë was never very
good at making things simple. She had too much respect for*

accuracy, and given the choice between a good story and sticking to hard facts, she would always opt for the facts. She's never been able to admit that a good story is sometimes a better way of getting the facts across, until such time as the listener is ready to swallow them without the sauce! She thinks everyone has an iron stomach like hers. Fortunately, I was never at a loss in the story department, as you well know: I rearranged the facts to suit myself, so that I could explain them to you. The males in each Family had to be changed regularly because the seeds of the mothers and males didn't blend just anyhow. Some weren't compatible and produced defective children (the males' fault, naturally). In order not to make mistakes in bringing seeds together, the new dottas had the marks of their Lines tattooed on each shoulder.

Antonë got rather bogged down trying to give a detailed explanation of the laws of genetics to a dotta barely seven years old. Mooreï, in contrast, showed me genealogical trees in the Book of Lines. All those trees with little rectangles instead of leaves, containing the marks of the Lines with the names of the mother and the genitor . . . (That was the day I learned you wouldn't have the same mark as mine on your right shoulder, since you were a Belmont.)

What fascinated me was the idea that if you ran your finger down a branch to the trunk, and down the trunk to the root, you could find your whole Line. Not as far down as Elli, because that was too far. (And was it in the earth—not in the sky? But Elli was the earth and the sky, Mooreï reminded me.) Even the first woman and the first man were too far . . . Oh well, Tula, at least your story and mine figured in the genealogical trees. And these stories were History with a capital H. *I was thrilled. Everyone's most personal story was at the same time part of the story of all the people who had come before. The seeds within me, although they wouldn't be ripe for years and years, held a little of the seeds of all the women of my Line. I touched my belly with somewhat awed respect. Being a Mother of Bethely also meant carrying the seeds of all the Mothers of Bethely. . . . And of Selva, too? How strange to think I had something of Selva in my belly!*

But after that, Mooreï left the technical details to Antonë. Oh, the drawings in the anatomy book! I tried to describe them to you like a map, do you remember? It didn't work very well, and no wonder. Also I found the whole thing . . . embarrassing. The male's seeds went in there? Through the little hole be-

tween our legs, right near the place where we made each other happy? To think that Turri and Rubio had been right, even half-right, was already too much. The male made the seeds come out of his pipe. They were collected, and someone injected them right away into several Red women with a syringe. It was called insemination, and Antonë tried to reassure me that it didn't hurt at all. But I wasn't convinced, and every time I thought of the syringe, I pressed my thighs together.

"Anyway," said Antonë, "the Mother doesn't make her children like that, she makes them directly with the Male." At which point there was a now-familiar blink in her light that meant, "Uh-oh—I've gone too far again." And she promptly sent me off to see Mooreï. For once Mooreï couldn't really simplify things. This was no knitting matter! It involved the very basis of faith in Elli, concerning a subject that came within a hair's breadth of the mysteries of the Celebration. One mustn't forget how the first woman and the first man had given birth to the human race, according to Elli's wish. Even if there aren't enough males now. (Another of Elli's wishes? Rather contradictory, Elli. But I didn't dare say so to Mooreï then, and I'm not sure I even thought it.) Anyhow, each Family had one Red who made her children in this way, with a male, and she was the Mother. It was one of her duties. Because Elli had divided Elliself in two at the Beginning to create the woman and the man, the Mother and the Male would briefly recreate Elli by somehow coming together again in the Dance at the Celebration. (Mooreï and her "somehows"!) Well, somehow it happened, and it was a great honor and a great joy for both the participants.

What bewildered me, I remember, was that Antonë appeared convinced she'd said something different from Mooreï, when it seemed to me they were really talking about the same thing. Mooreï laughed and was pleased with me, explaining that words have precious but strange attributes. "Sometimes the same word has different meanings for different people. Sometimes different words really mean the same thing. And sometimes different words mean different things; it would be too easy otherwise." Then she added, "What matters most to Antonë is the how. For me, it's the why."

Mooreï left me to figure out her whys and Antonë's hows for myself. But even Mooreï could be wrong—she'd imagined I thought like her, preferred her approach. But it wasn't a question of taking sides: I combined their points of view instead of keeping

*them separate, and saw the same story told in two different ways,
the how by Antonë, the why by Moorei.*

*I should have paid more attention, shouldn't I, Tula? I
should have remembered Moorei's remark. I might have realized
later that you and I were using the same words, but that we
weren't really talking about the same things any longer.*

10

"Elli's snowing!" The cry echoed through the Towers early in
the morning. It was an event: dottas and workas could leave
their tasks for a moment without being scolded and go to the
windows to look at the strange white world.

Lisbeï had never seen snow. For a while she ran around
the courtyard with the other dottas, arms outstretched, face
upturned, tongue stuck out to catch the flakes, but now she
was standing underneath the West Tower portico wondering
how she would describe snow in her notebook. Tula must be
able to see it too; perhaps she'd been out in the garden with
the other mostas, but no matter: Lisbeï had already become
accustomed to recounting her day in the notebook, even
things that Tula could have experienced herself. Snow was like
. . . like the sky falling on the earth. Not a bit like rain—with
rain you saw the clouds most of the time, and sometimes you
could even see the rain falling from a particular cloud, moving
like a slow curtain. Snow came at you from all directions, not
from anywhere special. It seemed to just happen, to come out
of the air instead of the sky, as though the air—that space you
could never touch—had decided to show itself for a while. But
although snow was solid enough when you looked at it (fascinating lace crystals loomed large in the magnifying glass that
Lisbeï now carried everywhere), it was so fragile. Just a touch,
and it melted.

Lisbeï recognized Selva's voice and instinctively hid behind a pillar. She must be late for her lesson, and Selva was
looking for her! But no. Wrapped in a fur-collared cape, despite the fact that Elli wasn't all that cold, the Mother had

come to look at the snow with Mooreï and Antonë. She had spotted Lisbeï. But she was smiling.

"How pretty it is," Selva remarked.

"Snow in Decemra!" Mooreï looked concerned. "In Bethely such a thing has never been recorded! We're down on the plain here."

"The climate is changing," said Antonë. "It's fairly clear when you look at the weather statistics for the last hundred years or so. I read several articles about it in Wardenberg. You might expect it in Termilli, where it's much higher. They've had two or three snowfalls each wintra for the last few years. In any case, judging by the abundant physical evidence and the oldest books, the climate in this part of the continent used to be colder. It's slowly returning to what it was."

"If this keeps up, we may have to think of its effect on plants and the things we grow," Mooreï mused.

"We'll develop other kinds of plants," countered Antonë. "Surely the process will be gradual, nothing like the upheavals of the Decline. We'll have time to get ready."

Selva was frowning slightly. "It might be as well, just the same, to bring up the question at the next Assembly. Could you help Mooreï prepare a dossier on the subject, Antonë?"

"Certainly."

Selva turned back to the courtyard. The snow had chilled the flagstones now and was beginning to accumulate instead of melting. "But it is pretty," she murmured, "so different."

"What's the Decline?" asked Lisbeï, gliding over to Antonë. With Antonë you had to strike while the iron was hot.

"It was long, long ago. Long before the Harems. There were lots of changes in those days. The climate changed everywhere, and here it got hotter. A lot of ice melted, and the level of the seas and oceans rose. There were vast floods. The world was very different before the Decline."

Just at that moment a big, blond dotta ran up, out of breath: two cavalieras were coming from the direction of Cartano.

They were already quite near: you could see them on the road winding through the apple orchard at the West Gate. Mooreï and Selva gave off a different feeling now, more tense. Antonë drew Lisbeï aside, close to the pillar, so that the Capta and her Memory could welcome these visitas properly. Lisbeï, as she watched the cavalieras enter the courtyard, asked Antonë, "Are they the new males?"

"I don't think so. They usually have more of a retinue than this."

But Antonë seemed preoccupied by the visitas, and Lisbeï decided to save her curiosity for another time.

The cavalieras stopped at the entrance to the West Tower, in front of Selva. Both figures were muffled in long capes that hid the emblems of their Families. Even their faces were hidden beneath the hoods, but when they alighted, a flash of blue showed between the folds of the first cavaliera's cape. She threw back the hood to reveal that she was indeed a Blue. She must be rather old, because she hadn't much hair on her head. Still, the face seemed quite young—a very ugly face, thought Lisbeï. Square, with thin lips and a lot of down-ward-pulling lines, especially where two deep folds ran from the sides of the nose to the corners of the mouth. And the skin was all rough and blotchy, with a funny, gritty look about the cheeks and chin. Or—yes, there were *hairs* beginning to grow there!

Lisbeï had no time to conjure up fearful thoughts of the Badlands and their Abominations. The other visita had thrown back her hood, too. The first Blue looked ugly, but this one appeared utterly alien to a young Bethely dotta. Perhaps it was the clothing: jacket, trousers, and boots in tawny, gleaming leather without a single color or Family emblem. Perhaps it was her height: she was slender and at least a head and a half taller than the ugly Blue, or Selva, or any of the others. And then there was her skin, smooth, unblemished, and black, really black. Bethely had all shades of brown, some of them quite dark, but nothing like this. The hair was black as well, crinkly and very short, hugging the outline of the small, oblong head. Could this be a male, Lisbeï wondered? No, it was just too different. . . . Could it even be a human being?

"Kelys!" said Selva. Her words held a rush of feeling, a mixture of surprise, joy, and relief. But the black head gave the faintest shake, and Selva seemed to subside. Nothing more was said. As though in unspoken accord, Selva, Mooreï, and the two visitas disappeared into the Tower. At the last moment Selva turned and beckoned Antonë, who followed the others into the entrance hall. Meanwhile the few dottas who had clustered around the visitas busied themselves with the cavalas, unsaddling them under the eye of one or two Reds and leading them off to the stables.

No one paid attention to Lisbeï. Quick as an arrow, she ran the length of the portico to the outside staircase that led to the back of the Library, and climbed as fast as she could to Level Four. She closed the many-paned glass door behind her and stood still a moment, panting as she brushed the snow off her hair and short cape. Then she went into the Library. As usual at this time of day, no one was there except the scribes —five big Greens who barely lifted their heads as she went by —and Tonia, the librarian for that semester, who answered her greeting absently. Once safely past these obstacles, Lisbeï began running again on tiptoe until she reached the map room, where a spiral staircase wound down to a third-floor storeroom, the first of a series opening into one another. They were filled with a jumble of things—archives waiting to be indexed or recopied, old paper for recycling, and various supplies. In the last storeroom was a steep ladder rising toward the ceiling, where a trapdoor opened into the room beside the Mother's office. Lisbeï sometimes used this shortcut on mornings when she was late for her lesson with Selva.

Lisbeï lifted the trapdoor silently, just far enough to peer around the room at floor level. Nobody. And the door to Selva's office was open! Luck was on her side. She pushed the trapdoor all the way up and crept to the door. Taking a chance, she glanced into the room.

Selva was seated, her profile three-quarters turned toward Lisbeï, reading a letter by the light of the gasole standing on her desk. She wore her bad-day air—days when Lisbeï knew it wasn't worth even trying to perceive her feelings, that an icy wall would block any attempt. A worried-looking Mooreï stood beside her. Antonë was a little to one side, silhouetted by the window. The ugly Blue was standing in front of the desk, hands clasped behind her back, legs slightly apart, waiting. Not only was she ugly: she didn't seem to have any waist, and the front of her blue shirt was absolutely flat beneath the triangular emblem of Cartano! The chair usually placed in front of the desk had been pushed back. The black creature was sitting in it, her body in a relaxed posture that contrasted strangely with all the others.

Selva finished reading the letter. Her expression hadn't changed. She handed the letter to Mooreï and folded her arms. Mooreï read it, and her face seemed to go all gray. She reached with her free hand for the back of the chair, as though she needed something to lean on. Nobody said a word.

After a while Mooreï murmured in a broken voice, "Oh, Elli!"

"Give Antonë the letter," said Selva. As Mooreï hesitated, Selva added sharply, "She's going to be our Medicina, she has to know."

Antonë took the letter and bent over beside the lamp to read. Her body stiffened and she gripped the paper, shaking her head as though she couldn't believe what she read. She threw the letter on the desk.

"Why didn't she say something?" she cried, her voice quivering. "Why didn't she speak at the last Assembly of Litale? Or even before?"

"She was a Bethely," said Selva, her tone cold yet vibrant, dangerous. "Bethelies don't complain."

At this moment a horrified Lisbeï felt a tickle rising in her throat, in her nose. She couldn't completely stifle the sneeze. There was a moment of general surprise, and then Mooreï walked over, grabbed Lisbeï by the arm, and pulled her over the doorsill.

Unbelievably, the Mother didn't even seem cross, but Lisbeï sensed that this was because her anger was too vast to be concerned with such trifles. "My first-living, Lisbeï," she said, vaguely sardonic, as though such an event was only to be expected.

The black creature unfolded itself and stood up in a single, fluid movement. The effect was hypnotic: an interminable body, so tall, so slim, sliding smoothly through the intervening space to kneel in front of Lisbeï, so that its dark face was almost on a level with her own. The creature didn't touch her. Its eyes were inky black in their perfect whites, the nostrils flared a little like an animal scenting danger, and its large, thick-lipped mouth opened to reveal teeth that were also very white—but this was a smile, and when the creature spoke at last, its tongue was very pink. "No, little Lisbeli, I'm not from the badlands. My name is Kelys. I'm a peregrina and an explora, and I come from a long way South where lots of people are more or less black like me. From Fusco. Do you know where Fusco is?"

Lisbeï stared back, speechless, neither surprised nor ashamed at having been caught out in her childish reaction of fear, but already conquered by that marvelous voice, slow and deep, a voice filtered through several layers of velvet, a voice she would always try to imitate from then on. And from then on she would never be able to separate this voice from Kelys's special presence—not a light, but a vast, ordered, peaceful emanation, different from any she had perceived until now.

"It's on the other side of the Tirannean Sea, near Lake Sahra," she said finally. Kelys nodded with a smile, and only then did she touch Lisbeï, a quick, cool caress on the cheek with the tip of a finger. She stood up.

Mooreï sighed. "Go now, Lisbeï."

"Why?" asked Selva. Everyone looked at her in surprise. She circled the desk, stopping in front of Lisbeï. "This is the future Mother of Bethely. She has the right to know—as much and more than the future Medicina. She won't be participating in Loï's dolore. Lisbeï, you love stories, don't you? At a dolore we tell stories about people who've died. I'm going to tell you a story.

"Once upon a time there was a Red who went into the Great Badlands. Nobody goes into the Great Badlands—you know that. But the young Red went because she was fed up with making babies that never came out of the garderies, babies that never even lived long enough to *enter* the garderies. She decided to go into the Great Badlands because she knew that when she returned to her Family, they would take out her seeds and sterilize her, to stop her from bringing Abominations into the world. She came home after two days in the Great Badlands. A day, a month, an hour would have been the same. They punished her and took away her seeds. She thought everything would be all right after that because she had no more seeds, seeds they should never have allowed her to keep on growing, even before her time in the Great Badlands, because they weren't any good even then. Do you understand, Lisbeï? They weren't compatible with any male seed. After her punishment, she tried to live as before. But nobody wanted to speak to her because she'd been to the Great Badlands. And they wouldn't let her look after other people's mostas in the garderies, or the dottas. She was very, very unhappy. At last one night she threw herself from the highest roof in the Capterie. She died."

The final word passed like a whiplash over Lisbeï's head. Once again she shrank back, although well aware that the story wasn't really for her, but for the others in the room, or perhaps for none of them, even though Mooreï at last replied, her voice broken. "She could have put her case to the Assembly. She could have written us. She chose not to act."

"Chose!" said Selva. "Did she choose to bear nonviable childreen year after year? She should have been declared Blue right away!"

"That's not what they do in Cartano. Loï knew it when she followed Tomma."

Lisbeï, fascinated, listened to the adults talking in their grown-up language about their grown-up world, using familiar words that seemed to say things she almost understood, but which remained just beyond her experience.

"Loï would have been an excellent gardiana. She'd have been excellent at anything. And all they could make of her was a renegada. The Cartanos killed her, as surely as if they'd pushed her from that roof!"

Selva's voice broke suddenly. Her body slumped, as though emptied of passion. She rested a hand on her swollen belly, a hand clenched into a fist. Antonë, alarmed, went to her. Selva waved her away, but the Medicina ignored this and took her by the wrist, feeling for the pulse.

"Why didn't they sterilize her and send her back to the Badlands? Or simply send her back here?" asked Antonë.

"They tried to deal with the circumstances as they found them," said Mooreï wearily. "Loï could have asked to come back here before. She didn't. And Juddites don't send away the Mother's compagna—it's not done."

Selva straightened, eyes glittering. "Juddites do lots of things now that they didn't do before, and it's high time to make them change, once and for all, even if they don't want to!"

Mooreï also straightened up, and said in a voice Lisbeï had never heärd, "That's enough, Selva. Shouting or jumping off roofs isn't going to change anything. We'll put the matter before the next Litale Assembly. We'll take it to the Assembly of Mothers if necessary. Reparation will be made."

"Tell that to Loï!"

"Loï has found comfort in the arms of Elli."

Lisbeï sensed the rising outburst in Selva. Suddenly the black Kelys stepped forward and slipped an arm around the Mother's shoulders. "It's time things changed, Selva. But Mooreï is right, too. It's a question for the Assemblies."

Selva's face crumpled as though she were about to cry. But she gritted her teeth and breathed deeply. "You must both be tired," she said. "You must have left at daybreak to get here so soon. Will you stay with us for a few days?"

The ugly Blue answered. Her voice was strange like everything else: very low, almost growling. "I'll leave now, if you don't mind. I'm expected at Lobianco."

"You were very kind to make this detour with Kelys," said Mooreï.

"It was the least I could do. Peace in Elli to all," muttered the Blue. She put out a hand to push back the chair—a big hand with square-cut nails and, to Lisbeï's amazement, black hairs growing out of the back and even along the fingers!

"Peace in Elli, Rico," replied Mooreï and Selva in unison.

Rico? What sort of name was that?

And all at once Lisbeï saw clearly, understood that this wasn't a *she* but a *he!* A Blue *man.* Who'd once been a male. She would have liked to get a better look at him, but there was no time: he strode to the door and disappeared.

11

Antonë to Linta

Bethely, 17 Marsa, 481 A.G.

Dear Linta,

I fully understand your decision. In fact, I expected it. The long spaces between your letters, and especially their content . . . well, that's why I wrote my last letter, after much hesitation. I may be obsessed by my research, but I'm not as blind and deaf to my surroundings as you appear to think. Don't take this remark the wrong way. I'm sad about it, as are you, and I bear you no ill will. I think we both knew from the start what really mattered for each of us, and that sooner or later we'd each go our own way. Maritna will be much better for you. Like you, I hope with all my heart that we can remain friends. Nothing that origi-

nally brought us together has changed or been destroyed by your decision, and it did me a lot of good to learn this from your letter. Anyway, we were friends before becoming compagnas. Of course I'll keep on writing—even more often than before, because then I was afraid of talking too much about my work. Since you say you're still interested, I'd be delighted to keep our correspondence going and have you continue as my enlightened (and fierce!) critic—a role you had given up. I regretted it, but said nothing about this, either. We were both wrong.

"The poison of shared silence." That's what Kelys told me in connection with Selva and Loï. I understand more clearly now why Selva never took a compagna. Luckily, we never let it really poison our relationship. But then we weren't raised in Bethely, and we hadn't lived for ten years in a Juddite Family such as Cartano. Do you realize that they don't even recognize the status of Mother's compagna? After ten years Loï was still their "ward." Incredible. And to have allowed her to procreate all that time! Since I'm now officially the Medicina of Bethely, I went next day to perform the autopsy. I won't go into my reception. I had every right to be there, and they couldn't go too far in Kelys's presence. I managed to make them give me the autopsy reports—as rudimentary as they are with Juddites—of each of her children. The fact that they didn't declare her Blue after the second, and the way they treated her the whole time is . . . monstrous, far more monstrous than any so-called Abomination.

To top it all off, at last month's Litale Assembly they had the gall to refuse to table the reports and make reparation! The case will come up before the Mothers next Juna. Selva is determined to submit it. I hope she'll be in a state to go herself. Her pregnancy is progressing satisfactorily, mind you, but you never know. It will be barely a month after the birth, and the trip to Caraquès is tiring, even though half of it is on water. But Selva won't hear a word against the project. However, I understand her attitude toward Lisbeï and the younger childe better now. She doesn't want the same thing to happen to them. Loï was her younger sister, don't forget. She must have been miserable when Loï decided to go to Cartano. To tell the truth, after having met Tomma, the Mother, I wonder how Loï could love her enough to make it worth living in Cartano. She certainly must have known the kind of life that awaited her. No doubt Selva was also rather mystified. But I do see why she made Mooreï and me swear not to let Lisbeï and Tula make contact again before Tula came out of the garderie.

Ah well, the heart has its reasons that reason. . . .

You see? I can even joke about love. I hope you're not offended. It doesn't matter what we call it; for me, the feeling that unites us is still love. The fact that we're no longer compagnas is a development of another order, on a different plane. Maybe I'm wrong to consider it less important, and maybe that's where we differ. But I know now that you can accept my shortcomings in this respect, because you know and understand the reason.

To get back to the dreadful Cartanos, they'll be forced to table the autopsy reports at Caraquès, because the Lines are involved. And I don't see how they can avoid reparations. Selva has made up her mind to make a cautionary example of this case, not only for Cartano, but for other Families in the region. I must say the Juddites in this part of the Province are particularly irritating. I've had some firsthand experience, as you know. They cling stubbornly to their traditions, even the most burdensome—not to say the most unpleasant or outright criminal (Loï's case). They're a dead weight that the others have to suffer. I mentioned that they sent the message, not by Kelys, but by a Blue man who was passing through, a Cartano who lives in Lobianco. (I'm amazed that any man would want to go back to the Juddites for an instant after being declared Blue!) It wasn't until I'd remarked on this to Kelys that I realized they intended it as an insult: their way of humiliating Bethely for Loï's "impious" behavior. I couldn't believe my ears at the Litale Assembly. They're always dragging their feet, not only for things that matter but for details, waving the Word in people's faces on the slightest provocation—that is, their narrow, petty interpretation of it. As far as they're concerned, Cartas must always take second place to the Word. Why, I wonder, did they bother signing them? (Some of them would no doubt answer that if they had been present when the Maerlande Carta was signed . . .)

To put it in a nutshell, our Northeastern Juddites are virtually enlightened philosophers by comparison. I could go on about the Cartanos for pages. I'm not exactly impartial, since they've just denied me access to their Archives for the third time, despite an explicit letter from the Litale Assembly. I think I'll follow Selva's example and have them up before the Mothers! (Just joking, of course. It's too soon. I want a complete and unassailable dossier on the Malady.)

Kelys looks on all this very calmly. After all her travels she's seen plenty—sometimes far worse. I wish you could meet her. You'd like her. For an explora who has so many finds to her

*credit, she's surprisingly modest. And the fact that she keeps on
exploring instead of resting on her abundant laurels makes her
even more attractive in my eyes, as you can imagine! Obviously,
she isn't any ordinary explora. Although she's the soul of discretion, to some extent she acts as the eyes and ears of Wardenberg.
I wonder what the Cartanos would have done if she hadn't been
there when Loï killed herself? I get the feeling they wouldn't have
hesitated to cover it up as an accident, to avoid reparations!*

*Kelys is going to stay here in Bethely until the Caraquès
Assembly. I'd hoped she would dissuade Selva from going.
(Mooreï is quite capable of representing the Family. She did it
when Selva was expecting Tula.) Kelys and Selva are old friends
—from as far back as Selva's becoming the Mother, I think.
Moreover, Kelys has an ability to persuade and pacify that far
exceeds anything Mooreï can do, and that's saying something!
She didn't even broach the subject, however. I guess it's because
she knows Selva so well, knows what Loï meant to her. She will
even testify for Bethely if need be. With her weight thrown in, the
Cartanos are done for, and they must know it. Maybe that's why
they wouldn't let me into the Archives: they knew they'd be forced
to, sooner or later, but they put a spoke in my wheel out of sheer
malice.*

*While I'm on the subject, we have a real gymna-maestra
now (instead of the graceful but highly ineffectual Karitee): Kelys
is teaching the taïtche to the dottas in the elementary and secondary cycles, and the parade to the others. What's more, she has
taken in hand the training of future patrollas, although some of
them must be privately cursing the day, given their aching muscles! If the mythical Abominations in the Great Badlands ever
take it into their heads to have a look at Bethely, they'll get a
rousing welcome!*

12

For the taïtche lesson, Kelys had subdivided Karitee's groups,
taking no more than six at a time. It meant working much
longer hours, but she didn't seem to mind. Lisbeï was physically lazy and embarrassed by her body, being already too tall

for her age. She had been very comfortable with Karitee's undemanding regime. For Kelys, however, she was ready to make an effort. She stood there with the other five on the mat in the gymna hall, at once excited and anxious. Kelys would surely ask them to show her what they knew how to do, and she had practiced the basic movements with Arië in their room the night before. She wasn't sure Kelys would be satisfied, however. The tall Blue moved with such efficient grace, so strong yet so supple. . . . One rainy day, the dottas had seen her crossing the courtyard in several bounds, leaping like a catte over a huge puddle to reach the shelter of the portico. Kelys hadn't even been out of breath.

The maestra observed her pupils one after the other, but said nothing. Then she touched them, examining a bone or a thigh, the joints of a foot, or the abdominal muscles. This done, she opened her large bag (the dottas were wondering why she'd brought it), and took out bracelets and bands studded with dozens of tiny, silvery-sounding bells. She attached them to her ankles, wrists, forehead, and waist. "Listen to me," she said mysteriously, and for a while stood perfectly still. When Lisbeï could no longer suppress a giggle, Kelys smiled and began to walk. Her arms went through the motions of the taïtche's first movement, her feet followed the invisible path on the matting, all in perfect silence.

There was a tinkling as she took other bands of bells out of her bag and handed them to Lisbeï, who had shoved in front of Tuina and now regretted it. "You try," said Kelys.

The little bells jangled furiously as Lisbeï, her body tense, tried to imitate Kelys.

"Try not moving, then," advised Kelys. She wasn't laughing, and her glance quelled the dottas' giggles.

This time it was a little better, but soon the tinkling started again, even though Lisbeï was sweating and almost not breathing in an effort to keep the bells still.

"I know how!" said Tuina.

Kelys handed her some bells, and a mortified Lisbeï watched Tuina take a very slow step, then a second and a third. Not a sound. It was just like one of the Capterie cattes stalking a birda. And then the bells began to jingle, and Tuina stamped a foot in frustration, sending forth a fresh carillon.

Kelys smiled at her. "It was a good idea. However, I think that if you really want to know how to move, you first have to know how to stand perfectly still. It's very, very hard."

She handed each of them a band and asked them to hold it with the tips of their fingers, their arms folded at eye level. At first all went well, but after a bit it seemed as though looking at the bells while thinking very hard about *not* making them tinkle made you feel like scratching the inside of your head. The desire to move was becoming unendurable—just barely to move, to drop that arm ever so little, rest on the other foot . . . and the bells tinkled mockingly.

"Don't think hard," said Kelys. "Think differently."

She explained how. Gather the whole body into a single thought that would then be no longer a thought, but the sensation of breath inside, outside, the flow of breath from nostrils to belly, the continuity of breath running down through neck, torso, and legs, and through the horizontal set of head, shoulders, pelvis, and bare feet.

"You can perceive each other," said Kelys. A bell tinkled as Lisbeï jerked, thinking of the light and of Tula, but Kelys only meant they'd sense the others out of the corner of their eye with "peripheral vision," as Kelys put it. If they paid close attention, they could hear the others breathing all along the row. . . .

And it was true. In Lisbeï's inner perception, the others' presence was clearer, smoother, calm, rising on a sort of rhythmical wave that she guessed was their breath, and beneath that the heartbeats.

". . . and if you close your eyes, you can feel the air between you, the air touches your skin and the others' skin, the air is between your skin and the others'. . . ."

And it's true. Lisbeï feels her skin become permeable, her flesh radiating through it like a halo, streaming outward until it touches the others' skin, the others' flesh. It feels very strange, as though she no longer had any limits to her body. Disturbing, after a while: she no longer really knows where her body is in relation to the others. She'd like to get back to her own body. But how? Her body seems to know: there is a kind of reverse motion, a contraction, a slow condensation. Somewhere behind Lisbeï's closed eyes a pink light rises, ever more intense, deepening to red, every shade of pink, every shade of red, from pink so pale as to be almost transparent white to a scarlet so deep as to seem black. She no longer hears the breath and the heartbeats of the others, only her own breathing. And what must be her own heart, this throbbing that makes her undulate like water, and she can feel the waves rolling outward from this center. . . . She is water, and she can hear herself trickling, running, cascading in perpetual motion, going, coming, with all the shades of red and pink and white surging and palpitating, sizzling and sparkling, pulsating in a dizzying whirl that is soon intolerable . . . all this movement, all this noise, and suddenly Lisbeï is terrified, she feels as though she's falling, she *is* falling without even knowing where she is, inside or outside, and she wants to scream but no longer knows how.

Something touched her, bringing her back to her body with a violent start, like waking from a dream fall. Yet her bells were silent. Amazed, she glanced around. The others had their eyes closed. She could see movement at the edge of her left field of vision, a calm presence. Kelys had circled the row of dottas and stopped in front of her. Very slowly Lisbeï lifted her head to look at Kelys. Still no tinkling. Black eyes in a black face observing her, indecipherable. A long arm reached out, a hand touched her cheek. Silence. Pale lips, almost violet compared to the black skin, stretched in a smile. And all at once it was the same as with Tula—no, much better, different but the same (wrote Lisbeï in her notebook that night, after much hesitation). So brief, so strong, as though the perception consumed itself in its own intensity. Lisbeï couldn't describe it for Tula, no matter how hard she tried. All she could remember was that . . . something happened with Kelys. Instead, she attempted to explain the strange, colorful visions (they must have been visions) that accompanied her efforts to keep the bells from tinkling. But the only comparison that came to mind was her feverish dream during the Malady—and this as a last resort, because she knew Tula hadn't had any such experience when *she* was sick.

Kelys took back the bells and asked all the dottas what they'd felt. No one appeared to have shared Lisbeï's experience, not even the first part, the impression of radiating out into the room and touching the others without doing so. She didn't dare speak of it. Kelys, not looking at her, said, "Did anyone have a feeling of falling asleep, or see lights the way you do when you rub your eyes?"

Lisbeï hesitated just a little too long. Kelys moved on. "I hope it will happen. It's rather odd the first time. You feel out of touch with where you are—inside or outside of your body. The trick is to hover just between the two."

Imagine a clock, Kelys continued. The big hand circles to

the right, reaching a point where it is so far to the right that it starts moving left up the opposite side of the clock face, the side that is no longer day but night. For an instant it is exactly between the two. . . . ("At noon!" "At midnight!" chorused the dottas.)

Lisbeï had the feeling she'd heard this argument before. Somehow she suddenly thought of the spinning lens, sphere and slice, sphere and slice, twirling until it inevitably stopped. Here it was the opposite: the hands didn't stop as long as you remembered to wind the clock. The opposite, but it seemed like the same thing.

"Not for the clock hands. But for humans, yes. You can learn to stretch out that moment. In order not to move, and then to move well without making the bells tinkle, you must concentrate until you find the point of equilibrium, a thread running between the outside and the inside, between the noon and midnight of mind and body, and you have to balance on that thread without toppling to one side or the other. That's the basis of the taïtche and the parade."

And the Dance of the Pairing. But the Dance would come later.

13

Once again Lisbeï's status in Bethely was rather peculiar. Every day she visited Selva for three hours, and the office became a schoolroom. Later there would be extra sessions with Mooreï and Antonë. She also had to spend two hours a day reviewing her lessons. Moreover, History was a means of teaching reading, writing, geography, arithmetic, and—invisible but all the more effective—ethics. Selva rarely spoke of Elli. Later, with Mooreï, the Word was usually entwined with History, but Lisbeï already felt they were rather distinct.

The rest of the time she was expected to do as the other dottas: perform chores for the captas, either in the kitchens or on the various levels of the Towers, and later in the gardens, the barns, or even the weavery. There was always work for everyone in Bethely. Lisbeï complained to her journal that she was treated like everyone else. But she wasn't really like everyone else: she'd had her tattoos long before the rest. Wasn't she the future Mother of Bethely, after all?

Selva and Moorei always made a point of demonstrating, either by word or action, that the future Mother of Bethely wasn't so very different from everyone else, but this salutary lesson passed right over Lisbeï's head. She wouldn't have minded some of the affectionate respect that surrounded the Mother and her Memory. She could perceive the feelings she aroused in adults: certainly neither respect nor admiration, but from some that kind of rough tenderness given all the little dottas, from others an amusement at times condescending, or a more demanding severity, maybe even something hostile.

The other dottas, especially the older ones, were either puzzled or annoyed, or else gave off an aura of what seemed like compassion, perhaps pity, which nearly drove Lisbeï wild. Didn't they realize she would be the Mother of Bethely, the Capta? Even so, she felt she could understand their attitude. When she was honest with herself, she admitted harboring a slight regret for those first weeks in the Tower when she had truly been part of Majda's team. Officially she was still part of the team, but in practice her new timetable prevented her from participating in a good many of the group's activities, whether work or play.

As time went on, everyone seemed to agree that Lisbeï could belong to any group, since she really belonged to none in particular. Despite the fact that she still shared a room with Arië, a rift had opened between herself and Majda's team. Not that she was isolated—but she was alone. She watched from the sidelines, observing the various currents of affection and disaffection that united and separated the other dottas. At night sometimes, after a long session of writing in her notebook, she would pleasure herself in silence, thinking hard about Tula.

Lisbeï didn't really suffer from being set apart. This, too, was "like the garderie." The familiar incantation brought her a kind of peace. Her perception of others might mean she could never completely forget her special kind of solitude, but it also enabled her to come to terms with it. If everyone felt that way about her, it just had to be the normal thing: it must be so, simply because it was. Occasionally she regretted being "different," and sometimes it even irritated or hurt her. But at such moments she thought it was wrong of her to feel this way. Anyhow, Tula would come out of the garderie one day, and everything would be all right again.

Her situation did have its advantages. At least Lisbeï was learning lots of fascinating things before everyone else. Unfortunately, she couldn't win acceptance with her precocious knowledge. In the early days, her peers didn't care much about information that had little to do with their daily lives in the Towers. Bethely dottas didn't usually begin their real education until their eighth birthday, although their various tasks in the Towers were already using and developing the elementary skills acquired in the garderies. When they turned eight, however, the fact of having survived the dangerous period of early childhood was officially recognized. Their shoulders were tattooed and their names entered in the Book of Lines. Later, when they, too, began lessons, they were annoyed with Lisbeï rather than envious. Of course, she could always congratulate herself on her knowledge, at least in the notebook where she spoke to Tula.

Lisbeï also did less manual labor than the others, but since a good third of her day was devoted to intellectual work, this was a very relative benefit. Nevertheless, she was allowed to roam around the Tower and later all Bethely, more often and more freely than any other dotta. She had her own itineraries and shortcuts for this or that errand or task. In this way she possessed Bethely better than she would have otherwise, almost as though she herself had created these labyrinths of passages, levels, and staircases, within which she discovered new connections and new complexities almost daily.

And then—not the least of privileges—she could ask grown-ups more questions than the other dottas, and they would answer more readily.

If this hadn't been the case, how could she have learned where Tula would go after leaving the garderie?

It took cunning and patience, but Lisbeï had acquired these early on. Innocent remarks, indirect questions led her to her goal, like the small wooden squares in the alphabet puzzle. Lisbeï found out when Tula was to leave the West Tower garderie, who would be her tutress, on what level and in which room she would be lodged, and who would be her roommate. The lists were drawn up in advance: everything in Bethely was well organized, and the management of new dottas was no exception.

Tula had been assigned to Lisbeï's Tower. This wasn't so surprising, since Lisbeï hadn't once mentioned Tula's name. Selva was willing to believe that Lisbeï had been distracted by her new life, and that the unforeseen bond would have frayed sufficiently in two years (an eternity for childreen at that age!) to remove any danger. Mooreï, although she had seen Lisbeï and Tula together, tried to believe it as well. If Antonë thought otherwise, she kept it to herself and followed Lisbeï's example in never mentioning Tula's name. In any case, Lisbeï hadn't extracted information from Selva, Mooreï, or Antonë, and felt no guilt about her subversive actions, although these three had taught her that such manipulation was wrong. Yes, it was wrong, but then everything involving Tula belonged to a separate world where only the rules made by Lisbeï and Tula applied.

Now there was nothing left to do but cross the days off her secret calendar and wait, filling a second, then half of a third thick notebook in the silent nights while Arië slept like a babie.

At last Tula came out of the garderie, on the very day and hour foretold. With her tutress and the two other members of her team, Tula passed by the foreordained place where Lisbeï waited, clutching a little note giving a time and place to meet, ready to be slipped into Tula's hand. Tula is coming, Tula, Tula looking almost the same, barely taller than before. How like Selva she is! (The thought rather upset Lisbeï, although she didn't know why.) And now Tula is on the point of seeing Lisbeï. The beloved presence is about to run joyfully to meet her—oh, if only Tula says nothing, doesn't react, no one will suspect a thing. . . . Now Tula sees Lisbeï standing in her path and . . .

Tula stepped around Lisbeï and walked on without a glance.

Lisbeï stood there, turned to stone, a half-raised hand concealing the scrap of paper so carefully folded in eight. She was dreaming. She must be dreaming. Someone gave her a shove, and her strangely independent body started moving again. Could she have made a mistake? Was that really Tula? That indifferent look? That absence of light?

She tried to remember, stomach churning, legs rubbery. Had she really sensed nothing? It had all happened so quickly. Yes, she had sensed something . . . her own joy rebounding vaguely in her direction, but there was nothing of Tula in it;

no, she had sensed nothing from Tula, only her own emotion, as though bouncing off a mirror, a smooth, hard surface, brilliant and horribly familiar. Selva! What had Selva done to Tula?

Lisbeï/Journal

Wardenberg, 4 Ellième, 496 A.G.

Last night I dreamed about the cherry orchard, Tula. It's been so long since I had that dream. Now I understand a little better why it was such a horrible nightmare and why I never told you about it. I detest you so much in that dream. Everything else is normal, except that . . . loathing when I look at you. Such a brief dream. Not even the other people in it this time, nor the well you used to fall into. Just you. You're picking cherries and I see you in the tree. I woke up sweating, as always, my heart beating as though I'd run the klim. But I didn't cry. I understood what the feeling really was, the feeling that always passed through from dreaming to waking. Not sadness. Anger, Tula, hate. That was why I used to cry in the old days. Hating you so much made me afraid, hating you so much that I didn't even want to recognize it. A nightmare: that was all I cared to know.

It took me a long time to admit Selva hadn't actually done anything, that it was you who had deliberately surrounded yourself with that barrier, that wall like Selva's. All right, it was your way of surviving. But I had to survive without you, too, and I didn't put up a wall! I wouldn't have shut you out! Or passed by next day with a polite, "Oh, hello Lisbeï," and then run off giggling with the other—I forget who—when she said something and mentioned my name. . . .

14

Lisbeï had found Meralda, Tallie, and Meï lodged on the same floor but in the north wing. Initially, Tallie and Meï had been assigned to one tutress, Meralda to another. By the end of three months, however, Meralda had managed to find or fabricate the "valid reasons" required by the Instructions for a transfer. (Meralda, as Lisbeï had discovered with jealous disbelief, was one of Mooreï's childreen! At least Mooreï didn't single her out for special attention, but still . . .) With Pia on Level Five, that meant the gang was practically together again. In garderie days the fact of moving down to the main floor among strangers, leaving Tula behind, had made Lisbeï gravitate toward Meralda's group, even though she'd remained an outsider. Once the group had reformed and mastered the intricacies of life in the Tower, the same force again brought Lisbeï within its sphere. She didn't really take the initiative, nor did they, but there was a tendency to clump the new dottas on one floor to do chores that needed many hands. Then there was the free time after meals, especially in the evening before bedtime.

Lisbeï had noticed that her new status, even though not officially recognized by grown-ups, gave her a certain interest in the eyes of the old garderie group, despite everything: an interest disguised as teasing or mockery, although it stopped short of explicit questions about what she did with the Mother, the Memory, or the Medicina. Still, interest was interest, and it conferred upon her a sort of condescending acceptance by members of the gang whenever she met them, either together or alone.

It happened four months after Tula's arrival. That day Lisbeï was picking fruit with Meralda, Meï, and Tallie in the cherry orchard on the East Esplanade.

"We've got helpers," said Meralda with a laugh. "Come over here, you pipsqueaks!"

Lisbeï's heart almost stopped as she recognized Tula's red hair among a group of little dottas. Four of them trotted obediently over to the tree where Lisbeï stood in full view, having just climbed down.

Tula and another dotta headed for a different tree.

Luckily it was sprinna, and soon it would be sumra. Luckily a dotta could bury herself in work, what with lessons with Selva, and now with Mooreï and Antonë. Picking, weeding, feeding the animals, working in the kitchens, cutting grass, running errands for this and that, anything to fill the endless days. Lisbeï, who used to love walking through the levels with a proprietary air, was afraid now, afraid of meeting Tula, of having those terrible green eyes—or gray or blue—glance at her carelessly. She knew now that Tula did it on purpose, that Tula blamed her for failing to meet her at night in the garderie. How could Tula be so cruel? (How could Tula be so *stupid?* But that idea never really took shape.)

Sprinna slipped into sumra without diminishing Lisbeï's pain, only wearing down her ability to behave as though it didn't matter. Until the day Meralda returned a book of tales Lisbeï had lent her. They could all use the Library now, but since they were allowed only a limited number of books at a time, the dottas circumvented the system by lending to each other.

The Red Catte's Tales. Lisbeï can still picture the book with its naive but colorful cover. It contained the story of the Princess and the Spirit in the Cave, with all the Spirit's riddles and not just the triple riddle of the Blood.

Arië was not in the room. Lisbeï was tidying her cupboard, and some of her things were lying on the bed. Among the clothes and clutter were the three diaries, their pages carefully glued together, two of them full and the third half-blank since Tula's arrival. How was it possible? Tula had come back and nothing had really changed, but it was all different, horribly different. Her heart used to sink each time she opened the cupboard. Those miserable diaries! She'd stuffed them under the clothes, but she'd known they were there. Should she throw them out?

The diaries were lying on the bed when Meralda came in. Lisbeï, eyes stinging with unshed tears, was staring at them. She made an effort to chatter normally and distract her visita, but Meralda's gaze had fallen on the papers.

"What's that?"

"Oh, nothing. My exercise books. For the Mother."

"Hey, can I look?"

Before Lisbeï could answer, Meralda had heedlessly picked up one of the notebooks and was about to leaf through it.

Lisbeï couldn't help herself. She dashed forward and ripped the notebook out of Meralda's hands. Meralda, now really intrigued, grabbed another clump of glued pages and shoved Lisbeï back long enough to read a few lines. She began to laugh, an insulting laugh. (An angry, disappointed laugh, as Lisbeï realized a long time later.) "Tula! Don't tell me you're still hankering after Tula! She doesn't want you and everyone knows it!"

For years Lisbeï would remember the thud of Meralda's head hitting the floor as they rolled on the ground. A dull thud, luckily, because of the braided bedside rug, but it reverberated through Lisbeï's body. She didn't hear what Meralda was yelling, her mind was blank, and she felt nothing except this inner burning that must be quenched by banging Meralda against the floor again and again. Something caught at the collar of her tunic, tried to pin down her arms. She kicked and thrashed, and suddenly there was a snapping sound and a flash of pain from somewhere in her right arm that shot through her whole body. Now she could hear again, and what she heard were Meralda's terrified sobs. And she could see again, see the pages scattered on the floor, crumpled and torn, see Meralda crouched over, holding her head and swaying back and forth, blood on her hands. See Mooreï's horrified face looking at Lisbeï, looking at Lisbeï's arm, which Mooreï had just broken.

Lisbeï tried to pick up one of the scattered diary pages, but a white wave of pain pushed her back to the floor. Strangely enough her one idea at the moment was *I must tidy everything away before going to the infirmary.*

In the infirmary they closed her off with screens. No one must speak to her. She was being punished. For having fought with Meralda.

"What happened?" asked Antonë, ignoring the injunction once she'd dealt with Lisbeï's arm. Lisbeï pinched her lips. She stared at the fingers of her right hand, curled over the plaster cast like alien things, not part of her body at all. What did she care about these questions from grown-ups who wanted to hear what they already knew, who wanted to hear you accuse yourself? They had Meralda, they had the diaries. Wasn't that enough?

"Meralda wouldn't say anything except that she'd read your private diary without your permission. She's getting the same punishment as you, for a month. No one else has read your notebooks, and no one will. They belong to you, Lisbeï, and therefore they mustn't be touched unless you allow it."

There were laws that grown-ups observed? Even for a dotta in disgrace? Lisbeï had a strong feeling that the Medicina was telling the truth, that she wanted to know more, not to punish Lisbeï further, but to understand. But Lisbeï couldn't, wouldn't say a thing. She wasn't going to let them take away what little she had left of Tula. Since Meralda had said nothing, she could do the same and remain isolated behind her screens like a plague victim. She had sensed the sharp disapproval following her and Meralda as they traversed corridors and staircases on their way to the infirmary. Now Lisbeï was as horrified as the bystanders: she had broken Maerlande's most important law, a law that had imbued the severe voices of gardianas with authority as they put a stop to the first scuffles in the garderie. *One does not raise a hand against a sister in Elli.* No grown-up had ever struck Lisbeï; no grown-up had every struck any mosta, any dotta that she knew of. She remembered the burning sensation and how good it felt to bang Meralda's head on the floor. She thought about the thud, the blood on Meralda's hands, and she felt like vomiting.

Lisbeï was being punished and no one must speak to her, but Selva came. She seemed calm, although enveloped in her usual armor. Lisbeï certainly wasn't going to tell *her* anything!

"Do you know what you should have done, Lisbeï?"

Silence—slightly surprised all the same.

"What should you have done, Lisbeï?"

"I should have got my team and Meralda's together," Lisbeï muttered finally.

"And?"

"If that didn't work, I should have fetched my tutress and hers. And after that the capta on our level. I shouldn't have taken justice into my own hands."

"Particularly when there was such a huge gap between the offense and the reaction!"

Lisbeï bristled once again. Was Selva also trying to worm things out of her? No, the Mother was simply stating her opinion—her judgment: "We'd still be in the Hives if we settled our disputes like that in Maerlande! We're not animals. I don't want my daughter, the future Mother of Bethely, to behave like an *animal*. Is that understood?"

Lisbeï nodded mutely. Again she was surprised, but for another reason: Selva's armor had opened slightly for a second, and the emotion that Lisbeï had fleetingly perceived was by no means anger. It was anguish, almost fear.

On Selva's heels came another visita: Kelys. Had they realized isolation wasn't as effective a punishment as being visited, being subjected to reprobation, feeling her own shame? Kelys seemed neither horrified nor disapproving, however. Her presence emitted the same calm, strong sensation as always. Her tall body folded itself elegantly onto the edge of the bed, and her hard, cool hand clasped the tips of Lisbeï's fingers.

"Are you angry at Mooreï for breaking your arm?"

"No." Of course not!

"She thought she'd never stop you. You know what would have happened if she hadn't."

It wasn't a question, but Lisbeï bobbed her head, sick with horror. They would have tattooed a black cross on her right hand, she would have been exiled to an Offshoot for months—or worse, they would have obliterated her shoulder tattoos, operated to sterilize her, and sent her into the Great Badlands, for she would have *killed* Meralda, and not really by accident.

"Why, Lisbeï? Do you know why you were so angry with Meralda?"

Lisbeï opened her eyes, full of reproach. Was Kelys also trying to make her talk? But Kelys said, "I'm not asking you to tell me. Just say whether you yourself know."

Lisbeï bobbed her head again. Because Meralda read her diary.

"Are you sure you really know?"

Forced to be honest with herself, although not quite understanding why, Lisbeï sniffled tearfully. Because Meralda had said that Tula didn't want to have anything more to do with her. Because it hurt too much to think that Tula didn't want her.

"Meralda hurt you and you wanted to hurt her back. Isn't that it?"

"Yes," whispered Lisbeï at last.

"Meralda hasn't said anything about what was in the diary. Do you know why?"

A thrill of fear brought Lisbeï out of her gloom. How did Kelys know . . .

"I don't know what's in your diary," said Kelys with a clairvoyance that was hardly reassuring. "I only know that it must have been something very serious, something you didn't want her to read. She could have said what it was. Her punishment wouldn't have been less—on the contrary—but she didn't know that. Have you asked yourself why she didn't tell?"

No, Lisbeï hadn't had time to wonder about Meralda's silence. She pondered the fact for a moment with a growing sense of amazement. "Because she didn't want me to be punished even more?"

Kelys nodded. Then, after a silence in which all Lisbeï's preconceived notions about Meralda crumbled and painfully kaleidoscoped into new, surprising patterns, Kelys spoke again. "Think about it, Lisbeli. Think about your reasons for being angry, and Meralda's reason for everything she did." She still held Lisbeï's fingers, stroking them pensively with the tips of her own, such strange fingers, paler inside than outside. "Lots of things make us angry, little things, big things. It's normal. You surely must have banged yourself somewhere, sometime, and wanted to bang whatever it was that hurt you? When people hurt you, it's so easy to blame them, to believe they really mean to do it and to feel like hurting them back. But most of the time they have some reason for hurting us. Often it's because they hurt, too. It's no excuse. But it explains things. Sometimes you don't feel the hurt so much if you understand. There are always at least two sides to an argument. Possibly even more."

Then, switching subjects with a speed that astonished Lisbeï and dissolved the lump in her throat like magic, Kelys asked, "Do you want to stay in the infirmary for long?"

The quicker she got out, the quicker the three more weeks of isolation would pass!

"I don't want you to, either," Kelys went on. "Did you know you're one of the best at the taïtche? When you're there, the group performs better."

Lisbeï smiled in spite of herself. She hadn't been too sure Kelys had noticed her progress. "It would be too bad if you lost ground by staying in the infirmary, wouldn't it? You should keep up your training in bed. Concentration can be practiced without moving. I broke my leg once—I must have been about your age—and that's what I did. It helped me pass the time. I remember being so keen to get out that I told my fracture to hurry up and get better. I did my concentration exercises, and at the moment when you see the red-pink light . . . oh, but I forgot, you don't see it—"

"Yes I do," blurted out Lisbeï, carried away by curiosity. "Sometimes," she hastily amended.

Kelys grinned. "Well it's easy: when I saw the red-pink light, I imagined it was the inside of my body and that I could see my fracture. And I told it to get better faster."

"Did it work?"

"I got out of the infirmary faster, in any case! I read somewhere that if you really want to get well, you do. Anyway, once you've had the Malady, you never get sick again. Perhaps you can mend fractures faster, too."

She stretched gracefully and Lisbeï watched, fascinated. It was almost impossible to imagine Kelys as a clumsy little dotta or an almost-person in a garderie.

"You've had the Malady?"

"Yes. Did you dream of red light when you had it?"

The question was put with such artless but flattering complicity that Lisbeï replied, "Yes," without a second thought.

The gymna-maestra merely winked. "Maybe that's why we're good at the taïtche!"

15

Antonë to Linta

I find it hard to understand Selva's reaction. The Bethelies aren't a flock of bleating ovinas—especially not Selva, not if I read her correctly when her armor slips! The same goes for the rest of Maerlande, such as it is. "One does not raise a hand against a sister in Elli," certainly, but it happens all the same. In any case, physical violence is merely the most obvious form of aggression. What do we call the Cartanos' treatment of Loï? Human beings are what they are, and all Garde's sermons haven't changed a thing. The slaughter among Harems and Hives surely contributed as much as Garde's sermons to the drawing up of the Carta, not to mention the impoverishment of the genetic pool!

There I go again. Forgive me. Yes, I know that the Word of Garde and her disciplas was essential for raising the collective consciousness that led to the end of the Hives, etc., etc.

As for our other non-ovina, Lisbeï began to eat very little and sleep a lot in the infirmary. Normal, you'd say, for someone who had nothing to do all day but think about her crime and the three remaining weeks of total isolation. Normal, except she slept too much. And she had increasing difficulty waking up. I had increasing difficulty waking her up! It began to look like a coma. The Malady coma, to be more precise. Rising temperature, speeding up of the entire metabolism . . . I couldn't make head or tail of it, and by the third day I was really worried. I told Kelys and she said, "Interesting. I've already encountered several such cases, a kind of relapse."

Well thanks for telling me! As you can imagine, I went after her like fleas on a hedgehog, trying to learn more. Kelys had wanted to become a Medicina when she turned Blue, but finally opted for being an explora. She has kept up her interest in biology, however, and genetics in particular. To cut a long conversa-

*tion short—we talked about it the whole night!—she thinks like
me that the Malady is changing. That we are changing. It's a type
of mutation, since we must eventually call things by their real
names and not let the Juddites confiscate the word "mutation"
to fabricate bogeymen for little dottas until the end of time. There
are mutations and mutations, however. This one clearly is not
"evil"!*

*Kelys has had the Malady too, Linta. And like all those who
have contracted it and survived in the last hundred years, she has
never been ill since. What's more, she's like us. There came a
point when she placed her hand on my arm: I perceived her, she
perceived me, and we almost embraced! She's like us, like the
dozen others I've mentioned, like Lisbeï, Tula, and Selva. Variants of the same mutation, Linta. No more shilly-shallying and
euphemisms, not with you in any case. Surely you're beyond that
now?*

*Anyway, there it is, the great news that I announced at the
beginning of my letter. I could add another important fact: according to Kelys, several of the relapsed cases she mentioned
showed an increased capacity for healing accidental wounds afterward. And it's true that Lisbeï's broken arm healed very
quickly. She came out of the infirmary a good week earlier than
expected.*

*This leads me to the following episode in the adventure of
Lisbeï and Tula. Apparently our efforts to separate them are
doomed to failure (Selva's efforts—rather inconsistent, actually,
since she put them in the same garderie to begin with). When I
couldn't wake Lisbeï from her coma, Kelys advised me to get
Tula. I was skeptical. But when little Tula saw her sister in a
coma, she became absolutely terrified and began shaking her and
calling her name. Lisbeï woke up, and the two of them fell into
each other's arms sobbing violently. You see, I was right: they
hadn't forgotten about each other at all.*

*I don't know whether I'll tell Selva about all this. I don't
mean about Lisbeï and Tula. (She's well aware of that, anyway,
and is no doubt pondering what to do! I hope Mooreï and Kelys
will advise her not to take any radical step.) I'm talking about the
rest—the mutations and their effects. When I reread all I've written, I realize that I've failed to see the most likely hypothesis, the
one that would best explain Selva's attitude. Since I touched her
for the medical examination, she's never spoken of it, although
she perceived me perfectly well. She hasn't changed toward me in
any way; it's just that every time I touch her, I encounter her*

armor. (And no, I don't know how she does it, or Tula, either. I can't ask Tula—she seems very distrustful of me.)

Selva—well, her mother was a Believra, not such an old-style Believra as to be a Juddite, but almost. Perhaps that's why Selva is so rational, so pragmatic. At the Caraquès Assembly, when I presented the autopsy reports on Loï's childreen, the Cartanos and other Juddites began to yelp, "Abomination! Abomination!" Selva didn't flinch. But perhaps, deep down . . . She must know that her two first-living resemble her (although I'm not sure she has seen Tula since the childe came out of the garderie). Would the term "mutation" reassure her? I doubt it. What do you think, Linta? What does it do to you, even now, when I use the word? Kelys tells me she sent up a few trial balloons in Wardenberg: nothing definite, just "speculation." She got a pretty skeptical reaction, but at least they didn't go into hysterics.

But that was Wardenberg. I'm not sure that the South, and particularly Litale, would be ripe for that kind of "speculation." Bethely—well, I don't know. Did I tell you that they say "change-lines" here? A delightful word, considering what it refers to, especially in Litale. But it's only for plants and animals. As for humans . . . Selva made it clear she preferred "aberration." The oldest Blues still say "Abomination" at times, but it's through habit, not malice. The general attitude is one of resignation, but they haven't relaxed their vigilance. Here as at home, they teach childreen to distinguish "good" insects and "good" plants from the changelines, except that here they do it very early on, at the garderie stage. When the wind blows from the Great Badlands, the childreen play a game in the weeks that follow. The winner is the one who brings the most changelines to the garden capta, and now they bring them to me for my collection. According to the Archives, there were several serious alarms in the old days, especially with insects. In general, however, Bethely seems to have made peace with its environment, although at the cost of unflagging vigilance.

The ever-pragmatic Bethelies have adopted and developed certain beneficial changelines. Take their mock rubber plant, for example, their fruit and vegetable cultivars, their hornless little wicows, or their big-footed ovinas with thick brown or golden wool. It happened well before Selva's time, what's more. Even the rigid Cemmelia agreed to close her eyes to what other Juddite Families frankly considered heresies, if not mortal sins!

*But that doesn't mean Selva has made peace with what she
and her daughters may be. I wonder if she even admits the possibility?*

16

Tula never spoke of the garderie directly, or of the months
and months spent without Lisbeï. And after the Meralda incident she had asked Lisbeï no questions. Everything began,
began again with their rediscovery of each other under the
astounded gaze of Antonë. Lisbeï did not give Tula her diaries: Tula didn't want them, although nothing was said. Day
after day she had to tell Tula things as though she'd just
learned them. This was how Tula wanted it, and it was better
this way. Lisbeï, too, wanted to forget about that time, about
the heartbreak of Tula's return and what it had driven her to
do. Someone else, not Lisbeï, had attacked Meralda. Each
time the memory tried to surface, Lisbeï pushed it away,
aghast. It was over . . . no, none of it ever happened! Tula
had never been that inaccessible, cruel stranger behind the
mirror-wall. It had been a dream, a bad dream, but now by
common accord they had awakened and would not speak of it.

There were lots of other things to share. The Tower, all
the Towers, the gardens and orchards, races on the Esplanade
road that ran through pastures on the site of the old fortifications, sumra swims in the Douve, upstream from the wharves
and warehouses where they'd watched barges being loaded
and unloaded before being floated down to Cartano or hauled
up to Collodi by blunt-horned water buffalas. Lisbeï and Tula
would tear home naked along the white road, dripping at first
but soon dry, whipping their tunics in the wind like flags.
There were the skeins of wool hung in multicolored hiero-
glyphs from pole to pole beside the dye shop. There was
autumna harvesting, gleaming rows of jams and preserves in
the cupboards, fruits and vegetables lined up to dry in the sun
beneath gauze-hung frames abuzz with frustrated bees. Later,
when they were bigger, there would be ovina shearing, harvesting at the Aigueli Farm to the south between the Douve

and the Wildwood, or at the Hill Farm lying at the foot of the range to the northwest, nestled in the tongue of the great horseshoe curve made by the river before it flowed back toward Bethely. And in the increasingly chill winters there would sometimes be the fun of sliding over the fleeting snow.

There was also the Book of Bethely, which fascinated Tula as it had Lisbeï—but because it opened up space rather than time. Tula daydreamed over the maps: all that was Bethely? So much more than three Towers! Bethely was a capterie that had once been a realm in the time of the Harems and Hives, taking in Collodi and Cartano and stretching as far as Nevenici on the edge of the Tirranean Sea to the southeast. Tula dreamed of the sea. One day they would go down the Douve as far as the sea. One day they too would leave Bethely and find out what lay across the water.

But they would be Reds, Lisbeï at first remarked, and Reds didn't travel, not Bethely Reds. And anyway, Lisbeï would be Mother of Bethely. The Mother could travel, but only to provincial Assemblies, or in alternate years to the great Assembly of Mothers and—

"We won't be Reds forever," interrupted Tula with a laugh. "And you won't always be the Mother. When your first-living is old enough to replace you, you'll be able to go wherever you like. It's in the Maerlande Carta. And then, or not long after, I should be a Blue and able to leave too. We'll be free."

Free. The idea had seemed rather odd to Lisbeï. How could you be *free* from what you'd been created for? Being the Mother wasn't a prison. And then to leave . . . that wasn't the future she dreamed of. What she imagined was a future with Tula in Bethely. Tula imagined being . . . anywhere with Lisbeï. The two things weren't so different, Lisbeï told herself at last. One day Mooreï had shown her a black-and-white engraving, a cube seen in perspective. "Is it hollow or full?" Full, of course, since the purpose of drawing it from an angle was to create the illusion of a free-standing object. "Look carefully." She studied the engraving, puzzled. Was it full? Or empty? And suddenly, in an invisible but instantaneous transfer, the black and white surfaces changed perspective, and the cube was hollow. After several tries she understood: a kind of deliberate mental twist enabled you to see the hollow cube, then the full cube. She burst into delighted laughter. It was a little like the spinning glass circle, sphere and slice at the same

time, or like Garde dead and alive, human yet Daughter of
Elli.

"Some people choose to see the interior of things, others
the exterior," explained Mooreï. "It's a question of viewpoint.
But we all see a cube, don't we? We all look at Elli's world
and each of us sees it from our own perspective. But you have
to try to see all the other perspectives at the same time, and
find a point of view that unites them."

The lesson had been initiated by one of those discussions
between Mooreï and Antonë that were more like arguments.
Lisbeï can't remember how it started. But she never forgot the
cube. She called it to mind each time Tula surprised her,
which was often—far more often than in the garderie. Tula
imagined being with Lisbeï no matter where, and Lisbeï imagined Bethely with Tula. Oh well, they'd be *together,* wouldn't
they? No-matter-where with Tula would still be with Tula.

But now it was Tula who wondered about the other side
of space, and Lisbeï who listened in silence, often feeling it
was better to say nothing, because another side of time might
have crept between them, the two years that mustn't be mentioned. The two years Tula had spent without Lisbeï and Lisbeï without Tula.

17

Antonë to Kelys

Bethely, 19 Juna, 486 A.G.

Dear Kelys,
    *Yes, we received your letter and present for Lisbeï just in
time. She was thrilled. Selva made no comment, but I get the
feeling she's not yet ready to get Bethely used to the Bretanye
custom of giving gifts to people on their birthday. Tula gave Lisbeï a big silver watch from Liborne, secretly acquired by me at*

the last Assembly Fair, and she also made a small bookcase with burnt-work decoration on the doors. The shelves will be filled in no time, since you and I had the same idea once again—books, an extravagant luxury for Litales! Mine were sufficiently educational to keep Selva from raising her eyebrows too high ("good" plants and insects of Litale, with ten beautiful color plates), but I must tell you that your Complete Works of Ludivine of Kergoët *would have met with a lot less indulgence if they'd come from anyone but you. Having one's own book is permissible, but novels! And romances at that!*

The modest morning ceremony went off quietly, and Lisbeï gave Selva the gift required by custom in Litale. I see the reason for it perfectly: you thank your genetrix. Lisbeï took a lot of trouble over weaving that scarf, considering how she hates manual labor, and Selva was gracious enough to show her appreciation—but without going overboard, naturally. I don't know if Lisbeï expected something more effusive; she didn't seem disappointed, in any case—but she controls herself so well now that I wouldn't really know without touching her. The rest of the day went by as usual, with lessons and a session in the Library. Still, this afternoon in the hottest part of the day, she was allowed to go to the Douve with the others and meet Tula.

I couldn't help thinking of our birthdays in Maroilles: my mother, my sisters, and me, surprises, laughter, sharing, and tenderness. Really—although I understand why Bethely and most of the Families here behave in this cool way, they don't realize the loss to themselves and the deprivation to their childreen.

But what did I gain in the end? Only that it seemed much harder when the time came to leave. . . .

You must forgive me. I think this is going to be one of "those" letters. I don't know why, but I spent the whole of Lisbeï's birthday in a state of vague anxiety. Or rather, I know perfectly well, and so do you. Still nothing. She's entering her thirteenth year and she hasn't had her first blood. She doesn't talk about it; no one talks about it much. If by an extraordinary chance someone brings the subject up (but not in front of Lisbeï, though, nor Selva!), there are ten voices ready to point out that some people menstruate very late and that it's not for nothing that sixteen is the legal age for . . . And then the voices fall silent and people try to change the subject. I myself couldn't tell Lisbeï any more than that, except for describing all the different reasons for a Green sometimes failing to become a Red. She must know them by heart now.

Except one. Except one, Kelys, and I still don't know whether I should tell her about it or not. Tell them *about it, Selva and Mooreï, because actually half the mostas contract the Malady here, and enough survive to make it entirely likely that the problem may arise again. I'm still not convinced by your argument. I know what you're going to say: I'm always brandishing figures, and yet here am I, refusing to believe them myself. Rather comical, isn't it? The only reason I can give is one I'm accustomed to ridiculing: intuition. Even if the sterility ratio hasn't risen these past thirty years among those who contracted the Malady very late and who survived, it's now slightly higher all the same. Just enough, just too much for me. Yes, I know: I myself am part of these statistics and not particulary objective about the question, as Linta is always telling me. But neither of you saw Lisbeï's expression only the other day, when Meralda received her Red necklace. (Another of those Litale traditions! At least at home we don't have to go through a public ceremony when we change status! Well, all right, we make a private ceremony out of the perforation of the hymen, whereas here it's merely routine. But just the same . . .)*

Kelys, the fact is that Lisbeï has been the Mother-designate of Bethely since leaving the garderie! If I, an ordinary dotta, was so upset by not becoming a Red, can you imagine what it would do to her? I'm sure you do!

And to Selva. And to Tula. You should have seen how Tula looked at Lisbeï the day of Meralda's necklace ceremony.

The more time passes, the more I think I was wrong to believe your figures and not follow my intuition. I should have at least spoken to them three years ago and given them more time to prepare. The time I wish I'd had—yes, I know: one mustn't try to relive one's own life through the lives of others, and "the sum of one individual's experience is really of no use to another." And all the other wise things you told me, that Linta told me, that I tell myself. If you were here, it would be easier to believe, I suppose. I miss you. I miss your strength, your light.

I'm faltering as I write. It's as though my mind were blocked. After all this time I'm still not used to it. I was so fiercely independent before meeting you, wasn't I? The travella setting forth in the desert, believing she'll never be thirsty or that she can recycle herself forever.

But I don't want to think about you only to avoid thinking of what I could say to Selva or to Lisbeï. Still, I'm not sure I'll tell them that it may be "a perverse effect of a fairly benign mutation." Would it help much at this point? It might do more harm than good. Not only might the Mother of Bethely be sterile, but a mutant to boot! Poor Selva would never hold up her head again. The Cartanos would expire with delight.

But you know, it's still the most likely theory: that somehow the same mechanism that speeds up healing in other cases interprets the changes of puberty as a malady and "cures" the subject each time menstruation looms (or once and for all, who knows?). That it may not do so systematically fits my theory: a secondary mutation. Oh, what I'd give for the kind of instruments postulated in the article by Seneca of Lletrewyn! You must have read it (in the last issue but one of the Exploras' Newsletter): she attempts a reconstruction of the kinds of apparatus used by the biologists who wrote the Sanctuary Fragments. If only we could prove (or disprove), once and for all, these cursed theories that I—we—have been dragging about for years! Perhaps Balte of Gualtière was right after all, and it would have been better to have started from scratch, never to have found anything from the Decline and especially the Sanctuary. Better not to have constructed or learned of theories without ever being able to test them clinically; better not to have discovered that the technology would exist if only we could build the industrial infrastructure to manufacture it. And better not to know that we can't do it because we lack the sources of energy and enough raw materials. It's too frustrating, and in the long run it wears the spirit down.

18

One day in early Septemra, a train of three large wagons stopped in the courtyard. Lisbeï was playing there with Tula after the midday meal, and now she and two other Greens were detailed to help unload the wagons. The sacks weren't heavy, and judging from the dry rustle beneath the canvas, there must be nuts inside. Lisbeï looked toward Tula to share her guess about the sacks' contents, but Tula was busy talking to a big Green with cropped brown hair. She seemed all excited. Curious, Lisbeï walked over. Who was she? Lisbeï had never seen this Green in Bethely, she felt sure, and yet she wore the Family tunic and emblem.

Tula turned to Lisbeï, grinning with delight. "It's Garrec, Lisbeï! Do you remember?"

Lisbeï stared at the Green for a moment. Suddenly something clicked, like the revelation with the cube, and she saw a Green *boy* although she didn't recognize Garrec. Of course! All the boys went to Malverde Farm when they left the garderies. It was a dozen klims to the west of Bethely—she knew this, but she'd only just remembered. And she knew that Blue men lived on Farms. There were even a few—very few—Blue men in the Towers, half a dozen at most. And once, when walking through the Library with Mooreï, she'd seen an unknown Red poring over maps spread out on a table. "Have you found what you were looking for, Fillip?" Mooreï had asked. Lisbeï had felt the same startled comprehension: she was looking at one of the new males-in-residence, Fillip of Westershare, whom she had already met in a corridor several times but never really *seen*. Now she realized that most of the unfamiliar Greens unloading the wagons were boys.

Tula threw an arm around Garrec's shoulders, and he smiled, shuffling from one foot to the other with embarrassment. "It's Garrec, Lisbeï. Surely you remember?"

Lisbeï shrugged. "Not really. We'd better get on with the unloading if we want to play afterward."

Tula let go of the boy, who hurried off to another wagon. Lisbeï turned on her heel and carried her sack to the portico, returning for another. Tula, after standing still for a moment, did the same. They worked side by side for a while without saying anything.

"You had Meralda and the others!" Tula blurted out finally.

The violence of her light left Lisbeï speechless. Then she reacted indignantly, protesting. It wasn't the same! And Meralda didn't exactly hug her when they met one another. (After their brawl, Meralda had been moved to the East Tower.)

"That's the point: it's not the same," said Tula with a logic that completely escaped Lisbeï. "Garrec was always nice to me. I was all alone and so was he. He loved stories, and I made him laugh. It's hard for a boy, all alone in the garderie." She set her lips in a tight line, grabbed a sack, and walked off.

Lisbeï watched her go, dumbfounded. Tula and Garrec in the garderie? Tula . . . and Garrec? Together? The thoughts came slowly, then faster, then with burning speed. Together how? What did they do together? Did Tula tell him about her, about all their secrets? What did they *do*?

How could she ask? She didn't want to ask! Tula might say nothing when she came back for another sack, and the incident would be over and done with. But no.

"Garrec cried almost every night after Turri and Rubio left. After all, their bodies may be different, but Elli made them that way, isn't that so? And if they didn't exist we couldn't make babies, could we? Why are they kept apart, anyway? Why can't they stay in the Towers with us?"

Lisbeï took the safest course and chose to reply to Tula's protest as though it were a real question. "Because they're being trained at Malverde."

"I know that, but what do they learn that couldn't be learned here? What are they being trained for?"

"For the Service."

It was the usual response, the one Lisbeï had received when she asked the same question. In her case she'd been shunted back and forth between Antonë and Mooreï, between genetics and genealogical trees. When the Green boys became Red males, they went to do their Service in other Families with compatible genes. Two years per Family. To do their Service really well, especially if they were chosen to be the Mother's Male, they had to learn a few of the Family languages: Iturri, Moski, Litali, or Frangleï. Some Families also taught their Green boys the history of the Families in which they were to serve, the geography, the Cartas, and "their rules, traditions, customs, and other idiosyncrasies not committed to writing." So Selva had said, after which she had meanly profited by the occasion to make Lisbeï look up "idiosyncrasy" in the dictionary. That was what Selva would have liked for the future Red males of Bethely, and in fact she was gradually making changes in the Malverde program. Green boys would actually have to know almost as much as the Mother, Lisbeï realized with some surprise when she first explained all this to Tula. Except that they could never be the Mother, naturally!

"You learn the same things, don't you? But you stay here," Tula stated.

"I'm learning *all* languages and the history of *all* Families," corrected Lisbeï with dignity, thereby giving herself time to think. Tula was right. The Green boys could have learned everything right here in the Towers.

Lisbeï was forgetting about the argument that had started the discussion. Tula, always sensitive to Lisbeï's shifts in mood, decided to follow suit as usual by asking the right question—or maybe the wrong one, or in any case the most unsettling.

"Do you think they learn the same things as you do with Antonë?"

Most of Lisbeï's lessons took place in Selva's office, under the aegis of the Book of Bethely. One morning shortly after her tenth birthday, she was sent instead to see Antonë in the West Tower infirmary.

The Medicina opened a padlocked cupboard, its contents hidden by frosted glass, and took out a number of long, smooth objects. At first Lisbeï thought they must be funny wooden sculptures, all the same shape but different sizes. But Antonë wouldn't have handled mere sculptures with such brusqueness, or set them down on the table with such a clear burst of resolution. She folded her arms, and in this unconscious imitation of Selva, Lisbeï thought she knew the source of this change in routine.

Right from the start, not only the future Mother but all new dottas learned about the things that every well-brought-up Bethely should know: dietetics, botany, entomology, agriculture, and animal wifery. The mechanics, laws, and problems of plant and animal genetics held no secrets for well-trained dottas. (Genetics, of course, meant the knowledge reconstituted from the Fragments, a point Antonë was always careful to insist on, once she had fully replaced the aging Marcella.) Dottas were allowed to watch ovinas being born, as well as chicks and kittens. Only Reds could witness human birth, but the process was pretty much the same, as Lisbeï could see from the anatomical pictures Antonë showed her.

There were differences between animals and humans, nevertheless. First and foremost was the fact that, despite various mutations, the animals hadn't been affected by Elli's punishment. They produced almost as many males as females. And although rutting was part of Elli's pattern, humans weren't subject to that kind of biological constraint (and a good thing too, Lisbeï had told herself after being taken with the others to watch a Bethely cavala being mounted by a stallion).

How did it work with humans?

"Elli's love brings them together," Mooreï had once said. Antonë had remarked sarcastically (and a dull pain had flashed through her aura) that this was outside her field and she was content simply to examine the operation of biological machines. Lisbeï hadn't paid much attention at the time. She must have been eight and accustomed to the amiable but persistent taking of sides in discussions between the Memory and the Medicina.

Anyway, dottas (and Lisbeï before any of her peers) learned at the time of their tattooing how humans made their infantes: with a syringe. And they all knew that love among humans had nothing to do with the production of children.

As to *why* humans made children . . .

"Well, if they didn't, you wouldn't be here to ask," Antonë had said. At first the irony had escaped Lisbeï. Reds made babies, who grew up to become mothers, who made babies; that was the familiar pattern of the world, the Tapestry of Elli, Mooreï had explained, having left her "knitting" in the garderie. But Lisbeï was beginning to recognize certain of Antonë's wry smiles as an invitation to push the question further, and so she had repeated it, curious to see what would happen.

"Women make children because if they didn't, the human race would disappear, and apparently it doesn't want to disappear. There is something in every human that urges her to reproduce," Antonë had said, suddenly and inexplicably bitter. But how was this so different from Mooreï's answer? In fact it wasn't nearly so satisfying. At least Mooreï had known what this "something" was: the desire of Elli, the pleasure of Elli in seeing Elli's creation dancing. Antonë's "something" had seemed uncomfortably like Turri's "because they have to!" of garderie days.

But the Mother didn't do things in the same way as ordinary Reds. The Mother made babies "with the Male"—the West Tower Male and no other. Neither Antonë nor Mooreï had been able to allay Lisbeï's anxieties this time. The Mother "Danced with the Male," a capital *D* kind of dancing. This happened at various times, and also at the Celebration. The Celebration was "the thanksgiving that we all offer to Elli on the night of the sumra solstice." Well, all right. But only Reds and Blues could take part in the Celebration. On that night the dottas went to bed early, exhausted by the preparations. They'd been busy since sunup, what with all those flowers to pick and then arrange around the great platform set up in the middle of the courtyard—flowers that covered every single board and made the platform appear to float on a sea of plant life. In the afternoon they were allowed to run around the Fair and gorge themselves on fritters and candy. As the crowning treat, they were given a whole goblet of Solstice Wine. How could they fail to sleep after that?

All Lisbeï's cunning had produced nothing very enlightening. The only thing she'd learned was that Reds and Blues Danced with the Mother and the Male on the night of the Celebration. You had to know the steps of the Dance by heart so as not to get in the way of Elli's Celebration, and that was why the dottas had to work hard at the taïtche and the parade. In exasperation, she had finally asked Mooreï point-blank. Mooreï had smiled solemnly: you had to walk before you could run, and Lisbeï would learn about the Celebration all in good time, when she became a Red. For once the fact of being the future Mother of Bethely earned her no premature knowledge.

"You'll be a Red before you're the Mother, Lisbeï. Don't be afraid; you'll know what you need to know when the time comes."

Why not tell her about the Celebration now? Was it really so bad to know about things before they happened?

Mooreï had laughed—unexpectedly, since the Celebration seemed to matter to her a lot. "Ah, Lisbeï, sometimes yes, sometimes no." And she had made a funny face that wrinkled her nose. "It's not a very satisfactory answer, I know. Just tell yourself that . . . the Celebration is a surprise. You don't want to know about surprises ahead of time, do you?"

Lisbeï hadn't been so convinced. In the garderie, if she hadn't imagined time and time again what she'd find beyond the garden wall, she'd surely have been sick with the fear and strangeness of those first days in the Tower, just like the other dottas—even if the reality had in fact been totally different from the stories she'd made up for Tula. But then, quite unbidden, the memory of Tula's long-awaited reappearance had sprung to mind, of how she'd rehearsed it hundreds of times, and how horribly different the reality had been.

Mooreï had watched her, hesitating. "There are things

you have to learn for yourself, Lisbeï," she'd said at last. "Supposing you had never seen the color purple. People could try to describe it to you, but it wouldn't be the same thing as seeing it, would it?"

"Supposing I'd never seen an Abomination," Lisbeï had retorted, unimpressed by Mooreï's logic. "If I were warned, I'd be less afraid on my first patrol."

Mooreï had knelt at that, with a loud rustling of her robe (now blue), and had taken Lisbeï's hands in hers. She seemed terribly upset. "Lisbeï, you mustn't be afraid! The Celebration is a great, a beautiful, a wonderful surprise. You mustn't be afraid of Elli!"

But Lisbeï wasn't afraid of *Elli!* She wasn't afraid of the Celebration, either. She just wanted to know what it was.

And now Antonë placed the wooden objects on her office table. "Since you are to be the Mother of Bethely, you must be prepared for the Celebration." She paused for a moment, then added, "And you'll tell no one about this, Lisbeï. It's only for the Mother of Bethely, and absolutely no one else must know. Promise?"

"Promise," said Lisbeï, flattered. She stepped up to the table to inspect the pieces of wood. They were slightly curved, one end a little bigger, the other circled by a sort of ring, with two symmetrical bulges and a small hole. Antonë must have perceived her rather anxious puzzlement, even without touching her, because the Medicina heaved a sigh and made an effort to calm her own emotions. She wasn't very good at it in those days, however. She picked up an anatomy book, opened it at the page on the male body, and placed a finger on a picture marked, "penis in erection."

"Same thing, in three dimensions," she said, pointing to the objects. "It's also called a 'phallus.' "

Lisbeï absorbed this information with polite interest. All right, so there was one word more to describe the male organ, as against a dozen for the female. It was perfectly normal. After all, this organ was basically one of Elli's clever tricks, making it easy for women to get the men's seeds—men's "genes."

Antonë explained very precisely how the "penis in erection" functioned for the Mother, and showed her how to use the little phallus. She told Lisbeï how to be careful not to hurt herself and even explained why she had to do the exercises. It was to get used to this kind of penetration.

Then, gritting her teeth as though in response to an objection that Lisbeï was surely not making, Antonë stated, "They train males, don't they?"

"You should have asked her how," said Tula when they met after lunch.

Lisbeï shrugged. She'd already explained: for the Mother, the males rubbed their penis and a liquid called "sperm" spurted out, rather like getting a pump going.

"They already know how to do that!" exclaimed Tula scornfully. "No one needs to teach them, for Elli's sake. There must be something else." Tula seemed unaware of Lisbeï's stupefaction and had already moved on to another subject. Could she try the phallus too?

"You're too little," said Lisbeï impulsively. "You'll hurt yourself. You didn't see how Antonë did it—"

"Well show me!"

But it wasn't the same. And anyway only the Mother of Bethely used the Male that way. Tula didn't need to train for it.

A wave of wounded disbelief emanated from Tula, and Lisbeï suddenly woke up. Was she refusing to share something with Tula? Of course she would share! When she'd promised Antonë not to tell anyone, she obviously hadn't included Tula! Naturally it was still "you and me together."

They found a quiet corner and began the exercises. It certainly was strange, this "penetration" (even with the small beginner phalluses and using the cautious, graduated approach recommended by Antonë). It wasn't much like their familiar explorations with a finger. And then the idea of a body attached to the other end of the thing . . . But that was exactly the problem: Lisbeï couldn't imagine it. The only body she could imagine so close to hers was Tula's, but that was completely different: they rolled over one another or caressed each other for the sheer *pleasure* of it! With the Male, there'd be this big, queer thing inside her, pushing in as though . . . as though it were going to fill every bit of space! She tried telling herself that she'd be getting what her seeds—her *chromosomes*—needed, the other half for making proper babies, but still it seemed like an intrusion. The funny thing was that she felt it would have been different with the insemination syringe. But with the Male . . . just to feel that body so close and that bit of it inside her . . . and more than that, surely: the foreign presence invading her, when until now only Tula's hand, Tula's light . . . But what sacrilege—how could she even think of the two at once, of coupling with the Male and making love with Tula!

When Antonë had discussed—argued—the matter with Selva, she had realized full well that techniques used in Progressista Families had as yet no place in Bethely. She might be ignoring Selva's orders, but she nevertheless preferred to stick to what she knew. She'd said nothing about pleasure. She herself had never wanted to take part in a Celebration.

Lisbeï and Tula tried the phallus and had to stifle an attack of helpless giggles, all the more intense because of the danger of being found in their hiding place.

The Celebration must be something else, they both decided. The phallus was a surprise all right, but "a great, a beautiful surprise"? No. Something more than that must happen between the Mother and the Male during the Celebration.

"Do you think they do it in front of everyone?" asked Tula, having pondered the question at length. "You said they made Elli."

Lisbeï could see the logic of this: Elli was all, both male and female, and by coupling in this way, Mother and Male could somehow recreate the unity of Elli. To make Elli, even in such a relative way, couldn't really be unpleasant, could it? The Mother did what she had to: it was an honor and a duty. But at the same time it was—well, a little *embarrassing*.

"We've got to stay awake for the next Celebration," said Tula. Lisbeï had reached the same conclusion, but she felt vaguely uncomfortable about it. Greens didn't take part in the Celebration. It was truly, truly forbidden. Still, she was the future Mother. . . .

The Celebration came and went, but Lisbeï and Tula were none the wiser, for they had succumbed to the soporific in the Solstice Wine and slept soundly through the whole thing.

Which of them thought of the next move? Lisbeï doesn't remember. They didn't always communicate with words. Ideas rose like half-formed bubbles that they nudged back and forth, the bubbles swelling as each added her questions, desires, and fears, until the idea materialized in words—words

that gave it meaning and direction. "The Mother's new Male
has arrived," Lisbeï heard people remarking in the corridors a
few months later. She and Tula knew that the Mother often
made Elli with the Male in order to get babies, not just on the
night of the Celebration. It was like Red women going to the
infirmaries several times during their fertile period. The bubble burst, and this time the idea that emerged pointed to
Selva's rooms.

Night. Sumra. Selva and the Male are together, as they
have been every night since the beginning of the week, for
Selva is fertile now. Her bedroom windows are open, like all
the windows of Bethely. Elli has been hot and humid all day
long. Selva's door is also open to catch the first cool drafts
that will begin moving through the heavy air in the night. The
door opens onto the short passage and private spiral staircase
leading to the Library. And ever since the incident with Meralda, Lisbeï's room has been at the other end of the passage.

Tula, having slipped noiselessly from her bed, is in Lisbeï's room. They haven't met like this at night for a long time.
The powers that be have given up trying to separate them, and
they see each other during the day now.

Lisbeï really shouldn't be uneasy: she's been noting the
comings and goings of Selva and the Male for the last two
weeks, and she's thought of everything—oiled the hinges,
tested for squeaky floor boards. She's tried to foresee all even-
tualities, even the ghastly prospect of being caught. But as
always when on the brink of reality, she wants to wait a while,
put off the moment when the balance will be tipped. An impatient Tula pulls at her arm. "Come on, or they'll be asleep!"

The passage is dark on this almost moonless night. A
faint light from a gasole in Selva's room makes the shadows
deeper. But it's not the shadows that stop Lisbeï. It's the
noise, a sort of faint, rhythmical creaking. Tula tugs at her
again. They hug the wall on either side of the open door.

Shadows move on the ceiling, on the walls. The lamp
stands on the floor beside the bed. On the bed itself they can
see a massive shape—lines, curves, glimmers that resolve
themselves suddenly into two naked bodies gleaming with
sweat. In the foreground is Selva, turned slightly toward the
door, eyes closed, face half-hidden by her disheveled hair.
Selva, on all fours, supported by her elbows. And the Male
. . . is he straddling her? No, he's on his knees behind her.
He's gripping her shoulders, digging his fingers in, and shov-

ing her hard, again and again. She's gripping the edge of the bed, it's the bed that's creaking. Her whole body quivers with each push, her arms, her breasts, her face. The Male is lost in the shadows above her. Only his hair catches the light now and then.

He begins moving faster and panting hard. And suddenly he falls on top of Selva with a kind of groan, a weird, throaty cry. She doesn't move, and he slides off her, lying flat on his stomach beside her. He's still panting. Are Selva's eyes still closed? Impossible to see, as the hair has fallen right over her face now. After a while she rolls over and lies aslant the bed, not touching the Male. "Goodnight Aleki," she says, her voice clear and cold. The Male gets up, picks something off the floor—his dressing gown. He slips it on and walks to the open door at the other end of the room, where another passage leads to his quarters. On the threshold he turns, his voice full of malicious triumph. "What one has to do to be the Mother!" He shuts the door.

Selva hasn't moved. After a long pause she rises. There are dark marks on her shoulders, hips, and thighs. She takes the lamp and puts it on her dressing table, sits down, and picks up her big tortoiseshell comb. Lisbeï can see Selva's face perfectly, alight in the darker oval of the mirror. Staring into her own eyes in the glass, pulling the comb unflinchingly through a tangle in the red hair, the Mother is weeping.

19

Lisbeï/Journal

Wardenberg, 3 Aprila, 490 A.G.

. . . but now I realize it must have been before. We'd never have gone to see a Blue man after that. Not me, anyway. Do you realize we never spoke of it? We never talked about boys after

that, either, except in the most carefully impersonal way. No, it must have been before, even before Antonë's lesson. I think it was your idea, since it's highly unlikely that I'd take it into my head to speak to a Blue man, even before. But perhaps you were thinking about Garrec. How would I know? Anyway, you were the one who came and fetched me, saying there was a Nevenici Blue man in the stables. I believed you wanted to get him talking about the sea. We were little, of course, but do you remember how gigantic he seemed? Broad and burly, hairy all over, and hands like paddles. But he was really pleased to see us, to see little dottas—almost childeishly pleased, I now realize.

He mopped his brow and pretended to frown. "Well, well, what have we here?" But he didn't tell us to go away.

"We've come to see the new foales," you said, and he smiled. He hadn't seen them born, of course—he wasn't allowed —but he was as proud as though he'd made them himself. He pointed out how beautiful they were, especially the white one. We talked a little about animals, and I was wondering how to lead up gently to the subject when you dived right in with, "What's Nevenici like?"

He looked surprised, probably at the change of subject. Then he laughed. But at the same time he was pleased and flattered. He sat down on a hay bale, grinning. His face was all sunburned and wrinkled; he had two front teeth missing and his hair was cut very short. Come to think of it, he can't have been so old, not even forty.

"And what do you want to know about Nevenici, little dottas?"

"The boats," I said. "The big ones that cross the Tirannean Sea. Have you seen them?"

"Yes indeed. I've helped build some of them."

I guess you wanted to know whether he'd gone to Afrike, but you let him tell us how the big boats were made in his Family. He was glad to talk about it. Glad and sad. A funny mixture that I didn't quite understand. After a while he stopped and looked at his big, callused hands. "But that was long ago, when I was a Green." And he sighed.

And suddenly, as he said it, I sensed such a sorrow. . . .

"Was it good when you were a Green? Better than now?"

He didn't answer right away, but he looked at you for a while and must have decided that it would do no harm to reply. "In a way, yes," he said. "I was home."

How could I have appreciated such a feeling then? Anyway,

*I felt his light was rather blurred, as with almost everyone except
you and Antonë and Kelys—and sometimes Selva, when she was
willing. But you seemed to understand that it was nostalgia.*

"Why didn't you go back?"

"I haven't the right."

*It was true: Nevenici was a Juddite Family, and they didn't
want their Blue men to return. I had overheard Antonë speak of
it to Kelys.* "It's really stupid," *she'd said.* "What are they afraid
of? Do they think they'll be raped?" *But since I didn't know what*
"raped" *meant, I merely sensed that Antonë had been crude on
purpose to shock Kelys. Kelys didn't turn a hair, of course.*

*As you and the Nevenici Blue had fallen silent, I decided to
take things in hand and ask a question that interested me.* "Is the
training after the garderie difficult? Is it true that Green boys
learn sort of the same things as the Mother?"

*He must have still been lost in memory, because he mut-
tered,* "Yes, yes," *rather absentmindedly, then stiffened a little.
My studiously innocent air must have reassured him, because he
smiled.*

"Not exactly," *he said.* "But when you travel a lot, you need
to know a great deal."

*Before I could think up another question that wouldn't
scare him off, you jumped in.* "Were you sorry to leave
Nevenici?"

*I was quite taken aback, and so was he, but probably not for
the same reason. He stared at you for a moment with his brown,
slightly opaque eyes, and then slowly, as though searching for the
words, he said,* "No. The new males are proud to go and do their
Service, little dotta. The males are the redeemers, the servants of
Elli, the ones who atone for the sins of the men of the Decline."

*I thought he was about to launch into a speech, but he
stopped suddenly, and I could sense an emotion like Antonë's
when she realized she'd said too much. I don't know what you
sensed. I was about to urge him to continue when you said pensively,* "But you're no longer a Red now." *The two of you looked
at each other, and a strange feeling passed between you, too
quickly for me to comprehend. He nodded as though pleased
with you and repeated sadly,* "I'm no longer a Red."

*With that, two Reds arrived and he stood up, suddenly em-
barrassed. I could feel it. I can't remember who the women were.
All I recall is the way they told him to stack the hay bales without
bothering to look at him. We followed them, but I looked back
and saw him lift a bale almost as big as himself and heave it on*

*top of the others. I knew what his body was saying: he was angry.
I didn't ask myself why. What I registered most was his strength.
I'd been told I was tall and strong for my age. I wondered
whether I would get as strong as that. I wasn't even afraid. But
that was before we'd seen Selva with the Male.*

20

Tula preferred lessons with Mooreï. She attended them with
other dottas her age, and did the same with Antonë and the
captas in charge of practical training—cooking, carpentry, and
Bethely's most important barter commodity, rugs and fabrics.
She wasn't much interested in Antonë's classes. To tell the
truth, they were dull at that period, for Antonë fed the dottas
facts and figures as though it were now terribly important for
the young Medicina to prove that the living world was a machine—a complex machine, of course, but one that would
yield up all its secrets to systematic examination. That was the
year that Kelys came in the wintra. But she and Antonë were
almost never seen together, like magnets that could never
connect.

No doubt Tula preferred the ambience generated by
Mooreï because of the Memory's inner peace, her certainties.
Although Tula couldn't perceive these as clearly as Lisbeï did,
nor even as clearly as she perceived Antonë's fragile stiffness,
still she liked the Word better than biology. Tula, it seemed,
wasn't troubled by Antonë's light, nor Mooreï's, and even less
by Selva's since she had rarely encountered the Mother at
close quarters. Of course Selva's mirror-wall, so like Tula's,
was something the two dottas wouldn't discuss. Tula accepted
her shared resonance with Lisbeï without a second thought:
they were like that because Elli wanted it. She couldn't see
why anyone would consider the Word and biology as opposite
poles, as Antonë implied. The Word was obviously more complete. Lisbeï, with her penchant for seeing things from various
angles at once, now found herself in the odd position of up-
holding a point of view she didn't really support. Like Tula,
she didn't consider the Word and biology as opposites—they

complemented each other. Nevertheless, her fertile imagination immediately produced objections to Tula's certitudes, even though she agreed with her.

Tula threw up her hands. How could you be on both sides at once? That's how it had to be, Lisbeï tried to explain. The Capta must try to see all the different points of view and bring them together. Well, Tula remarked, that wasn't exactly what Selva did! The discussion ended in short order. The two of them found it hard to talk about Selva in any way.

The fact was that, for Tula, Mooreï's cube was either hollow or full.

"It's both things at once," protested Lisbeï. "What changes is our point of view when we look at it." And right away she began to wonder what happened when nobody looked at the cube. Tula shrugged slightly and replied that there was always Elli, everywhere, all-seeing. So perfect was this answer in assuring the continued existence of the world that Lisbeï couldn't find a thing to say against it.

Possibly this wholehearted faculty for believing only one thing at a time was what made the taïtche so hard for Tula. She had no trouble slipping into the light trance that followed Kelys's breathing and concentration exercises. In this she resembled Lisbeï and a few other dottas of her generation. But she couldn't stop there. Where Lisbeï soon learned to balance on the thread between the inner and outer sides of her body, Tula kept on slipping toward the exterior. The frontiers of consciousness and body melted outward, and Kelys had to interrupt the first session because Tula had fallen into a sort of coma. After that she could only continue training by making use of the mirror-wall. At least in this way she was able to go through the basic movements without a mistake, and even executed them with an easy grace that gave the illusion of mastery. But she knew and Lisbeï knew that she was somehow applying the letter, not the spirit, of what Kelys was trying to teach them. They agreed tacitly not to speak of the taïtche to each other.

When she started training with a partner for the parade, however, the tables turned. The taïtche taught you to know the boundaries of your body and to situate it exactly in its own space. You brushed the boundaries of someone else's space very briefly and immediately returned to your own. The parade, by contrast, taught you to reach out toward your partner's space, to touch it, mold to it. And now Lisbeï couldn't get free of her thread. If she did . . . But after a while she had to give up, heart pounding, sweat pouring down her body, concentration shattered. Something had drawn her back into herself, she knew not what or how, for her memory was a blank.

Lisbeï was coming out of the showers after the session, thoroughly downcast, when the long-legged gymna-maestra caught up with her. "Wait a minute, Lisbeli," said Kelys. She would always use this pet name, even when Lisbeï was a grown woman. Kelys led her back to the exercise room, sat down on a mat with supple grace, and waved to Lisbeï to do the same. She seemed to meditate for a moment, then smiled. "It seems we have a small problem."

Lisbeï stopped herself from snorting sarcastically. A small problem! She wasn't capable of performing the parade! She, the future Mother who would one day have to Dance before all Bethely at the Celebration, was incapable of performing the parade!

"I say we," continued Kelys as though she hadn't noticed Lisbeï's reaction, "because I had the same kind of problem. It seems you can't always be very good at both the taïtche and the parade."

Lisbeï had straightened up and was looking at her with incredulous hope, already full of gratitude. Kelys could help her, of course Kelys was going to help her!

"Do you remember the first taïtche session, Lisbeli? At the very beginning, when you felt yourself moving outward? You learned to shorten that phase a bit too well. And now you suppress the impulse without even realizing it. That's where we have to start. Will you try doing it with me?"

Yes indeed, Lisbeï would to it with Kelys! And at first there'd been no problem. She was able to get back to the first phase of the taïtche, especially with Kelys and her calm presence, so perfectly . . . ordered. And when Kelys began to slip into the phases of the parade, Lisbeï thought that all would be well here too. All you had to do was open yourself to the fluctuations in the other's presence and imitate them. It was very simple—let the echoes play back and forth, changing little by little, quickening from resonance to resonance like the light between two mirrors and—

And Lisbeï found herself kneeling on the mat, shaking, her throat burning from an unheard scream. Kelys caught her up and cradled her for a while, and when Lisbeï could at last perceive the other's light, she knew by Kelys's slightly sad resignation that the gymna-maestra could do nothing for her.

Kelys didn't even try to tell her that she should have developed a mirror-wall, as Tula had done for the taïtche. It, or something like it, some inner configuration, was needed to perform the parade well, but Kelys knew that Lisbeï wouldn't manage it. Lisbeï would have been amazed to be told that it was the very fact of perceiving this mirror-wall that had made her break off contact with Kelys, as she had done earlier with her practice partner. Lisbeï wouldn't have understood why—and of course she would never be able to train for the parade with Tula.

At last, in despair, Lisbeï decided to sidestep the concentration exercises and make use of her usual perceptions of those around her. For some reason it was less difficult when not in a trance. She could filter her perceptions and control them sufficiently to adapt her movements to her partner's. But she always moved just a bit too much or too late. The gap was to shrink through relentless training, until it became imperceptible to any but the eye of a very attentive observer such as Kelys—or Tula.

Like the taïtche, the parade disappeared from their conversation.

21

Antonë to Linta

Bethely, 14 Marsa, 487 A.G.

Dearest Linta,
Your letter did me a lot of good. Frankly, I often had to fight back the tears as I read. We are better friends than we ever were compagnas—and perhaps, as you once said, we never should have become compagnas. I feel you understand what's happen-

ing better than I do, better than Kelys. At least you have no
motive for pretending not to understand. She's too perceptive in
every sense of the word not to understand my state of mind. She
must have decided, for reasons that she intends to keep to herself, to behave as though she didn't comprehend. As far as she's
concerned, we've given each other what we had to give, and
that's the end of it. She still keeps quietly out of my way. When
she can't avoid a meeting, she's as nice as can be, even sincere
about it, which obviously makes the whole thing even harder to
bear. There's no talking to her, though. Anyway, she's leaving
next week on her new expedition.

Enough. One letter full of wailing and gnashing of teeth is
permissible, but not two. You've had your say on the subject. I
agree, I knew it all along, but it's so much more convincing
coming from someone else, especially you. I'll keep on mulling it
over and try not to let my emotional outlook harden. But it's
difficult. Think of me, my sweet, and pray for me if you will. (No,
I didn't smile on reading that last line. I was moved, very moved.
Thank you for being there.)

News, news. Well, nothing much to add on that score. The
Assembly is looming, and everyone is beginning to get fidgety,
especially if this is their first time attending the Games. It was
only in '72 that Litale agreed to send dottas to the Games, and
the thought of the journey—never mind the Games—has the
little ones in a tizzy. You can't walk down a Green corridor in the
evening without hearing music or recitation. The workrooms and
gymna halls are never empty. Also, people are edgy about the
question of admitting the youngest Blue men and giving the
Green boys a greater part in the Games. There is a rumor that
some Families (nasty Progressistas, naturally!) began training
Green boys and young Blue men as soon as they knew that the
motions had been tabled last Novemra. The speculation is that if
the Assembly adopts the Wardenberg motion, they will insist on it
taking effect right away and enter their participants in all the
trials allowed.

A lot of fuss for nothing, in my opinion. I'll be very surprised
if the Wardenberg motion gets through. As usual, they've only
proposed it to give more moderate motions a chance. What
amazes me (and of course delights me) is that anyone can still
fall for this old ruse. The Lletrewyn motion might pass. . . . But
no, that's my scientific bias talking; it's too technical, too clut-
tered with figures. More likely the Kergoët motion will get
through. Anyhow, we'll be lucky if the Assembly only lasts for the

*usual month. Then the approved motion (or better still a synthe-
sis of various motions) will go back to the provincial Assemblies.
The Progressistas have certainly stirred up a veritable beehive (or
should I say Greenhive?) that isn't likely to stop buzzing very
soon.*

*In any case the Green girls who'll be in this year's Games
are forever talking about it. And not only the Greens, of course.
It's interesting to see how people take sides and especially to
speculate on why they do. I'd have thought they'd all be against
the idea. But no: it seems that the fact of living with boys in the
garderies has made the dottas and youngest Red women more
tolerant. Or more open to discussion, at least. It's barely fourteen
years since Bethely opted for this change—since Selva, in her
hesitation-waltz with progress, introduced boys to the garderies. It
was one of her first official acts as Mother. But she's still wavering about letting older Green boys visit the Capterie more often—
for festivals, anyway, although certainly not for the Celebration!*

*I really don't know whether Selva will rise for the yes or no
side in the final Assembly vote. She has her very own way of
proving me wrong. I know that Mooreï is generally in favor of
Green boys being allowed to do more (on strictly religious
grounds, which I find—well, amusing, or else somewhat troubling). Not only does she favor it for Green boys and young
Blue men, but for adult men, Red and Blue, and not just in
the Games but in the Assemblies. Not even the most rabid
Progressistas go this far! But she won't be the one voting at Serres-Morèna. Too bad. For once we're on the same side, even if
not for the same reasons!*

*The childreen can't agree—I mean Lisbeï and Tula. That is,
Tula has made up her mind: she's for it, like Mooreï. Lisbeï as
usual swings between pro and con. I get the feeling she might be
against the idea. (Don't ask me why. They were brought up in the
same garderie!) But she loves Tula too much to be at odds with
her for long. It's a rather worrying prospect, should Tula not go as
a ward to Angresea at her first blood, which should occur any
day now.*

*They've made the classic arrangement: Lisbeï's first Male
must be an Angresea, and Twyne, the Angresea Mother's fourth
childe, must come to Bethely as a ward. Neither Lisbeï nor Tula
know this. I'm surprised Selva hasn't told them yet, since the
agreement was ratified at the last Assembly of Mothers. Perhaps*

in spite of everything, Selva herself isn't looking forward to telling them. All I hope, from the bottom of my heart, is that she has the salutary cowardice to let Mooreï do her dirty work!

22

As Antonë read over her letter to Linta, she was struck by another explanation of the Capta's curious silence. Lisbeï would be fourteen in Juna, the very month of the Serres-Morèna Assembly. She still hadn't had her first blood. Perhaps the Mother of Bethely wanted to keep her options open. With a heavy heart, Antonë sealed her letter and left it with the courria. She went on to her botany class, which included Tula's group.

What was wrong with little Tula today? She seemed to veer between a highly excited state and one of complete somnolence, either laughing too loudly as she whispered with her neighbors, or floating off in a fog. Antonë walked by her at the beginning of class and sensed the mirror-wall swing into place with a suddenness that came through almost like a sound—the click of a lock. She'd never been able to gain Tula's complete confidence, that she knew; but usually the childe felt no need to protect herself like this. What was going on? Had Tula done something wrong, or was she contemplating mayhem? Better ask Mooreï if she'd noticed this unusual behavior.

The theoretical part of the class passed off without incident, apart from a general squirming—something Antonë was resigned to: it would be like this until the Games. She marshaled her small flock in preparation for a trip to the herb garden on the South Esplanade. The dottas had difficulty keeping quiet as they walked through the Library behind her. As the group started down the main staircase, nearly deserted at this time of day, the childreen surged around and in front of her. It must be a dare or some new game, Antonë realized as the dottas shouted out numbers and jumped down the stairs, two, then three at a time. Tula's red head disappeared around the bend in the staircase as she cried, "Four!"

Alarmed, Antonë pressed forward, shouting at the children to stop. But when she reached the ground floor, she found them in a group, consternation written on their faces. They separated in guilty silence to let her through. Tula sat on the tiled floor, wax-white beneath her disheveled hair, holding her foot and trying not to grimace. At the sight of Antonë she tried to stand, but to no avail. She bit her lips and turned even whiter.

"Stay still," ordered Antonë, kneeling to untie the sandal laces. "Karlina, get me some ice from the kitchen if there's any. Sentaï, bandages from the infirmary, and Martie, bring a chair." The ankle was already swollen, but nothing appeared broken. It might just be a crack rather than a break. . . . "She fell down a whole flight," said someone in vaguely admiring tones, "head over heels all the way."

Concussion? Possibly a skull fracture? Antonë quickly examined Tula's pupils, but they seemed normal. "We'll see about all this in the infirmary," she muttered. The remark had been made under her breath, but as she stood up, she registered some surprise at the brief flash of—terror? despair?—something, anyway, that had shot through Tula before the mirror-wall clicked unsteadily into place. After all this time, was Tula still frightened by the terrors of the garderie?

Once they reached the infirmary, she began to undress the childe to examine her. Tula was as stiff as a poker. When Antonë started to remove her underpants the childe clutched at her hands. Then suddenly she became a rag doll, and Antonë thought for a moment that it was shock. But the mirror-wall had melted too, and she could sense Tula's despair and resigned misery.

Brown and red spots on the white cotton. Blood.

She told me that she'd realized it just before class and hadn't had time to change, wrote Antonë to Linta three days later. *What would she have done if I hadn't noticed? Hidden the fact? For how long? Of course I didn't ask her: she wouldn't have answered. I asked her if she wanted to tell the Mother herself first, as is the custom here. Frankly, I don't know whether I was all that surprised when she said yes.*

I was a coward, Moorei told Lisbeï. *I didn't ask how the childe took the news.*

So. What I feared, what in fact everyone feared, has hap-

pened. Tula, now well past eleven, is a Red—more or less normal. Lisbeï, the Mother-designate of Bethely, is still a Green at nearly fourteen.

I said nothing about the possible link between sterility and a late occurrence of the Malady. What's the use? Two years from now Lisbeï will either have menstruated or be officially Blue. In either case, knowing there might be a further possible reason for her failure to menstruate won't help. But I don't know if I'll be able to look her in the eye from now on.

Everyone's waiting for Selva's next move. Not that anyone has much doubt about what she can do.

The Mother of Bethely did what she had to. Officially, Lisbeï was to be Mother-designate until her fifteenth year. Tula would discreetly begin an accelerated education program with Selva. Lisbeï would keep on with her studies, since there was hardly any difference between the education of a Mother and her Memory. As for the Angresea agreement, nothing would be said to Lisbeï or Tula. Selva and Mooreï opened intensive negotiations that lasted until the Serres-Morèna Assembly: Bethely would support the Kergoët motion on the Games if Angresea would postpone the exchange for two years and no questions asked. Nobody alluded to Lisbeï's problem, and Selva was grateful to the Mother of Angresea, who clearly knew all about it. Selva did not mention, however, that she'd intended to vote for Kergoët all along.

After the inner Family council in which these decisions were reached, Antonë wrote to Linta again. *What is Selva up to, I wonder? Does she think this will give her two oldest a chance to succeed where she and Loï failed? And yet she knows perfectly well that even half sisters can't be compagnas without attracting opprobrium in the Province (especially if one of them is prematurely Blue), and that it's anathema for a Mother. Of course, you and I agree that this tradition is utter idiocy. What possible harm can it do to the Lines? I ask you! But that's the way it is. Maybe Selva is deliberately defying tradition again, but more openly than before. For the past sixteen years she's stretched Litale customs a little at a time, but often. Perhaps now she's decided to burn her bridges. The Angresea agreement is a pretty thundering statement of intention, even under the nicely traditional guise of an exchange of wards and the new Mother's first Male. Why not pick Kergoët or, better still, Verchères? Both are equally compatible with Bethely, genetically speaking, and they're moderate Progressistas—well, more moderate than An-*

gresea, anyway. But, and this is a big but, Kergoët and Verchères aren't building ocean-going ships, and they've always voted against Western exploration. You certainly can't criticize Selva for not taking the long view!

And in a way Selva is acting for the best. She's keeping Lisbeï and Tula together and saving the Angresea agreement. She hasn't said so, but one must suppose that if Tula becomes official Mother-designate in two years, Ylene will take her place in Angresea. Ylene will be eight by then, the minimum legal age. She'll only have known the garderie here, practically speaking, and she'll certainly find it easier to leave than Tula would have.

Selva is forgetting just one thing: to date, neither Lisbeï nor Tula have really agreed with the way people want to arrange their lives.

2

Bethely

487–489 *A.G.*

1

The light from the setting sun blinded Lisbeï as she climbed out of the pit. She pushed back the earth-smudged curls that kept slipping out of the kerchief knotted around her forehead. Meï's figure stood silhouetted against the apricot sky. Of course they'd sent Meï. Why not Meralda while they were at it? Lisbeï didn't need to see Meï's face to guess at her worried yet disapproving expression.

"Tell her I'm coming. I'm going to wash up a bit first."

The young Red pursed her lips, deprived of the scolding she'd no doubt been primed to administer. "The Mother said *right away.*"

Lisbeï gave her a quizzical smile. "My mother probably wouldn't appreciate dirt in her rooms, would she?"

Without waiting for a reply, she began carefully replacing the boards over the excavation. As she straightened up, she glanced at the Red with studied amazement—what, still here? "Run along and tell Selva. Go on!"

She turned her back on the messenger and stalked off toward the calm expanse of the Douve, catching up her satchel near a pile of earth and rubble as she went.

Meï was determined to have the last word, as usual. "The Mother won't be pleased!" she shouted before scurrying off. Lisbeï kept going as though she'd heard nothing. It wouldn't make much difference anyhow. The Mother was never pleased with her.

All the same, she was rather annoyed with herself for letting the time slip by. The afternoon was nearly over, and the shadow of the Towers stretched beyond the grazing areas on the Esplanade to the Douve and the ball field. The three Towers stood tall against the western sky—flat, black rectangles edged with the lace of outside staircases spiraling with mathematical precision on a gold background. The sunset wouldn't be much, though: no clouds building cliffs and seas in the heavens. An ordinary sunset in an ordinary sprinna sky at the end of a day that was . . . not entirely ordinary, thank Elli! As she had hoped when she began clearing, the conduit uncovered by the cave-in led somewhere. She was positive she'd vindicate her theories by discovering one of Bethely's ancient subterranean passages. Legends weren't just legends!

Energy flowed back. She peeled off work clothes that were stiff with sweat and soil and crouched down beside the water. The surface was smooth, motionless: the locks upstream were closed. She washed quickly. A little dirt remained under her fingernails and bits of earth clung to her tangled hair. But you couldn't keep *the Mother* waiting any longer, could you? Mustn't overdo it. She had surely stayed longer than the allotted two hours. Lisbeï dried herself off with the towel brought for just this purpose and slipped into a clean tunic and slacks. They were rather wrinkled from sitting in a ball in her satchel. Loathsome green clothes! If she had any choice in the matter, she'd have torn them to shreds. Anger overwhelmed her once more, and she threw her satchel roughly over her shoulder. Two hours late? So what! The world wouldn't stop turning. After all, you could take your time when training to be a Memory, couldn't you? The past wasn't going to run away overnight. The Library and its Archives would be there in the morning. If only it were just the past! But there was also the present, those interminable figures for Farm production and inventories and accounts! You could certainly be two hours late for the chore of totting up those rows of digits yet one more time.

(But the Library and Archives hadn't always been there, observed the part of Lisbeï that couldn't resist arguing, even against herself. The past *could* disappear, or at least be blurred in legend—like the underground passages of Bethely.)

And be rediscovered! If only she could keep on digging . . . No, tomorrow—if she weren't punished for the rest of the week.

Tomorrow, no matter what!

She could have retraced her steps toward the main entrance, crossing the Esplanade directly to the West Tower, but instead she followed the curve of the Douve, making a wide circle by the South Tower. This added only five or six minutes. She did it on principle. Six o'clock really had come and gone, and the workas returning from the gardens and the paper mill straggled in little groups along the road. Among them were two or three Reds crossing the little bridge. They greeted Lisbeï by name. She muttered an answer and walked faster. Of course she had no idea who they were. But who did not know Lisbeï these days in Bethely?

Rather than follow them on the road to the Esplanade, she continued along the path beside the river until she reached the South Garderie. She stood there a while, fists jammed into her pockets, looking at the high, ivy-covered wall behind which the little mostas laughed and played in another world. Was she now nostalgic for her days in the garderie? Days when she'd been no one, an almost-person? She knew nothing then and could dream of everything. And the world had been complete, because she was there with . . .

She began running as hard as she could, and it must have been the wind in her eyes that brought the tears. She rounded the circular garderie wall, left the path halfway up the hill, and cut across the wide terreplein, scattering caprinas and ovinas as she went. She scrambled down the other side and headed for the Towers, zigzagging between piles of straw and bales of hay, past the warm, strong odors of the South Tower barns, faster and faster now, running as though she were late, as though it mattered, for the benefit of any Reds, Greens, or Blues who might be watching. *See? I'm hurrying, the Mother is waiting, am I not an obedient daughter?* In reality she ran for the mere sake of running, for the ambiguous pleasure of arriving out of breath and being able to say to Selva, who wouldn't be taken in for a moment, "I ran the whole way."

Selva didn't answer. Her red head, hair screwed back, remained bowed over the thick ledger, and the steel pen continued scratching across the page. Lisbeï kept up her act, gulping air, wiping her forehead, shifting from one foot to the other. She was used to Selva's tactics. It was all a question of who would tire of the silence first. It wouldn't be Lisbeï.

"You'd have to run pretty fast to make up for those three

and a half hours," said Mooreï, rising from the hidden depths of a large armchair.

Selva was cheating! She'd got Mooreï to give the lecture!

"I lost track of time," said Lisbeï with false joviality. But because it was Mooreï, she added, "There really is an underground passage, and it's heading for the South Tower!"

A flash of interest shot through Mooreï's calm aura, but Lisbeï realized she was wasting her time. She wasn't dealing with Mooreï now, but with the Memory of Bethely, speaking for the Mother.

"Your digging mustn't impinge on your work, Lisbeï. It's the second time this week."

But this was part of her work! She was going to be the Memory of Bethely, wasn't she? Bethely's History was her field. Something had to be added to the Archives once in a while, didn't it?

So Mooreï had argued when trying to convince Selva to allow digging after a subsidence had revealed the tip of the underground passage. But not any longer.

"It's only part of a Memory's work. And you'd have to know everything already in the Archives before thinking of adding more."

Lisbeï kept dancing from one foot to another. It wasn't fair having to answer to Mooreï. She refused to get into a fight with *Mooreï!*

"After all, two hours . . ."

"Three and a half," said Selva. Lisbeï turned to the Mother, almost relieved, but the red head was bowed over the ledger still.

"It's a matter of principle, Lisbeï," continued Mooreï. "Do you think you can have your way all the time?"

"I found a replacement for . . ."

"You had no business finding a replacement. For the last two weeks you've spent every free minute in that hole and . . ."

Well, free time was free time, wasn't it?

Mooreï came over and took her by the chin. Lisbeï could sense the compassion that hung about her like a desolate fog. She stiffened, and Mooreï let go of her chin. "Lisbeï, we've discussed this a dozen times."

So why begin again?

"Enough!" snapped Selva. This time she meant it. She rose and came round the desk to confront Lisbeï. "You're not

a law unto yourself, Lisbeï. This so-called archaeological dig is
finished and done with. You will spend your free time doing
everything you've let slide, beginning with taking your turn in
the gardens and kitchens. No more replacements. Tomorrow
morning you will report directly to the captas, who will keep
me informed. Is that clear? And you will go back to the chorale and resume your other training."

Lisbeï couldn't contain herself. "I won't go to the
Games!"

"You're registered."

"You can't make me."

"You'll make yourself! Have you no sense of decency, for
Elli's sake?"

"There's no rule saying I have to take part just because
I'm registered!"

The two fell silent for a moment, hackles raised as they
confronted each other. Suddenly Lisbeï could sense Selva's
pained anger, sharp as the smell of burnt bread, but she was
too furious herself to take any pleasure in it.

As usual it was Mooreï who tried to mend things. "You're
the best archa in your age group, Lisbeï, the third-best in
Litale. And you sing so well. Surely you're not going to give it
all up?"

"She knows her duty perfectly well," said Selva, returning
to her seat. "She's the first-living and the Mother-designate."
The cold mirror-wall was distinctly there again.

"A Blue!" Lisbeï exploded at last. "A Blue, Blue, Blue!
I'm a Blue, and I have no duties!"

"You'll be a Blue officially next Juna. Meanwhile, until
Tula has been named, you are still the Mother-designate of
Bethely, and you will conduct yourself accordingly. You may
go now."

Selva's voice had the merciless cutting edge that Lisbeï
had come to recognize. It had always made her yield. Until
now.

"Everyone knows," she cried hoarsely, her voice really
shaking now (but it didn't matter, she wasn't listening to herself, wasn't playing games anymore). "You can't force me,
you have no right. Everyone knows I'm sterile!"

There. The word was out. She'd said it at last. She turned
on her heel, shrugging off Mooreï's hands outstretched to
touch, to calm her. Lisbeï grabbed the door handle, feeling as
though she could have wrenched it from its socket rather than

turn it, ripped the door from its frame, the wall from . . . and she rushed out into the corridor and on toward the spiraling outside staircase.

There were people in the corridor when Lisbeï burst out of Selva's office. She paid no attention. There were always people in the corridors of Bethely, always somebody going somewhere doing something. Sometimes she imagined the Towers being transparent like Antonë's ant terrarium. It was just the same, all these blue dots, or red, or green, forever moving in all directions. There had been a time when this incessant activity had fascinated her, when the adult world and its certainties had been a desired goal. One day she would have all the answers to all the questions and be as powerful as the Reds and Blues. But answers were like fireflies: when you caught them, their lights went out, and there was always another lighting up just a bit farther on. Power . . . who really had power in Bethely? Not Selva, not the Mother. Nor Mooreï, who would have been more worthy of it. Nor Antonë nor Kelys nor any of the captas. The Family Assembly, then, the delegates of the Reds and Blues? No. Everybody. Nobody. Tradition with its stupid rules was the true mistress of Bethely, this invisible shell that everyone always carried around, preventing them from really seeing their surroundings.

Just as she was about to push open the glass door to the outside stairs, Lisbeï halted. The sky was already darkening, but the gleam of the setting sun still caught one facade of the East Tower, lighting up row upon row of molten orange mirrors, broken here and there by the black gap of an open window. She began to descend the staircase into the dark well of the court. In childhood days, she used to see crossword patterns on the Bethely facades, used to imagine them as messages to be deciphered. Night used to bring different messages: "I am awake despite the late hour," or "Someone is with me tonight," or "I'm sleeping." But she used to find messages in everything when she was little, or else she'd invent them so she could tell Tula.

Do we invent the messages the world sends us? Or are they there always for us merely to decipher? "Elli's design in the pattern of the Tapestry," Mooreï had said in answer to these childeish questions. But Elli hadn't built Bethely. Elli was too distant, Elli's time was not really human time. No, another message was hidden in the giant crossword of Bethely's windows. When had Lisbeï really noticed it? She doesn't remember, although she recalls the instant of comprehension, the moment when everything had clicked into place, much as the illusion of perspective, the illusion of the hollow cube had suddenly become clear.

All at once she saw Bethely in perspective *in time.* She was gazing at the East Tower facade from her bedroom, staring unthinkingly at the rows of identical windows, wider than they were high, and the red brick set in the gray walls where all the windows had been made smaller. Suddenly a flash of illumination linked the familiar sight with the pictures in the Book of Bethely. The Towers were ancient! Older than the Mothers, older than the Hives or even the Harems. All these societies had occupied them, transformed and adapted them, but the Towers themselves came from much further back, from a time when people could construct perfectly rectilinear buildings of fifteen stories or more, with all those wide (too wide) windows so incredibly wasteful of energy—but that was normal in the Decline, for the Towers must date at least from the Decline. . . .

Not much was left of the original buildings, apart from the skeleton. The inside and outside had been renovated several times, but the general aspect had always been preserved for the very reason that the frame placed uncompromising restraints on change. Even the Hives, so anxious to wipe out the past, had not razed the Towers in order to start from scratch as they had so often done elsewhere. The task would have been too daunting, it was customarily said.

Lisbeï had another explanation: the women of the Bethely Hive who had risen up against their Queene had been born in the Towers, as had their mothers, grandmothers, and great-grandmothers before them. Probably they'd forgotten how old the Towers really were, blinded by familiarity just as women were today. Isn't it strange to think we forget the thing that has shaped us most deeply, perhaps just because we have taken on its shape ourselves?

Lisbeï had felt comfortable in Bethely once, like a hand in a well-fitting glove. But that time was long gone. What called to her now was the other Bethely, the subterranean Bethely. Each time she emerged from her excavation, the Towers and their occupants seemed farther away. The present inhabitants seemed no more sensitive to the past than the

Hive women who had tried to destroy it. For them, what existed now had existed always. But what did their present matter? What did Selva's narrow view of a Memory's task matter? Or Mooreï's, even hers! A Memory's true task was to bring the past to light, not embalm it in interminable copies, lists, and inventories. The real memory of Bethely wasn't on the Archives shelves or in the great Book. It lay somewhere beneath the basement, where only maintenance teams and gardianas went. It lay in the darkness of underground passages, walled tunnels that ran beneath the Capterie, forgotten in legend—another, obscure Bethely running deep like a root, far from the sun, burrowing into the real past, the past of questions, not answers.

A voice from the heavens broke into her thoughts, calling her name. The voice, not the name, brought her to a standstill, her hand gripping the railing. She could feel the shuddering of the spiral staircase as Tula scrambled down from Level Four.

"I thought you were in the Library—I was coming to get you for dinner!" Impatient pleasure dissolved into concern, then reproach. "You were still in your hole? You've just come from Selva's office? Did they punish you?"

With a brief shrug Lisbeï started down again, flattening against the wall on the Level Two landing to let a gaggle of little Greens go by with their laundry hampers. Was Tula going to ask what she'd found in her *hole* now? She couldn't stand it, this benevolent curiosity, this way Tula had of always being so *considerate,* of talking about anything and everything except what mattered, of being with her in every way except the one that counted! Lisbeï felt like shouting, as she'd just done with Selva, but she had a muddled sense of the impossibility of shouting at Tula. She mustn't start. (Tula knew it too, Tula who refrained so prudently, who revolved around Lisbeï with such caution.) One cry in Tula's presence, and everything would topple, Lisbeï would be swept in a direction she had no desire to follow, not yet. Better to be suspended in this odious silence of deliberately meaningless words than to be confronted with the question that had only desperate answers: *And now?*

"Are you coming to eat?" asked Tula. "I've got to go to first sitting." Her voice dropped a little—ever so little—but she had to finish. "I've got a training session with Kelys right after supper."

All right, go and dance with Kelys, go and train some more to be the Mother!

"I can't. I've got to go to the barns," lied Lisbeï with quick invention. Was Tula's disappointment tinged with relief? It was hard to tell among those murky shadows that blurred the outline of her aura.

"Afterward, then? You've got to tell me what you found today."

"Selva said I had to report to the captas. They're sure to give me work for the whole evening."

"What about tomorrow morning at breakfast?"

(Don't think about how in other days they'd have met in the night, punishment or no.) "Fine," called Lisbeï over her shoulder, jumping down the last two steps. She headed at a run for the South Tower, pounding along too fast to stop at the barns. Why not keep going for a bit—no one had said she must go to the barns anyhow, and here was the white-pebbled road climbing toward the Esplanade and passing through the pastures, the cherry orchard, the sweet-smelling rows of flowers where late-working bees still buzzed, and here was the pile of earth and stones and the boards over the entrance to the conduit, and who said she had to obey? She was a Blue, she could do as she liked, she was free.

2

The pungent smell of damp earth filled the gloom at the foot of the ladder as she gropingly lit the gasole. She climbed back up and pulled the boards over the excavation from inside. If by chance anyone was looking for her, there'd be no telltale light. She put the pickaxe into the wheelbarrow with the spade and gasole and trundled along, slightly hunched, as she descended the steeply angled conduit leading to the underground passage.

It may have been an air vent. Beneath the deep layer of soil surrounding Bethely, patiently accumulated and fertilized by generations of people, lay a strata of stones, bits of irrecuperable metal, and chunks of various ancient materials that time had not yet destroyed—the residue of the nameless city on which the Towers, the only visible relics, had once stood. Lisbeï had immediately recognized the nature of the rubble mixed with the soil and had soon cleared the conduit's circular opening. All that had barred her way was a huge half-disintegrated grating through which the soil had sifted to form a compact earth wall at the lower end. The conduit must open into one of the underground passages that supposedly ran beneath Bethely (and even between Bethely and neighboring Capteries, if tradition were to be believed). She'd had a tough time convincing Selva to let her keep digging.

When at last the wall of earth had been breached late that afternoon, a strange, indescribable odor had assailed Lisbeï's nostrils—the dank smell of stagnant air, sealed off for . . . how long? She had attacked the wall of earth with renewed energy. When she'd finally been able to pass the gasole through the opening, there hadn't been much to see: walls rising to a vaulted ceiling, covered with something discolored by time—tiles perhaps—with the occasional damp spot that glinted silver in the lamplight. Instinctively she'd thought, "I've got to tell them!" Then she'd remembered she wasn't really supposed to be there and wondered about the time.

But time wasn't a problem now. She cleared away enough earth to make the opening passable, checked her pocket for her compass, and weighed the lamp in her hand, trying to estimate how long the fuel would last. Three hours at least. She gathered up spade and pickaxe and climbed through the hole.

The passage was at least ten meters wide, but the ceiling was fairly low. A checkerboard of tiny tiles, greenish white and dirty brown, covered the floor. Large rectangular cavities in the ceiling must have contained some form of lighting. The passage ran straight forward into the darkness. South-southeast. Lisbeï started walking, counting her steps in an attempt to keep track of the distance. She must be . . . under the Esplanade now . . . under the courtyard . . . under the dairy. Nothing much to see, no corridors branching off, no doors, not even a rusty pipe. The occasional little pile flattened by time: leaves, earth, the bones of a few small rodents. Somewhere there must be another surface opening.

Was that a wall ahead? In the weak light of the gasole it was hard to tell, but the passage did seem to come to an abrupt halt farther on. Lisbeï slowed down, disappointed. Had she taken all this trouble just to come up against another wall? But as she got nearer, hope returned: bricks, crude masonry much more recent than the passage itself. And when she knocked hard, she could feel the wall vibrate. She put the lamp and spade down and raised the pickaxe, braced her feet well apart, and struck the wall with all her might. A shower of masonry fell away, leaving a gap about a meter wide. Lisbeï smiled in triumph as she picked up the gasole again. When the dust settled, she leaned through the opening. The vault seemed to continue from the other side of the opening, as did the floor, but new walls had been built, making the corridor narrower. Storerooms? These walls seemed more carefully constructed than the masonry partition, with stones set in cement, and much thicker, judging by the dull echo when she knocked on one. But there were no doors! Storage bays without doors? Walled up?

Suddenly, in a dazzling focus of comprehension, she knew: not storerooms. Cells!

She backed into the middle of the passage, heart pounding, throat constricted. The last stone in these walls had been laid 489 years ago. By smoking torches, workas had pushed wheelbarrows and wielded trowels while the stern-faced Chief looked on, surrounded by his female soldiers. Women, *women* had cemented the final stone, and women had watched them do it—and darkness had closed forever on the six Compagnas. It was the day after the great march organized by the Juddites following Garde's first execution and first resurrection.

So it was true, *true!* The Compagnas had really been walled up alive in Bethely, in subterranean passages. That was why their cells had never been found. The basements of present-day Bethely weren't the same thing as these deeper levels! There must have been entrances to the real subterranean passages at one time, but the Harems had walled them up, sealed off their crime and their shame. Oh, to think of Selva's face when Lisbeï proved she'd been right in believing the underground passages existed!

A sobering thought occurred to her. What if the cells were empty? If the legend were only half-true? But in that case why would the cells be sealed?

For others, maybe, not the Compagnas? After all, Harem justice had been indiscriminately merciless.

Lisbeï's rather awed respect for this wall, this tomb, began to fade. She knocked on it again at intervals covering several meters. It did seem very thick. Perhaps she could open a cell from the side, from the wall she'd breached first. It had crumbled at one blow. She checked and found she'd been lucky that first time. On either side of the breach, the masonry was backed by a much stronger stone wall.

With a sigh Lisbeï rolled up her sleeves, spat on her hands, and began to hack at the wall.

Two hours later (judging by the weight of the gasole) Lisbeï at last heard a different sort of thud. A few more blows —and the pickaxe hit air. Lisbeï staggered, awkwardly retrieving her balance. Her legs shook, her back ached, and her ears rang.

She stood still, catching her breath. Then she attacked the hole with her hands, tearing her nails as she enlarged it. But what did a few scratches matter? She was a hair's breadth from her goal. When the gap was big enough to tilt the gasole through, she crouched in the niche she'd hacked out and pushed her face up against the opening.

The air hung dry and odorless. The bare floor was decorated by the same dingy checkerboard mosaic, the same ceramic tiles covered the vaulted walls.

But in the corner of the ceramic wall and the stone masonry . . .

Lisbeï closed her eyes and opened them again. Beside the stone wall lay a dark pile. Fabric, thick-looking, soft. On the near side the lamplight caught a yellowish-white object, something spherical . . . a skull?

Lisbeï set to work once more with redoubled energy. She hadn't much time. A space large enough to wriggle through, that was all she needed. She scraped her arms and knees as she squirmed past the rough opening.

She knelt by the dark pile. It was some kind of robe or cloak made of felt, stretched out full length. The skull lay half-hidden beneath the hood, and the sleeves were folded across the cloak. She lifted one sleeve gently. Something rolled against her knee and tinkled to the floor. A tarnished metal ring, gold-colored. She rubbed it against her tunic. A crudely engraved double spiral, the double helix of Elli. Lisbeï felt a lump in her throat. She folded back the other sleeve. A bone fell away with a brittle click as the whole arm came apart and the knuckles, invisible until now, slid out of the sleeve.

Lisbeï felt sick with helpless compassion. She opened the cape to reveal the symmetrical curve of the rib cage. Nestled in the pelvis lay the rectangular object—the bulge she had noticed beneath the felt. It was some sort of large purse made of brown leather, attached to a belt that must have been worn next to the skin.

The leather thongs, stiff with age, broke as she tried to undo them. She lifted the purse flap. Inside was something that looked like a book, perhaps a thick notebook. Hands trembling, she nudged it gently out of the purse, fearful it would dissolve into dust.

It was a fat notebook with the pages held together by a metal coil! Clearly from the Decline. The thick blue plastic cover was still fresh despite a few small cracks. The paper inside was very worn, even dog-eared in places, like a well-thumbed book. The first page yielded nothing. The second contained crowded lines of figures grouped in a seemingly random way. The numbers were painstakingly formed, like a childe's. And there was a lot of blocking out—entire sections blackened line by line. It went on like this for eight pages, then changed to handwriting, a finer, more slanting hand, less deliberately careful, occasionally illegible—but words, clearly words. Not Litali, though.

Lisbeï summoned up her taïtche training. Breathe in, breathe out, fill your mind and spirit with the rhythm of breathing. Her hands stopped shaking. She reached for the pendant magnifying glass she always wore around her neck, and quickly scanned the pages as Mooreï had taught her to do with the most ancient Archive documents, not trying to comprehend, but merely to pick out familiar constructions in the words and sentences. It looked like some kind of Old Frangleï.

Lisbeï glanced anxiously at the gasole. Time had run out. She opened the notebook again, at the end this time, just to get an idea. The writing had changed completely. This wasn't really very legible, either, since the ink was rather faded. But there was no mistaking it this time: Old Litali, unusual spelling but fairly recognizable. When the lines stopped dancing before her eyes, she began to decipher the first one: 3 . . . 145 . . . of the Harems.

The meaning suddenly leapt out at her: 3 *January* (the old name for the month now called Ellième), 145 *of the Harems*.

The gasole began to flicker, and Lisbeï, startled out of

her reverie, scrambled from the cell with the notebook. For the last half of the underground passage she had to feel her way in the dark.

3

I, Halde of Melorney, bear witness before dying that I have seen the Voice of Elli dead and that I have seen her living. The Voice of Elli called to me in the night, and I saw her before me. I touched her breast, and the wounds were gone. Glory be to Elli, who will make us as the Voice of Elli, Glory be to Elli, Life Everlasting, Glory be to Elli.

Lisbeï had slipped like a thief into her room and was feverishly deciphering the first words of what was to become the Testament of Halde. She remembers how wildly her heart pounded, how her whole body shivered with nervous excitement, and how she had to grit her teeth to prevent them chattering. Excitement soon turned to unbounded stupefaction. Halde was indeed one of the martyred Compagnas, as Lisbeï knew from the Appendices of Hallera. But what she had written in her notebook differed in every way from what Lisbeï, like all Maerlande dottas, had learned since childehood.

The official History was this: toward the end of the Harems, Garde and her Compagnas had brought the Word of Elli to the slave-women. The Word had given them succor, restoring their courage and dignity. Gradually they had organized themselves around the nucleus of Juddites—so-called after a discipla who had paid for her courage with her life during one of the first peaceful demonstrations in the Bethely Harem. The movement had spread from Harem to Harem, rising like a tide with the journeys of Garde and her Compagnas. The Harem Chiefs had suppressed all demonstrations with ferocious cruelty until the day Leandro, Chief of Bethely, had captured Garde. He'd had her shot. But three days later, Garde had reappeared to lead the huge demonstration organized by the Bethely Juddites. In the course of the demonstration, six of the Compagnas had been captured, and Garde had been killed again. She had risen once more, this time after five days, reappearing to lead the second demonstration, the one that had toppled the Bethely Harem.

Garde had never been seen again. She had left her disciplas with the enigmatic legacy of the Promise transmitted by the sole surviving Compagna, Hallera. One day, said the Promise, all human beings would be like Garde: no longer would they fear death, for it was part of Elli's plan that they all become like Elli. But the victorious women of the Hives, still infected with the poisonous violence of the Harems, had rejected Garde's message and had persecuted the disciplas until peace and tolerance triumphed at last.

Halde's account drew a quite different picture, at least for part of the story. Garde had indeed brought the Word of Elli. She had been executed by a firing squad in Bethely and had been resurrected afterward. However, she had not returned to lead the great demonstration but to *prevent* it, to stop the Juddites from inciting a massacre—for the Juddites had not been Garde's first disciplas, but her enemies! Not only did they disbelieve the Word of Elli, they had delivered Garde and her Compagnas into the hands of the Bethely Chief!

The Juddites had long been in a state of rebellion. They wanted to seize power from the Harem Chiefs and wreak vengeance for their years of oppression. They hadn't the patience to wait for a pacifist victory—in fact they didn't believe in non-violence. The Word of Elli had lived on in secret among the Harem women since the regime began. Juddites were forever persecuting Believras in the despicable little *wars* that the Harem women waged among themselves under the indifferent or amused eyes of the Chiefs. The Juddites had actually been part of the Harem armies! There had been Juddites among the drugged, fanatic killers used by the Chiefs to fight other Chiefs.

Garde had converted a few of them, however, and they had converted others. They had tried to influence those Juddites who wanted to wage war against the Harems. They didn't succeed. The first great protest had ended in a bloodbath in which most of the disciplas of Bethely had been massacred. And according to Halde, the Compagna Hallera was among those walled up in the underground cells! The Compagna *Fedra* was the only one whom Hallera had seen escaping with Garde.

The Harems had never really persecuted Elli's followers. A pacifist religion suited the Harem leaders perfectly—something for which the Juddites had always reproached the disciplas. But the triumphant Hive women had brutally suppressed Believras. As a result the Word had gone underground. It took another century—eighty-seven years, to be exact—before the Word regained its influence and the Hives one by one abandoned their harsh rule to become the Capteries of Maerlande. But this transition was sometimes violent, and once again the bloodiest changeover took place in Bethely. Markali, the last Queene of the Hive, was brought to justice. During the great trial, the daughter of Hallera produced documents left her by her mother (Hallera's Appendices as they came to be known) and glowingly affirmed the divinity of Garde, a Garde who had twice died and risen.

Of course all this wasn't in the notebook—the Notebook, as Lisbeï now thought of it—especially not the second dying and rising of Garde after Halde's capture. As the Compagna waited for death, she had only sketched briefly the events leading to her present plight. But Lisbeï didn't think of this that night as she blinked with fatigue beside her reading lamp. She was still in a state of shock. Garde was part of her daily life, as for so many: the sort of fabled figure that, once discovered in childehood, one never questions—something that later becomes too much a part of one's inner and outer landscape to elicit wonder in adolescence or adulthood. From her earliest days, Lisbeï had loved the story of Garde because it blended History and legend rather than setting them against one another, as happened all too often. But what fascinated her most was how Garde's history and legend bore out Lisbeï's private intuition—something that had occurred to her when she had spun the magnifying glass, and later on when she had gazed at Mooreï's illusory cube. For despite Hallera's Appendices and the formal recognition of Garde's divinity, Garde must be mortal *and* divine because she had died *and* risen. Garde was on both sides of the line, so to speak—she provided a threshold, one of those magical places of passage where you could make the leap from the everyday reality of pro and con to alight on the thread between the two, the vantage point from which you could see the unity of the world. When you balanced on the thread, some apparent contradictions ceased to exist: you had the power to rise above them, to resolve them. It was an experience dear to Lisbeï, this resolution of contradictions. It filled her with joy—a joy always too brief, for it was only in performing the taïtche that she could sustain it.

Now, as Lisbeï looked at Halde's Notebook, what she saw wasn't so much the familiar story of Garde, despite Halde's variants, as the confirmation of her intuition: legend could be true, story could be History. And she, Lisbeï of Bethely, was the first to know this truth. On the morrow it would spread, radiate outward from her. She probably had in mind the image of light pushing back the darkness rather than the ripple from a stone disturbing quiet waters. Not for an instant did she dream anyone could question her truth.

The gleam of first light awoke Lisbeï. She had fallen asleep hunched over her work table. Her eye immediately fell on the Notebook. With a thrill—and now a little anxiety—she wondered what to do next. "Tula first," urged the old instinct. She'd been too excited the night before, in too much of a hurry to decipher Halde's testament. Now . . . yes, in spite of everything it had to be Tula first.

She slipped into Tula's room across the hall. Usually she winced at the thought that so little physical space separated them, and all for nothing. But there was no such feeling now. She shook Tula gently. Beneath the mop of red hair a sleepy eye opened a slit, then widened.

"Lisbeï!"

"Shhh!"

"Lisbeï," Tula repeated softly, sitting up in bed. "What's happened?" Her eyes were wide with horror.

Lisbeï followed Tula's gaze and realized that she still wore her work clothes, covered with soil and dust and stained with blood where she'd unconsciously rubbed her torn fingers. She laughed gently. "Nothing! Yes, lots of things, but I'm not hurt."

"Tell," ordered Tula. It was the old habit, the magic formula that brought them together at night in the garderie. The thought touched Lisbeï without pain for once—this was a timeless moment outside their individual stories.

"Tell" indeed . . . Where to begin? Never before had she lacked time to put her ideas in order for Tula. In desperation she opened the Notebook and read what she had deciphered.

Tula listened, hanging on every word as in the old days, and then they communicated with each other instantly, one finishing the sentence begun by the other. A magic moment, truly, and one that would endure. In the thorny desert of Lisbeï's last months in Bethely, there would be this most unexpected miracle, entirely unlooked for: she had Tula once more. Almost. And almost to the end.

"We've got to talk to Mooreï first," said Tula after she'd considered what Lisbeï had just read.

"Why Mooreï?" Lisbeï had vaguely imagined she'd go to Selva first thing in the morning and place the Notebook in front of her—"There!"—and after discussing it, she and Selva would jointly compose the letter announcing the news to all Maerlande. Was Tula, the adventurous Tula, now saying, "Wait"?

"Think of the consequences," said Tula.

What consequences?

"The Juddites," added Tula patiently.

What about the Juddites? And then shreds of Selva's teaching began to filter through the ecstasy of discovery, things Selva had taught Lisbeï when she was destined to become the Mother, things she'd banished from her mind for nearly two years. Tula meant today's Juddites. They would definitely not be pleased to learn that the Juddites of old had fought against Garde. That some of their number must have lied about the tradition, falsified both History and legend. The position of present-day Juddites, entrenched in their strict fidelity to the Word, intractable gardianas of tradition, would not emerge unscathed from such a revelation. Litale was above all a Province of Juddites. Bethely's position within Litale was a delicate and unusual one. It drew strength from having played a significant role in Maerlande's History, in being a holy place, the site of the Pilgrimage of Garde. But it was somewhat isolated because of its moderate religious stand and even more by its recent excursions into Progressista changes.

But wouldn't all of Bethely be behind Lisbeï and the truth? The Juddites couldn't overcome such a united front!

Mooreï's reaction should have alerted Lisbeï. Surprise, fervent wonder—Lisbeï had expected nothing less as she began her story. But as she continued to read her transcription, she sensed Mooreï's growing uneasiness. When she had finished, the Memory sat mutely for a long time, so deeply lost in thought that she appeared to be in a trance. "We'll go and show all this to Selva," she finally said. Then, with a gravity that Lisbeï had rarely observed, she added, "I can't deplore your discovery, Lisbeï. If it happened, it was because it was meant to happen. But we might be tempted to be sorry. Truth is not a tender mistress."

Nor was Selva a tender mother. Before Lisbeï could explain her discovery, she had to listen to an exasperated diatribe on her disobedience. She fully expected Selva to dismiss her without a hearing. Mooreï insisted, however, and Selva managed to calm down sufficiently to listen to Halde's testament.

"Juddites betrayed Garde and her Compagnas to the Harems? Do you realize what you're saying, Lisbeï?"

Selva displayed neither wonder nor fervor, and very soon lost her sense of amazement. In fact she appeared to be furious. But for once she never thought of hiding her reaction, and Lisbeï perceived that the Mother was *afraid*.

"Who cares about the Juddites?" Lisbeï burst out. "Garde really died and came to life again in Bethely. We have firsthand evidence with the Notebook, the testimony of one of the Compagnas walled up alive. Isn't that what 'matters'?"

"Evidence?" Selva said. "Evidence?" She sat down again abruptly, as though at a loss for words.

Did she mean the Notebook wasn't evidence? What more could she want!

"It's not true simply because it's written down, Lisbeï," said Mooreï. "I thought I'd taught you that History is not a science. It depends too much on human testimony."

But until now the whole history of Garde had rested on the testimony of the Compagna Hallera, hadn't it? Testimony collected and put forward at Markali's trial. And wasn't that also the source of the actual Word?

The tones in Mooreï's emotional aura took on a confused coloring for Lisbeï—a confusion that was to recur frequently in the coming months. "It's not the same thing," muttered the Memory, but her tone was hesitant. Mooreï too was afraid, Lisbeï realized with consternation and astonishment. Was it because Halde mentioned Hallera as being among the imprisoned Compagnas? Halde was mistaken, that was all. Halde herself said in the Notebook that she hadn't really seen what happened in the heat of battle. Mooreï shook her head at this and said nothing.

Only much, much later was Lisbeï to realize that for Mooreï, the Garde described by Halde was suddenly much too real, too human yet too unmistakably divine in her resurrection, as confirmed by the Notebook. Mooreï felt her faith teetering on the brink of a dangerous threshold.

4

Antonë to Linta

Bethely, 2 Maïa, 489 A.G.

. . . and despite all my affection for Lisbeï, I can only conclude this notebook must be a fake, the result of misplaced piety run rampant. We have literally nothing but the so-called Halde's word for all these revelations. The notebook is a Decline artifact, but such notebooks can still be found today. We have no reliable way of dating the material any more than the remains found in the cells. What we actually see are six female skeletons, in accordance with tradition, in tunnels beneath Bethely, again according to tradition, in cells where they were probably walled up alive— all according to tradition. But there we stop. At first sight the skeletons consist of three adults, including "Halde," and three childreen. This alone would be enough to make it doubtful they were really Garde's Compagnas.

As for Halde's statements, they could very well be a case of mythomania fed by despair and delirium. Tradition tells us that the risen Garde appeared to Compagnas, but we aren't told their names. And as though by chance, this "Halde" claims to be the first to have seen Garde. As for her vilification of the Juddites, it is now established that a covert revolutionary movement existed at the end of the Harem era, and that it staged several demonstrations that met with bloody reprisals before the final uprising. Knowing the brutality and unscrupulousness of the women of the time, it's very likely some of the revolutionaries might have infil-

trated the Juddites. Their aim would be to use the movement for their own ends, and they might have been ready to scuttle the pacifist campaign led by Garde, her Compagnas, and her disciplas, since it ran counter to their own agenda.

But who can say what passes through the mind of a poor wretch who is slowly dying of hunger and thirst in a walled cell?

Anyway, I really don't know why I waste time discussing the possible truth of Halde's statements when I've always thought the very story of Garde absurd. Two deaths and two resurrections—I ask you! Once perhaps, but twice? I never trusted the Hallera documents. This sudden "historical proof" sanctifying the revolt against the Hives was all too convenient. The idea of a divine messenger who would come to save women was already in the air in the early days of the Harems, as has been shown. It's perfectly possible that such a "savior" was reinvented in the last days of the Hives, taking the actual historic figure of Garde as its focus—I certainly don't deny she existed! This needn't have been for purely political motives. Indeed, the most likely theory is that the idea was a collective creation, arising from the desperate desire for freedom and peace motivating the women of that era— in other words, a myth fabricated by Hallera and her colleagues, and grafted by the Juddites onto Garde's heroic death, a real event but with no resurrection. This doesn't detract from Garde's martyrdom or from the selfless nobility of the sacrifices made by her followers, nor does it affect their message of peace. It wouldn't be the first time that History and faith met in a charismatic figure of this kind, if one is to believe the few extracts of the Gospel to survive. That "Son of God" sounds uncannily like our "Daughter of Elli," don't you think? He didn't resuscitate himself, but he performed miracles and gave his people the Promised Land—and since males had the upper hand in those days, the phenomenon naturally coalesced around a male figure.

But you already know my arguments in support of this theory.

I hope the storm will soon blow itself out and Bethely will get on with preparations for the Assembly of Mothers. In all conscience I can't give this letter to the courria until a decision has been reached. It'll be worth the wait for you to read the whole story at one go, without a single "to be continued."

I'm sorry you can't come to Bethely. They have a reputation for doing things on a grand scale, and the Pilgrimage of Garde should be especially splendid this year, what with the Assembly being held right afterward. But here they are, trying to get rid of *the stone Lisbeï has tossed so carelessly into their pond. Really, the very year when Bethely is hosting the Assembly! She couldn't have timed her discovery worse if she'd tried! Or better? Whether she's Red, Blue, or Green will hardly matter if ever this unlikely story reaches the Assembly.*

Oh, what a dreadful thought has just entered my head—no, obviously she couldn't have forged the notebook or faked the underground passage, the cells, or the skeletons. Poor Lisbeï. She's absolutely convinced the notebook is true, and she's seething with rage because the others can't make up their minds at this point, except for Tula, and you can guess what Tula thinks. They haven't yet told the Family Assembly about the find.

Kelys, who has a knack of turning up just when you need her, arrived the day before yesterday after lunch. Her expedition near Puyvalense isn't going too well, so she's decided to terminate it and take a rest, she says. I hope she can knock some sense into them all. We went and looked at the site. There was one queer detail: the walls are very thick, about half a meter. In three of the cells, the wall giving onto the corridor had been chipped away from the inside, quite deeply, in fact. It happens that these are the cells where the smallest skeletons were found—the chil-dreen. One of them had sewing scissors, but I can't believe she could have dug through half the wall with them! Even taking into account the energy of despair. Anyhow, the others had no tools at all, only personal objects. Apparently they weren't searched before being immured. "Halde" had an ink bottle and a small traveling gasole as well as the notebook, which is how she wrote her testament. Perhaps, after Garde's "resurrection," such an aura of terrified superstition surrounded the Compagnas that no one wanted to touch them.

Kelys is examining the notebook in the Library with Mooreï. When she's through, we'll move the skeletons and study them more closely. I'm glad I didn't do anything until she got here. Kelys clearly has the requisite knowledge, far more than Mooreï, myself, or Lisbeï! There'll be an inner-council meeting tonight to take stock. Yes, believe it or not, Kelys of Fusco, the presumed eyes and ears of Wardenberg, is invited to the meeting. But she's always been asked whenever one was held during her stay. As I mentioned, she's a very old friend of the family.

And yes, I saw her again and managed to take it in my stride. She doesn't change—she's still beautiful, and I find it hard to realize she must have turned forty-seven last Ellième.

*She's as luminous as ever and just as amiably distant. But it
doesn't hurt me the way it did in the old days. (Old days! Three
years . . .)*

5

Inner Family councils took place in one of the small conference rooms in the Library. The room overlooked the main
courtyard. Gasoles now hung on the wall in place of the old
candelabras, and a massive table almost filled the room. Its
ancient wood surface bore the traces of many meetings—
lines, vaguely geometric shapes, and even initials. No one had
ever thought of getting rid of these marks. It was said in
Bethely that the table had been there in Hive days and that
you could find the initials that Markali, the last Queene, had
scratched in the wood when she was just a little Princess, unaware of her fate.

The table was round, as befitted equals, but at least one
seat differed from the rest—a tall-backed chair covered in
Bethely colors. Selva already occupied this seat when Lisbeï
and Tula came in. Kelys sat opposite. Tula took her usual seat
on Selva's left—Lisbeï's place until a year ago. Antonë always
sat down in any one of the half-dozen remaining chairs. When
she arrived, she went and sat beside Tula, ignoring the space
beside Kelys.

Mooreï came last, bearing a sheaf of papers, and sat on
Selva's right. She looked around the table and sighed. Her
voice was husky with fatigue, but she pronounced the ritual
opening with conviction. "Let us gather ourselves in Elli. May
Elli guide us in her peace."

Selva cut short the required moment of welcome with a
slightly impatient "Peace to all in Elli." She wasted no more
time in preliminaries. "An important discovery—perhaps one
with grave consequences—has been made in the underground
passages of Bethely. A notebook has been found that might
have belonged to one of Garde's Compagnas. Mooreï and
Lisbeï have been busy translating excerpts. Kelys has taken a

quick look. We're here to listen to their reports and decide how to proceed. Mooreï?"

The Memory tapped the sheaf of papers edgewise against the table to straighten them. "We translated passages rather at random so as to get an approximate idea of the general content," she said at last, frowning slightly and not looking at anyone. "You know the notebook contains not only text, but figures. I'll tell you what we've found, and then pass out copies of the translations we've done, mainly from the last part."

Lisbeï tried to catch Tula's eye, but Tula, sitting very straight in her chair, was looking at Mooreï with solemn concentration. They had spent the day together copying everything out six times. Their fingers were still covered with ink. Selva had made it clear that absolutely no one else would be allowed to see these translations for the moment.

"The notebook appears to have been written by three different people," Mooreï went on. "Kelys thinks it dates from at least two different periods. One writa produced the short first section made up entirely of figures—probably a code. We've decided to put it aside for the moment, and anyhow, it's impossible to date it. The middle section may have been written by a second person. This takes up two thirds of the remaining pages and seems to be written in a very unusual form of Old Frangleï. The third writa calls herself 'Halde of Melorney,' and has written only a dozen pages at the end, using an Old Litali fairly comparable to that of the end of the Harem period in this region."

Mooreï glanced around the table. "A combination of various linguistic details—spelling, turns of phrase, vocabulary, and so on—is what makes us think these were two separate authors writing in different periods. Kelys places the center section in the middle of the Harem period. Our samplings are too few, however, for us to be sure about these dates."

"All right," said Selva. *Get to the point,* implied her expression, which hadn't changed since they sat down. Antonë had straightened up, but seemed more disconcerted than amazed by Mooreï's comments. Kelys, with her usual nonchalant grace, had slung a leg over one of the chair arms and was leaning on an elbow, chin in hand. Her placid black face gave nothing away.

"The middle section seems to contain several versions of well-known tales and legends," Mooreï went on. " 'The Dancing Queene,' for one, and 'The Hundred-Armed Giantess' for another. Also what seems to be a version of the Word."

Lisbeï tried to suppress her impatience. They were more like stabs at *creating* stories, what with the deletions, insertions, and false starts . . . not stories being recopied, but stories being written. Well, they'd probably get to that later.

"The vocabulary in the last part is limited, and the syntax pretty elementary. This supports the theory of a second author. She sketches Garde's betrayal by the Bethely Juddites, Garde's first death, her own meeting with the risen Garde near the Great Badlands, and their conversations during the return trip to Bethely."

Mooreï kept her voice completely neutral. "Here are our attempts at translation. Read them for yourselves."

Lisbeï handed the papers around the table, then sat down and looked at her own sheets, but it was a mere formality. She knew exactly which passages to cite in support of her arguments—in fact, she'd circled them in red that morning. She looked at the others and tried to read the emotional nuances behind their silent perusal. Tula went through the material slowly and very methodically, as though she hadn't spent hours copying it out. Antonë skimmed the pages, leafing back from time to time with a start and a frown. Selva let each sheet fall to the table as she read, sighing occasionally—although whether she was exasperated or overwhelmed was difficult to say. Kelys had read the material through quickly and was now rereading each sheet like a solemn scholechilde, chin cupped in hand. Mooreï was leaning against the chairback, eyes closed. She seemed exhausted. Lisbeï studied the drawn features and dark circles under the eyes, feeling puzzled and slightly remorseful, although a little annoyed as well. Mooreï of all people should have been delighted! Wasn't this yet another proof of Garde's existence? And if Garde had insisted on not being called "Daughter of Elli" but "Voice of Elli," if she had told Halde that she was human, what difference did it really make? She *had* risen again, hadn't she? Divine *and* human, couldn't Garde have tried to find the best way of teaching the truth to the Harem women? The Word wasn't Elli, any more than the territory of Bethely was the Family. Garde's Word was simply that: words, the way in which she'd . . . translated Elli for human beings. If there were two versions of the Word, it was fascinating rather than depressing, wasn't it? Especially if they differed.

The silence had altered. No one moved. They'd finished and knew the basic facts. Now what?

"Let us be perfectly clear from the start," announced Selva. "We're not here to decide whether or not the notebook's contents are genuine, but how we should deal with the discovery. The Assembly of Mothers is taking place in a little over a month, right here. As you know, Nevenici has tabled a motion for pushing exploration in the South—submitted at the last possible moment, of course. We, however, support exploration of the West, along with most Bretanye Families. In other words, we've stepped completely outside our traditional alliances. We're facing some particularly difficult palavras, and we'll need every resource we can muster."

She glanced around the table, stopping briefly at Lisbeï without giving her time to open her mouth. "In my view we simply haven't time to deal with this beforehand at our Family Assembly. A month won't be long enough to reach a consensus on the nature of Lisbeï's discovery or how we should consider it, let alone what to do about it. We can't broach it in the Assembly of Mothers unless we've come to a unanimous position within the Family first. And we can't run the risk of a leak. In my opinion, therefore, we can't tell the Family. Nor the Assembly of Mothers."

"What!" gasped Lisbeï.

"The irrefutable facts that we can offer the Family or the Mothers amount to six skeletons found walled up in underground cells, plus one notebook. All the rest is based on the allegations of a self-styled 'Halde of Melorney' whose identity can't be confirmed. These allegations contradict a well-documented historical tradition four hundred years old. It levels serious but absolutely unfounded accusations against the Juddites."

"Unfounded for the moment," interposed Tula. Lisbeï was still speechless.

"That's precisely my argument," said Selva, smiling at Tula—a joyless smile. "*For the moment* nothing proves the truth of the notebook. On the contrary, there's a great deal to disprove it. To begin with, only three of these skeletons belonged to adults. . . ."

"No," said Kelys.

Selva's mouth hung open for a second. Everyone turned to look at Kelys. "Antonë and I have given the skeletons a closer examination. The skull sections are fully knit: these are adult females. They've even borne childreen." She twisted slightly toward Antonë, who merely nodded.

"Adults the size of six-year-olds? It's impossible!" exclaimed Lisbeï. "Or . . . are they dwarfs?"

"The skeletons show none of the malformations you'd expect in that case," said Kelys.

How could she be so calm? You'd think she was . . . enjoying herself!

"Tiny adults," Mooreï said.

"Garde's Compagnas were meant to be adults, weren't they?" remarked Tula hesitantly. She too had sensed Mooreï's distress and, like Lisbeï, couldn't fathom it.

"Halde says she met Garde near the Badlands," said Kelys. She was looking at Mooreï. "There's a tradition that says Garde herself came from the Northeast, as well as three of the first Compagnas."

"An apocryphal tradition," said Mooreï in a low voice.

"There were mutants?" queried Lisbeï. "Mutants among Garde's Compagnas?"

Mutants! *Abominations!* But of course! That was why . . .

"That's why the Juddites—" began Tula.

Lisbeï turned toward her with an exultant laugh and completed the sentence: "—falsified the tradition!"

"Kindly refrain from taking assumptions for proof," said Selva icily. She appeared to have recovered from Kelys's revelation. "In any case, this isn't the sort of theory that would please most of the Assembly."

"It doesn't have to *please* the Assembly," retorted Lisbeï, rage rising again. "Facts are—"

"For the moment it's a theory, not a fact," Kelys cut in. "It will be very difficult to prove. I myself have never heard of such mutations."

Lisbeï stared at Kelys for a moment, unable to speak. What was Kelys playing at? Bringing a new factor into the discussion, then backtracking? Kelys stared calmly back at her.

"I'd like to remind you once again," continued an exasperated Selva, "that we're not going to decide on the truth of the notebook, the skeletons, or anything else!"

"How can we make up our minds about whether or not to tell the Family or the Assembly of Mothers if we don't decide this question first?" murmured Mooreï. But she bowed her head and said no more.

Selva turned back to the others. "I'd like you to try to picture the reactions we'd get if we went into the Assembly with this story. And, let me remind you, without the unanimous support of the Family."

"Why not?" protested Lisbeï. But she knew she didn't mean it and dropped the objection. It had taken over three months to get a Family consensus on the question of greater participation by Green boys and young Blue men, the year of the Serres-Morèna Games. That hadn't been nearly so thorny a question as revising four hundred years of History.

"Lisbeï is the Mother-designate until June nineteenth. As such, she will open the Assembly, since we're the hostesses this year. She tells the delegates of her discovery, of the notebook—"

"I could simply read the part written by Halde," remarked Lisbeï.

"Better still!" said Selva sarcastically. "She reads it. The Believras hear that the Daughter of Elli never said she was the Daughter of Elli, and that Hallera—the same Hallera who is the cornerstone of the entire body of tradition concerning Garde and the Word—may be an impostor. Furthermore, the Progressistas are told that Garde is opposed to the use of technology, and as a crowning touch the Juddites are informed that they betrayed Garde, persecuted her disciplas, and falsified History and the Word of Elli. Or rather—"

As she talked, Selva had risen and walked over to the window. She turned abruptly. "Or rather, she tells them that the *Bethely* Juddites betrayed Garde, that the *Bethely* Juddites falsified History and the Word of Elli."

"We aren't Juddites now!"

"But we are Bethely, Lisbeï. Why is that, do you think? Because the Juddites of Bethely brought about Maerlande."

"Neither the great deeds nor the sins of the mothers shall be visited upon the childreen, Selva," Mooreï said gently. "The Bethely of today is no more responsible for the acts of olden-day Bethely than are present-day Juddites for the acts of the old Juddites. It's an argument that wouldn't stand up for very long, if indeed it were used at all."

Was Selva *blushing?* The Mother came back to her seat and sat down.

"But you're right about the other point," continued

Moreï. "There's something in this testament of Halde's to upset everyone."

"But if Believras can't stand having their faith questioned, what's that faith worth?" asked Antonë.

"The same as the lack of faith that unbelievras don't like to have questioned?" asked Kelys, apparently speaking to the air.

Antonë turned on her with lightning speed. "I'm a skeptic, that's all. As long as there are other possible explanations—"

"You'd like to be forced to believe," said Moreï, observing Antonë with a kind of tenderness. "Elli has made us free to believe in Elli or not, free to choose. Are you afraid of your freedom, Antonë?"

Antonë sat still for a moment, her emotions fluctuating violently, but not with anger. With stupefaction? Lisbeï had no time to ponder the phenomenon. She was wondering whether she ought to knock on the table to bring everyone back to the real subject of the meeting, when Tula began to speak in her steady voice.

"Anyhow, whether it upsets everyone or not is no argument. You want us to think of the consequences, Mother Selva, and yes, of course there will be discussions and disputes and difficult revisions and changes. But had Compagnas or disciplas decided not to tell the truth because of the possible complications—such as their *deaths*, to start with—where would we be today? Antonë and Kelys are also right, each in her own way. If your belief isn't strong enough to stand up under questioning without fear, then you'd better change your belief. I think we ought to tell the truth to the Family and the Assembly, even without Bethely adopting a unanimous position."

She stopped abruptly and bowed her head. A brief silence followed.

"Hear ye, hear ye," murmured Kelys.

"The truth," said Selva crossly, after a pause. "What truth? A few facts, some unproved allegations, and a mountain of theories. A long way from 'truth'! What I see in all this is that if we announce it at the Assembly opening, we'll unlock the floodgates of endless palavras. No one will emerge the stronger for it, and the motions tabled by Nevenici and ourselves—or Lletrewyn—will be delayed. And these are things that really matter. For all the Families, for all Maerlande.

It matters *now*. We must begin Western exploration. Things will soon become unbearable otherwise, and the consequences . . . You've seen Antonë's population curves. This is more urgent than finding out whether Garde considered herself a Daughter or a Voice of Elli, or whether the Hive Juddites or the Harem Juddites, or both, lied about what happened!"

"More important, Selva?" Mooreï's solemn tone held a reproach. "It's important in a different way, but *equally* important all the same."

"If famine breaks out in the next few years, it won't be Garde who feeds us," remarked Antonë.

"If famine breaks out in the next few years, our choice will be determined by what we are and what we believe we owe each other." Suddenly Mooreï was speaking in a ringing voice that Lisbeï had never heard. "And we are our faith, we are the Word, yes, even you, Antonë, even the most progressive of Progressistas. The whole of Maerlande has been shaped by the heritage of Garde. Not only the Word, but the Service and the Dance of the Celebration. They are part of us and govern our behavior every bit as much as the rate of population growth or the percentage of arable land." And then Mooreï seemed to shrink and become the old familiar Mooreï, who smiled at Antonë and said, "I know it's always tempting to simplify the truth. But not by mutilating it, Antonë. That would be a fatal simplification."

"The truth again!" exclaimed Selva, letting her hands fall on the table with a thud. "But what truth, for Elli's sake? And wasn't it you who taught me that not all truth should be revealed at just any time to just anyone?"

"But this isn't just anyone!" protested Lisbeï. "It's the Assembly of Mothers."

"But it does seem inopportune, in fact," remarked Kelys, rising as she spoke and stretching gracefully. Lisbeï watched her silently, as did the others, somehow aware that this was the aim of the exercise, but incapable of being angry with Kelys. "There's not only the question of Western exploration being delayed or even postponed. Other Families have motions that must seem just as important to them. We're talking about the Assembly of Mothers: some people have been looking forward to it for months in the hope of resolving their problems. They won't be in a frame of mind to consider such grave questions as those raised by Halde's testament. I think

Selva is right: it would be better to wait until after the Assembly."

"It's not as though we'd say nothing at all," Selva added, happy to find support where she'd apparently given up hoping for it.

"Really?" retorted Lisbeï. "And what are we going to tell the Family?"

"Later!" Selva shook her head with returning irritation."I've already explained. We'll tell them everything later."

Lisbeï, too indignant to speak, sensed Mooreï's resigned acceptance and Antonë's approval. Kelys nodded approvingly as well.

Tula raised a hand as Lisbeï was on the verge of exploding. "What you mean is that we, the people in this room, are deciding what the others can hear and know?" she said slowly. "We are deciding for all the Reds and Blues and Greens, not only in Bethely but in all the other Families? By what right? This isn't how Bethely is supposed to work, nor Maerlande."

Selva's mirror-wall reared its hard, brilliant surface. The Mother considered Tula for a moment, taking in her genuinely shocked disbelief. She gave a mirthless smile. "Imperfect choices in an imperfect world," she said. "Learn."

6

Antonë to Linta

Bethely, 4 Maïa, 489 A.G.

My Linta,
Because of Selva's decision, from now on my letters can tell you nothing about what's really happening here. But I hope that one day you'll be able to read all this, and I'm sure you'll understand.
*   I can see why Selva made her decision and still think it was the right choice, but at the same time I can't help understanding*

and sharing the resentment of Tula and Lisbeï. I feel guilty knowing what I know while the rest of the Family remains in ignorance.

In short, the official story is that Lisbeï found nothing of interest in her hole. The entrance has been sealed. She's been punished for having spent too much time there and is back doing her chores and training for the Games. I thought (and feared) she would make a fuss, but she didn't. Perhaps, like Tula, she's still too upset by the way the council has twisted the Bethely Carta. Tula has resumed her training with Mooreï and Selva for the role she'll be taking on after Juna 19, when she's officially declared Mother-designate of Bethely in the Assembly and takes Lisbeï's place beside Selva in the debates. Neither one has said a word about all this since the inner-council meeting. I don't know whether this is a good or bad sign for Tula. Her emotional wall is constantly in place these days. As for Lisbeï, Selva appears to have poured balm on the wound by giving her permission to copy out the entire Notebook (it deserves a capital N!). Kelys is delving into the oldest Bethely Archives, looking for—what? If the Bethely Hive Juddites invented the second Garde out of whole cloth after their ancestors had obliterated all trace of the first, they certainly won't have left a confession anywhere!

True or false? Halde's Garde or Hallera's? Both true, both false? I don't know. I don't know what I believe—or what I don't believe. Mooreï's remark still echoes within me. "You want to be forced to believe." And it's true. I'd felt it was possible and plausible that Markali's trial was rigged with the help of Hallera's daughter, in order to entrench Garde's divinity and the Word, both so vital to the creation of the future Maerlande. That was enough for me—then. And it still is possible and plausible, even more so now because Hallera herself may well have simply been a liar. I should be strengthened in my disbelief, but instead I have doubts. Why? Halde's testament can be contested with almost the same kind of arguments I've always used against Hallera. Can't it?

Kelys is researching Archives from the end of the Hives period. There's a tradition—she says—that Markali and Alicia were friends or compagnas, one having chosen the way of Evil, the other of Good. A classic story of the Hive days. There are dozens of tales and romances on this theme. Alicia organized the trial from which Markali emerged without the death sentence. If they were secretly in collusion, that would explain it. But why would the Juddites suddenly make an effort to establish the di-

*vinity of someone they'd massacred (if we believe Halde) a hun-
dred years earlier? The revolution that toppled the Hives came
from within—that much we know. Some of the Juddites converted by Garde at the end of the Harem period may have kept
her memory alive despite all the persecution. They might have
revived it at the end of the Hives, not hesitating to use a subterfuge. For them, the end would justify the means: they wanted to
speed up the process of change without too much violence. And
in fact they succeeded. Maerlande came into being, we're here
today, and things are fairly peaceful.*

*In that case the first Garde, Halde's Garde, would be the
"true" one. The true Daughter of Elli. Who didn't want to be
called that. Truly divine and human, dead and resurrected.*

*But if a trick was played once, why not twice? That's what
also bothered Mooreï: if one Garde is false, the other is inevitably
suspect, no matter which one we want to think of as "true."*

*Which brings me back to Mooreï's "you want to be forced to
believe"—or disbelieve. Everyone around me believed Garde was
indeed the Daughter of Elli, and I saw it as being more likely a
trick. And now, when I envision the possibility that both Gardes
may be false, I immediately begin thinking that at least one could
be genuine! Yet there's no more "evidence" that it should be the
first Garde, apart from Halde's testament, so why should the
absence of hard evidence in one instance make me want to believe, when the abundance of proof in the other made me doubt?
I can't believe I'm doing this out of sheer contrariness!*

*I'm totally lost. After the council I spent the whole night
talking it over with Mooreï. She had also seemed troubled during
the meeting—but not now, not really. Wait—yes, she is troubled
by the idea of accusing the Bethely Juddites of skulduggery at the
end of both the Harem and Hive periods. She's thinking of the
political consequences in the medium and short term, and she's
thinking of the effect on others' faith. She's thinking of Tula
(who's getting a rather harsh lesson in what being the Mother
really means), and of Lisbeï, whose desire for the truth and respect for knowledge are being violently rebuffed. Of Selva and
her future relations with her daughters and the Family. Of the
Family itself, when it finds out that it wasn't told the truth right
away. But Mooreï is no longer troubled on her own account. Do
you know why? Because she knows in her heart of hearts that
Elli is and that Garde told the truth in her Promise. She knows
because she has Danced at the Celebration, because she still
Dances. The answer's always the same, it's yours and all the*

other Believras' whom I've asked. (And Kelys's too, although she's no Believra, despite everything.)

And I have never Danced, never wanted to Dance, never even been present at the Dance. Do you remember all my arguments? Out of respect for others' beliefs, out of disgust for that all-too-familiar frenzy, or out of self-respect, or for all sorts of reasons. But the fact is, I never wanted to try. Not with you, not with anyone. What was the point, since I understood what happened, the mechanics of the operation. . . . Isn't that right?

But Mooreï is so sure. And I, suddenly so unsure. What if I had really missed something? If the Dance was more than mere ritual and mechanics?

(Garde doesn't even mention the Dance, if Halde's testimony is to be believed!)

But if Garde really came to life again, if Elli really existed . . .

And according to Mooreï, if I Danced I would know. Know it's true.

But if I were so keen on being forced to believe, why am I still afraid? All I need do is Dance at the Celebration next month and I'll be forced to believe.

Or perhaps not. There are many who Dance without believing. Mooreï herself reminded me of this. I'd still have to choose, though. And I can't, can't take the step, the leap to faith. Yes, I am afraid. Of what, I'm not too sure. Of my freedom? I was shaken when Mooreï made that remark in the council, although I really have no idea why. What did I think she meant, what was it that affected me so? There ought to be some domino effect of revelations after the first shock, but there's been nothing.

My readiness to credit a Juddite plot concerning Garde stems from wanting there to be no shadow of a doubt—yes, wanting to be forced to believe. Also, because I don't like the Juddites. They would cry "Abomination!" if I made public my knowledge about the Malady and its effects. They'd point the finger and call me an Abomination, and you, and Lisbeï, and the others. Well, not all Juddites would be so vitriolic, but some would. Is this why Halde's account suits me better than Hallera's? Because it denounces the Juddites?

That too—again, I'm only human. And Garde . . . Halde's Garde is so very human. Is that why her divinity seems to me more plausible than Hallera's pious certitudes? I must have a contradictory streak after all.

7

One morning, a few days before the end of Maïa, Kelys came looking for Lisbeï in her room. Lisbeï had permission to use the breakfast hour to copy the Notebook. After her own breakfast, Tula would hurry in with a tray of food before rushing off to work with Selva and Mooreï, who'd been keeping her nose to the grindstone. Once the discovery became public, the Notebook and everything else would inevitably go to Wardenberg, which had the most expert researchas and the best-equipped Library. Lisbeï would be a Blue by this time but not an explora; therefore, Bethely couldn't claim any exclusive rights from her find. Of course Bethely would receive a copy of the Notebook. Selva, however, had remarked that Lisbeï needn't wait: if she wished, she could copy the Notebook right away. Lisbeï fell to work at once. Selva was pleased to see that her daughter had succumbed to this diversionary tactic, and Lisbeï was pleased to see Selva thought it had worked.

Kelys straddled the second chair in the room and studied Lisbeï, who had resumed her task after opening the door. It was a particularly difficult passage in almost illegible writing. The choices she made at this point would influence the later translation. Mooreï had advised her to note down all the possible spellings suggested by words that didn't make sense at first glance. It added to her task, but it would probably help later on.

Ten minutes went by. Kelys still hadn't spoken. She sat there, radiating calm and a slight amusement. Finally Lisbeï couldn't contain herself another moment. "Can I do anything for you?" she asked with exaggerated courtesy.

"How about coming for an outing?" responded Kelys, not the least flustered.

"I'm supposed to work in the laundry this morning."

"I've taken care of that. You're free for the day."

Oh really? "Does Selva know?"

"Selva won't mind when she finds out."

Lisbeï stared at Kelys, who spread her hands, pink palms upward, and widened her eyes in complete innocence. "No strings attached!" She stretched out a long black finger to stroke Lisbeï's cheek. "How defensive you've become, little Lisbeli."

What was there to say? "You betrayed me"? Too melodramatic, even if that was what went through Lisbeï's mind each time she thought about the inner council and Kelys's attitude. She put her pens and papers in the drawer, along with the precious Notebook, and locked it.

"Walk where?"

"Ride. Just you and me."

This was all Kelys would say, Lisbeï realized. She got out her riding gear.

Assembly visitas hadn't begun to arrive. Wicows and ovinas grazed as usual in the flat circle left by the ancient fortifications. All the fencing on the South Esplanade had already been removed, and now workas were busy with the West Esplanade. A good many athletes would arrive with the Mothers for the Games. Since the Pilgrimage of Garde followed the Juna 21 Celebration, the remaining fencing would probably come down to make room for the flood of campers. Animals brought by the visitas would be taken with Bethely cattle to the eastern pastures in the Douve's huge loop. Carts from the Farms had been trundling back and forth since dawn and would continue to do so for several more days. Everyone customarily brought her own provisions, whether for the Assembly, the Games, or the Pilgrimage, but Bethely had a tradition of providing sumptuous hospitality, particularly for an Assembly of Mothers.

The giant Assembly tent hadn't yet been raised at the West Gate, but the masts had been there for two days. The huge canvas sections had arrived, although at present the dottas were busy applying the final touches under the watchful eyes of the capta-seamstresses. The nearly two thousand emblems of Maerlande Families had been embroidered long ago, but at each Mothers' Assembly others were added for the new Offshoots that had sprung up in the four-year interval. Lisbeï remembered the year the Provincial Assembly had taken place in Bethely. The pricked ends of her index finger and left thumb had felt like pincushions.

To Lisbeï's surprise, Kelys turned the head of her great roan alezane to the northeast. She had her shotgun stuck in the saddle holster, although she hadn't said anything to Lisbeï about bringing a weapon. She must have seen Lisbeï's stare, because she smiled and patted the mother-of-pearl stock. "Just habit. We aren't going all that far."

But they were going all the same. Toward the Badlands.

Until Kelys came on the scene, the land outside Bethely had been simply a matter of words and colored patches on a map. "Those are the Great Badlands," Mooreï had said the first time, her finger following the dotted blue line bordering the big black blot to the north and east of Bethely. "Beyond this border, the air, water, and plants get increasingly poisonous the farther you go."

Maerlande maps were dotted with black or gray spots, some tiny, some big. These were badlands too, but not the Great Badlands. Before the Decline, before the water had risen and reshaped the continents, these spots had been the densely populated regions of olden-day countries—or even whole countries in themselves, like the Great Badlands. Too many people making too many things and creating too much garbage, much of it toxic, and spreading it everywhere, sometimes by accident, sometimes through ignorance or stupidity. Now these regions or countries were the haunts of Abominations (according to the horror stories that tutresses recounted to the dottas, who listened spellbound as chills ran down their spines). "Mutants," Antonë used to say with that curious flash in her light, sad and angry, before reminding Lisbeï about her lessons in genetics.

"Renegadas," Mooreï had sighed the day she showed Lisbeï the map. She hadn't explained what renegadas were, however—this was before the Loï affair. Little Lisbeï had stared at the black spot, a terrifying fantasy suddenly darting through her mind. Would Mooreï's finger become black and poisoned if it touched the spot? Unaware of the danger, Mooreï continued her lecture: the gray spots weren't so poisonous as the black ones (not so "contaminated," Antonë would say, not so "polluted"). Only exploras ventured into badlands, and since only Blues became exploras, there was no danger of hurting the babie-seeds. Why did they go? Because there were "Decline artifacts" in the badlands, objects and information about the past that could be useful and weren't necessarily contaminated.

And that was all there was to know. Lisbeï had soon formed an opinion on the subject of the Great Badlands, also called the Bethely Badlands, although the Family laid no special claim to them. It was a sort of "nowhere-land," a great emptiness that by its very contrast reaffirmed the existence of the only place that really mattered: Maerlande. And for the young Lisbeï, Maerlande had somehow been only a setting for Bethely. She would have considered it almost normal had Bethely been encircled by black. It would have satisfied her desire for symmetry far more than these irregular blue patches—lakes and seas far bigger than the blue ribbon of the Douve, far too big to be anything but mere words. And then there were the brown patches, the mountains. You could see some of them when you looked northeast from the highest floors in the West Tower. There were also very high mountains in the Great Badlands. Finally, there were the green patches, plains like the one around Bethely. But seven-year-old Lisbeï, barely out of the garderie, had puzzled over the idea of Bethely's immensity: how could it fit into that tiny round spot on the map?

Mooreï had explained that the map simply represented the places, just like the names given to things. Lisbeï had found this far more interesting than the map itself or the Badlands. It was comforting to know you were surrounded by Maerlande, but when you thought about it, Bethely was quite big enough. Just the West Tower was already quite big enough! At least for now. Little Lisbeï had contented herself with the idea that Maerlande was the other side of Bethely, just as the moon was the other side of the sun.

And then Kelys came. Kelys, a peregrina from "outside," "elsewhere," words that almost took on the magic sparkle of garderie days before Lisbeï had learned she must live "outside" without Tula. Kelys herself had plenty of sparkle in Lisbeï's eyes without the charm of an exotic origin, but for Tula it carried immense prestige: Kelys came from across the *sea!* She badgered Kelys mercilessly for stories, and Kelys always willingly obliged.

Tula would never go anywhere now—except to Assemblies, but that hardly counted. She could leave once her days as Mother were done, but not before. They could both leave . . . and yet, watching her with Selva (they looked so much alike now, with their bound red hair and milky complexions), Lisbeï thought of Mooreï. The Memory had been a Blue for several years, yet she'd never shown the least desire to leave Bethely except to accompany Selva. Lisbeï often wondered if they'd really let her and Tula leave one day—never sure whether by "they" she meant Selva or Bethely.

But they'd never let Tula go away with her after what she was thinking of doing. They wouldn't even let her become Tula's Memory.

"What do you want to do, Lisbeli?"

Lisbeï jumped, but Kelys wasn't reading her mind; she merely meant "when you're officially a Blue."

"I'll be Tula's Memory," Lisbeï replied, trying to quell her pounding heart. As though Kelys didn't know!

"No—what do you *want* to do, Lisbeli?" said Kelys patiently.

How clear Kelys's light was today! There was no mistaking it. She really wished to know what Lisbeï wanted to do with her life, it mattered because she really loved her. Lisbeï suddenly felt a hard lump in her throat as, moved and ashamed of her suspicions, she murmured, "I don't know. I haven't thought about what I'll do after . . ."

"After what?"

Lisbeï caught herself, shuddering inwardly. No, she must not tell, she couldn't, not even Kelys. She hadn't even told *Tula!*

"After what, Lisbeli?" persisted Kelys, frowning slightly. Once again her love, anxiety, and desire to help enveloped Lisbeï like a heady aroma.

Lisbeï stiffened. No. She mustn't talk about it. For their own good, to protect them.

"Have you ever thought about being an explora, Lisbeli?" asked Kelys. Lisbeï was grateful to her for not pressing the previous question. "Your first translation of Halde was very good, considering you've had no special training as a linguist. And to have discovered the underground passage . . . to have thought there might be underground passages and to have followed through with your idea—that's part of being an explora."

Lisbeï had never thought of it in this way. She pretended to consider the possibility. Well, yes, even just pretending, there was something to be said for the profession if it included that kind of thing—finding what was lost or hidden, bringing the past to light. But there were also all those journeys. Tula now—Tula would have made a good explora. She sighed. "No. No, I don't think so."

Kelys smiled. "Too bad. Shall we race to the woods?"

From one race to the next, as the morning and then the afternoon drew on, they made their way to the stony plateau from where the great blue-stained stones could be seen in the short grass, marching across the hills. When Kelys nudged her alezane forward, Lisbeï remained where she was. Kelys turned back with a crooked smile. "You're not risking anything now, are you?" As Lisbeï stared at her, disconcerted by the ironic gleam that accompanied the smile, Kelys became serious. "The danger begins way beyond the blue stones. They were put there over three centuries ago. Badlands can change, even Great Badlands. Surely you know that?"

But the patrols had again reported fresh and unknown animal tracks last year. They were far too big for a normal ursa. The Great Badlands were much more polluted than any other: everyone knew that. This was why patrols barely crossed the blue stones when gathering samples of soil and water, as well as plant and animal specimens. And why renegadas were sent there.

"You have tradition, Lisbeli, hearsay, and then there's reality, what you go to see for yourself."

"Have you been to see?"

"How do you think I found Loï?"

Lisbeï brought her mare up with Kelys's mount, interested in spite of herself. "Were you the one who found Loï? You went looking for her?"

"No. I was on my way to Bethely. It's shorter cutting through the Badlands from the Cartano road. You gain a good hour."

Loï hadn't got very far. Perhaps a klim past the blue stones. It was still far if you remembered that the Juddites considered one meter enough to contaminate you. Maybe she'd thought of going even farther on that day, or of staying in the Badlands. But she'd stopped in this spot and lit a fire because she probably didn't care whether or not she was found by whatever lived in the Badlands—didn't care whether she lived or died right then and there.

Kelys's face hardened, as did her light. She dismounted and lifted the food satchel off her saddle, then sat down with her back resting against one of the stones. After a moment's hesitation, Lisbeï did the same. It was true, after all: she certainly wasn't risking a thing.

For a while they ate in silence. Lisbeï couldn't keep from starting at the least sound that rose above the buzz of insects —the cries of birds, or the creaking of branches beyond the line of stones.

"Relax, Lisbeï. Don't you trust me?"

It was said lightly, but with a slight cutting edge. Lisbeï looked up from her sandwich, and Kelys laughed, teeth flashing white in her dark face. "Oh, I know: I betrayed you. I betrayed both you and Tula. But mainly you."

Lisbeï lowered her head, not knowing what to say. Kelys was admitting that a special bond existed between them, but seemed to deny it in the same breath!

The long, slender fingers lifted Lisbeï's chin. "Should I have 'betrayed' Selva, Mooreï, Bethely, and my duty to the Mothers? All that for you, Lisbeli?"

Common sense whispered the answer, and Lisbeï muttered, "No," a little ashamed to feel that other emotion within saying, "Yes!"

Kelys must have sensed it too, for she became serious. "Should I have betrayed myself, Lisbeli? What would you do if I asked you never to talk of it, of the Notebook, to anyone?"

Lisbeï looked at her again with alarm. She chided herself inwardly for her stupidity, however, and weighed the question. "It might depend on your stated reasons."

"No reasons. Only that it would harm a lot of people if you talked, beginning with me."

"It won't hurt anyone!" Lisbeï bit her lips—too late. "When it's made public after the Assembly," she added.

"No—suppose I asked you now to . . . destroy the Notebook, for example."

"Destroy it! But why?"

"Because there might be things in it that compromise me. Or my Family. Just a supposition, Lisbeli!" she added with a thin smile in response to Lisbeï's reaction. "Let's pretend, all right? Let's pretend the existence and revelations in this Notebook are very important to you, and that it's very important for me to get rid of it. No—let's say for Tula! Tula asks you to destroy it. What would you do?"

But Tula would never ask her to do such a thing!

Kelys nodded. "That's right: Tula knows there are parts of you that you can't give up without losing your identity. And when you were no longer yourself . . . well, in a way Tula wouldn't be Tula either. Do you understand?"

Lisbeï forced herself to take a bite of sandwich and swallow the mouthful along with the lump in her throat. Yes, she understood. And no, of course Kelys hadn't betrayed her. Any more than Tula could ever betray her. Or she, Lisbeï, betray Tula.

But wasn't she now preparing to betray Tula? By not telling her?

No. She bit deeper into the sandwich. It was for Tula's protection.

Or maybe to prevent Tula from asking her to give up her plan? But the thought was instantly obliterated. To *protect* Tula.

Kelys ate too, staring in the distance at first, then fixing her gaze on a red-and-yellow butterfly that had alighted on a nearby blade of grass. She leaned over slowly and held a finger in the butterfly's path. The insect climbed onto it and stayed there, gleaming like a jewel on the black skin. From time to time it fluttered its wings.

"Tula," mused Kelys. "Have you ever wondered about the bond that links you to Tula? Or to Antonë? Or to me? The way we can perceive emotions?"

Lisbeï was speechless for a moment. With Tula it simply *was,* always. Elli had made them that way, Tula had said, and Lisbeï had adopted this answer. The others, especially Kelys, whose light could disappear and reappear at will . . . They had never brought the subject up before—not Antonë, not Kelys, until now.

"What about you?" countered Lisbeï, feeling on the defensive without knowing why.

Kelys laughed and the butterfly flew off. Lisbeï sensed more clearly why she'd felt defensive. It hadn't been a real question. Kelys had in fact thought about it; Kelys no doubt had an answer.

They looked silently at each other; then Kelys smiled, a different smile, a little sad, a little serious. "We've all had the Malady, haven't we?"

"Yes," replied Lisbeï. What was Kelys driving at?

"We never get sick now, and our injuries heal quickly. It's not only we three, Lisbeli. Lots of other people are like us. The Malady didn't used to have this effect. It's changed. And it's changed us."

Kelys leaned her head against the blue stone. "Mutations aren't confined to the badlands, Lisbeli. They began long ago, before Maerlande, and they are going on in Maerlande right now. Most mutations are harmful, and you die sooner or later. Others—well, they aren't fatal. Like the mutation that produces more girls than boys. Still others are new, like us." She looked steadily at Lisbeï as she spoke. Her eyes and her light were *watching*.

Was Lisbeï meant to be afraid? To cry "Abomination" while making the sign of Elli? Kelys must know her better than that! "Or Garde's Compagnas," she said, taking another bite out of her sandwich.

"Or Garde's Compagnas," Kelys acquiesced. But she was still watchful.

"It's the Tapestry of Elli," concluded Lisbeï—and she truly believed it. What was Kelys trying to say?

"The Tapestry of Elli," agreed Kelys again. She had hesitated a little before speaking. What was that in her light? Disappointment? Surprise? Amusement? The sudden sparkle seemed to combine all three. It died down, and Kelys went on gravely. "There's another effect. Sometimes we never become Red."

Ah. *That's* what she was driving at. Lisbeï examined her own reactions without speaking. She wasn't angry, not even surprised. Was she relieved? Not being Red wasn't a . . . "punishment." Why did she think of punishment? What would she have been punished for? She brushed aside the thought with the emotion. It was a genetic mutation. A genetic accident. Well, it could have been worse. She could have been stunted, no bigger than a mosta at the age of forty like the poor Compagnas, or worse still, armless or deformed in other ways that didn't kill but meant you had to live in the big house near the Hill Farm with the handicapped people who simply couldn't be integrated into life in the Towers.

"Does Antonë know?" What a question! Of course she must. But why hadn't she said anything?

"Yes, she knows. But it's not automatic. I've had chil-dreen, for example."

Kelys? For some unaccountable reason, Lisbeï found it hard to imagine Kelys as a Red. The explora gave her a crooked little smile. "Several children."

Lisbeï thought for a moment, then attacked her sandwich again. "Unfavorable mutations will eliminate themselves if the carriers don't reproduce," she said between mouthfuls.

"That's true," said Kelys. She must have been impressed by Lisbeï's calm, for she remained silent for a while. Then another butterfly, a rather uninteresting white one, began to flutter around them.

"It must be a little like butterflies," Kelys said dreamily. "Us—among us," she explained, sensing Lisbeï's surprise. "Male butterflies can find females over immense distances because the females emit a . . . scent that we humans can't perceive, but it's powerful enough for the males to pick up klims away. Something called 'pheromones.' Humans emit them too, but people don't perceive them consciously. In our case, however, we do, or something like it. Apparently we can also control the process."

Lisbeï sensed a vague but growing apprehension. Fear: she was afraid! But . . . the wave of anxiety subsided as quickly as it had come, leaving her panting, muscles tense. Kelys smiled innocently.

"You?" Lisbeï stammered incredulously. "It was you who . . ."

The black head bowed wordlessly.

"How do you do it?"

"I don't know, really. Our emotions produce physical changes, as you know. I do the opposite, I suppose. I imagined that I felt great fear and your body perceived it in mine, or emanating from mine—sensed the physical changes stimulated by fear. I do it almost automatically now. But at first I tried it with the taïtche, the concentration of the taïtche. Do you remember when you broke your arm? Like that. I had a friend with the same thing, and we tried to develop our control of what we . . . emitted and received. You must have done this with Tula when you were little, and with Selva and Antonë, too, but without realizing it."

They might try it now, she and Tula! But Lisbeï's excitement evaporated instantly. Surely not now. And after the Assembly . . . Resolutely, she steered her thoughts away from the subject.

"Although with Tula it's a bit different," Kelys went on, seemingly unaware of Lisbeï's emotions. She spoke pensively. "Like Selva. The mirror-wall . . . The emissions may cancel each other out. Antonë is yet another case. She needs to touch, to make physical contact." Kelys appeared to shake off her reverie. "Yes, there are variations, but—"

"—but all linked to the Malady. Which is not a malady," concluded Lisbeï.

Kelys nodded. She had been able to finish her sandwich while talking. Lisbeï finished eating, too, and held out a hand to touch the rose-streaked peach Kelys offered her.

"Is that the reason you brought me here? To tell me this?"

Kelys did not relinquish the peach at once. She contemplated Lisbeï with great, liquid eyes, brows slightly raised as though she were also asking herself the question. She let the fruit go. "Yes," she said, "among other things."

But what other things? She would leave it to Lisbeï to guess.

8

Lisbeï/Journal

Wardenberg, 23 Ellième, 492 A.G.

She asked me if I remembered her, remembered our first meeting. As though I could forget! But she said no, the first *meeting, and opened the top buttons of her tunic to show me the necklace.*

She was the one I'd talked with just before the Assembly opening! But you don't know about that—something else I didn't tell you.

I had managed to get away from the reception they'd organized for the Baltike Captas, do you remember? You saw me slipping out and gave me a wink. I didn't feel sleepy. I'd had trouble sleeping for several nights, and that night—on the eve of the Assembly—I knew I wouldn't be able to close my eyes. The idea of staying alone in my room didn't appeal to me. The more I reflected on what I was about to do, the less sure I felt about it. Was it a good or a bad thing, I wondered, your being so busy the last two weeks? I would have loved to tell you everything, and yet I really wanted you to know nothing. I decided to have a look around the Fair. It was mask night, no one would notice me. Of course, I hadn't had time to make a mask, but Elli was chilly, and I wore my hooded cape over my green outfit.

In other years we used to make the rounds separately, you

and I, meeting afterward. We often noticed the same things, re-member? This time neither of us had the leisure to tour the Fair —not together, in any case. I don't know if you noticed that necklace. It was cloisonné *red and blue enamel, with red pre-dominating: a row of six-point stars. Its Baïanque* artisana *was inordinately proud of it, displaying it separately on a little stand in front of the other jewels—rings, bracelets, brooches, and combs. They were all gorgeous, but the necklace was something special. Not "gorgeous"—that was the point. Its workmanship was as delicate as the others, but it had a sort of . . . strength, a dignity, like a Mother's Necklace. Other objects had caught my eye, too. There was that polished ebony statuette from Tor-remolines, two symmetrical figures—*paradras—*their fingertips just touching. I thought of Kelys the moment I saw their slim lines. And in a Liborne stall there was a copper sextant engraved with images of the sea. Even if there'd been time to get ready for the Exchange that year, I'd have had nothing comparable to offer. But that wasn't why I was wandering around the Fair, anyway. I wanted to take my mind off my troubles, to leave no room for thinking about the things that had been bothering me.*

Night fell, and some of the artisanas *closed up their stalls. Looking at the West Esplanade from the fairground, I could see the tent village lighting up from within like giant colored lanterns in a field. The Towers were also lit. This was the hour we used to wait for, the hour when the grown-ups went to dinner and left the Fair to the little Greens. The dottas ran about excitedly, and the air rang with their shouts and laughter above the music. I felt as though I were floating through it all in a bubble of silence. I drifted over to the platforms where acrobats, jugglers, and story-tellers held sway. Childreen's stories, as usual at this time of day —Cyndrella, the Bethely version. Do you know, I've found twelve different versions in the Archives here? The story had already begun. It had reached the part where the nurse-sorceress finds Cyndrella in tears in her corner of the kitchens. It's only in our Southern version that she's a* nemdotta *and that her mother, the wicked old Hive Queene, hasn't recognized her because she is the childe of a disgraced Drone. The Cyndrella marionette had the black circle prominently displayed on her shoulder: nobody's daughter. Poor Cyndrella, now a slave and condemned to do the hardest, dirtiest jobs! (When Mooreï used to tell me the story, she'd always include everything I hated doing in the kitchens.) Anyhow, there was Cyndrella, weeping in her corner. It was the day of the Choosing, and naturally a nemdotta like her hadn't the right to go to the festivities.*

Cyndrella's shoulders heaved pitifully while the storyteller sobbed out her tale beside the stage. Then in came the nurse-sorceress. She waved her wand, and poof! the black tattoo disappeared. (And it really did, oooh, aaah! It took us some time to figure out the ink-and-solvent trick, remember?) Another wave of the wand, and there stood Cyndrella, splendidly clothed. The childreen were enchanted and totally unaware of the sleight of hand involved. (We're not used to having the story acted out for us in Bethely!) They shouted with amazement when the pumpkin turned into a cavala. "Pass yourself off as the Queene of Milane. Nobody knows you here because you're nobody," said the nurse, vanishing amid a string of little explosions. The puppeteers were awfully good. In the gasole light you could barely see the puppeteers' eyes. With their hooded clothing and gloves, they faded into the dark backdrop as they manipulated the life-sized dolls.

Now it's the ball scene. Cyndrella makes her Choice. She gets her male, and as we're in Bethely, she leaves the stage with him. (They're more explicit in Wardenberg. I was absolutely shocked the first time.) Cyndrella comes back to dance with the other Queenes. The new Queene—a sister, but ignorant of the fact—has noticed Cyndrella's cleverness during the Choosing. Charmed, she invites her to dance. Midnight chimes, and Cyndrella flees, losing a sandal. Things turn out as usual, but each time it's wonderful, isn't it? The young Queene gives Cyndrella her Family name and the right to bear childreen. That was our favorite part when we were little: "From this day thou shalt be Cyrina."

It was then that I became aware of her presence. She'd been behind me for quite some time but probably didn't choose to be noticed. I sensed someone watching me. My instinct was to move away as though I'd noticed nothing. But it was impossible because she was like us—you, Antonë, Kelys. And she knew I was like her—the resonance was unmistakable. Curiosity impelled me to turn around. Her mask—a scarlet birda with a silver beak —only hid her eyes. She was shorter than I and very slender, but I didn't think she was a Green. Her resonance was too . . . dense, too complex, a little like Kelys's. I could barely make out her features or guess her age in the glimmer of the gasoles. I have an image of keen-edged bones, however. But most of all I noticed the black froth of curly hair over her brow. And her eyes, their irises enlarged in the shadow, though not enough to hide *their pale color. She smiled. It was an invitation—this was mask night, after all—but more than an invitation because of the resonance.*

I'd never been at the Fair on mask night without you. I wondered whether she realized how much older she was than I. She took me by the arm and drew me gently toward the stalls that still had their lights on.

"Have you already chosen your Exchange object?" she asked.

I said no, I'd not had time to prepare anything.

She halted in front of the stall with the enamel necklace. "I have chosen." She began talking in rapid Iturri to the artisana.

I'm better at reading Iturri than speaking it, even now. At the end of the discussion she lifted her hands to her neck, slipping them under her cape to remove something. I saw it was a necklace of pale garnets set in copper, a Mother's necklace.

Naturally the artisana was astonished. Then the masked stranger said something else I couldn't really catch, something about "love" and "death," and the artisana smiled gravely as she accepted the Exchange.

Afterward the stranger took me to the refreshment booths and offered me a goblet of hot sanagra. We talked. About the Fair, the necklace, the Games, the music that had struck up over by the entertainment platforms. Her accent was Bretanye, clearly, but it no longer mattered much how old or who she was. Even though I wore no mask, I felt liberated. For a moment I was no longer really myself. When I try to look back now, it seems rather like a dream. So detached, unrelated to my anguish of the preceding days, my anguish about the events of the morrow. It was . . . like Cyndrella. What with the resonance (and possibly the sanagra), I felt I'd known her for ages, and yet everything about her was so new! It was a strange experience. We continued walking around the Fair, talking now of Bethely, of Litale. . . .

I can't exactly remember the thread of the conversation, but at one point the topic of the Assembly came up. She mentioned something about change, comparing Maerlande to a huge soup pot on the back of the stove. Every year there's an Assembly to let off steam—steam from the Provinces, steam from Maerlande. It made me laugh. Do you remember what we compared it to? Something more like a plant or a new flower each year, a new branch. And suddenly it all came back: the Assembly, change, yes. Of course she sensed the shift in mood and asked what was bothering me.

*You see, Tula, after all that time I needed to talk to someone
so much. There was the resonance, and I'd drunk a little too
much sanagra. And anyway, I didn't really* tell *her. I asked her if
she was afraid of change. Just to test her a little, because she was
a Mother and would be in the Assembly the next day.*

*"And you?" she queried. I was afraid, and she sensed it
clearly. "Why?" she added. "Are there great changes coming?"*

"Yes," I said.

"For you only?"

*"For everyone." Now I could feel the seriousness of her
resonance, as though she understood.*

*"I admire bringers of change," she remarked, "because it
takes a great deal of courage to make things change." As I said
nothing, she went on. "Personally, I like surprises. I also like
. . . to do the surprising." And she laughed. Oh, she knew who I
was; I realize that now. How, I don't know, but she did. I didn't
think about it, though, since all at once I felt less afraid. Because
she wasn't a bit afraid, you see, not of anything. Standing beside
her at that moment was like standing next to the spot where
lightning has just struck, its charge still hanging in the air along
with that indescribable smell and a sort of hair-raising vi-
brancy. . . .*

*At the Assembly opening next day, Selva introduced us.
Guiseïa of Angresea, but I hadn't known this the night before. If
she was wearing the necklace, it was hidden beneath the collar of
her robe. I didn't see it.*

9

Lisbeï's declaration stunned the newly opened Assembly. Before she'd even finished reading, the gathering exploded in an
uproar. Shouts from those who wanted to silence her, protes-
tations from others who wanted to hear her out, and, right
beside her, venomous indignation from Andrea of Lichterey,
the Assembly Capta . . . and the resonating tumult of
Selva's incredulous fury, Mooreï's desolation, Tula's sharp distress. The session was adjourned until the afternoon, allowing

time to circulate the translations she'd copied while pretending to copy the Notebook.

The memory of that morning is a complete blank for her, apart from a sense of dazed relief, the relief felt by survivors of an earthquake. She saw no one until the Assembly reopened, having been shut up in a small room in the Library right after the adjournment. When a Lichterey Blue led her wordlessly back to the Assembly tent, Lisbeï no longer really wondered what to expect. Let things happen: that was the very reason behind her decision to tell the Assembly everything.

Selva and the others had counted on the slowness of communication: the news of the Notebook would gradually get about, distance would weaken reaction, and delay would give everyone time for reflection. But the Assemblies were there for just the opposite purpose: to give people and ideas a real chance to meet and interact during the palavras, without the misleading security of distance and the dangerous illusion of objectivity. Selva must surely be wrong not to have greater confidence in the Family delegates. Didn't the Word say that the Dance of Elli consisted of movement and change? Lisbeï *had* to tell it all, without delay. She owed it to the frail relics of the Compagnas, to Halde and her message, a message that had been destined to share the second death of oblivion, but which, like Garde, had been resurrected. Lisbeï felt responsible for their fate. She was the knot that tied the old thread to the new: Garde's story now passed through her, and along with Halde she was the link in a chain that she had no right to break or even distort. As Tula had repeatedly said during their few conversations since the inner council, the end was in the means. It was Garde's teaching: too much prudence, too much manipulation—and too much distrust—could only distort the final truth.

But what truth? By the evening of the first day, Lisbeï could no longer tell. The Notebook seemed unreal. Several times, listening to some cunning explanation of how she might have lied, she found herself twisting Halde's ring on her finger, as though to reassure herself that she'd really seen the Notebook, really read the words she'd deciphered. . . . (She'd said nothing about the ring to anyone except Tula and had kept it as a deserved talisman.)

There were plenty of insinuations. Who was making these spectacular revelations? An adolescent well versed in languages and History, perfectly capable of fabricating the

Notebook from beginning to end. Poor childe, nearly fifteen and still a Green, although as Mother-designate of Bethely she retained a seat in the Assembly for a few days more. Perhaps this was a pathetic way of grasping at the status she was so soon to lose. Indeed—and here Gileyn of Nevenici turned a smile of false sympathy toward the sector of the tent where Selva sat, impassive but inwardly fulminating—these revelations appeared to take Bethely itself by surprise. Young Lisbeï had told no one in her Family, which in itself was enough to cast serious doubt on the truth of these allegations.

Selva didn't rise to defend Lisbeï, who was sitting close by, nor did Mooreï. Tula surreptitiously clasped her hand, and Lisbeï could sense her desolate anguish. Like Selva and Mooreï, Tula would remain silent. But wasn't that why Lisbeï had kept all knowledge of her plans from them? Tula, like the others, could truthfully say she'd known nothing of Lisbeï's intentions. Then why had Lisbeï felt so hurt and bitter about their silence?

The disputes—they couldn't be called palavras—raged on for two days. Delegates hurled arguments back and forth, availing themselves of all the contentions she'd foreseen and many she had not: to begin with, arguments for and against the authenticity of the Notebook, the skeletons, the site, and the translations, but gradually shifting to Hallera's documents, Markali's trial, and everything the delegates did and did not know about the Bethely Hive, the Bethely Chefferie, and the Great Badlands. "What do the Great Badlands have to do with this?" "The Notebook says that . . ." And back they'd go to the Notebook, the translations, Bethely's hidden motives and Lisbeï's unavowed ambitions, back and forth from morning to night, barely halting for meals and even then prolonging the quarrels of the morning or afternoon.

On the third day, after the silent offering to Elli that opened each session, Antonë asked leave to speak for Bethely and demanded a Decision.

Nearly 480 years earlier, a Decision had recognized the divinity of Garde, putting the seal on the definitive Word and acknowledging the Hallera Appendices. It was therefore fitting that a new Decision should now be invoked. She, Antonë of Maroilles, proposed herself as Arbitra. She would withdraw immediately to begin meditating.

A profound silence fell on the Assembly after Antonë had gone, as though suddenly the delegates had all been called to order and had themselves undertaken to meditate for a moment. In a single stroke Antonë's proposal had crystallized and exorcised all negative emotions. Soon the Mother of Lletrewyn, followed by several others from Bretanye including the Angresea Progressista, rose in approbation. The rest of the Assembly soon followed suit. The principal of the Decision was adopted, and the Assembly was adjourned until the morning—time for the auditantas to be named or declare themselves.

A Decision wasn't something to be set in motion lightly, as Antonë had reminded her audience in a clear, calm voice. Lisbeï's revelations transcended the Family interest, *all* Families' interests, because they ultimately touched the soul and conscience of each individual. That was why Antonë had withdrawn at once to the hills of Bethely, and why each of the auditantas would also retire to fast and meditate in solitude until the final moment of the Assembly, when the actual Decision process would begin. And that was also why Lisbeï would be given into Kelys's care, there to remain in virtual seclusion for the rest of the Assembly.

Later Lisbeï would better understand the nature of the Decision and the burden Antonë (of all people!) had taken on. Not only Antonë, but the auditantas who volunteered or were named by Family delegates or others who knew them. It meant months if not years of commitment. After hearing the testimony of all the interested parties present in Bethely, the Arbitra would stay there while the second phase began. The auditantas would visit each Family, listening without comment to each of those who wished to speak. Once they'd formed an opinion, the auditantas would return to Bethely, there to submit their views and the testimony from all Maerlande to the Arbitra. She would then decide, answerable only to her soul and conscience, and her choice could change the faith, thought, and lives of hundreds of thousands of people.

Alone with Kelys in the Library or her room, Lisbeï wasn't too sure what awaited her in particular. Never for an instant had she thought a Decision would be invoked. She'd been caught completely unawares, like the whole Assembly (or almost, with the exception of Kelys and Guiseïa of Angresea). Of course she understood the basic structure of a Decision: one Arbitra, twenty auditantas, the long closed-door sessions that would end only with unanimous agreement. But the reality was something else.

"It's different every time," said Kelys. "Everything depends on the subject of the Decision and those who are called upon to make it."

In any case, Lisbeï would be one of the "pieces of evidence" examined by the auditantas. She too must meditate. This was why she'd been put in isolation with Kelys to watch over her. Kelys shouldn't have spoken to her and, indeed, after a few days said nothing except what was strictly necessary. Lisbeï used the Mother's private staircase to get from her room to the Library, never meeting anyone on the way. "You must be alone with your own decision," said Kelys at the outset. "I'm only here to remind you of that."

So Lisbeï would have to prepare her defense, read and reread the Word, the Appendices, the minutes of Markali's trial . . .

"No, Lisbeli. Nobody's going to attack you. Together, you will all seek a truth that holds for everyone."

Lisbeï couldn't help being impressed by so solemn a process and strengthened in her resolve to be worthy of her fate, worthy of Halde and Garde. The Assembly would last the full month that year. As the days passed—an interval so curiously detached from the normal flow of time, yet spent in familiar surroundings—Lisbeï felt her convictions crumbling, convictions that had already been shaken by the Assembly's initial explosion. The concentration of the taïtche was to be her salvation. She lost (or found) herself in the taïtche, aware of Kelys hovering at the edge of her perceptions and of the rippling modulations in her aura—so many messages that she could try to decipher and might legitimately attempt to answer, because they were wordless.

Faces: that is what Lisbeï remembers most about the Decision. The faces of the auditantas who interrogated her for a whole day. Names she knows—they were mentioned in the minutes, and anyhow, she has only to consult the Archives to find them. But she has trouble linking them with the faces. The Blue with the loud, hoarse voice, almost comical in an ethereal woman with childlike features: Siffrèn, Gloster, or Westershare? Westershare, surely. She was a Progressista. Gloster and Siffrèn were Traditionalista Families, like Bethely. How commendable of the Juddites not to have named an auditanta of their own—or reprehensible, since it amounted to admitting they weren't capable of being unbiased enough to participate in the Decision. One had come forward on her own, however: Domenica, the Memory of Carésimo born in Juddite Lichterey (she wore a patch over her left eye and spoke with deliberate slowness).

Faces, yes. She remembers faces and the clear atmosphere of peace and simplicity among all these women, gathered for several weeks in complete isolation. They met in the wooded hills north of the Highland Farm, where their tents were scattered beneath tall walnut trees. The meetings took place in the open under the spacious blue sky of Jula, lasting late into the warm nights, serenaded by piping froggles from the ponds below the hills.

Lisbeï had never known deserted places. Even when she used to meet Tula late at night, there was always a light still burning in some window, a figure crossing the courtyard, or even the mere presence of the Towers, with the implied pressure of human voices and human bodies accumulated in time and space. On the Farms at harvest time she'd been surrounded by a crowd of other workas, laughing and shouting, and the traffic of big carts in the wake of clanking machines drawn by buffalas. In the evening the Farm was full of people —a miniature Bethely. And by the blue stones there had been Kelys.

But the hills of the Decision were silent. Yet not quiet. Here she felt a kind of anguish and at the same time a vague exaltation, a sense that things might assume another perspective in this space where human History had left no mark. She saw nothing but the ever-replenished traces of nature left to itself since time immemorial. Later she would realize her naïveté. There wasn't a place in Maerlande that didn't bear the mark, visible or invisible, of previous ages, a History delving so far into the past, beyond even the Decline, that it was almost terrifying to think of the successive generations on this land, shaping their fields, roads, and cities, a hundred times vanished, a hundred times recreated. These woods were merely a phase, perhaps a little longer than others, in the cycle of deaths and resurrections.

It was probably for all these reasons that Antonë had chosen this spot. But Lisbeï couldn't ask her, for the Arbitra wouldn't speak before, during, or after the hearings, any more than she'd intervene in the palavras. Her voice would only be heard on the day of the actual Decision, after all the auditantas had stated their opinion at length. At that moment the time would be ripe in the soul and conscience of the Arbitra, standing where human and divine forces met, to choose in the name of all.

Lisbeï had thought that once the auditantas had heard and questioned her, the virtual seclusion would be over. Officially her isolation had ended. The Assembly, the Games, and the Pilgrimage of Garde were done with at last. Where tents once dotted the Esplanades, wicows and ovinas grazed again. Everybody made a conscious effort to talk of trivialities in Lisbeï's presence, but she fully sensed the suppressed curiosity and censure that lay behind such small talk. Sometimes there was even ill will, but more often it was a vague rancor, the vexation of sleepers suddenly awakened and trying to recapture sleep. Some appreciated the significance of the jolt given the Family Carta, others disapproved, but all agreed in thinking Lisbeï the prime mover in this cascade of troubles. Or almost all. In the Library one day, Meralda planted herself in front of Lisbeï. She was right, said Meralda (speaking very fast, although stammering a little) to tell the whole truth. Then she fled, leaving Lisbeï agape. But a single voice against the silent chorus of Bethely was too little to make a difference.

Lisbeï had resumed her tasks as apprentice-Memory under Mooreï, who was busy exhuming dusty Archives from the time of the Hives, but she realized that as yet she hadn't the training to be of any real help. She was still barred from the underground passages, where a team of recuperatas worked methodically under Kelys's direction. If she had been honest with herself, she would have admitted that toiling away in the tunnels with Kelys's exploras would have bored her. Lisbeï considered things that were labeled for display in glass cases to be relics of a dead past that remained dead for her. Words were what stimulated her curiosity, and this was why the Notebook fascinated her. Her links with the past lay in the lines written by hands that had once lived. Objects touched her less, except where they could be used again and given new life, like Halde's ring.

Lisbeï felt she was losing ground, that Bethely was moving on while she herself stood still. She had thought without much enthusiasm of doing her three months' tour of duty in a patrol, since she was now a Blue. Selva had said bluntly, "Not right away." Mooreï had elaborated on this curt dictum. "Do

you want to give people the idea you're punishing yourself?"
Or that we are punishing you? But of course Mooreï didn't say
so. Was this what Selva had in mind? But among other things
Selva was very taken up with becoming pregnant by the new
Male who had settled into the West Tower. She avoided talking to Lisbeï as much as possible. The absent Antonë was
trying to come to a Decision. And Tula . . . Lisbeï's coura-
geous revelation had pushed the official designation of Tula as
future Mother of Bethely into the background, to say nothing
of Lisbeï's own entry into the ranks of Blues. Tula's workload
had doubled instantly, since apart from her daily chores in the
Tower she had to spend many more hours with Selva and
Mooreï. Although she tried to see Lisbeï at least once a day,
Selva arranged things so that she always had too much work.
The sisters had almost no time to talk, and anyway what Tula
was now learning, Lisbeï already knew. On the other hand,
Mooreï's Archives and Kelys's tunnel had produced nothing
very spectacular. Lisbeï and Tula finally contented themselves
with saying little and just being with each other and catching a
bit of breath, often at the end of the day.

They used to climb to the top of the West Tower and
watch the sun go down, waiting for the perfect instant, so
brief, in which it was easy to believe that the sky was a molten
lake, an inland sea, a gulf, and that the masses of scarlet cloud
already merging into violet-blue formed a distant coast. Opposite lay unknown archipelagoes bathed in a sea of gold or
liquid copper, or perhaps even lava, a benign lava in those
lands where details blurred but contours shone with almost
painful clarity. It seemed one had only to advance, to scale the
uplands and foothills of the sky, and suddenly there would be
beauty, forever.

And on one of those evenings, seated beside Lisbeï in the
long silence, Tula said, "You should leave. Go to Wardenberg."

Had they talked of other things before? Did they afterward?
There's a blank in Lisbeï's memory. All she sees is herself
seated on the windowsill in her room later, contemplating the
nocturnal well of the courtyard, while the thought of jumping
drifted lazily across her brain. She knew she wouldn't, of
course; it was a game, a histrionic way of expressing her despair to herself, but at the same time it would be so easy, so

quick. . . . Yet after a lengthy pause, how ironic to be surprised by one of those long yawns that seem to come from the belly and spread to the tips of your fingers, leaving your body quivering with pleasant lassitude. And then to close the window with a shrug, almost amused, almost disgusted at feeling so plainly alive, at this absurd evidence of life that made any idea of a deliberate end equally absurd.

Go to Wardenberg. But that wasn't really what Tula said. *You should leave,* that's what she'd said. Go anywhere, Wardenberg being as good a pretext as any. Leave; the destination didn't matter. Leave Bethely. Tula hadn't taken her hand, something they always did when they wanted to convince themselves by sharing their feelings more deeply. Tula wouldn't mention it again, and Lisbeï would be alone with her distress and her dark fantasies.

"You want me to go." That was how Lisbeï began her imaginary conversation with Tula each night. Even at the outset Tula never said, "No," and they did not fall weeping into each other's arms. Throughout the year in which Lisbeï had at last accepted the fact that she'd never be a Red, the story of the flight-to-the-sea-together-in-the-night had reached and overshot its mark. No longer did it soothe: it had become a source of pain, almost of humiliation. The naïveté of its worn-out plot was so apparent. . . . At first it was Tula who rebelled against Selva, refusing to be Mother and organizing their escape—after all, it was Tula who wanted to see the sea and who'd imagined their future far from Bethely once they'd become Blues. As time went on, the story shifted to the opposite pole, and now it was Lisbeï who persuaded Tula to flee with her. Sometimes she went so far as to imagine Tula as Mother of Bethely after her first Celebration, and had her moping about the Tower for days, pale and thin. Then one night Lisbeï awoke to find Tula at the foot of her bed, watching her. Tula tried to run away, but Lisbeï caught her and made her admit her horror of being Mother with the Male, and they hugged each other, sobbing, before fleeing to the South.

But all these carefully honed plots had collapsed forever with one short sentence from Tula. Lisbeï was forced to invent other stories, of course. It was terrifying to listen to Tula's brief words reverberating in the emptiness of that devastated landscape. . . . But how hard it was! She had to begin with the words Tula had *not* said, try to imagine a conversation (yet another) that had not taken place.

"You ought to go to Wardenberg."

"You want me to go?"

"Of course not!"

And there, for a long time, Lisbeï stalled. Then, as often happened when she told herself tales, curiosity about the other side gradually overcame her unavowed aim of creating a story that would give her pleasure. She suddenly glimpsed herself through Tula's eyes—but Tula as imagined by Lisbeï: to see yourself as another, without actually being another. What could Tula have to say—what argument could she put forward to justify Lisbeï's leaving?

"You want me to leave."

The only response that allowed the conversation to proceed was, "No, but you must."

The rest came more easily. "Why?"

"Because there's nothing for you in Bethely. . . ."

There's you! But this retort drove the conversation into a dead end that Lisbeï didn't even want to contemplate.

"Do you really want to become the Memory, keep inventories and file Archives until your dying day? No. You're simply doing what Selva wants; she doesn't feel like wasting the time and effort she's invested in you, even if you are a Blue."

"But we'd be together! I could put all that training to good use—to help you."

And we'd be together.

Lisbeï couldn't resist the logical progression of the conversation and finally had Tula respond, "Is this how we'd want to be together?"

Lisbeï hung her head and Tula took her hand, saying quickly (avoiding the reef of an answer), "Being a Memory your whole life would kill you. Think about it. You're not cut out for it. You'd be untrue to yourself. Wouldn't you rather keep on learning and make other discoveries, like you did with the underground passage and Garde?"

"For all the good it's done me! The whole of Bethely considers me an Abomination!"

"Exactly. Do you think you could stand it much longer?"

That and everything else, Lisbeï sterile, Lisbeï who should have been Mother . . . They didn't say these things in so many words, but simply looked at each other in silence for a long time, buoyed up by the same wave of loving understanding. And yet, captivated in spite of herself by the play of contradictions, Lisbeï went on. "Why would it be so different anywhere else?"

"If you study in Wardenberg, you'll become a recuperata, that'll be your *job*—making discoveries—and no one will criticize you for it then. And you might finish translating the Notebook, take part in research on Garde . . ."

"I could do it just as well here."

"You can only learn to do it properly in Wardenberg. You could come back here afterward to continue the dig and consult the Archives."

"Yes, but . . ."

The imaginary conversation hit a stumbling block with this "but," and Lisbeï couldn't get past it. She felt her subsequent arguments were mere pretexts, disguised pleas: "But what will Selva say, but will they really accept me in Wardenberg, but *I don't want to leave, I don't want to leave you, I want to stay in Bethely!*"

"But you can't stay," said the voice that was neither Tula's nor Lisbeï's now, as it seemed to have acquired a sort of life of its own in the course of the conversation. "Selva won't say anything, except for the form. In her heart of hearts, she never liked seeing you and Tula together, and now that Garde has brought you closer, she thinks it's not a good idea to have you in Bethely, especially as Memory. You might have more influence over Tula than she would. And you'll be very favorably received in Wardenberg. You've had the education of a Mother and a Memory, you're a Bethely. Just think: the eldest daughter of the most influential Traditionalista Family of Litale, in Wardenberg! And you discovered the Notebook: that can't be overlooked. Being a recuperata isn't so terrible. Kelys is one. Anyway, it'll only last long enough for you to repay the cost of your studies in Wardenberg—three or four years. Think of all you'll see, all you'll learn, all the people you could meet and all the places you could visit. . . ."

But at this point the voice became Tula's once more—Tula who had so dreamed of traveling before Bethely closed in on her. It wasn't fair! And Lisbeï was back to the "yes, but" that stifled her with helpless terror. Leave Bethely! It was like tearing off her own skin. It was impossible: Tula couldn't ask such a thing of her!

She did not ask it, but it had to be. Tula knew it, Lisbeï knew it, and at last they wept in each other's arms (Lisbeï wept alone in bed, hugging herself) and uttered passionate declarations, sometimes even making love, desperately, "one last time." But soon Lisbeï was no longer capable of simulating Tula's presence, Tula's hands on her. It had been too long since they'd been together in this way, and it was too sad, even when Lisbeï found pleasure in it—especially then, in fact, for tears would well up, dangerous tears: the fictitious Tula was too difficult to recreate after that. No, better to have them fall asleep together, exhausted by their mutual tears. At dawn, without waking a Tula who was pretending to sleep, Lisbeï would gather up her things, saddle her horse, and set off on the western road, alone in the early-morning chill.

The month of Austa passed in this way. After the harvest, the Farm feast, and the final picking—no, after the jams and preserves had been done . . . Lisbeï put off the moment again and again. And then in mid-Novemra the recuperatas and Kelys announced they were returning to Wardenberg. A report and inventory had been submitted to Mooreï. What could actually be concluded from such data? If Wardenberg taught you how to draw the necessary conclusions, it was almost worth going there to check it out.

Suddenly Lisbeï heard herself saying, "I think I'll go with them."

"You'll see the sea," said Tula after a short silence. She took Lisbeï's hand, and neither of them said another word.

Lisbeï didn't leave on horseback in the small hours of the morning, but in a light covered wagon in the early afternoon. Three weeks later, having passed from wagon to horseback to ferry, she saw the sea at last. Not the sparkling blue expanse that Kelys had told her about, waves curling with foam over which one sailed through the light toward the Southlands. Autumna was well advanced, and as often happened at any season in the northwest, Elli was raining—not a grand, raging storm but a fine, insidious drizzle. Lisbeï would never forget this interminable voyage on the flat, gray sea that separated Bretanye from Baltike and Wardenberg. Barely a sea: little more than fifty meters deep, less in places. When the weather is calm, you can see the drowned lands and their ruins. She would recall the mounting anguish during those two windless days, the boat moving forward at a snail's pace amid puffs of steam, that immense void all around, the bleak, leaden flatness of the water, the suffocating sky, almost as dreary as the water . . . Impossible to imagine the other side of the sea: it

was too vast, too smooth, too inchoate because of its very
uniformity. Impossible to imagine the future. Lisbeï's mind
flew to the past, to other waters, the spring rains of Bethely,
and the main courtyard. Not level but concave and uneven,
with a dozen large depressions like spokes in a wheel—run-
nels to carry water from the base of the Towers to the center
of the courtyard and into a drain beneath a big grill, and from
there into the invisible network of smaller drains leading to
the Douve. One day Tula and Lisbeï along with other dottas
blocked the grill to see what would happen. The gray puddle,
popping bubbles because Elli was raining hard, spread out
from the center of the yard, slowly gaining on the circle of
sodden little girls, covering first one tile, then another, always
chasing the retreating bare feet. And Lisbeï suddenly thought
of the tides in the seas she'd never seen, inundating the coasts
and islands and continents with the same silent patience,
places that no one would ever see again. In a flash she had
imagined the water rising over Bethely itself, and the game
Tula had suggested was no longer fun. Blues were beginning
to open the windows to see what was going on in the courtyard, and Lisbeï darted forward to clear the grill. The water in
the middle was up to her calves. Tula and the others helped
her, and afterward they had to do cleanup duty for the rest of
the week . . . and all at once the memory of Bethely, so far
away, overwhelmed Lisbeï, and she hid in a corner of the boat
to weep.

3

Wardenberg—
Amsherdam—
Belmont

489–499 A.G.

1

Lisbeï to Tula

Wardenberg, Decemra 24, 489 A.G.

Dearest Tula,
I arrived safely, as you see. Kelys found me a small room right away, on the third floor of what they call a "pension" on Level Two of the Citadel. I had some idea of what Wardenberg would be like from Kelys's descriptions and the engravings in the book she brought me last year, but as you can imagine, it's very different when you're actually here.
Wardenberg is quite unlike Bethely.

And with this Lisbeï stopped and sucked the end of her pen, staring through the mottled glass of the window at the blurred wall opposite, the only horizon visible from her tiny room—on the third floor of Pension Number 12, South Quarter, Second Quadrant, Level Two of the Citadel: she had simplified things a little for Tula. There wasn't much else she could simplify. After a week in Wardenberg she felt everything needed explaining, and she was far from having all the answers, in spite of Mooreï's lessons.

Wardenberg was a peninsula about a hundred klims square at low tide, and a much smaller, rocky island when the tide was in. It had always been a fortified city, and this was why it had been able to fend off the Hives after taking in the surviving Chiefs as they fled, as well as their families and the warrias who'd remained loyal. The Harem people weren't all drugged fanatics as certain Southern Families would still have it. Moreover the Chiefs themselves weren't all monsters, as Mooreï had explained to the young Lisbeï. The Harems had already begun to change when the Juddite revolution broke out. ("They had begun the slide into decadence," wrote Balte of Gualtière, the Hive historian.) Some of the Chiefs were less cruel than others, and their slave women weren't all subjected to harsh treatment. Some of the women hadn't had much sympathy for the lethal extremism of the Juddite revolutionaries and had preferred to follow their Chiefs or their compagnas who had stayed with the Chiefs. Many more had no choice, however. But whether of their own free will or not, these women had swollen the already large population of Wardenberg to create the most populated agglomeration in the North of the continent. Nearly four hundred years later it was the only thing resembling a "city," as much for its high density as for its numbers: nearly fifteen thousand people of whom at least twelve thousand were permanent residents.

Bethely had never equaled this. More than ten thousand visitas passed through the capterie during the Assembly of Mothers, the attendant Games or the Pilgrimage of Garde—but not all at once. Lisbeï hadn't seen much of even this influx; she'd been isolated in the West Tower until the end of the Assembly and hadn't taken part in the Games. The Pilgrimage finished on the fifteenth of Jula, and she'd seen only the final stage. By then there hadn't been more than three or four thousand.

Wardenberg was something else, although not the ant-heap Lisbeï had expected. There was a great deal happening, and all of it far more varied than in Bethely: the underground steel mill with its workshops, the photographic-plate factory, and the printshop; then there was fishing and shipping—the loading of raw or finished products destined for the "Coast" (as the long stretch of rising land opposite was called) and the unloading of incoming boats. Farming, of course, and general services—maintaining the fleet of carracks, boats, and barges, as well as keeping the city functioning, along with its factories and workshops. But as in Bethely, working hours were spread out over the whole day and also staggered by quadrant and

quarter. And since the population was far greater, not everyone worked all the time. In Lisbeï's South Quarter, linked to
the mainland at low tide, the daily influx of workas was nevertheless immense. Most of the terraced farms were on this
portion of the island, and workas also passed through it to
reach the fields of the Coast.

*You see people all the time, but it's not so much that, as
knowing you're in the midst of such a crowd,* she wrote in this
first letter to Tula. *You'll tell me Bethely gives you the same
sensation, but there's a difference between two and twelve thousand people—and not just in quantity. It's as though quantity
became quality beyond a certain threshold. The effect changes.
Somewhere in your head there's a constant pressure because you
know* there's *such a crowd—the constant movement, the smells,
and the noises outside. You feel there's a constant hum. Funny,
isn't it? Wardenberg was never a Hive, but it buzzes like one.*

Wardenberg was certainly never a Hive. The Citadel ramparts had never been torn down, nor had the inner breast-
works, which made each of the three levels a sort of closed
city, cut off from the others if access was blocked. Ramps and
stairs had multiplied with time, but for each level there had
originally been a single entrance, easier to defend and safer to
withdraw from. To tell the truth, even the demolition fanatics
of the Hives would probably have thought twice before trying
to raze Wardenberg to the ground or even make any radical
changes. (Bethely was rather similar in this respect, though it
predated Wardenberg.) Within the Wardenberg walls, every
conceivable kind of structure was grafted onto the ramparts,
and these sprouted yet other buildings, higgledy-piggledy.
Even before its isolation by the rising waters, the city had
proliferated uncontrollably, spreading outward into every
nook and cranny, then upward. Lisbeï had thought she'd
learned the meaning of the word "labyrinth" in the network
of corridors and staircases of Bethely. But after getting lost a
dozen times on the rather short route from her pension to the
Schole Library, she realized "labyrinthine" could describe un-
dreamed-of topological complexities.

Wardenberg had indeed never been a Hive. Moreover it
had soon ceased to be a Harem, and yet it had inherited much
from both regimes. In the course of its years of isolation,
however, it had become a distinctive society, differing also
from Maerlande, which eventually replaced the Hives. In fact
it joined Maerlande only some twenty years after Alicia of

Bethely came to offer (and obtain) peace. Wardenberg used these twenty years to prepare for opening up, and Maerlande did the same. Integration took place fairly smoothly, and three centuries later there were few signs of the long isolation —at least as far as the neighboring Families of Baltike and Bretanye were concerned. For someone from the South, however . . .

Wardenberg is very different from Bethely. How could she begin to explain? To make it *live* for Tula—to make her aware of all those differences hitting her like a storm of hailstones. Unexpected differences—ones that had never occurred to her, and ones she'd come to realize only after some thought, since they had touched her unconsciously. Smells, for example. Her room faced South toward the island's fields, organic recycling cisterns, and the methane tanks. When the wind blew from the Coast, it brought the familiar odor of compost mingled with the smell of salt water and seaweed, a strange, disconcerting smell that came from every direction at high tide. When the wind blew from the northern part of the island, even stranger smells wafted southward from the ventilators of the underground works—whiffs of things like charcoal, slag, and sulfur. She felt unsettled on those days, irritable without knowing quite why. The smells short-circuited her consciousness and reminded her that she wasn't in Bethely. Eventually she realized this, but she never got used to it.

As in Bethely, but far more so, spatial organization determined human organization. People lived in families and sub-families linked to quarters, quadrants, or levels—and not classed by age, trade, or color. For years Lisbeï had been accustomed to the daily human landscape of green, blue, and red, seen yet unseen, always in the same proportions: about twice as much blue as red, about twice as much red as green (except in the totally green garderies, but these didn't count because they were away from the Towers). Within this spectrum the shades varied little. In Wardenberg, however, the range varied infinitely, from delicate green to orangey-red to almost midnight blue. But the most distinctive difference was the fact that not everyone wore their status color prominently displayed. It took Lisbeï several days of deliberate reflection to realize this constituted yet another source of her constant uneasiness. At first she thought it was a matter of style and cut. In Bethely they didn't vary these factors much. Clothes were cut and sewn in the workshops of the East Tower, and patterns were the same for everybody. If you wanted to give your garments a personal touch, it was usually in the form of various appliqués. But accessories made the real difference—brooches, bracelets, necklaces—and the craftsmen of Baïan-que and Serres-Morèna always did a brisk trade at the Pilgrimage Fair.

People wore lots of accessories in Wardenberg, too, in addition to numerous escutcheons, insignias, crests, and other relics of a vanished military tradition. (Lisbeï's neighbor on her third-floor landing always wore a W surmounted by the ankh of the Defensas somewhere on her clothing, her ancestors having belonged to this early warria caste.) Wardenbergs usually had their clothes made by the seamstresses of their quarter, or of another quarter if they preferred some other style. There were fashions that swept the city at regular intervals, leaping from one level to another, one quadrant to another. Of course clothing was constantly recycled—a constraint from the besieged past that had fitted in well with the thrifty habits of Maerlande. Almost everything was recycled in any case, and it was just possible that the most inventive ways of resuscitating material had originated in Wardenberg.

Wardenberg is very different. In Bethely . . . It became a formula in Lisbeï's confidences to Tula, replacing their childish "like the garderie," or the phrase "as in Bethely" that she'd initially hoped would help her deal with the shock of novelty. She'd held on to the reassuring theory of ever-larger boxes invented long ago, although it had gone through many transformations; but now it held no comfort. Elsewhere was not "like Bethely but bigger." Elsewhere was . . . well, different, and so she wrote: *Dearest Tula, Wardenberg is very different.*

There was the way the place was arranged, of course—the fountains, the courtyards, the steep little squares, the stairs and terraces, and small bridges over canalized streams running down to the cisterns on Level One. (A deep stratum of impervious rock created artesian pools that had made Wardenberg self-sufficient, even when cut off from its farming resources on the Coast by the neighboring Hives.) Then there were the tortuous, narrow streets winding between houses, small restaurants, and shops, enhanced by miniature hanging gardens and balconies. A bend in a stairway would reveal a sudden jumble of gabled roofs covered with shingles or with varnished, patterned tiles in the colors of the local quarter and occasionally of Wardenberg: orange, green, and black. It was a bit like the Assembly Fair, but much, much bigger, thought Lisbeï as she searched for a meaningful comparison for Tula. Far more permanent, naturally. There were no commonrooms for eating except in the Library and the scholes. This was how the besieged Wardenbergs had combatted the leveling pressures of confinement, Lisbeï eventually realized. People ate in their own rooms and prepared their own food in the kitchen of their "block" or "building," or else they "paid" to eat in one of the little restaurants found in every Quarter. In the first few months she was to find it very hard to manage the "budget" allotted by the Schole to its students, constantly forgetting the little books of chits to be signed for Family accounting purposes.

I eat lunch at the Library every day. It isn't like Bethely, of course. The Library is actually a rather motley cluster of buildings on Level Three, at the very summit, not far from the Mother's Residence. People tend to refer to it as "the Schole," in fact, and everyone understands, even if there are scholes in the quarters for the Greens.

As Wardenberg had never been a Hive, the Archives accumulated during the Harem era had never suffered the ravages inflicted elsewhere. Even at the beginning of the Harem era the Library had been well stocked. Moreover the fleeing Chiefs had all brought a good portion of their own Archives with them, and many Families came to the Wardenberg Library to consult relevant documents for the Harem period—documents missing from their own collection that they didn't want to bother copying. Around these various Archives and their updated appendices had gathered cohorts of researchas who gradually formed the Schole of Wardenberg, which eventually became an irreplaceable center for training and study. Recuperatas, exploras, historians, and other aspiring scholars came here, paying for their stay by giving the Wardenberg Family part of their eventual finds— metal and other recuperable materials, as well as documents and artifacts that contributed to the work of the scribes and the Schole or further enlarged the Archives. It was a self-expanding, unique, and historic place, a shrine of knowledge. (And it was also a place where would-be Memories habitually spent some time, this being the convenient fiction put forward by Selva in allowing Lisbeï to leave.) People therefore visited

Wardenberg, and as there were numerous such visitas, it had became a trading center. This brought even greater numbers to trade goods and information, increasing Wardenberg's knowledge and connections apace. Sheer weight of numbers seemed to be the only reason for Wardenberg's present role—a mere snowballing of habit on the slope of time.

Wardenberg was also the only Harem that the Hives failed to conquer, although strictly speaking it hadn't remained a true "harem" for long. You could admire its resistance to the Hives, but this was also a matter for reproach. Maerlande's collective consciousness had come to regard the Hives as bad, but not nearly as bad as the Harems. At least the Hives had been the result of the first liberation of women, and they had given birth to Maerlande. The Harems, by contrast, were the shameful heirs of the Decline, an ancestry that the Wardenberg Family was never allowed to forget.

Last but not least, Wardenberg was a society that had lived in isolation for nearly a century. Despite every effort, it had become highly inbred. Lisbeï, when trying to imagine the place, had supposed she would see a fair number of deformed or handicapped people compared to Bethely. Then she remembered the Family had a policy curiously resembling that of both the Hives and the Juddites. Accidents or "aberrations" were eliminated far more methodically than anywhere else. The reason was fairly obvious when you thought about it: "useless mouths" had been judged an encumbrance by a besieged Wardenberg. Because the siege hadn't been as total as generally believed, however, the genetic pool hadn't been irreversibly diminished—and besides, with a bigger population there had always been a greater number of males. The Hives around Wardenberg had soon given up hope of a military victory. It was too unlikely and too costly, and they had enough trouble dealing with other Hives. Night raids, on the other hand . . . Wardenberg, too, had tried to steal males from other places, although when the undeclared war between the city and the neighboring Hives cooled off a little, there had been exchanges: males from the Hives for women from Wardenberg. It hadn't been enough, though. When Alicia had made her peace proposals, there was resistance from some, the Juddites being especially adamant in arguing that the various Lines in Wardenberg must be highly defective and would sully the purity of the Lines developed by the Hives. Alicia had easily refuted this by retorting that the so-called purity of the Hives was in fact a fatal impoverishment, and they would all have died out if common sense hadn't got the better of fanaticism (with the help of the Word, naturally). Even the "impure" Wardenberg Lines and males were much too precious to be rejected. In the end there was agreement on a progressive mingling of Lines, carefully supervised for an observation period of thirty years, in other words two generations. Now, even more than three hundred years later, Wardenberg's Lines were generally considered far from stable. Accepting Wardenbergs was always considered a bit of a gamble.

But this island capterie wasn't just an unrivaled center of knowledge, either past or present. It was a unique center of heavy industry. The dam and hydroelectric power station on the Coast had been the source of power during the Harem period, but the Hives had destroyed the facility. After Alicia, Wardenberg had got it operating again, and instead of manufacturing weapons had turned the underground works into factories producing tools, farm implements, methane compressors, and a lot of other useful machinery. Not everyone made use of these, of course, since Families were supposed to be as self-sufficient as possible in every field but procreation. It was a tradition established in Maerlande's earliest days: self-sufficiency in food, initially, but also in everything else. For this reason many Families, and not all Juddites either, had decided not to harness the hydroelectric potential in their rivers. It would have made them too dependent on heavy machinery and those who supplied and serviced it. Rather, like Bethely for instance, they had opted for the more direct mechanical energy furnished by waterfalls. There was a widely popular saying among all the Families, be they Juddites or Progressistas—a saying less frequently heard in Wardenberg: "If we did without it in the time of the Hives, we can get along without it now."

Still, sayings notwithstanding, there was no denying Wardenberg's importance in the Maerlande trading network, and some looked askance at its preeminence, even though it was equally obvious that Wardenberg relied more heavily than any other Family on exchanging males and young Greens—the only desirable and acceptable form of dependence, and one that was considered the very cement of Maerlande's unity. With nearly five hundred Red women to be inseminated every year, Wardenberg needed at least twenty males in residence.

Its rate of male births was high (each year an average of seven Green boys became Red males and entered the Service circuit). These males weren't considered as reliable as others, however, and couldn't be exchanged as easily, a circumstance that applied to the Family's best female Greens as well.

What a complex place it was! All that, and more: the invisible networks of respect, admiration, and curiosity that linked the Family to Maerlande, not to mention the envy, resentment, and mistrust. The Capta and her Memories had been aware of this from the start. No Wardenberg motion was ever passed in Baltike or Maerlande Assemblies, nor were any proposed. Wardenberg worked in other ways, through the Progressista Families of Baltike or Bretanye, with which it had contracted ties of common interest, or through individual friendships.

Kelys lives in Sygne's Residence when she's in Wardenberg. She wanted me to join her for dinner there the day after we arrived, but I was too tired . . . .

Kelys wasn't fooled, but she said nothing. Lisbeï didn't want to be stared at like a strange beast. It would be a private dinner where she couldn't hide her identity, since everyone knew about her—well, the Mother and her Memories, anyway. When registering, she'd already met the Schole Capta, Ireyn, who was also Second Memory. The identity of Blues registered at the Schole was confidential, and Lisbeï knew hers would stay within the four walls of Ireyn's office. Still, she was thankful Kelys had gone with her, since her presence certainly shortened the mandatory interview.

"Lisbeï, from Bethely," said Ireyn—a rather lanky Blue in her forties with big, large-veined hands. A raised eyebrow, nothing more, when Kelys explained that Lisbeï wanted to train as a recuperata. Then the ritual question, "Under what name?"—since Blues could choose their future names if they wanted. Lisbeï hesitated. But although she might have given up Bethely, she didn't have to give up her own name. "Lisbeï, from Litale."

At least she could pass unnoticed in Wardenberg. Now that she was officially a Blue, she needn't wear the Bethely emblem. No one would ask for her Family of origin or even her name if she didn't volunteer it. In Wardenberg she needn't even wear blue. But it was such a relief after all those years of green that she couldn't forego it.

No one asked her anything. This was the rule for Blues

throughout Maerlande, but in Wardenberg it extended to everybody. Another relic of the days when the fortress-city's population had been even greater, without hope of leaving, and where the limited space had given rise to a unique and jealously defended idea of private life. You could be alone in Wardenberg if you wanted, even in a pension where nearly forty people shared the facilities. They didn't avoid you, since there was really no place to go; it was the courtesy of silence, of glances that didn't linger.

After those last months in Bethely and the journey with Kelys and her recuperatas (although Lisbeï didn't say as much in her first letter to Tula), it was wonderfully sweet to be alone in this way, anonymous, and yes, free. When she became aware of her pleasure in solitude, and (as she realized on rereading the letter) of the delight in questing and discovery revealed in her descriptions of Wardenberg, she was ashamed. She couldn't send Tula such a letter! But then the only letter she could send was the very one she didn't want to write: a letter of despair, regret, and possible reproach, a letter that she'd tried to exorcise by turning it into a travel story. She scanned the half-dozen sheets covered on both sides and, with a sigh, began to recopy them, neutralizing the emotional content.

Dearest Tula,

The journey went well, and I'm here at last. Kelys has found me a room in a pension on Level Two of the Citadel. Wardenberg is very different from Bethely, as you can imagine. I registered at the Schole without any difficulty, and I've begun studying. There's a lot of work. . . .

2

With Selva and later with Mooreï, Lisbeï had studied Maerlande. It was part of the future Capta's tasks, in addition to all the chores she shared with other dottas. Although hydraulic power now enabled machines to do a good part of the work, you still had to learn how to do everything from scratch, as people had done in the days before machinery, and on top of that you had to learn how to run and repair the machines. By the time a Bethely Green was twelve, she knew what she did best and had generally learned to like it, even though she'd be doing various jobs throughout her life, switching each quarter or each year.

A Mother's specialty, however, was her ability to be truly Bethely, to know all about it—how it had functioned in the past, how it functioned now, and its place in Maerlande. And that meant knowing all about Maerlande: History, geography, and above all everything concerning the Families—their Lines, their tendencies, their Cartas, their principal trading products, and of course their languages and regional dialects. How else could she represent her Family properly in the Assemblies and talk to the other Mothers and delegates?

Between her seventh and fifteenth year, Lisbeï had therefore studied Maerlande. During the past two years, however, she had virtually ignored the subject on the pretext of learning to be the Memory. Its present and her own future no longer counted. It was Bethely's past that engrossed her, the past of obscure legends, dusty Archives, and underground tunnels.

In Wardenberg, Maerlande began to take on another reality, as much in the hidden panic of her first days as in the frenetic studying that would steady her in later months. Wardenberg seemed like a microcosm of Maerlande. This was what she had in mind when she used the term "capital," newly learned, to describe the fortress-city, although she knew perfectly well that Maerlande was a fairly loose federation of Provinces, themselves a federation of Families.

"No, no," said the slightly quavering voice of Carmela of Vaduze. "There's no capital of Maerlande, little one. Capitals were before the time of the Harems, long before. We're all 'capital,' although some Capteries seem a little more so than others. Each has an equal voice in the Assembly. Wardenberg doesn't decide for Bethely, or Cartano for Nevenici, does it?"

The old word was useful, Lisbeï tried to explain, but the elderly Blue shook an admonishing finger. "The word is inexact. It can be dangerous to use inexact words."

"It's only a word," protested Lisbeï.

"But by using inexact terms, our ideas will be gradually polluted and transformed."

She was ready to agree with her Tutress. After all, who knew the power of words better, having taken such care not to say certain words to Tula? But she couldn't resist trying to see the other side of the argument. "Mightn't it be a good thing for ideas to change sometimes?"

The old woman pursed her lips indulgently. "Probably. But you're not able to judge unless you're aware of how the words we use affect our emotions and therefore our ideas. The Harems 'had colonies,' the Hives 'had Swarms,' and Maerlande 'created Offshoots.' You might think them all the same, but the meaning of the general word 'offshoot' in other facets of our lives shapes our whole relationship with these outlying branches of our Families. It transforms them, and they transform us in turn, in a way that has nothing to do with 'colony' or 'Swarm.' "

Lisbeï smiled. She felt on home ground: the power of words, their shifting relationships with what they described, with the people who used them—the end and the means, to put it in a nutshell.

Carmela of Vaduze reminds me a little of Mooreï. Not physically, since she's tiny (although you should see her lifting piles of dictionaries!). She has gray hair and not much of it, and she's missing a front tooth. It's her way of talking and her "ambience." (Tula would understand the quotation marks.) *She knows an incredible number of facts, which I suppose is nothing for a Tutress of Ancient History. She's always calm and smells of frangipani. It's delicious—except it makes me hungry when we meet too near mealtime.*

Carmela would not be the only object of Lisbeï's game of likenesses, a game that lessened her homesickness a little, despite everything. But at first Carmela was the only person she saw regularly. Other students faded into an anonymous fog, as did the people in her pension. Only two faces emerged a little from the fog: those of the proprieta (a jovial, stocky Blue named Merritt, with a large, wine-colored birthmark on her face), and Cardèn, the cook in the restaurant where Lisbeï ate lunch.

Kelys had helped Lisbeï deal with Wardenberg for the first two or three days, registering her in the Schole, taking her to the pension, walking around the quarter to show her the eating places, and explaining how to use the quarterly "credits" issued by the Schole. Then Kelys disappeared. Lisbeï didn't know whether to resent being left on her own or not. Perhaps it was better to make a clean break, to jump in just as they did in Bethely when learning to swim in the Douve. Learning to keep your head above water in Wardenberg wasn't really so dangerous—not from what Lisbeï could see at the moment, anyway.

Early each morning she rose, dressed, breakfasted at her usual restaurant on a "bought" roll with fruit and cheese, and walked to the Schole (getting lost on the way, to say nothing of negotiating the maze of Library corridors once there). She met her Tutress and went over the books and papers consulted, lunched hastily in the Schole commonroom, and studied, sometimes staying late in the evening. At first she went straight back to her pension by the familiar route. It took her some time to venture off the beaten path—to make Wardenberg *hers*. Funny, in Bethely she'd never been afraid to explore. She wasn't *at home* in Wardenberg, that was it. She had no link with the place or the people, with those women streaming by her each day. Since leaving Bethely, she'd lost her way—she was indeed *lost*. Bethely had seemed intolerable without Tula (or with Tula inaccessible and cool, which amounted to the same thing). But the searing fibers of her body cried out to her each day that she'd left her skin in Bethely, far to the South, and that this might be even worse (was it possible?) than having left Tula behind.

After her third week in Wardenberg, the sense of freedom settled once more into solitude as new habits became routine. Her unhappiness faded only in the evening when she climbed the stairs to her room and dipped her pen in the inkwell to write: "Dearest Tula." They were week-long letters, covering a dozen sheets on both sides by the time she took them down to the harbor on the weekend. They might have been even longer, since she generally wrote something every day. But paper was limited, and sometimes she was too tired when returning late from the Schole.

Tula didn't write much, even in the beginning. Lisbeï's letters were accounts rather than correspondence and didn't really lend themselves to answers. Anyway, they came at such a rate . . . Tula had nothing but Bethely news to tell: births, pregnancies, the trivia of everyday life—how many Greens had left the garderie that month, what wards were being sent away or were arriving. Nothing was happening in Bethely. Tula was preparing to be the Mother, and that was all. How could Lisbeï help being disappointed by the slimness of these two- or three-page letters that arrived so sporadically from the South? Soon her own letters became fewer and fewer, and increasingly laconic. The novelty of Wardenberg had worn off, and what she really wanted now was to tell Tula her thoughts and her feelings, to go over all those memories that sprang up the minute Tula's name came to mind.

Tula kept on not really answering. The correspondence eventually subsided into an impersonal exchange every three months, retailing neutral information or, on the contrary, adopting a painfully jovial tone.

Lisbeï went on talking to Tula, nevertheless. She couldn't have jettisoned such a lifetime habit even if she'd wanted to. She kept on writing, telling Tula the intimate details of her days. She would have done this even if Tula hadn't replied at all. Like the carefully preserved notebooks she'd filled since leaving the garderie, these other letters were her only link with the whole past. To tell Tula her innermost thoughts, and, in order to do this, tell herself about herself—it was the only way of coming to terms with the strange world in which she now found herself. These true letters to Tula accumulated with ritual regularity in a drawer, then in another. One day Lisbeï acquired a large notebook and wrote in it from then on. It wasn't yet for herself that she confided her thoughts, dreams, and daily anecdotes to the notebook, but it was no longer for Tula. Not really.

3

"No, Litale," said the Tutress, "I don't think tales and legends can be used as indicators of this type, and proverbs even less. Or only in very specific instances. Anyway, they aren't much help, and we have plenty of other indicators, far more reliable in tracking down possible sites. Maps, geographical and historical data in the Archives, that's obvious. But mostly topology, the nature of the terrain, the vegetation . . . There you have clear, objective data. Exploration is first carried out on the actual terrain."

Lisbeï swallowed her "yes, but." She could sense that the group believed she'd already slowed down the lecture enough. Anyway, although Edwina of Carlsbad wasn't exactly a Juddite (no self-respecting Juddite would be teaching at the Wardenberg Schole), Lisbeï had noticed you didn't actually have to be one to hold fairly intransigent views. Better not to point out that the underground passages in Bethely had been a legend. She'd simply be attracting attention again, and she'd already made herself conspicuous enough with her too-frequent "yes, but." Anyway, Edwina was right. If the South Esplanade hadn't caved in and revealed the entrance to the conduit, Lisbeï would probably never have been able to put her theories to the test, verify them in relation to the terrain. . . .

"There's been too much systematic destruction," the Tutress continued, "destruction of sites and documents. And in many cases, the various human groups that occupied the territory since the Decline have been too far apart in space and time. Traditions and legends about ancient urban and industrial sites have had too many opportunities to get lost."

"And inversely, some stories are found throughout the territory," chimed in Bertia, the Blue from Carrères.

"Right," said Edwina with a little smile of approval. "Several local variants of the Hundred-Armed Giantess story contain almost identical references to her city of origin. But where was this city? Did it ever really exist? If so, which variant gives the true site?"

Marcie, another Blue sitting beside Bertia, nodded. "We'd get some rather odd results if we took legends literally, wouldn't we? A giantess—well, there are some documented aberrations in the early Hive period. But hundred-armed? That's pretty farfetched."

Several of the other students laughed. The Tutress had clasped her hands behind her back and was monitoring this exchange. The pause enabled her to steer the seminar back on course.

"The Giantess's terrifying hundred arms are obviously an exaggeration of certain types of aberration that have almost disappeared now, although you still find children being born with more than five fingers or toes on a hand or foot, especially in Litale. There's some connection—it would be foolish to deny it. Take the archaic Pimpernella Cycle of tales, with their continual transformations of girls into boys. This confirms the fact that the low percentage of male births has been a constant factor since the Decline. The Harem women adopted the tales and added to them, because being a woman was a terrible thing then, and many women must have dreamed of being men instead. The Hive women took over the tales in turn and reversed the sexual roles, just as they did with so many other things. Pimpernella changes from a boy to a girl—"

"And from a girl to a boy when she feels like it, what's more!" remarked Marcie.

"And now these tales are dead, so to speak, for all practical purposes. They've settled into a definitive form and won't change. Nobody tells these tales much nowadays, and certainly nobody feels any urge to add to them or invent similar stories. No, if the legends and tales that have come down to us indicate anything, it's the psychological past, the subjects close to the minds and hearts of the people who invented them. And we still need to know exactly when such texts or oral traditions appeared—not an easy thing, if indeed it can be done at all. It may be an interesting exercise, I agree, but for historians, not recuperatas."

And recuperatas were not historians. The briefness of the required period of study with Carmela of Vaduze had made this clear to Lisbeï. It had been cut even shorter by the fact that she had already been given a Mother's and Memory's training in Bethely and knew far more on many points than the Schole deemed necessary for a recuperata. Exploras explored, discovered possible sites, and brought back data. Recuperatas dug, photographed, dismantled and removed the finds, and labeled them. Then came the historians, and that even more specialized type known as evaluatas, to determine the value of the find. And the evaluatas' criteria differed significantly from the historians' ideas. As Lisbeï was to realize after the Belmont discovery several years later, metal and technological or scientific information were much more valuable than works of art or nontechnical books.

Kelys was a historian and linguist just as much as an explora and recuperata—in addition to being virtually a medicina, a gymna, and probably a lot of other things that hadn't had a chance to surface during her sojourns in Bethely. But Kelys was a special case, Lisbeï had found. And anyway, Kelys was first and foremost a recuperata, and an excellent one. That's what had enabled her to pay off her debt for four years' study in Wardenberg so quickly. If Lisbeï wanted to become a historian, she'd have to wait until she'd done as much.

Lisbeï sighed and tried once more to concentrate on Edwina's exposé and the aerial photographs of the Entraygues site before exploration—a typical case of terrain-oriented technique leading to a discovery. The darker patches of vegetation, the shadows showing depressions or contours, all indicated the site of underground ruins, undeniably with far greater precision than hearsay about subterranean tunnels between Bethely and its neighbors. At least with this kind of technique there was the fun of going a little way up in a balloon before getting down to the actual digging. The experience had delighted Lisbeï—not so much the take-off and ascension as the change in perspective. To see the countryside from above, to see so far, as far as the curve of the sea on the horizon! Lisbeï quite forgot the turmoil in her stomach. She could hardly help thinking of the Tapestry. Elli's view of Elli's creation must be a little like this. How vast and peaceful the land looked, and how little space the human world occupied!

"What soil type, Litale?" Edwina's tone made it abundantly clear that this was the second time she'd spoken. Lisbeï tried frantically to remember the beginning of the question. Soil type for what? For some kind of vegetation, probably. . . .

"Acid," breathed Fraine from across the left-hand aisle.

"Acid?"

Edwina grunted to show she wasn't fooled, but accepted the answer. Lisbeï smiled at her savior, and Fraine gave her a surreptitious wink, then assumed a deadpan expression as Edwina turned around to look at her group of students.

After her two months spent exclusively with Carmela of Vaduze, Lisbeï had been assigned to a group of a dozen students who found themselves together most of the time with their various Tutresses. Not all of them intended to be recuperatas or exploras. Ysande of Gers, a homely, good-humored Red of twenty-five, was a Wardenberg ward attending the classes out of mere curiosity between two Service periods. She was an unassuming Believra, a rather peaceful personality who resembled a sort of future Mooreï. Livine, a recent Wardenberg Blue, had the characteristic straight blond hair and blue eyes of the Family. She planned to be an evaluata. She had a habit of touching you when she spoke, as though to reassure herself about your reality—or her own. Fraine was a small, stocky blond with sparkling brown eyes in a round, freckled face. She'd just become a Wardenberg Red and hadn't begun her Service, but already she looked ahead to a career as an explora-recuperata, taking advantage of her last year of full freedom to get a head start. Of course, she'd have to wait until she became a Blue to use her knowledge. Fraine wasn't fond of waiting.

These three had stood out from the group right away, since they were the first to speak to Liskeï. Ysande had said hello on the first day and greeted her at each class. Later, Fraine had sat down beside her in the refectory, so clearly relieved at finding a familiar face that Lisbeï couldn't help smiling in response. Another day Livine joined Fraine. Lisbeï's good manners prompted her to respond when people spoke to her. Little by little, at mealtimes, before or after classes, or as they were coming and going from the Schole, she got into the habit of having frequent conversations—the meaningless but socially necessary kind, rituals in which you can take part almost automatically without being really involved—talking of the weather, the day's menu, the exasperating or comical oddities of this or that Tutress, or the latest news of importance in the levels or the quarters.

There were others in the group: three other Blues (the one from Carrères, Amily of Kergoët and Marcie of Anglade), and two other Reds from Wardenberg who were nearing the end of their Service and still weren't sure what they'd do once they became Blues, although they were fairly interested in Archives management and maintenance. And there were two or three Blue men. In fact, the Schole had a noticeable number of them, as Lisbeï had very soon remarked. Often they came from the Citadel, although plenty of other Families were well represented. Some of them were simply curious, but the majority came for training—technical for the most part—or to update their skills in the light of new discoveries, with the exception of metallurgy, of course.

Pure research wasn't officially forbidden to Blue men, but few of them took an interest in fields that might have caused the slightest raised eyebrow—History, linguistics . . . On the other hand, Blue men could be artists or artisanas without hindrance, as long as metallurgy wasn't involved. This was the case with certain types of jewelery, for instance. It was no doubt too bad, since some were excellent artisanas, in Wardenberg and elsewhere. But of course it was out of the question for men to be involved in metallurgy any more than in the related manufacture of weapons, wasn't it?

The presence of Blue men in the Schole may have been surprising, but Lisbeï was much more astonished at finding

Red males—a fact she enlarged upon in this letter to Tula. There's even a Red male in our group! A Verchères who hasn't been chosen yet. They're apparently letting him study at the Schole while waiting. His name is Dougall and he's seventeen. Very shy.

Lisbeï was about to add, "like Garrec," but changed her mind. Still, Garrec and the episode with Tula had sprung to mind the moment she'd perceived the young Red's aura. Verchères was considered the most traditionalist of the Progressista Families. Dougall never spoke first, and when the other students took the initiative (usually students from Wardenberg or Kergoët) he answered with eyes lowered, a mixture of embarrassment and deference that Lisbeï found both disconcerting and a little comical. Fair, slight, and narrow-shouldered, Dougall had a blotchy complexion and black eyes with persistent dark circles that gave his face a hunted expression. He always wore a long-sleeved tunic with the cuffs tightly fastened.

There are several Red males in the Schole, not only from Wardenberg. I never thought males could go anywhere other than into the Families that had chosen them. In fact, she'd never wondered what males did who weren't chosen right away or who were between choices. *There must be nearly three thousand of them in Maerlande, after all. The one from Verchères is studying to be a recuperata. Are Blue men recuperatas? I'll find out.*

They were far more numerous than Blue men who chose to be exploras, she discovered, but even so it was a very unusual occurrence. Exploration and recuperation aimed at recovering useful technologies, particularly those connected with metal. Through a kind of exasperatingly irrational osmosis of ideas, men steered clear of these activities—a circumstance on which Lisbeï commented pointedly.

Other names, other faces were added to the human landscape that slowly became familiar. But they remained just that, names and faces—Merritt, Cardèn, or Cyse and Tonyn, who shared the pension landing. They all called Lisbeï "Litale." Each new Tutress had asked the ritual question, "What should you be called?" After hesitating the first time, Lisbeï had responded, "Litale," as was her right. Fortunately she was the only one in the group or in her pension from that Province.

When the meeting finished that day, Fraine and Ysande

came over to Lisbeï, who was busy filing the precious photographic plates in their large boxes before returning them to their section in the Archives. Fraine cleared her throat.

"A small party is being organized for Ysande's birthday. Could one possibly attend?"

How stiff they were! Lisbeï was beginning to get used to the indirect and impersonal manner of speech in Wardenberg, where the formalities were always observed—sometimes even between close friends. Yet another legacy from the siege days. *Could one possibly attend:* an invitation out of mere courtesy? Their auras conveyed another message.

Lisbeï's special perceptions had always fluctuated in relation to the people around her. She'd learned how to block her perceptions, more or less, when there was a crowd. This wasn't like Tula's mirror-wall—more a deliberate forgetfulness, a barrier between her consciousness and her perceptions. Most of the time she no longer distinguished between what she absorbed through her special sensitivity and what was revealed, as it was for everyone, through mimicry, gestures, and tone of voice. She only remembered her peculiar ability when she came upon a similar aura—Tula's, Selva's, Kelys's (or Antonë's, but hers was less clear)—or when people's behavior contradicted some powerful emotion, as was the case now with Fraine and Ysande.

Lisbeï made a deliberate effort to perceive more clearly. Yes: anxiety or fear, uneasiness anyway. Were they afraid she would accept? But Fraine added, eyelids lowered, "One would consider it a great pleasure," and Ysande echoed her. Their sincerity was unmistakable.

Although only sixteen, Lisbeï had nearly reached her full adult height. She was tall by any standard, but particularly in Wardenberg, where people were shorter on the average than in other Families. Fraine, still an adolescent, barely came up to her chin. Ysande wasn't much taller, although five years older than Lisbeï and already having borne three living children. She was—well, an *adult*. What could possibly intimidate her about a young, sterile Blue from Litale?

"It would be a pleasure to come," Lisbeï replied, drawn out of her habitual reserve by surprise and curiosity.

Her letter to Tula that week merely gave a brief account of the session with Edwina at the Schole. It wasn't the first time Lisbeï had put forward the idea in class: stories were perhaps just the other side of History. Reactions varied.

Sometimes people (like Marcie) made fun of it, or else they explained patiently (like Edwina) why it was virtually irrelevant. And sometimes she received an astonished stare that plainly asked where in Elli did she get such ideas? Only Carmela of Vaduze smiled, more at Lisbeï's earnestness than her ideas, however. "History is made in terms of calendars, little one—the Harem calendar, the Hive calendar, and ours," she said pensively. "But stories are timeless."

Where do stories come from? Have you ever wondered, Tula? Maybe not, since I was the one who did the story-telling. When you were little you thought I made them up. But I didn't, not always. It wasn't the gardianas, either. "There's an island in the heart of the world where the Mother of all stories lives. She's very, very old—ageless, rather, since it is she who has given, is giving, and will give birth to all stories. She throws them to the wind, like seeds, and when they touch the earth, they take root." According to Carmela, that's the tale they tell in Wardenberg to account for stories—a sort of variant of the Tapestry of Elli, in fact. But it's charming, don't you think? And at least it explains why stories spring into being, as though ready-made.

Lisbeï chewed on her pen for a moment, gazing into the distance. In the second part of Halde's notebook there were stories that seemed to be in the process of being born, full of crossings-out and fresh starts. . . . Come to think of it, didn't it contain the story of the Hundred-Armed Giantess? She'd have to check, but Selva had confiscated the few translations she'd done in Bethely, and the Notebook was under lock and key in Wardenberg until the Decision was over. There were plenty of copies: Antonë, whose silent retreat had lasted over a year now, must have one, and so must each of the twenty auditantas. In any case, no one else would see them before the Decision.

I went to have a peek at the Pimpernella Cycle, which I'd never seen, and guess what? "The Princess and the Spirit" is part of it, in quite a different form (the Spirit comes out of a bottle, and the cave opens from the top, by a trapdoor). Only the three Riddles of the Blood are the same. Instead of "warrias whose arms grow as fast as they are cut off," the Princess has children whose wounds heal as fast as they happen. Of course, she wins too, in the end, but she doesn't go back to the cave, and the Spirit evaporates from boredom in his bottle.

It's true that it constantly mentions girls turning into boys, first Pimpernella, then her sisters, then their daughters. Edwina's interpretation seems reasonable. When being a woman means being a slave forever condemned to forced labor, I suppose it's some consolation to make up stories about changing into a man. Still, it's odd that all those Harem storytellers never imagined Pimpernella getting together with her sisters to overthrow their tyrannical masters. But perhaps the Harem Chiefs wouldn't have allowed that kind of story to be circulated, and only the most "unrealistic" tales had the right to survive. . . .

There's another common factor throughout the Cycle that struck me, and you'll see why: they're always talking about the good health of Pimpernella and her family. They're never sick, they get horribly beaten but recover very quickly. (There's even a story in which one of Pimpernella's daughters is considered a witch because she hasn't had the plague like everyone else. They try to burn her, but it doesn't work very well, and they have to keep adding wood to the fire.) But there was no Malady in the Harem period. Antonë says the first cases appeared about a hundred years ago, and that the mortality rate was nearly a hundred percent at first. The nonfatal variety developed only about forty years ago.

Here's a case, perhaps, where reality and fiction meet. It would've been normal for the Harem storytellers to make their heroine and her surrogates almost indestructible if you look at it from Edwina's viewpoint—that is, if these tales are essentially a way of compensating for reality, taking into account the incredible harshness of mere physical life for women (and for everybody, in fact). Arms that grow again and wounds that heal instantly are quite understandable from this viewpoint. The phenomena are given a dimension of fantasy, but at the same time they're completely logical.

The idea captivated Lisbeï, who chewed dreamily on her pen again for a moment, then resumed her letter. *There's something fantastic about it yet at the same time completely logical. You could go a long way with such a formula—although it could be done from a perfectly realistic standpoint as well. Those who develop the Malady are practically never sick afterward, and you can easily extrapolate from there and take it further and further from the starting point of what Kelys . . .* No, she'd never told Tula about her conversation with Kelys beside the blue stones of the Badlands. She carefully crossed out "Kelys" and replaced it with "Antonë." *What Antonë also called mutations. IF the Malady is really a benign mutation, and IF the survivors are equipped with greater ability to throw off other ailments or even to heal accidental wounds faster—as would be the case with my arm and your foot, for example—why not imagine it going further? With the passage of time, increasingly favorable mutations would develop and our descendants would be like the childreen of Pimpernella. Not with arms that grow again, but . . .*

But why not? Was there any *qualitative* difference between repairing bone cells more rapidly and growing a whole new arm? Was this a case where quantity, pushed to the limit, became quality? But tales surely weren't concerned with this kind of problem. *Not with instant new arms, but with slow-growing ones, like a lizard's tail, for instance. This phenomenon already exists in nature! After all, if our bodies know how to repair the skin around a cut because there's a blueprint somewhere, they could do as much for an arm or a leg. It would take longer, that's all. And it would no doubt require the raw material, too, since you get nothing for nothing and you have to create the new arm out of something. You'd stuff yourself, and the body would take the energy it needed. Otherwise the body would have to feed on itself for energy, and you'd lose an arm to grow another!*

Tula would have liked this story in garderie days. It was just crazy enough and just logical enough. That image of an arm growing out one side by consuming the other . . . but no, logically the whole body would contribute energy by burning matter. And then what? You'd get terribly thin, be nothing but a bag of bones! No, too inefficient. The body would have a better system, it would shrink as it worked, feeding on the excess skin and bone. The person would be smaller in the end, but she'd have two arms. Perfect! And inversely, the more you ate, the taller and bigger you'd get. Elastic creatures! And there's your Hundred-Armed Giantess! It would even account for the difficulty of Pimpernella and her cohorts turning into taller and bigger *men*. But you'd have to add eating binges to the tales—and while you were at it, why limit the transformations to men; why not cavalas, ursas, or even butterflies!

Probably not butterflies. Where would all that excess matter go? An intense combustion? No. Mustn't forget Antonë's lessons. The mass would remain constant, allowing for the amount converted into the energy needed for the transformation. An ursa or cavala, but nothing much bigger than the original body. Unless it simply stuffed itself to bursting, which is always possible, but let's be reasonable even if we are crazy!

Anyway, how could you *think* if you were a butterfly? How could you turn yourself back into a human? IF, of course, this all emanated from the brain. The choice would be limited to animals big enough to have a brain the size of a human's—or almost. . . . . And if they had offspring in their animal form, what would they be like? Animals? Humans? A bit of both? In what proportions? Lisbeï burst out laughing. Really, this was too much. . .

How would such a creature get *born,* to begin with? How would it grow in its mother's womb? If the mother changed while pregnant, what would happen to the fetus? You had to presuppose the mother wouldn't or couldn't change herself for nine months. Perhaps she could make the babie grow faster. But in any case, how would you raise such a childe? Who would raise it? Creatures with such a capacity for transformation wouldn't need protection from the weather; they could eat almost anything. . . . . And they wouldn't need each other for protection from animals, either. But it's for all these things that societies are created, isn't it, Carmela? Creatures like that wouldn't need to form a society. They'd be completely autonomous. No society, no culture, no group to raise childreen. But they'd have childreen, all the same, if the generative instinct is as strong as Antonë said. Informal groups to raise the childreen? But if the childreen are endowed with the same capacities, perhaps they won't need adults, perhaps they'll be self-sufficient from the day they're born. . . . .

Lisbeï raised her head, astonished to find it was dark. What in Elli was the time? She shook her head, incredulous and amused as she looked at the blackened sheets of paper strewn over the table. Carried away by her stories again!

But the days of the garderie were long gone. Tula wouldn't have much patience for this sort of thing now. The future Mother of Bethely surely had plenty of other matters on her mind. Lisbeï sighed and reread what she'd written. Rather puerile fantasies. But she would cross out none of it. From the beginning she'd decided never to delete what she'd written, except for a word here or there. She thought for a moment about how to bring the thread of her letter back to earth, then started writing again.

Obviously, if the storytellers who invented Pimpernella tried in imagination to compensate for the lack of male births, as Edwina suggests, they didn't think it out properly: if all the girls became boys, we wouldn't be much further ahead! In fact these

Harem women had already developed the Hive mentality: change by total reversal, thinking it will solve the problem. We've gone beyond this mentality, and that's why the Pimpernella Cycle is "dead," as Edwina put it. We have a different way of thinking today.

Really? Lisbeï studied her last sentence skeptically. She'd had an inkling in Bethely, but living in Wardenberg and seeing it through a stranger's eyes showed her more each day of how the past survived, even when it had changed almost unrecognizably. All those customs and traditions, in theory as "dead" as the Pimpernella stories but in reality still alive, drawing their authority from their age, from force of habit. Like the upcoming festival in mid-Aprila of Ister, the Baltike avatar of Ilshe, and the eggs that people gave in dozens of different forms. Or the festivals at the end of Decemra, with their wreaths and bright decorations, and the children's choirs in the streets—a reminder that the new year once began at this time, in the month of *January* according to Halde's testament, rather than with the winter solstice in the beginning of Ellième. With a yawn, Lisbeï closed her inkwell and put away her pen. The gasole was almost out. She'd talk to Tula about all this tomorrow. The oddities of Wardenberg were a more suitable subject for a future Mother, and some of Mooreï's books were indeed out of date.

Ysande lived on Level One in the Sixth Quarter of the West Quadrant, with the family to whom she'd been confided as a ward seventeen years ago. According to Maerlande custom, this was the date you celebrated as your birthday, and according to Wardenberg custom, this occurred in the same month as your actual birth date. The ward's arrival in her host Family was arranged this way.

Lisbeï found the idea of "family" with a small *f* strange, as was the knowledge that the word had such different connotations for Fraine or Ysande. In Wardenberg, when you wanted to speak of the Citadel as a whole, including its territory and Offshoots, near or far, you said "the Family," and everyone knew it was capitalized. But if you said "my family," it meant the Sub-Line to which you belonged, that is to say all people who lived in your quarter, and more precisely those who lived in your "bloc," "building," or "house." Ysande's family building consisted of four stories obviously built at different times. They seemed to be climbing one on top of another, or around and over each other. It was all very curious but rather pleasant, decided Lisbeï after some reflection. The inside reminded her a little of Bethely. It corresponded to the mental picture she'd had as a childe of the first four stories of the West Tower, especially the Third, where the Library was, with their labyrinth of winding corridors, doors, trapdoors, hidden staircases, and shifting levels.

She was greeted by a volley of giggling little Greens who led her to the next floor. Some were really young, four years old or maybe less. Lisbeï noticed that the stairs were made wide and shallow. Was this done on purpose for the small Greens? She now knew that garderies strictly segregated from the rest of the community were a feature peculiar to Litale. Already she had seen childreen in the street who would still have been invisible mostas in Bethely. In Wardenberg they trotted off each day to the little neighborhood scholes of their quarter, known as "Klinescholes." She hadn't yet seen the littlest mostas, the babies, because they remained at home until they were three. There were none in Merritt's pension, which housed only Blues foreign to Wardenberg.

There are babies *on Ysande's floor—not only those of her immediate sisters and her compagna, but her own! She came to meet me carrying a babie of barely two under one arm and holding another by the hand. (They call it "a baby" in Wardenberg. How odd. Frangleï is really an archaic language!) Ysande's place is a veritable garderie: I saw at least a dozen little ones between two and five years old. Three others of seven to nine, including a boy, were off at the Klineschole. Ysande's three sisters are six or seven years older, and the two oldest, Luci and Karin, are expecting babies in two and five months respectively. They have a high rate of survival in this Line (this Sub-Line, or Sub-Sub-Line— well, this "family"). But still, how can they live with those tiny childreen all the time? They must have lost fifteen, if not more . . . We didn't discuss it, not on a first visit. It's not the kind of subject you discuss with a foreigner, particularly in Wardenberg. In any case, they must have noticed my discomfort—or my surprise, at least—because they sent me up to the party on the third floor right away. Ysande came up a little later after nursing her youngest herself—breast-feeding! My head's still spinning. This must be the greatest difference between Wardenberg and Bethely!*

And yet the general feeling hadn't been so unfamiliar after all. Was it a different means to a similar end? She'd had a sense of warmth, affection, sharing. . . . Less obvious than in Bethely, perhaps? But more . . . personal? You could tell at a glance whose childe was whose, quite apart from possible physical likenesses. What she couldn't discover was any trace, either on the faces or in the auras of the family, of the loss of all those little ones in infancy. Living as they did with their childreen from birth, could these Wardenberg women be as hardened to loss as their Bethely counterparts?

But it wasn't her astonishment at the childreen that imprinted this first evening with Fraine and the other student guests on Lisbeï's mind.

Several guests had already arrived when she entered the large room. It was abundantly decorated with wreaths and gasoles. Outside, the light was fading as the Aprila afternoon drew to a close. She recognized the younger half of the Schole group—little Dougall, sitting silently in a dark corner, and a few others whom she'd seen around the Schole with Fraine or Ysande. There were about a dozen other Wardenbergs whom she didn't know at all: several young Reds like Fraine, three or four Blues who seemed fairly young too. People were already engaged in lively conversation, and she noticed several empty bottles standing around, although the generous trays of food had hardly been touched. Someone helped Lisbeï off with her coat and took the satchel containing Ysande's present. Someone else placed a glass firmly in her hand—it contained a sparkling wine, no doubt the famous Wardenberg Zirfell. You could only drink it here, since there weren't enough terraces in the Zirfell Commune to grow sufficient grapes for an export wine trade.

Lisbeï found herself surrounded by strangers at the end of a large, low sofa pushed against a wall, under a set of windows with colored panes. At least she had the sofa arm to lean on; her head was already buzzing with the proximity of so many people and the noise of conversation, even taking into account the subdued voices of the guests. Wardenbergs were customarily soft-spoken, and no one shouted after the age of four—no one who was well brought up, at any rate, and in this respect everyone in Wardenberg had impeccable manners. Having to live in each other's pockets for a century teaches people to reduce possible causes of friction.

It was a new experience for Lisbeï, her first real outing in society since her arrival five months earlier. She wondered whether she'd been right to accept the invitation. What in Elli could she say to all these strangers, or even the people she knew? Talk about the Schole and their studies? Hardly a suitable subject at a party. About life in Wardenberg? She knew too little about it, and her perspective was certainly too foreign. The safest thing was simply to listen and only to speak when she was spoken to—and even then, to reply with great care.

But perhaps Fraine and Ysande had warned the others about Lisbeï's reserve, or else the infallible Wardenberg politeness protected her. In any event, she was merely asked whether she'd like some wine and hors d'oeuvres (yes, it would keep her hands and mouth busy), and what did she think of the latest play at the Blue Court (she hadn't seen it). Otherwise, people seemed satisfied with a nod or a shake of her head, according to the subject under discussion in her vicinity—a greater share in the Bretanye boat building for Western exploration, for example (the principle of such a venture had been approved by the Assembly of Mothers in Bethely, and the details were now being argued out in each Family). Or the right length and trim for the thick, sleeveless overtunics that were all the rage in Wardenberg this wintra. With the help of the Zirfell she was beginning to sink into a pleasant somnolence when the word "Decision" floated toward her from across the room through a momentary lull in the conversation.

Now *there* was a subject that really interested her! Lisbeï left her sofa, although with some regret, and navigated a little unsteadily toward the opposite wall. She leaned against it with studied nonchalance, near a group of Reds and Blues who were in fact discussing the Decision, as well as the Notebook and the Assembly.

And "her."

Lisbeï didn't immediately understand who this ever-recurring "her" was. It must be Halde. An unfamiliar young Red considered "her" as at best the victim of some manipulation, and at worst a lying forger. Another young Red—Fraine —was defending "her" hotly as a champion of truth.

"And it's surely not for want of trying. I'm sure she had her whole Family on her back. . . ."

"Then they knew about it?"

"They must have. I'd be surprised if you could dig a hole that size without anyone being the wiser, especially in a Family like Bethely!"

Lisbeï started violently, then changed position to cover her involuntary reaction.

"I mean she stood firm, in spite of everything. Think about it a little! In her situation . . . But no one could muzzle her. . . ."

No one tried to muzzle me. They knew nothing about it!

"If it hadn't been for her, and her alone, the truth would never have come out!"

They didn't want to hide it forever, just until after the Assembly!

"Even the Juddites' hysterical remarks . . ."

Hysterical? They weren't really hysterical. . . .

"Bethely's cowardly silence . . ."

Cowardly, cowardly . . . they had their reasons. . . .

"But really, Fraine, how can you approve of what she did? She embarrassed her Family, delayed important palavras, and prompted a Decision about something that may be a pure forgery! And why? Because she couldn't be the Mother and wanted her revenge!"

The Zirfell had a lot to do with it, I'm sure. I felt they weren't really speaking about me. And anyway they couldn't talk about me as though I weren't there, when in fact I was, could they? I'd completely forgotten they didn't know my real name. I was—well, stupefied, but fascinated, too. It was the first time I'd heard my story told by someone else. There was a story in Wardenberg, and probably all over Maerlande, and I was a character in it. At times I felt like shouting, "No, it wasn't like that! I wasn't like that!" Yet I could see things from their side, too—from the viewpoint of the Red who was against me and Fraine, who was for me. And they were both wrong!

Or were they both right? (Lisbeï hesitated; no, she wouldn't scratch this out.) *But I feel that neither "Lisbeï" was the real me.*

She paused again. No—it was ridiculous! She knew perfectly well the Notebook wasn't a forgery. But it was true she'd embarrassed her Family and that she'd done it . . . not to get revenge, of course, but . . . she'd known full well what she was doing, hadn't she? She'd *known* the awkward position she would create for Bethely by revealing everything. She wrote slowly, *Or perhaps both Lisbeïs were real?*

Now at last she could be totally honest. *I was very frightened when I stood up to speak at the Assembly opening, but it wasn't totally fear that I felt. There was pleasure as well—the*

*pleasure of telling the truth and telling it right, despite the others
and their prudence. At last I can own up to being partly the
character invented by the unknown Red, as well as to being
Fraine's Lisbeï. But this second Lisbeï is harder to accept, too
flattering, too heroic, too sure of herself, a bit like Hallera's
Garde, radiating strength and goodness, absolutely certain of everything. What merit is there in that? Halde's Garde, as far as
I can remember from the translation, is far more human, far
more real . . . and as a result her divinity is more so, too.*

Tula would understand that she wasn't comparing herself
to Garde. It was just another illustration of the paradoxes that
fascinated her, like Mooreï's cube—when extreme opposites
suddenly touch.

*They continued their discussion for a while, and then Fraine
turned to me and asked what I thought. I should have been
ready for such a question, but I'd had something to drink and
had rather forgotten who I was. The Arbitra would decide, I said,
and I could feel how disappointed they were.*

*"But you, what do you think, Litale? The Arbitra doesn't do
our thinking for us, she's simply the first to choose, that's all."*

*Kelys had told me pretty much the same thing. What did I
think about it? It was a pretty odd question to ask myself—
perhaps the Zirfell again, but even now I find it odd. Because
when I try to put my feelings aside, I'm not really sure what I
think. If I were a Litale Blue who'd never become a Red, like
Lisbeï but not Lisbeï, what would I think of it all? Impossible to
know, obviously. But under the influence of the Zirfell I tried
anyway.*

"I believe she didn't quite realize the consequences. But
what else could she have done?"

"One never knows all the consequences. Nobody would
ever do anything if they did know," said a Blue whose name
Lisbeï didn't recall.

"She could have warned her Family, all the same," said
another.

"Her Family!"

The outburst of hate and distress that accompanied this
muffled cry was so intense that it pierced the Zirfell-induced
fog. Lisbeï looked around to see who had spoken. Dougall?
She hadn't noticed him join the group, but there he was, a
little to one side as usual.

"Do you think they knew?" asked Fraine, unaware of the
emotions overwhelming the young Red.

"Whether or not they knew doesn't change a thing. Families are absolutely indifferent to questions like that. All they care about is how many heads of cattle they have for trading at the Choosing Time. Since Lisbeï couldn't be part of the herd, they dumped her."

There was a silence. Lisbeï, slightly disgusted, would have liked to dismiss Dougall and his outburst with an inward, "He's drunk," and continue the discussion as though nothing had happened. But she was too close to him and perceived his emotions all too clearly. Such rancor, such suffering . . . it couldn't be directed at Bethely. Dougall wasn't speaking of Bethely.

"We're not cattle," she said finally, watching him attentively. It was hard to read his expression in the dim light. His emotions sent a much clearer message, and she turned her attention to his aura again. Yes, that was the key word.

"Cattle," Dougall repeated. "Males, wards, they're cattle."

He was desperate now. He knew it was wrong to keep on this way, but he wouldn't stop. He took a sort of painful, perverse satisfaction in doggedly proceeding. He wanted . . . to hurt himself? Why? Because he hadn't been chosen yet?

"I never considered myself cattle," said Ysande slowly. "Since I'm able to give Maerlande childreen, I give them; it's the least I can do in return for what I get. I surely gained in the exchange when they sent me to Wardenberg."

The group wasn't reacting as Lisbeï might have expected. They were astounded, yes, and felt uncomfortable as she did, but not totally . . . well, scandalized. They obviously couldn't perceive Dougall's emotions, but they were ready to listen to him as though he weren't merely disguising a personal wound in a general theory.

"Even so," said Fraine, "one childe every two years for fifteen or sixteen years . . ."

"Facts are facts," said another nameless Red. "Too many die, and there aren't enough boys. You can't get around it. There are things we can't control. We have to live with it."

"It could be worse," someone else remarked. "The fertile period could last longer. At least we can begin living after fifteen years."

"*You* can begin living!" said Dougall.

To Lisbeï's astonishment, no one reacted to the violence of this remark. People seemed to understand. Understand what, though? When males became Blues, they were as free as others.

"What's to stop you from living?" she asked, genuinely curious.

Now it was the others who were surprised. Livine touched her arm. "That's right, you're from Litale," as though it were an excuse.

But all she meant was, "You haven't had much opportunity to meet males." There are a lot more of them in Wardenberg, it's true. Not only their Greens and pre-Service males, plus the twenty or so males-in-residence, but their Blue men. Did you know almost all their Blue men come back to the Family? Then there are visiting Blue men at the Schole and elsewhere. All told, there are always at least four or five hundred men in Wardenberg —a staggering figure. And the most striking thing is that they don't live apart, like our Green boys and Blue men, but in the quarters with everyone else. So obviously they are a more usual sight. The women know them better. Ysande, for example, knows the donor of her latest babie—knows him outside the Service, I mean. It seems this is often the case, and no one thinks anything of it.

But with Dougall she had been slow to understand. She had merely thought the others knew something she did not, something that made them more tolerant toward the young Red male and toward men in general.

"What stops me from living?" said Dougall. "What stops us from living? The Service, of course! Being a Red and not being chosen. Or being chosen and having to leave all the time. Becoming a Blue with nowhere to go. Being good for just one thing, and good for nothing afterward!"

"Dougall, that isn't true," protested Ysande miserably, and Lisbeï felt it wasn't the first time they'd had this conversation. "We all contribute to the Tapestry—before, during, and after, all the time! What you do in the Schole, what you learn, everything you are, that isn't 'nothing'!"

"Not for you, maybe," muttered the male.

"The Verchères Family let you come to the Schole, after all," said Fraine.

"They *let* him, yes, because they had their collective arm twisted!"

"But the fact is, he's here," insisted Fraine.

"And if ever he is chosen, he'll have to go. Anyway, he can't study the subjects he really wants."

Men were never communicatas, of course. Suddenly the conversation had veered to the subject of all the things men couldn't do and why. If the male Greens and young Blues were allowed to take part in more of the Games, why couldn't they be admitted to all the nontechnical sections of the Schole? Yes, but where would it end—were you going to let them become Memories? And as Lisbeï was taking part in the discussion—still somewhat inarticulate in Frangleï—some of the group noticed how she used the feminine forms for men where they would have distinguished between the genders: patroller, explorer, or child, for example. Lisbeï remarked to the others that Frangleï contained more archaïc forms than other Maerlande languages. Livine, half joking, retorted that Frangleï simply had less contradictory relics from the Hives and their fanatic determination to remake the world from scratch. "Why do we say, 'Elli is raining,' but elsewhere use the neuter 'it'? And why are some terms masculine instead of everything being feminine?"

"Because after the Hives, people began taking the past into account again," said Lisbeï, sounding calmer than she felt. (Really, she thought, why do I persist in adopting positions that aren't mine? She agreed wholeheartedly with Livine on the subject of Maerlande's linguistic anomalies. She had merely started out to say the Wardenberg variety was different, nothing more!) "In the long run it's usage, not decrees, that have shaped our languages. Perhaps these masculine terms will end up being feminine again. And I don't see why you couldn't say 'Elli is' instead of 'there is.' "

They were moving further away from the subject of Dougall, much to his relief. He seemed suddenly self-conscious about his own daring. Historical/linguistic considerations were certainly less compromising. Dougall displayed a fund of knowledge in these matters that surprised Lisbeï. She noticed something else: two vertical marks on the inside of his wrists, a little darker than the normal skin color, revealed when he rolled up the sleeves of his tunic to offset the heat generated by the crowded room and their animated discussion. It was only later, in telling Tula about the evening, that she realized what the marks must be.

Wardenberg is so different. I don't think I'll ever get to the bottom of it. Each time I begin to get used to it, I discover another layer of weird new things. It's a bit discouraging. And as Dougall is always with us now, even outside the Schole, I can't simply forget about him. Perhaps it's like your experience with Garrec. Except that in the garderie it wasn't really like growing up with Greens, the way they do here. But you see, I understand better now about how you used to talk of Garrec, or boys, or men generally. You didn't do it often, but it always upset me. . . . Like the time you wanted to visit the Blue from Nevenici, remember? Only now do I understand why. It was after . . . or was it before? I can't remember now. A moment ago, I thought it was after we'd seen Selva with Aleki, but now I realize it must have been before.

But you couldn't be afraid of Dougall. He was too shy, too unassuming, too . . . unhappy. And you did become accustomed to having a boy around, a man. (What did you call an eighteen-year-old Red male who hadn't been chosen? A young man?) His presence occasionally made Lisbeï feel awkward. How ought she to phrase things when he was there? After Ysande's party she'd become acutely conscious of Wardenberg's confusing speech patterns. Here people used the feminine form customary throughout Maerlande in the Frangleï for "All are equal in Elli," but on the other hand they said men were discouraged from becoming mediciners or historical researchers. She finally decided to adopt the current usage, but she would never feel comfortable with it. She didn't like contradictions that failed to reveal themselves as illuminating paradoxes.

That evening at Ysande's seemed to have set off a chain reaction. People came up to Lisbeï much more often now. Not just Fraine, Livine, or Ysande, but the other students in the group who'd been at the party. Would she go to dinner at Marika's tomorrow? How about joining Jiadule at the Blue Court? What were some good reference works on the Hives? Could she lend them her notes on this or that book (which they seemed mysteriously aware of her having read). Or else it was, "Litale, could you help me translate this passage from Old Litali? I can't make head or tail of it." Everyone was less formal and expected her to be the same, although such is the perversity of things that she now had difficulty shedding the carefully learned Wardenberg formulas. Anyway, without quite knowing how or why, she seemed to have passed some test, some initiation.

How strange it seemed! For the first time in her life oth-

ers were seeking her company, and these "others" were not
Tula. People asked what she thought, although they didn't pry
and still called her "Litale." And, yes, she used the familiar
pronoun and had read the books, could advise, lend her notes,
or help translate. Now she took part in History and language
seminars as well as the recuperata classes. The Tutresses, surprised or annoyed, had reservations about this, but as her
work didn't suffer, they let it pass. She was a Blue, after all.
Yes, she'd be pleased to go to the theater, thank you, or dine
somewhere, sing in the Schole choir (she'd almost forgotten
how much she liked to sing), or go for walks afterward on the
ramparts. Once sumra returned, she was taught how to sail
the round-bottomed little boats that skimmed the waves before the wind. She learned how to dress, do her hair, paint her
face and hands with intricate designs for the festival of Ister
that ushered in sprinna in Wardenberg. And she even learned
how to dance—the ordinary dances performed in Bethely, but
which she'd never really learned or practiced because she was
too busy learning to be the Mother.

But not the Dance of the Celebration. Lisbeï spent her
first Wardenberg Celebration holed up in her room, wax balls
in her ears to block out the noise that, on this night alone, was
permitted within the Citadel. She spent the second Celebration in her pension as well, alone with a bottle of Zirfell after
refusing Fraine's invitation. That was the year Tula officially
became the Mother of Bethely, although she would only
Dance with her first Male the following year.

4

Guiseïa to Toller

Wardenberg, 23 Elliéme, 492 A.G.

Dearest Toller,

Guess whom I met yesterday at the Wardenberg Concertalle? Our Bethely friend, little Lisbeï. She sings in the Schole Choir. I shouldn't call her "little"—she's a good head taller than I am. The program was delightful. Meroë of Aspughi: the Ballad cycle as originally written—a capella. And all at once this voice soared in the last movement of the third—you know: the magnificent solo lament. It was a beautiful contralto, full and rounded, just held back the necessary fraction, with a subtle and mournful vibrato. . . . I was enchanted. During the intermission I looked at the program. "Soloist: Litale." So, a Blue. But I wasn't thinking of Lisbeï at all, you see. Then the superb voice appeared again in the finale, the fifth, with that deep, velvety resonance. . . . Rather like Kelys's voice, come to think of it. But the singer was invisible in the middle of the Choir. I went to congratulate the group with Sygne afterward. And there she was, surrounded by the rest. She saw me looking at her. I don't think she recognized me at first. Once she did, however, she tried to slip out.

Her friends had recognized Sygne and were determined to introduce Lisbeï to her. They seem very proud of her and call her "Litale," although some of them must guess her real identity. They introduced her to Sygne, then to me. She didn't bat an eyelash. Good external control; not so good internally, though, but she probably hasn't had our training. Not with her mother, in any case, and probably not even with little Tula. I would have thought Kelys would have seen to it, though.

We chatted amiably about the concert, how good it was, and so on. She blushed—and it wasn't affectation. She seems perfectly unaware of her talent. I remember her as being lively and intense, yes, but not really pretty, or only the prettiness of a clumsy colta. She's changed a lot in two years, though she still has that exotic look that struck me in Bethely—high cheekbones, matte olive complexion, lustrous black curls, and great bronze eyes. . . . And then that piquant contrast between her charm and her complete unconsciousness of being so attractive. Actually, she seemed rather embarrassed by her tallness amid all those tiny Wardenbergs. She always stoops a little and tries to efface herself—and you know how good our kind is at doing that! But she hasn't enough training to be really successful.

We decided to end the evening at Sygne's Residence. I made a point of getting close to Lisbeï and asked her if she remembered our first meeting. Of course. I showed her the necklace. She stared at me with those great eyes, beneath those very uncharacteristic eyebrows—for Bethely, that is: you know the kind, "like two raven's wings" as they say in the old books. But nothing about her is very Bethely. Too bad the alliance didn't take place as originally planned. I'd have loved to see the childreen produced with her and our Maxime. Her little sibling Ylène is very different. All the half-sisters are different, although Tula's a bit like us.

Lisbeï recognized the necklace, and it all came back, at which point she became horribly embarrassed. I could have put her at ease, but I was curious. And then she surprised me by bursting into laughter. More ironic than humorous, mind you, but I didn't think she had it in her. The Lisbeï of three years ago certainly had no sense of humor, or else hadn't had the chance to develop it.

You're familiar with Sygne's evening parties. Not a gastronomic feast, but it was all done with that exquisite Wardenberg courtesy. Sygne's drawing room has been completely redecorated since I last visited her. I chatted with various people about the Choir, Meroë, the upcoming programs, the Schole's work, and of course the Decision. You should have heard the outburst and the arguments of those who approved! Comforting—especially the reaction of three who seemed closest to Lisbeï, and your little Dougall of Verchères, as a matter of fact. He seems to have survived the culture shock of Wardenberg. It's heartening to see how he's blossomed. He talks to the others almost like an equal, as long as he knows them well. Lisbeï—well that's another question. She always seems a little constrained in his presence, and he shrinks back into his shell.

Lisbeï's closest friends must know who "Litale" really is.

When they discussed the Decision and the talk veered to the subject of her revelations in the Assembly, they either avoided looking at her or made a point of asking her opinion. She herself was as quiet as a mouse, of course. She buried herself in an armchair behind a glass of rosé wine, maintaining such a neutral stance that it would have been almost comical if I hadn't perceived her aura. The whole business has affected her deeply, I think, and it will for a long time. I wonder if she's aware that her identity isn't such a secret as she'd like to think?

Antonë's Decision seems to be fairly popular here. Perhaps not for the same reasons that may have influenced Antonë, but still . . . It's so diplomatically phrased that everyone can find something to approve, whether Believras, Progressistas, or even Juddites. "We must understand the two facets of Garde better and therefore gather and study all the pertinent data." And then, "All Archives in all Families must be open to researchas," although the latter are to be "under a vow of silence on all matters not pertaining to these facets." A good strategic move.

Knowing Antonë, I doubt that the rolling prose and clever conclusion could have been the sole result of an inner struggle between faith and disbelief. But do we really know Antonë? Her sudden about-face caught me completely by surprise, though it's just typical of such a fervent disbeliever to swing the opposite way. When you look at it from this point of view, it's astonishing she didn't pronounce on the Notebook's contents, or on Hallera's Appendices. "Halde's Testament and the other Bethely discoveries are genuine. We must therefore decipher the Testament."

All Lisbeï's friends were eminently satisfied with the Decision. They never doubted it would uphold the Notebook's authenticity. But who ever thought otherwise, apart from the most fossilized Juddites of Litale? They probably won't be convinced, but now the Decision will force them to open their Archives. As for the Notebook, the Schole copyists have been working night and day since the terms of the Decision reached Wardenberg. There's already a waiting list of several dozen names, including "Litale," I suppose. Kelys reappeared in Wardenberg several days after the Decision was announced, Sygne told me, and she already has a copy. She'll stay here all wintra long. Maybe she'll actually organize the interfamily association of researchas we talked about last autumna.

I'm surprised Antonë didn't reserve the Notebook for specialists. It doesn't seem characteristic—this willingness to make the Notebook available to anyone who wants a copy. Who knows what Halde's Notebook contains? If Garde came from the Bad-lands . . . or if the three tiny Compagnas also came from there. . . .

If, if. What difference will it really make to our concerns? If Antonë finally decided to make her research on the Malady pub-lic, then it would matter to us. But I really have no idea what stage she's at, or in fact anything about her research after these three years of total silence. I wrote her in Bethely, and her answer is probably waiting for me in Angresea. I only hope she hasn't turned completely into a Believra who's seen the light, so to speak.

Well, I still haven't told you the last of my meeting with Litale. Of course, I turned on the charm the whole evening. I'm nothing if not consistent, as you know. She took it all in. How did she react? Disbelief, rejection, fear—in general, total confu-sion. One really wonders what in Elli she's been doing in War-denberg all this time. But no, I know what she's been doing on that score: nothing. I tried to gauge the kind of relationships she had with her three friends, but it's all very chaste, though Fraine would like it to be otherwise. I don't think Lisbeï has an inkling —her head's probably still full of Tula. Touching. Exasperating but touching. But exasperating.

So much for happenstance. Chance often plays a significant role—but it's too bad one can't always rise to the occasion, isn't it? But perhaps Lisbeï and I will meet again when she's a little more grown-up. After all, Angresea is beginning to get on very well with Bethely, what with three new wards from them, and five of ours living there. Maxime will be Tula's first Male. . . . And you'll be visiting Wardenberg soon. With the fleet going into pro-duction, I'll have good reason to come here again and drop in on Lisbeï in passing, won't I? She still has two years to go before becoming an apprentice.

I'm leaving tomorrow. Perhaps there'll be a letter from you waiting at the Capterie. I'm longing to see you. And the childreen too, especially Sylvane. Generally everything is going well. Rowène's latest experiments seem conclusive, but it's impossible to be sure until we've tested them longer on a large enough num-ber of people. You know the kind of problems we're up against in this respect, however. And the fourth boat was about to be launched in the shipyard when I left Angresea for Wardenberg. When I hear from you about your dealings in Entraygues, I'll tell

*you more about mine with Sygne—and with her wily Memories.
Until we meet, my beloved,*

Guiseïa

5

It was sprinna once more, a chilly season very different from
sprinna in Bethely, with fleeting patches of blue (but such a
delicate blue), fitful bursts of sunshine, and hesitant flowers.
But sprinna nonetheless.

Lisbeï would never get used to the cold, wet wintras of
Wardenberg that required you to live shut up indoors for
nearly five months of the year. But in Wardenberg she felt
confined even outside, despite the little trees, the verdant balconies, and the hanging gardens so carefully tended by the
green-thumbed denizens of the Citadel. From her first month
there she had resumed her taïtche exercises in the gymna hall
of her quarter. Going to and from the Schole wasn't enough
for her impatient body. When wintra ended that first year, she
went for solitary walks on the beach around the Citadel at low
tide. Her Schole friends found it a little odd when they heard
of it, but some of them ended up going with her—Fraine as
much as her first pregnancy would allow, Livine and even
Ysande, who hated physical effort. But they let her race the
incoming tide alone.

And now it was her third sprinna in Wardenberg, and she
longed to go *out*. Walking in the streets and stairways, or even
on the strip of uncovered sand at the foot of the rocks—that
wasn't going out.

"Maybe it's time you did your patrol service," remarked
Kelys. She was in Wardenberg to consult precious documents
in the Schole, in preparation for a new expedition. The idea
surprised Lisbeï at first, but it gradually seemed more and
more sensible, not to say attractive. You usually joined a patrol on becoming a Blue, and the quotas agreed upon by each
Family would soon have sent Lisbeï to the Badlands frontier if
she'd stayed in Bethely. But in Wardenberg there were

enough Blues to allow more flexibility in arranging the patrol roster, particularly for students in the Schole.

Lisbeï went to find the capta in charge. A patrol would be assembling in Amsherdam in ten days, made up of Blues from Baltike and from Wardenberg and its Communes. Since Lisbeï was in excellent shape, she could forgo the prior training. Perfect. Lisbeï informed the Schole, went to pick up her equipment, and pored over maps. Amsherdam wasn't all that far away, especially by boat, but she wanted to visit the Sanctuary and continue her way by land. It would take a little longer.

"You want to go along the Coast?" said Fraine, wrinkling her nose—although this didn't stop her from accompanying Lisbeï, along with Livine, as far as the Sanctuary.

Wardenbergs felt ambivalent about the Coast. It probably arose from having had to look at it in the distance for a century, knowing the Hive warrias could come at any moment. But it was also *outside,* a space where you could live normally, a possible freedom. The present inhabitants of the coastal Communes of Zirfell and Keilloch clearly had a less romantic view. But in the minds of Wardenbergs, it still offered a dangerous yet seductive prospect.

The Sanctuary was along the Coast, slightly inland to the east, in the Commune of Zirfell. (Lisbeï had researched the various uses of the word "commune" to find its connotations, as old Carmela had advised her to do. She still preferred "Offshoot." "Of course you would," said the old Blue, smiling.)

Seen from the Coast at high tide, Wardenberg floated on the sea like a big, two-cornered hat. The northwest corner was the site of the original Citadel, now Level One. The smaller point to the southwest had been engulfed by the Citadel's growth. At the beginning of the Harem period it had been leveled and turned into arable land by the patient transfer of earth.

A similar technique had been used on the Coast, where the terrain belonged to the same chain of rocky hills as the Wardenberg island. Gardens and small fields formed an intricate mosaic clinging to the most improbable slopes by virtue of a system of terraces that had been lovingly constructed and maintained for centuries. However, the climate had been getting colder in the past twenty years, particularly in northern Maerlande. Wardenberg and other Baltike (and Bretanye)

Families had spurred the development of greenhouses. At Zirfell on the southwest slope of the Coast, most of the terraces grew vines. Each square inch of land had been wrested from the ancient hills, but there were no greenhouses. The terraces on the northwest slope, by contrast, like those of Wardenberg opposite, glittered in the sun like countless dragonfly wings.

Zirfell was the site of the power station, fed by the falls on the Pughe River—you pronounced it "Push." Here stood the dam once destroyed by the Hives. The river ran through the Wardenberg forest, a resource guarded, maintained, and replenished by a swarm of maniacally dedicated forestas. Wood was vital to fill the pulp and charcoal demands of Wardenberg. Although old paper, fabric, and farming by-products were systematically recycled, it wasn't quite enough for the Schole's paper needs—the Schole being Maerlande's biggest consumer. Charcoal was essential to Wardenberg's steel mills. Both the steel and paper factories caused much criticism. It was impossible to prevent some pollution from the underground steel plant and adjacent workshops, and the cutting of trees for the paper mill meant deforestation, even though limited. There were those who didn't hesitate to reproach Wardenberg for these misdemeanors, although these same critics were quite ready to use the utensils, tools, and the books produced in the process.

In the year 152 After Garde, in a little clearing at the foot of a rocky outcrop, a team of woodcuttas had found the entrance to the Sanctuary while checking the aftermath of one of the minor earthquakes that sometimes shook the region. They fell into it rather than found it. Beneath the humus in the clearing lay a rusty grill that had been further weakened by the earthquake. It collapsed under the weight of one of the woodcuttas (a fall of fifteen meters—a miracle that Elka, the woodcutta in question who thus made her entry into History, came through with nothing more than a broken leg). Like the Bethely find, the Sanctuary was an underground complex. The Decline people were decidedly mole-like in their outlook, judging by the way they frequently burrowed into the ground to build. Maybe they were afraid of the sky and the artificial lightning that, according to tradition, flashed across it. Or perhaps the surface area, already threatened by the rising waters, was so overpopulated that they could only go downward to find space. But who really cared to understand the madmen of the Decline? It was enough to make use of the materials they'd crammed under the ground—particularly the metal, since the people of the Decline had finally exhausted all the surface mines, like many other resources, in order to build these subterranean structures.

Once inside the Sanctuary (after digging a staircase from the conduit), the recuperatas had found themselves in an underground complex very different from the one in Bethely. It began with a short, narrow passage, a corridor lined with exceptionally hard cement, and a layer of plastic material made to look like ceramic tiles. The woodcutta who fell from the heavens had seen a light at the bottom of the hole. Small panes of frosted glass set in the walls lit up when she touched them as she tried to get up. They remained lit while her friends came down to help her, but went off when they left, only to light up again when they returned with a team of recuperatas. But the lights went out for good shortly after this. Whatever remnant of power had fueled them, it was now completely exhausted.

The recuperatas used the air vent until discovering another entrance, one the Hive women had also found and blown up to block further entry. The corridor was blocked by rocks and earth, but despite the rubble, they could see points of light and feel air circulating. By drawing a map of the corridor and plotting its course above ground, they managed to find a small depression filled with rocks and overgrown with bushes and trees. They could free the further side of the corridor more easily now, and it was soon cleared.

They didn't get very far, however, as the corridor ended in a square hall about ten meters wide. At least twice before, early Maerlande recuperatas had come upon halls with the same marks of destruction: a wall covered with smashed screens above a large, sloping shelf that must have been a control panel, because here and there were the remains of a lever, a switch, or a sliding contact protruding from the tangle of melted plastic and metal. Black smoke smudges and dark streaks stained every wall, and in the center of the hall lay the charred remains of burned material: a lot of plastic, but many books as well. Whoever lit this pyre hadn't bothered to watch it burn out. A few pages (about a hundred in all) were in near-perfect condition. They represented several different languages, already far removed from the current languages of Maerlande, and it was generally quite impossible to tell when

· they'd been published. Even so, most of the pages had eventually been deciphered. Of these pages or fragments, the greater part dealt in quite a matter-of-fact way with numerous areas of knowledge that were apparently commonplace during the Decline—archaeology, chemistry, astronomy . . . There were only three groups of connected pages. The first, a dozen sheets that must have been part of the same chapter, though disjointed, referred to climatology and the Great Tides of the Decline. Eight others summed up the theory of evolution, although there were numerous gaps because of missing pages. And there were thirty nearly consecutive pages of a chapter on genetics. Its particular thrust was how and why fewer men were born than women. Normally the ratio should have been about equal, but mutation occasionally distorted the ratio. At some undefined period, probably before the actual Decline, these mutations had affected the chromosome that determined the sex of childreen, and the male/female birth ratio had completely altered. Of Elli or the punishment of males for having sinned against the natural order of the world, there was no mention.

The "Fragments," as they would come to be known, caused a furor among the Juddites, who rose in a vociferous body to denounce this abominable heresy. While they were at it, they castigated the recuperatas for their sacrilegious activities, a phenomenon they had been eyeing with increasing distrust for the past thirty years. Out of this and subsequent debates emerged the Proto-Progressistas, who fought the Juddites' position tooth and nail.

A Decision was called for. The recuperatas and the Fragments emerged victorious. The men of the Decline had triggered their own destruction, and the contamination caused by their irresponsible activities had resulted in human genetic material being altered. Elli had used the natural order of things to inflict punishment. Knowledge, change, and recuperation of Decline artifacts were not Abominations. If these things had occurred, it was because they were threads in Elli's Tapestry (the very argument Mooreï had used for the Notebook). The Dance of Elli could easily include the progress of evolution, whether for plants, animals, or humans, as well as the melting of the icecaps and the genetic combinations.

Maerlande was really born of this Decision, Antonë had told little Lisbeï when recounting the history of the science of human reproduction. Mooreï preferred to date Maerlande's

·

origin from the Decision ratifying the Word and Garde's divine nature. As usual, Lisbeï thought they were probably both right.

The underground hall of the Sanctuary was sealed at one end by an exceptionally thick armored door made of some impenetrable alloy. With their limited technology, the recuperatas had no way of getting through, nor could they find any mechanism for opening it, although there must have been one. They solved the problem by piercing the wall beside the door. Apparently the Decline builders had never thought of this possibility, merely lining the wall with a ten-centimeter layer of lead within hard concrete—not easy to pierce, but not impossible either.

The armored door stayed where it had always been, beside another door installed by the recuperatas in the rebuilt brick wall. There must have been many smithas who looked longingly upon this massive but irretrievable treasure trove of metal. Another and similar door faced it from the opposite wall of a second square hall—an absolutely empty space with ceramic walls punctured by puzzling orifices. They sounded the walls. There was rock behind the facing, but after working steadily at it for a whole day, they had hardly chipped it. Explosives would have been too risky for the rest of the structure. They tried sinking a circle of exploratory wells but came up with nothing.

The Sanctuary: some thirty meters of corridors, two square halls, and two doors of irrecuperable metal (but the recuperatas retrieved the metal in the walls). Why "Sanctuary" though? It was in memory of the Arbitra of the Decision, Megan, a moderate Believra of Gloster. After her Decision she continued living there—a hermit who died at a ripe old age. Lisbeï, in searching through the most ancient Archives, would later find the term "saintes." There was no real cult of saintes in Maerlande, not in this sense; it didn't fit in with the deeply personal nature of faith in Elli. But Megan of Gloster was no doubt the closest thing to this idea.

When visiting the Sanctuary, they left their cavalas at the foot of the slope ("horses," said the sign in good Wardenberg Frangleï) and climbed upward through the trees. The path had been beaten smooth as stone by generations of visitas. The last hundred meters really were stone, two and a half centuries of footsteps having long since pulverized the thin layer of humus. The staircase descended from a housing about two meters high, just a wooden roof resting on varnished brick walls. Lisbeï would have expected a more solemn approach than this simple lean-to. A little farther on they encountered the Arbitra's house, its round logs weathered by time. It was just as it had been, a respectfully maintained memorial. The original clearing had been landscaped as a small park, with grass, white-flowered shrubs known as "pretty-by-night" (the flowers were closed for their noon visit), and varnished wooden benches where visitas could catch their breath after the climb. In the underbrush around the clearing they caught glimpses of blue, red, and a little green—visitas picnicking.

The stairway fell away steeply. They had to hang on to the banister tightly. There was no lighting—probably on purpose—and so they descended through the gloom toward the luminous rectangle in the corridor beneath, to emerge at last in the light of bygone ages. Although there was frequent grumbling about waste, the lights were powered during visits by several klims of underground wiring laid by Wardenberg electricians between the Sanctuary and the Zirfell hydro plant.

The illumination struck Lisbeï as unpleasantly white and glaring. She had grown up with the blue-green flicker of gasoles, and Wardenberg had been the same. There, electricity was used only for the underground steel plant and its workshops. Once a year it was turned on for the Celebration, although the Juddites muttered against such sacrilege. Here in the Sanctuary it was too bright. There was an air of almost disappointing newness in its lack of mystery; the shadowless outlines gave the place a flat, barren look.

Of course the metal doors were impressive, gleaming cold and naked in the glare. They lacked the idiosyncrasies of doors, however: hinges, a lock, a handle—there was nothing but the metal surface set in its frame. ("And you can't even slip a needle into the join!") The floor and walls had been cleaned long ago, and some effort had been made to "restore" the wall of screens and the control panel with a painted imitation. The painting was continually being updated as fresh discoveries supplied new details about how it might have looked.

They moved into the next hall, going through the ordinary door that opened in the ordinary way—an almost ridiculous effect, with its brick surround and wooden panels, when viewed beside the inscrutable metal portal of the Decline. Or touching, perhaps terrifying, this brutal encounter of two vastly different technologies from two such distant epochs, so irremediably ignorant of one another. Maybe the contrast was deliberate. Maybe not. But it must have been this that created the hush when visitas entered the Sanctuary.

The Fragments had been mounted in sloping glass cases, accompanied by enlarged copies to make reading easier. Lisbeï bent forward, fascinated. The printed characters were still perfectly clear after all this time. But she soon forgot the letters, surprised by the familiarity of certain words.

"But this is Old Frangleï," she exclaimed. "It has the same variants as the Notebook!"

"Yes, it is Old Frangleï," said the Blue who acted as guide. "What notebook?"

"The Notebook . . . the Testament of Halde," replied Lisbeï, correcting herself. That was now the official name.

The Blue frowned. "It's supposed to be in Old Litali."

"No, that's the third part," chimed in Fraine. "The second part is in Old Frangleï."

"Well, you don't have to live in the Decline or the end of the Harem period to know how to write Old Frangleï," said the guide with a shrug.

Lisbeï caught the dryness of her tone. It puzzled her, this sudden . . . anger. "What do you mean?"

"I mean the Decision didn't convince me," replied the Blue abruptly. She made an effort to recover herself and to respond politely, if not amiably. "Would you like to stay longer, or do you want to go back up now? There'll be a crowd soon. . . ."

"What do you mean, didn't convince you?" said Fraine.

The Blue turned toward her with a look of ironic resignation. "Since it has convinced *you,* apparently, we won't discuss it if you don't mind."

Courtesy prevented them from pressing the point. Lisbeï and her friends looked at the rest of the glass cases and then went back up, leaving the hall to other visitas. The crowd really was increasing, now that the lunch hour was over.

Fraine was silent for a while, then burst out, "No one ever said you couldn't discuss a Decision!" They were walking down to the spot where they'd left their cavalas. "What about the Decision of Megan, about the Fragments? She must agree with that, mustn't she? Would she agree to discuss it?"

"It's her right, Fraine," said Livine. "Anyway, the Decision of Megan didn't deal with the same sort of thing. You can't compare them."

"Why not? The Juddites of that era had religious motives for wanting to prevent the Fragments being accepted, and Megan handed down her Decision with this in mind. She said that the advancement of learning wasn't incompatible with faith in Elli."

"Antonë said more or less the same thing."

"Exactly! And learning progresses by questioning, doesn't it? Elli has left us free to question the plot of Elli's creation, free to explain it as best we may. To refuse to discuss it is to reject Elli's freedom."

"You always exaggerate, Fraine."

"No, I don't! There were discussions after Megan's Decision, and they're still going on. Weren't you and Ysande doing exactly that the other day? Weren't you asking her why Elli was also still punishing women nowadays by letting fewer boys be born than girls, when it was actually *men* who chose to use their freedom by altering Elli's creation, and anyway, the sins of the parents aren't supposed to be visited on the childe? And didn't you point out that the Decision of Megan was meant to have taken care of this very question? Well?"

But Livine had no intention of letting Fraine's leaps of logic confuse her. "Decisions don't settle questions once and for all, and I never said they mustn't be discussed. Only that we have the choice of not doing so. It's our freedom, our responsibility, and we have to live with it. That's what Ysande said. We're not *punished* because we're not *guilty* of the Decline's past choices, although we are *responsible* for what we do *today* in order to live with the consequences of those choices. By the same token, if the men of the Decline introduced irreversible changes to the Tapestry, it was their choice. If *we* do the same, that's our choice and our responsibility. The Service is our creation within the creation of Elli. If we want to change the Service, we're responsible for weighing all the consequences. . . ."

"You can never weigh all the consequences! When something isn't working properly, you have to change it, even if you can't foresee all the consequences. You learn as you go. Nothing would ever be changed, otherwise. And what about changes over which we've no control? If they're for the worse, it's our duty to avoid or reverse them, even if they've been put in our way by Elli. Elli wants to see how we'll behave. Since

Elli has created us free beings, Elli can't foresee all our actions. Elli doesn't necessarily know where the Tapestry is going. We're weaving it at the same time, we're making Elli while Elli is making Elliself. That's what change and evolution are. Imperfect choices in an imperfect world. Even Garde said so, didn't she?"

Imperfect choices in an imperfect world. Lisbeï knew now that this adage wasn't the sole property of Selva. It was in common use throughout Maerlande. Fraine's voice and emotions had taken on a slightly aggressive tone, slightly anxious, too. As they walked along, Lisbeï reflected on what lay behind the young Red's ideas, although Fraine probably thought she was speaking of something quite different. But the sense came through clearly: her first childe hadn't survived and she was very frightened about what would happen in her second year of Service, which began in two months. Livine must have remembered this, too, since she steered the conversation onto firmer ground, a less personal aspect of History.

"Perhaps," she said. "But the ways in which we manage to adjust do develop with time, keeping pace with changes in the Tapestry. The Bethely find was a change, and the Decision a way of responding, first individually, then collectively. The Blue in the Sanctuary is responding to the Decision by not talking about it, and you by wanting to discuss it. She can choose not to; you can choose to do so with others who want to discuss it, and that's all right, isn't it?"

The conversation flowed on, but Lisbeï had stopped listening, reminded of her own choices and their consequences. Two years ago she'd thought Maerlande would return to its old self once the Decision was handed down. Or almost. And this despite the fact that she'd seen the reactions of Selva and Mooreï, heard the tumult in the Assembly, and witnessed the auditantas questioning themselves and herself during her testimony near the Highland Farm. But she'd believed or had wanted to believe Maerlande would return to its tranquil life after the Decision, like the pond once the stone has sunk and the ripples have subsided. Now she realized it was no metaphor for reality, or not an accurate one, for the pond was never quite the same afterward. Although the Tapestry of Elli was being constantly reshaped, it moved only forward in time. And Maerlande would never be the same "as before," either —not for hundreds of thousands of very real women, very much alive, whom Lisbeï suddenly encountered in the person of this anonymous Sanctuary guide.

The young Lisbeï (as she began to see herself with two years' hindsight) would no doubt have been enchanted at having thus inaugurated a new plot in the personal stories of each individual, as well as in their collective History. She would have been proud of her pivotal role, of her power over these stories. The Lisbeï of today felt the responsibility, almost regretting her refusal to obey Selva . . . But you couldn't go back. And anyway, the Lisbeï of today had paid the price, had exiled herself from Bethely, hadn't she? For her, too, nothing was the same. She wasn't going to beg Bethely to let her come back, either. That would amount to admitting she'd been wrong when she'd simply told the truth. Changes that came in the wake of truth couldn't be for the worse, could they? The beginning was the end; the end was in the means. Could it be wrong to tell the truth straight out rather than letting it filter through and manipulating it by manipulating those who received it? Now it was up to all of them to decide what to do with this truth.

In one of the books recommended by Carmela of Vaduze, Lisbeï had found an expression describing a procedure of the Decline or perhaps earlier. The "Judgment of God." The old Blue had asked her to compare it with the Decision. The Decision had none of the barbarity of two champions in mortal combat! Then she began to understand. It was a sort of sacred court meant to rise above the petty machinations of human beings by calling on divine intervention to distinguish the truth. The Decision differed *in nature* from the Assemblies and their interminable palavras that only stopped when everyone had been convinced—at least in theory. It was an act of faith ("a gamble," some said) in the human conscience—even when faith in the light of Elli was lacking. Not all the Auditantas had been by any means Believras.

Later Lisbeï would believe that Decisions were also meant to bring new threads to the plot of the Maerlande story, the Families prodding themselves into evolving further. Whatever the Decision, however, it couldn't guarantee the direction or success of Maerlande's subsequent evolution. Once a Decision was announced, people had to learn to live with it, to accept it in soul, in conscience, and in complete freedom of opinion.

And if some of them didn't want to talk about it, that was their right, as Livine had said.

6

The Commune of Amsherdam was in the process of being established at the edge of one of the rare, almost white patches on the map of Maerlande, on Bretanye's eastern frontier. Deep ruts scored the last ten klims of road as it climbed through an otherwise impenetrable undergrowth. Sprinna was just beginning to cast a light dusting of half-opened leaf buds over the woods. At the top of the rise you came out on a large, pear-shaped basin with a small river looping through it. The Commune could barely be seen from the hills, except for the unnaturally regular shape of the plots of cleared land beside the water, and the gardens and fields already greened by the warmer temperature below.

The site had been chosen for its microclimate. A few hundred Blues of all ages, from Wardenberg and other Communes, were busy constructing what would be the Capterie and its outbuildings, as well as the little dam upstream that would later supply the necessary energy. A nearby copper-beech wood hid their tent village.

When Lisbeï arrived, she found someone to direct her toward a cluster of five log cabins on the edge of the river. Still riding her cavala and leading two pack mules, she went over to them. A blaze of daffodils surrounded the cabins, and a mat of vines covered part of the silvery wood. They must have been there a long time. Three Blues sat on the veranda of the largest cabin, their faces masked by the shadow.

"Reinforcements," said one from the depths of an armchair.

"Well, goody for them," said another grumpily from the next chair.

"Are you the patrollas?" asked Lisbeï, disconcerted.

"No kidding?" sneered the third Blue, seated on the floor with her legs stretched out.

The cabin door opened, and the three Blues straightened up a little, although they made no effort to rise. A small, stocky figure appeared in the doorway, then emerged to reveal a woman in her forties with clipped gray hair, wearing dark leather trousers and jacket. Blinking in the sunlight, she advanced toward Lisbeï.

"Peace in Elli. I'm Nance, capta of the Amsherdam Patrol."

"Peace in Elli," replied Lisbeï, relieved. She dismounted. "I'm Litale. I hope I'm not too late. There were floods near Osberg."

"Litale, eh?" The woman put out only one hand and Lisbeï took it, managing to remember the Wardenberg custom in time. Nance's fingers closed over hers like a delicately controlled vice, and Lisbeï suddenly thought of Kelys, perhaps because this woman displayed the same aura of assured strength. "We're waiting for four others," continued Nance. "Myne will show you where to put your things. When you're finished, come back here and we'll do an inventory of your rations. Gerd and Kolia will unload the mules."

The three Blues rose lazily. Lisbeï stood by. She'd have to wait to match faces and names. The young Blue who'd been sitting on the verandah floor came and took her cavala's reins. Myne. As Lisbeï passed by the mules, she glimpsed a pair of hands unfastening the pack straps. The right hand had a large black cross on it. Gerd or Kolia? Lisbeï glanced surreptitiously at Myne's hand on the reins. Nothing. Only later, in the common showers, did she see Myne's shoulders and the black stain covering each of the Family tattoos. By suppertime Lisbeï had distinguished Kolia and Gerd—Gerd had the tattooed hand and was older than Kolia. Like Myne, both came from Wardenberg.

Four more Blues were expected. Lisbeï awaited their arrival with some trepidation. It had never occurred to her she'd be doing her patrol with exiles. The patrol served this purpose as well, but it was one of those bits of information that lay dormant in her mind because she'd never encountered the reality. For violent or repeat offenders there was internal exile to begin with, then exile in an Offshoot. Before the next stage in a nonlethal badland, the offender was "exiled" to a patrol. *I should have thought of it, having been in Wardenberg,* she confided to her journal. After two years she'd begun to see beyond the Family's customary courtesy and had noticed the number of hands with different tattoos. *Suppressed violence is always just beneath the surface. Too many people in too small a space—or perhaps in too many different boxes. The past weighs too heavily on people's lives: Upper Town, Lower Town, quadrants, quarters, subterranean workas, field workas, "proprietas" and "tenants," North Island and South Island, the ancient castes, the families with a small f. A century of containment creates such divisions. Inherited quarrels still linger, even though their causes have faded from memory. The "instability" of Wardenbergs isn't only genetic.*

The four other Blues came from Baltike Families, however. Sairle and Linde, both from Capanagh, were compagnas. Berte and Megyn came from Oslova and one of its Communes. All four were the usual type of patrolla—over thirty, veterans of fifteen years' Service, each with half a dozen children to their credit. They had just finished their prerequisite training and were full of goodwill, though not particularly excited by the prospect of patrol. The mixture of exiles and ordinary patrollas was surely no accident, Lisbeï decided, noticing that Gerd was assigned to Berte and Megyn, Kolia to the other two. She herself and Nance formed a support team for Myne. Gerd and Kolia were perfectly aware of what was happening, as the tough, sarcastic tone of their auras made quite clear. Myne—well, Myne didn't care about anything. The others noticed only her sulky silence, broken by the occasional acid remark. Lisbeï, however, was aware of the suffering that burned within. There was a heavy gloom about Myne's aura, like the persistent smoke of an invisible, unquenchable fire.

Here as elsewhere, the rule of discretion forbade prying questions. But though Lisbeï didn't know the details, she and the others were aware of Myne's burden: she had killed, without premeditation, in a fit of rage or jealousy. She regretted it —oh, how she regretted it! No chance of backsliding there. Once she had served her time, she'd be able to return to her Family if she wanted. But Myne didn't want this. She didn't want anything at the moment. Or perhaps she wanted to feel nothing, wanted to be dead.

Lisbeï thought of Loï. Of the fight with Meralda. Of the story she used to tell herself just before leaving Bethely, the story in which she convinced or forced Tula to flee with her into the Great Badlands, just far enough and long enough for them to have to be sterilized once they returned, to be rene-gadas, but Blue and free. . . .

Myne had no use for Lisbeï's compassion with its shades of horror and shame. She responded with silent rejection to all Lisbeï's timid overtures in the days preceding their departure.

The group didn't stay in Amsherdam long. It was simply a meeting place. ("Amersherdam is getting too civilized," as Nance put it.) They headed east for a new, permanent camp on the edge of a territory colored pale gray on the maps. There they went through the usual patrol routine: mapmaking, taking regular samples of soil, water, flora, and fauna. And all the rest—the nature of this "rest" having dawned on Lisbeï somewhere along the way. Wardenberg had allotted her a month's rations; the patrol lasted three months. Patrols, like Families, had to be self-sufficient as far as food was concerned. They would eat off the land. There was little likelihood of finding enough nuts, roots, or fruit in the sprinna months this far north. They would hunt.

Bethely had been almost completely vegetarian. They ate eggs, but there was no question of consuming the pescas in the Douve, or the hens, ovinas, or wicows. They were far more useful alive. "Apart from their usefulness, they're *living beings*," Mooreï had pointed out after Antonë had remarked on the why and wherefore of animals in response to one of little Lisbeï's endless questions. Antonë had looked as though she were bursting to reply to Mooreï's comment, but she'd said nothing, and Lisbeï had adopted the Bethely credo without further comment. Later she had learned that other Families, even in Litale, didn't share this view, but she shelved this piece of information under the mental category of "other Families, other customs." Differences were something to be aware of and to accept, not to criticize. Lisbeï had never eaten meat, even in Wardenberg. And of course she'd never hunted. She'd shot at moving targets while training, but never at *living* targets. She knew in an objective way that the capta-veterinarian put very sick animals out of their misery, but it wasn't the same! It wasn't *killing*.

On the site of the new outpost they built the first log cabin, the storehouse for all their dry and concentrated rations. Nance then proceeded to give them a little lecture. Antonë would have approved, Lisbeï felt. Now that they were

Blues, said Nance, they were no longer dependent on their Families, even though some might go back once their patrol duty was over. They were there to learn to survive. Human beings were part of nature. ("Part of the Tapestry," said Lisbeï to herself—an automatic reaction that had survived even Wardenberg.) They were no more and no less important than other animals.

Cavalas ate grass, spidas ate insects, and carnivores ate meat. "And humans are omnivores," Nance went on. "That means they can eat almost anything, which makes us more adaptable than most other animals." With a wide sweep of the arm she indicated the half-cleared space around them, the thick woods, and the leaden sky. "You're here to learn to adapt. To survive. No matter what the circumstances."

Lisbeï sensed Nance's intention before the Blue moved, but even so the lightning quickness of the attack caught her off guard. She found herself nose-down on the grass, her arms pinned behind, and a knee in the small of her back.

Nance helped Lisbeï to her feet, and the unexpected strength in her grip was a further surprise in a woman who barely reached Lisbeï's chin. Keeping a firm hand on Lisbeï while the others looked on, scared and wide-eyed, the stocky Blue added softly, "Including circumstances like that."

But first they built two more cabins as shelter from the rainy chill of this northern region, since no one welcomed the prospect of spending three months under canvas. Each morning they went through the taïtche, although their real training only began at the end of the first month, after the Baltike Blues had fully hardened their muscles. They had established contact with the other patrol station to the south and divided up the territory to be covered. And by this time, as Lisbeï noted with a mixture of humor and anxiety, their rations had nearly run out. She was the only one really worried by this. She tried to hide her anxiety, but Gerd and Kolia, who had seen her Bethely shoulder tattoos and knew the Family customs, teased her about it.

Lisbeï didn't like to think how merciless they would have been, had they made the connection between her and the famous young Bethely Blue who'd been involved in the Testament of Halde. It was enough that she was the youngest in the group (Myne was two years older), appeared too knowledgable (she'd made the mistake of speaking Slavoï to the Baltike Blues, among other things), and performed the taïtche too well (she'd never thought of it as something you could do "too well" . . .). Anyhow, after a month it was pretty clear Gerd and Kolia would have found some pretext for picking on her.

This didn't bother Lisbeï, who was more than used to being set apart in some way or other. In fact she watched the two Blues with what almost amounted to fascination, alert to the contradictory but unconscious emotions that shot through their auras. Would they have left her alone, she wondered later, if she'd reacted more conventionally? If she'd lashed out? They didn't pick on Myne, of course; there were limits to what tattooed hands could get away with on patrol, especially for Gerd, who'd coolly announced that she got into fights easily. Kolia—well, she was harder to figure out. She didn't say much and seemed content to follow Gerd's lead. Kolia, however, was careless, lazy, and muddle-headed, characteristics that might prove dangerous for those around her. One of the cabins had nearly caught fire during her tour of kitchen duty in the second week.

Gerd and Kolia, though separated during the day, gravitated to each other whenever the various patrols returned to the post, especially at night. They didn't make much effort to conceal their lovemaking. One night, as Lisbeï came back from the latrine, she noticed the gasole burning in their cubicle. A naked Kolia was crouching near the door, rummaging in her bags. She stood up when she heard Lisbeï enter. In her hand were two oblong objects, vaguely familiar. Kolia shoved one under Lisbeï's nose, mistaking her expression. "Like to try?" she whispered, grinning sardonically.

"Forget it," hissed an invisible Gerd, equally sneering. "She hasn't a clue what it is!"

"A phallus," said Lisbeï involuntarily. She sensed a shift in Kolia's emotions. Astonishment, grudging approval, uneasy curiosity.

Gerd stuck her head through the gap in the leather curtain. "Hey, Litale, you've got hidden talents!"

Lisbeï was appalled. Surely she'd given herself away this time. But the two Blues didn't appear to make the connection between recognizing a phallus and the training of a future Mother. Kolia stroked Lisbeï's cheek with the polished wood, her tone changing as she repeated, "Like to try?"

"No!" But she couldn't help being curious. "You like it?"

The question and its evident sincerity took Kolia aback. She'd been about to deliver a caustic comment on Lisbeï's indignant refusal. Instead she shrugged one shoulder and seemed to catch Lisbeï's sincerity in response. "Why not? It makes for a little variety once in a while."

"But they aren't pervertas in Litale, Kolia," snickered Gerd.

"What's perverted about it?" said Lisbeï without thinking. Unusual, yes, and rather ridiculous. But perverted?

"Come on, we'll show you," said Gerd. There was a hint of menace in her voice, of a summons. But Kolia's aura shifted to mockery once more, although with something like regret. "Oh no, not good little Litale!" She gave Lisbeï a broad wink and slipped behind the curtain. The gasole went out, and Lisbeï stood in the darkness for a moment, listening to the giggles, then the sighs and groans. As she tiptoed to her own cubicle, she sensed Myne was awake. Was it despair or envy that kept her from sleeping? Lisbeï couldn't tell.

The following day was a day of rest—or a day with no patrol duty, not in the morning, anyway. They spent the time entering the results of the previous days' reconnaissance tours in the log and training for the parade.

It had been clear from the start that Nance's idea of the parade wasn't what was practiced in the Families. Contact was the aim, contact and victory. "Adversary," insisted Nance when the word "partna" was mentioned. Lisbeï, more than anyone present, understood the psychological switch in attitude that the term "adversary" was meant to provoke. But she simply couldn't manage it. Nor could the others, for that matter. The first morning of training consisted mainly of a demonstration by Nance. The instructa chose Lisbeï to work with, she being the tallest and most fit. And Lisbeï found herself on the ground again. Discussion followed. It certainly wasn't the first time Nance had done this with a group of patrollas.

"One doesn't raise a hand against a sister in Elli," argued the trainees. It was perfectly plain. Then how could there be two different laws, one for Families and another for the Patrol? (Each of them probably thought of Gerd and Myne, who had been assigned to this particular patrol for that very sin.) Nance's answer was equally clear. If one raised a hand against a sister in Elli—and there might be extreme cases where it was called for, as they all finally agreed—it was a good idea to know how to do it properly.

"But it's not the same!" protested Sairle, thoroughly upset. "You want to teach us how to . . . to . . ."

"To kill," finished Gerd with cool malevolence.

"Is that what you think?" replied Nance. The others were struck dumb by the unseemly casualness of the capta's response. That was all she said. She put a stop to the discussion and handed out patrol assignments for the afternoon.

After that, each training session included demonstrations by Nance of various holds. A little more strength or length in these holds would make them lethal. Then she would pick an "adversary" and attack her persistently while the others tried the exercises with less than convincing results. Her friendly, "You're dead!" was heard each time an adversary let down her guard and found herself pinned to the ground. Any attempt at further discussion, however, was cut short.

On the morning after Lisbeï had come upon Kolia and Gerd in the night, Nance picked Gerd as her partna. (Perhaps "object of her demonstration" might have been a better way of putting it!) Lisbeï was paired off with Kolia. She was shorter and slimmer then Lisbeï, and such a hopelessly inept fighter that Lisbeï couldn't even begin to take the session seriously. Neither could Kolia, obviously, since, with a puzzling mixture of malice and determination, she clung to Lisbeï instead of breaking away whenever she had the chance. She emerged from a final tussle holding Lisbeï's ripped tunic. Lisbeï sensed the flash of triumph and realized this had been Kolia's aim all along. Kolia stepped back, waving her trophy and ogling Lisbeï, who stood half-naked in her cotton tights and leather breast-shield.

"What happens, Nance," Kolia taunted, "when you're disarmed by the beauty of your adversary?"

"You're disarmed," replied Nance drily, having just finished off Gerd for the umpteenth time. She walked over to the pile of equipment and picked up two batons, handing one to Gerd and tossing the other to Lisbeï. "Take Lisbeï, Gerd!"

Gerd jumped in front of Lisbeï. Nance had rarely coupled the two, though they were fairly evenly matched, Lisbeï's height being offset by the other's weight. Gerd appeared to be Nance's best pupil. After a week's training she'd even declared they ought to be using real weapons instead of wooden dummies: then they'd have to take the training seriously. Lisbeï disliked having her for a parade partna. Her aura was impenetrable, a bit like Tula and the mirror-wall—but not at all smooth. Gerd's defensive barrier heaved and throbbed as though restraining something, rather like a door held shut with great effort against some wild surge of energy.

When Gerd fought, however, this sensation of suppressed violence underwent a puzzling transformation, melting into a trance. Not the parade trance, though. The lids of Gerd's closely-spaced eyes drooped slightly, and her long face with its protruding jaw took on a dreamy expression. The contrast between Gerd's languid exterior and the sudden concentration of her inner violence distracted Lisbeï.

Now, from the edge of the practice circle, Kolia tossed the tunic at Lisbeï. Nance caught it in midair. "Do you think there'd be time to get dressed if the post were attacked?"

Attacked by whom? The thought had barely entered Lisbeï's head before Gerd attacked, baton flailing. Lisbeï stumbled backward, caught completely off guard. Gerd whipped the baton along the ground, making her jump, then whipped it back to knock her off balance. A jab in the solar plexus laid Lisbeï flat on her back, gasping for breath. She dimly heard Kolia's excited voice before a heavy, hard mass fell on her. The weight reeked of sweat and rage and something else, something she remembered sensing in someone, but whom? Then Lisbeï was fighting for air as Gerd's baton pressed down on her throat. Her left hand, thrown up for defense, was imprisoned beneath the weapon. Her right arm was pinned between her abdomen and Gerd's body, which bore down with every ounce of weight . . . but what was Gerd doing, why didn't she stop, she'd won, *what was she doing?*

An inexplicable burst of strength shot through Lisbeï's panicked body. If there was any will behind it, that will came from her body. Her right leg hooked Gerd's left, her left hip thrust itself upward and twisted Gerd off and over so that Lisbeï now straddled her. And Lisbeï was calm. She could sense the raging whirlpool of emotions in Gerd, but she herself was very calm. In what seemed like slow motion, she wrenched the baton away and twisted her adversary's arm, pinning it against Gerd's back and deliberately pushing her face into the turf. When Lisbeï felt Gerd beginning to suffocate, she leapt off and back, out of reach. Gerd lay there for an instant, not moving, then stirred a little. Kolia came over and helped her up. Gerd sat on the ground, stunned, her face grass-stained. A few steps away, Lisbeï stood panting, amazed to find her body not trembling. She became aware of the others, of Nance gazing at her and holding out the tunic, her head slightly thrown back. In approval.

"You chose," was all Nance said that night when she queried her. Disconcerted, Lisbeï bowed her head over the tunic she was mending. Chose what? To defend herself? To stop short of choking Gerd?

"Gerd will end up in a badland," remarked Linde, who was listening as she mended the tunic Sairle had inadvertently torn in their training bout. Nance gave a little sigh and nodded.

"Is this why you don't want us to use real weapons?"

"No," said Sairle, answering for Nance. The others looked at her, and she cleared her throat. "It hasn't anything to do with weapons, really." She put a hand over her heart. "It's there. Knowing that it's possible . . . that you *can* do it. And that you choose not to, when it isn't necessary."

Nance nodded again, this time with a curiously sad little smile.

The image of Meralda's blood-streaked face suddenly floated before Lisbeï. And the white pain of her own broken arm. To choose . . .

"But if Gerd is sent to a badland, what's to stop her taking off before she's served her time?" said Megyn abruptly. They all looked at her, surprised by such a different train of thought.

"Nothing," said Nance. "But if she doesn't bother anyone wherever she ends up, what's the difference?"

"Even so, it's never seemed . . . well, fair," muttered Megyn.

Nance's sad little smile resurfaced. "Imperfect solutions in an imperfect world."

"Anyway, her tattooed hands are a dead giveaway," remarked Berte. "If she tried anything, it'd be the Great Badlands for her. . . ."

The Renegada Traverse, the wicker basket in which the condemned were placed, weaponless, rationless. The descent, pulley wheels creaking as the basket dropped slowly down the face of the fault that cut the Traverse in two. A face of sheer rock, impossible to climb. Lisbeï had never witnessed the sight, but a novel by Ludivine of Kergoët had provided a vivid description. The top of the Traverse was on the near side of the blue stones, and so was much of the area at the foot of the cliffs, but that made no difference: there was nowhere to go but northeast into the Great Badlands. The two nearest passes through the Divide were at least five days' walk over rough terrain, and each had a permanent Patrol station. In any event, either the deadly pollution or the wild animals would get you before long. Only in Ludivine's novels did the unjustly sentenced renegada come stumbling into the Amberger Pass frontier post, there to die in the arms of her beloved. No one had actually ever been seen emerging alive from the Badlands.

"One does not raise a hand against a sister in Elli." No, the Badlands did the humans' killing for them. What would Garde have said? And if the Traverse hadn't existed, what would the Families have done with renegadas?

There was an uncomfortable little silence.

"Well, the fact is it *does* exist. The Hives blew up a piece of the mountain for this very purpose, and that's why we send the renegadas over the cliffs," said Linde at last. "I suppose we'd have found some other spot from which they couldn't get back. Anyhow, Garde's disciplas helped draw up the Maerlande Cartas. Garde would surely have approved. The Badlands represent the madness of the Decline, and it's . . . fitting that people whose behavior is an ancient madness should be sent there. If they weren't, what's to stop them doing whatever they like to others for as long as they want? Would you be prepared to deal with them, Litale?"

The remark produced some smiles. If it hadn't been for Sairle (and later Myne), who shared the fruits of the hunt with her, Lisbeï would have always gone hungry these past two months. A few days earlier, she'd been helping Myne and Nance remove animals from the snares. Skinning, gutting, cooking, and eating the animals was bearable when they were already dead, she'd found, but this time it was different. A small rabbit was still alive, despite the fact that some other animal had given it a vicious neck bite before presumably being scared off by the approaching Blues. Lisbeï forced herself to remove the rabbit. The animal's heart was beating wildly beneath the blood-spattered fur. She must kill it: the animal was doomed anyway. Lisbeï held the condemned animal, felt the warm flesh quiver with life, and envisaged step by step how she would finish it off. One hand grasping the head, the other the body. A quick twist and . . . But she couldn't do it. *She couldn't do it!*

Myne took the animal and broke its neck with economic

precision. She stroked the ears, at last immobile, and the soft fur on the skull. Looking up, she met Lisbeï's eyes and for once didn't turn away. "Sometimes you've got to do it."

But that didn't apply to people, not at all! Even Myne, who after all had already killed someone, wouldn't suggest . . . executing renegadas! There was no question of "you've got to" with humans!

All at once Lisbeï thought of Antonë and her occasional black moods of sadness. There were times when Medicinas were faced with "you've got to." Babies severely handicapped at birth, each breath a needless torture since they would die in a few hours anyway. The fatally ill for whom the Medicina could do nothing more and who asked her to end it all . . . Lisbeï had never really thought about it. Greens never went into that part of the infirmary, and no one talked to them about it.

Is it really so easy to simply ignore what you don't see? There was Loï, but I was too young. And Meralda . . . Well, Meralda is a case in point. And there were so many ready answers in Bethely, so many shields. "One does not raise a hand" . . . and even "The Tapestry" . . . But once you begin breaking down the shields . . . If one can raise a hand, if one has to, sometimes . . . But why do you have to? And why will Gerd end up in a badland one of these days, or Myne probably avoid such a fate? Because they're like that in the Tapestry? And me—does the same apply? In that case, how was there any "choice" for me, as Nance said? Because Elli doesn't know the pattern before we've created it?

In the first weeks after her return to Wardenberg, Lisbeï was repeatedly amazed to realize she'd been gone such a relatively short time. Only three months. How could she have learned so much in that brief period of patrol?

7

Lisbeï looked around for Fraine, but the young Red hadn't arrived. The only one of their group already in the lecture hall was Dougall, and since he'd come before anyone else, he had naturally gone to the back of the hall. Lisbeï made a point of going over and tapping him on the shoulder. "Peace, Dougall." He started, blushing a little as usual. Gathering up his things, he followed her to a seat in the first row.

None of the speakers had appeared at the semicircular table facing the audience. Lisbeï had hoped for a visit from Kelys once she'd reached Wardenberg, but all she'd had was the lecture circular slipped under her door with a "yes?" scribbled across it in Kelys's big, clear hand. Since childehood, Lisbeï had become accustomed to Kelys's sporadic comings and goings and had made up her mind not to let it upset her.

The hall began to fill up. Were people drawn by Kelys's reputation, or by the quality of the speakers as a group? Maybe they came because, for the first time in Wardenberg, a panel was going to discuss the Notebook—correction: Halde's Testament. People were probably attracted for all these reasons, plus their curiosity about the association formed by Kelys. The speakers of the evening were all members. But what a mélange! A research association that combined Juddites, Believras, and Progressistas on a subject like this was a gamble as spectacular as a Decision, to say the least!

Familiar voices. Fraine, Ysande, and Livine. Dougall moved over and Ysande sat down with a grunt. Her new childe was due soon, and she was huge. Fraine, although also pregnant, revealed only a slight bulge as she sat down beside Livine in the row behind Lisbeï. She pulled her chair closer in order to whisper in Lisbeï's ear. As Lisbeï turned to greet them, she saw the hall was a mass of color—blue mostly, as expected, but a good proportion of red, plus a sprinkling of other colors typical of Wardenberg. There was a relatively large number of men, mostly Red males, but that was normal. Even in Wardenberg, males usually had strong religious convictions. For them, too, the Decision and the purpose of this meeting were important.

The speakers filed in together. Kelys brought up the rear, tall and lithe as always, her short hair lightly touched with gray. A brief hush always greeted Kelys's appearances in Wardenberg. They'd heard about her, of course, but they were used to much paler complexions, the blending of Lines being relatively recent here.

The buzz of conversation faded to silence, and the oldest speaker, Carmela of Vaduze, came forward to give the ritual benediction. "Let us gather in Elli. May Elli guide us in Elli's peace."

"Peace to all in Elli," murmured the audience after the required moment of silence. Lisbeï leaned back, apparently nonchalant. Then why did she feel an undercurrent of anguish along with her excitement? It was the first time anyone had spoken publicly of the Notebook, and her first opportunity of hearing how research was progressing. She knew studies of the Notebook had been going on during the three years of the Decision. Kelys had stopped at the Schole several times between explorations to investigate the Archives brought from Litale by the fleeing Harem people. Nevertheless, public discussion of anything connected with the Bethely find was forbidden until the Decision was final, and Kelys wouldn't have broken this rule even if Lisbeï had asked her.

The program listed four talks: one on the site and its surroundings, one on the skeletons and the things found with them, and two on the Notebook itself—a linguistic analysis and an evaluation of the contents. Davie of Belmont gave the first talk, illustrated by numerous photographs, topographical charts, and blackboard diagrams. Since the Assembly of 489, Kelys and others had explored the underground passages several times. These occasionally ran a considerable distance from Bethely, although there were numerous cave-ins. They certainly dated from the Decline and possibly earlier. This was no surprise, nor was the proposed dating of the masonry cells —the end of the Harems, fairly close to the period mentioned by Halde.

There were a few surprises in store, nevertheless. Carmela of Vaduze began her talk. The tiny stature of the skeletons created a stir. And their clothing differed from the usual archaeological finds for that period in Litale, the thread being much finer and the weave much closer. The felt of their hooded capes was covered—or rather impregnated—with some substance that made the garments almost waterproof, a kind of resin, probably pulverized under high pressure. The small sewing kit came from Wardenberg, as did most of the metal objects, but the trademarks dated from at least eighty years prior to the date mentioned in the Notebook. The Notebook itself was a Decline artifact, but the researchas hadn't enough similar material from other digs to establish its exact origin. Carmela gathered up her papers and photographs with a nod of finality. Her talk was over. A murmur of thanks rose from the audience. Some clearly wanted to ask questions, but Carmela had made it clear at the outset that the question period would come after the talks.

Now it was Kelys's turn. Her study of the handwriting in the three parts of the Notebook indicated there were only two people involved—one for the first two parts, although writing at different periods of her life, and Halde for the last part. Kelys then went on to discuss the linguistic features of the second part. Where and when had it been written? She distributed sheets showing comparative details about Old Franglëi. Lisbëi ran her eye over the paper. Nothing new there, anyway, except a clear indication that the variant in the second part was even more archaic then she'd thought, and of a type found mainly in eastern Maerlande. Oddly enough, some of the spelling and vocabulary only matched the kind found in scattered sites predating the Harems.

Domenica of Caresimo rose to speak. She had been one of the auditantas. Lisbëi saw she had aged since their first encounter. Her hair had turned almost completely white. Her single eye squinted shortsightedly over her lorgnon, almost disappearing in the folds of her eyelid as she contemplated the audience. She spoke even more slowly now, in a low, hoarse voice that gave her words a compelling, almost hypnotic quality.

Domenica hadn't dealt with the second part of the Notebook, but with the end, the Testament of Halde, which she had translated. She'd also begun a detailed study of the Appendices of Hallera, as well as the Word before and after the Decision of Karillie, which had called for the Appendices to become part of the Word. She would be studying all commentaries on the Word attributed to Garde or her Compagnas. Not only that: she'd also be looking at the tales, legends, and proverbs based on the Word that were current in Maerlande. It was a question of determining which written and oral material was closest to the dates under consideration, establishing the general compatibility of all these elements, and perhaps in the long run reworking the entire Word accordingly.

Lisbëi sat up. At the same moment she felt someone touch her shoulder and heard Fraine whisper, "That's for you!" She nodded and focused sharply on Domenica's words. Alas, Domenica's research plans were more interesting than any insights she'd managed to derive from studying Halde. The audience already knew Halde's version didn't jibe on all points with the current form of the Martyrdom and the Resurrection; nor did her portrait of Garde correspond to Hallera's description. It now appeared that Halde herself, to judge by her style, differed from the general conception—hardly a major discovery.

Feeling restless and disappointed, Lisbeï stifled a yawn and shifted in her seat. She had hoped to hear something about the second part of the Notebook, and apparently no one had made an effort to study it. Hadn't Kelys found something in the Archives confirming the events described or implied by Halde? Something might come out during the question period. Lisbeï wasn't sure she'd say anything herself, though. She could trust Kelys and probably Domenica not to reveal her identity, but too many questions and too much evident knowledge of the subject might compromise "Litale."

Domenica closed her file and bowed her head. The audience broke into a murmur of thanks.

"Question period is now open," said Carmela, resting her chin on her hands as she scanned the hall. "We'll deal with Davie's talk first."

A series of highly technical questions followed. Then someone from the back of the hall asked, in an embarrassed but resolute voice, about the possibility of fraud. It was a predictable question, which Domenica demolished with the inexorable precision of a grinding tool.

"The second subject?" queried Carmela, her eyes moving over the audience. They stopped for a moment at Lisbeï. Carmela smiled, but Lisbeï shook her head.

"Kelys," a man's voice said from the back of the hall, "you've been careful not to give us any conclusions about the linguistic aspects of the Notebook's second part. Does that mean you haven't any?"

"I have theories, but no conclusions." Kelys revealed her white teeth. "You can draw your own conclusions, Toller."

The name was vaguely familiar, but Lisbeï stopped herself from turning around. Kelys clearly knew the man.

"You've established the fact that the language of the third part is associated with an area bordering on the Great Badlands," the voice went on. "Would this confirm the possibility of Garde and some of her Compagnas having come from the Badlands?"

"As a case in point, yes," said Kelys, smiling again.

"Impossible!" came a very young female voice.

"Where in the Great Badlands would they have lived?" exclaimed another.

"Maybe they passed through," urged a third, "but they didn't live there!"

"Surely the Daughter of Elli could live where she liked," protested another male voice.

"Or maybe the Great Badlands aren't as contaminated as we think," added Kelys, "or not on the outer reaches, at any rate."

Now the audience was astir. Lisbeï expected to hear someone utter the word "abomination," or the more polite "aberration," but no one did, though several certainly thought it. Domenica of Caresimo appeared to be the only Juddite in the hall, and apparently she had no comment to make. Didn't anyone grasp what the exchange between Kelys and this man Toller implied?

"What connection would Halde have with the writa of the second part?" asked Fraine suddenly. "It seems this writa came long before Halde, at the very start of the Harem period. How did Halde come by the Notebook, anyway? From what I understand of the linguistic data mentioned, it would appear to come from the Badlands, isn't that right? It could have belonged to one of the three Compagnas. . . ."

"It would have been found in another cell, in that case," interposed Livine.

Halde's Testament mentioned possible sources of the Notebook on two occasions. Domenica had already cited one, though it wasn't the most telling. Lisbeï felt almost paralyzed with tension, her fingertips icy, her chest constricted, just like the first time she'd sung solo in the Schole Chorale. She wanted to speak, she was afraid to speak. . . . To her great surprise Dougall's voice suddenly rose, a little hesitant and muffled. She could barely see him beyond Ysande's swollen belly.

"Wasn't there a citation just now that—well, seemed to say Halde got the Notebook from Garde herself? Garde gave Halde her personal effects before the demonstration, didn't she?"

Kelys nodded. "Yes. But there's no mention of the Notebook."

Lisbeï held her breath. Surely Kelys would quote the other bit! The one that *spoke* of the Notebook. But the explora stared impassively at Dougall, her long, slender hands folded in front of her. She wasn't going to say anything! It was just like the inner-council meeting in Bethely: one step forward, one step backward! What was she up to now?

A woman's voice spoke up. "Garde can't be the writa of the first two parts," said the voice, calm and sensible. "The Old Frangleï in the second part dates from the early Harem period, about fifty-five years before the events described by Halde according to the established time frame."

"Anyway, what's the connection between the two Gardes?" asked a man's exasperated voice—a different one this time. "That's what we should be asking ourselves, not all this nonsense about these Notebook parts! Halde's Garde is in her thirties, Hallera's in her fifties. It's ridiculous! Why would the Daughter of Elli have an *age*!"

"Because she had a human body," said the slow, solemn voice of Domenica.

"That's not the point," someone remarked.

"Yes it is! The Decision implies the two Gardes are genuine. But they can't be!"

An excited chorus of approval greeted this remark, drowning out Fraine's "Why not?"

"It's too soon to raise this point. . . ." Carmela commenced. Her voice was surprisingly forceful for so frail a body. But the audience had clearly swung over to a rebellious mood, or perhaps the unknown man's protest had encouraged those who'd been silenced until then by the more scientific tone of the meeting.

"We've got to discuss it!"

"The Decision says—"

"It does *not* say the two Gardes are genuine! It doesn't even say one of them is! Only that Hallera's Garde has been deemed authentic by a Decision!"

"But the Notebook—"

"Is declared authentic, yes, but only in the sense that it dates from the right period and was indeed written by Halde. But Halde could very well have falsified the Garde material!"

Always this stupid argument! Lisbeï seethed with exasperation as she watched, half-turned in her chair.

"As Carmela was saying," came Kelys's voice, soaring effortlessly above the fracas, "it's far too early for this kind of theorizing. The Decision encourages us to throw as much light as we can on every aspect of Garde. Nothing more. Anyone who wanted to air her opinions could have done so in front of the auditantas. That was the time for it. For anyone who didn't, this present meeting is not the proper place."

The hall fell silent, and Kelys lowered her voice. "Now is the time for facts, for questions about research methods. Have any of you questions about these?"

"Do the researchas come under the heading of facts or methods?" called a sarcastic female voice.

Carmela and Kelys exchanged a quick glance. Kelys nodded to her.

"Both," said the old Blue.

"In that case, I've got a question about the fact and the method of Kelys. Kelys of Fusco has stayed in Bethely for regular periods over a number of years. She's an expert linguist specializing in archaic tongues as well as a recognized historian. She has a compagna in Bethely—from time to time, anyway. One Antonë of Maroilles who—"

Inarticulate protests burst from every quarter of the hall, but the female voice rose higher: "—who lives in Bethely. A startling discovery concerning Garde is made by Lisbeï, also of Bethely, a pupil of—guess who?—Kelys and Antonë, and the said Antonë calls for a Decision and puts herself forward as Arbitra. Then after the Decision—"

The hall was in an uproar, but shouts of "Let her speak!" could be heard above the protests. The tumult subsided and the woman continued.

"After the Decision Kelys of Fusco organizes a researchas' association for the purpose of touring Maerlande, setting forth the so-called facts, and eliciting new *facts*." The voice dripped sarcasm. "What does it suggest to us about such facts and methods, if you can call them that?"

Again the audience protested, but not so vociferously as before. Lisbeï noted this with disbelief and alarm. The protests died down, and the audience waited for Kelys to respond. She spoke without any show of emotion.

"I wasn't in Bethely when the discovery occurred or during the preceding months. As for my methods and results, anyone can check them by taking the Notebook and doing the same work."

A male voice rose, clear and precise. It was the man who'd spoken at the outset. "Those involved in the Bethely find have gone before the auditantas. It's not necessary or fair to go over this part of the Decision."

A murmur of approval ran through the audience, but the

dissident female voice was not to be silenced. "Antonë was in Bethely, though, as well as this little Lisbeï."

In a flash Lisbeï found herself on her feet, turned to face the audience. "I am Lisbeï of Bethely," she heard herself say. She looked for the woman who'd insulted Kelys and Antonë. It must be that narrow-faced Red staring at her with hostile surprise. "During the past two years I've often asked myself whether I did the right thing in speaking out at the Assembly. But if we in Maerlande have reached the point where we'd rather think people were lying than question our own entrenched beliefs, then I was right and I'm not sorry. At least I'll have let all this poison surface for everyone to see."

She sat down and folded her arms, trembling. Was it rage or the relief of at last being able to tell that other truth—her name? She didn't know. She felt arms enfold her, a head pressing against her neck. Fraine. Then a hand on her arm. Ysande. In the drawn-out silence she lifted her eyes to meet Kelys's gaze, Kelys with her head slightly tilted, perhaps in gratitude, perhaps in approval.

Wardenberg, 4 Juna, 492 A.G.

After the meeting some of us ended up at The Dancing Princess with Kelys—Fraine, Livine, little Dougall. Ysande was too tired. Then there was the man called Toller, apparently an old acquaintance of Kelys. A Blue with no Family emblem. He avoided talking about himself, but you could tell he came from Bretanye —not because of any accent, but occasionally he used telltale expressions or turns of phrase. He's been a Blue for a dozen years at least, judging from some of the things he and Kelys said, and yet he's only in his midthirties. Dougall knows him, too. I got the impression Toller and Kelys made it possible for Dougall to be admitted to the Schole. Quite an influential fellow for a Blue; Dougall seems ready to kiss the ground beneath his feet!

How can I describe him? His thick blond hair is practically white. It must be from the sun. The hair is short in front but fairly long in the back, as is the fashion in Wardenberg at the moment. He's got one of those severe-looking faces: strong jaw, aquiline nose, high cheekbones, and a firm mouth. And as for his eyes, they're very strange: deep-set beneath bristling eyebrows, and very pale blue or gray in color, rather like sammoye eyes, those dogs

*bred in Baltike's far north. I say "strange" because in certain
lights they look like two pools of emptiness. He has a clear,
pleasant voice and makes a point of choosing his words carefully. Very calm, very controlled. A little too much so. One wonders what he's controlling! But at the same time he strikes me as
being very much at ease, and he calls the Capta of Wardenberg
"Sygne," just like Kelys. In any case I can only guess, since people's personal history certainly wasn't the subject of conversation!*

Indeed it wasn't. No one alluded to the fact that she was
no longer "Litale," but Lisbeï of Bethely. She sensed the emotion and satisfaction in Fraine and Livine, however, and could
see the almost maternal pride in her friends' looks (even Dougall's). It made her realize it hadn't been much of a secret
from them, nor perhaps from others. How could she have
been so naïve? And why did they let her go on pretending to
be Litale for so long? That was why they'd accepted her?
Accepted Lisbeï of Bethely—Lisbeï-champion-of-the-truth,
the rebel, the heroine of the story that Fraine or Livine or
even Ysande had built around her (and maybe Dougall?).
They'd accepted her on a misunderstanding.

"Not at all!" protested Ysande. "At least only partly. But
that's partly you, too. Isn't it?" She smiled at her friend.

Ysande was lying in bed, her face as white as the pillow-
case except for two pink spots staining her cheeks. It was
three weeks following the famous lecture, and Ysande was
slow to recover from a difficult birth. The babie had barely
survived and even now might not live long. Lisbeï visited
Ysande every day with Fraine or Livine, and sometimes on
her own. The large house with its fanciful architecture had
become a second home. The small Greens were very quiet
these days and tiptoed along the passages near Ysande's
room.

How had the topic come up? Lisbeï usually chatted about
the Schole or retailed the latest Wardenberg gossip. But today
she'd suddenly found herself harking back to the lecture. Perhaps it was because she'd been officially invited to join the
Haldistas (as they were already called) although she wasn't yet
a researcha or even an apprentice-recuperata. Ysande was
delighted.

"Of course you'll accept!"

"Not yet. I'm not sure—"

"What do you mean, you're not sure? You're interested
in the Notebook, aren't you?"

"Yes, but—"

She couldn't quite understand why, but she preferred working alone on her translation. Anyway, it was mainly the Notebook's second section that interested her, though the first was intriguing too. (Those numbers must surely be a code!) But she and the researchas had differing reasons for their interest, she felt, and what with one thing and another, she'd argued herself into the notion of a misunderstanding.

"But me no buts," insisted Ysande. "You overestimate other people's imaginations. Their idea of you is important, I grant you, but do you think a false idea could survive almost constant contact for long? We're all capable of seeing someone for what she is, even if we're not as perspicacious as you."

Lisbeï raised her eyebrows. Perspicacious? As far as she knew, she'd never displayed her peculiar sensitivity in Wardenberg. In Bethely she'd been with Tula, Mooreï, Antonë, Kelys, and Selva almost exclusively. But her group in Wardenberg showed no trace of the "special empathic faculty," as Antonë described it. She'd had to pay closer attention here, that was all. They found her perspicacious? It must be her capacity for listening when Fraine or the others told her of their dreams, hopes, and fears. She herself rarely spoke of her own hopes and fears, keeping them for her letters to Tula and later for her journal.

At first her friends' confidences had embarrassed and disconcerted her, though it was all very flattering. But it became so fascinating that she soon forgot her surprise at their choice of confidante. Their revelations were a story, and she would lose herself in contemplation of its plot, its contradictions, omissions, and possible hidden meanings. If she spoke at all, it was to suggest variants, possible interpretations. Because of being more or less consciously attentive to the storyteller's emotions, she knew when to say a word and when to remain silent, and she learned to relate to each of her friends on their own terms.

She had no wise answers for direct questions, no counsels to give—her experience of life was too limited. Instead she questioned herself and made others do the same, made them see another side of their fears, hopes, and ideas.

For Lisbeï, it was such an instinctive process that she couldn't imagine anyone using it as a deliberate strategy. (She'd have been very skeptical if someone had suggested she was using it as a kind of mirror-wall, the barrier she'd never been able to erect.) Her friends appreciated her interest and her talent for listening. The real misunderstanding was that in those days she was far more interested in the story than the teller—but perhaps her friends didn't know this.

"Lisbeï, you've got to accept the Haldistas' invitation. Whatever you may be, your fate is linked with the Notebook. Discovering it and revealing its existence the way you did must surely be significant. There must be a pattern to it all."

Ysande was a simple Believra. When the Tapestry altered without reference to one's humble self, it was fate. If one caused it to change, willingly or not, this too might be fate: "All is in Elli." In the first instance, you did your best to absorb the change, wondering if you might have had a hand in it after all, however unlikely it might seem. In the second instance you studied the consequences carefully (if you had time) and pondered why you'd been instrumental in changing the Tapestry and how it all fitted into the pattern, into Elli's design.

Ysande and Fraine had frequent and lively arguments about the Tapestry. Fraine, despite her dualist leanings, didn't go so far as to adopt the extreme Juddite positions. The young Red considered herself a Progressista and had been extremely piqued when Lisbeï had pointed out how close she came to the views of her pet antagonistas in this regard. Good and evil: like Fraine, the Juddites saw them as opposing forces in the universe, though their idea of the source of evil was rather fuzzy. Did it originate with Elli or with some external, equally powerful force? Again like Fraine, the Juddites considered Elli to be ignorant of part of Elli's creation. But this was because Elli had made the mistake of endowing humans with free will. Oh, Elli could make *mistakes*? If you pushed the Juddites a little on this question, up reared the Flawed One, nameless but generally male. Elli, they said, had not corrected this mistake because Elli respected Elli's own laws. Elli was therefore obliged to put up with the continual outrages perpetrated upon Elli's creation ever since.

The logical outcome of this argument for the Juddites— and one loudly touted—was their insistence on as little change as possible and then only with the greatest caution. They clung to each letter of the Word, constantly quibbling, determined not to budge. One of the most frequently recurring themes was the Juddites' conviction that Elli had made a mistake in creating matter in general and the human race in particular. If the human race disappeared from the face of the planet, it wouldn't necessarily be a bad thing. Look at what humans had done and were still doing to the world in which they lived!

At this point the Juddites again came close to the most austere Progressistas, who argued that the human race was a failure, a botched design, an evolutionary flop that should have been content with a dignified exit from the Tapestry. Unfortunately, it seemed determined to reproduce itself even under the present difficult conditions—conditions that must surely signify something about its ultimate fate.

Fraine was to bring up this argument repeatedly after Ysande's death, several weeks later. Again and again it resurfaced—when Fraine produced a second stillborn childe a few months after this, when the third died two years later, and even when she'd been officially declared Blue, the year of her twentieth birthday.

8

Ysande had been dead for two weeks when Lisbeï found a letter from Tula waiting for her on her return from the Schole. It dated from the previous month. Among the dull trivia of Bethely and the days of Tula-the-Mother-to-be, she found the following passage:

One of the new males has arrived in Bethely. He's a Kergoët-Wenzel called Andre, which means "man." Funny, isn't it: a man called "man"? Selva chose him at the last Assembly. It's a good Line. They make lots of males. He's rather old, though, nearly twenty-nine. When they get to thirty their sperm is sometimes less effective, and then you never know, it can happen so suddenly. Oh, well. His production record is impeccable in the Families where he's served, and anyway, it's a useful alliance. That's why Selva picked him over Gualientès. Now Kergoët will trade part of their preserved goods for our fabrics. He seems nice enough, though. . . .

Lisbeï dropped the letter on the table. What did she care about new males in Bethely! Why did Tula mention it? Might as well tell her about that Angresea Male while she was at it! The Male with whom Tula would be Dancing for the first time at the Celebration. But she'd said nothing about it, nor would she, of course. Just the way she no longer mentioned the famous Dance she'd begun to train for with Kelys, the year of the Bethely Assembly. Forbidden ground, reserved for Reds and the Mother, the Dance of the Pairing!

Lisbeï rose, went to the open window, and stood there contemplating the geometric patterns of the rooftops in the warmth of Juna. The smells and sounds of Wardenberg eddied through the evening air. Elli was still alight. People were busy hanging garlands of small colored lights along the narrow streets and staircases. They weren't illuminated yet, but their very presence seemed to heighten the feverish atmosphere of the Citadel two days before the Celebration.

In the rest of Maerlande the Celebration was a strictly Family affair, but in Wardenberg it attracted visitors from neighboring Families. Fortunately many of the city's temporary residents, especially those attending the Schole, went back to their own Families for the holiday, thus restoring the balance somewhat. The Schole closed for two weeks, allowing time for traveling before and after the celebration.

Wardenberg's festivities were far more entertaining than the Bethely equivalent. There were music and drama festivals, and a local version of the Fair. Instead of being confined to one specific area, this Fair took place in all the shops and eating places of the Citadel, spilling out into the wider streets, the squares, and every available flat space. Then of course there were the Family Games held on the Coast, including all sorts of water sports. Lisbeï had passed most of her time at the Games during her first Celebration in Wardenberg, particularly as several Greens from Ysande's and Fraine's families had taken part that year. The second Celebration had been spent at the music festival, since Lisbeï belonged to the Chorale and the Orchestra. She'd promised herself the drama festival this year, but Ysande's death made everything seem gray and futile.

In Bethely, when a youngster over eight died accidentally, or when a Red died in childbirth or a Blue died of old age or some illness, the departed's closest friends gathered for the dolore. Each of them evoked some memory she felt to be meaningful, and together those present tried to reconcile the sometimes contradictory pictures of their vanished friend.

They tried to understand how the broken thread of this life fitted into the ever-renewed Tapestry. In Wardenberg there was a similar custom. The "mourning." Curiously enough, at Ysande's mourning Lisbeï had been unable to evoke much—despite her penchant for telling stories—apart from describing their first meeting, with Ysande smiling as though at an old friend and saying, "Hello, Litale." At this point Lisbeï had burst into tears.

Fraine, usually the life of the group, no longer cared for the theater or anything else. Her whole emotional force was taken up with trying to swallow the helpless rage that had gripped her with Ysande's death. And fear, fear that grew as her own belly swelled. Livine spent almost every minute with her. Lisbeï hadn't had a problem with Fraine's first pregnancy, but this time she fretted at having to listen to her, kept saying the wrong thing, and felt awkward simply sitting there saying nothing. Fraine saw it and was hurt. To spare her further pain, Lisbeï avoided seeing her as often as she used to, outside of Schole, feeling a little less guilty because Livine was so faithful in keeping Fraine company.

Neither of them intended to take part in the Celebration festivities, and Lisbeï found herself alone in Wardenberg once more. She chose to be alone, in fact. Others in the group, not as close to her as Fraine and Livine, had invited her to go with them. She'd declined. Dougall had left, having at last been selected for Service at the end of Maïa. He had departed for Escarra in an aura that told of mingled regret, fear, and hope. But Lisbeï needed no one to walk with in the Citadel these days. She no longer lost herself in its labyrinthine ways, and in any case she didn't want to walk around the Citadel. She had taken a few books out of the Library and fully intended to put all this free time to good use. There were passages in the second part of the Notebook that still defied translation, and she would certainly spend her time more profitably working on them rather than wasting her funds in the shops.

Lisbeï/Journal

Wardenberg, 21 Juna, 492 A.G.

I've just finished a translation of the Notebook's version of "The Hundred-Armed Giantess." It's very close to the Fersheim variant, the oldest known version. The Notebook version is transcribed rather than retold and is clearly based on an oral recital. For example, there are notes as to audience reaction (laughter, the fairly ritual questions, and so on). If this tale was collected during the Harem period, especially early on, it's difficult to imagine how the person who wrote it down gained access to the Harem women. Judging by the storyteller's remarks and commentary from the audience, the latter were evidently pregnant or fertile women. But we know the Harems kept them apart, under pain of death if they should leave or be seen. The annotations all indicate that the writa heard what went on, and I tend to think she was present but separated from the others, perhaps by a thin curtain. Why? How? The Harem authorities would hardly allow collectors of folklore to wander around their gynaecea! Anyway, there weren't any collectors of folklore. The most likely explanation would naturally be that the writa was a Harem woman who later escaped. She must have been a privileged individual since she knew how to write—one who watched over the others in fact.

All very well, except the supervisas were supposed to be unshakable fanatics. Anyway, is it likely one of these ferocious creatures would have been interested in gynaeceum tales?

Perhaps she was spying for her masters? It's a possibility. But no more likely than the first hypothesis, and in any case I don't like it. I much prefer my idea that the Notebook belonged to Garde and that she was the first to write in it. Still, I have to admit the theory seems fantastic, with nothing to prop it up except Halde's testimony. And even Halde said nothing about Garde actually writing in the Notebook. On top of it all, there's the time lapse between the writing of the beginning and the end of this second part. (Why do I want it to be Garde so much? Because she'd have liked stories the way I do?) But of course the Notebook isn't supposed to be for my enjoyment, after all.

Well, I'll have to shelve that theory along with the others until I've translated more text. We'll see whether or not the rest confirms my idea.

The sound of the Citadel bell clanging wildly caused her to lift her eyes from her notes. The outgoing tide. The luminous square of the window showed softer colors now, rose-tinted. Sunset already?

She put down her pen, stretched, yawned, and rubbed her eyes. Her shoulders ached. She had kept her nose to the grindstone all afternoon. Pretty silly of her. She pushed her papers aside, her head still buzzing. The Notebook always left her in this excited state. But when everything was put away, she regretted stopping. What was there to do now? She couldn't start in again right away. Eat something, maybe? At least the kitchen would be empty. They must all be out swimming.

At the bottom of the stairs she stopped instead of turning right toward the kitchen. She wasn't really hungry. She could easily take a short walk, or even go for a swim—why not? She climbed the staircase four steps at a time, donned a short tunic that salt water wouldn't harm, and went down again.

The wreaths were alight and the little lamps stood out from the shimmering sky like precious stones: unusual blues, greens, yellows, and reds. Rare colors, brighter than nature, *electric*. They formed shining archways beneath which Lisbeï let herself be swept by the crowd, descending to Level One and onto the wide quays encircling it.

The tide was beginning to ebb, and already a crowd had gathered in the water. People clambered down staircases, jumped or were pushed in from the quays, shrieking with laughter—especially the little Greens, some fully dressed, some in light tunics, and some stark naked. The sea was still chilly at this time of year, and a wind had sprung up. The setting sun no longer warmed the bathers as they emerged from the water, and they quickly made room for newcomers, spraying them as they shook the water from their bodies. Traditional greetings were exchanged: "All in Elli," "And as Elli." They followed the sea over the spongy sand as the water retreated from the quays. Everyone who wanted to observe the tradition would bathe, leaving the sea to retreat to the horizon, carrying with it all the impurities of body and spirit. They would go home to shower, put on their holiday clothes, and dine copiously, especially those who were to Dance and had been fasting all day, as custom required before the Celebration. Sumra solstice: the night when the two halves of Elli became one.

The night of the Celebration, which Lisbeï had spent in her room for the past two years, all windows shut.

But after showering with the others in the pension and going back to her room, Lisbeï could hear them laughing and calling to one another from floor to floor. She looked around her little room, vaguely irritated at the sight of the Notebook copy on her table and the neat pile of notes. Why should she shut herself up again? Shut herself up from what? She'd turned eighteen a week earlier. Hadn't she earned the right after all this time to know what happened at the Celebration? She resolutely took out her handsomest tunic-dress, the white one Fraine had given her last year for her birthday, with the double eagle of Wardenberg embroidered in gleaming thread on the breast and back in her favorite shades of blue and violet. It had never been worn. She checked her belt purse to make sure she had enough funds and went downstairs to mingle with the joyous and, for once, noisy crowds streaming through the Citadel.

The gray stones of the Citadel were shot with scarlet. A minor eruption in the distant Feloyt chain a few days earlier had combined with the ever-present clouds above the sea to produce quite spectacular sunsets. The geology Tutress for Lisbeï's group had explained how volcanic activity and earthquakes might be among the long-term consequences of the melting ice that had changed the face of the continents over a thousand years earlier. The Earth, disturbed in its sleep by human depredations, still quivered and groaned. . . . And yes, the climate was changing again and so would the Earth. As ice thickened once more over the poles and mountains, the waters would keep on receding. The land submerged so long ago in the Decline would reappear; the seasons would go on changing, and the plants and animals dependent on them would move to new latitudes or perhaps evolve into new forms. One cycle in the Dance of Elli would come to an end as another began, and no one could tell exactly when the beginning and end would occur. Somewhere within the delicate equilibrium of the elements, a threshold would be crossed, something would have shifted—something the Believras called the Love of Elli, and everything would kaleidoscope into new patterns that would take generation upon generation of humans to decipher.

This hidden relationship of fire and water over time fascinated Lisbeï, as did the mutual fulfillment of earth and water. All things, or almost all, in the Tapestry of Elli touched the fate of the rest in some way or other. How comforting to be part of such a consistent universe, but how disquieting to be so ineluctably responsible. . . .

As in Bethely, the actual Fair began to shut down at sunset. The smell of succulent food wafted out from the few eating places still open. The gasoles had been turned off, leaving only the torches with their strong odor of resin and the garlands of lanterns to light the Citadel in the hours preceding the Celebration. The little Greens scampered through the narrow streets and galloped up the staircases, their shrill shouts and laughter reverberating from the walls. Every once in a while the wind carried a burst of harmonious sound from Level Three, where the music festival still had a few hours to run. Soon the Greens, drowsy with Solstice Wine, would go home. It was the same all over Maerlande. Lisbeï felt dizzy with the onset of one of those migraines that sometimes overwhelmed her in the midst of a crowd. This Celebration crowd was especially disruptive, and she found it more difficult than ever to shut out the huge, excited aura enveloping her.

She stopped in front of a stall where an artisan was putting things away, her heart gripped by the unexpected sight of the bright materials with the Bethely trademark clearly visible. No, she mustn't think of Bethely, not now, not tonight! She turned away resolutely at the same instant that a well-known voice cried out quite near her, "Lisbeï!" It was Marcie, one of the Blues in her Schole group, with her inseparable compagna Bertia and two middle-aged Reds who were strangers to Lisbeï. On this Celebration night they wore tunics of solid red, though with typical Wardenberg flair these were embroidered with ingenious variations on the ancient blacksmith emblem. "Would you like to come with us?" asked Marcie after introducing the two Reds, whose names went right out of Lisbeï's head a minute later. She hadn't any real reason to refuse and so fell in with the quartet.

Great pools of shadow interspersed with flickering torchlight or rainbow constellations of lanterns: this is how Lisbeï remembers Wardenberg on that night. The familiar landmarks had melted away. She felt lost in the Citadel after following her friends up and down stairs or along winding streets, past terraces and shops, from one level to another. Shapes and colors of dreamlike vividness sprang out from the darkness at each turn. A gymnata spun within a circle of silent spectators. Seemingly lighter than air, she played with the sequined and feathered ring, tossing it tirelessly upward. Her body leapt and twirled beneath the sparkling wheel—a slender, adolescent body, almost naked, gleaming in the torchlight. A group of very young Reds gathered around a shadow play. Two storytellers manipulated lacy, perforated wooden templates while a third punctuated each episode with sharp flute trills. It was "The Tale of the Lost Princess," a Baltike variant inserted in the Princess saga after the point where she finds the treasure in the cave. She has gained the Cave-Spirit's friendship. With the Spirit's help, she gives birth to magic children whom nothing can harm, but she herself loses her way trying to get back to them in the Cave. The shadows flickered on the walls as the story unfolded, and some of the youngest Reds, caught up once more in their childhood, took up the dialogue between the Princess and her Wicked Hive Queene. The story was as familiar to them as Lisbeï's Bethely version was to her. She longed to hear it all, but her friends dragged her off toward other fragmentary images framed in the chiaroscuro of the narrow streets. Now came a farandole of masks, false beards, huge mustaches, bristling, frowning eyebrows, and gaily painted papier-mâché phalluses. And all at once grotesquely protuberant figures danced toward her shouting incomprehensible words, their voices metamorphosed by the masks. She stood still, paralyzed with shock. But the farandole circled the two Wardenberg Reds and began singing and beating them with the phalluses. The Reds tried to grab the bright objects, laughing until they could hardly breathe.

Other Families, other ways, thought Lisbeï. The Bethely Celebration had far more decorum. But she wasn't in Bethely now. Tula was in Bethely. Tula, who this night would become the Mother, Tula who would lead the Dance for the first time with her Male! Lisbeï tried not to think about it.

But a voice spoke from behind. "They're a lot more reserved in Litale, aren't they?" She turned around. A man's voice, Toller, Kelys's friend or a relation of some kind. How did you say "friend" when it was a man? He was wearing a long, tawny jacket with no emblem, the jacket of a wandera, a peregrina, because he *was* a kind of peregrina, a . . . travella like Antonë who visited Maerlande Families, but he had never settled anywhere the way she had. His eyes seemed black in the shadow. He smiled rather sarcastically at Lisbeï.

Marcie and Bertia stood by curiously. Lisbeï was about to introduce them, but the two older Reds apparently knew him very well and even seemed glad to see him. The oldest told him her firstborne had recently become Red and was taking part in the Games as well as the parade, and had a good chance in the races. Toller was visibly pleased by this news, although he looked as though he couldn't quite place the Red. Had he done his Service at Wardenberg at some point? Marcie, not one to be reticent like Lisbeï, didn't hesitate to ask. The Blue nodded. "With Sygne," interposed the Red proudly. Lisbeï hadn't known it was a matter of pride. The Mother's Male was used by other compatible Reds; what was so remarkable about having childreen of his Line? But this was Wardenberg. Other Families, other ways.

They chatted a while longer, the Red asking whether Toller was staying at the Residence again. Yes, he said, and something strange passed between them, something . . . complicitous? He excused himself after this, saying he must join friends on Level One. Toller walked off in one direction, Marcie and her friends in the other.

Lisbeï tagged along, and after a while realized they were heading for Level One. A lot of people were going this way, in fact. They wore only light tunics and robes, despite the night chill. Red and blue and every color but green, the tide of Wardenberg celebrantas flowed down to the port. Others watched them pass, either in silence or with a murmured blessing. Faces swam briefly out of the shadow: a sad-eyed old woman, a frowning young one beneath an outlandish red hat, two craggy male faces, two men with brush-cuts—two Blues who could celebrate Elli if they wished, but who would not join the flow. They had the right, though; why did so few avail themselves of it? And in front of them stood another man wearing a tawny leather vest, a man with thick, pale hair, pale eyes, a face she recognized only after it vanished, and the pale eyes had seen Lisbeï, too. Toller, once the Male of Sygne of Wardenberg. She forgot him as soon as she set foot on the quays.

The flow didn't halt here, but streamed down the steps to the strip of sand and shingle left by the retreating sea, now invisible in the distance. A brazier glowed on the sand—no, it was the platform covered with torches, greenery, and flowers. (The petals and leaves would be buried next afternoon in the small gardens and terraces of the Citadel, and in the fields and vineyards of the Communes. The sea would have engulfed the denuded platform.)

Lisbeï had lost her friends while she lagged behind. They hadn't noticed, and she hadn't called to them. Now she walked slowly along as the crowd of celebrantas flowed by. No more masks and painted phalluses. No more shouts and laughter. If anyone spoke, it was in hushed tones. But soon all voices fell silent. Lisbeï was far away from the platform, but she could see it clearly, silhouetted on its pylons in the night against the backdrop of the Citadel. Behind the flaming torches the mass of the Citadel rose blackly. The garlanded arches and wall sconces in the narrow streets no longer twinkled and flickered in the night, and the windows were dark. Only the stars and platform torches would light the Celebration, joined this night by the moon rising white and swollen above the Citadel's pointed roofs.

Despite the great silence, a soft rustling ran through the crowd. Lisbeï sensed, then saw, movement beside her. People were turning one to another, and now her right-hand neighbor touched her on the arm (Lisbeï sensed the haze of fervor in the aura) and handed her something, a large goblet, gleaming silver in the moonlight. A dark liquid, smelling strongly of balsam, glimmered in the bottom. Was it merely pleasant or inebriating? Impossible to tell. But no doubt she had to drink some and pass it on to her left-hand neighbor. The liquor was both harsh and sweet; her teeth ached, but it slid down her throat, rich and hot.

Three times from three different goblets: one for the Woman, one for the Man, and one for Elli who is the beginning and the end. The goblets pass haphazardly from hand to hand. Where they begin or where they end, nobody knows. Perhaps the same goblets reappear after being filled anew, following other paths—like Elli, the beginning, the end. But soon all the celebrantas will drink, and the circulating goblets will weave together all the threads of the living warp around the still-deserted platform.

Lisbeï, unfamiliar with the ritual, has drunk more than three times now, and her head is spinning. Or is it because of the crush of near-naked bodies, the enormous sense of expectation swelling and quivering like an almost palpable fog above the crowd? She feels parched, hot, and what's that roaring in her ears? Is the sea returning already? No. The burning sensation stabs through her body, a burst of red fire breaking in successive waves in time to her heartbeat . . . but is it her heart? It's beating inside, outside, seething through her veins and over her skin. All sensations become knife-sharp, transfigured and painful in their plenitude: the colors washed pale by the moonlight, the distant torches on the platform, the smell of the invisible sea still permeating the sand, the radiant heat of close bodies and their sudden musky, greedy odor. And the brazier within her unexpectedly bursts into flame with a blinding ardor, sweeping away every other sensation.

That was the moment they used to kill them, the males who'd become sterile—the moment when the heat of the drug exploded and shot through their bodies, beating against the constraint of skin and finally bursting forth in a cry of joy, cruel and timeless. Here and there in the crowd, random cries rise as the drug takes effect at different moments. When the males, the worthless males, used to cry out in the ecstasy of their Goddess, the Hive priestesses slit their throats. But now when the cries multiply and grow more shrill, it isn't blood that responds to the call, spattering the flowers on the platform, but two naked, gleaming figures. Lisbeï feels a knot of heat within her body, imploding and devouring itself rather than blossoming into a shout, and she groans *Tula?* almost inaudibly as she bites her lips and tastes the insipid blood while far, far away in Bethely, Tula and the Male are undulating toward one another in the first figure of the Pairing.

Lisbeï feels herself undulating too, feels a body undulating but not her own or perhaps it is thousands of bodies—she no longer feels them around her but in her and she in them, she is all the celebrantas just as they are the Mother and the Male. She shuts her eyes in horror, struggling with all her might not to let go of the slender thread linking her own body and spirit. She lifts her hand to her mouth and bites it viciously until the pain cuts through her trance and she can hear again—hear thousands of bare feet hammering the ground in time to thousands of rhythmic pantings—and until the pain opens her eyes to those thousands of bodies moving together, gliding, bowing, and stretching like a single body in the figures of the Dance.

She moves too. Moves to avoid them. At first she tries to move with them. But she can't, she doesn't really know how, despite the resemblance to the parade. She steps backward, forward, stopping and starting, and oh! the solitude of her lurching gestures within the great body of the Dancing crowd. But little by little she reaches the edge of the Celebration and steps beyond it onto the cold sand, beyond the powerful, dark, and joyous aura of collective desire.

She runs. Over sand, over shingle, slippery rocks, paving stones, anywhere, just running and murmuring convulsively, "Elli, Elli." It is a prayer: *Elli, spare me; Elli, pardon me,* but you don't ask things of Elli, and she has nothing, nothing to offer Elli except the scarlet veil before her eyes and the rumble of fever in her flesh. She runs through the moon-slashed shadow as though she can escape the drug coursing through her, escape the voracious pit of desire that only the Dance, the Pairing can fulfill, yet how would she know this, she who has never been a Red, never learned the Dance? She runs, her lungs on fire, runs beneath the milky gleam of the moon and now suddenly it is dark, she stumbles and falls.

She lies there panting, each breath tearing her lungs. The burning void within is devouring her. She tries to listen, to see where she might be, but all her perceptions are distorted and magnified, a dark, lacy sky moving above her (trees?), a pulsating buzz (insects?) . . . And the beating of her huge heart shakes the whole Earth. She shuts her eyes to find not peace but a hazy fire of pink then red then blackish-crimson flames endlessly sputtering. Like an unseen panic, and she wants to see what is seething so within her and yet she mustn't open her eyes or all will be lost. She must keep them closed, must watch her crumbling body, powerless to comprehend, to act, must feel the spiral of her perceptions tighten about her consciousness, choke it off, extinguish it . . .

And then a liquid, quivering sound washes over this shrinking universe in long, whispering waves—*lllliiiiiissssbeiiiii, llliiiisssbeii*—and suddenly another universe materializes at the limits of her own, at first just a speck, but then swelling to a surface, the surface of her skin, a hand on her shoulder and another light, another aura, urgent and strong—*Tula?*—an infusion of life, and the light fills the void, reverses the lethal spiral, extinguishes the fire. Lisbeï does not open her eyes. She puts her arms around the body of her savior, drawing it close. Not Tula, too large, too hard, different, and she knows all too well Tula is far away, that on the platform bleeding with flowers and flames Tula is gliding toward the

Male in the final figure of the Pairing, and Lisbeï lets herself
glide, too, as the limits of these bodies, hers and this other,
become faint but still distinguishable in the mounting wave of
light within her, and within is without is within and the waves
leap against each other, with each other, shooting upward
through the light.

9

Lisbeï awoke to find herself at the foot of the water tower in
the little park surrounding the Residence. No wonder she'd
collapsed: she'd run without stopping all the way from the
Port to the top of the Citadel! Someone had covered her with
a tawny-colored jacket. She recognized it, although she'd
have known who left it anyway. Invisible birdas twittered in
the trees, and the sun, already quite high, filtered through the
trembling leaves of the globe-birches. Lisbeï gathered the
shreds of her beautiful dress around her, knotting the ends to
create a semblance of clothing and anchoring it all with her
belt. Then she threw the jacket over one shoulder and, without thinking, began walking up the path to the Residence.

There were no sleepers wrapped in each other's arms, the
way there were in Bethely in those last years when she used to
wander through the eerie silence and immobility of mornings
after the Celebration. She doesn't remember very clearly what
she was thinking as she followed the path. Blurred thoughts,
neither images nor ideas, darted through her exhausted mind
like furtive fish in troubled water. She had almost Danced. So
this was the Pairing. She had seen it, at least. The illuminated
platform, the bright shapes of naked bodies beneath the
moon. On this morning three years ago *she* would have been
the Mother. The bittersweet smell of the oily liquid gleaming
in the proffered cup. The pleasure. Why had no one ever told
her of the pleasure of the Celebration? The tearstained face
of Selva floating in the dark glass, and the rage, the shame,
the despair that had swirled about the small room. Lisbeï and
Tula, speechless, going back to their separate cots and never,
never talking about what they'd seen.

And you, Tula, did you feel pleasure with your Male?

Later, trying to write it all down, she would have to stop here. The magical release of putting things on paper wouldn't work. Three scratched-out pages of attempted description, and then the sudden tears, incomprehensible, surprising tears, and the certainty of having truly lost Tula this time without knowing why. The letter ended there—the first letter she would write without even pretending it was intended for Tula.

A small Green of about ten opened the door to her uncertain knock. All at once she wondered what she meant to do. She stood in the entrance hall, a large room with well-polished paneling. The Capta's household was astir despite the Celebration, and breakfast aromas wafted toward her. The little girl had ash-blond hair, very white skin, and pale, oblique eyes squinting in the sunlight. So striking was the childe's resemblance to Toller that Lisbeï couldn't speak. The childe stared at her for a moment, then politely held out both hands, offering the greeting customary on the day after the Celebration. "Happiness in Elli, compagna; will you take breakfast with us?" All were welcome in every household on this day, in Wardenberg as in Bethely.

Their hands touched, and both the childe and Lisbeï quivered, shaken by a brief and intense resonance that faded as Lisbeï let go. The two gazed at each other for an instant, then the childe turned, motioning Lisbeï to follow.

In the large common room the faces around the oval table turned toward her in smiling welcome. Sygne was there, slim and blond, back for the Celebration from Foloten, where the Baltike Assembly had taken place that year. To her left sat her mother and second Memory, Ireyn, the Schole capta. On her right sat Utika, her compagna, first Memory, and "cousine" as they said here. Childreen of assorted ages stopped their chatter to stare curiously at Lisbeï, as did two young Red women seated among them and the Blues who were doing the serving. Across the table from the Mother sat Toller, holding a spoon to the open mouth of an infante barely a year old.

Apart from Ysande's household, Lisbeï hadn't visited many Wardenberg families. Livine's family had Juddite views and considered her virtual leap from Green to Blue a disgrace; on the few occasions she'd been in that household, Lisbeï had noticed how different the atmosphere was from the friendly rough-and-tumble of Ysande's dwelling. The childreen were off by themselves, and the adults paid little attention to them unless the older Greens in charge couldn't impose discipline. Adult irritation or indifference toward childreen seemed to be the rule, and Fraine had confirmed it, explaining this was often the case in Wardenberg. No doubt this attitude masked a great deal of feeling, but the children perceived it as a barrier. Fraine's family affections were for her sisters and cousines, not the mother or "aunts" of the preceding generation. It was the Wardenberg way of staving off the all-too-certain threat of grief at lost children. Very often the adults would keep their distance even after the critical age of childehood had passed. Lisbeï thought back to the gruff but genuine affection of the Reds and Blues—even the gardianas—for all Bethely children. Perhaps the Litale system wasn't so bad after all. . . .

But never had she seen anyone but a woman take care of children! And here was Toller, turning back to the infante, clearly used to the task of feeding small childreen, while the infante in question howled lustily at the sight of the spoon just out of reach.

"Lisbeï," said Ireyn, adroitly intervening before the newcomer's silent gaze at Toller and his spoon of mush became downright rude. "Welcome in Elli. Come and sit down."

Did they all know? Did they all see that . . . ? With a superhuman effort, despite the ringing in her ears, Lisbeï managed to explain without stammering that she had found the jacket in the park and had seen Toller wearing it.

"Yes, he said he'd met you," said Sygne, completely matter-of-fact. "How kind of you to bring it back. But sit down, you must be hungry."

The only free chair was beside Toller. She sat down, her legs suddenly weak as she realized she was ravenous. The Celebration had this effect, as she knew from having witnessed the mounds of extra food prepared in Bethely for the occasion, and in Wardenberg too. One of the drug's side effects, maybe? Or was it all the energy dissipated in the Dance? But she hadn't the strength to even pretend to be rational, not right away. Later she'd try to work it out. For the moment she was too hungry.

And so, half-naked in the shreds of her beautiful dress, she spent the day after her first Celebration in the household of the Wardenberg Capta. Somehow she found the strength to hold her own in the friendly chatter about life in the South,

Bethely, her studies in Wardenberg, the Kergoët Assembly and the concerns of Baltike, the music festival, the unofficial results of the Games . . . Now and then Toller chimed in, but mostly he played with the childe on his lap. He appeared to share the infante's enthusiasm for the spoon, picking it up and handing it to her each time she promptly tossed it back onto the floor. When the children left the table, taking the babie with them, he relinquished his small charge with evident regret—a regret felt equally by the abandoned infante, judging by her noisy exit.

Lisbeï was invited to dinner—she refused—and asked whether she'd attend the music-festival finale next day—probably—and whether she was planning to take part next year—maybe. At last they let her get up to go.

Toller accompanied her to the door. "I simply told them I'd lost my jacket," he said, not looking at her. Was he embarrassed? But no resonance emanated from him beyond this strong will to control his emotions. They reached the door, and Lisbeï, despite the ridiculous nature of the question, despite its rudeness (but what was one more impropriety on this totally strange morning?) couldn't help herself. How many of Sygne's childreen were his? He was silent for a moment, as though estimating her ability to take in his answer. "Just the oldest, Gudrun, and the second, Emelyne." And then, with his quick wry smile. "But I'm on excellent terms with the Capta of Wardenberg and her family."

The smile vanished. "Lisbeï," he said, his voice suddenly urgent and serious, "never drink agvite unless you're about to Dance or if—" he hesitated an instant, "don't drink if you're alone at the Celebration. That drug has some really dangerous effects and could even be fatal if . . . if you aren't taking part in the Pairing. All right?"

She had a clear sense of an aura resonating with anxiety and sorrow and tinged with bitterness. Then it disappeared as though it had never existed. Lisbeï stood staring at the Blue, her mind full of the confused memories of the previous night, memories that refused to sort themselves out. The light, yes, she remembered it distinctly, she hadn't been dreaming: the same bright evanescence she sensed with Kelys, with Tula, better than with Tula—but she pushed the thought aside. With a *man*? The *light* with a man?

As he looked at her, his expression once more impassive,

she grasped at what he'd been saying and said the first thing that came to mind. "Agvite. The Hives' drug?"

He looked briefly surprised (or perhaps taken aback) and then slightly amused. "It was your first time," he muttered to himself. "I should have known."

Yes, he went on more clearly, yes, it had been the Hives' drug and earlier the Harems' as well.

Lisbeï was familiar with the drug. Every History book mentioned it. She knew how it was made and what it contained: the essence of a hallucinogenic mushroom and several distilled plant oils. It had rendered the Harem and Hive warrias especially devoted to their masters and later to their mistresses. The recipients became highly responsive to suggestion, and then there were the aphrodisiac side effects (if not short-circuited by some other suggestion), which increased the user's dependence.

But Lisbeï hadn't known that agvite formed part of the Celebration ritual. The Pairing was a *Mystery,* the only one in the worship of Elli. (She'd recognized Mooreï's word in an ancient tome at the Schole and had found it appropriate after Carmela had explained its context.) No one mentioned it, except among initiates. In the months preceding the Bethely Assembly, Tula, for example, had simply learned the figures of the Dance and nothing more. There'd been nothing else for her to tell Lisbeï. "They all said nobody could talk about it until afterward, and only with people who'd taken part in a Celebration," she'd said. "The others can't understand." Tula was embarrassed because Lisbeï had already told her she wouldn't Dance once she'd been declared a Blue, or if she did, it would only be when Tula herself led the Celebration.

Aware now of her ignorance and remembering the cause, she looked away from Toller. She too was embarrassed, even irritated. Was she supposed to thank him? Instead she heard herself retort almost accusingly, "You weren't at the Celebration yesterday."

"I no longer Dance." He frowned slightly as he said it. "Thanks for bringing the jacket back. Good day, Lisbeï." He turned on his heel and went back into the Residence.

Lisbeï walked along the narrow streets toward her pension. Only the big striped cats of Wardenberg, with their curious corkscrew tails, watched her pass as they began to warm themselves on balconies and doorsills. The pension was silent. She went to wash, alone in the showers for once, then returned to her room. She wavered between the table and the bed, unable to make up her mind, then sat down to write the letter to Tula that she would never finish, the letter that was not to Tula, a letter to be slipped into the drawer with all the other, unsent letters.

She wept long into her pillow and at last lay staring at the ceiling, exhausted. She tried to sleep but couldn't stop her whirling thoughts. Rather than let them resurface in tears, she decided to concentrate on what she had just learned, imitating that other Lisbeï, the observant, sensible historian.

What had prompted the use of agvite in the Celebration ritual? Wasn't it one of the most obvious signs of past barbarism? It was already astonishing enough to realize that the Hive women had preserved this symbol of their enslavement, considering how eager they were to obliterate all trace of the Harems. Balte of Gualtière had an explanation that Lisbeï had tried to digest without much conviction: the very fact of agvite being a symbol of their slavery was what led them to keep it, first of all to show they were free to use it as they wished, and then to turn the tables on the males by subjugating them through the drug, a situation they viewed as the essence of justice. And then the drug heightened the warrias' performance—made them feel invincible, insensible to injury —an element not to be scoffed at, given the Hives' almost constant internecine warfare. But Lisbeï had hardly been insensible, had she? She was willing to believe in the power of suggestion, and there were plenty of documented instances, but *her* sensations had been heightened to a frightening degree. What suggestion would be strong enough to wipe out such a huge jump in sensorial sensitivity? A jump that would have been disastrous for warrias . . . But probably interesting from the erotic standpoint, since this was meant to be the only so-called side effect. No mention was made of any lethal effects, nor of the need to compensate for lost energy by eating a great deal.

Perhaps the agvite used nowadays was mixed in quite different proportions to take account of these possible effects?

If she asked about the drug, would she get any answers? The manufacture of agvite must be part of the actual ritual and therefore a taboo subject. But after all, she had taken part in the Pairing—well, almost. No one need know she hadn't

stayed until the end. All in all, she now knew what the Celebration consisted of.

She remembers how triumphant she felt at the thought,
yet how disappointed. Where was Mooreï's "beautiful big surprise"? You drank a drug that made you nearly crazy, you
jigged up and down like an automaton, and then when the
Mother and the Male . . . made Elli . . . (Sygne, now she
thought of it, the tranquil, amiable Sygne with whom she'd
just breakfasted, had . . . ?) But Lisbeï hadn't stayed that
long. In all honesty she had to admit she was only guessing.
What she guessed was that, under the influence of autosuggestion stimulated by the drug, the celebrantas shared in the
encounter of Mother and Male, becoming Elli with them for
an instant . . . and it all ended in an erotic orgy, just as Lisbeï had supposed for years now, ever since finding naked
sleepers scattered over the meadows and orchards of Bethely.
And that was the Dance.

Surely not. There must be more to it. Could that be all?
Mooreï wouldn't have been so certain, so serene. But Selva
definitely wasn't sure or serene, and she was the one who'd
Danced until this year. Perhaps the experience differed, depending on . . . on what? The Male with whom one made
Elli? Maybe pleasure wasn't always part of it. Maybe she'd
imagined the pleasure. It must have been autosuggestion, and
probably the effect of the drug. She'd have to find out more
about agvite.

She could consult Schole documents on the origin of the
actual ritual. How did it happen that the peaceful worship of
Elli could incorporate a ceremony so obviously derived from
the sprinna sacrifice of sterile males by the Hives? Of course
the context was different, but the similarities were too numerous to deny. It was an adaptation, a recuperation from the
Hives, like so many other things: the calendar, the Litale garderies, the choice of the feminine as the dominant gender in
all languages (with the exceptions in the Frangleï spoken in
Wardenberg), the renaming of certain animals, certain plants
. . . the list was a long one. And then the Hives themselves
had recuperated plenty of things from the Harems, transform-
ing or adapting them, as the Harems had in turn done with
. . . Successive human societies weren't as cut off from one
another as the Hives (or Edwina of Carlsbad) had thought.
The thread was never entirely severed. Even when it became a
very minor thread, drawn exceedingly fine beneath the main

warp of the Tapestry, it survived. And it was thus that humble tales and legends, proverbs, games, idioms, and even nonverbal behavior, carried a hidden legacy.

It was with a thrill of surprise and pleasure that Lisbeï later discovered the mention of a drug with similar effects, penned by the unknown writa of the Notebook's second section. This writa called it "neopsylocin" and totally disapproved of its use by the men of the Harems.

The Schole would be closed for another week, but the Library had reopened the day after the Celebration. The portress, an old Blue called Olcya, was becoming familiar with Lisbeï's work habits and opened the door without comment before going back to her interminable knitting. Lisbeï had once come upon a fragmentary reference to a legendary woman who wove and unraveled the same piece of cloth to stave off some unknown event—her death, perhaps, thought Lisbeï when she saw old Olcya.

Lisbeï liked getting to the Schole early in the morning, liked the empty corridors and the deserted staircase, the feeling that for a few hours the Library belonged to her, with all its books, documents, and archives. She had long ago established a favorite workplace, a small room with a single window overlooking a tiny garden two stories down. The garden appeared to have no entrance, and yet it was very well kept, as were all gardens in Wardenberg.

The first place to do serious research on the use of agvite was Hallera's Appendices—the original along with contemporary commentaries. She needed at least five major dictionaries and a dozen dialect indexes. Commentatas had come from all over Maerlande, and the Compagna Hallera, a native of eastern Baltike, had used an archaic version of Slavoï that was difficult to understand.

Maerlande had not done away with the Hives all at once after the coming of Garde, despite her gospel of peace. ("Garde the Second," as Lisbeï and many other Haldistas now referred to her.) There had been three years of sporadic warfare, interspersed with equally sporadic negotiations. The trial of Markali and her warrias had only taken place seven years after the events that would later be the subject of the first Decision. The actual Appendices hadn't been assembled and assessed for purposes of the Decision until 122. These were a mélange of notes recording the oral confidences of survivors of Bethely demonstrations, as well as letters and bits of text written by Hallera, tentatively dated prior to 42 After Garde, although the date of her death hadn't really been fixed, and even her burial place was unknown. But it was Hallera's memoirs, recounting the Daughter of Elli's brief passage on Earth, that held the greatest interest.

Not all the material in the Appendices had been considered a valid addition to the Word, however. What had become the Word, after the integration and fusion of many fragments, was the account of the world's creation by Elli, plus Garde's transmitted laws of human behavior as expressed in numerous parables, and the Promise. The approved Appendices contained the story of Garde's martyrdom and resurrection as well as the account of her last days with Hallera, the only surviving Compagna, and the Disciplas of Bethely. This account mentioned details of what would eventually become the Celebration. Garde and Hallera had shown the Disciplas how to come together in Elli so that they might comprehend the full scope of the Promise, and Garde had asked them to repeat this ceremony in her memory.

This was the origin of the taïtche and the parade, and of course the Dance and the Celebration. But there was no description of the ceremony as such and therefore no mention of the drug. Hallera's text already forbade those who had experienced the Celebration to reveal it to the uninitiated. It had to be learned through participation, not study. If anyone, even then, had been amazed at the use or effects of the Hive drug in the Celebration, they never committed it to writing and discussed it only with other initiates. Any deaths resulting from the use of agvite had been kept secret.

The decision of Karillie had been called for because different versions of the Word and the ceremony were in circulation, and the threat of conflict among various groups had arisen. More specifically, many Juddites opposed the presence of a male at the Celebration. The way in which the original ceremony with clearly female partnas had evolved into the Pairing, where the Mother danced with the Male, was a direct result of this Decision, linked to Hallera's commentaries. The Decision concluded that Garde had been able to give only an approximate demonstration of the ceremony to her Disciplas, since they were all women at the time. The Word made it fairly clear, however: Elli was all—male and female among other things, and a male should therefore be the partna of the chosen woman in the Celebration of the Promise. It took a good thirty years for this article of the Decision of Karillie to be fully accepted, nonetheless. By this time it was well established that only the Mother of a family could be this chosen woman.

The Decision also set aside many fragments of the Appendices as apocryphal. The nature of these fragments could only be guessed from the auditantas' testimony, since they had been subject to wholesale destruction after the Decision—an act subsequently regretted and described by historians as an unfortunate survival of the Hive mentality. A few fragments came to light here and there, discovered by chance in some Family Archive because they had slipped in among other papers. These precious relics were sent to Wardenberg.

The accepted Appendices included many fragments describing Garde at firsthand, or through her words and acts. The Decision of Antonë didn't account for the differences between the two Gardes. In relation to Hallera and the testimony of Markali's trial, the personality of the "second" Garde was perfectly consistent: she had known what she wanted and had expressed it in peaceful but strong terms. The other Garde, by comparison, seemed to have been in a highly exalted state and, to be frank, at times a little mad. This second Garde had taught her Compagnas the rudiments of the taïtche and the parade (and practiced with them regularly, according to Halde's description of their last days together). But she had never required them to keep silent on the subject —on the contrary. And she had said nothing about the Dance, the Pairing, or agvite. . . .

Lisbeï wasn't looking into that aspect, anyway, but into the use and effects of the drug. She was hoping to find at least some disguised mention in the auditantas' commentaries. There might be something in remarks concerning "a practice inherited from the Hives," made by Galice of Ermenonve and Justice of Trevise, although their disapproval seemed to hinge more on its coming from the Hives rather than its potential physical threat to the users.

Lisbeï hadn't expected to find much about the drug in the accepted Appendices or the vanished apocrypha, as seen in the auditantas' commentaries or surviving fragments. The accounts of Markali's trial produced more plentiful evidence— in the form of incidental remarks, since the drug wasn't the subject of the trial. Its "illicit" use had occasionally resurfaced (Lisbeï now understood the real meaning of the term) over a period of at least twenty years after the Decision of Markali— years in which the oldest Hive survivors had died off or been converted. Such massive disintoxication couldn't be done from one day to the next.

The only noteworthy detail in the existing Apocrypha was the fact that Ariane, Hallera's daughter, appeared to consider Markali and Alicia as sisters—probably the origin of this persistent legend. No wonder these fragments had been included in the Apocrypha! Oddly, in several of the fragments, Ariane seemed to speak of herself in the masculine, as did Hallera herself and several others—proof of the fragments' lack of authenticity.

It was late at night by the time Lisbeï finished her research and put away the documents and books, satisfied she had done her homework thoroughly. No stone had been left unturned, a principle Kelys had instilled in her.

The following day Lisbeï plunged into the available documentation on the drug as used in the Harems and the Hives. All the sources said the same thing, and nothing new could be gleaned. A single account, which was impossible to date (and was therefore considered unreliable by the historian who cited it) described the physical effects of the drug as including a high fever, sensory hallucinations, a feeling of splitting in two (but not the horrible shattering sensation experienced by Lisbeï), and quick death by "a general overheating of the vital systems" if the subject, excited by the sensations, engaged in "intense physical activity." This hardly seemed likely, unless people's reaction to the drug had changed, since the Hive warrias went into battle after using the drug, and the celebrantas Danced and made Elli. And anyway, Toller had told her in no uncertain terms not to take the drug if she didn't intend to Dance or if she was alone.

How did he know that, by the way?

This time she couldn't stop herself from wondering about the very nature of the man—something she'd been able to avoid until now. He was like Kelys, like herself. Like that disquieting Red, Guiseïa, the Mother of Angresea. And like Tula—although Tula wasn't quite like the others. All children of the Malady, mutants. She really had no difficulty accepting Kelys's remarks in this respect, or what Antonë, as she now realized, had often suggested. It was only logical that men would be equally affected. She shouldn't have been surprised.

But did this mean Toller had undergone the same experience as she had? If so, and since he'd been the Male of at least the Mother of Wardenberg, how had he survived his Service? Or was this precisely his reason for becoming prematurely Blue? But no, one *couldn't* possibly be declared Blue without being proved sterile. How long had his Service actually lasted?

From there it seemed perfectly natural for Lisbeï to look up the Wardenberg Lines, Sygne's and Toller's. This wasn't being indiscreet: he had answered Marcie's query readily, even if he didn't wear his Family emblem.

Angresea.

Lisbeï sat staring at the ship and waves of the insignia in the square containing Toller's name, along with brief details about his Line. Of course the name had been familiar. Toller of Angresea. The "twin brother" of Guiseïa of Angresea. She'd seen his name when looking at Angresea documentation in Bethely, when Selva had at last spoken of the planned alliance. She had even mused briefly on this twin birth and the strangeness of the implied relationship, particularly between a girl and a boy. But how unlike they were! Except for the color of their eyes . . .

The Book of Lines contained nothing about Toller's reasons for becoming a Blue, of course. For such information she'd need to consult medical records after demanding his permission, as was the rule. Unthinkable. But this wasn't the thing uppermost in her mind. She was thinking of Maxime of Angresea, who would have been her first male if she'd become Mother of Bethely and had led the Celebration the year of her sixteenth birthday. In the end she really *had* Danced, and with an Angresea. It was rather comical. Then why were there tears in her eyes, why was she sure she could never tell Tula?

Perhaps in a spirit of defiance, Lisbeï decided the only way to learn more was to ask Toller point-blank about the effects of the drug, since he seemed so knowledgeable. At the Residence they told her he was working at the Schole. That he was a temporary *Tutor* at the Schole in a technical section—optics! There couldn't have been more than a dozen Blue men teaching in the Schole. She waited for him to emerge from a seminar. As might be expected, nearly half of his students were Blue men and Green boys. Seeing Lisbeï standing at the laboratory door, Toller raised his eyebrows but seemed neither irritated nor embarrassed, whatever his memories of the Celebration incident. Nor did he appear disconcerted by the direct question she put to him once they had the corridor to themselves. "Yes, I had the same experience," he said, very calm.

Clearly, he wouldn't go into detail, but Lisbeï really wanted to find out whether he knew what he was.

"You developed the Malady late?"

He smiled briefly, as though he knew perfectly well what she was trying to get at—the only sign of any emotion. It was very strange. When Tula or Selva had wanted to hide their feelings, they had raised the mirror-wall. With Kelys, emotions had always been there, but Lisbeï now knew the peregrina could control them pretty much at will. Toller had no perceptible barrier; he just didn't seem to be there. From what she could remember of her two encounters with Guiseïa, it had been the same.

"You too," he said, his tone almost indulgent, as though conceding the point. "And Antonë, Kelys, and a few others."

She decided to shift her approach. "Have you known them long?"

"Antonë spent a few months in Angresea. Kelys is an old friend of the Family. She's the one who explained things to us, before Antonë."

Us? "About the drug?"

"About the drug, too."

"Is there a connection, then?"

"Yes."

They continued walking along the corridor. Guiseïa was like Toller, and the "us" must refer to her. Had Kelys mentioned the Angreseas in Bethely? Lisbeï couldn't remember. Was she the one who advised Selva to arrange the alliance? And was Antonë aware that Kelys knew them well? The Medicina had never mentioned the Angreseas either. But in any case, Antonë had never referred explicitly to the link between the Malady and the mutation. Did she know about the drug's special effect? She had never Danced. . . . Suddenly a brief anguish shot through Lisbeï. But no, surely Tula had been warned. Kelys had trained her for the Dance, and since Kelys knew about the drug, she had surely told Tula. Perhaps the effect differed with the varying mutations? Antonë was one variant, Tula another, Selva too. . . .

"How long have you known?"

"Always. Not always about the drug, though. We were barely ten years old."

She felt an inward shock: it must have been before she was born. Toller—and therefore Guiseïa—were thirty-three. Had they tried the drug as children?

The Blue responded to a surprise she didn't bother to hide. "We were very daring," he said.

At this she thought of Tula, and all at once their own feats of daring seemed awfully tame. She continued walking and said nothing.

"I wonder if Antonë will make her research public now," said Toller abruptly. His thoughts had obviously followed another track.

"What research?"

"On the Malady and its variations over the past hundred years. The last time she wrote us about it, she was beginning to amass a considerable amount of data. In my opinion, she's had enough to go public for some time now. But she's been putting it off because she wanted to be really sure. . . . You know Antonë. And then came the Decision. She almost never writes about her research in her letters, now."

The two letters Lisbeï had received from Antonë since the end of her self-imposed silence had nothing to do with the Decision. She talked mainly about events in Bethely and of her memories of Wardenberg, where she'd studied medicine. Antonë had never written her before, but Lisbeï clearly sensed this wasn't the pre-Decision Antonë. She was more at peace, as though delivered of some burden. Antonë had spoken of Mooreï, too. Well. When Lisbeï compared these few remarks with Mooreï's (the Memory had written regularly every three months since Lisbeï had left Bethely), it was fairly clear where Antonë had found some of her new serenity.

"Antonë never really told us anything about her research," said Lisbeï, slightly annoyed at having to make such an admission.

"I believe your mother has a rather ambivalent attitude toward anything to do with mutations," said the Blue, as though it were a matter of public knowledge. Lisbeï's first impulse was to protest, but she was too astonished. How could she have missed it? She had only to remember how she herself

had been treated in the garderie when she tried to speak
about her special perceptive faculties. What must it have been
like for Selva, alone with such faculties a generation earlier
(Loï hadn't been like Selva, according to Kelys), and with a
mother who had in many ways been virtually an orthodox
Juddite?

It was still strange to think of Selva as anything but the
Mother or the Capta. Selva as a *person*. Selva a little girl or an
adolescent with her half sister Loï and her mother, the difficult Cemmelia. Strange to see Selva in the light shed by
Toller's words, to have to admit Selva had excusable reasons
for her attitude, to reflect that she might have been far worse.

"She isn't the only one," Toller went on, as though talking to himself. "In any case, Maerlande has more urgent concerns. . . ."

Lisbeï felt herself acquiescing, shocked to find she was
agreeing to the same strategy of prudent silence she'd
thwarted so spectacularly three years earlier in Bethely. But
no, it wasn't the same. . . . Why—because she was more personally involved? Because *she* was what the Juddites might
call an "Abomination"? A rather suspect argument. For the
sake of the Notebook she had been willing to be called a liar,
a forger, a manipulated half-wit; what could be more directly
involved than that? Perhaps it was different, now, because she
wasn't the only one involved. There'd been Tula and Antonë,
Kelys, Selva, the two Angreseas, and probably many others. . . .

But within her was that other Lisbeï who wasn't convinced. Selva and Mooreï, and Kelys, and Antonë had been
subjected to the same suspicions—she'd exposed them to the
same suspicions.

But she hadn't really thought her discovery would be attacked. She'd been naïve.

And was she now so worldly-wise? If so, in what light did
it place her actions of three years earlier?

She had become grown-up enough not to try to avoid
such a question, but she hadn't as yet the maturity to find a
satisfactory answer. She felt suddenly uncomfortable, but
luckily Toller changed the subject.

"Anything else you want to ask?" His voice was friendly,
though not devoid of irony.

"Were there many children like you born into the Families where you did your Service?" She was surprised at the

sharpness of his reaction—Toller kept his emotions under such control. His expression hardened as he looked away. She could see the jawbones tighten briefly, hear the cold voice.

"It's a recessive characteristic, apparently. But I don't know them all."

So Sygne must have had it somehow, because that childe the other day—was it Gudrun or Emelyne? Why was he angry? Surely Blues were allowed to talk about childreen? Was it because he'd become a Blue prematurely? Was it perhaps a very hard thing for men to accept, sometimes? She remembered the Nevenici Blue and the occasional remarks in Wardenberg about the profound religious convictions of many Blue men: the redeemers, the servants of Elli. . . . But Toller didn't give the impression of being a *Believer*.

"I didn't mean to offend you," she murmured, embarrassed.

"It's normal. You're a woman, and from Litale."

She stared, dumbfounded. "So?"

"So, women know their childreen. Males don't, especially not in Litale."

It took Lisbeï a little while to realize she had misunderstood the Blue's sudden irritation. What hurt him wasn't his inability to produce more childreen: it was not *knowing* them. What an odd idea! But she realized Toller was right and that she'd truly hurt his feelings because of her unawareness. It had never occurred to her that men might want to know their childreen. "Their childreen." The very expression was bizarre, and yet the childreen were theirs, too, in a way. But to know them . . . the idea was . . . well, a bit ridiculous, no? She'd never thought about this aspect of things, but a normally fertile Male could be instrumental in producing several hundred offspring. During his two years' Service in Wardenberg, Toller himself must have produced . . . at least fifty, if not more! To want to know them—well, why not want to look after them while he was at it!

But that's exactly what he was doing when I went to the Residence. I felt like laughing after my initial shock, seeing him there, spoon in hand, with Sygne's latest babie. I was more scandalized than amused, now that I think about it. A man can't be a . . . gardiana. There's no such thing as a male gardiana—gardian, I suppose—and not just in Litale.

He'd looked pretty handy at it, though.

And after all, there weren't any Green boys or young Blue

men in the taïtche events at the Games, five years ago. (There weren't even Green girls from Litale in the Games before 472!) And a hundred years ago, Blue men weren't allowed to attend the Celebration, not even in Wardenberg. I suppose things are changing.

The conversation lingered a while on this subject—not on childreen, I mean, but on the situation of men in general. All in all, it certainly is a bundle of contradictions. If every human being is equally important in the Tapestry of Elli, why do we treat them as though they were . . . less equal? Not letting them participate in the events involving defensive and offensive skills, nor in the patrol—well, that's understandable. But why no representation in the Assemblies?

And then the Schole. We talked about Dougall and his wanting to be a communicata—communicator, I guess—but in fact Toller meant himself. Technology interests him, and he's very talented. He wouldn't have been taken on by the Schole as a Tutor if he weren't. But I really think he'd have liked to be a Memory. It would have admitted him to Assemblies, and that's why men can't be Memories.

"A word that doesn't need a masculine form in Franglei," he said. *But why use masculine forms, anyway? There are only three men for every hundred humans, and even this is a statistic. In reality it's generally even less.*

The fact is, there are just too few men. But this isn't a logical argument for denying them greater scope. There were also fewer men during the Harem regime, but then it was women who lacked power. The Hives turned the situation upside down, like a lot of other things. Since we have criticized several of these about-faces engineered by the Hives, why not this, which runs contrary to the Word itself?

Lisbeï would write several pages in this vein that night. The question came to mind each time she saw Toller at the Schole during his month of tutoring. He'd advised her to have a look at the Wardenberg Archives. Some of the Harem chiefs had expressed "very progressist" (Toller's term) opinions on the status of their women, particularly the one who had opened the Citadel to Alicia. Lisbeï had consulted the Archives, but she could hardly agree about these "very progressist" opinions. However, he was the only person with whom she could talk things over. Fraine was becoming increasingly distressed about her pregnancy, and Livine was correspondingly anxious. The other members of the usual group were

more busy than ever preparing for their future explorations.
Even Dougall had left. There was the Notebook, of course,
but it wasn't the same. She tried hard to look at the question
from the male point of view, but she simply couldn't manage
it. It was just too difficult. She was too intrigued by the other
side of things in general to give up, though, especially now
that she realized what a *very* strange point of view it was,
stranger than all others. Or was Toller himself a particularly
strange man? It was possible.

Little Dougall obviously can't be considered a valid com-
parison. He wasn't brought up in such a Progressista Family as
Angresea, in the first place. And then he's so much younger,
completely inexperienced. Of course, I have to admit my own
experience with men is pretty limited! The garderie trio, Rico of
Cartano, an almost equally brief glimpse of the adolescent Gar-
rec, and the Nevenici Blue . . .

Aleki.

Lisbeï's pen hung immobile above the paper. What did
she really know about Aleki of Felden?

That he had been brutal. Angry. That he had hated Selva
at least as much as she detested him. That he had gladly hurt
her (and then she remembered: like Gerd during her Patrol
days).

And that Selva had submitted to him.

But how could Males possibly be allowed to behave like
that in Maerlande?

They weren't allowed, of course. Other Mothers weren't
as proud as Selva and didn't hesitate to complain if a Male
maltreated them in the Service. Such Males were punished,
and the Family where Aleki had served after Bethely had indeed lodged a complaint. It wasn't the first time: he had been
sterilized on the spot; his family had been publicly repri-
manded at the Baltike Assembly and had been forced to make
reparation to the injured Family. Aleki had departed for the
nearest badlands without the slightest show of remorse.

Lisbeï learned all this from Kelys, who had resurfaced in
Wardenberg a few days later. Not from Toller. Maybe he had
touched her that Celebration night, but she'd never dream of
talking to a man about something she couldn't even discuss
with Tula! And anyway she wouldn't—she couldn't—relate
the events of that night to the memory of Aleki and Selva.

What really happened, anyhow? Toller had touched her,
yes. The revelation of his light had helped her return from a

black, spiraling pit. But had anything more occurred? At first she'd thought so, but now she doubted it. She doubted it more each time she met Toller. His invariably easy manner with her, and most significantly his concrete presence, made her doubt. Perhaps the idea of an Angresea coupling with her to make Elli, satisfied some latent but persistent regret about not becoming the Mother of Bethely, but she didn't fool herself for a moment. She was no longer a childe, now.

10

The enclosed back terrace of The Dancing Princess, the restaurant where Lisbeï and her friends liked to congregate after classes, gave onto Level One. From there they looked down on the multicolored roofs with their varnished tiles, descending in stages from the terrace to the invisible wharfs. Beyond lay the sea, gray, blue, or green according to the season. In fine weather you could see huge, dark patches where the submerged land rose near the surface. Unless the windows were blurred with raindrops, there was always one of the group who would stare out to sea, musing aloud on the hidden treasures of the depths. Today it was Livine.

"Nonsense. Everything must be rusted to bits," said Fraine sulkily.

"And there are mo-o-onsters," added Marcie in a cavernous drawl.

"You can laugh," interposed Bertia, "but did you see the dolphine they brought in the other day? The teethmarks?"

"Arbaletas could be adapted for underwater use."

"It's already possible to work underwater," chimed in Livine. "We know how to make diving suits. It's not that complicated."

"But what about deep-sea diving?"

"We wouldn't have to go all that deep."

"Too many things could go wrong."

"Things could go wrong in a badland, too."

"You're not likely to drown or get the bends."

"Oh come on, Livine!" cried several voices, protesting at

her obvious insincerity. "What about contamination?" asked one. "Yes, and aberrations?" added another. "And wild animals. Surely you've seen the stuffed animals in the Bestiarie?"

"And the renegadas," said Fraine a moment later.

There was a brief silence. Then Marcie took up the thread again. "To make a long story short, nothing is safe, and everything's getting worse. Alas, we exploras and recuperatas are doomed!" Laughter greeted the comic foreboding of her last words.

"Not everything is getting more dangerous," remarked the levelheaded Bertia. "In fact, the badlands are becoming less and less contaminated."

"And more and more explored," said Livine obstinately. "So we ought to try the sea."

"We are. The Western Fleet will be ready next year."

"I mean *under* the sea! The continental shelf is closer to home."

"We'll go," said Kelys. "But it makes more sense to explore the continents first, doesn't it?"

As usual, her steady, melodious voice, so rarely raised, restored calm to the discussion. Almost.

"And when we've explored this famous Western Continent and filled it with Communes, what then?" said Fraine. As usual when in an argumentative mood, she spoke with eyes lowered, apparently absorbed in watching her hands. She had taken a sheet of paper from her Schole things on the table and was tearing it into ever smaller shreds.

"Even if the fertility period is really increasing . . ."

"It's increasing. The Schole has the figures for anyone to see."

"It'll take time!" said Marcie.

"*If* the continent is habitable."

"A continent that big—"

"—might actually be a gigantic badland," stated Lisbeï.

This brought a roar of protest. In any case, not even Lisbeï believed it. She made it a principle to keep reminding people of other possibilities, nevertheless. When the tumult had died down a bit, she continued stubbornly. "It could be a badland with a population that might take a dim view of our arrival. Who knows how they've evolved?"

"Well we won't know until we go there," said Livine, encapsulating the general opinion.

"Let's not panic, anyhow," said Marcie, checking to see if

any cider was left in the pitcher. "*We* won't be on board the ships. We'll be working our backsides off to repay Wardenberg for our education. Did you know it takes an average of six and a half years now, instead of the five required fifteen years ago? And that's for the contracting captas. I haven't even figured it out for team members. It's really time to find something new to explore!"

"Oh, but they haven't uncovered everything yet, have they, Lisbeï?"

She greeted the smiles without anger, though Fraine flew to her defense. "Certainly not with the techniques available at the moment!"

"Don't worry," persisted Marcie. "Lisbeï will wander all over the land brandishing *The Red Catte's Tales,* and sites will spring out of the ground all by themselves!"

Even Lisbeï had to laugh at such an image. "Marcie, your laziness will be your undoing! I never said it wasn't necessary to pick up a spade. Only that there were clues no one has followed up yet."

"You could always have another try at convincing Cedryn!"

This time Lisbeï's smile was a bit forced. Her first year in the field had been something of a disappointment. She'd had the bad luck to be apprenticed to Cedryn of Schuiten, a particularly unimaginative recuperata who did everything strictly by the book: studying old maps for the most likely sites, exploring, locating, analyzing the terrain on site, and digging trenches or sinking wells every meter. Cedryn thought of herself as a Progressista because she only accepted hard facts. Lisbeï had spent several weeks trying to make Cedryn admit that her definition of hard fact was perhaps rather narrow. It was useless. And the first time Lisbeï had suggested applying her own theory to an actual site had been the last. It was absolutely out of the question for one of Cedryn's apprentices to waste her time like that. But what was the point of being an apprentice if you couldn't try new things? "When you're in charge of your own expeditions, you can amuse yourself as you please. For now, dig."

And yet Lisbeï had been positive she was right. She had assembled all the data on her own legendary underground passages in Bethely, clearly demonstrating that all the clues were there if anyone had taken the trouble to recognize them before the actual discovery. Kelys, however, had discouraged her from submitting this work to the Schole, reasoning that Lisbeï would be unable to answer the objection that it was easy to see the clues *after* the fact. She would need to demonstrate the reverse. But after her stint with Cedryn she'd be obliged to spend time repaying her debt to Wardenberg. Could she let herself get deeper into debt by heading profitless expeditions just to prove her theory? It would make more sense to enroll in the team of a recognized—and lucky—recuperata such as Kelys, and to share in the finds. She hadn't actually spoken to Kelys about it, but there shouldn't be any problem.

From the start, Lisbeï had decided not to ask Bethely for help. Anyway, she'd also have to pay the Family back, which came to the same thing, or worse. At least Wardenberg had a credit system that made it possible to evaluate exchanges somewhat more objectively. Why, in the name of all that was reasonable, didn't the whole of Maerlande adopt it? But the Juddites had always been solidly opposed, along with a good many Believras and even some Progressistas. They considered the system a legacy of the Harems and the root of all evil, utterly impervious to the argument that Wardenberg didn't seem to be doing too badly. But in any case Wardenberg never carried any weight with the Juddites. The others (including Kelys, much to Lisbeï's surprise and dismay) argued that a common currency system would be an irreversible step toward centralization, requiring a bureaucracy and attendant agencies —something that Maerlande had tried to avoid ever since its inception. Centralization had partly accounted for Wardenberg's power during the Harem period, for example. (Wise in this as in other matters, Wardenberg had never insisted on its system being adopted elsewhere.) The disadvantages of other options—a currency for each Family or Province, with rates of exchange—were so cumbersome compared to the advantages that they weren't worth thinking about. It was enough to have to keep track of Lines in the Books! The current barter system was based on long-established values. Everyone knew them by heart by the time they ceased to be children, and it worked fairly well. For the moment it answered most Families' needs, and no one was going to change it just to please the radical Progressistas. Lisbeï didn't think herself a radical Progressista as such and usually held her peace when the discussion reached this stage.

"It would be worth trying, all the same," said Livine

dreamily. She was still musing on the subject of the tales and their possible clues. "Just once, to see if it worked."

"An expedition for nothing?" queried Bertia.

"I'd do it," said Fraine defiantly.

"So would I." A masculine voice, behind Lisbeï. She turned around.

"Hey, Dougall!" said Livine, grinning.

Fraine pushed back her chair and stretched out an arm to grab another from the next table. A middle-aged Blue woman and a plump Green girl of about twelve, both wearing traveling clothes, were seated at it. Without turning her head, the Blue lifted her bag from the floor onto the chair.

"May we have this chair?" asked Fraine.

Now the Green lifted her bag onto the chair too, looking Fraine straight in the eye as she did so.

"Look here . . . ," the young Red began, her voice already shaking.

"Forget it," said Dougall. "I'll stand."

"Take my chair," said Lisbeï, standing up and turning to face him. "I was beginning to feel a pain in the butt in any case."

He was still a little shorter than she, but he had filled out and his skin had a healthy color. He was wearing wide blue trousers and a sky-blue shirt and had a travelling jacket slung over one shoulder.

"Blue, Dougall?" said Fraine.

"It's been official for a month." He still hesitated, but Lisbeï pushed her chair toward him.

The Blue woman at the next table rose. Her young friend did the same. They picked up their bags and stalked off.

Fraine grabbed one of the deserted chairs and dragged it noisily over to the table. "Thanks for the chair," she called, her tone biting.

Lisbeï stared at the retreating offenders. It was unbelievable. She had never seen such hostility toward men in Wardenberg before. Polite indifference, yes, at the worst. Open hostility, never.

"Sit down, Lisbeï," said Fraine slowly, her tone dangerous. Her hands were again busy shredding paper onto the table, though they shook a little.

"I don't care," said Dougall, almost as though it were true. "I'm a Blue now."

"Did you see their emblems?" said Livine in a shocked

voice. "The Green was from Nevenici, in any case. What are Juddites like that doing in Wardenberg?"

"There's a big delegation from Litale at the Assembly Games this year," said Kelys tranquilly. "Are you coming back to the Schole, Dougall?"

He won't return to our group, though. We're two years ahead now, but he'll try to catch up. He hasn't been idle during his Service. Paradoxically, he seems far more sure of himself now that he's a Blue. Lisbeï hesitated, but decided not to cross out this sentence. Toller certainly wouldn't be offended by such a remark. He himself had said in a letter that becoming Blue hadn't been a catastrophe, but rather a liberation. At this stage in their correspondence, Lisbeï hadn't been particularly taken aback. She had come a long way.

After a month of tutoring, Toller had left Wardenberg. She'd been surprised to get a short letter from him a few weeks later, giving his present address (he had changed addresses often that first year) and asking whether she'd continued her "mental voyage in the land of men." More astonished and amused than shocked, Lisbeï decided to answer, and they had kept up a patchy correspondence. Lisbeï thought each letter would be the last, but in the end another always turned up from somewhere in Maerlande. In the second year the envelopes bore the Angresea emblem. Often they contained reading lists, generally rather moth-eaten titles attributed to the Decline, or works in the Wardenberg Archives dating from the hundred years' isolation, dusty tomes that almost no one looked at. *Have you decided to undertake my education?* she had written at one point, half-serious and a little annoyed. However, curiosity always drew her to see what the books were about. She didn't read everything, but enough to cut into her Schole work at times—though it was always a welcome diversion from the boredom of the exhaustive reports Cedryn insisted on after each small practice expedition.

"You need it," he had replied. The nerve of this Blue! But even though his letters were short, they always raised some interesting point or other, often discomforting ones that Lisbeï found impossible to ignore once he had aired them. After she had looked at things from his point of view, she couldn't refute his arguments. And then it was so strange to have a correspondence—even a sporadic one—with a man she hardly knew, when all was said and done. But more especially with a *man*. It had a touch of something pleasantly . . . out of the

ordinary. And anyway, he sometimes gave her news of Bethely from another perspective, different from the views of Mooreï or Antonë—or Tula. It was always interesting to compare and to view Bethely through other eyes: the same, yet different.

In fact, most things Toller wrote about gave her a new perspective. Often she felt they were speaking of the same thing but accentuating different aspects. The Service, for example. Women did their Service, too. The fact that they did it within their own Family made no difference—and furthermore, as Fraine remarked one day in one of her bitter outbursts, characteristic since Ysande's death, it was the women who had to bear the childreen and sometimes die from them. And Green girls were sent as wards to other Families. Lisbeï was no longer shocked to hear complaints about the Service, not after four, now nearly five, years in Wardenberg. And in her opinion, the Males had no more to complain about than Red women.

Nevertheless, she had been shaken by the incident in the restaurant. This wasn't something theoretical, something in a musty document. Although her perception of Dougall's emotions had been confused, his reaction was very real, like Livine's and Fraine's—especially Fraine's. Poor Fraine: she would have liked nothing better than to be declared a Blue right away, but tradition condemned her to one more try with a different Line. Males, however, could be declared Blue after their first tour of Service, sometimes after no more than a year if the inseminations didn't take or if pregnancies didn't go to term. At least that was the rule in Baltike and Bretanye. Litale itself was beginning to change in this respect, even if only to spare Reds the trial of useless pregnancies. Bethely had been a moving force in such change, with Selva bringing up the question at every Assembly since Loï's death. So who had more to complain about?

Lisbeï chewed on the end of her pen (she'd better get a new one soon) and then went on with her letter, writing of Dougall and how he'd changed. *He showed me some sample translations of the Notebook he'd done, usually with the same results as mine, except in passages where we were completely at odds. But his interpretations have something. Too bad he can't present them himself to the Association.*

And why not? replied Toller a few weeks later. But Lisbeï's audacity had its limits. To pass off Dougall's translations as her own, as she had offered to do, was already bold enough. Her interpretations and theories were already viewed with a fairly skeptical eye by the Association whenever she had the nerve to make them known! Of course, a Blue man had a perfect right to consult and try to translate the Notebook. "Access for all," decreed the Decision of Antonë, and that obviously included men. But men couldn't be members of a research association—to be more exact, men weren't members of any association. Yet plenty of future Males received more or less the same education that had made it possible for Lisbeï to skip at least a year in the Schole. There didn't seem much point in giving them such an education if they couldn't make use of it once they became Blues. And in the case of someone like Dougall (and Toller, too), it was clearly a sheer waste of talent.

That "why not" kept up an annoying buzz in her mind over the next few months. It became more persistent than ever when the Association journal refused to publish her essay on the variants of three tales included in the second part of the Notebook. The editorial board dismissed it with the comment, "Frequently unacceptable conclusions based on questionable interpretations." When she indignantly showed it to Kelys, the latter threw up her hands in mock regret.

"I'm not on the editorial board, Lisbeï."

"But you founded the Association! You're a member! Why did you let those old idiots be named?"

Kelys raised scandalized eyebrows, and Lisbeï blushed. They were all respected researchas. Old but respected. Respected for work done quite some time ago, but respected nonetheless.

"You must admit the results have been fairly disappointing since they were named. The Association produces practically nothing of importance—just a lot of nit-picking studies on this or that linguistic variation, but as for the *content* of the Notebook . . . Is this what you and Carmela had in mind when you formed the Association? Surely not!"

Kelys contemplated her silently, her aura vibrating with amusement. They were in the enormous room allotted to the peregrina in the Residence. Lisbeï strode back and forth one last time, then collapsed into an armchair, defeated. "All right, so patience isn't my strong point. And some of my conclusions . . . are daring. But it's not forbidden to *think*, is it?"

"In those fields it's merely inadvisable to think too fast," said Kelys.

"Too fast! But you did read the essay! Wouldn't you have published it?"

"I would, yes. But . . ."

"But you're not on the editorial board. Yes, I know."

". . . there's nothing stopping you from publishing it somewhere else, Lisbeï," finished Kelys, catching her unawares.

"Oh really? Where? *The Recuperatas' Gazette* wouldn't take it: I'm not yet an official member, and anyway, it's not at all their line."

"It doesn't hurt to try. What about *The Exploras' Newsletter*? Or start your own magazine, the . . . *The Haldista Independentas' Tribune*—how about that? You're not the only one to have her articles rejected. You might even ask Dougall to contribute."

Kelys was clearly amusing herself.

"Why not?" said Lisbeï.

But first she waited until *The Exploras' Newsletter* had also refused her essay.

11

One day Lisbeï met her father. She didn't call him this. There was no such word, even in Wardenberg. It existed only among the oldest Harem relics to escape the ravages of the Hives, and in Decline documents. In fact, Lisbeï didn't name him at all, not even in her journal. The man is simply "he" throughout the pages devoted to the incident.

One day Lisbeï met . . . her genitor. Selva's ex–first Male—and for many years an ex–Male, period. He was a fifty-ish Blue, rather short and broad-backed, with a big florid face, brown hair going gray and thin on top. She would never have met him if he hadn't sought her out, or hadn't wanted to have a look at her, at least. It happened at one of the controversial lectures sponsored by the "Independentas" in Wardenberg at the end of wintra 495. He was seated in the front row, unremarkable and at first unremarked, a Blue among others. She noticed him staring at her all through the lecture, his expression occasionally shocked, but more often skeptical, amused, a little indulgent. After the lecture was over, he stayed for the question period, though he said nothing. He kept on watching her, wearing virtually the same expression as before, as though he were curious to know how she would handle the sometimes virulent criticism of some members of the audience concerning her comparisons between various versions of the Word—the Hallera version, for instance, or the version after the Decision of Karillie. . . . One of her provisional conclusions met with a generally sour welcome: Hallera's version, like her letters and all her other writings, drew far too heavily on elements from the Harems rather than Hives, and even included elements from the Decline. Close linguistic analysis revealed that beneath Hallera's Slavoï—and beneath the Old Litali of her daughter, Ariane—the expressions and the syntax were definitely characteristic of the Old Frangleï current in Baltike at the time. Other curious details emerged from the comparison. It seemed that the technique of artificial insemination appeared in Litale (and especially in Bethely) very near the end of the Hive period. And this technique had initially been rediscovered and used in Wardenberg. Alicia had traveled to Wardenberg to propose peace. What if Ariane had been a Wardenberg agent? Or Hallera herself—who could tell?

These last theories met with an even cooler welcome, particularly in Wardenberg.

The strange Blue, however, listened quietly to the discussion, merely shaking his head now and then with a vaguely incredulous expression at moments when the debate degenerated into a shouting match. When the hall began to empty, he would have left without a word had not Lisbeï, as usual highly irritated by the exercise, suddenly asked him what he thought of it all. She was too close for him to think she meant anyone else, but he registered surprise at being asked for an opinion.

"I don't know," he said.

"What do you mean, 'don't know'?" exclaimed Dougall with a smile. These lectures excited him, too. "You have no opinion?"

"I just came to see," replied the Blue, a little embarrassed at being singled out. Only Lisbeï's closest friends remained: Fraine stacking chairs with Marcie and Bertia, Livine gathering up the papers, and Dougall, who now asked angrily, "See what?" Since the series of lectures began, inevitably at least one member of the audience had objected to the idea of a Blue man meddling with things that were none of his business. This time it had been two Red males.

The strange man lifted his chin in Lisbeï's direction.

"The famous Lisbeï of Bethely?" asked Lisbeï acidly. Nobody seemed prepared to forget her role in discovering the Notebook, whether it was to congratulate her or—more often —to criticize her for the way in which she'd announced its existence.

"Lisbeï of Bethely-Callenbasch," said the Blue, adding almost apologetically, "I am Erne of Callenbasch."

At first Lisbeï didn't understand. When she recognized the name, her first impulse was to burst out laughing. The Blue's murky aura throbbed, vaguely indicative of hurt feelings. Lisbeï tried to put on a straight face. "Forgive me. It's such a surprise."

What was I supposed to do? To say? Should I do or say anything special? Or just let him look at me until I remarked, "All right. You've seen me; now you can go"? And then I thought of Toller and of what Kelys had told me—how his childreen in Wardenberg were important to him, especially the last, Emelyne, because she was the last childe he had made. I was the last childe of this strange Blue, in a way, or one of the last, since he had been declared a Blue right after his Bethely Service. I asked him to sit down for a moment. The others had moved off politely; it was almost funny. "Do you live in Wardenberg?" I asked. No, he was just passing through. "Do you stay in Callenbasch?" Yes, most of the time. There was a certain lack of subject matter. But he didn't look stupid. Really, I didn't need to coddle him this way. "So you wanted to see me?" I asked. "Yes," he replied simply. "I haven't made many famous childreen." He smiled a little shyly. All in all he seemed very nice. I asked him to join us for dinner—Dougall, at least, would be pleased if he accepted the invitation. The Blue surprised me: he accepted.

They went to Fraine's place. Since finally becoming a Blue at the beginning of the wintra, she had her own apartment on Level Two. It had become the gathering place for the Wardenberg "Haldista Independentas." But Livine was the cook. "We'd starve to death if I did the cooking!" was to be Fraine's joke during Lisbeï's expedition.

Lisbeï watched the Blue surreptitiously during the meal,

all senses alert, but he was perfectly ordinary in this respect.
She perceived no more with him than she would have with
Livine or Dougall—no more, no less.

*"A recessive character does not surface when the gene is
present without its corresponding activator." But considering
how intensely it has "surfaced" in me, I would have thought the
genitor himself would already be an active mutant. Apparently I
owe it mostly to Selva.*

What a stupid idea! It's half and half. . . .

Nevertheless, her satisfaction in writing this had been
very real. After a moment's thought, Lisbeï was obliged to
conclude indulgently that childhood fictions die hard. To remind herself of this, she added *No, Lisbeï, women do not actually make childreen all by themselves.*

Selva had made her with this innocuous Blue. Her first
Male. He must have been . . . let's see, in his thirties. A Red
at the end of his Service, and apparently amazed at having
contributed to the creation of a childe like Lisbeï.

"I needed agvite each time I went to her," he finally told
her. Or told himself. It was very late, and the Zirfell had
flowed copiously. Marcie and Bertia were trying to remember
all the words of some bawdy song from Harem days. Dougall
was asleep, curled up on the Bethely shag rug Lisbeï had given
to Fraine. Livine was dozing, her head on Fraine's knees, and
Fraine had decided to finish off the Zirfell.

Lisbeï and the Blue found themselves seated on the cush-
ions of the wide window seat, perched above Level One and
its dully glistening rooftops. The half-moon was about to set.
Did she question him? She can't remember—probably not.
But he had begun to reminisce, perhaps because, like most
people who confided in Lisbeï, he had felt her interest. She
doesn't deny she was interested. And he had drunk a great
deal.

*Luckily for him, agvite isn't a really addictive drug! He used
to take so much that he'd wake up in his bedroom without remembering what had happened.* "Too bad, I guess, since when
we ate breakfast in her rooms next morning, Selva was very
friendly." *(Selva ate breakfast with her Males in those days? The
imagination boggles!)* "I was rather embarrassed, actually," he
went on, "since I couldn't remember a thing. The trouble was,
she wanted to talk." *(About what, in Elli's name! He didn't say.)*
"And I've never been much of a talker." *(He has improved with
age, then!)* "By that time I was thoroughly fed up with being a

Red. I couldn't manage it anymore—well, barely. If it hadn't been for the agvite, I'd never have made it with Selva. It was getting to the point where I couldn't see a Red woman without wanting to run." (Well, it wasn't as though he'd been forced to make Elli with every compatible Red, as in the Hive days!)

At this juncture Lisbeï became aware of how frequent her asides were becoming. How unlike her! She always tried to transcribe conversations as objectively as possible. Her asides were definitely not objective. True, the Blue had irritated her with his peevish tone, or was it a plaintive call for sympathy that she sensed?

In a word, if he were to be believed, with a bit of luck I might have been Tula.

Lisbeï looked at what she'd just written, a little surprised, and then added, *Or I might not have existed at all if this worn-out old Red hadn't been able to lay his hands on some agvite. Aren't you only supposed to drink it at the Celebration? Where did he get it?*

"Kelys," had been the astonishing reply. "That tall black woman, Kelys—I think that's her name. She got the picture. Very understanding for a woman. Of course, she was a Blue, and sometimes it helps. You see . . ." He had given a drunken, hiccupy laugh. "Without Kelys you might not be here."

Kelys was due to arrive in Wardenberg in two days. But Lisbeï had no chance to question her on the subject of Erne of Callenbasch, for Kelys never turned up. Instead, a brief message came a few days later, informing Lisbeï that a circular had been discovered in the Maestera Archives in Escarra—one of the famous circulars of the Bethely Harem announcing the capture and execution of Garde and her Compagnas. Naturally she was going to have a look at it. The following week Lisbeï at last wound up her lecture series and gave herself the luxury of a few days with the Notebook as a reward. And here she stumbled upon the passage mentioning "neopsylocin" and other clues that would lead to her own discovery at Belmont. She had better things to do than recall the half-drunk confidences of an unknown Blue—a man she wouldn't have thought of calling "Father," even if she knew such a term existed.

12

It was Coralle, a young Blue from Baïanque, who had first come across a mention of the circulars while looking for something quite different in the Wardenberg Archives. Ironically, she wasn't even a Haldista!

The reference turned up in a packet of tattered letters, a correspondence between Wardenberg and the Harem of Kilermere across the strait. Where, asked Kilermere, were the posters that Wardenberg was supposed to print and distribute? Unfortunately the letter was almost in shreds and the date illegible. Still, the rest of the packet made it possible to assign the right period: between 140 and 145 of the Harem regime. From the letter it could be deduced that Bethely had ordered a run of several hundred posters showing a photograph of Garde after her execution, as well as the names of the Compagnas walled up alive. Kilermere was responding to a circular sent earlier to all the Harems, advising them to use the poster as a means of putting an end to persistent rumors of the rebel's resurrection.

Coralle was doing some rather dull research on the kinds of foods eaten at the end of the Harem period. Lacking sufficient data from the local Harem records, it occurred to her to go through the correspondence between Wardenberg and its neighbors, on the off chance of finding something—food having always been a great subject of conversation in Wardenberg, even before its isolation, when it became a dramatic obsession.

But instead of comments on the quality of pescas in the strait, Coralle found a mention of the circular. Lisbeï couldn't help thinking Elli's sense of humor had got the better of decorum in this instance. Pescas indeed! Coralle didn't even realize the significance of her find. Absorbed in her own research, she put the letter on her discard pile. Only later, when talking to another student who planned to rewrite the history of the Wardenberg Presses, did Coralle mention the letter. Luckily the friend was honest and didn't use the discovery as her own.

Now began a feverish search in Wardenberg for the

poster. The Hives people had undoubtedly destroyed any copies they had come upon, but if a copy had survived at all, it would be in Wardenberg. If even just the circular was found, it would be enough! It would be the first irrefutable proof of the Testament of Halde, or at least confirmation of the first Garde's existence. If nothing else, it would substantiate her execution by the Bethely Harem.

And now here it was: a copy of the circular, found not in Wardenberg but in the depths of Escarra! This time the hand of Elli was less evident. The Memory of Maestera, one of Kelys's old Scholemates, was actually looking for the document. Since Coralle's discovery a year and a half earlier, she had begun going through her Archives with a fine-tooth comb, looking at everything presumed to date from before the Hives, including material from early Hive days. For once, blind and unremitting patience had paid off—an exception that didn't prove the rule, thought Lisbeï, stubbornly committed to following hunches.

Because of this confidence in intuition, born sixteen years earlier in the West Tower garderie and corroborated by her discovery of the underground passage, Lisbeï had no hesitation in placing her faith in the Notebook—or rather in the unknown author of the second part. "The-one-who-may-have-been-Garde," as Lisbeï always thought of her. According to Lisbeï's interpretation, this writa suggested the existence of a large site in the Belmont territory. The "neopsylocin" mentioned by the Notebook in relation to the Harem drug had been manufactured, apparently at the end of the Decline, "in Bellemont." There was no mistaking the Old Frangleï preposition: "in" meant "inside," and given the Decline mania for burying everything, it *must* mean "underneath."

How could this writa be familiar with such an obviously scientific name as "neopsylocin" and its production locale during the Decline? Supposedly—particularly at the end of the second section—she had been writing eighty years before the Harems' demise. But this didn't bother Lisbeï. She also brushed aside the fact that Belmont, to say nothing of its badlands, had been one of the most dug-over terrains since the beginning of Maerlande. There must be a site, and if no one had found it, this only meant it must be deeper than the rest. Most of all, it meant no one had thought of looking for it.

"So what have you in mind? Digging up the entire Belmont territory with spade and pickaxe, a hundred meters down or more?" Marcie was clearly skeptical.

Even Livine and Fraine were puzzled, though Dougall was interested. But everything Lisbeï said, thought, or did always interested Dougall. However, when Lisbeï unveiled what she considered her decisive argument, none of them displayed the enthusiasm she'd hoped for.

"Oh no, not another tale!" groaned Marcie, lifting her eyes to the heavens.

"Tales in the plural," corrected Lisbeï. "At least let me explain!"

"Go ahead," said Dougall.

The others acquiesced with a sigh. They were slumped over the table at Fraine's place. They sighed again when they realized the three tales in question were from the Notebook, apparently part of a series resembling the Pimpernella Cycle. Heads shook ruefully as they listened to Lisbeï's list of variant locales from one tale to another. They sat up to take notice, however—Dougall before anyone else—when she continued with a comparative list of details from versions current in the Belmont territory.

"Twelve correlations?" queried Dougall. He looked the list over. "You're sure? The spelling is different in at least five names."

She had foreseen this objection, however, and went on with a comparative list of place names. Twenty. Twenty-three if you stretched it a little.

"All right. Pimpernella's main hiding place is located, in twenty instances, at the foot of a hat-shaped hill, or a cap-shaped hill, or a hill shaped 'like a snake that has swallowed an elephant,' " remarked Bertia, still skeptical. "So what's an elephant?"

"Something that looks like a hat?" replied Marcie, giggling helplessly.

"Be serious. What kind of hat or cap?" said the sensible Livine. "We have dozens of shapes today, and it must have been the same back then."

Lisbeï pulled out sheets of paper on which she had copied various documented shapes of hats or caps from early Harem days and the few believed to date from the Decline. Marcie hooted with laughter as she turned the sheets every which way. "A hill shaped like a bowl of fruit?"

"The shape underneath the fruit," said Lisbeï, forcing herself to be patient.

"In the shape of an empty plate," said Marcie, trying to keep a straight face. "A hill with a hollow on top?"

"No," said Fraine. "If it's like a snake that has swallowed something, it must be a more usual shape, like this, for instance." She rested a finger on a stove-pipe hat.

"A mesa, you mean? There aren't any in Belmont," noted Dougall.

"It might be more to the point to find out what an elephant is," said Bertia. "It is some sort of object, a fruit, an animal?"

"It must be a small animal," said Lisbeï. "Snakes aren't vegetarians."

"But who knows how big the Decline snakes were or what they ate?" whispered Marcie mysteriously.

"Cut it out, Marcie." Fraine scowled. "We'll have to look into the Decline animals."

The others agreed.

"Oho! So you're convinced?" exclaimed Marcie.

"Looks like it," replied Dougall, grinning.

Two days later Marcie arrived at the group meeting with bad news. Elephants, it would seem, were huge beasts as tall as a house. "It would take a pretty big snake to swallow an elephant," she concluded.

"Ah," mimicked Livine innocently, "but who knows what those Decline snakes—"

"We're talking about *tales*!" protested Lisbeï. "Of course they exaggerate. What do elephants look like, anyway?"

"It's not very clear from the fragments I found. Feet like tree stumps in any case, big ears, and a 'trunk' on the head." She sketched an egg propped up on four solid legs, with donkey's ears on either side of a boxlike protuberance.

Lisbeï felt rather discouraged. No hill could look like this, even in the wildest tale!

"Perhaps it just means the snake is distended because of swallowing a large prey," murmured Dougall, "in which case the hill would be like dozens of others anywhere you care to look."

"Maybe we should see what we can find under 'snake,' " suggested Fraine, aware of Lisbeï's disappointment.

"Or keep on looking under 'elephant.' That 'trunk' must surely mean something else," said Livine.

In the end it was Fraine who knocked gleefully on Lisbeï's door late the following night. She was clutching a copy of a fragment found when checking out "snake." "It's in a book for childreen, about someone who draws pictures instead of telling stories because she's trying to fix something in a desert. There's another childe—or maybe a child—pestering her for stories about animals. But since she can't really draw, she puts the animals inside boxes because boxes are easier to draw. To make a long story short, one of the fragments shows a 'hat' inside something called a 'boa constrictor'!"

Lisbeï looked sleepily at Fraine's sketch of a snake distended by something with two humps.

"A hat isn't an elephant, surely?" she said, unconvinced.

Fraine said nothing for a moment, then, "They're tales; you said so yourself."

There was a kind of twisted logic in Fraine's urging, especially at one in the morning. They decided to take the sketch to the next meeting.

"A hat is definitely not an elephant," stated Marcie firmly.

"But it's a pretty characteristic shape for a hill," remarked Livine. "Two humps, one slightly higher than the other."

"Isn't there a word crossed out just before 'elephant' in the Notebook?" asked Lisbeï, suddenly seeing the light. She ruffled through the pages of her recopied translation. "Yes: 'swallowed a (something scratched out) an elephant.' Maybe Fraine is right. Tales often have arbitrary shifts like this: the crossed-out word might be the Old Frangleï *chameau* or camel, looking very much like another Old Frangleï word, *chapeau* or hat. And there is"—she searched through the other sheets with growing excitement—"a kind of hat that would do!"

"Bor-sa-li-no," said Marcie, looking at a drawing with a puzzled expression. "Well, the shape is right, anyway."

And Pimpernella almost always approached her hiding place from the same direction. A little cross-checking enabled them to establish that the hill was seen from the east. In the same way they were able to pinpoint the likely area as the northernmost sector of the Belmont badlands. ("Oh no, not the rocky hills!" groaned Marcie.) And what with cross-checks, educated guesses, and going over everything repeatedly, Lisbeï finally came up with a sufficiently convincing case, in the group's opinion, to be submitted to the Wardenberg Exploration and Recuperation Funding Committee. The committee members were polite enough to hear Lisbeï out before collapsing with laughter (or to be more precise, indulging in a lengthy chuckle, which for such respectable matrones amounted to the same thing).

"Lisbeï," said Alwyne, the first to pull herself together and probably the most understanding of the lot, "don't you think you've already run into enough debt by continuing your Schole studies after your two years' apprenticeship and especially with the *Independentas' Tribune*?"

Alwyne was one of Sygne's closest aunts, and Lisbeï had met her several times when visiting Kelys at the Residence. Finding her on the committee had given her a gleam of hope, but now she doubted whether she'd get anything more solid than sympathy. She wondered whether she ought to point out that her friends worked on the *Tribune* too, and therefore bore part of the debt. It was probably better to say nothing: Edwina of Carlsbad was also on the committee. At the end of her year as the group's Tutress in exploration technologies, she had reproached Lisbeï for being a bad influence on the others.

And it was probably better for Lisbeï not to remark that, with what she already owed, a few debts more or less hardly mattered.

"She might ask Bethely to underwrite this funding request," began Rosyle, the other Wardenberg Family member on the committee. There was a gleam in her eye.

Lisbeï had wondered who would be the first to think of it. "No," she said firmly. She already had rejected the idea of asking Bethely for help in her own name, and she certainly had no intention of having Bethely indebted to Wardenberg on her account! Even if she asked Selva personally (which wild cavalas couldn't make her do), and even if Selva wanted to help her, which was even more unlikely, the Family would quite rightly refuse.

Alwyne started to say, "In that case, young Lisbeï—"

"This project is absurd," interrupted Edwina. "It doesn't even look like a reasonable gamble."

Lisbeï felt like shouting, "That's exactly why!" But she kept quiet. She loved paradoxes and believed in them, but she had finally realized most people weren't likely to share her views, apart from a few Believras such as Mooreï. And no one on the Wardenberg Exploration and Recuperation Funding Committee could seriously be called a Believra.

Feeling desperate, she wrote Kelys in distant Escarra. It was at least "a reasonable gamble" to presume that Kelys wielded some influence in Wardenberg. If Kelys backed her project, and perhaps if she agreed to ask for funds on Lisbeï's behalf . . .

Not only did Kelys back the project; she returned from Escarra (with the famous circular) as soon as she received the thick file containing Lisbeï's proofs and arguments. And not only did she agree to request the funds, but she offered to lead the expedition and pay for the equipment herself.

"Then you think I'm right!" cried Lisbeï, overjoyed.

The tall black settled more comfortably into her chair. "I can afford to think people should be allowed to try—at least once."

It wasn't exactly a vote of confidence, but coming from Kelys it would do.

Every recuperation expedition had what Kelys amusingly referred to as a "vulnerability window": the moment just before the expedition was officially announced. Once the locale had been pinpointed, the ideal procedure was to take test samples, particularly soil and water. If you were caught in the act, so to speak, the local Family might decide to organize its own prospecting team. However, it also would have to make an official statement of intent to the Capta of the Assembly of Mothers, and the upshot might be a race to make the crucial announcement. When badlands were involved, however, there was less likelihood of being found taking samples.

Fortunately this was the case with Lisbeï's hypothetical site. The Belmont badlands were pretty well harmless, since the various Decline pollutants had been fairly mild to begin with here, and now had almost disappeared. Because the terrain was generally rocky and barren, with nothing more than a few scrawny trees to offer, the Belmont Family and its Offshoots hadn't been in a hurry to claim them. Kelys sent in her usual scout, a taciturn, stocky Blue with the pretty but inappropriate name of Dulcie. She would fix the location of the site and take the necessary samples as discreetly as possible. Indeed, she had no trouble finding the hat-hill—a respectable protuberance, she told them, covering an area of five hundred square meters. Marcie groaned in agony.

Samples taken, especially of running water, showed a slightly higher acid content than was normal for the surrounding terrain, as well as the presence of metal oxides. Marcie looked unconvinced. "It's hardly conclusive."

"But this sample is from a stream originating in the hill," remarked Livine. "If the underground structure had been damaged by an earthquake—"

"Hasn't been an earthquake in Belmont for a hundred years," said Bertia. "Very stable area. Continental shield. I checked."

"If I wanted an underground complex to last, that's where I'd build it," announced Dougall, trying to bolster Lisbeï's confidence. "There may have been very minor earthquakes and subsidence."

"And since no one ever goes there, who'd know if anything had occurred in recent years?" concluded Fraine.

"So we're off?" asked Marcie. "Oh my poor hands!"

Fraine gave her a quizzical smile. "Don't worry, we'll bring along lots of gloves."

All the Independentas were to take part in the expedition. "But you don't realize what a chance you're taking," protested Lisbeï. "If we find nothing, you'll have wasted all that time and effort and landed yourselves with new debt. I don't want to drag you into this."

"You're not dragging us," said Livine. "It's our choice."

"Why, I wonder?" murmured Lisbeï.

"What do you mean, why?" said Fraine reproachfully.

"What! Why?" added Marcie, pretending to be puzzled.

"What are friends for?" Livine smiled.

Bertia concluded this chorus with a laconic, "Yep."

Lisbeï looked at each in turn, caught up in the warmth of their emotion. *Friends.* In the six years they'd known one another, she'd never really thought of them this way. They had been . . . the people who had accepted her in their studies and amusements. Compagnas, co-workers, colleagues. When they had shared in setting up the *Tribune* at their own risk, or in organizing the Independentas and the lecture series, she had thought it was out of intellectual conviction, not personal affection. They were the real "group," in any case, and she saw herself as being more or less tolerated, somewhat peripheral, even after they knew her identity and she had become

Lisbeï-discoverer-of-the-Notebook for them. Ysande had tried to make her understand, but her voice had been silenced too soon. . . .

What a lucky thing the group wanted to take part! Kelys hadn't planned an expedition that year, and her usual team was unavailable, apart from Dulcie. Once the Belmont expedition was announced, new recuperatas had to be enroled. Unfortunately, though Kelys's name might be a drawing card for some, the project description discouraged a good many. Ellième was nearly over, and they couldn't wait much longer.

"How can forty people dig a terrain five hundred meters' square?" protested Marcie. "It'll take years—if we live that long!"

"Maybe we'll find people in Belmont."

"In early sprinna? That's when they begin sowing!"

"We could offer better terms by reducing our own share," suggested Livine.

"But they'll merely say a bigger share of nothing is still nothing," said Fraine, echoing the reasoning of several prospects.

"We can't give up!" cried Livine.

Kelys, half-hidden in an armchair, remarked in her cool voice, "Enroll men and offer them good conditions."

Enroll *men*? Blues? The only good condition they could offer was a partnaship in the contract. But men were never enrolled as partnas! If men worked on an expedition, it was as hirelings.

"Dougall is a partna in this one," remarked Kelys.

Lisbeï realized with a start that she'd *forgotten*! So had the others. None of the prospective enrollees had any idea Dougall was a partna. The question hadn't even come up.

They all turned toward Dougall, who seemed to shrink into himself a little.

"Don't worry," said Lisbeï involuntarily, "of course you're included. It's just that . . ." She hesitated. Would he be offended? "We'd forgotten you were a man."

He looked at them one by one. "Do you mean to say . . . I'll be registered in the contract as a partna?"

"There's nothing officially forbidding such a thing," noted Kelys, nonchalant as ever.

"If it isn't officially forbidden, then . . ." Fraine paused.

"It's feasible," concluded Livine.

Lisbeï, who had begun to reflect on her impulsive words,

realized with astonishment that the others had apparently accepted what Kelys had merely put forward as a hypothesis. She turned to Kelys with a "but" on her lips. Kelys looked steadily at her, and the impassive black face seemed to say, *But what?*

But what, indeed? Nothing had ever stopped men from taking part in exploration or recuperation expeditions, apart from narrow and habitual interpretations of tradition.

"We need sturdy people," said Lisbeï, giving in. Men were generally a little stronger, physically speaking. That at least would be an advantage.

The other two were beginning to take in the significance of their decision. Would any Blue men be interested, anyway?

"I'll take care of it," said Kelys, slowly unfolding her rangy body from the armchair.

Nearly two weeks later, the expedition set off for Belmont. Most people thought it was a waste of time, and only Kelys's participation had kept the critics relatively subdued. The sixty or so Blue men who had responded to Kelys's call for volunteers would join them in the field. How had this call gone out? Lisbeï had no idea. There must be some kind of discreet network among Blue men. Logical. Yet rather strange. It was an . . . *uncomfortable* idea, wrote Lisbeï in her journal, then immediately added, *But why?* Such networks existed among Blue women, particularly among recuperatas and exploras. But Blue men were so rare in these activities that it was hard to imagine why they'd need a network. She voiced the question aloud to a newly arrived Blue man.

"To find out which Families need experts, and in what branches," answered Duarte, as though it were a matter of course.

Not all Blue men with good technical skills were employed by their own Family. Some preferred to become traveling experts. And to take apprentices.

Lisbeï's eyebrows rose in amazement. "What about the Schole?"

"Some Blues would rather be assigned to men," replied Duarte, his face impassive.

She sensed he was watching her, and she controlled her slight start of shock—and annoyance. Who did this Blue think he was? Toller's sermons were already bad enough—but no, that was unfair. Toller never preached in his letters. Nor was

Duarte preaching now. He had no need. His mere presence
was . . . disconcerting enough.

He was one of the Blue men who'd arrived at the site
alone or in small groups during the second week of Marsa. He
was the last—a taciturn brown giant in his forties, accompanied by a young Blue of barely twenty. When he presented
himself to Lisbeï and Kelys, he made it clear he and Sergio
would leave the dig at the end of Maïa (if the dig lasted that
long) to attend the Entraygues Assembly. Then he said, "We
have a mutual friend," and handed Lisbeï a small envelope.

I recommend them. Signed, Toller.

Duarte was not a native of Bretanye, however, but of
Escarra. Sergio was from Termilli, almost next door to Lisbeï's
native Bethely. He seemed an unlikely recruit for a dig: rather
thin and delicate. "Don't worry about him," Duarte assured
her. And indeed, his fragility was more apparent than real.
His naked body revealed the muscles of a racer who could go
the extra klim. He didn't have much to say for himself—one
of those southern Blues who were pathologically shy and always made Lisbeï think of Garrec. But Duarte spoke for him.
Duarte very soon spoke for all the other Blue men on the
team.

It's a thoroughly curious phenomenon to watch, wrote Lisbeï in her diary, to which she always gave a precious moment
at the beginning or end of the day, no matter how tired she
was. *I've never seen so many men together all at once, all of
them Blue, all working on the same thing. At harvest time in
Bethely there were never more than four or five per farm. They
almost disappeared amid the Blue women and the Green girls.
They did whatever the capta assigned them, just like everyone
else. This is a little different, though—nothing but digging and
banking the earth walls. The strongest take on the heaviest work,
and since there are a lot of men, they're the ones who do it. After
all, that's why we enrolled them. What's interesting is to see how
the work has been shared out. We were already organized in
teams by the time the last Blue man arrived, and it was Duarte
who assigned the men to our various teams. I don't quite understand how it got done so fast. He's not especially qualified. Is it
because he's the oldest? Or—and this is even more bizarre—
because he's the strongest? Are men, among themselves, still at
that stage? (A curious expression, by the way, "men among
themselves.") I thought this archaic outlook had disappeared
with the Harems. Or rather, with the eugenic programs of the*

Hives, which attempted to eliminate men who were too violent or too strong. (From the standpoint of physical size and strength, Duarte is very definitely an anachronism.) In any case, he took charge of assigning the men to the existing teams. They were good choices, and we ratified them. Kelys is the only other person I ever saw assume such immediate authority without doing anything particularly notable. It's clear she has worked with Blue men before, and she seems perfectly at ease in their company. More than they do with her, or with us.

Or us with them. It was easy to forget Dougall was a man: we didn't live with him all the time! Of course we don't live with these men all the time, either: they're camped about a hundred meters from us. But in fact we work all day with them. When Elli began to get hot in the first week, and we all began to strip off our jackets, tunics, and shirts . . . We never gave it a second thought. I suppose if I'd been from Nevenici, I would have thought twice about it, even after seven years in Wardenberg. But if I were a Nevenici, I would not have gone to Wardenberg. Anyway, we stripped, and after a while it began to dawn on us that they all seemed somewhat embarrassed, even Dougall. When it came time to wash at the end of the day, we went ahead to use the river running by the camp, and they went next. The pattern was set that first day and remained unchanged.

Might this be another silly reason why there are so few male recuperatas? It doesn't bother me that much, nor the others. Perhaps it's because in the Bethely garderie we were always together, even in the showers. Wardenberg women are even more accustomed to having men around. Among the women from other Families, only two broke their contracts right away when they saw the Blue men.

Does it bother the men? In order to spare them . . . Well, perhaps . . . But it would still be silly, wouldn't it?

Dougall in particular seemed very disturbed. He had quite naturally set up his tent beside the rest of the Schole group. After the other Blue men arrived, he paid Lisbeï a visit. At first she couldn't understand his problem. "But you can set up your tent wherever you like, Dougall!" Then she realized he wanted to stay with the group, but felt he ought to join the other men. Lisbeï had no idea what to advise. She sent him to Kelys, who took pity on him and chose in his stead: he pitched his tent among the men.

"What was the problem?" said Lisbeï when Kelys told her of this.

Kelys looked at her doubtfully. "Do you think you could imagine your roles reversed, with you in Dougall's place?" Before Lisbeï could answer, she threw up her hands. "No, forget it. Merely a rhetorical question. Believe me, this was probably the best solution."

Dougall didn't look very happy, nonetheless. And why a rhetorical question? But after trying to imagine their roles reversed, Lisbeï was obliged to admit she probably couldn't imagine things from his perspective. She wouldn't have had a problem: she'd have joined the other Blue women, of course!

Kelys nodded, looking very much like someone who'd just proved her point.

As of the first week on the site, Kelys persuaded everyone to begin and end each day with a taïtche session. It was a good way of getting ready in the morning and of relaxing in the evening. Women and men together. The Blue men were excellent at performing the taïtche, noted Lisbeï with some surprise. At first many of the Blue men and some of the Blue women who'd enrolled in Wardenberg seemed uncomfortable with the idea. "No one's forcing you," said Kelys. But by the end of the first week, everyone took part in the exercises except Sergio—not because he didn't want to, but because the taïtche made him fall into a sort of coma, said Duarte as the young Blue stood in front of Lisbeï and Kelys, his head slightly lowered.

Like Tula? But Lisbeï hadn't noticed anything special. . . . Impelled by curiosity, she went over to touch Sergio. He shrank back, and Duarte stepped between them. To defend him? Lisbeï stood very still, her hand still extended. She was amazed. *Afraid?* Sergio was *afraid?* But of what, in Elli's name?

"Sergio doesn't like people to . . . touch him," said Duarte, his voice a little muffled.

"It's all right," said Kelys in her calm voice, and the atmosphere eased a little.

When they had walked away, Lisbeï turned to Kelys. "He's like Tula? I didn't sense a thing."

"More like Antonë."

"Have you touched him?"

"No," said Kelys.

It wasn't very important, anyway. What was more interesting was the way Duarte stepped in, the almost threatening luminescence quivering in his aura.

Maybe Sergio is one of his childreen—one of his children, rather, mused Lisbeï in her journal that evening with a touch of humor, though she was also intrigued by the story that had sprung to mind with the incident. She was prepared for such a phenomenon, having seen Toller with Sygne's little ones. It wasn't unthinkable to attribute this kind of defensive reflex to a man protecting a childe—*a child* (what a nuisance this masculine form is!) It would be extremely odd but not inconceivable. *After all, what's to prevent a Blue man from looking for his . . . productions? Any more than a Blue woman from looking for her genitor?*

Here Lisbeï substituted an exclamation point to emphasize her amusement: *. . . her genitor! But it's not really a situation you can turn around, Kelys. Men may sometimes want to know their childreen, if I can credit Toller, but the opposite? No. Anyhow, in the case of Duarte and Sergio, you'd have to check their tattoos.*

Her story evaporated on the first afternoon when everyone took off their shirts. Duarte was a Gualientès-Teysseres, and Sergio a Termilli. They couldn't have known each other long, either; Sergio had been a Blue for four years at most.

"Have you many Blue men friends, Dougall?" asked Lisbeï during a pause when the team had just finished with a particularly stubborn tree stump. The cavalas were also taking a break as they cropped the short grass farther down the hill.

He hesitated. "Not many, really," he said at last.

"Toller?"

He seemed embarrassed. "I don't see him often," he muttered.

No doubt Toller was more a benefactor than a friend, an equal. Lisbeï nodded and added, "But what about Wardenberg, in the Schole?"

"Not really." Then, as though by way of explanation: "I was with our group most of the time."

True enough, they're all together as Green boys, but as soon as they become Red, they start circulating among Families for their Service, never staying more than two years. It must be difficult to keep up friendships under those conditions, given the average number of Blue men in each Family. When they in turn become Blues, only some of them go back to their Families. Others can't, thanks to the Juddites, and keep wandering from place to place. Some go to Wardenberg, but not for long, and are off once more after their Schole training. A good many Blue men actually live in Wardenberg, nevertheless, even though they don't belong to the Family. Still, I can see now that Dougall hasn't had much chance to make friends.

We *are his friends, is this what he meant?*

Well, I suppose he's right. But it must be a bit odd for him. . . .

Perhaps that's what Kelys meant, the other day.

The expedition established the most likely areas where they might have access to a buried complex, taking into account the lie of the land, the variations in chemical concentrations revealed by water runoff, and the experience of Kelys and others as to what one might expect in underground structures. They also took into consideration the few descriptions of Pimpernella's hiding place common to almost all the Belmont tales as well as those in the Notebook. The structure must rest on a stratum of granite running through the hill. The western slope was more eroded than the rest and revealed the exact line where the top of the granite stratum began. The base of the structure might reasonably be supposed to be at this level. Unfortunately, they hadn't the slightest idea of the structure's length and breadth, although they could make an educated guess at its height. The base of the hill formed an oval running almost north-south. The hypothetical structure must run east-west, so as to make air vents and entrances as short as possible. The digging zones consisted, in decreasing order of probability, of the east slope, the hollow between the two humps, and the west slope. Luckily, the order of probability corresponded to the order of feasibility, since the east slope wasn't as steep. They would dig there first. ("Thank Elli!" said Marcie fervently.) The steep west slope with its rockfalls would be a last resort.

Kelys had estimated the average depth to which they would have to dig on each site. If they were to try to hit the top of a domed structure in the hollow, they would need trenches ten meters deep at the very least. The half-dozen underground structures discovered to date had been domed, but it might not be true of this one. But working in from the east slope, they would have to cut through at least a hundred meters horizontally and some half-dozen meters vertically, after the initial clearing with explosives. This would mean going through a layer of soil followed by a layer of brittle shale above the granite. Here, however, the work would be much easier, since they were looking for conduits or passages running at right angles to the slope.

Lisbeï watched the workas strung out along the dig line, the Blue men wielding powerful pickaxes in front, the Blue women following with shovels and wheelbarrows. The hill rang with the sound of tools from dawn to dusk. On hot days they took a three-hour break to escape the sun. For the moment the weather was fairly good. Following a week of heat, the sky had turned gray, although a few small rainfalls had made them fear the worst. ("And what can be worse than rocky terrain?" Marcie had asked the company at large as they sat by the river that evening. "Mud!" the rest had chorused.) But normal sprinna weather had returned at the beginning of Aprila: blue skies, the mornings a little chilly, gentle clouds, and a few threatened storms that never materialized.

"Tired?" asked Dougall solicitously, straightening up as Lisbeï had just done.

"No. I was only thinking that if we don't find anything, we'll have to put everything back the way it was."

"We'll find something!" said Dougall.

He started digging again, and Lisbeï did the same. She was beginning to have serious doubts about her flash of intuition while translating the Notebook. What with fatigue, and the fact of having found absolutely nothing as yet to support her theory—not a single artifact, not even a crumb of matter that wasn't native to the terrain—she was assailed by objections to her theory, by other possible interpretations. . . .

"Stop thinking!" said Fraine at the midday break, seeing Lisbeï silent and preoccupied.

"And dig," added the irrepressible Marcie, raising her tumbler to the memory of Cedryn.

The sound of voices rose suddenly from the side of the hill where the men usually gathered to eat. Angry voices. Lisbeï ran after Kelys and caught up with the long-legged explora.

The men parted to let them through. In the middle of the circle Dougall was staggering painfully to his feet, his lower lip bloody. Duarte was looking at him, head lowered, fists closed, his aura a dark cloud. Sergio was seated on a rock a little to one side, head hanging, arms folded across his chest.

Kelys went to help Dougall and led him away. Lisbeï stood speechless, her heart beating like a drum. She folded her arms and took a deep breath, drawing herself up to a height that would have impressed most people, but not Duarte.

"Duarte?"

The massive body seemed to collapse all of a sudden. The anger had vanished, leaving only shame and chagrin.

"It's my fault," said Sergio weakly. He hadn't lifted his head. "I shouldn't have. Tried. To explain to Dougall . . ." He stopped talking, as though the effort to talk had been too much.

"Explain what?" Lisbeï glanced around the circle of silent Blues. They looked away. Their faces and bodies told more than their clouded auras: shame, embarrassment, pity, anger, resignation.

Duarte straightened up a little. "Ask Dougall," he said, and went over to sit on his heels beside Sergio.

In her tent, which was also used as an infirmary, Kelys had finished with Dougall. "Just a scratch," she said without turning as Lisbeï entered. "A split lip, some teeth a little loose."

"What happened, Dougall?"

"He tried to hit Duarte."

Dougall? The gentle, tranquil, even somewhat timid Dougall had tried to hit Duarte?

"What did he do?"

The young Blue was slumped on a stool, hands dangling between his knees, head lowered in an agony of shame and despair. He straightened up a little to look imploringly at Kelys, who shook her head and turned away with the blood-stained compresses.

"He told me I was jealous," he muttered finally.

Lisbeï couldn't think of a thing to say. Her mind was a blank. Jealous. Dougall. Duarte. Jealous of whom?

Sergio?

Lisbeï sat down abruptly on Kelys's stool. Total stupor— that's what she remembers. Dumbfounded at not having thought of it earlier, of never having even wondered. It was there, however, it had been there all along, but in one of those inert, disconnected areas of her mind that mobilized itself with sudden, blinding knowledge. Men among themselves. Greens, Blues—what did they *do* among themselves? Reds. She hadn't thought of any Reds but the Mother's Male. But all Males weren't "the Mother's Males," even if they all were capable, must be capable, were trained to be capable . . .

She looked at Dougall. He almost looked away, then stared back at her, hopelessly, pleading. Dougall: Blue after just two years' Service. There was something else she should have been able to understand, but she was missing some essential clue and didn't know how to find it.

"Were you jealous, Dougall?" she asked gently, watching his reaction.

"No!" Anger, denial, disgust.

Fear?

"What did Sergio try to explain?"

Seeing him hesitate, she added, "They told me to ask you."

He hung his head again. "It wasn't anything . . . bad. Just that you could . . . even when you were a Blue . . . with a Blue woman . . ." He stopped, as though choked by what he had said.

Lisbeï was completely baffled. She thought she was beginning to understand, but she had lost her.

"But I'm not jealous of them!" shouted the young Blue hoarsely, startling Lisbeï. "Not of that! It's . . . impious. Sacrilege. Even for Blue men!"

"What *are* you talking about?" exclaimed Lisbeï, rising in exasperation.

Her outburst shook Dougall, who stared at her a moment and then—no, surely he wasn't going to *cry*! Yes, mute tears, his eyes fixed on her.

She crouched down beside him, tried awkwardly to take him in her arms, murmuring encouragement. She hadn't seen anyone cry since Ysande's death. Even then, it had been Livine who had hugged Fraine while Lisbeï, a captive of her own powerless rage and heartbreak, stood by, paralyzed. Now Dougall clung to her wordlessly, his whole body trembling. She lost her balance beneath his weight, and they both tumbled to the floor. Lisbeï began to pick herself up, ready to laugh, relieved to be able to laugh. Surely Dougall would recover himself, too. At least he wasn't crying. Suddenly his aura seemed different, more condensed, more intense. But he didn't let go of her, he continued to press himself against her, eyes closed, with a sort of . . . obstinacy?

She pushed him away, gently at first, then firmly. He resisted. Then suddenly he let go and rolled over on his back, his arm covering his face.

Thoroughly mystified, as well as worried and exasperated, she knelt beside him. "Dougall? Say something. Explain."

There was a short silence, then he spoke, his voice different, devoid of intonation, dead. "You don't know. You don't understand."

Well that was just it: she wanted to understand. Why didn't he explain?

He sat up with sudden agility. Startled, she moved back. He must have taken it for something else, because he murmured, "Oh no, no, never . . ."

He stood up, wobbling a little, and ran a hand through his hair. He touched his lip with a little grimace, turned on his heel and went out of the tent.

Toward noon next day, Dulcie and Duarte found him wedged between two rocks in the bend of the river.

As a childe Lisbeï hadn't shared in Loï's dolore, for she had not known her. But she knew the ceremony had taken place, even if it had been Loï herself who had snapped the thread of her life—an action some people seemed to think very grave and even reprehensible. Never, however, had she taken part in a dolore for a man, whether Green or Blue (Bethely, praise Elli, had never lost a Red in Service). Her inveterate curiosity about what men did had been answered with, "They remember among themselves."

Now, overwhelmed with grief, she sat in Kelys's tent listening to the water dripping slowly from the table where Dougall's sodden cadaver had been laid. Her one coherent thought was *the dolore*. Would she and the others take part? Shouldn't they take part in his dolore, Fraine and Livine and the others in the group? What could she *say* at Dougall's dolore? "It's my fault, I should have understood something, but I didn't know what—I didn't understand and I still don't." No: it was Dougall's dolore, not hers. "He thought I knew, thought I understood, but he was wrong."

Something stirring in the light and shadow caused her to

look up. Someone had lifted the tent flap. Kelys, silhouetted in the doorway, a deeper shadow.

"Don't look for someone to blame, Lisbeï. I had sent him to join the men. You didn't know."

"What? *What* didn't I know?"

Kelys strode over and took her in her arms, her aura a hard hollow of compassion—bleak, resigned, with a faint red glow of anger. "He couldn't tell you, and it wouldn't be right for me to do so. The men might, if they wanted to. Duarte and the others. They were the first to take him in."

"Take him in?"

"Some men perform a sort of . . . dolore sometimes, when a group takes in a new Blue man."

But dolores were for the dead!

Kelys nodded. "It's also an attempt to restore snapped threads, to be born again in Elli."

Lisbeï was speechless. To be born again . . . when one is still alive? Was this how Blue men saw themselves?

After a while Kelys continued. "He went to see them before going to the river. They weren't able to stop him." She stood back a little from Lisbeï and studied her carefully. "Do you want to go and see them?"

"The Blues? Duarte? Would they agree to that?"

"One can ask."

Lisbeï nodded. She felt utterly torpid. Vague thoughts crossed her mind: "If they refuse?" But Kelys's aura of determination seemed to make the question unnecessary. Outside Fraine waited with the other three, all equally overcome. Kelys motioned them to follow. Several other Blue women from the team watched them go by, hesitated, then fell in behind. These were the Blues from Wardenberg.

The Blue men had gathered outside Duarte's tent. They fell silent and parted as they saw Kelys approach with the small group of women. Lisbeï found herself standing in front of Duarte. His clothes were still wet; he hadn't changed after bringing Dougall back. She knew Kelys wouldn't ask the question. It was up to her. She looked at Duarte, her head tilted back, eyes squinting in the bright sunlight. He was waiting. No anger, no rejection. Simply waiting.

"We were . . . Dougall's friends." She stopped. This single sentence had exhausted what was left of her courage.

The colossus watched her calmly, tipping his head slightly sideways.

"The mourning," said Fraine suddenly from the group of women. She left it at that.

Duarte's brown face registered some surprise, a hesitation amid the calm. "You want to take part in the mourning?" The words came slowly.

"Yes," said Lisbeï, encouraged by the emotions projected by the group behind her. The men looked at one another, heads turning this way and that, a current of uncertainty and some hostility running through them.

"Let them come," Sergio said tonelessly. "Too much silence."

Duarte turned to him with that aura of mingled pleasure and surprise, his customary reaction whenever Sergio spoke. But the young Blue fell silent again, as was his wont.

The other Blue men were very still, watching Duarte. Would he again decide for them all?

Duarte nodded. "Too much silence." It was an admission, an acceptance.

At sundown they gathered around the bonfire lit by the men —even the women who had not followed Kelys and Lisbeï earlier in the day. The table had been brought close to the fire. On it lay Dougall's body, clothed in blue. A body at peace now, its hands folded across the breast. The women and men sat down in a half circle, the flickering silhouette of the table between them and the fire. Alone or in groups, they had meditated all day long on what they would say.

Lisbeï still had no idea of what to say. There were hundreds of images in her memory, surely, hundreds of gestures, words. . . . Which of them should she have understood, which of them showed she had not? She couldn't tell. Even that last conversation in the tent . . . No, it didn't capture Dougall, but rather her own ignorance, impatience, and lack of awareness!

Perhaps she should simply try to say what Dougall meant to her. But what *did* he mean to her? He hadn't been "a friend," not really, despite her use of the word that morning. He had been part of the decor at first, an oddity. Gradually he had come into focus—a face, a name, a voice, always a little removed from the others. Then she had almost forgotten about his maleness, and he had become part of the group. . . . But not a friend like the others. What word could express their relationship? What had they really shared, just the two of them? The Notebook. Was he a Scholemate, then? A colleague? Did the clue lie in his incredulous joy at her proposal to present his efforts at translation under her name to the Haldistas' Association? No, it couldn't be. That wasn't Dougall, that was herself, yet again.

Dismayed, she realized she couldn't even remember when she'd first seen him—really seen him. Perhaps she should speak about that. Could she talk of such a thing at Dougall's mourning? If she'd had her journal for that year, she could have looked for the first mention of Dougall. But she had to rely on memory alone, a memory overflowing yet deceptive. She couldn't fix the shifting images of Dougall. No sooner had she called one up than it drifted away, to be replaced by images of Bethely—but why Bethely?

After a while she closed her eyes in exhaustion, letting herself sink into a sort of humming, semiconscious state. She had spent a sleepless night, tortured by inexplicable anguish, turning their last conversation over and over in her mind, rising to scratch incoherently in her journal, and lying down again to stare into the dark. At dawn, when someone had come to tell her Dougall had disappeared, she'd been unable to shake the irrational certainty of some catastrophe. And then, toward noon, Duarte coming into camp with Dulcie, leading his great red cavala with Dougall's streaming body hanging over the saddle . . . The rocks hadn't torn his face much—just a triangular purple dent over the left eyebrow, the blood washed away by the river. It gave his face a puzzled yet childelike expression. Childelike. She had always tended to call him "little" in her journal despite the fact he was a year older. She'd been careful not to do it in front of the others, though. But being taller wasn't the real reason. Little Dougall. Not because of any special affection . . . Childelike. *Childelike.* What had Dougall, the little Green, been like? There were no garderies in Verchères, but the boys were brought up apart from the girls. . . .

She woke with a start. Evening was drawing in, and Kelys was crouched beside her, Kelys, solemn and calm. It was time, time for the dolore, time for Dougall's mourning.

The women spoke first, the Blues in the group—Fraine and the others. "You knew Dougall before we did," Duarte said. "Tell us about him first."

There was a long silence. But Lisbeï wouldn't, couldn't

begin. She still didn't know what to say. The images that had followed her in and out of sleep, of Bethely and the garderie, were completely irrelevant! She didn't know why Dougall was dead, didn't know what to say about him, and she couldn't make up a story, not for a dolore where the true picture of a life must be found. Nor could she describe just any image that sprang from memory; she sensed it would be somehow mendacious, and she couldn't lie to Dougall now!

"The first time I touched him . . ." Livine's voice trailed off uncertainly. "When I speak," she resumed more confidently, "I tend to touch people. I know it's rather annoying, and I've always tried to get rid of the habit. But the urge is too strong. The first time I talked to Dougall and touched him—well, I don't know what we were talking about, but I clearly remember touching him, because he gave a start and I apologized, explaining that it was one of my shortcomings. 'No, no,' he said, 'I don't consider it a shortcoming.' And he told me how he used to do the same thing when he was little and how he'd been trained not to, but he didn't mind my touching him at all. He was . . . he was pleased that I touched him as I would anyone else."

Shifting firelight, silence, and Marcie's voice rising, resolute.

"He would have liked to be a communicata. He said that, one day. Well, not in so many words, but we all understood what he meant, I think. It was just before he heard he'd finally been chosen. We were talking about different sorts of training, about what was the most interesting job. And he said, 'Communicata.' I must have laughed—I have the habit of laughing for no real reason. It was just so . . . bizarre, the idea of a man being a communicata at all, not him in particular. And anyway, it's not a job I think of as particularly interesting. We discussed it afterward, but he didn't say much. Lisbeï asked him at one point what he found so attractive about it, and he said, 'Helping people talk to one another.'"

Marcie suddenly stopped, as though she'd been prepared to say more but had thought better of it.

Bertia told of how she'd quarreled with Dougall. After Ysande's death Fraine had been very irritable, ready to lash out at anyone. Particularly at Dougall, who answered back every time. His behavior exasperated Bertia, who told him to leave Fraine alone when she was in that mood—especially him. Of course she meant to say "a man," meaning what would a young Red male know about such things, about babies who kill you and don't even stay alive themselves, and what with Fraine having to bear two more after her first one had died. Dougall got angry, and so did Bertia. He walked out, slamming the door. (Dougall, slamming a door!) Only then did she realize it was her "especially you" that had infuriated him, even though she didn't quite comprehend why.

Again, silence, then Fraine's voice, a little hoarse. "Dougall was a Red who didn't really want to be one. He was afraid, not in the way I was, but afraid all the same. He was brave, though, much braver than I. When my third babie died, he came to see me at home, undaunted by the presence of my sisters, cousines, aunts, even my mother. He said nothing, even when I made the same old nasty remarks. He put his Blue necklace on the bedside table and waited for me to keep quiet. Then he said, 'We are more than our Lines.' Exactly what Ysande used to say. I've never worn his necklace, but I still have it. Perhaps he could have been a communicata. We never really talked about it, but he knew. He understood. He, too, loved Lisbeï."

Silence. The luminous shadows dancing. Vague bits of blue tunic, half a face, a hand. The smell of fire and smoke uncurling in a sudden gust of wind. The shattering into glittering fragments of all those Dougalls whom Lisbeï knew without really knowing, without wanting to recognize them, without being able to . . . Her own voice rising, slightly unsteady, speaking words that held no real surprise.

"He reminded me of Garrec. And Turri. And Rubio. The boys in the Bethely garderie. There were three of them, but they were like one person. One, and always off to one side, but I didn't want to pity them because I, too, was alone."

4

Entraygues —
Angresea — Bethely

499–519 A.G.

1

That year the Assembly of Mothers took place at Entraygues, a medium-sized Capterie in east Bretanye conveniently near Litale and Escarra. It was a region of fertile plains, marshy woodlands teeming with fish and game, and a number of long-eroded, primeval mountains covered with forests. This lush countryside surrounded a stretch of badlands, a wasteland of flat desert and scarred uplands. Most of it was still shown in darkish gray on maps. Old documents commonly referred to these badlands as the heart of a densely populated region at the time of the Decline, possibly a *megapolis* such as those mentioned in surviving fragments—agglomerations that had covered tens of square klims with stone, asphalt, and concrete, after which the builders had burrowed beneath the earth in search of more space. As it turned out, the amount of contamination registered in these badlands confirmed the old maps. Flora and fauna were still rare and often deformed, and expeditions had to be limited to a fixed number of weeks, otherwise the exploras put their health and possibly their lives at risk.

The presence of these badlands was something of an embarrassment, yet the Family was also rather proud of them. Several very useful finds had been made there, and though badlands didn't belong to anyone in particular, a small portion of the material recovered went to the Family with the closest territory. Some of the objects that had come to the Family in this way were exhibited in the great hall of the Capterie. The one that fascinated Lisbeï most was a portable clock, about the size of a small brick. The clock face consisted of a black rectangle with large, luminous, ruby-red figures that changed at regular intervals—or rather, new figures formed themselves out of the old by ingeniously combining a limited number of straight segments. The figures were very angular as a result: 112305, which you had to decipher as eleven hours, twenty-three minutes, and five . . . six, seven, eight, nine seconds—the blinking shapes were hypnotic.

Lisbeï realized she had been standing utterly still in front of the clock face for a good minute and a half, trapped in that ever-fleeting yet strangely fixed moment of time. She preferred her own big pocket watch or the round-faced clocks in the Bethely Tower or the Citadel. The slender hands crept imperceptibly around the space that was time, this circle where a segment of human life could be clearly marked off. *Almost* half past seven, *more than* seven minutes, *already* quarter to eight.

And you could see eight o'clock, too, and eleven o'clock, midday/midnight, the whole day, all days, the same on the round clock face, different in life, a duration of time that you could foresee or look back on, but not this infinitesimal, eternal present that dribbled time away along with the concentrated consciousness of the watcher, prisoner of a rectilinear race toward a goal never reached.

The slow passage of the pointed hands had its own inexorable rhythm of ever-returning hours, but at least you had the choice of forgetting to wind the clock! And you could see the hours recurring—midday-that-is-midnight. In the Belmont volumes, opened at random in a feeling of panic (all those books!), Lisbeï's eye had caught a line of poetry. After a determined effort, she had deciphered the line. It came from one of those Decline poems, the kind in vertical blocks of roughly the same size, most often separated by a blank line and written in very early Old Frangleï, even older than the language of the Notebook. *The Thirteenth returns . . . Once more she is the first.* A note at the bottom of the page (those Decline people had to explain everything, even poetry) seemed to connect this line with the figures on round clocks. How strange to think these same people had abandoned their round-faced clocks for numbers with no past or future, numbers that flipped on the screen with a contagious fragmentation of time, and by the same token, of spirit. . . .

"And it's still working," said the voice of Duarte behind her.

For him, the fascination lay in the fact that the object could still function after so many centuries. Yes, this too was fascinating, but in a rather terrifying way. Machines still intact and alive when their inventas had long since vanished. How these people must have detested their machines, even while endowing them with this near-immortality they themselves would never possess! An immortality relying on sun power, nevertheless. It had merely been a lump of black plastic with a dark screen when taken from the dig at Entraygues two centuries ago. The diggas had left it in the sun with other seemingly useless objects. What a surprise it must have been to see the figures blinking! In the Great Hall of Entraygues, the clock had been set on a pedestal where the sun lingered longest.

"Too bad our site didn't operate on the same energy source," Lisbeï acquiesced.

I was so relieved when Kelys shouted up from the bottom of the elevator shaft that all was well, Lisbeï had written after the first day of exploring the underground site at Belmont. *She really took an awful chance going down on her own like that, even though she had more experience than anyone in the group. And then everything stopped. Luckily, the Decline people went in for emergency staircases as well. And we had gasoles. It was rather like the discovery of the Sanctuary: just time to reach it, to see how it must have looked in the Decline, then no more light, no more power. Frustrating. Kelys thinks things were activated only by the presence of human beings, in order to save energy. But like the Sanctuary, there was hardly any energy left after all these years. If we hadn't happened on the conduit, if we'd had to dig all the way to the main tunnel, we might have found no power at all. Who would have thought they'd put the entrance right at the bottom! But perhaps the terrain was different in that epoch.*

As it turned out, "that epoch" predated the Sanctuary. This would become clear several years later, when researchas had finished cataloguing and indexing all the artifacts from the site, the books, the paintings, the sculptures, and the strange, grotesque, or ugly objects that must also have been considered works of art since they were found with the others. The books would allow them to estimate the construction date of the site—"the Museum" as Kelys had immediately dubbed it, explaining the meaning to the other diggas.

None of the books bore a publishing date later than 2120. But when was that—"2120"? 2120 in relation to what? In relation to a vanished history. If you combined the Maerlande, Hive, and Harem calendars, taking 0 as the year when the word "Harem" first appeared in surviving texts, the present year was 623. Proto-Harems had existed earlier: there was scattered evidence of occupation dating back even 150 years earlier. But the ravages of the Hive people and the continual recycling of Decline ruins made it difficult to be precise.

"Rather surprising the Entraygues people should have kept this object." This time it was Kelys behind her.

Yes, indeed: the clock dated from roughly the same period as the contamination in some of the badlands. The incongruity of this Family keeping a possibly contaminated object had struck Lisbeï when she and her group met the narrowly traditionalist Mother of Entraygues. Marcie had proposed a theory: the Entraygues people had never seen eye to eye with their neighboring Progressista Family; perhaps the Mother of the time had thought the clock would make a lethal gift. Kelys had found the idea highly amusing. "Apparently no one in Entraygues has suffered from it, anyway," she'd retorted, "although it's been gathering dust for over two centuries!"

Now Fraine, who had gone round the Great Hall with the others and was casting a last, doubtful look at the display windows, asked Lisbeï, "Has this given you any idea of what you'd choose?"

"Not really. What about you?"

"Not the slightest."

How was the unprecedented Belmont find to be assessed and shared? From the moment the group had seen the underground chambers, the numerous problems had been obvious. Kelys had suggested taking their difficulties directly to the Mothers' Assembly. Basically, one twelfth went to the Family on whose territory any find had been made. Another twelfth went to Wardenberg for housing, copying, and conserving the documents. One third went to the contracting explora, plus one sixth for her Family of origin if it still supported her, as in Lisbeï's case. The rest went to the partnas and others enrolled in the project. No problem there, as long as only recuperable materials were involved. It was the "useful" artifacts that made things difficult—mainly a question of their usefulness in terms of possible technical advances. So-called "useless" artifacts still had potential scholarly value, but it was something of a gamble. Books and written documents had first to be deciphered and translated. Only at this point could their potential usefulness be assessed, and then their value. It could all be very time-consuming.

By a sort of natural sedimentation, slow and unseen, the original books and documents always ended up in Wardenberg, and evaluation was often based on Wardenberg research —hence the traditional twelfth portion finally allocated to this Family by the Baïanque Assembly of 171 A.G. A system had eventually been developed for assessing technical and scientific works. So far, exploras had never discovered a whole Library of intact works not immediately recognizable as scientific or technical documents. What precious information did these books hold concerning the people who had buried them, the Decline, and no doubt many other subjects? Who could tell? How could such things be assessed or divided?

And no one had ever discovered a "museum" of art works.

Luckily for the exploras, the site abounded in recuperable materials, especially metal: bookcases, pedestals, various cupboards, and a good proportion of the structure's removable parts, such as staircases and platforms. The historians would want to preserve the site in its original state, and there would be frequent tussles with the recuperatas. As usual, the recuperatas would win, and the historians would have to make do with part of the first floor. To tell the truth, however, the historians would only object for the principle of the thing. All the Museum floors were as alike as two peas in a pod, its builders clearly governed by the need to store the maximum number of artifacts in the minimum amount of space. Most surprisingly, however, there was no sign of the pharmaceutical plant to which Lisbeï thought she'd found a reference in the Notebook.

All things considered, those who favored the Wardenberg credit system, or at least a prudent extension of it for general postdiscovery negotiations, would have weighty arguments on their side. Kelys had immediately foreseen this.

With only three weeks left until the Entraygues meeting, the deadline for submitting motions had long since passed. Still, Kelys judged the Belmont find important enough to warrant asking for the special procedure set up after the Decision of Antonë. She had signed the application for funds, but had insisted that Lisbeï alone sign as contracting explora for the dig, with Kelys herself heading the list of project workas. How fortunate: Bethely, the (respectable) Family of the contracting explora, would approach the current Capta of the Assembly; an independenta like Kelys of Fusco couldn't have legally done it.

The Belmont carrier pidges flew off with their urgent messages, arriving almost simultaneously at Bethely and Selonges. Kelys knew the Mother of Selonges well enough to suggest using this shortcut. At the same time, a communiqué about the Belmont find and the emergency motion went out to Mothers on the point of setting out for Entraygues. The motion asked for new rules for assessing and sharing discoveries of this type and magnitude.

Lisbeï and her troop of Blues were already celebrities when they reached Entraygues. Moreover, Lisbeï was unofficially free of her debt and of Wardenberg: Kelys was absolutely sure of this, whatever the final sharing arrangements.

During her two-year apprenticeship, there had been times when Lisbeï used to let herself dream—times when the rain leaked through the tent and she couldn't get to sleep on her thin mattress. In one of her dreams she discovered an amazing site and returned to Bethely in a blaze of glory, laden with treasures. In another, she made some staggering breakthrough connected with the Notebook and went back to Bethely, again in a blaze of glory though none the richer. Now, with the ironic twist that sometimes occurs when dreams become real, in one stroke she had discovered an amazing site linked to the Notebook and would be showered in glory and riches. It would be a long day before she saw Bethely again, however—but she didn't know this.

The Bethely delegation had been in Entraygues for only two days when Lisbeï and her group arrived. Tula would get there even later, on the eve of the Assembly. She was very pregnant and had traveled by boat, a slower but more comfortable means of transport. Tula hadn't wanted her Second Memory to speak for Bethely, and she herself would probably represent the Family's interests more effectively—Mooreï was becoming more and more conciliatory with age. Selva would have been perfect, but Selva was ill.

Lisbeï had not known Selva was ailing. Mail didn't get forwarded to the badlands, and she hadn't been back to Bethely for ten years. Oh, there'd been letters from various people, Kelys had told her the news, and she'd even had a visit from Antonë the year before, right in the middle of the "Independentas" controversy. It was a completely personal support visit, since an Arbitra had no special authority after a Decision.

The letters and Kelys's reports had given Lisbeï a pretty clear idea of how Mooreï, Antonë, Selva, and even Tula had changed with time—how their personalities had developed, that is. But she'd never imagined the physical changes. Kelys seemed almost immutable, apart from the snow spreading slowly through her crinkly hair. Antonë was only thirty-five when she came to visit, and Lisbeï had mostly been struck by the changes in the Medicina's personality. But Selva ill, old, slowing down . . . She was only forty-two!

"She never really recovered from the last babie two years ago," sighed Meralda. Despite her Red status, she was now Mooreï's apprentice-Memory and Tula's assistant at Entraygues.

Yet another childe, one who might never leave the garderie. And for what? Had Selva wanted to remain a Red longer than Mooreï and prove to all Maerlande how amazingly fecund the Bethely women were? Mooreï had refused her insemination turn at thirty-eight, as was her right since she was two years over the official age limit. And here was Tula, eight months pregnant and forced to undergo this exhausting journey!

"Oh, Meralda," said Kelys, appearing out of nowhere and startling the young Red, "shall we get to work? Time's getting on. . . ."

They had to put the finishing touches on the motion to be presented by Bethely. Officially Lisbeï wasn't supposed to have anything to do with it. She had decided to take this convenient fiction literally and had told Kelys she wouldn't take part in the work sessions with Meralda. In the end, whatever the fate of the motion in the Assembly, what counted was her freedom—freedom from Wardenberg for her, Fraine, and the others, with all their debts repaid. They'd probably have a surplus, too—little enough individually, but they'd all agreed that in a lump sum it would make a sizable contribution to the *Tribune*. They were determined to use the Belmont find as a

means to keep on jogging the elderly researchas in the Schole
out of their rut.

Lisbeï studiously ignored Meralda's disappointment and
headed for the Fairground between the Capterie and the Garesche River. The Entraygues Capterie stood in the center of
an almost circular tongue of land formed by a wide loop in the
river. It wasn't much to look at: the usual Hive architecture,
small, identical two-story structures arranged in staggered
rows around a central building where the Mother and her
immediate family lived. Apart from two extra stories, even
this building had nothing special about it. Luckily, a lush
growth of clambering roses and vines covered most of the
walls and hid the dreary sameness. The defense-works once
surrounding these buildings had disappeared. The only real
reminder of the Hive women's warlike fantasies was the flat-
topped mound resembling an ancient terreplein on which the
Capterie stood.

Stalls and trestle-tables leaned against the mortared
stones that now reinforced the almost vertical slopes of the
mound. They skirted it and then straggled in exuberant disor-
der as far as the Garesche River. Beyond, on the other side of
the mound, the Games field also stretched from the wall to
the river. In the heat of early Juna the water was full of bathers splashing about and skiffas sliding upstream, propelled
against the current by young rowas. Entraygues was to hold a
regatta. There'd been one in Wardenberg, too, though not in
Bethely. Every Family that could muster a big enough stretch
of water held swimming and boating events as part of the
Games. Lisbeï felt tempted to try the water and wandered
down the path to the river. Fraine and the others had said
they'd spend the afternoon there. Maybe she'd find them, although she'd been busy with her diary longer than expected,
and Meralda had delayed her even further.

She found them on the old towpath, towels thrown over
their shoulders, tunics damp, hair still wet. Two of Duarte's
youngest Blues were heading back with them to the Fair:
Marek from Entremer, dark and broad-shouldered, and the
fair-haired Toome (odd name!), supple and athletic of body—
he'd gone Blue after only a year's Service, a typical example of
the "nonstabilized" Wardenberg.

Clusters of bathers were still wending their way to and
from the river. Like boats avoiding a reef, they skirted Lisbeï's
group at a respectful distance, turning to look as they passed.

Fraine smiled hesitantly at Lisbeï. "Would you like some real company?"

As people arrived in Entraygues for the Assembly, the news had spread. The famous Lisbeï-of-the-Decision was getting herself talked about again. This was the persona by which most people in and around Entraygues had known her. When the Baltike and Bretanye Families arrived, a second persona joined the first. Lisbeï-of-the-Independentas. Now a third was emerging, Lisbeï-of-Belmont, whose involvement with the Notebook bridged the gap between the first two. And there would be a fourth: Lisbeï-of-the-Blues, as yet an unknown figure, for Duarte and the other men had entered Entraygues separately, breaking up into small groups.

There were droves of Blue men here for the Assembly festivities. Most of them ended up on the Games field, as might be expected. They had been coming in ever greater numbers to provincial Assemblies and the Assembly of Mothers ever since young Blue men and Green boys had been allowed to enter the Games. "To encourage them," Marek had said. This might be true for many Blue men who were there, but not all.

Duarte and his group had virtually disappeared since their arrival. Lisbeï supposed they must be in the Blue men's tent village on the far shore of the Garesche, putting the finishing touches on the motion they'd present at the Assembly —*if* they were allowed to do so.

The unreality of it all suddenly struck Lisbeï. Perhaps it was the deceptive familiarity of the river, the hum of the Fair behind her, the memories of Bethely sumras that flooded back, submerging the events of the past two months. Had she really agreed to help Duarte and his group? Had *Kelys* agreed? Kelys hadn't wavered when Duarte turned to her and asked, "What will Wardenberg say about it?"

"Wardenberg will hear it at the same time as the others," she had replied tranquilly. She'd say nothing to Sygne. No Blue had doubted Kelys's word, for most knew her by reputation at least. In the stories men told each other, there existed another Kelys: in the semicircle of mourners on the night of Dougall's dolore, it was Kelys who had spoken after Lisbeï, Kelys who had described the ashen-faced Dougall brought to her by Toller one night in Wardenberg, so that the deep wrist slashes could be stitched and the incident kept quiet. A sixteen-year-old Dougall, overcome with desperate rage at not being chosen, rage against the other Reds, the Mothers, his teachers, everyone, a rage so sacrilegious, so inexpressible that he'd been driven to turn it on himself.

"Too much silence," Kelys had said in the end. "Too much silence among yourselves, too much silence between you and us. Tell us about Dougall, Duarte."

One after another, the voices pierced the flickering darkness around the flames. Nameless, faceless voices, the voices of men floating up into the night. After a while, despite the stupor of grief, Lisbeï realized this couldn't be just Dougall they were talking about. The Green seeing a cavala for the first time in his life when he left his garderie—this couldn't be Dougall. Verchères had no garderie and no cavala stock farms. But at Termilli, yes, even if it was Duarte speaking rather than Sergio, Duarte describing the young Green going up to the cavala, marveling at the soft, quivering nostrils, the hot breath on his outstretched hand, the powerful, quiet body of the huge creature . . . then the brusque shoving aside: Reds aren't allowed, it's too dangerous—but he's still only a Green, couldn't he just make them run around the paddock, just feed them? No. And was this Dougall, this ecstatic young Red, the newly chosen Male? Now his life has real meaning, he'll be the true servant of Elli, he'll Dance with the Mother, redeem the sins of the Decline! He's in luck: the Family was kind to him, this Mother is neither too young nor too old—though what does it matter, since he can see Elli in all Mothers, always. He practices fervently, training for hours each day, his body instinctively moving through the figures of the Pairing from the moment he slips into a trance. He prays morning and night, performs the ritual learned in childhood, the endlessly repeated prayer, concentration, kundali—for of course he has always been a good childe of Elli, and his phallus can stay hard and erect for hours if he wills it—no, if *Elli* wills it.

But perhaps this is Dougall, this young Male silently sobbing as he comes back from the Mother's chamber. He has tried, how he has tried to give her pleasure the way he'd learned! But she has pushed him violently away, stared at him as at some sort of revolting insect, hissed softly, venomously, "Don't do that again!" It could be Dougall, this young Red doing his Service, who always finds the Mother with her Red compagna when summoned, because she wants to be lubricated to lessen the pain, and because she doesn't want him touching her, naturally . . . and the compagna staying the whole time, and afterward the Mother crying in the arms of her compagna, who strokes her hair and eyes him with disgust.

The voices coiled and spiraled into the night as the fire spat out its dying sparks and settled down like a sleepy red beast with staring, hypnotic eyes. This can't be Dougall who overhears the Doctor speaking to her assistant as he leaves the infirmary. "This one doesn't produce much now. He'll soon be finished." She's right, but not in the way she thinks. Finished, can't do it anymore, *can't do it anymore*. At the Celebration, with the drug, he could surely do it—but he isn't the Mother's Male, he wouldn't be given the drug. Here, like this, in the small meditation room of the infirmary, he produces less and less. If he could have some of the drug, just a little, the way he had with the teachers in the beginning . . . He is terrified. Elli must be punishing him for that thought and for his months of misery, anger, and resentment. He's more careful about his food, does all the prescribed exercises, and meditates for hours. All virtually useless. He'll soon be a Blue anyway, not because he's sterile, but because he's *impotent*.

Dougall, not Dougall, perhaps Dougall—but they were all really talking about Dougall just the same, just as it was Dougall whom Lisbeï saw when she thought of Garrec. The tiny Green crying in a dark corner of a garderie because he'd found out Elli punished boys—this was Dougall, or Rubio, Turri, Garrec. All living together but each alone in his silence. The other boys can't be, mustn't be, friends. They must only think of Elli, no one else. Each Green boy alone in his sin because sometimes, during meditation, the images evoked fade before the face of a loved one, a familiar body, another forbidden boy whom it would be sacrilege to love. Alone because Blue men don't usually live with Families and are too far away or sometimes too jealous, like Reds when they aren't the Mother's Male. Alone even when he, too, becomes a Blue, alone with the shame of his wretched body conditioned since childhood, a body that can't forget and continues to desire . . . to desire the Mother—but he is a Blue man now and can't possibly talk to a Blue woman, can't possibly tell her . . . and never, never more will he dare Dance at the Celebration.

Dougall. This could have been what Dougall, the young

Green, the young Red, had endured, what others were still enduring, what Dougall would no longer endure. Dougall: Duarte, Sergio, Marek, and Garrec, Turri, Rico of Cartano, the Blue from Nevenici, and even Aleki, the fierce Aleki of Felden, and all the others—those who flee to the badlands, those who are sent there, those who kill themselves. Those who kill others.

And while this litany of great and small agonies spiraled into the gloom above the fire-glow, another slowly filtered upward, the voices of women, echoes of other scenes and memories, all different, all the same, Lisbeï's included—the memory of Ysande smiling and her face nearly as white as the pillow, of Merritt lashing out against an old grievance: "They lead the good life, they don't have to bear childreen and care for them, they don't have to die because of them." No, not in the same way. Cardèn's voice overheard in the shop one day: "I'm going back tomorrow," and Lisbeï knowing what she meant, sensing the mixture of lassitude and resignation, the syringe, the waiting, the disappointment mingled with relief, and "I'm going back." Ysande just before her last babie was born, huge, deformed, her expression always slightly strained. The puffy scar (never before seen, though often imagined) across the abdomen of a woman in the pension shower. Loï shivering by her small fire in the Badlands, Loï on her roof, ready to jump. And Selva, a block of ice, reading the letter from Cartano.

Selva's searing agony, the marks on her shoulders and breasts, her tears after Aleki. Tula who would never cross the sea until time had robbed her of the will to go. And Lisbeï-who-should-have-been-the-Mother, who had lost Bethely, who could never have been Tula's compagna in any case.

But those were memories she kept to herself.

Resigned but resolute, Lisbeï continued on her way toward the river, accompanied by Fraine. She owed her this tête-à-tête anyway. The day after the mourning, they had buried Dougall close to the river. By unspoken agreement, work hadn't begun again until the next day. Instead, on the day of the burial, they had silently done a few domestic chores, sharing the burden of a knowledge communicable only by glances. Lisbeï had spent the day writing in her journal, transcribing everything she could remember about the night of mourning.

Without a single commentary or question, without a "yes, but."

When work resumed, Lisbeï fell back into her old habit of watching, trying to catch any word or gesture that might reveal a change between Blue women and men in the various teams. There seemed to be little difference, unless it was the occasional added awkwardness. Were they quicker to smile and dissipate it, then? Perhaps. She felt a little disappointed, noting in her journal, *Real life moves more slowly than stories, even though it may resemble them sometimes.*

Later Lisbeï would also make a note of Kelys's response when she asked during a break, "Did you know all that?" Kelys had understood her meaning perfectly: *Should I have known all that?* She'd thought for a moment, then replied, "Part of it, one knows part of it," suddenly using the impersonal form current in Wardenberg. "One sees another part, but one doesn't always think about what one sees. Not so much at Wardenberg, anyway; a little more elsewhere. But one can learn."

Now, as Lisbeï stood by the river, she truly saw Fraine, saw how Livine had always seen Fraine. But Fraine had never broached the subject of Livine, and Lisbeï had to admit to a guilty sense of relief.

The two of them sat down on the grass, dangling their feet in the water. Lisbeï didn't want to swim now. Anyhow the afternoon was practically over, and a swim would only have been a way of delaying her talk with Fraine. For a while they watched the other bathers. The Bretanye Greens, their training session over, let their skiffas drift with the current, oars held high or trailing in the water. Distant laughter and breathless cries wafted over the river.

"After all, what difference would it make if men had their own events at the Games?" said Fraine, opening with a safe subject. Lisbeï was ready to follow her lead and wait, even though they had discussed this with Duarte and the others on the journey to Entraygues.

"No difference in the short run, probably. . . ." Lisbeï couldn't see what difference it would make, even in the medium or long term, but something bothered her. Would it really solve anything to have separate events? Weren't men already isolated enough? Marek had said half a loaf was better than none.

"The Green boys and young Blue men already take part

in some of our events. Do you want these to be separate, too?" asked Fraine, pressing the point.

A silence followed. Even the women and men Blues in Lisbeï's troop hadn't been able to agree on this. No, said some, yes, said others, and a minority of one, Toome, said everyone ought to compete together in all the events, under the same conditions as Blues and Greens did now: equal height and weight. At this, both sides protested vehemently.

"After age fifteen the difference is too great!"

"It's questionable even for Green boys and girls."

"Certainly not for all events, in any case!"

Cavala events were admissible, but Green boys and young Blue men shouldn't be allowed into the shooting or anything to do with defensive skills.

This was the insoluble question. All the other events in the general gymna category, or contests of artistic and technical skill in singing, sewing, making jewelry, sculpture, architecture, or horticulture had the same underlying aim. The Games offered a chance to show off the physical and creative skills of Family Lines, and of Greens who would not only grow into robust Reds, but could later become architectas, researchas, gardenas, or other useful workas. Tests of skill and accuracy such as archery or similar events showed only one thing: aptitude for the Patrol. And the Patrol was every woman's obligation, without exception. Each must do her stint of surveillance on the limits of various badlands.

"Every *woman*," Dulcie had stressed, adding sententiously, "Men and arms don't go together."

Duarte and the other Blues had let this assertion pass. *Because they go too well together.* The old Hive proverb inevitably resurfaced whenever the subject of Green boys and Blue men entering combative games arose in Maerlande—or the Entraygues Assembly when the time came. It was a difficult argument to refute.

What about the rest?

"Not the parade!" (Dulcie, adamant.)

"Why not? We're taught how to Dance. Why not the parade?" (Marek, unruffled.)

"But the Dance isn't part of the Games! It isn't a contest! The parade is different." (Dulcie and her friends, stubbornly reiterating this rather lame argument.)

It is different. Lisbeï found herself paying more and more attention to this remark. "How is it different?" she would later ask the Assembly, as she had asked Dulcie that night. You Danced in Elli, yes, you lost yourself in Elli in order to make Elli a part of yourself (mostly through the use of the drug, but she wouldn't say that in the Assembly). Inversely, you always remained distinct from your partna in the parade, even if the aim was for each to become the reflection of the other, to complete the other as perfectly as possible. "So how could a man and a woman be partnas in the parade?" someone would say. What about men together, then? The parade required strength, endurance, grace, and agility, as did the Dance. In fact, the parade was a preparation for the Dance, something you trained for as arduously as for the Patrol. If men could Dance (as no one would deny), then they could parade together. Their training took them directly from the taïtche to the Dance, but this was simply a tradition that could be changed like many others.

Here the rationalization began to wear thin, revealing underlying prejudices. Juddites (like Dulcie, though she really wasn't a Juddite) would launch into a somewhat irrelevant, not to say repetitive argument that had already surfaced at Serres-Morèna. How compatible were the Games with the Word? Just how far did the Games foster a competitive, aggressive spirit that ran contrary to the teaching of Elli? Seen from this standpoint, any participation by men was definitely out!

"It's a question of being the best for Elli, in Elli, not of triumphing over others," Duarte would riposte in the Assembly. The colossus could be quite eloquent when he wished. All men could be, it seemed, if they got the chance. "Nowhere does the Word say Elli created us all the same, like bricks! Elli loves and cherishes all of us, but for different reasons, because of different qualities. Trying to do better what we already do well is perfectly consistent with the Word. Every Believra seeks her own way of satisfying Elli, doesn't she? In the peace of Elli, no one way of seeking or achieving is better than another." (Duarte could quote the Word by heart as well as anyone.)

Deprived of this argument, the Juddites would finally reveal their deep-seated fear: if men were allowed to enter the parade, where would it end—even if they weren't competing with women? ("*Against* women," was the actual expression, betraying their sentiments even further, since those who paraded *against* others were never the best.)

The Juddites would then trot out the old Patrol argument. Men were weaker than women—not in body but in mind and spirit. Their habit of violence was too ingrained, and even the Hives hadn't been able to eradicate it from their genes. Did people want another *man-made* Decline? ("Those Juddites and their antiscientific fantasies!" groaned Antonë whenever she heard this. "Violence is surely not part of the genetic code.")

The Memory of Fontbleau would rise to ask whether the Juddites were really in a position to speak of violence in these terms, since their ancestors had fought for the Harems, created the Hives, and caused Garde's death—at which point the discussion was to degenerate, that afternoon, into a shouting match over the Notebook. Lisbeï, though seething inside, would listen in prudent silence as the argument raged on.

Earlier, on the road to Entraygues, Duarte had answered Dulcie's concerns about the parade in a conciliatory tone. "Well, at least it would be possible for men to enter the other events, wouldn't it? Young Red males and Blue men separately—that would be the most reasonable suggestion." "The most likely to get Assembly approval," was what he'd meant. He'd apparently taken it for granted that the motion would be tabled.

"It's a start, anyway," said Fraine, interrupting Lisbeï's reverie. "It's what they want for the moment, isn't it? You're always thinking too far ahead."

Was there a hint of reproach in her last words? An implied *you're always thinking too far ahead and don't see what's under your nose*? Too far into the future, too far into the past . . . No, it was Lisbeï who reproached herself for the way she'd treated Fraine. And yet she couldn't stop herself from retorting, "But farther in the future means they won't just take part in the Games but in the Assemblies as well."

"Well, why not?" retorted Fraine, more for argument's sake than anything. But Lisbeï had no intention of letting her penchant for imagining the other side corner her into arguing against something she actually believed in more than Fraine! Anyway, this wasn't what they were really talking about.

"It'll be an interesting development, I suppose," she said, stopping the discussion in its tracks. A brief silence followed. Fraine neither replied nor changed the subject, and Lisbeï finally gave in. "What did you and Livine decide in the end?"

Fraine glanced at her, then looked back at the river, embarrassed yet grateful for the opening. "We'll exchange vows on the eve of the Celebration."

"Oh, that's good!"

The young Blue turned toward her and Lisbeï smiled, thinking once again that she must ask Kelys how to project emotions. But Fraine seemed to sense her sincerity, for she too smiled, eyes shining. Then the smile faded, leaving a pensive, slightly melancholy expression in its wake. "And you, Lisbeï?"

Has there never been anyone, will there never be anyone? Lisbeï understood perfectly what Fraine meant. What could she say? She didn't know if there would ever be anyone. And no, there hadn't been anyone since Tula, but she didn't want to talk about Tula. Was it wrong to prefer being alone to only half caring for someone? To using someone just for pleasure? Fraine would have probably suffered far more from this than from Lisbeï's innocent indifference.

Innocent? Really? wrote Lisbeï that night, raising a skeptical eyebrow. *Probably no more nor less than with Dougall,* she decided after a moment. But on reading the entry over she added, *definitely less innocent than with Dougall.* Still, it wasn't the same thing, and anyway, Fraine was a survivor, as she had told Lisbeï while they sat talking by the river. Lisbeï, unable to answer Fraine's question, had replied with a seemingly unconnected apology. "I'm sorry." But Fraine must have seen the connection, because she had touched Lisbeï's hand and said, "I'm here." Perhaps she meant, "I love you all the same, I'll still be your friend." It didn't matter what Fraine actually said, for Lisbeï had sensed the affection and strength behind the words. Her throat tightened, and she surprised herself by murmuring, whether in gratitude or shame, "I don't deserve it." Fraine almost sounded like Ysande when she replied, "You're not the only one to decide what you deserve."

After that they sat in silence and watched the river, at peace with each other at last. Their trains of thought must have been very different, however, for Fraine broke the silence with the dreamy comment, "In a way, it must have been good before the Decline, with as many men as women. Everyone didn't have to be inseminated, and women could decide not to have childreen if they liked, since there were always enough to keep the Lines healthy. And it must have been the same for men. If they wanted to keep to their own sex, they could probably do that too. . . ."

Somewhat astonished, Lisbeï pondered the past as depicted by Fraine. And could men be with women if they wanted? "Probably," said Fraine, but she obviously hadn't thought it through. The theory didn't necessarily imply *women* wanted to be with men in that way! Mothers, perhaps? But there weren't any Mothers in those days. Still, this suggested another idea that suddenly filled Lisbeï's thoughts. *Since it's sometimes harder for the Mother's Male once he becomes a Blue, or so they say, are there Mothers who . . . develop a desire for men when they no longer Dance directly with them at the Celebration, when they're no longer Mothers? Can one desire men? For pleasure? Logically, yes. Why not? Logically, the reverse of a proposition is also possible. Could one push logic to absurd limits and imagine Mothers unhappy at the departure of one particular Male? Mothers who'd become Blues looking not for one special Blue woman, like Parsia and Nylla in one of Ludivine of Kergoët's books, but for a special Blue man.*

Clearly, "Why not?" could cover some very different cases. However, this particular query smacked too much of pure logic to be convincing, at least for Lisbeï. "Don't you think it's a bit risky for us to try to imagine how things were before the Decline?" she countered, deliberately pragmatic. Fraine agreed, of course.

Lisbeï subsequently recalled this conversation as she deciphered *La Princesse de Clèves* with its heroine tragically torn between her incomprehensible love for one man and her duty toward another. But that was much later, when the shock of the *romances* of Belmont (they later called them "novels") had begun to wear off—at least for her, if not for the rest of Maerlande.

2

Two days to go before the Celebration. The interminable discussions over the new way of evaluating and sharing recuperable discoveries were winding down. It was then that several historians rose in the Assembly to ask that the works of art in the Museum (Kelys's expression had been immediately adopted) be kept together for all to see, in a place safe from the whims of any one Family or individual. Perhaps the members of the Belmont expedition could be compensated by asking Wardenberg to make a global evaluation of the materials used in sculptures not made of wood or stone. As for pictures and other objects difficult to evaluate, couldn't they be assessed according to criteria generally used in barter?

"But who'll be in charge of creating this . . . new Museum?" queried Ireyn of Wardenberg. "How will it be done? And who will buy . . . barter for the works first? Will each Family contribute?"

Ireyn wasn't serious—her tone of voice made this clear—but the Kergoët delegate took her literally and rose to speak. "Why not? That's more or less what we did for the Patrol and the Western Fleet. With so many artifacts involved, it's absurd to think of dividing them up between the members of the expedition. Wouldn't it be better to keep them together in a special place as a visible reminder of the Decline?"

And where would this special place be? (The voices were from Escarra.) Wherever its location, it would be within the boundaries of some Family or other. Would this Family volunteer, or would it be chosen? By whom? And for what? Not just for the enormous task of building, but for maintenance, conservation, organizing tours . . . This wouldn't be some tiny Sanctuary, after all. Showing these works properly would require a huge installation. Who would compensate the Family for its expenses? An association of Families? An association transcending Families?

The very idea of a transcending power had the Juddites up in arms. What! Were these objects of the *Decline* to be used as a pretext for forcing Families to abandon some of their independence, so dearly purchased? These things belonged to the *Decline*, and there was no reason to treat them with greater reverence than any other recuperable artifact— on the contrary. Not only were they completely useless, but the hands and minds that created them were those of the *Decline*. (The voice of Maine, the Memory of Nevenici, sounded the word like a death knell.) The fatal contamination —spiritual if not physical—had surely passed into whatever they'd touched. In Maine's view, they should have been destroyed.

The Assembly didn't waste too much energy in refuting the Juddites' predictable wrath. In any case, the Nevenici tirade was merely for form's sake. The artifacts certainly wouldn't be destroyed—they all knew it, especially Maine, but she had to speak for her Family, not for herself. Then to everyone's amazement, Tula of Bethely took the floor and stated that Maine might have a point—there might indeed be something dangerous about the works discovered at Belmont. Lisbeï was stunned. She was about to protest when a hand stayed her arm: Kelys, her aura at once amused and curious.

"Yes, a spiritual danger, not a physical one," continued Tula. "This is perhaps what a discovery of this size represents, and maybe we should consider it first of all. Until now we've never recuperated anything but fragments of the past, bits and pieces that didn't bear much relation to one another, for the most part. Whatever unusual or disquieting revelations they might hold always had a limited impact, and we invariably had time to assimilate whatever it was without too much difficulty, even when it touched the deepest chord. . . ."

This was a clear reference to the Notebook. A murmur rose in the Assembly. Tula waited until it had died away. "With the Belmont discovery we have not only objects, but books, even though these aren't being discussed at present. It may be that the whole Decline, or large parts of the Decline, will suddenly be revealed to us. Fortunately, it will take a long time to decipher the books. I say 'fortunately,' because time can serve as a buffer, as it has in other circumstances, minimizing the shock of knowledge that is too strange and, given its origin, possibly perverted. The effect of encountering such objects, such pictures and sculptures all in one place would be overwhelming. Who knows what critical threshold might be crossed in the minds and hearts of the viewers? No, the only way to cancel out or at least mitigate the effects of the Decline's spiritual miasma, possibly harbored by these objects . . ."

Quiet laughter rose from the Bretanye ranks. "The Decline's spiritual miasma?" whispered Lisbeï, unable to believe her ears but staggered by Kelys's obvious approval. "Don't tell me you wrote her speech!"

"Oh, I just made one or two general suggestions," replied Kelys, not the least ruffled.

"Don't laugh!" Tula went on, once silence was restored. "We may not agree with the Decline's idea of art, but you've all seen the few photographs taken at Belmont. Is there one among you who wasn't touched by some object? Some work?

Moved, shocked, taken unawares, maybe horrified—but touched, all the same. And afterward, as we left, weren't we all either upset, depressed, or dumbfounded?"

This time the ripple of murmurs had an approving tone. Was this why Kelys had insisted on selecting most of the subjects photographed herself?

"Just imagine a whole building filled with such objects—and I'm not speaking of the considerable cost of this Museum, as you call it, or the material and technical problems of building and maintaining it, so clearly outlined by my neighbors from Escarra. No, the only way to exorcise these objects, these works, these relics of the past is definitely *not* to gather them in a single place. Nor is destroying them any better. The Hives would have, but we aren't so easily frightened anymore. What we must do is share them, not only among the members of the Belmont expedition and the other rightful claimants, but among all the Families, and even within Families, so that everyone can have an object if they want. In other words, we should circulate them in the bartering network. In this way, they'll become ours—they'll take on *our* values. In fact, we must give them new life, a chance at redemption as we ourselves have had the chance. They may be the products of the Decline, but so are we through the Harems and the Hives. Let us never forget it! But, unlike us, Elli wanted these works to escape the ravages of time so they might reappear in the Tapestry, untouched by the events that had shaped our destiny. Just think: each of these works was probably created by a single individual. It's up to each of us to reintegrate them one by one into the thread of our lives—the thread of Elli."

All thought of protesting, all astonishment faded. Lisbeï listened as Tula's last word echoed within her. A dolore—a memorial grieving. A vast dolore, not for the Decline, but for those who lived and died in it, a grieving that was a rebirth and would last as long as the works passed from hand to hand in barter. Yes.

Tula sat down, clearly relieved. She found it difficult to stay on her feet for long. The silence spun out a little, then Marine of Lletrewyn rose to speak.

"Each of the works must be photographed, and the photographs must be reproduced and circulated. It will take a very long time, but in my opinion delay is a positive factor."

"These works are sure to change hands more than once," added the Memory of Maestera in a pensive tone, "passing from person to person throughout Maerlande—the kind of exchange that takes place at the Celebration. And it will go on for years and years."

"And the things received in barter the first time round can be put into some sort of common fund to pay those doing the photographing, indexing, handling, and so on," chimed in Kergoët.

"Hmph. What you mean is, most of it will go to Wardenberg," grumbled one Cartano. Nobody paid much attention, since Wardenberg was already compensated for the Schole's work, and this would amount to roughly the same thing.

There was a definite future tense about all these remarks, as though Tula's motion had already been put to the vote and passed—as indeed it was at the end of the day, along with a motion from Gualientès proposing that the members of the expedition, and others with a vested right, be allowed to choose first without giving something in exchange. After all, the contents of the Museum represented a substantial slice of what they would have received under normal circumstances. Consulted, as was the custom, the beneficiaries quite thankfully agreed on the fairness of this solution. Most of them, beginning with Lisbeï, had been rather daunted by the prospect of sharing all these objects among themselves. She much preferred them to be alive and circulating throughout Maerlande than dead and lying in a heap in some Museum. Even so, she had an urge to say, "Yes, but . . ." She felt there was a hint of collusion among the speakers (except for the Juddites, of course). And it wasn't just Kelys and Bethely. She held her peace, however. There was nothing forbidden or reprehensible about discussing matters outside the Assembly, exchanging opinions, or even sharing the same views on a given subject. Within limits, there were subtle distinctions between strategy as such and actual lies. She needed to believe it, thinking back on her understanding with Duarte and the others.

Everyone was in fine humor as the day drew to a close. Even the Juddites were caught up in the general air of satisfaction, and several went up to Tula afterward to congratulate her on her foresight and wisdom. She greeted their remarks with a tired smile and remained seated in the Bethely section, waiting for the crowd to thin out before tackling the stairs down to the floor of the Assembly tent. Lisbeï looked across at her for a moment. She wouldn't bother Tula now, she decided. She could talk to her later that evening. Someone had just passed along a note, an invitation to Lisbeï to attend a reception for the expedition members.

Lisbeï had barely exchanged two words with Tula since her sister's arrival late at night on the eve of the Assembly. They'd met in a crowd next morning during the opening session and had embraced awkwardly after a hesitation on both sides. Lisbeï knew why she herself had hesitated: Tula looked so much like Selva, a young, vulnerable Selva, so pale beneath her red hair, so fragile with her swollen belly—a delicate eggshell that might crack at the slightest shock. As to why *Tula* should hesitate, Lisbeï wondered. After all, they hadn't seen each other for ten years. Tula had changed physically, but so had Lisbeï. She was a head taller than Tula now. Suddenly she'd felt huge, awkward, conscious of her wide shoulders, her long legs, her callused hands, and all those muscles hardened by four months of almost uninterrupted digging. Ten years. Was it possible? She had been able to live through ten years without Tula. Did her hesitation contain a shred of embarrassment, of shame at having done so? Perhaps this was why Tula had also hesitated. "You and me, together." Not together, as it had turned out, and both of them had survived. What was left of all those promises, all those dreams, all that pain? Two strangers who had looked at each other for a moment without moving and then embraced, simply because this was the thing to do, what was expected of them.

And then the first week of the Assembly . . . the receptions, the breaks between discussions, always surrounded by a crowd, always separated by people, because Tula was the Capta of Bethely, because everyone wanted to meet each other before the Celebration, to engage in a flurry of arrangements and ententes, settling everything so as to approach the Celebration with a more serene heart.

Today was Lisbeï's birthday. Tula had sent her a gift the day before (a handsome compass, silver and inlaid enamel), with a short note: she had to attend the reception for Litale Families. And people wouldn't understand if she stayed away for a birthday—she didn't even say so, it was a matter of course. She added something in slightly different writing, as though after a long pause. "There'll be something else for you tomorrow." What did she mean?

And tonight at the Entraygues reception there'd be another crowd of people. People Lisbeï knew—but that was just the problem. They were merely names for Tula—*if* Tula remembered her letters and could conjure up the names of those who shared Lisbeï's life, her life without Tula. . . .

Lisbeï slipped though the press of bodies, heart heavy and eyes averted to avoid meeting anyone's glance, to escape the trap of some inane conversation, of having to be Lisbeï-of-Belmont or Lisbeï-of-the-Notebook, or Elli-knew-what-other-Lisbeï. She got out of the tent without incident and followed the crowd downhill to the Fairground. All Assembly members had the same impulse once formal sessions were over. Before repairing to their tents to freshen up and get ready for the social rituals of the evening and night, people took a little stroll back into childhood. They lingered among the stalls of the Exchange, dreaming of what they could get, give, or be given. But, as in other years, Lisbeï had no one to shop for and nothing to offer. Perhaps she could use the photographs of things she might choose from the Belmont treasure: a painting of a young woman with a big, rounded belly, but dressed in blue—heavy, archaic clothes—and reading a letter in the twilight. And a little statuette in green stone, creamily pale and cool to the touch, a sinuous-armed, almond-eyed dancer with an enigmatic smile on her round face. "Is that all you want?" people would say later, surprised. But she'd decided to trust the instinct that had made her stop in front of this painting, this sculpture, when going round the Museum with Kelys and the expedition photographer. Such rows and rows of stuff. It was overwhelming. (Tula had been right, "overwhelming" was the word.) Her attention had been caught by other works afterward, but they all merged into a sort of fog. These two items were the first, and they stood out more clearly in her memory.

Kelys would choose a small bronze, an open hand. In the upturned palm lay two human bodies, a man and a woman entwined. The hand was definitely masculine, but if the unknown sculptor had caught this faint intuition of the Dance of Elli, one couldn't really blame him for being a man.

Lisbeï recognized the voice before the face, despite the passage of four years. Not that the face had changed—the hood thrown back revealed the same finely chiseled countenance beneath the tangle of black curls, the same large, light, almond-shaped eyes. The gentle glow of the gasoles smoothed away whatever wrinkles there must surely be by now. Forty years old, at least . . . almost the same age as Antonë or Selva. The realization came as a surprise to Lisbeï.

The Blue gave her a wry smile. "Are we doomed only to meet at Assembly Fairs?"

"There was the Wardenberg Concertalle."

"I mean on the quiet, anonymously like this. You say 'incognito' in Litale, don't you?" She knew perfectly well, considering her excellent Litali.

Lisbeï looked her in the eye for a moment, trying to imitate Kelys's tranquil equanimity. She was getting better at it all the time. Like Kelys, too, she had the advantage of height, particularly now. And yet this woman didn't seem short; she was so vibrant, like a whip or a bowstring . . . and her light also vibrated, dazzled the beholder—*electric,* that was the word; Wardenberg had given Lisbeï the adequate expression for what she felt in the presence of Guiseïa of Angresea.

The Blue stared back at Lisbeï, head slightly tilted, a mischievous gleam in her eye. The necklace, its red and blue glimmer half hidden, still circled the brown throat. But this was no longer a Mother—at least not technically, since her second living daughter, Coreyn, now bore the title. It was Lisbeï who first looked away, masking her defeat by running her fingers through her hair and gazing around at the Fair.

"Will you exchange something this year as well?" Lisbeï felt she'd achieved a suitably nonchalant tone. It annoyed her to think Guiseïa probably saw through it all. Why should Lisbeï feel hostile? This woman had never harmed her. She'd been the Capta of Angresea, but it wasn't . . . her fault, thought Lisbeï—a rather absurd way of putting it, but it brought her unexpected reaction into focus. Maybe the Capta of Angresea was some other woman, like Lisbeï-of-Belmont or Lisbeï-of-the-Independentas. The Capta of Angresea . . . her relations with Bethely, everything Lisbeï had learned from the news and rumors concerning the quiet but stubborn Progressista, this woman whose destiny had been altered by the accidental death of her younger sister, the designated Mother—none of this should have had any place in Lisbeï's dealings with the "incognito" Blue, to use her expression, the woman who was now watching her. Who was also Toller's twin. How did this fit in with all the other identities? Lisbeï found it especially difficult because Toller had never spoken or written of it, and she couldn't imagine being related to a man in this way. She was about to ask impulsively whether Toller was at the Fair too, but stopped herself, remembering Guiseïa hadn't yet answered her first question.

"How did you guess?" The Blue smiled and reached into a voluminous cape pocket. She drew out a packet and pulled back the fine, glossy fabric in which it was wrapped, revealing a slim leather strap studded with glittering stones.

"Cyndrella's sandals," said Guiseïa, at once amused and indulgent. "I couldn't resist. They're for my third daughter, Sylvane. She collects them."

Yet another Guiseïa: the attentive mother with several childreen to think about. Lisbeï couldn't help smiling at her own discomposure, and, as often happened, this rueful self-awareness brought back her poise. Guiseïa, no doubt sensitive to this change of mood, continued in an unembarrassed, neutral tone, merely a woman in the middle of an Assembly Fair chatting with another woman whom she'd like to know better.

"What are you going to do now?"

For an instant Lisbeï had a dizzying sense of *déjà-vu,* the feeling that once again she would have to remain silent about certain plans, as she had ten years earlier.

"Return to Wardenberg?" continued Guiseïa.

Lisbeï realized the Blue was referring to a time beyond the end of the Assembly (the end, this time, not the beginning . . . for Lisbeï and Kelys had decided with the others that this would be the best time for them to intervene). She heaved a sigh and started walking, not even bothering to notice whether the Blue followed her. "Yes. After Belmont is wound up, of course."

"Of course."

Of course. No triumphant return to Bethely. How could she have seriously entertained such a childeish fantasy, anyway? Later, much later, and only maybe, would she return to Bethely. First there'd be Belmont, the photographs, the books, cataloguing, assessing, sharing . . . And then, the Independentas, the *Tribune,* and yes, Wardenberg. A few trips, surely, to meet other Independentas who'd made themselves known through letters and articles. And doubtless there would be conferences to organize. And as a treat, the occasional chance to decipher the Notebook.

"You don't seem exactly thrilled at the prospect," remarked Guiseïa. There was no mockery—rather a sort of solicitude.

"It's just fatigue."

"Yes," replied the other pensively. "The campaign was quite a strain. . . ."

Lisbeï stopped abruptly. Guiseïa turned, and the two women stared at each other for a moment, Guiseïa somewhat surprised at first, then concerned, then smiling, almost in excuse. "Kelys," she said.

With a returning sense of irritation, Lisbeï began walking again. So Kelys was talking about her behind her back? Kelys knew this woman, this ex–Mother of Angresea, well enough to talk about her, to tell . . . "What did she say, exactly?"

"I knew Dougall, too."

Lisbeï realized she couldn't keep on being annoyed. Guiseïa's sad voice held too many undertones—no, not undertones, it was simply a statement of fact, but one that suggested to Lisbeï so many possibilities that she found curiosity getting the upper hand. "Did you know him long?"

"I met him the year he was passed over. Poor boy."

She seemed sincere. Why would she pretend, in any case? She was a Progressista. And more important, she was Toller's sister. She probably shared his views on men's lives.

The two walked slowly on, their steps matching. Not a word passed between them, but this shared knowledge had suddenly created a bond in the midst of the crowd. Soon they reached the broken glimmer of the river. Reflections quivered on the dark water. On the opposite bank a great fire had been lit, and black silhouettes crossed back and forth in front of its tawny glare. Snatches of music floated on the wind—the sharp ripple of flutes, the insistent clack of castagnas, and the staccato beat of guitars thrumming to the frenetic rhythms of Escarra. The men were dancing among themselves in their camp across the river.

"Have you ever seen Escarra people dance?" asked Guiseïa, her voice pensive.

Yes, their waists tightly encircled by wide sashes, backs arched, heads held high, the scornful yet imperious clapping, the fingers in perpetual motion, the faces aloof even when the dance was most wildly explicit. Of course, only the women of Escarra danced in public. Until this very night Lisbeï hadn't realized the men of Escarra also performed these dances.

Suddenly a presence loomed beside them. Kelys.

Guiseïa didn't seem particularly surprised. Perhaps just slightly annoyed? "They're dancing," she said simply.

"They're getting ready," was Kelys's reply.

"Duarte's made a decision, then."

"Yes."

They fell silent. So much said in so few words. Lisbeï felt her irritation rising again. Duarte recommended by Toller, Guiseïa Toller's sister, all these people at Entraygues—and she'd never for a moment put two and two together and realized Guiseïa could already be informed, that the former Capta of Angresea *must* be aware of what was afoot. Were there others, other Captas ready to support Duarte's request on the final day of the Assembly, unaware, as Lisbeï had been, that they were party to . . . to what? A conspiracy? Was this the word for it? Or was it a "movement"? Lisbeï's imagination bubbled with possibilities, wiping away any wounds to her self-esteem. So: it had been decided. Was it Dougall who made Duarte decide? And yet when Duarte arrived at the dig, he was on his way to Entraygues—or so he said. Perhaps he hadn't really made up his mind at that point?

This, however, wasn't the question Lisbeï put to Guiseïa. "Do you know Sergio as well?" she asked.

Guiseïa nodded. "During his first year of Service in Escarra, in Gualientès, he was kidnapped by renegadas. Duarte and Toller brought him back." That was all she said, apparently confident Lisbeï would have no trouble imagining the rest of the story, or at least *some* story. And yet it was the type of story Lisbeï would never have believed possible. Renegadas? Renegadas kidnapping Reds? But whatever for?

"It's happening more and more in the South," said Guiseïa, misunderstanding Lisbeï's amazement. "Sometimes they're organized."

And the patrols were there to keep watch on badland limits, not to go in after anyone, even renegadas. Even *organized renegadas*.

"But the patrols . . . ," Lisbeï murmured, voicing her thoughts.

"That would be the solution, Lisbeli?" countered Kelys, "More patrols?"

Lisbeï hadn't thought this far ahead. She was still trying to come to grips with the idea of organized renegadas. "But why would they kidnap a Red?"

Kelys looked at her for a moment, saying nothing. "Elli didn't make us naturally resigned to our fate, Lisbeli," she said at last. "If Elli had, Garde would have had no reason to come among us."

It's happened before, thought Lisbeï with a start. Renegadas have fled without intending to die or to come back like Loï—and they weren't sterilized. To kidnap a Red for . . . In the *badlands*?

The imagination boggled. Such hate, such despair, such utter contempt. And there were real renegadas as well, the kind who killed, or ones like Aleki who were *sent* there, who stayed there. Organized renegadas.

Lisbeï stared across the river at the black silhouettes dancing in front of the fire. She thought of Dougall, of Fraine, who sometimes during the second year of her Service alluded to . . . She thought of Loï, who had indeed escaped. And of Gerd, of Myne.

"No," she said quietly in answer to Kelys's question, which still echoed in her mind. "Increasing the number of patrols certainly isn't the best solution nor the only one."

Something moved beside her: Kelys turning to Guiseïa with approval, Guiseïa skeptical. Had they made bets on her reply? Lisbeï was amazed by her own ignorance—all the more so because this ignorance lay at the very heart of her perceived wisdom, of things she'd always taken for granted. She turned to the two women.

"My education needs a complete overhaul, doesn't it?" For some reason, she suddenly thought of Toller.

Guiseïa looked surprised but delighted.

Kelys was merely amused. "No, just to be completed," she said with amiable nonchalance. She jutted her chin out at the scene across the river. "Would you like a closer view?"

"Is it possible?" asked Guiseïa in astonishment.

"Now it is," was Kelys's reply.

Several hours afterward, Lisbeï remembered the Entraygues reception and Tula. But it was far too late.

From the moment Lisbeï rose to speak in the Bethely stand on the last day of the Assembly, everything went according to plan. Duarte was with her, enveloped in his hooded blue cloak. The main subjects of interest to Bethely had been dealt with, and Tula had departed a week after the Celebration. Meralda was left to take care of other business and gain experience. Lisbeï had been both disappointed and relieved, for though she hadn't found a chance for a serious talk with Tula, neither was she forced to explain why she wanted a friend with her in the Bethely stand on that final day. Tula would have wanted to know, but Meralda asked no questions.

The Assembly Capta scanned the tiers of seats for form's sake before putting the traditional question to the delegates. She was clearly on the point of pronouncing the farewell blessing, and it was with unconcealed surprise and dissatisfaction, expressed in a deliberately audible sigh, that she gave the floor to this latecomer. Lisbeï quickly ran through the brief opening words that had been rehearsed, then sat down as Duarte in turn rose and threw back his hood. The Assembly was thunderstruck. Duarte wasted no time. Before the shocked silence could turn into angry murmurs he began to speak, his loud, gravelly voice carrying to every part of the tent. He even got through his initial proposal without interruption. "We move that the Games, and particularly the parade, be more accessible to Green boys, to all Blue men, and to all Red males not in Service."

Exclamations, shouts, and protests greeted the motion—phase two, all according to plan. Duarte silently folded his arms and bowed his head. Lisbeï stood up and did the same, and so did Meralda—after a brief hesitation, so brief as to surprise Lisbeï. Then the entire group of Blue women from the Belmont expedition followed suit, rising in their Family stands where they had asked permission to witness the Assembly closing. Gradually, throughout the Bretanye and Baltike stands, a scattering of red and blue figures also rose—those who had known of this motion, such as Guiseïa, or who had an inkling, such as the women of Lletrewyn, or who were simply ready to allow a Blue man as much right to be heard in the Assembly of Mothers as anywhere else.

The uproar died down, and—again according to plan—Duarte was able to plead his case, though not without a certain amount of interruption. Arguments and counter-arguments, fresh waves of protest, questions, further arguments, objections, all of them foreseen . . . Perhaps Lisbeï found it all so routine because, at each halt on the road to Entraygues, she, Duarte, and the others had tried to anticipate every contingency. This was a palavra much like any other: more lively, of course, and provoked by a *man,* granted—a last-minute palavra most Assembly-goers would have cheerfully foregone, but a real palavra for all that.

The groups' worst fears didn't materialize. No one tried to throw Duarte out. (If a Juddite attempted to propose a motion to this effect, her voice was quickly drowned out by the general tumult in the surprised and curious Assembly.) Duarte was allowed to speak freely despite interruptions. When, toward the end, a voice was heard expressing shock and asking that the Blue be punished for daring to transgress Assembly rules of procedure, hardly anyone responded. Never before had such a thing happened. Were they going to prolong the Assembly even further in order to decide his punishment? In any case, he obviously had accomplices, said some. How long would it take to decide *their* punishment?

Not accomplices, said others, *partisans,* fairly prominent women allies. Many of his arguments made a lot of sense. What else could he have done, anyway? The very fact of having to act in this way showed that Assembly procedures, and perhaps even Family procedures, were clearly inadequate. Protests greeted this statement, but less vigorously than Lisbeï had expected. Were people merely tired, or were they seeing the light? Perhaps one led to the other. . . . In any event, the whole subject would have to be discussed in individual Family Assemblies. It was more to the point for delegates to return to their own Assemblies than to sit around in Entraygues, debating a punishment that the Families might veto, should they decide the Blue was right.

To everyone's relief there was a grudging consensus, and by eleven that night Crisanne of Selonges pronounced the blessing that should have freed the delegates at ten in the morning. In the flickering torchlight, the members of the Assembly made their way through a waiting crowd of mute Blue men, several hundred strong, and beyond them a crush of spectators, curious, perplexed, worried, or angry. Discussion had raged outside as well as inside the tent, with women and childreen, Red, Blue, and Green, going at it hammer and tongs while the Blue men stood by, scrupulously silent as planned. The discussion kept on long after the delegates had left the tent. That night in Entraygues, no one got to bed before dawn.

I didn't think it would be so easy, wrote Lisbeï in her journal. She was dropping with fatigue as she wrote, but conscious that she had probably witnessed a historic moment. Faintly amused, she noted a tinge of disappointment in her surprise. What had been initiated this day would surely bring far greater change to Maerlande than the Notebook, yet the odd thing was that the Assembly had not been nearly as fiercely resistant toward Duarte and his supporters as toward herself, ten years earlier. Why? She was too tired to speculate and merely noted the fact.

On the morrow, however, Lisbeï found herself assailed by some of this same fierce resistance, much to her chagrin. A group of Juddites, but also some more moderate Believras from Litale, took her aside and made their feelings clear. She noticed a similar sentiment in the occasional remark or glance in her direction on the Fairground and the Games field.

Lisbeï could have returned to Wardenberg with Fraine and the others, or gone back to the Belmont site with the expedition's Blues. The latter would continue working and keep an eye on things while waiting for reinforcements. Neither prospect tempted her, however. The very thought of all those rows of books, all those stacks of pictures, all those heaps of heteroclite objects depressed her. Bethely was probably out of the question. And Wardenberg—no, not right away! She felt like . . . like a change of scene rather than returning to stale, familiar things. And so with relief, almost gratitude, she accepted Guiseïa's invitation to spend a few weeks in the Capterie of Angresea.

3

Like Wardenberg, Angresea had never been a Hive, though for very different reasons. The women of the Harem of Angresea had razed the Chefferie to the ground, after which they had settled inland. They had divided their numbers between Kergoët and Lletrewyn, far from the existing coast. Their reasons for doing so became evident when one approached the Capterie from the southwest at low tide. The road, well maintained and paved with flat stones and pebbles, climbed the steep Morbriand range in wide loops, then followed the narrow summit running above a sheer drop of grey-pink rock that fell away toward the sea. This smooth, slightly concave wall was clearly the work of human engineering.

The sea disappeared as the road snaked briefly over the Raz range, then followed the clifftop again in a barely perceptible curve. Ahead, on the Cape of Angresea at the end of the road, rose the terraced quarters of the Capterie. Beyond this the road ran along artificial rose-grey cliffs once more, culminating in the Cape of Brezblüt. Here it veered sharply to the northeast to meet the Kergoët road. The Hive women had not wanted to be forever contemplating the vanished power of the Decline—a power capable of constructing these cliffs, these dikes nearly eight klims long, designed to stop the rising waters from flooding the interior. The same power had graded the lowlands to the east into a gentle slope rising steadily from the foot of the Trélaz range to the top of the dikes.

The morning after her arrival, Lisbeï understood this retreat to the interior even better. In olden times, the Bay of Angresea—which of course hadn't been a bay then—had been walled off from the sea by an outer dike thirteen klims long, running between the Raz and Brezblüt promontories. At high tide this eroded dike now became the Reefs, foaming, lethal, and passable only at the Melourèn Gap to the north, or in fine weather at the narrower Sans-Jeane Needle. At low tide the ruins of the former dike cut off the west of Angresea like the lower jaw of some gigantic sea monster, with the narrow Gaps looking like the unequal spaces of two lost teeth. Within the jaw, between the ruins and Angresea, the receding waters revealed a plain dotted with the remains of what must have been a large city between the Raz and Brezblüt capes. One could still make out the ground plan of buildings that had been slowly demolished by generations of recuperatas. Mud and kelp choked the structures. Here and there rusting skeletons encrusted with barnacles jutted out of the mud, relics of ancient metal structures and machines, or the hulks of boats.

Guiseïa and her household (as the immediate family was called in Bretanye), lived in the Molten Tower, the larger of the two round towers overlooking the northwest segment of the Port. The other, the Dys Tower, housed the Library, the laboratories, the workshops, and at the summit, a lighthouse with a circling beam that swept the bay at regular intervals. Angresea had its own small hydroelectric plant, of course, built across the Lletrewyn. The river emptied into the sea just south of the Batlerie (or the "Batelerie" or "shipyards" as they were variously called in Angresea). For some ten years now, the Capterie had been involved in building boats for the Western Fleet.

There had actually been a port at the Brezblüt Cape, a submarine port in a manmade cave never quite emptied by the tide—just one more example of the Decline's obsession with the depths. The whole peninsula was riddled with tunnels, although the entrances had apparently been blown up long before the Harem era. The remains of the submarine port formed a giant grotto lined with walls of some apparently nonrusting metal—irrecuperable, alas! Lamps set in the metal still shone after all these centuries, their light a vague luminescence at high tide, becoming stronger as the water level dropped.

"It's forbidden," said Guiseïa, smiling, "but almost all the children go there at least once. Part of the grotto is still above water, though the entrance is submerged. You've got to be able to hold your breath." As she said this, her aura took on a faintly nostalgic quality.

The childreen of Angresea were even more visible than those of Wardenberg. Twice a day mostas and dottas streamed down to the waterfront to harvest the oyster beds and shrimp nets uncovered by low tide. In reality, Angresea had proportionately fewer Greens than Wardenberg (and they rarely wore green)—but then Angresea had less space, even though the Capterie, built during the first twenty years after the Hives, rather resembled a miniature citadel with its terraced levels connected by ramps and stairs.

The childreen were all the more noticeable for the virtual absence of grownups. A third of the adult population worked in the Batlerie, and another third in the fields and orchards spread over the rolling plain that stretched from the south bank of the Lletrewyn to the Trélaz and Raz mountains. The rest worked in the low buildings of the cannery near the hydro dam. Mouth-watering but sometimes contradictory aromas (fish and strawberry jam, for example) floated up on the east wind. The cannery was Guiseïa's pride and joy, an asset in the Family's brisk bartering with the rest of Bretanye. Neighboring Families brought a large part of their fruit and vegetable produce to be preserved here, and in exchange provided workas for the Batlerie and the fields and orchards of Angresea.

Guiseïa considered the much-vaunted self-sufficiency of Families an anachronism, and felt it was time to move on. All

Families depended on one another for the Service and the Patrol, and no one had any regrets. Why not extend the existing network to production relations, or trade goods that were as vital to Family economies as males and wards? Why keep on manufacturing almost everything within each Family? Why not get those who made the best fabrics, or the best preserves, or the best tools, to do it for all the others? Why not systematically exchange these specialized products? It would save time and resources.

"Save time and resources for what?" asked Lisbeï the first time Guiseïa and she discussed the matter.

"To study, to travel, to . . . well, to make the most of life . . . to learn, most of all." Guiseïa pointed to the darkening night sky where the first stars were beginning to twinkle. "There once were humans among those stars. Haven't you ever wondered what it would be like to go there?"

"Difficult if not impossible, even if we could reassemble all the necessary knowledge."

"Why not?"

Lisbeï smiled at this echo of Toller's words. But she sensed Guiseïa's genuine passion and answered seriously. "We'd have to reassemble a whole technology as well, and we haven't the raw materials or enough sources of energy to do it."

"Electricity, recuperation. Better management of existing resources."

"Most of which would go to fuel such a project, to the detriment of everything else. And it wouldn't only be energy resources but human resources, too. One Family wouldn't be enough."

"We could get together. It's been done for the Western expedition."

"But this would be something else entirely. The scale is completely different, Guiseïa." One of those instances where the quantitative becomes the qualitative. "Little by little the whole of Maerlande would be altered by it, and for what? To satisfy the curiosity of a few?"

"To make contact again with those who are perhaps still living up there."

Lisbeï didn't even bother to reply: Guiseïa was fully aware of how flippant such a remark was.

But Guiseïa went on, more serious than ever. "Who knows what we could learn up there?"

"Lots of things, probably, and that's why Wardenberg is already trying to make navigable balloons."

Guiseïa shook her head, her expression quizzical. "One step at a time. Is that your philosophy, Lisbeï?"

"Why not?" retorted Lisbeï, the corners of her mouth twitching.

Guiseïa burst out laughing. "Well then, why not admit we can *begin* to change the Family trading system and the way each Family organizes its labor? If production weren't so fragmented, there'd be fewer tasks for everyone."

"You mean less variety and more specialization." Lisbeï frowned. "There's an old fragment in the Schole that mentions a man, an astronomer, who fell into a well because he was watching the stars instead of paying attention to what was in front of him."

"And?" queried Guiseïa, disconcerted by this apparently abrupt change of topic.

"The men of the Decline and before could enjoy the luxury of not thinking about everyday matters because they had women to serve them, just like the Harem men. The astronomer's maid had to fetch water from the well: she couldn't have fallen into it by mistake."

"But we're no longer men's servants, Lisbeï!"

"No, but with or without men to serve, we still have to fetch water from the well. In a way, it seems to me you're proposing we return to a similar situation. In the name of 'efficiency,' some of us will be stuck doing the same things all the time so that others can be free."

"Others whose talents aren't being put to good use."

"But as Families are now, the drawer of water can dream of the stars if she likes—when it's not her turn to go to the well. In your system, she could never dream."

"But perhaps we could do something besides just *dreaming* of the stars. Nothing ventured, nothing gained."

Lisbeï looked skeptical. "Isn't this a disguised version of 'the end justifies the means'?"

"Absolutely not! There are plenty of causal relations in the world, after all. If I want to eat fish, I have to go fishing, don't I?"

"There are different *degrees* of cause and effect, Guiseïa. Fishing to feed oneself is one thing, changing a basic Maerlande system for a doubtful benefit is another. Imagine having to do the same thing all one's life. . . . No, you have to let people at least choose for themselves. All of us have to decide on the ends. Which are inherent in the means."

Guiseïa heaved a sigh of comic exasperation. "Do you have to make everything a moral problem?"

"Yes, because it all hangs together."

"The Tapestry."

"The Tapestry," admitted Lisbeï, seeing the humorous side of the situation: herself and Guiseïa, fifteen years her senior, in the position of Mooreï vis-à-vis Antonë.

They were walking along the wide avenue of plane trees that skirted the waterfront between the two towers. Lisbeï had been in Angresea for two days, and Guiseïa hadn't nearly finished showing off her Capterie. (Lisbeï had immediately noticed Guiseïa's free use of the possessive pronoun, and she wondered how Coreyn, the official young Mother, coped with this.) Guiseïa had just taken Lisbeï to see the lighthouse, with its ingenious mirror mechanism. The top of Dys Tower provided a magnificent view of the Reefs at low tide. Local legend had it that the mud-covered city in the bay had been Ys, swallowed up in a single night by the Great Tides in retribution for its sins. The only just person in the city, Melourèn, a woman, had blown up the dike.

"Impossible," countered Lisbeï. "The whole region would have been flooded. If the breaches were deliberate, they must have been made after the second line of dikes was built."

"And I thought you liked stories!" Guiseïa laughed.

"Nevertheless . . ." Lisbeï stopped, unable to explain to Guiseïa how she could appreciate the charm and mystery of legends while analyzing them logically, in an attempt to find some link with an actual historic event. Guiseïa, by contrast, could look at things from only one perspective at a time. It was a trait Lisbeï had noticed on their journey to Angresea—a pleasant trip of two weeks, taking them from Entraygues to northwest Bretanye.

For example, Guiseïa naturally didn't believe the vitreous stones set in the walls of the Molten Tower had been melted by celestial fire, a calamity attributed by legend to the Decline. The stones actually came from a nearby site, a small volcano some twenty klims off in the Morbriand mountains. The Lletrewyn Capterie also had "molten stones" in its walls. But as far as Lisbeï was concerned, a concrete explanation didn't cancel out the figurative one. For example, there was abundant evidence of the Great Tides as a historical reality, both on the Angresea coast and in southern Escarra. There, the Capterie of Baïanque stood on an artificial rock that resembled the outcrops of the region far more closely than the dikes echoed the natural cliffs of Angresea. Had it not been for such compelling proof, however, one might easily believe the Great Tides to be merely a figment of the imagination. Lisbeï had found a reference to the city of Ys in an old textual fragment that alluded to it as though to a legend dating from well before the Decline. Time, in this case, had made reality of a legend—not for just a single city, but for thousands, for a whole civilization. Now, with the Molten Tower and Dys Tower, reality was gradually turning back to legend.

Lisbeï found this reversibility of things pleasing. She had been given a generous run of the Archives, and during the first weeks of her stay in Angresea she took an almost childelike delight in pinpointing where legend and reality switched places. The cliff to the north of the Capterie had come to be called the Noire Dame, that to the south the Suave Dame, and the Raz was the Rase Dame—a trio of ill-fated lovers, or so the tale went for the childeren of Angresea and the region. But the intriguing thing was the imaginative transposition into modern Frangleï of what must have been perfectly prosaic names for the dikes or dams in Old Frangleï.

"That takes away the charm," objected Guiseïa.

Not at all! On the contrary, it was . . . more moving to witness how each human society interpreted its environment in terms of its own dreams or nightmares. No one knew what the Harem people had invented to explain the dikes, for the Angresea Harem had been annihilated. Wardenberg had no relics that might provide a clue. The Hive people had fled the vicinity of the three "Dames," but had preserved the memory of them for posterity by spinning them into legend, turning them into figures in a sombre drama of love and vengeance. Just imagine—if Maerlande should in turn vanish, who knew how visitas in some distant time might interpret its relics— something like a map of present-day Angresea, for instance, with these curious names?

"What visitas?" asked Sylvane, trotting in circles around Lisbeï and her mother like an eager Sammoye puppy, covering ten times the distance of her elders as they strolled forward. "If Maerlande vanishes, that means the whole human race has disappeared."

A curious remark from the lips of a dotta so full of joy and good humor. But she was probably parroting some grownup. Angresea harbored a number of Progressistas who were pretty skeptical about the future of the human race.

"There must surely be people on the Western Continent, Sylvane," said Lisbeï. "Anyway, it was just conjecture."

The adolescent pulled a face. She took after her mother when it came to imagining things for the sheer fun of it. Indeed, she took after her mother in almost everything, as far as character went. Physically, Sylvane was a conundrum. On seeing her for the first time, Lisbeï had been reminded of the disbelief she'd felt at learning Toller was Guiseïa's twin. *But they don't look at all alike!* The same was true of Guiseïa and her childe. It was as though Toller's physical traits, latent in Guiseïa, had emerged as strongly as possible in her third dotta. And yet the childe was an Angresea-Fontbleau mix. The straw-blond hair, the almond Sammoye eyes, the clearly defined chin, thick eyebrows . . . She'd be pretty later on, just the same. Now, at twelve and not yet a Red, she had a merely coltish charm. She was lively and clever in her mother's rather abrupt way.

Guiseïa adored the childe and clearly favored her over her other offspring. Lisbeï watched with interest how Coreyn, in particular, reacted to this. She soon gave up the possibility of spinning a story, however. Neither the youthful Mother nor Guiseïa's other two dottas still living in the Molten Tower seemed to take the slightest umbrage at this preference. Everyone adored Sylvane, and Toller did too, although "Uncle Toller," as the youngster always called him, was somewhat more restrained in his affection. Sylvane didn't appear to have the heightened perceptions of either her mother or Toller, however. The difficult period of early childhood had passed without any major problems. Sylvane hadn't had the Malady —but then she was robust and hardly ever caught cold in the winter damp of Angresea.

"A sturdy little working cavala," said Guiseïa, ruffling the girl's hair. The first time Lisbeï heard this, she had to be reminded that cavalas, not water-buffalas, were used to haul ploughs in Angresea. She was taken to see one of these "working cavalas," an enormous beast such as was never seen in Litale. The hooves were almost bigger than her head.

"Why, it's a veritable . . . elephant!" she exclaimed, at

once astonished and amused. Then it was her turn to explain all about elephants.

"I don't see the connection," said Sylvane bluntly, a tiny, serious-faced figure standing beside the great cavala. Lisbeï had no trouble convincing the childe that there wasn't much connection between her and a working cavala, either, even a little one—if there *were* little ones.

"What tale today?"

Lisbeï swiveled to meet Toller's gray gaze. He was smiling. Anyway, she'd no reason to feel guilty. Guiseïa had opened the Library door and indicated shelves and cupboards with a wide sweep of her arm. "All the tales, all the accounts, all the deep, dark secrets of Angresea's past are here," she had said, her funereal tone belied by the wicked gleam in her eye. "Or since the foundation, at least. Dig away."

"Everything?" Lisbeï had said.

Guiseïa had stared at her, the gleam fading, then looked around the silent Library. Like the Bethely Library, it was usually empty in midafternoon, except for the staff. After a moment she had sighed, her eyes returning to Lisbeï. "Why not? Papers are just papers. One can make them say lots of things, but in themselves they say nothing. Nothing that matters, in any case."

Of course Lisbeï had taken exception to this, thinking of the Notebook. But Guiseïa probably had something else in mind.

"No," she had said in response to Lisbeï's protest, "when the living voice has faded, the breath . . . there's nothing left." Then she had smiled the characteristic, crooked little smile that Lisbeï was coming to know. "Perhaps," she had remarked, her tone sincere, "I trust you."

"I'm too curious, too fond of tales."

"For you, tales are a means to an end," Guiseïa had said then. It was the Capta of Angresea, in fact if not officially, who had looked at Lisbeï, evaluated her. "You like to *understand*."

And her expression had changed to one Lisbeï knew all too well—knowing, seductive, and just insistent enough to signify that despite everything one wasn't deceived by one's own desire. "You're like me. Like Toller."

She's wrong, wrote Lisbeï, vaguely annoyed by the episode without understanding why. *We're very different.*

Possibly they were both right, but for once the idea occurred to her only later.

Toller had evinced no surprise at seeing Lisbeï dismount from her cavala in front of the Molten Tower. She hadn't had to tell him about Dougall's death, praise Elli, nor about events at Entraygues. Guiseïa never moved without a cage of pidges. Toller and the rest of the household had therefore waited for the travellas at the head of the great semicircular staircase. There had been a flurry of embraces and cries of greeting (very disconcerting for Lisbeï, considering how Guiseïa would have been welcomed at Bethely). The immediate family had been introduced all at once, beginning, rather oddly, with the youngest: Joane, Martinika's firstborne infante (Guiseïa's oldest girl bore the exotic Iturri name of Martinika); Liet, Guiseïa's last childe—"the babie," a plump, five-year-old mosta who had seemed quite happy to be hugged about the waist like a sack of potatoes by Sylvane; Gawain, her next youngest, tall and strong for his eight years (Twyne, her fourth childe, was a ward in Bethely); Sylvane, of course; Mireyne and Alane, Rowène's last childreen, two Reds of fifteen and thirteen; and Coreyn, who had appeared unoffended at being introduced as "my second childe," though she was officially the Mother of Angresea.

Martinika hadn't been named Mother because of the particular system for selection in Angresea and most Bretanye Families, which called for the choice to be ratified by the Family Assembly. Martinika was a tall Red, sweet-natured but shy, whose features were hard to remember after a first meeting. Just turned twenty-one, heavily pregnant, and studying to become Coreyn's Second Memory, she seemed to share a perfect love with Ylene.

Ylene was the same age as Coreyn—eighteen—and as a pupil of Angresea had been introduced to Lisbeï right after the young Mother. *Would it have seemed more odd to have Guiseïa say, "And your sister, Ylene"?* Lisbeï wondered in her journal. *But Guiseïa didn't bat an eyelash as she introduced my young half sister like any other ward. It was the best solution, really. Still, we stared at each other rather hesitantly until Ylene, with an amused smile, held out her hands. She was glad to meet me at last. When I left Bethely, she had just graduated from the garderie. There was no resonance, no light like Tula's, nothing.*

But a thoroughly likeable young Red, I must say, and a real Bethely: red hair ("hot enough to light a fire" as they say here), milk-white skin, aquamarine eyes . . . with the big nose and mouth of the Gloster Line, however. The overall effect isn't unpleasant, although a bit strange.

After that I was introduced to the Mother's Male—Coreyn's first, Odrigo of Serres-Morèna, a quiet, pretty man in his early twenties. Then came Rowène, the older sister of Guiseïa and Toller. Like Martinika, she'd been passed over for Mother, but for obvious reasons: she's the Family Medicina, obsessed with research—the archetypal Progressista! Last of all came the oldest in the family, Edwayne, Guiseïa's grandmother and the First Memory of Angresea, officially at least. She's a frail old Blue now, but must have been something to see in her youth. Even with her slight stoop she's as tall as I am. Terribly shortsighted (with glasses like bottle-bottoms), and a rather quavery voice. I don't think I've ever met anyone so old: she's seventy! They're a long-lived bunch, these Angreseas. Everyone speaks to her in the formal second person. She's the one who brought up the household when Bruwyne left her official Mother's necklace on the table beside the infante Yolde's cot—a pretty offhand way of designating one's childe as a Mother, to say the least—and disappeared into the anonymous crowd of Blues.

That must have been the necklace Guiseïa exchanged at Bethely when she and Lisbeï first met. Her Mother's necklace. Bruwyne's necklace, a piece that had surely been in the family for generations. Lisbeï could picture the antique design. And then it must have been Yolde's—but not for long. Guiseïa had probably removed it from her dead sister's neck. . . . No, if anyone took it off, it would have been the Medicina, maybe even Rowène at that time. A less striking image. Still, it had the makings of a story.

The Angresea documents hitherto consulted by Lisbeï had revealed no such fascinating details. Nor, of course, had they contained the minutes recounting how Guiseïa had *persuaded* the Family Assembly to name her as Mother. Actually, it had been done with Edwayne's aid and Rowène's support, but contrary to Bruwyne's explicit wish. This had been expressed in the letter to her own mother, Edwayne, designating Yolde as her successor. So there'd been a letter! But Bruwyne hadn't been there to present her case—clearly a tactical error. Although she had become a Blue the year after Yolde's birth, her sudden departure had been a surprise; yet according to the Bretanye Carta, Bruwyne was strictly within her rights in stepping down, even if Yolde wasn't yet a Red. Bruwyne had not only renounced her option to continue as interim Mother, however, but exercised her right to leave the Family. Other Provinces, other Families, other Cartas. In Litale, a Blue was automatically disqualified from continuing as Mother. It would have been interesting to find the letter. . . .

Toller sat down across from Lisbeï and reached for the papers she was reading. After a quick scan he pushed them back at her. "Hmm. The tale of Bruwyne. A night to remember."

"You were there?"

"Incognito."

The word startled Lisbeï. She looked hard at the Blue, searching for a trace of irony in his expression. Nothing, of course. Like Kelys, Toller sometimes made an art form of impassivity. The trick was in the voice, the inflections. If one weren't sure of having heard right, there would be no other clue. Lisbeï had a way of dealing with it—it seemed the only safe thing to do, either with Kelys or now, with Toller: she took everything at face value and pressed on with her own idea, asking direct questions until she got either a clear refusal or an answer. This technique ran counter to everything she'd taught herself in Bethely and had retained in Wardenberg despite all the odds. Now, however, she'd become somewhat accustomed to Toller.

"The letter was lost?"

"Destroyed. Deliberately, in a fit of rage."

"Guiseïa?"

"Yolde. She didn't want to be the Mother."

"But Bruwyne considered Guiseïa too ambitious."

"Bruwyne," said Toller evenly, "didn't want an Abomination for the Capta of Angresea."

"But that wasn't in the letter," replied Lisbeï after a pause, trying to equal Toller's noncommittal tone.

"No. But in any case, the other arguments were just as valid."

"Bruwyne was like you two?"

"Like Antonë. Or Selva, rather, but a lot more intolerant. Not a word was spoken on the subject. But she found us with Kelys, the time we tried the agvite."

"And Kelys explained things?"

"Kelys had more scruples in those days. Or less—it depends."

Kelys-of-Angresea seemed somewhat different from the other avatars Lisbeï knew. Guiseïa, Toller, and practically the whole household were familiar with Kelys because she'd spent ten uninterrupted years in the Family. Lisbeï let the remark pass, merely noting it in her journal without comment. After her experiences at Belmont and Entraygues, she felt nothing about Kelys could surprise her. In fact she was more intrigued by what Toller or Guiseïa had revealed about themselves in discussing Kelys. There was a world of shared curiosity, pleasure, and pain, at once familiar to her in the context of her relationship with Tula and yet singularly odd each time she recalled who really were these accomplices, these inquisitive beings, these friends. No one had ever tried to separate Guiseïa and Toller. From the moment Kelys came to Angresea—they were about five then—both had received the same education. Bruwyne had somewhat grudgingly approved. It was a Mother's education, for in Bretanye all children in a household were eligible. Except boys, of course. Didn't anyone in Angresea object?

Toller smiled a little. "Boys in Angresea aren't considered so important that they have to be excluded all the time."

This sounded rather like Lisbeï's own argument regarding Green boys in the Games. However, hearing the argument on someone else's lips, she remarked, "But elsewhere they are." Of what use was Toller's education in Angresea?

"It helped me keep on good terms with the Mothers for whom I did my Service, at least."

"That's what future Males are trained to do, anyway."

"They're trained as future Males. I was primarily *educated* as a person."

Then how did he submit to his training as a future Male? Badly, she supposed. . . . But Lisbeï kept this question for her journal. When one edged near this kind of topic, Toller's message was unmistakable: nothing doing.

Lisbeï already knew that all the Bretanye Males were sent to the same place for their education—a sort of schole called La Baillie, on the limits of Lletrewyn and Verchères. Lanik, Rowène's only boy, would soon be leaving it to begin his Service in Escarra. Visitas were permitted, and when Lisbeï saw it, she was impressed by the obvious antiquity of the place. It must certainly date from pre-Decline days. Neither the Harems nor the Hives had touched it. Why not, she wondered? Like many buildings of the Decline, it offered a ready-made quarry of durable, dressed stone. Fear, perhaps? Simply because such durability was considered supernatural? The Hives had so completely cut themselves off from the past, as well as from the traditions that might have provided some explanation, that they had become even more superstitious than the Harems. The stones were sealed with some sort of transparent coating (plastic?), which had protected them from the weather. La Baillie must have been a revered relic even during the Decline, and this accounted for its conservation.

The building consisted of wings forming an elongated cross (rather like the hobskoch figure of the Northern Provinces—was there a connection, perhaps?). At the smaller end of the cross rose a square tower. Flying buttresses supported the walls, reminding Lisbeï of some of the Hive fortresses, but this was the only familiar feature amid a wealth of intriguing architectural detail: the rose-shaped opening above the main entrance, with its stone lacework and bright-hued panes, their intense colors echoed in the tall, tapering windows; the enormous pillars and high, criss-crossed vaulting in the main section . . . A kind of garden lay within the intersection, surrounded by a walkway lined with small, carved columns. The three other wings housed dormitories, refectories, meditation and gymna halls, classrooms, and Tutresses' lodgings (a few Tutors' lodgings, too, this being Bretanye).

The stone cluster breathed tranquillity. Perhaps the same was true of the Bethely Green's Farm in Malverde, but Lisbeï had never visited Bois-Malverde. La Baillie stood in a small valley surrounded by great chestnut trees. It was said that Elli was closer in such places, far from human clamor.

"Elli is neither farther nor closer," Toller said. "Conditioning is more effective when the subject isn't distracted, that's all."

Toller is different in Angresea, Lisbeï had noted early in her stay. Less distant, less often hidden behind his mask of calm, less controlled. Guiseïa too, as a matter of fact. Still vibrant, but in a lower register. It was probably to be expected. They were at home, after all. *Would I be different in Bethely?* Lisbeï thought for a moment, wondering why she hadn't written *will*. Since Entraygues, she'd found it very hard to imagine herself returning to Bethely. She left the sentence as it was.

The day began like any other. Lisbeï woke early to the shrill
whistling of a pair of swalles nesting between two stones just
beneath her third-floor window in the Molten Tower. She
liked being awake before anyone else, watching from her window as the sea gradually brightened with the dawn, and seeing
the Port with its boats asleep at high tide (in Jula people
fished at nightfall, with lamps), the calm water barely rippled
by the wind, the white line of the Reefs on the horizon becoming sharper each minute, then the Brezblüt coast with its pink
cliffs flaming to crimson, and finally, as the sun rose in the sky,
the shadow retreating from the farthest extremity of the Noire
Dame, slowly revealing its smooth, unnatural curve. The landscape changed completely at low tide: the bay shore shifted
perspective, the dike soared thirty meters above the muddy
plain dotted with seaweed-draped carcasses and formless hill-
ocks too regularly spaced to be natural. The ruins offered a
curiously appropriate response to the artificial cliff, its lofty
curve intact.

How different it was from Wardenberg! There Lisbeï's
room had looked out on the rooftops. Ysande's room, later
Fraine's, had overlooked the Port. Wardenberg was only a
pretend island, each ebb divulging its true link to the mainland. The Port faced the mainland shore, and the seldom-used
quays on the seaward side of the island were a sign that the
Citadel, for all intents and purposes, turned its back on the
sea.

Angresea, on the contrary, confronted the sea. Lisbeï had
never experienced such a feeling of sheer space in Wardenberg, where at low tide you could see the rocky mass of the
mountain and the surrounding plain. The Wardenberg sea was
an intruder from afar, an unlawful occupant of land it should
never have encountered. In Angresea it was at home, even at
low tide with the debris of the city and the teeth of the old
dike almost closing the horizon. Beyond the line of the broken
dike, the open sea had always glittered in the distance. Naturally the Angreseas built ships, naturally they had become the
prime movers of the Western Fleet. Looking out from the
Molten Tower at dawn, as the revolving beam of the lighthouse atop the Dys Tower faded to a luminous blink in the
sunlight, you could easily capture the immense sweep of the

horizon and be drawn in imagination beyond sky and water, yearning to set forth.

What caught Lisbeï's imagination was not the voyage to the West, however. She had always let Fraine and the others discuss its organization, its problems and perils and how they might be faced. It was the arrival that she imagined. She even liked to speculate on the exploras returning, heralding not only a habitable continent in the West, but the existence of people already living there. Her imagination almost outran itself in conjuring up all the possible forms and consequences of such an encounter. New languages, new customs, a whole other History—and a flock of new stories as well! She let herself be carried even further, trying to imagine the different world in which the childreen of Ysande and Fraine would grow up. (But in the end, of course, Fraine had no living children.)

It wasn't the material changes she had in mind so much as what happened when a badland was officially opened: gray spots would disappear from the maps and new territories would take shape in each person's mental landscape. Where there was nothing, suddenly there would be something, a new thread in the Tapestry—no, a whole new *design* in the Tapestry! The dimensions of the whole world would be subtly enlarged, and people's minds and spirits would also have to enlarge to accommodate this changed world. The prospect was exciting, and yet you couldn't ignore a twinge of misgiving, of resentment, as when you long to sleep late and a hand shakes you. She turned away from the window with a small sigh. Maybe she could come back to Angresea in two years to see the Fleet set sail, but Elli knew when they might return and with what news. There were other possible stories in which proof of a Western Continent might be a source of eternal sorrow and regret, even of horror in each Maerlande heart. . . .

Lisbeï dressed quickly to the raucous cry of scigullas circling in the sky. Since Belmont, she had kept up her habit of at least a fairly regular morning session of taïtche. In Angresea she used the top of the Molten Tower, running barefoot up the spiral staircase to warm up her muscles. The messenger pidges were kept there, and she listened to their persistent cooing while waiting for her pulse to slow down, then began the series of familiar movements as she slipped slowly into the trance. Kelys had taught her and the others how to "program" (queer word!) one's body-clock. When she emerged at the preordained moment, it was time for breakfast, and she could go down to the dining room (the Angresea term for the refectory) without any grumbling from the kitchen.

This morning the dining room was empty. The large table was already set—this being the evening task of the younger childreen. The tick-tock of the big clock echoed in the silence. Nearly eight o'clock. Lisbeï was slightly late. In the kitchen, pots and pans were steaming on the two big stoves but there was no one in sight. She went into the deserted hallway and was about to call "Hello?" when she heard the tearful hiccuping of a babie on a distant stair, then footsteps, voices. At last a gaggle of childreen appeared, herded along by the cook, Ermyne, a stocky Blue in her forties with polished red cheeks. Like the childreen, like Liet, whose sobs were now subsiding and who had stuffed a hand into his mouth, Ermyne had been crying. She stared at Lisbeï, then seemed to recognize her. "Sylvane," was all she said in a mournful voice, waving vaguely toward the staircase.

Lisbeï rushed upstairs to the second floor where the childreen slept. The dottas each had her own room, although the mostas slept together. As she reached the corridor, she was just in time to see Guiseïa come out of Sylvane's room and close the door behind her, wavering drunkenly as she leaned back against the wall, eyes closed, hugging herself tightly.

"Guiseïa?"

Guiseïa turned her head and opened her eyes, watching Lisbeï approach.

Did Guiseïa see her? Lisbeï could not be sure and reached out a hand to touch a bare arm. "Guise?"

Was it the diminutive that did it? Guiseïa seemed to repossess her body. A dull glint appeared in her tired eyes. "Sylvane," she muttered hoarsely. "The Malady."

Lisbeï entered the room. After a moment Rowène turned her head to look at her, then returned to her immobile contemplation of Sylvane. During the night the girl had thrown off all her bedclothes and taken off her nightgown in an effort to cool down. Now she lay naked on her back, soaking wet and unconscious, her diaphragm rising and falling with each quick, shallow breath and her ribs clearly visible beneath the drops of sweat on her skin. Toller, as rigid and unemotional as a tree trunk, stood at the foot of the bed gripping the wooden bedstead.

Lisbeï shuddered. She wouldn't dare touch Toller. "We must wait," she murmured futilely. Out of the corner of an eye she saw Rowène nod. Time seemed to stand still, and then she heard herself saying, "Does the Memory know?" Their despondency deepened a shade. No, the elder didn't know. She was always the last to rise—the privilege of old age. "I'll go," Lisbeï mumbled and escaped from the room.

Guiseïa was no longer in the corridor but on the stairs leading to the main floor where old Edwayne lived. When Lisbeï caught up with her, she continued her descent, moving mechanically. She was empty, a wasteland that would have silenced Lisbeï even if there'd been anything to say. Guiseïa knocked on the Memory's door and walked in without waiting, leaving the door ajar. In the shadowy room a figure sat up with a rustle of sheets. The old woman was awake and feeling for the curtain cord.

"Grandmother?" Guiseïa moved toward the bed, not even blinking when sun flooded into the room, lighting the mound of pillows and Edwayne's anxious face. "Grandmother." The voice was that of a little girl, incredulous, imploring. "Sylvane has the Malady." She dropped onto the bed and curled up against the old woman with a rasping cry. The old woman folded Guiseïa in her arms—surely a long-familiar gesture—the bony fingers knotted in the black curls. Edwayne's eyes, nearly blind without their glasses, tried to make out the still figure of Lisbeï standing beside the door. "Toller?"

"No, it's me," said Lisbeï, approaching the bed with a heavy heart. "Toller is with the childe."

Edwayne reached out with one hand, fumbling on the night table for her glasses. She put them on and stared thoughtfully at Lisbeï for a moment, then looked down at Guiseïa, who hadn't moved or made a sound. The old face bore a curious expression. The slightly trembling hand came to rest again on the curly head. "Elli is taking back the thread that should not have been," she murmured.

Guiseïa's whole body jerked violently. She sat up slowly. "Don't say that," she hissed, suddenly compact, hard.

The old woman's arms dropped, and she leaned back on her pillows. She wasn't afraid, not even sad, she was . . . very calm, resigned, with a vast weariness, a certitude, like someone who has long been running to escape something and who stops and turns, knowing already what she will see, close behind.

For a moment Lisbeï thought Guiseïa was going to hit the old Memory. Instead she got up, her hands curled into fists and pressed against her chest as though in an effort to restrain them, then swung around and left the room. As she swept by, Lisbeï was buffeted by a violent wave of suppressed emotion, of rage, of terror—of guilt.

4

Sylvane was strong. She held on for five days. The fever neither rose nor dropped, having jumped to the maximum at the outset and remained stationary right up to the end. They brought a bathtub into the room and put the childe in it. The ice had to be replaced every fifteen minutes. They used up the entire salt stock stored in the Molten Tower. What else could they do? Nothing. Wait. Pray? People didn't pray in Angresea, not in Guiseïa's house, anyway. Wait. Fall asleep with exhaustion, seated on a chair beside the bed, wake with a start to find that only a few minutes had gone by, that nothing had changed, that one must wait.

Lisbeï has disjointed memories of those five days, those five nights. Martinika, hands resting on her huge belly, supported by Ylene leading her gently toward the door, urging, "It won't help. You'll only do yourself harm. Come." Guiseïa mechanically going about the business of the Capterie, her inner being always closed, like a fist. Rowène closeted in her laboratory, incapable of remaining idle, concocting substances to relieve fever and inflammation. Sylvane unable to swallow anything, with the fever like a brazier on which she was being visibly desiccated. Toller, his chair pulled close to the bed, holding a pair of tiny sandals with rhinestone-encrusted straps, turning them over and over.

The other childeen had gone to stay with their half sisters and cousines in various lodgings in the Capterie. Unfamiliar Angreseas came in groups of two or three—never the same people—standing silently in the hall of the Molten Tower, then departing without a word once they'd been told there was nothing new to report.

On the day before Sylvane's death, Rowène made a desperate effort to restore her body fluids with a "drip." It consisted of a tube made from animal gut and soaked in boiled mock-rubber sap, hooked up at one end to a similarly waterproofed fiber sac that had been filled with a distilled solution of water and honey, then tightly closed. At the other end was a hollow needle inserted in the forearm and held in place by a bandage. The sac was suspended from the top of a tripod higher than the bath-bed, the solution being forced into the veins by gravity. The speed of the drip was controlled by a small metal device, a kind of graduated tourniquet.

The solution had no perceptible effect.

Edwayne hardly left her room. Perhaps she was praying. Lisbeï, bringing her something to eat, would find her seated beside the window thrown open to the quivering Jula heat, or lying fully dressed on her bed in the shuttered shadows. She ate very little and said almost nothing. On the fourth day, when Lisbeï was coaxing her to finish a bowl of broth, she murmured, "I am punished. Did you know, little one, that we could be punished for what our childreen have done?" She spoke with childelike surprise. As night fell on the fifth day, before Lisbeï had found the words to tell her of Sylvane's death, Edwayne, sunk in her chair, said, "Too long. I've lasted too long." She turned slightly toward the window, where the lingering light of the sun was now fading, and closed her eyes with quiet finality.

During the afternoon the join between the tube and the "solution" sac began to leak. While Rowène was repairing it, Lisbeï had held Sylvane's arm, despite the jiggling tube, to keep the needle and bandage in place. All the while, as she was touching the childe, she could sense Sylvane's light, the dwindling glimmer, the distant resonance now perceived for the first and last time, that of a childe who had contracted the Malady very late, far too late . . . a childe whom the Malady, instead of changing, was now killing.

"After all this time!" said Toller, the evening of the double funeral. The three of them—just Guiseïa, Lisbeï and Toller—were in the large living room after a dinner that no one had really touched. The youngest childreen were still lodged else-where. The young Serres-Morèna Male had stayed tactfully in his rooms. Martinika was devastated, and she, too, kept to her quarters under the watchful eye of Ylene. Rowène was again closeted in her laboratory, studying the results of the autopsy.

The pain of the actual burial had been heightened by the blazing sun, the heat, the irony of living things. But why would nature weep for Sylvane, whom it had killed, or for Edwayne, who had lived so long? Only the immediate household stood at the graveside, except for a few representatives of the Family and someone from each of the three neighboring Offshoots. This was an unexpected novelty, but Lisbeï was too tired to bother making comparisons. She wondered when the dolore would take place, whether there would even be a dolore or a mourning or whatever they called it in Bretanye. No one had mentioned it, and she hardly dared ask. Perhaps it took place only when there were enough Believras. There didn't seem to be a single one in Angresea—no one to sing the Word while painting the ritual symbols on the coffins, no one to drop seeds on the faces and bodies of the white-shrouded corpses. Only this silent file of people, all black-garbed as they wound along the path to the field of the dead. As the bodies were placed in the earth, the mourners at last broke the silence with songs and blessings, but even these held no sense of re-lease. This was how they were in Bretanye. As if they were punishing themselves, but for what?

At least they planted flowers on the graves.

Lisbeï, ensconced in an armchair, held a glass of cordial that Guiseïa had handed to her. Light-headed with utter ex-haustion, she didn't dare touch it. She had reached this point in her rather disjointed reflections when Toller sent his glass crashing into the cold fireplace.

"After all this time!" Fury and disbelief shook his voice.

"The Malady . . . ," began Guiseïa.

"She shouldn't have had the Malady! Not at twelve! Kelys told us she wouldn't get it!"

"Kelys?" said Lisbeï, slow to react.

"She was here when the babie was born. She came back every year," said Guiseïa.

"Sylvane *was* normal!"

"Well, Kelys isn't infallible," muttered Guiseïa. She closed her eyes and leaned her head against the back of the armchair. "You touched Sylvane near the end, as I did," she added, her voice ragged with fatigue.

"It was *us,* not her!"

Guiseïa shook her head wearily. "Oh, Toller . . ."

"You'd rather think like Edwayne? Elli's retribution?"

"You have no right to say that," said Guiseïa, her eyes still shut, her voice devoid of passion.

"Why not?"

"Because she was my childe, too."

In her journal, later, Lisbeï wondered when she had—not guessed, not sensed, but *known* the answer.

Guiseïa came into Sylvane's room. She'd walked rather than run from her office on the ground floor. She went over to Toller's armchair. He hadn't budged since Rowène had removed the useless drip apparatus with its needle and bandage. She knelt as though her legs were collapsing beneath her and said, oh so softly, "Best-beloved," taking Toller's dangling hand and pressing it to her cheek. She stayed with him, looking at the small body.

That was all Lisbeï had seen and heard before shutting the door quietly behind her. Of course there had been other clues: the physical resemblance, Edwayne's words, the abortive light she had sensed in Sylvane, and also the way Guiseïa and Toller moved or stood when they were near each other, never touching, and the way they looked at each other, and surely a hundred other things, although none of them taken alone revealed anything. Nor was it necessarily this final clue that had suddenly jostled the knowledge into her conscious mind. It was a revelation beyond time, the figure in the Tapestry, the whole design springing to view in all its detail. And that night, when Guiseïa and Toller recounted the story in their duet of grieving, Lisbeï realized that the pattern she had intuitively grasped was very close to the reality.

He's just passing through. It's a long time since he's seen her, and he rather hopes to find her pregnant—misshapen and unrecognizable. But she's as slim and vibrant as ever, despite being the mother of two, despite being the Mother. He talks of this and that; she replies, knowing he really speaks of something else. Who suggests a walk on the Noire Dame? She, he, it doesn't matter. They say nothing as they walk along the road in the afternoon heat, and this silence draws them together. Then the familiar path down the rocky cliff to the smooth sea, slack between tides. A scigulla, perhaps, high in the luminous sky, its wings like two hands waving good-bye. She takes off her red dress. (She had put on a red dress that day, she'd known he was coming, had perhaps wanted protection from herself.) She takes off the red dress and there is nothing underneath. (She had known very well.) He looks for the marks of childbearing on her thighs, her belly, her breasts, and finds barely a trace. Does he hesitate? He, too, undresses. She holds out a hand, touches his cheek lightly, then turns and dives.

He dives too. Ahead of him is the trail of bubbles and the undulating body in the green coolness. Down he goes, plunging away from the daylight toward another light, past the smooth, round rock that marks the way. A few strokes more—will he make it or will the darkness close in on him as it had the first time, retreating to reveal the terrified face of Guiseïa, Guiseïa's mouth on his, her white body trembling? But he's no longer a thirteen-year-old, he has the chest, the lung capacity of an adult.

He hoists himself onto the ledge after her. In the subterranean, submarine grotto he stretches out on his back to breathe, listening to the gentle drip of the water from their bodies, eyes lost in the perpetual play of light over the roof of the cave. Lamps still shine on the walls after all this time. After all this time.

He lets the silence grow. He knows he shouldn't, that each passing moment makes their shared visions more palpable, but his throat is too tight. She turns toward him. Her hair falls over her face as the water held in the curve of her body streams off. He tries not to see the stirring of her breasts.

She rests her head on his neck and slips an arm about his waist, saying nothing. He doesn't want to say anything, either. After a moment she stands up. In the mirror of the metal wall at the back of the cave, her silhouette stands up too. Reality and reflection take his hand, pulling him toward the wall. Their reflections look back at them, and she steps in front of him, singing softly, "Elli looked upon Elliself, Elli saw Elliself, And from eternity was born the Night, And the Day . . ."

But their mirror-images don't coincide the way they did in childhood games. The outline of his body is like a halo behind hers, shoulders, torso, hips, and his face above her face. After all this time.

She turns and presses herself against him, he enfolds her in his arms, his penis burning against her cool skin, and he is lost, lost in the contact and he can no longer choose who he is and he glides in her and she in him in the old, dizzying spiral.

Afterward, watching the water lap against the walls, perhaps she says, "I have to start receiving my Male tomorrow." *(Yes, she doesn't even use his name, Maxel, or the surname Fontbleau. Just "my Male, tomorrow.")* He lifts himself up on one elbow to look at her, trying to be shocked, but he knows deep down that he isn't, and she knows he isn't, and that's all right, it has to be like this, their Line, his and hers, that will begin with him and her, their secret, their revenge, their forbidden childe.

Then he leaves while she waits. In Sylvane's beginning as in her end, Guiseïa waits for death or life, and it will be life: her belly swells. And perhaps she's afraid. Perhaps one day she tells Edwayne everything or Edwayne guesses, for those two are her childreen far more than they have ever been Bruwyne's. And now Edwayne waits too, death or life. The childe is born, born alive, stays alive, survives two, five, twelve years, normal, ordinary, marvelously ordinary, their childe.

"And now," murmured Guiseïa, "after all this time, she's dead."

At the end of an interminable silence, Toller stood up, eyes averted, and walked slowly out of the room, back bowed, arms pressed to his sides like an old man who feels the cold. Guiseïa lifted her hand a fraction, but no more. Lisbeï knew that it was not really the dolore for Sylvane that she had just heard, but for themselves, their grief for two young Reds who no longer existed, their grief for all those memories of secret triumph that had kept them alive and together, memories that were becoming regrets, remorse that would now gradually drive them apart.

Two days after Sylvane and the Memory Edwayne had been laid to rest, life pretended to resume its normal course. Martinika was about to give birth and kept to her rooms most of the time. This withdrawal had little effect on the daily routine. Toller could easily assume the tasks of Memory with Coreyn, and in any case Guiseïa still managed much of the Family's business. Rowène, however, was left to handle the youngest childreen's lessons almost single-handedly, since Toller had shared the burden until now. Lisbeï offered to help, and Rowène accepted the offer with laconic thanks. The two oldest childreen were no problem for Lisbeï, but to teach a boy as well was a new experience. Eight-year-old Gawain was just beginning his lessons, but his curriculum contained more subjects than even the final year of Lisbeï's Bethely garderie. Reading, writing, and arithmetic, of course, but also history, geography, natural sciences, biology . . . and (surprisingly enough) the rudiments of the Word. (Lisbeï half-jokingly evinced surprise at finding the Word on the Angresea curriculum, but Guiseïa merely shrugged. "He'll do Service with Believras too, you know." Like his sisters, Gawain had never been discouraged from asking questions. In fact he was more curious than they, for in Angresea as in Bethely and everywhere else the daily environment provided far more ready answers to Green girls than boys, a point Lisbeï noted in her journal with new insight.

Lesson time soon became the only part of the day when she felt at peace in Angresea during these few weeks. There was something reassuring in the essentially simple and familiar questions asked by the small girls and Gawain, and in her complete confidence at being able to provide satisfactory answers. With adults, with Guiseïa and Toller, it was quite different. She'd been too exhausted the night of the burial, too caught up in the violent emotions neither had attempted to hide—and too fascinated by the story that was unfolding. She had said nothing. It was only when she wrote in her journal next morning that a sense of deep uneasiness filled her, a sentiment that recurred each time she thought of their story in the succeeding days.

Neither Guiseïa nor Toller said anything. They didn't even talk to each other at first. As the days went by and their distress was gradually attenuated by routine, they were often thrown together in working with Coreyn. Yet they seemed to have devised a tacit system of avoiding one another everywhere else. Meals brought the whole household together, but mealtime conversation was easily confined to innocuous topics. Nevertheless Lisbeï had a growing sense that Guiseïa and Toller were watching her more than each other. Being a guest, she still had plenty of opportunities for meeting them separately, although the heavier work load caused by Edwayne's death made these occasions less frequent than in the early days of her stay. The subject of Sylvane's unorthodox parentage would have to be broached sooner or later. With a twinge of cowardice, Lisbeï hoped it wouldn't be up to her.

Guiseïa gave in first. One hot afternoon in Austa, as Lisbeï was thinking of cutting short the day's lessons in favor of going to the beach with the childreen, Guiseïa walked into the classroom and said, "It's much too hot to work." Soon they met again on the shingle cove south of the Port, where everyone in Angresea went to swim. Nearly all the Greens and young Reds were there. As in Bethely, things weren't as strict in sumra, but in any case childhood went on much longer here. Serious work in the Capterie began only after fourteen. The laughter and the splash of divers echoed against the Capterie walls and mingled with the sound of the surf. A few of the older ones had taken out small boats with triangular sails and were racing each other along the shoreline. Others, farther out, practiced criss-crossing and sharp tacking, their sails continually in danger of luffing as they lost momentum in coming about. No wonder Angresea had dominated the sailing trials in Bretanye for years! The littlest children had tossed water over a sandy stretch among the pebbles in order to draw the traditional double-crossed hobskoch of the North, chanting in unison the nursery rhyme that accompanied each toss of the marker.

Instead of speaking at once, however, Guiseïa went for a long swim with Lisbeï, cutting smoothly through the water, her body powerful and supple despite its slenderness and the pregnancies that had left their mark without deforming her figure. Guiseïa waited until they were back on the shingle beach, stretched out in the shade of the breakwater at some distance from the others. Lisbeï had closed her eyes and was beginning to drift off when Guiseïa spoke at last, resolute beneath the affected irony.

"So you didn't take flight." Guiseïa used the Frangleï familiar form *toï*.

Lisbeï couldn't remember who initiated this verbal intimacy or when, but it had happened during Sylvane's illness. With an inward sigh, although in fact she was relieved, Lisbeï sat up and leaned her naked back against the rough stones of the breakwater.

"I didn't think you'd run off, in any case," continued Guiseïa.

"What did you think?"

"That you'd protest. With conviction."

In fact, the protests in Lisbeï's journal ran to several pages, in which she'd already spilled out the better part of her stupefaction, her indignation, and her attempts to comprehend Guiseïa and Toller's appalling story. After Belmont it was probably easier to understand, all things considered, if not approve. She'd already rehearsed various versions of this conversation, with herself speaking for Guiseïa or even Toller.

She had the sudden impression Guiseïa had done the same: it
was in her aura, this mingling of resolution, exasperation, and
vague amusement—*let's get it over with*. They could dispense
with the tortuous preliminaries.

"It isn't as though you'd done it on purpose to begin with.
But to let the pregnancy . . . to keep her . . ."

"It was a gamble," Lisbeï had answered for Guiseïa in
one of her diary conversations. *"Let Elli have Elli's way. Nothing might have happened, or the fetus might have miscarried
early without anyone being the wiser, or at any time during the
nine months. Elli could have killed her at any time, couldn't
Elli? Punished us at any moment, then or later, at the birth or in
the months following. But Elli didn't choose to take her then, so
I kept her."* But it was highly unlikely Guiseïa would have
deferred in this way to a deity about whose existence she appeared to have tangible doubts. Or had her lack of faith begun
then?

"It was Toller's childe," murmured Guiseïa. "And Kelys
had told us it was possible for us to have normal childreen.
The first time it happened, we were still Greens, but we were
terrified just the same. Of course she guessed. She went over
our Lines with us and showed us there was a reasonable
chance of a childe being normal."

But surely Kelys hadn't given them her blessing?

"No. But she understood. She'd seen us grow up together. I don't think she was even very surprised at what happened. A little sad and worried, but not surprised. Not . . .
angry either, really."

"And the second time?"

"It wasn't the second," Guiseïa remarked with a crooked
little smile. "But no, not that time either. She reassured me,
stayed with me through the whole pregnancy. She was the one
who helped me give birth."

Kelys. Decidedly nothing about Kelys would ever surprise
Lisbeï after this!

"I think she was curious to see the result, too," added
Guiseïa. In earlier times Lisbeï would have reacted indignantly to such a supposition. Not now. She looked at it from
every angle and had to admit it was very likely. Kelys always
had several motives for every action, Lisbeï was beginning to
realize.

They sat in silence for a while. "Anyway, I didn't designate her as the future Mother," Guiseïa muttered finally, as though to excuse herself. But to whom?

"You assumed a terrible responsibility all the same," Lisbeï said, incapable of keeping the severity out of her voice. "Not only for the childe, but for all her childreen and childreen's childreen, for the whole of Maerlande, in fact. The Lines aren't there for nothing!"

"Lines! Service! Do you still not see what they do to us? Do you still defend them?"

Lisbeï felt the bitter violence overwhelming the other's aura, but resisted it. She knew Guiseïa wasn't being honest. "You never became a true renegada. You're working for change through the Assemblies and elsewhere."

"But too late for Toller!" Guiseïa seemed less bitter now. "Too late for me . . . and for our mother and so many others. Don't you really see?"

There was an almost pleading note in her voice. And all at once I did see. She wanted me to understand, to forgive her. To say . . . that I didn't blame her, despise or hate her for what she'd done. It wasn't so much Sylvane she wanted to talk about. It was herself and me. Us . . .

This wasn't at all the conversation Lisbeï had imagined. She turned away, suddenly uneasy, murmuring, "Yes, yes, I understand. Even so . . ."

Guiseïa's aura shrank back, disappointed. "Well, the damage was contained, anyway, wasn't it?" she remarked with black humor. "The childe is dead. She'd never have become a Red or brought a babie to term. She would have become a Blue right away." Guiseïa spoke aggressively now, looking defiantly at Lisbeï.

There was a brief silence, then Lisbeï raised her eyebrows with studied calm. "Aren't you going to tell me why?"

Guiseïa stared at her, taken aback. "You want to know?" Her slight, appreciative smile lacked warmth.

"You want me to know."

Again a pause, and then Guiseïa sighed and turned away to watch the patches of color sailing over the shining sea. "I need . . . to talk about it, you know. Toller, well—" She couldn't finish. What was the point of pretending anymore?

Lisbeï sensed the great lassitude and sincerity of her appeal, and this time she did not resist. She touched Guiseïa's arm with frank sympathy.

"When he left the first time, I almost . . . well, I

thought about it, at least. I wasn't serious, though. I was young. Anyway, I didn't do it. But time went by. He became a Blue shortly after the childe was born. He came back. I'd had time to get myself in hand. Being a Capta sorts out your ideas a bit, I guess." She looked at Lisbeï for a moment. "There are ways . . . of not conceiving. Did you know?"

Lisbeï thought Antonë had mentioned it, but this wasn't at all what they were talking about. Sylvane wouldn't have been the Mother in any event. But for a normal young Red in good health to prevent *artificial insemination* from working . . . well, no, she didn't know. But there was a drug. Rowène had developed a drug apparently, after years of determined research. It wasn't exactly a way of preventing insemination from taking, but of preventing the fetus from reaching term.

"You mean *voluntarily* inducing an abortion? Of a *normal* fetus?"

"In the first place nobody knows whether they'd have been normal," snapped Guiseïa, once more on the defensive. "And yes, voluntarily. It would have been the only way of having her declared Blue. Would you have preferred her to have children?"

"Did you tell her? Did she agree?"

Guiseïa's silence was an admission.

For a minute Lisbeï couldn't speak either. At last she murmured, "She didn't know." A sense of horror overwhelmed her. "And she wasn't going to know, either. You wouldn't have asked her opinion."

"What else could I do?" Guiseïa's voice was low but intense, torn. "It wouldn't have hurt her. She wasn't in any danger."

"How do you know? Because you and Rowène had already tried the drug?"

"I tried it," whispered Guiseïa. Then, her spirit of revolt rising again, she cried, "I already had four children living! I had Gawain and Liet afterward. Those fetuses might never have survived anyway! And I wasn't going to test the drug on someone else, was I?"

"Well, I'm glad you had the relative decency to restrain yourself," said Lisbeï drily. She couldn't help it. She wanted to be understanding, but there were limits!

Guiseïa crumpled. Lisbeï perceived the painfully reverberating shame, despair, and returning rage. It was impossible to ignore them, though she tried. She breathed deeply. What had happened, had happened. What had not happened, had not. And anyhow, the childe was dead. "The thread that should not have been," Edwayne had said—that and the whole awful pattern that had woven itself around this thread, ever more deformed because its very source was twisted. But it was inevitable. Guiseïa had spoken truly. Had she any choice, once she'd chosen to let the childe live?

She could at least have given the childe the chance to choose.

But she'd wanted to protect Sylvane.

She'd wanted to protect *herself* and probably Toller, too—to keep the childe's respect and love for them both.

All that, and everything else—circumstances Lisbeï could barely imagine at the moment, but which she would subsequently set out clearly in her journal: Guiseïa may have subconsciously wanted to punish herself and Toller through the childe . . . or to purchase her salvation, or maybe both. But whatever the truth of it, Lisbeï couldn't maintain her indignation that afternoon on the shingle cove, couldn't go on judging Guiseïa. She fully understood Guiseïa's dilemma, sensed all too well Guiseïa's lacerating anguish.

And she couldn't help wondering what the drug was. How did it work? Weren't there side effects? And how did they ever conceive of such a thing in the first place?

"I really can't remember now," said Guiseïa. "You'll have to ask Rowène. She explained it to me, but I'm no biologist. The drug comes from a vegetable base, in any case. It started with a discussion between Rowène and Kelys about the interpretation of some fragment of text dating from just after the Harems, something about the various ways in which the women could resist the masters in certain Chefferies."

Several plants appear to have been used for this purpose. According to Kelys, it was more a question of magic and probably had no effect whatsoever on fertility. Rowène disagreed and decided to prove Kelys wrong. It became a kind of running joke between them, except that Rowène was completely serious. She researched the kind of plants Chefferie women would have been able to get hold of. She acquired these plants and experimented by successive elimination, testing them on mice as is done for potentially useful plants from badlands. In the end even Kelys got involved and began to do her own research, and between the two of them they succeeded.

However, Kelys had no idea the drug was being tested on

an actual human being. Once the mouse tests had produced positive results, she had conceded the point to Rowène and thought about it no more.

"Would you have told her you were administering it to Sylvane?"

"She would have guessed, I suppose."

"And said nothing?"

"And you? Are you going to denounce us?" Guiseïa's words had a touch of mockery, but she was serious.

Lisbeï thought for a moment. "Do you intend to use this drug on others?"

Guiseïa shook her head with grim humor, though it wasn't directed at Lisbeï. "Good question. No, not for the moment."

"What do you mean, not for the moment?"

"It's too soon," said Guiseïa, more assured now that the conversation was back on the level of global strategies. "But when the predicted demographic explosion gets going, it may be time to consider it. When you've had four surviving childreen, including a boy, is it really necessary to keep on having them until you become a Blue? Either they won't survive—in which case, what's the point of conceiving them—or else they'll survive and add to the population problem. I can't believe the Lines aren't diversified enough now or that we need to keep on enlarging the genetic pool!"

"If the exploration of the Western Continent is successful, the Offshoots will reduce the number of available Lines. . . ."

"To begin with, but if the period of fertility continues to expand, it won't really be a problem."

Lisbeï was unconvinced. She sensed her own antipathy to the idea of preventing the birth of *normal* children.

"Consider it in the long term, Lisbeï. Even if the Western Continent—and that's a big if—or if all the badlands become habitable . . ."

"In the *very* long term!"

"It doesn't matter. There's a limit to available space. We can't envisage infinite population growth."

"We need boys."

"There are plenty of boys! Nearly two thousand each year aren't in Service!"

"They're from the less acceptable Lines."

"Lines that will get better with time." Guiseïa shook her head. "Lisbeï, it's not you thinking. It's Litale."

And she was right! Of course I might equally well have said that Bretanye or Angresea were speaking for her, but nevertheless it was true—for both of us. She had her proofs, I mine, the Juddites theirs, the Believras too, as did everyone who had never questioned things because they grew up with them. But there comes a time when you can't avoid questions. The Tapestry includes change. And it doesn't stop changing just to please us, or because we're uncomfortable with the idea and are willing to go only so far and no farther. Once things get started, there's no holding back. And that's exactly why we've got to try to envisage all the consequences now. Except that we can't, not really, as Fraine had said. So what then?

"There's a way of envisaging the long term that is really an escape," was all Lisbeï answered. (She was suddenly struck by what this meant if applied to herself.) "We're dealing with the here and now. Anyway, I fail to see why the use of this drug would be more legitimate or morally acceptable in fifty years, simply because the world's material situation might have changed. The end wouldn't justify the means any more then than now. We can't brush aside laws when it suits us."

Guiseïa looked very put out at this but made a visible effort to contain herself. "No," she said finally. "Imperfect choices in an imperfect world, as they say. And it will be up to each to decide for herself."

Something Sylvane would have had no chance to do. Lisbeï bit her tongue. Another idea had occurred to her, something better than useless recrimination. "And Toller?"

"What about Toller?" Guiseïa raised her eyebrows, disconcerted by the question.

"Did you tell him about your plans for the childe?"

"Yes."

"And he agreed?"

"Why wouldn't he? He himself decided . . ." She hesitated, then went on resolutely, "to become a Blue before his time. He didn't want to make childreen he would never get to know. Especially after Sylvane. And particularly when he could spend time with his childreen in Wardenberg. The idea of doing Service in Families where he might not even be allowed to *see* his children . . . No, Toller agreed."

"He became a Blue before his time?" Lisbeï was incredulous. "He took a drug too?"

Guiseïa's laughter was slightly bitter. "No. Rowène says that in all logic the principle should work for males as well, but probably with some other drug. The male mice didn't long survive the one she'd developed. Anyway, it's easier for males to stop. What do you think the Service rules are meant for— the nutrition, the regimen? It's not just for the fun of making their lives miserable, whatever people may think. Their systems are much more easily thrown off balance than ours. After the fourth or fifth ejaculation, there's not much left." She broke into laughter again, and her laugh had something unpleasant about it. "That's another way for Mothers to prevent conception, isn't it?"

She saw Lisbeï's expression and abruptly softened her tone. "But of course, how would you know?" she murmured. She stretched, her joints cracking. "Well, to make a long story short, that's how Toller arranged to be declared Blue. The amazing thing is that more don't do it. One must suppose they, too, have a sense of duty. But on the other hand, we don't know how many actually manage to become Blue before their time."

"But if he was still . . . fertile when he'd been declared Blue . . ."

Guiseïa mistook Lisbeï's alarm and stupefaction. "He abstained," she said drily, although a little sadly as well.

With you too? The thought flashed through Lisbeï's mind at the same moment as a dozen other impressions—Toller's voice in Sygne's Residence at Wardenberg, when he said, "I no longer Dance." And what he might have meant when he said, "I'm on very good terms with the Mother of Wardenberg." But above all she was thinking of the night of the Celebration.

Lisbeï realized that Guiseïa was observing her, puzzled and no doubt sensing her uneasiness, her sudden dismay, her relief as she exclaimed inwardly, *Well, it's a good thing I'm a genuine Blue!*

But most of all Lisbeï realized that Toller had said nothing to Guiseïa about their encounter on the night of the Celebration, seven years earlier.

When Lisbeï climbed to the top of the Molten Tower for her exercise next morning, she found Toller waiting for her amid the persistent cooing of the pidges. When she leaned on the parapet beside him, eyes on the Port below, he immediately said, "You told her nothing."

Although he spoke with his usual formality, he had lost his impassive manner over the past week. It would never return. His uncertainty and, above all, his lassitude came through to her with perfect clarity.

She tried to resist. "Neither did you."

Toller nodded, effectively silenced.

A little ashamed, Lisbeï added, "I said nothing because— well, I don't really know what happened."

He studied her in that disconcerting way he had of assessing people before saying something important for himself or for them. He looked away first. "I said nothing because nothing happened." The disbelief he sensed in Lisbeï made him look at her again. "Oh, the drug had the usual effect, on top of its special effects on us under such conditions. . . ."

She could sense his effort to keep looking at her and forced herself to be calm. "Well, what happened?"

"I saw you walk toward the beach with the celebrantas. It made me . . . uneasy, so I followed at a distance, saw you leave and break into a run." He gave her a wry little smile. "It was hard work keeping up. You're certainly tough. I thought you'd collapse much sooner." Lisbeï was aware of the returning uneasiness beneath his determination to tell his story. "I finally caught up. To find out what stage you'd reached, I had to . . . touch you. Make contact, I mean. Open up to you. But when it's someone like you or Kelys or Guiseïa, I can't . . . I find it hard to control myself. I'm lost—I lose myself in the contact."

"You mean the *light*?" said Lisbeï, her desire to understand overriding caution.

"It's a light for you?"

She'd never really talked about it with anyone, not even Kelys when they were on the Badlands limits. With Tula it had been just a fact of life to begin with, like the color of the sky, not something to talk about. Then, after the incident with Meralda, it had become a mutually avoided subject because of the mirror-wall.

"It's a bit of everything, but I got into the habit of calling it light because the first time . . . Anyway, I always feel I can *see* them better, I mean the people who have it too, as though they were . . . in a better light. It's a light, but a kind of resonance as well."

"With me it's a sense of contact," said Toller, his uneasiness suddenly overtaken by curiosity. "As if my whole skin . . . Guiseïa too. They had to keep us in the same cradle, and that's why they never really tried to separate us later on, either. As we grew up, it faded somewhat. Kelys taught us how to cope, luckily. She worked very hard at it. But . . ." He stopped abruptly.

She remembered Guiseïa's half-confiding remarks and recalled her own adolescent dreams, when looking up Angresea's history, about the possible intimacy between twins. But to be twins *and* to be like this—well, it was a bit frightening. To be lost in the sense of touch . . . How could they bear being apart?

"To continue," said Toller, his voice hard-edged, "you were well on your way. With the drug, I mean. I touched you. It's what Kelys did with us, made physical contact. To begin with. Then I couldn't stop myself from sharing your sensations —in my own way, that is. But there was no . . ."

Lisbeï sensed Toller's uneasiness again and felt her own dismay suddenly cross a threshold: it was ultimately comic, the way they were pussy-footing around the actual word!

"Penetration," she said aloud. She sensed Toller's surprise. "Antonë," she added.

"Oh." He smiled hesitantly. "Well, yes, there was no penetration. And that's why I said nothing to Guiseïa."

"And nothing yesterday evening."

"Neither did you, yesterday afternoon."

Lisbeï couldn't prevent a smile at hearing him echo her own words. But the smile faded at the thought of what lay behind it. "Would she . . ."

Toller finished for her: "Be jealous? I don't know."

"And that was another reason for saying nothing."

"Yes."

There was a pause. All at once she felt the laughter bubbling up and let it come. The idea was so absurd! Jealous? Of whom, exactly? Of what? The Blue smiled in turn, but there was a bitter twist to the smile. Lisbeï stopped laughing. Curiosity overcame prudence again.

"And you, would you be jealous?"

"Of you and her?" He shrugged—a less than perfect return to the old impassiveness. "I've no business being jealous."

That was no answer. I didn't realize it at the time—didn't

*want to. I didn't think of the possibility of a whole other side to
this conversation. Did he? Guiseïa and Toller, Guiseïa and myself, me and Toller. "Of you and her?" he asked. He might have
said, "Of her and you." Would that have been closer to the
mark? Jealousy between men and women—it is such a . . . bizarre idea, it is hard to envisage. . . .*

Envisage what? Lisbeï couldn't imagine very clearly. It
was too alien. She merely noted down the rest of the conversation. Somehow they had eventually slipped into a discussion
of Angresea research into the mechanics of refrigeration, but
she couldn't remember how they got there.

*At first we talked of Guiseïa and how she'd never taken a
compagna. For some reason this made me think of Selva. She'd
never taken one either, but that must have been because of Loï
and surely not one of her Males! I don't know whether Toller was
confiding in me. He seemed to be talking to himself or at least
pretending to—maybe it was the only way he could tell me things.
I know he talked of Sylvane, of the train of circumstances that
had led Guiseïa and him to transgress. . . . "We were more
militant when we were young," he said. There was some bitterness in that remark. Irony, too, and a great deal of sadness.*

"Aren't you militant now?" I asked.

*He understood, of course, and smiled again. "We didn't
plan to educate you, you know. It was more a . . . joke, really."
(He didn't say who had shared the joke.) "Dougall was in your
group and told me about you. And then, you're one of us, and
Kelys had also told us about you."*

*After that we wandered onto the subject of Kelys and how
she never blamed them for what they did, now or in the past. I
thought this was a roundabout way of asking me whether I
blamed them. But why would I? How could I? What if Tula had
been a boy, or I—or both of us, for that matter?*

"I'm not capable of judging that kind of thing," Lisbeï
murmured, suddenly bitter too. "What do I know of love,
anyway? There's never been anyone."

Toller said gently, "Tula." Sensing Lisbeï's amazement
and indignation, he added, "You spoke her name that night."

How they ever moved from this to the problems and
promises of refrigeration, Lisbeï could not begin to remember.

Lisbeï's journal would soon turn to a completely different
subject, however. Two or three weeks earlier, Lletrewyn had
forwarded to Angresea a trunkful of old documents dating

more or less from the dispersion of Angresea women into the
Hives of the area. It had been discovered in the Commune of
Greymarshe. When she got around to examining the contents
as a welcome diversion, Lisbeï happened on a photograph.
Although the accompanying documents were in very bad con-
dition, they seemed to show that the photograph was a dupli-
cate of the original one of Garde sent to the Wardenberg
Press by the Bethely Harem.

5

Stellane of the Bethely Harem was among the survivors of the
great peaceful demonstration organized by Garde's disciplas.
She had fled the Juddites and their growing persecution of the
followers of Elli, then fled again before the revolutionary
wave of the Hives, finding refuge at last in Angresea. Here
disciplas welcomed and hid her until the Harem of Angresea
itself fell before the triumphant Juddites, its chief massacred,
and its women arbitrarily dispersed among the other communities of the region. What had become of Stellane then? Had
she survived in hiding, like so many disciplas? Or had she
been discovered and put to death, as had happened to so
many more? The few notes found with the photograph in the
same, tattered envelope said nothing about Stellane as a person—her age, for example, or other details. The fact that the
photograph had survived suggested that she had survived as
well. Still, it might equally well have been preserved by other,
more fortunate or cautious disciplas. Apparently Stellane
hated the Juddites with a ferocity ill suited to the disciplas'
nonviolent philosophy or the caution necessary to their survival.

Stellane's comments concerning the Bethely Juddites
corroborated Halde in all respects. They had betrayed Garde
and handed her over to the Chief of the Harem. But at this
point the two testimonies diverged, which was no surprise.
Since Halde had been walled up right after she and Garde,
along with other Compagnas, had been captured, she couldn't
have described subsequent events. Only Hallera's account had

survived. Garde's second death and second resurrection, her triumphal march at the head of the peaceful demonstration—
    Hadn't happened.

There it was, on thick, crackling paper. The carefully traced words were unmistakable. The demonstration had been manipulated by the Juddites and had ended in a bloodbath. The disciplas and their message of nonviolence had been completely discredited, and the most violent revolutionary faction had taken over. The result was victory for the Hives and persecution for believras in Elli—believras who were dispersed and demoralized because there would be no Second Coming for Garde, the Voice of Elli. Garde—executed, risen, seen by Stellane and Halde. Garde, once more brought before the firing squad, her corpse burned on a pyre this time, while the Compagnas were walled up alive. But she did not reappear. Garde had not risen a second time, had not led the demonstration before vanishing forever, leaving behind the Word and her teachings for her disciplas.

The photograph, yellow with age, is nevertheless very clear. It shows a woman seated on a wooden bench facing the camera, her back to a brick wall. You can tell it's a woman, because her breasts are visible through the torn shirt. She is wearing ripped breeches—possibly of leather—and soft boots covered with stains of some sort. Her legs seem strangely bent. Her captors must have broken the knees. The woman's hands are bound in front with heavy manacles. There are dark patches on the exposed skin—face, arms, chest, and knees (these must be bruises, Lisbeï realized). Two grinning, bearded men flank the figure, holding her by the shoulders. You can't tell how old the woman is. Her head sags to the left, hanging back a little, and the mouth has fallen open slightly. One eye seems to stare at the camera while the other is hidden by midlength hair. Too pale to be blond. White. Clearly, if the soldiers hadn't been propping her up, she'd have collapsed. The woman in the picture is exhausted, half-unconscious. Or dead.

The weight of the photograph in her hand. Oddly enough, it's Lisbeï's most vivid memory of this first glimpse. A picture reproduced on a metal plate. She held it in both hands, but it suddenly seemed heavy as lead, and she had to put it down. Not for an instant did she doubt the identity of the woman in the picture. It was Garde, and she was dead. There was no gainsaying such evidence. You couldn't imagine her being alive, let alone resurrected. The details were too real, too material—the checks on the torn shirt, the bits of decoration on the boot flaps, probably colored beads . . . Once Lisbeï had examined the photograph with a magnifying glass, she noticed the grim bullet marks. "Not much blood, considering the number of wounds," said Guiseïa later. Lisbeï, once the first shock of horror had passed, thought the corpse must have been washed, then dressed again, thus making sure the victim was recognizable.

Dead. Dead. Lisbeï tried to think of the Notebook, of Halde's stubborn, triumphal cry from the brink of her own death. "I saw the Voice of Elli dead and I saw her living. . . ." But Stellane had also seen her living—and the consuming fire. Garde, no longer dead *and* risen, but risen *and* dead. Why was the sequence no longer reversible? Why, when put this way, did the ancient paradoxical truth no longer exist? Dead, alive, and dead once more. A one-way process toward death, and when you reversed it, the first resurrection . . . no longer made sense. An enigma at best. A mistake, a fraud —any theory was more likely. The thread on which Lisbeï's belief had so easily balanced was stretched to a hair's breadth by the weight of this photograph. She sat down abruptly, as though falling, and for a while no one said a word in Guiseïa's office, where she, Guiseïa, and Toller had gathered.

Guiseïa was the first to move, rummaging in a cupboard and returning with a bottle and some small glasses. She poured out an amber liquid that Lisbeï drank without tasting. Toller had picked up the bits of paper and was squinting in an effort to decipher the faded ink.

Later Lisbeï in turn finished reading the few commentaries left by Stellane, written in a state of dazed exaltation. When Garde came back from the Badlands, she was already aware of betrayal, even before Halde told her. Garde had known perfectly well she was walking into a trap on her return to Bethely for the demonstration. There had been a sense of sublime despair about her (the same words used by Halde), and Stellane had heard Garde whisper, "If I die, Elli may hear me more clearly in death than in resurrection."

Afterward Stellane tried to persuade herself that Garde hadn't really died the second time, that she had vanished in order to be with Elli once more. But Stellane had never successfully explained why Garde had left her disciplas to be massacred, or why Elli had allowed the Word to be defeated and persecuted by the Juddites. Stellane, whatever her end, must have died in despair.

Later Lisbeï asked the obvious questions and gave the obvious answers. Her theories about Hallera, the collusion between Ariane, Alicia, and Markali, Wardenberg's involvement, all were probably much nearer the mark than she'd believed. The nearly bloodless revolution that had spelled the end of the Hives had been as much the product of secret political dealings as of the ringing victory of Garde's underground message, or of the disciplas' faith in the truth. When these had been mere theories, Lisbeï had accepted them quite comfortably. But to accept them now, to perceive this meeting of sacred and profane as coexistence without contradiction was, she now discovered, impossible. She noted her dismay in her journal, feeling that a vital gift had vanished or been wasted. When had she lost her equilibrium on the fine thread between paradoxes? It couldn't just be the photograph, those few pieces of paper, or Stellane's ancient agony. It must have begun earlier. At some moment, without being aware of it, she had crossed a threshold.

Do we each have a limited reserve of resilience, a limited capacity for belief in several things at once without each destroying the others? I must have unknowingly exhausted my reserves. Because I told myself too many stories that were contradicted by reality, perhaps, or that had different endings, endings I'd never imagined. Maybe Dougall's dolore was the point of no return. Or Sylvane's death. Or maybe it happened somewhere between the two, on the road to Entraygues? In Entraygues? Or was it much earlier, in Wardenberg? Could it be Wardenberg itself? Wardenberg, so pragmatic, so reasonable in its certitudes.

Maybe we cross several thresholds, each time regaining a kind of equilibrium, yet after a time, after too many changes, we can no longer recover it. . . .

Is this what growing old means?

Two days later, Kelys arrived. She knew nothing of the photograph, yet was aware of Sylvane's death. But Kelys had been at Belmont supervising the Museum work site. How could she have heard? "Some news travels fast," said Kelys brusquely. Guiseïa and Toller seemed satisfied, but Lisbeï found it perplexing. She had no chance to ask about it, however: she was too taken up with answering Kelys's questions. Kelys wanted to know every detail surrounding the childe's death. She spent nearly a day closeted with Rowène's autopsy report and then with Rowène. Lisbeï had the impression that if Sylvane hadn't already been buried for two weeks, the restless Kelys would have had her dug up in order to perform another autopsy herself.

"She shouldn't have," murmured Kelys in response to Lisbeï's astonished and somewhat shocked comment on her persistent questioning. Kelys passed a hand over her face. She seemed suddenly old—not physically, but her aura gave off a sense of heavy exhaustion, a slowness . . . a little like Edwayne in her final days. "Had the Malady, that is. Died of it. She shouldn't have." It wasn't so much surprise as guilt.

"You mean it could have been prevented? You could've stopped it?"

Kelys hesitated, then, with a deep sigh, seemed to pull herself together. "It's the first case of its kind." It wasn't really an answer; perhaps she was speaking to herself. "The mutation is still evolving."

"Or else it's simply due to Sylvane's origins," Lisbeï couldn't help remarking. Was Kelys trying to deny her responsibility? But she hardly seemed to grasp the accusation implicit in Lisbeï's remark and merely shook her head. "No?" queried Lisbeï. "But how can you be sure?"

Kelys looked up this time. She sat in silence, contemplating Lisbeï. "It might be," she said at last. "There's no way we can really know, is there?" The old impassiveness smoothed the lines on the black face. As with Toller, Lisbeï had to make an effort to catch Kelys's tone and detect the emotion behind it. Regret? Remorse? Sadness, certainly. An immense, tired sadness, so much akin to what Lisbeï herself felt that she ceased to ask questions. After all, what did she know of the story in which Kelys, Guiseïa, Toller, and the little dead girl figured as main characters? Almost nothing. And she had no business prying or inventing possible scenarios. She had no right at all to be curious.

"What are you going to do with the photograph and the documents?" Kelys asked abruptly, much to Lisbeï's surprise.

"The papers belong to Angresea," she said hesitantly, almost overcome by the prospect. Until now, she'd avoided the question of what to do next. Wasn't it enough to have discovered the papers, the photograph? She no longer put much store in signs and portents. So far, her life had been

given meaning by a kind of faith, even if it was more an aes-
thetic need than her childehood faith in Elli. But now . . .
There could be other reasons, all quite accidental, as to why
the thread of her life had again become entwined with Garde
—or one of Garde's disciplas, at least. A dozen different stories, perfectly plausible trains of circumstance to account for
events, quite apart from divine intervention. But she would
not imagine them. She was here, the papers and the photograph were here, and Kelys was right: she could no longer
elude the question.

And the answer was easy enough. Somehow or other,
sooner or later, she'd announce the discovery. Except that
now she felt sure it wouldn't matter much, though she was at a
loss to explain why. It would be more out of principle than
conviction that she'd state . . . what exactly? Not "the
truth," in any case. Another section of Halde's Notebook
would be corroborated, another section of Hallera's Appendices would be placed in doubt. But there would never be any
certainty about what really happened. None of these accounts,
no matter how materially authentic, offered irrefutable proof.
They were simply stories—Halde's, Stellane's, Hallera's—neither more nor less plausible. Belief in some rather than others
could only be arbitrary. There were too many facets to the
same underlying story, and instead of corroborating, they can-
celed each other out. Who would be foolhardy enough to
request a Decision? It would simply be a repetition of Antonë's experience. People would argue about the authenticity
of the papers and the photograph, but as for their real significance . . .

*Garde dead, resurrected, dead again. Who could, who
would dare decide whether a second, unseen resurrection had
taken place or not? Was there a divine Garde who moved in
mysterious ways? Or a human Garde who hadn't really died the
first time? Delusion? Illusion? What did it matter? Had Garde
sacrificed herself in the mistaken conviction (and contrary to her
teaching, in fact) that her blood would somehow contribute to
final victory? Had Garde possibly been a Juddite, or been
manipulated by the Juddites, perhaps a willing pawn in some
long-simmering plot—but there I go, imagining things again, and
I shouldn't. Still, it has to be one or the other: Garde human or
Garde divine. I'm no longer capable of imagining it differently.
My only comfort now would be Antonë's remark before the Decision: in the long run it's irrelevant whether Garde is human or*

divine. What counts is what we've made of her and what she's made of us. But then again, isn't that just a way of saying the end justifies the means? I don't know. I just don't know anymore.

I do know what I've lost, however. What can I put in its place? One or the other? Garde human or divine? I can't choose. Oddly enough, before I saw the photograph, there was virtue in not choosing, not even thinking of choosing. But now it's distressing to be unable to choose. Before there was a . . . plenitude, and now I feel there's a void, that I should choose. But why? And above all, what? If Garde could rise once, why not twice? If she had the power, why choose to die? "The better for Elli to hear her"? Why wasn't Elli listening? Listening to what? Or why would the death of the Bearer of the Word be more effective than her resurrection? Anyway, why would Elli listen or not to Elli's creatures? Elli created the Tapestry and the Universe, and left it to recreate itself eternally according to Elli's laws. No, Garde was merely human, that's all. Forced to consider her freedom and her responsibilities like the rest of us, whether we're Believras or not.

And what about the Promise? You shall *be as I am. You shall be as Elli. Mortal? Immortal? But in Elli's creation there is no law that says humans can die and be resurrected. Is Garde divine, then? Is this a mystery, a deliberate twist in Elli's own laws? But for what purpose?*

I can't choose to believe that, either!

In a way, I envy Hallera for being able to hold to her version of Garde—to fabricate her own version of Garde—and to have had powerful enough reasons for doing so. Not me. I must cling to my thread, not because I don't feel the need to jump, but because I can't decide which way to jump! I ought to write Antonë, ask her how she managed . . .

She called for a Decision, that's how. I couldn't do it. I'd spend my whole life making up my mind!

Well, then, a throw of the dice?

No. I'd have to decide why I chose to gamble. Is "chance" Elli? I don't know.

Anyway, would I abide by the result? I know I wouldn't.

There is a blank space after this sentence in the journal entry, dated the day after Kelys's arrival in Angresea. The journal continues on the opposite page without any change in date.

I'm in the garderie with Tula. We're not little anymore, but we're playing hobskoch. For some reason I feel uneasy. I look at the hobskoch spiral drawn in red paint on the tiles. We're not in Bethely, we're in . . . Belmont? In any case, there are shelves everywhere. Or big trunks piled one on top of the other. There are no other players, but people are watching. Selva, Mooreï, Kelys, probably Antonë. I don't look round, because the game has begun. Tula is wearing a long red dress, and she hitches it up to jump from segment to segment. I think to myself that she shouldn't be dressed like this. I'm wearing blue, but I'm the one who should be wearing red. Then I remember that Tula's the Mother of Bethely, not me. I feel the audience's disapproval boring into my back, but still I don't turn around. I watch Tula throw the chip, jump from segment to segment, return, throw the chip farther. It annoys me: I want to have a turn, too. Each time she lands on a segment, I sing the Old Frangleï rhyme right through instead of just one verse at a time: "Très sainte, viens-t'en, aime les Vertes, saisis-nous vite, presse!—Holy one, comest-thou, love the Greens, catch us quick, press!" I have to sing it very fast, because if I don't Tula will fall.

I'm crouching beside the painted red spiral, and I'm afraid: it's too red, too shiny, it's not paint, it's blood. And suddenly I realize I'm not singing the magic formula anymore, and Tula has stopped with both feet in the center segment, and now it's the double-cross hobskoch of Bretanye, and she's looking at me reproachfully but it's not my fault. It's the blood.

There's a huge, transparent lid, and Tula's walking round and round it. A bit like the cherry-orchard dream; all of a sudden there's a well, and Tula is about to fall into it except that it's like a cover, a cover over the opening to the underground passage, but it's ice and it's too thin. Tula is terrified, she knows she'll fall, but she steps onto it anyway, steps onto the circle, the cover, the ice, but that's not Tula with the white hair stiff with sweat, I see her breasts covered with bruises underneath her open, checked shirt, and I quickly shout, as loud as possible in a kind of crazy Old Frangleï, "Très enceinte va-t-en haine ouverte c'est ta fuite laisse—Very pregnant go away open hatred it's your flight leave!" and I know that's not right, I should have gone into the hobskoch to look for Tula-who-is-Garde (and someone else, but who?) but I can't get in, I'd have to step over the line, and that's not allowed, everyone's looking, and if I disobey I can never be the Mother. I force myself, I hold out a finger to touch the red line, I rub my finger, but the red won't go away, my finger is bleeding, and I'll die if I don't find the right answer because now there's a voice asking me the riddle of the Spirit, "What is red without and blue within, life when it runs and death when it runs, and remains whole even when cut to bits?" And I watch my finger bleeding and I know the answer, everyone knows the answer, it's "blood" but I can't say it, I can't, I say "Garde," Tula falls into the well and I'm glad, glad!

But it's not over. In the circle there is Garde-who-is-Tula, and I must dance with her for the Pairing. I'm about to throw myself into her arms, but all of a sudden I think that maybe it isn't Garde-who-is-Tula. I hold out my hand and she does the same. It's a reflection, it's Ilshe, I try to draw my hand back because I know I'll disappear if our hands touch. But they don't. I seem to be in a big glass bell-jar. I tap the wall, but there's no sound, and Garde says sadly, "You and I, Lisbeï, we're not the same." And now it's Tula again, facing me, standing perfectly still but receding, her chest is bleeding—no, she's shrinking, shrinking to a mere dot. . . . She disappears, and I wake up shouting her name and start to cry again, what is it, what's making me have such dreams, what does it mean?

Again there is a blank space followed by a different, chaotic writing. *I'm going back to Bethely. I must go back to Bethely.*

Mooreï's message announcing Selva's death arrived the day after. It was dated Austa 25. The Angresea pidge had taken three days to return to her perch atop the Molten Tower. On Austa 28 there is no entry in Lisbeï's journal. It resumes the day after she reached Bethely, Septemra 7. Before fever, delirium, and then coma took hold (in her rambling, Selva had talked to Loï and strangely enough to Erne of Callenbasch), her last lucid words had been, "Tell Lisbeï she was always my favorite."

Beside this note in her journal, Lisbeï has written simply, "How lucky for me."

6

"Once more, Tamino. That's better."

The small Green boy caught the feathered ring that Tula tossed to him. He rubbed an arm against his forehead, took several deep breaths, and walked back to the marker on the big, round carpet that was the training area. Eyes momentarily closed, he concentrated, stood on tiptoe with his arms curved in the graceful launching stance, opened his eyes, and shot the ring into the air at the same time that he bounded forward in a series of leaps and arabesques that took him to the middle of the circle, there to catch the ring and throw it up in the air again.

"Breathe, Tamino, the rhythm!"

Tula sketchily mimed the breathing and movements, naming each figure under her breath and commenting rhythmically: "Good, good," and "Higher, get the ring higher!" Her red hair, short in the front, clung to her forehead in dark, damp ringlets. The gymna hall was very warm on this Septemra afternoon, even though it was late and all the doors were wide open. Despite the heat, about thirty Greens, girls and boys between nine and thirteen years of age, were practicing enthusiastically. There was a gymna meet planned for the following week with Cartano—one of many meets held throughout the year to help select Family teams for the Provincial Games. And now the Bethely boys were training with the girls. Tonight a dozen boys would share a meal with the girls in the East Tower and sleep in the tent set up in a field along the East Esplanade. On the morrow they would work side by side in the orchards and continue their shared practice sessions in the afternoon. And early next week they would travel together to Cartano. They would only return to the Green Farm in Malverde Wood after the meet.

How often Lisbeï had visualized her return to Bethely— though not on the actual journey: she'd been too exhausted in the evenings to do more than fall asleep like an animal as soon as her head hit the pillow. But at Wardenberg and before the Entraygues Assembly, she had pictured this moment. Bethely would be different: that she expected, though exactly how was rather hard to conceive. It had never entered her head that the most striking change would be the sight of two young Green boys, cotton singlets clinging to their sweating bodies, parading together in a corner—or the others whom she'd taken for girls at first, mingling with girls in the gymna circles.

She'd foreseen the unfamiliar faces among the Green girls and young Red women, of course, as well as the missing faces among the adults. There would be new, virtually unrecognizable adults whose names were familiar. There would be—and this she knew from the Entraygues Assembly—Meralda, the apprentice Memory, by Tula's side. There would be an older Mooreï and a mellowed Antonë, but she hadn't imagined Bethely without Selva.

Lisbeï had arrived with Kelys and Toller late in the evening. No one expected them, not until a week later, at least. Seeing the light burning on the Third Level office, Lisbeï had gone up and pushed the door open. Tula's red head turned inquiringly. For an instant Lisbeï had been dazzled by a vision of Selva, and in this same instant she had realized for the first time that Selva was truly dead and that she would never see her again. Tula's gray-green eyes had filled with tears, the same surprising tears that stung Lisbeï's eyes, and then they had hugged each other tightly, a long embrace of shared light, all reserve gone, Tula's body pressed against her own, a body strangely different in the distended and still-flaccid breasts and belly of a woman who had given birth just a month earlier. But then Lisbeï had expected Tula to be different. She'd seen her at Entraygues, and however constrained and brief their encounter, there could be no further disappointment on that score.

In the main, Bethely looked pretty much the same: gardens, orchards, the Esplanades and Towers, the noises, smells, colors, and the rapid, musical speech. . . . Perhaps the place wasn't as big as she remembered, the Towers a little less tall, the halls a little less wide. . . . And yet she'd been fifteen when she left—an adult as far as size went, anyway. But the way she'd pictured Bethely was drawn from older memories that would forever assume different dimensions.

The boy finished his turn and stood still in front of Tula, panting and smiling triumphantly. She smiled back, imitating and exaggerating his panting. "Breathing, Tam, breathing! But you're doing much, much better." She stroked the boy's cheek. "That's enough for today. Run along."

The delighted boy bowed briefly to Tula, then to Lisbeï, and walked off jauntily, the tiny bells of his feathered ring tinkling against his thigh. Lisbeï looked sideways at Tula. Did the silvery sound revive the same memory for her, the first taïtche lessons? In any case, the bells were something new in Bethely acrobatics: they helped time the movements for the fluid performance of the various figures.

Kelys watched in silence, apparently lost in thought. It

was Toller who spoke. "A Maestera, isn't he? I didn't see the tattoo, but . . ."

"Yes," replied Tula. "Excellent sense of balance and very good spatial orientation. Still a bit young for the parade, but I think he'll be very good at that, too."

"What about the taïtche?" asked Kelys.

"He's like me," said Tula, "not so bad, perhaps, but"— she broke into laughter—"he falls asleep."

Lisbeï looked for the slim, retreating back, but it was lost among the other Greens. She hadn't noticed anything particular. Like Sergio, then. Another one who had survived the Malady in his own way.

The circles gradually emptied as the practice session came to an end. Near the main door some Greens were talking excitedly to the two gymna mistresses. Those who had just finished their acrobatics gathered near Tula. She excused herself and went over to speak to the youngsters, rapidly handing out comments and advice, ruffling the hair of one or two, giving another a pat on the bottom, and sending the lot off to the shower. One laggard, a slender, brown little girl, nonchalantly executed a double backward somersault, bowed with a big smile in Tula's direction, and ran to join the others. Tula shook her head, laughing. "What a little show-off!"

"Angresea," said Toller. (Elli! Did he always check every tattoo? What a sharp eye he had!)

"My first, and my first-living," said Tula with evident pleasure. "Cynria," she added.

Something in the intonation, or perhaps in Tula's aura, caught Lisbeï's attention as she gazed at the doorway where the last Greens were straggling off. Tula had been looking at her, but now turned away. The childe was her first-living, barely seven years old and out of the garderie at four—after the Malady as was the new policy at Bethely. The future Mother. Well, what of it?

And suddenly, with a guilty start, Lisbeï remembered Cynria (or Cyndria, the Litali name for Cyndrella) at the moment in the story when she is recognized by her sister, the Queene. It was also the name given the childe that was Lisbeï's gift to Tula as they exchanged seeds in the days before tiresome biological facts had dissolved their garderie make-believe. Surely Tula had written about the birth of her first childe? But Lisbeï hadn't noticed, must have forgotten the name and their old story, even before leaving Bethely.

Tula was already walking toward the doorway with Guiseïa and Toller. Lisbeï caught up with them. The Towers glittered in the light of the setting sun, and the veering wind brought whiffs of the stable. From the open windows of the Fourth in the East Tower came the rhythmic click of looms echoing among the other Towers. Bethely, so familiar, and yet all at once Lisbeï felt herself a stranger. Cynria. Perhaps it meant nothing. An amused recollection, perhaps, nothing more. Seven years and all those letters to say nothing. She tried to remember Mooreï's letters, Antonë's, Selva's. But it was no use. They merged in her mind, all alike, all confused with Tula's letters, to make one long, unvarying letter, always talking of things in and around Bethely that didn't interest her. Was the childe like Tula? Had Tula sometimes visited her in the garderie? Had she sat vigil when the Malady struck? Did she take care of the childe herself? And the others? There were two others, Madeli, who was . . . let's see . . . three? And the last childe, or child, Reno, in the West Tower nursery. Had Lisbeï been invited by Tula to the Green practice, along with the other two visitas, so that Cynria could be shown to her?

Would she find a moment to ask Tula these questions?

Lisbeï hadn't had a minute alone with Tula since her arrival two days earlier. Mooreï and Antonë had of course been much in evidence, or else there'd been Kelys, Toller, or Meralda. Or Sanra, the other living half-sister who'd still been in the garderie when Lisbeï left for Wardenberg. Sanra, now living in the West Tower and looking very much like her Westershare progenitor. She was nearly sixteen, a young Red with a green thumb, according to Antonë, who finished the introduction with the smiling comment that everything Sanra planted bloomed "indecently." In fact, the newcomers had been bombarded with information on Sanra and countless other subjects, supposedly for Toller's benefit. Like Lisbeï, he no doubt saw through this polite subterfuge but listened and watched attentively all the same, asking questions just as though he knew very little about Bethely, as though his niece Twyne had not been a ward there for the past five years. How much longer would Tula treat them like visitas?

Toller I can understand. And even Kelys. Tula never had the same relationship with her as I did. But me! Is that her way of reminding me that she's *the Mother of Bethely? Her way of telling me that once gone, I can't come back?*

Lisbeï halted her pen in its furious race across the page. Did she want to come back? To stay? In all honesty, she had to admit she'd only just thought of it. After Mooreï's message —why was it signed by Mooreï and not Tula? Had Tula not wanted to send it? No, that was stupid. Tula must have had plenty of other things to deal with, that's all. Anyway, the message didn't ask them to come. It was she, Lisbeï, who'd decided to leave for Bethely, caught up in a dizzying anguish that was inexplicable to the others, but which no one questioned—an anguish that propelled her across Maerlande in record time, but only because she hadn't wanted a chance to think about . . . what? They'd left at dawn, riding, walking, changing horses, jumping onto ferries, riding off again, falling asleep dog-tired at the end of each day's journey. Neither Kelys nor Toller had protested. And yet such haste was ridiculous. Selva's burial and dolore were already over when the pidge had reached the Molten Tower. And she couldn't escape the memory of the dream—for now Lisbeï could admit that she had been fleeing the dream rather than going to Bethely for . . . what? A confirmation, an explanation . . . a refuge?

But Bethely was not and could nevermore be a refuge. And as for speaking to Tula, how could she, what would she say? "Tula, I had a horrible dream; you were dying and it was my fault but I was glad"? That wasn't really the case; that hadn't really been Tula. It had been one of those twisted dream tales where present and past mingle. "Random brain activity," Antonë used to say, but the little Lisbeï had never really believed her then or now. The dream was too clear, too intense, too undiluted even in the light of day, its inchoate murmurings persistent at the edge of consciousness. Not a dream of ill omen. Of course not. Selva had already died when Lisbeï had the dream. Anyway, the dream wasn't about Selva, was it?

Lisbeï had been doodling in the margin of her journal as her thoughts wandered. A spiral. The hobskoch of course, the Bethely hobskoch. She drew the twelve segments inside the coil with their corresponding signs—meaningless, just like the accompanying rhyme. Mostas had faithfully transmitted them from generation to generation, however, and apart from a few variant decorations, they could be recognized anywhere, even though the shape of the hobskoch differed from north to south. Games. They too were a heritage, humble but determined survivors. Whoever had invented the games remained as anonymous as the spinnas of stories—even more, perhaps. Where had this one come from? She'd have to try to establish the earliest date, a task even more daunting than trying to date tales! Who cared about cataloguing games? *Hobskoch,* Lisbeï began to write with a confused sense of urgency about this digression from her earlier train of thought. *Halde's Notebook had hobskoch drawings. Whoever wrote the second part was also interested in games and tales. In my case it's the reverse: I became interested in tales and games because of the Notebook. Or maybe the Notebook provided a focus for an already existing interest.* "Crystallized it," *as Guiseïa would say.*

But there was no escape. The hobskoch connected to the rhyme, and the rhyme to the dream with its nonsensical words still ringing in her ears: *"Très enceinte, va-t-en, haine ouverte c'est ta fuite, laisse*—Very pregnant, go away, open hatred, it's your flight, leave." What struck her most wasn't so much the nonsense as the fierce joy it had evoked in her in the dream— but this was even more absurd.

Exasperated, Lisbeï deposited her pen in the inkstand, screwed down the top of the inkwell, and closed the journal without even bothering to check whether the ink was dry. "I'd better get some sleep," she muttered, knowing all the while she'd never been so wide awake. It was late, nevertheless. The South Tower clock had chimed eleven some time ago. The corridors were silent, and Bethely slept or was about to sleep. She couldn't help thinking of all the nights she herself had gone tranquilly to sleep, cradled in the capacious and certain arms of Bethely. Nor could she help thinking how different it was now, how stifling, all of a sudden, how sharp her need to go out—but where? In Wardenberg she'd felt like this. Often, after the first few months when she'd become familiar with the Capterie's labyrinths, she would find herself walking the narrow streets and stairways alone in the night. Was it the same now in Bethely? She wasn't at home here, either. This was no longer her place. It was . . . Tula's place.

She is in the darkened corridor, resolutely putting aside the host of memories, the hundreds of similar moments in days gone by . . . gone by. Just to walk, noiselessly. It is cooler now, and the doors onto the exterior staircases are open. Outside, the velvet night, the sprinkling of fading stars. Somewhere behind the dark mass of the Tower, the rising moon. Nocturnal smells and sounds floating on the air, their intensity heightened in the gloom, as though all the other senses are anxious to prove the superfluity of sight. The steps of the spiral staircase vibrating beneath her weight as always, and in the courtyard the penetrating fragrance of fruit and herbs drying on wire trays. Between the East and South Towers, great white phantoms trailing from the laundry lines: sheets. Everything familiar, nothing the same. Involuntarily Lisbeï lifts a hand to her throat, where the magnifying glass dangles as a pendant, worn like a jewel ever since Fraine had it mounted for her years ago. Has she lost everything, then—even Bethely? Tears sting her eyes as she curses herself under her breath for a sentimental idiot. She gulps air, and the knot in her throat loosens a little. Her step firm, she crosses the courtyard, not even knowing where she is going. Is she still running away? *Open hatred it's your flight.* There's no connection. Forget it.

Now she was standing in front of the open door to the gymna hall. Beyond the threshold, light from the windows streamed into the cavernous space, slashing zebra stripes over the floor. She kicked off her sandals and walked forward on the soft, braided mats. She hadn't done her taïtche today—nor yesterday, nor the day before, not since leaving Angresea. Well, better late than never. She took off her night tunic and began the warm-up, only to stop in the middle of the cruci-form-stretch, realizing that someone was watching. A woman. Who slid reluctantly out of a doorway and moved toward her. Tula. Part of her was surprised, but Tula must have had diffi-culty sleeping and had heard her slip out of her room across the corridor. For Tula to be awake at this hour and to have followed her was somehow . . . appropriate.

Lisbeï completed her stretch, eyes fixed on the approach-ing figure, then, with methodical care, finished the sequence. Tula stopped a few steps away, and Lisbeï paused for the required interlude before the breathing exercises and the ac-tual taïtche. Tula let the moment pass without speaking. Lis-beï closed her eyes and began to inhale and exhale, forcing herself to take three complete breaths and gamble that Tula would still be there. She opened her eyes. Tula hadn't moved. Nor had her aura changed. It was a perceptible presence, al-though distant—the kind of reserve that Lisbeï had become accustomed to with Guiseïa and Toller. Tula had learned more subtle defensive tricks than the mirror-wall. (With whom? It didn't matter.) Lisbeï went on with her breathing exercises, moved into the first figure of the taïtche, and waited for the gentle tingling that heralded the beginning of the trance. It would surely be difficult, with Tula to distract her. . . . Even so, she plunged into the trance, forcing herself—a strange sensation: she hadn't known you could *force* it like this. . . . And now she had the impression of becoming porous, yes, of filtering out through the pores of her own flesh, seeking the frontiers beyond which this awareness of the body begins to fade, there to turn, to draw in, to condense her consciousness into the pink luminescence. . . .

But at the frontier she found Tula's body, Tula, in a trance too, or something very akin to it, although she hadn't visibly performed the exercises. Had she finally found an equivalent to the taïtche? Stop. Stop thinking, let your body think, move. Move with Tula's body, with the shifting frontiers of Tula's body unfurling to touch Lisbeï's space, as in the parade. But this can't be the parade (don't think) only this slow undulation of one toward the other, this slow . . . infusion of one in the other, but who is the other? Too late to hold back the question, too late to stop its crystallization into a hard black core that grows heavier in the luminous space that is Lisbeï (or Tula?) and the luminous space shrinks, faster and faster, darker and darker, heavier and heavier, until it is once more a body locked in flesh, and it's Lisbeï, her heart pounding, looking at Tula and Tula looking at Lisbeï with a face contracted by . . . what?

"You," said Tula, her voice low and intense. "You can't, can you? You've never been able to, have you? Just let me be there, just let me be with you, just . . ."

She shook her head, her mouth open as though choking. She *was* choking. With anger? Was it anger that contracted her face and crushed her aura about her like a clenched fist? Dazed, Lisbeï stared at Tula, feeling a tiny, growing spark of anger in response, a spark that she forced herself to extinguish. What was happening? She hadn't done anything and neither had Tula.

"We never could . . . parade together, that's all. What's the matter with you?"

"*You* never could, not with anyone. You just couldn't admit there were others! Gathering everything in toward yourself is a lot easier, isn't it?"

Tula? Was this Tula speaking? Tula of the mirror-wall,

Tula of the silences, Tula of you-should-go-away-to-Wardenberg?

"What choice did you give me?"

"I had nothing to give! I was trying to breathe, to exist far enough away for us to touch each other!"

Tula's voice broke, but she went on. "You've never understood. Selva was right. You've never understood."

The spark ignited and grew, and a terrified Lisbeï heard herself say hoarsely, "Selva?"

"You were always her favorite. You were so much alike. But she understood, she really did."

"Understood what?"

Tula's only response in the gloom between them was a despondent half shrug. In an instant Lisbeï had crossed the space between them, taken her by the arms, and was shaking her. "You wanted us to touch, we're touching, I'm here, speak to me!"

Tula twisted away, freeing herself with astounding strength. Lisbeï tried to grasp her again, but Tula dodged. Again. And yet again. "Touch me," she said in a voice that should have been mocking, "touch me." Lisbeï leaped at her. Tula slipped aside. "You can do better than that, Lisbeï." Voice strained, eyes glinting in a patch of moonlight. Disconcerted, Lisbeï attempted a more sophisticated hold, but again Tula eluded her. And again. A rhythm began to take shape, an increasingly familiar rhythm. Attack, parry, parade. The old memories of training for the Patrol. This is a parade, too, yes, with its breathing, its concentration on the body of the other . . . and since Tula is the other, it's impossible not to seek her light at the same time, not to dilate one's own light toward her, even without the trance, because Tula's body is so near, yet at the slightest touch it slips away again, its light retracting, fading to the hard, hated gleam of the mirror-wall, and now there's no one there but Lisbeï, all alone again with the spark of rage igniting deep within her and rising to the surface. . . .

Tula stood perfectly still. She was there, very near, her head thrown back because Lisbeï was much taller, much bigger, much heavier—but Tula wasn't afraid, and Lisbeï's ears were ringing, her fingers tingling, her muscles contracting as though to . . .

She shambled backward.

"You can't touch me," said Tula, very calm, very tired. "Isn't that it? Are you too afraid to find I've a solid existence of my own, that I'm not like you? I suppose it's my fault. I believed you for too long. 'You and me together.' 'You *are* me' is what you meant. And when I began wanting *not* to be you, then you didn't want to be with me."

What was she saying? You are me—no! Well, yes, but in both directions, reversible, if you're me, I'm . . . No? Suddenly Lisbeï felt weak and began groping blindly for something to lean against, but found nothing. Her knees buckled, and she sat down heavily on the ground, gasping for breath. She'd come so close, so close to hitting Tula.

"I wanted to be with you," she protested feebly. "You're the one who told me to leave."

Tula sat down too, hugging her knees and resting her chin on her arms. A gleam of moonlight silhouetted her features in the shadows. "Long before that, Lisbeï."

"In the garderie? But I couldn't come. . . ."

"Not that." Tula sighed. "It's true, though. I was angry at you for that as well, and it wasn't really your fault. We should have . . . talked about it."

"You didn't want to!"

"You should have made me!"

They glared tensely at each other for a moment, then Tula relaxed a little. "You see. That's it. That's what it was. We were together too much . . . in the wrong way, and not enough in the right way. Oh, it's my fault as well, I know. When I finally did understand, I should have—well, written. But it was too difficult after all those years of silence. Those letters. When I came back from Entraygues, I was distraught. I had sworn I'd speak to you, and the only chance we had— well you weren't there, and yet I'd said to you . . . I thought you'd understood. You see? We've always assumed the other understood. Because of the light. I often used to wonder, if I'd been . . . normal, or if we'd both been normal, would it have been better? We'd have been *forced* to speak to each other. I watched you with your friends and I was . . . sad. Not jealous, really, but sad. Because you were never like that with me. You never really tried. But it was only to be expected, I guess. With me, you were too sure."

"Sure of what?"

"That I was like you. And in fact I *was* like you, like you wanted me to be. For most of the time in the garderie. How could I have resisted? Even afterward, there were times when

I couldn't . . . It was only later, when you'd gone, what with
trying not to feel all those others, that the mirror-wall . . ."

"What on earth are you talking about?"

They stared at each other again. "You didn't know," said
Tula at last. She took a deep breath, held it, and exhaled.
"You were influencing me, Lisbeï. You were suffocating me.
You're far stronger—your light is far stronger than mine.
When you really wanted something . . . I found the same
thing with Kelys later on, and that's why I've always had mis-
givings about her."

"But I never did it on purpose! I don't even know how
Kelys does it!"

"I know that," replied Tula. "Now, anyway. And so do
you." After a moment she got up with a slight groan, her
hands on her lower back. "Not quite in condition yet, even for
a pseudo-parade," she muttered with wry amusement.

Lisbeï stood up too and pulled on her tunic. Together
they crossed the bars of light falling on the braided mats and
went out. The moon-washed courtyard was cool beneath the
enormous, shimmering orb riding atop the West Tower. It
would shrink as it rose higher. Lisbeï remembered that she'd
left her sandals in the gymna hall, and that Tula was barefoot
too, had in fact followed her unshod. She felt a lump in her
throat as she said, "You'll be cold."

"Don't worry, I'll be all right," Tula replied.

They walked as far as the outside staircase. Lisbeï
thought of other nights with Tula, but had no idea whether
Tula was thinking of them. She ought to ask, but she dared not
—it was too soon.

*All at once it was as though we'd just met, as though Tula
were a stranger. I couldn't have any preconceived ideas, couldn't
assume anything . . . and it wasn't so bad, after all. We walked
past the paving stone with the hole in it, and she put her foot in
the hole—although it wouldn't fit the way it used to, of course. I
rested my hand on the pillar beside the tile, on the place where
we had carved our initials, and we smiled at each other. We
would always have the memories. All the memories. The only
thing is, we must tell them to each other to see whether they jibe
or not. We shared the memory of the tile, at any rate.*

They walked side by side up the stairs and along the corridor, stopping in front of Tula's door. Tula pushed the door
slightly ajar to let a slice of light into the corridor. She turned
toward Lisbeï. "We have so many things to tell each other. It

makes me dizzy." She made a mock-horrified face. "Tomorrow?" She raised her arms and slipped them around Lisbeï's neck, and Lisbeï bent over to receive the kiss—brief but without the slightest inner reserve.

"Anytime," said Lisbeï. "We'll have the time—we'll take the time."

She stood still momentarily, eyes on the closed door. She was absurdly happy. It seemed as if this were the first time Tula had kissed her. In a sense, it was the first time.

There was no point in even pretending to go back to her room. There'd be no sleep for her tonight, she knew. On the outside staircase she hesitated, then began to climb upward to the top of the Tower, running on tiptoe. After the tenth floor she slowed down, but she felt strong, light, filled with inexhaustible energy. She wanted to laugh, to cry, it was all one! Arriving at the top, winded despite her rush of energy, she skirted the water tanks and rested her elbows on the parapet. No sea at Bethely. Only the silver ribbon of the Douve and the rolling hills and meadows. But it was Bethely, and at last —even if she hadn't come back, because one couldn't really come back—she had arrived.

The minutes slipped by, and after a while she resumed the interrupted taïtche. It was a way of calming down, of retrieving the thread of that night, the same night as before, and yet so different. The pink luminescence came almost at once, turning to red, scarlet, and finally the luminous black of the trance. She let herself slide into the familiar inner rhythms— the breathing, the pulsing, the electric sputtering—and had the impression that if she wanted, she could almost have controlled these rhythms, shaped them to her will much as she shaped the external figures of the taïtche. She could see these inner rhythms as clearly as the wall of the water tank outside her body, or the parapet of the Tower, or the motionless figure. . . . She knew it was Toller, and she didn't care if he watched her, watched *with* her, perhaps, as the new landscape revealed by the trance unfolded.

There was a marvelous clarity in the depths of this inner landscape. For the first time she could penetrate its continuous flow of motion, distinguishing reliefs, symmetries, radiant knots of strength . . . but what were those two knots, dull, dark and dissonant? Two inert zones where there should have been that sizzling of electric sparks, that tingling of life as elsewhere. Knots that she must undo, that she could undo.

But how? Move . . . no. Even the movement of the taïtche had become superfluous, and her body became quite still. Will . . . *will*. The will to be even further within. Yes, now she could see that the knots were made up of countless other, smaller knots and that within these there were still others, but they weren't really knots they were . . . tiny closed doors, and all she had to do was open one to begin with . . . like this. And now they were opening one after another, like dominoes falling, emitting successive bursts of light to which the whole landscape undulated in response, changing its rhythms and slipping into new, kaleidoscopic configurations or swirling like water, but water that had kept all the glittering lights, all the ripples of the wind, all the waves.

Lisbeï opened her eyes. Above her spread a sky of deep blue quivering with unborn light. She was lying on the ground. Soon it would be dawn. She must have slipped unconsciously from the trance into sleep. She smiled. Toller was sleeping in a huddle between the parapet and the water tank. She stepped over the sleeper without waking him.

Nevertheless, in the days that followed they did not talk about the past. They didn't even try to talk much. To begin with, it was enough just to occupy the same space peacefully—joining Tula for breakfast, for instance, in what had been Selva's rooms. Sometimes little Cynria would join them as well, coming in before lessons began, clutching her notebooks. When the childe came in the first time, she'd given Tula a hug—clearly a customary gesture—and Tula had pushed her gently toward Lisbeï, saying, "This is my sister." Lisbeï watched the childe coming, this Bethely-Angresea who in fact resembled neither Family but rather, by a somewhat ironic twist of genetics, Lisbeï herself: black, curly hair, brown skin, hazel eyes. She was already tall for her age. And the light—perceptible only when the childe put her arms around Lisbeï's neck, a small light, confident and joyful as hers had never been. "So you're my *aunt,*" said the childe. "Isn't that what they say in Wardenberg?" Lisbeï hugged her, laughing—the Frangleï term sounded so odd in the Litali sentence. "But we don't say it here," she remarked, partly for Tula's benefit, to which Tula replied, "Why not?"

Judging by the number of "why nots" that Tula had instigated in Bethely without any squalls, they were probably far more alike now, after ten years apart, than if they had stayed together. During these days the thought occurred often to Lisbeï, who was both moved and amused by it.

When breakfast was over, Tula generally settled herself at her desk, and soon Lisbeï made space for a table and chair by moving the Book of Bethely to an adjoining room. She had decided to recopy Stellane's papers and translate them with greater care, a way of giving herself time to think about them, about what she would do.

On that first day Mooreï and Meralda joined Tula. Lisbeï rose and began gathering up her papers.

"What are you doing?" Tula asked.

"I'm going next door to work." A few days ago she'd have stayed put, defiantly waiting for Tula to tell her to leave.

Tula looked keenly at her for a moment and smiled. "Would you leave the door open, as long as it doesn't bother you too much?"

When the voices in the office ceased, a red dress moved into Lisbeï's field of vision. She raised her head: Meralda. She seemed merely curious, but Lisbeï knew it was more than that.

"What are you working on at the moment?"

"A translation. Old Harem documents. Yet again."

"For the *Tribune*?"

"Probably."

"I receive the *Tribune*. Did you know? An exchange with Kelys. She sends it to me."

"And do you find us convincing?"

"I've always been convinced where you were concerned," said Meralda.

Lisbeï felt the reflex rising, felt the inscrutable but encouraging gaze—her best imitation of Kelys—with which she would contemplate Meralda, giving her plenty of rope to hang herself. She compelled herself not to do it, not to turn away. "I never did much to deserve it."

Meralda's smile became less guarded. "That's not the way it happens."

This time there was no need to fill the silence.

"Are you staying long?"

"I don't know," Lisbeï heard herself say. A movement drew her eyes toward the office door. Tula was leaning against the doorjamb, arms folded—not to defend herself, as Selva had, but to *consolidate* herself. Lisbeï realized it now and suddenly understood that the difference wasn't so great, unless there was perhaps a shade less suffering in Tula's stance. Possibly Cynria would never experience the need to cross her arms at all. . . .

"I don't know," she said again. "Not very long." This qualifying remark was meant not only for Meralda, who had seen her look toward the door and knew without turning around who was standing there, but for Tula, who had overheard the tail end of the conversation—and for Lisbeï herself, who had discovered the answer in the very act of speaking. She repeated, "I don't know. Probably not very long." Meralda nodded almost in unison with Tula.

The afternoon was devoted to Family tasks. With two Memories, Tula felt she could dispense with constant supervision of paperwork. It was important for her to share in the everyday life of the Towers rather than waiting for meetings of the Family Assembly to find out people's moods and needs. Now Lisbeï followed her around without a qualm: Tula behaved like the Capta because she *was* the Capta, not because she wanted to rub salt in the wound. Anyhow, it was easier for them to talk as they went the familiar rounds, slipping into the old ways, past and present mingling smoothly as they noted this or remembered that.

As this first afternoon drew to a close, they passed through the infirmary in the East Garderie. Tula wanted to keep an eye on the current measles outbreak. Antonë was satisfied for the moment, as not a single mosta had died. She took everything that happened in the garderies very much to heart, even after all this time.

"They're trying out a vaccine in Wardenberg," remarked Lisbeï.

Antonë nodded. "And if it works, they'll have to convince everyone to use it and to depend on Wardenberg for their supply."

Of course, not all Families could build themselves a Wardenberg laboratory, and certainly not for a single product such as a vaccine. Lisbeï nodded in turn. "A tough job. I can already hear the Nevenicis yelping."

"Ah, but our able Capta will see to it," said Antonë, patting Tula's arm.

Tula made a face. "I very much doubt if I can persuade them to let Wardenberg take charge! If several Bretanye Families produce the vaccine, it might work. Toller was telling me that Angresea is doing research, too."

"On refrigeration, not vaccines," interposed Lisbeï.

"But they could produce vaccine as well. Refrigeration will be an asset, if I understand correctly. Anyhow, Wardenberg won't try to monopolize the discovery, I'm sure."

"They're not crazy," agreed Lisbeï.

Antonë was listening to this exchange, and Lisbeï, suddenly noticing her amused expression, quirked an eyebrow at the Medicina. Antonë looked as though she were trying to find the appropriate maxim. "Time passes," she said at last, "no matter what."

"Times change," said Tula as though it were the same thing. "Times and people."

"Perhaps some people simply take longer to find themselves."

"Depending on the times," countered Tula, and Lisbeï had the impression that they'd had this discussion before.

"Depending on the time, on the duration, the *length* of time," insisted Antonë. "Statistically speaking, everything can happen, given enough time."

Lisbeï burst into helpless laughter. "Still the same old Antonë, spouting statistics."

"Statistics aren't incompatible with the Tapestry," said Antonë. "Or maybe you think they are, now?" She was calm but attentive, an echo of Mooreï. It would have been funny had the subject not touched a raw nerve for Lisbeï.

"I don't know," was Lisbeï's belated reply. She observed with astonishment that the admission was less upsetting—less distressing—than it would have been a few days ago. This was an admission of ignorance, not of paralysis. Somewhere she had crossed another threshold. Was a new order, hidden in the apparent gratuitousness of the universe, possible once the old order had unraveled? Possible, yes. New configurations that would reveal themselves, new equilibriums on new threads? Or on the old thread renewed? The times were changing, people were changing, perhaps because they were penetrating some immutable truth ever more deeply. She echoed Antonë's words: "Time passes. And our own time is . . . changing. Because we are our time. That's History: we change, it changes us. . . ."

"Not serially, but at the same time," chimed in Tula.

Antonë threw up her hands. "Well then, we're agreed!"

"Except that it's the other way around. In your own particular time, your 'duration,' human History is a special case, whereas in our . . ."

"There only is human time," said Antonë with a hint of mischief.

"There's Elli's time, the time of Elli's becoming," concluded Tula stubbornly.

"Isn't that the same thing?" queried Lisbeï, half-serious.

Antonë and Tula swung round. "Of course you'd say that!" said one. "It's a long time since I heard it!" said the other. And they all broke into laughter.

"Let's ask Mooreï," said Antonë. "That should top it off. I'm dying of hunger. What time is it?"

It was time for the first dinner in the West Tower, as a matter of fact, and the group crossed the court. Antonë and Tula were playfully discussing what Mooreï would have to say, and of course each imagined her producing different arguments that amounted to the same thing. Lisbeï half listened, more attentive to her Bethely surroundings—the autumna light so in tune with her warm feelings for Antonë and Tula, the seemingly random dance of all these red, green, and blue figures toward the West Tower. Antonë was right. Duration was a spiral, and it had a direction. Tula was right, too, and for each human being the Tapestry was endlessly recreated where the spiral's movement and the individual's time intersected. It was . . . like the hobskoch figure some small Greens had drawn in the courtyard near the West Tower door—a southern hobskoch whorled like a periwinkle shell, but bearing the same symbols as the northern double cross—the same hobskoch, at different junctures in the spiral of time.

Impelled by a surge of childish joy, Lisbeï jumped into the small central circle, avoiding the words carefully written in chalk. Here the childreen wrote BETHELY. The final big half circle that you had to jump over without touching a toe to the ground was THE BADLANDS. (In Angresea the half circles were of equal size at each end of the double cross. Rather inexplicably, you started at ILSHE, over which you jumped at a single bound to arrive—quite logically—on ELLI, where you jumped with both feet once your counter had landed in that segment.) Lisbeï skipped quickly through the snail-like hobskoch, her strides growing ever larger as the segments widened, until her last jump was a huge swing to gain momentum and soar over the Badlands.

"Bravo!" cried Tula, laughing and clapping.

"Anyone could do it with those legs," grumbled a young Green. Lisbeï was about to invite her to show what shorter legs could do, but checked herself, stunned. Perhaps it was the way the childe had drawn the symbols in the twelve hobskoch sections, but when you stood behind the final half circle, looking back so that the overall pattern was upside down, some of them looked uncannily like square digits, a little like the small solar clock in Entraygues. 13, 20, 1, 16 . . . Lisbeï had drawn the symbols herself often enough to have noticed (as had generations of players), that some of the signs looked like a 5 or an S, and that the ninth sign, with two circles side by side, was usually drawn as an 8 on its side ("the sign for infinity," Antonë had told her). The lengthwise symbols had always been read as *M–O–R* ("Amor sans A," said the dottas, aping their Old Frangleï teachers, and Lisbeï had accordingly adapted it to "mort-santé"); and those at the end were *S–E,* which they used to hiss, snakelike.

"What is it?" asked Tula, coming over to Lisbeï.

"They look like digits," murmured Lisbeï, trying to rationalize the strange feeling that had overtaken her.

"Why, so they do: thirteen, five, twenty, one, *M, O, R* . . ."

There are times when dissimilar elements come together, and suddenly a spark is struck. All these elements carry within them some unknown but identical, incendiary significance. Suddenly they fuse within us. Some invisible chemistry crystallizes everything in a flash of illumination, a bolt of lightning as they say, a stroke of irresistible intuition. Afterward we try to reconstruct the process, we say "it was obvious," but we're wrong, it wasn't obvious at all. It became *obvious. And the consequences of this bolt of lightning change our previous and subsequent awareness—our future, but also our past. And it's painstaking work to reconstitute this flash of intuition in detail, to retrace, in linear series of words, the utter certainty that some short-circuit in time and language has produced. We must try, painfully, to go back, to* remember *what we* knew . . .

Lisbeï already felt the flash of certainty fading—the certainty that had shot through her on hearing Tula *say* the numbers that she herself had only read. But she would remember, she would try to explain to Tula and Antonë, then to Mooreï, Meralda, Kelys, Toller. The series of numbers in Halde's Notebook, the hobskoch, the rhymes, the symbols, Garde. "Garde, Garde," she would say, hardly knowing what she meant, but with the profound sense that this name was the link, the unwinding thread, the key.

"A code!" cried Toller, illuminated in turn.

A childish code, Kelys remarked later, with a sardonic smile. But what could one expect of an eight-year-old childe?

7

When I grow up I'm going outside to look after the people there. They say I should leave them in peace, but the people aren't in peace, they hurt, they hurt one another and they kill one another. I know because I've seen it. It's not good. If it's not good for us, then it isn't for them either. Even though our people say the outsiders are different, I know they're like us—they're people, and we've no right to let them die in total ignorance. I won't tell them everything. You have to be careful. But I'll tell them with riddles or else seeds, like Tom Thumb, so they can find their way. Not seeds—the birds eat those. Things that really last. I'll have to find things that really last, because the people live such a short time on the Outside. . . .

This passage, now decoded from numbers to letters, came from the very end of the first part. After that the childe had given up the code (and probably the Notebook, too) for other ventures. But she hadn't forgotten it. She hadn't forgotten it when she taught childreen the symbols of the hobskoch spiral. Where or when did she have access to Harem childreen long enough or often enough for the tradition to take hold? It would remain an insoluble mystery. Had she any hope that the key would one day be recognized for what it was? Probably not. The spiral was more like a knowing wink back through the years to the small girl whose coded journal began thus:

This is my diary! Hudo won't read it because he doesn't know the code, and so he'll leave me alone. Hudo is bad, he's ugly, he can't do anything right, and I hate him.

The entry was much scratched out, probably because the childe hadn't much experience with her code as yet. Having vented her spleen on the infamous Hudo, she moved on to subjects worthier of a secret language, beginning with herself, naturally.

My name is Garde. I am eight years old. My mother's name is Lia. My father's name is Abram.

She went on to name a gaggle of sisters and brothers, cousins, aunts and uncles—or rather brothers and sisters, uncles and aunts, the masculine form taking precedence. It was written in a version of Old Frangleï even more archaic than that of the Notebook. Later, when Lisbeï had translated some of the Belmont books written in this language, she would realize that the little Garde's writing—and probably her speech—resembled these works rather than the rest of the Notebook. The childe seemed to manipulate feminine and masculine pronouns and endings with an airy freedom, not only for the adults who opposed all contact with "outside," but for adults in general.

Her family seemed a prolific one, and her parents' generation was particularly numerous: two whole pages of names or possibly first names. The childe had probably practiced her code in this way, because the scratchings-out became far less frequent afterward. The ratio of women to men was difficult to estimate, though there seemed to be an impressively large number of men. Names didn't help much, though. How could you tell the sex of a Lantkéou, Jude, Torre, or Roger? The long list ended with *and Grandmother.* No doubt this was the matriarch of her Line, and as such the only grandparente worthy of mention. Of other forebears there was not a word.

Garde then launched into a description of her village, Lakewood, that soon became rather perfunctory: log houses, a lake, cows, sheep, and goats (all ancient names expressed in the archaic genders), lakeside gardens (irrigated, judging from the description), and neighboring villages, some of them hostile or, at any rate, to be kept apart. *You can't visit them—the people are a bit crazy.* The next passage was among the many blocks of text at the beginning of the Notebook that had been carefully crossed out. According to Lisbeï's theory, the adult Garde had obliterated certain overly revealing details that would have made it easier, for example, to locate the villages. Either she had feared her Notebook would fall into the wrong hands and had blotted out these sections before going Outside, or it had been done later (perhaps she planned to give Halde the Notebook, but this they would never know), since there were similar blocked-out passages in the second part.

This second part, Lisbeï was now utterly convinced, had been written by Garde. The opposing linguistic arguments fell by the way as the first part was deciphered. The childe Garde's community had been cut off for quite some time, but it seemed to have harbored occasional fugitives (Harem people "from the Outside"). The childe had picked up a more evolved language from these women, and this accounted for the comparatively recent varieties of Old Frangleï used by the adult Garde. It also accounted for the time gap between the period of her Old Frangleï and the Old Litali of Halde. It might explain some other mysteries as well: the person recounting certain tales was indeed Garde, but the material was certainly based on accounts by Harem fugitives. . . .

It fitted in neatly with Lisbeï's other pet theory that some of the tales, dating linguistically from the early Harem period, had been conceived rather than transcribed by the writer of the Notebook's second part. The tales, the proverbs, the hobskoch: all things more durable than seeds. But what were they meant to convey?

"Why are you so determined that it was Garde who initiated these stories or the hobskoch?" protested Tula. "Why wouldn't they merely be stories she'd heard and transcribed, like the others?"

"The key to the code," observed Toller.

Tula, brought up short, considered this point. "For the hobskoch, yes, if you insist," she conceded with a nod.

"What's this 'if you insist'?" exclaimed Meralda—not only aware of the latest Notebook research, but also as fiercely eager to defend Lisbeï's theories as Lisbeï herself. "I'd be more inclined to say Garde initiated the tales, 'if you insist,' but definitely the hobskoch. Who but Garde could have initiated the hobskoch symbols?"

"Someone who also knew the code?" offered Kelys.

"But why?"

The explora shrugged a shoulder. "In memory of Garde?"

"During the Hives period, you mean, the disciplas."

"It's a possibility," said Tula.

It was time to intervene, Lisbeï decided. "Why would Garde have taught her disciplas the code in the first place? As a secret language for communication? But it's a childe's code, Kelys, you said so yourself. More to the point, however, would she have taught them the code without anyone mentioning it later?"

"No one ever mentioned the Dance or the drug," Kelys pointed out.

"Beginning with Garde herself! That's one of Hallera's fabrications."

"There's nothing to prove Garde stopped writing in the Notebook just before giving it to Halde," remarked Kelys. "On the contrary, it would seem she'd stopped writing some time before, otherwise she would've used the form of Old Frangleï current in Halde's era. She could very well have developed the Pairing ritual without writing anything down, and, as Hallera says, she might have passed it on orally to her disciplas."

"Well, Hallera may mention it, but Halde says nothing about it in her account of their last night with Garde."

"But if Hallera's aim was to establish and consolidate the worship of Elli, she might very well—for didactic reasons, let's say—have based her account of the last night on several other meetings where the ceremony actually took place, even though it didn't on that final night."

Lisbeï had a sharp retort on the tip of her tongue, but stifled it: they were spinning a web of theories upon theories —what Carmela of Vaduze called "the third degree," a sardonic allusion to a form of torture inflicted in some of the Chefferies. But then again, Kelys was only carrying out a systematic examination of all the possibilities—exactly the sort of thing she herself did when others were too sure of their cases. She suppressed a smile: well, it was obvious now where she got some of her bad habits.

"Anyway, it doesn't matter particularly," Lisbeï urged aloud. "The significant thing is that the childe Garde lived in a badland. There are only two such areas that haven't yet been fully visited, let alone explored: Callenbasch and our own Great Badlands."

The silence that followed this remark lengthened as each person present yet again envisaged the consequences of this theory, the first that Lisbeï had articulated after decoding the little Garde's journal.

"But if these people are still living there, why don't they come out?" asked Mooreï with something close to anguish.

Antonë appeared to take the news better than Mooreï. She had studied the photograph and listened without comment while Lisbeï summarized Stellane's fragments and read her own hasty translation of the Notebook's opening pages. Was she unconsciously assuming the obligatory silence of an Arbitra? But Lisbeï sensed that the Medicina was not really troubled. Antonë had felt it her duty to keep an open mind, even after the Decision, and she had remained flexible enough to welcome these new facts without feeling threatened. How she interpreted them was something else, but in any case, she'd keep such interpretations to herself. In the initial silence that had followed Lisbeï's summary, all she'd said was, "Well, Garde still has things to teach us." One thing was certain: this Antonë would not ask for another Decision.

"It looks pretty clear to me," said Meralda in answer to Mooreï. "These communities want to keep strictly to themselves."

"After more than four hundred years? They must know the Harems are defunct as well as the Hives, and that we're not a bunch of wild animals."

"If they're communities of Aberrations?" murmured Tula, frowning.

"Garde was normal," interposed Lisbeï.

"Garde died and was resurrected," said Mooreï, her voice shaking a little.

"And died and was perhaps resurrected again," finished Antonë, more calm than Mooreï.

Lisbeï raised her hands to forestall the discussion she saw looming. "That's not the point, for the moment. A divine Garde could very well have *chosen* to come from the badlands as a means of highlighting her message of peace and tolerance. If she was human, the fact wouldn't lessen the significance of her message—on the contrary. But whether divine or human or both, that's not what we're talking about here. In my opinion we don't know enough to reopen such a discussion. It's the communities in the badlands that are important. And I think the badlands of Bethely are the ones involved. The only way we'll find out is to go and see for ourselves."

"But those are the Great Badlands!" protested Tula. "No one has ever come back!"

Lisbeï looked at Kelys, but Kelys said nothing.

"If they're really as polluted as the patrollas say, nobody could live there now. Nor, with all the more reason, in Garde's time. And yet . . ."

The atmosphere of anxiety and doubt emanating from

the others was beginning to eat away at the tenuous thread of Lisbeï's initial intuition, the certitude that had illuminated her mind after transcribing the journal. Nobody was questioning the content of the journal. It was the location of the communities described by the childe Garde that raised doubts. A badland, certainly. But the Great Badlands? The journal offered no proof of this, or else the adult Garde had made sure there was none. Stellane confirmed Halde's statement: the resurrected Garde was coming from the direction of the Great Badlands when the Compagnas met her. But neither said that she *was from* the Badlands. She *might* simply have taken one of the shortcuts Kelys had mentioned. The tiny adults whose skeletons had been walled up in the underground cells *might* have come from other badlands.

"Which simply means they're *not* our Badlands," insisted Tula. She'd opposed Lisbeï's exploration project from the start, and now that discussion was veering back to this subject instead of the contents of the Notebook, she found it easier to assert her views. Lisbeï tried not to feel betrayed each time Tula raised a fresh objection. Tula must be afraid for her safety, but it was exasperating, all the same.

"Aberrations are certainly described in the Notebook," remarked Antonë. "These people 'at once old and very young,' who die in a state of decrepitude at forty-five . . . And those she calls 'Seti' seem close to dwarfs."

"The three walled-up Compagnas," added Mooreï softly.

"Pretty harmless mutants, when you consider the reputation of the Great Badlands," Lisbeï pointed out.

"Exactly! So why would they have such a reputation if it weren't true?" retorted Tula.

"Because it suited the communities, and they fostered it," came Toller's clear voice, much to everyone's surprise. They all turned to look at him. "Which would mean there are actually vast areas in the East that aren't contaminated, or only mildly so."

Tula shook her head stubbornly. "But they won't be empty, in that case. Worse, they'd be occupied by aberrations who wouldn't want anything to do with us."

"Who didn't want any contact in Garde's time, but . . ."

"Who haven't sent any embassies since, either!" snapped Tula.

"Or else the Badlands are inhabited by renegada communities," interjected Kelys, leaning nonchalantly against a wall, as she had throughout the discussion.

All heads now turned in her direction.

"If the Great Badlands are habitable," she went on, "you're *sure* to find renegadas. Perhaps there'll be the communities Garde spoke of, possibly communities of descendants of Harem and Hive fugitives. But there's no doubt about the renegadas. And they'll be the really irrecuperable kind: the most violent, the most hostile."

There was another silence.

"No!" protested Lisbeï. "With news of that dimension, some of them would have run the risk of coming back, of exchanging such information for their reintegration into society."

"To keep such news from getting out, a good many renegadas, women and men, would have killed," replied Kelys coolly, "not to mention Garde's hypothetical communities."

"Better still!" exclaimed Tula. "Badlands occupied by hordes of renegadas! But the whole idea is absurd! No one's ever come back, because the area is too polluted, that's all!"

"If there are communities of hostile renegadas, as Kelys suggests, perhaps we should know more about them," said Antonë pensively. "It would be especially vital for Bethely. We'd be the first to suffer."

"It would be vital for the whole Province," admitted Tula, "but that's a job for patrollas, not exploras."

Lisbeï, worried by the turn of the discussion, tried to steer it back to her point. "The patrols are not supposed to go far *into* the badlands, and certainly not for that kind of thing. I think a small, unobtrusive group will be a better reconnaissance tool. If the communities are still there and we find them, they'll feel less threatened. If they're renegadas—well, either way it'll be easier to pass ourselves off as renegadas too."

"Don't use the future tense as though the whole thing had been agreed upon, Lisbeï!" protested Tula. "I know that game. I don't believe for a minute that our Badlands are concerned, and I'm not the only one here!"

Lisbeï forced herself to remain calm. She'd hoped it wouldn't come to this, but if Tula was determined to play the Mother, she could remind her that there were limits to a Mother's authority. What Lisbeï did with her life was her business—even if she had to go against Tula. Wasn't it Tula who'd said that they were different, two distinct people?

"This isn't an inner council, and I wasn't asking your permission. I can go. It's my absolute right as a Blue. I'm not dependent on Bethely now."

"Go alone?" queried Kelys, still cool.

Lisbeï stared, dismayed at the implied objection where she had looked for support. "You don't believe me this time, do you?" she muttered finally. "You think that the Bethely Badlands aren't the ones in the Notebook."

Kelys moved away from the wall and pulled a chair up to Tula's desk. She straddled it and hugged the back, resting her chin on her arms as she studied Lisbeï. After a moment she lifted her head, her face resigned. "What I think or don't think doesn't really matter. I can't choose for you, Lisbeli. If you decide to go, I'll go with you."

"But why, if you think I'm wrong?"

"Because you're not an explora, Lisbeli, and I have been one long enough to know that I can survive renegadas," replied the black woman after a short pause. "Can you?"

That was a question I'd already asked myself, Lisbeï wrote that night. *What could I say? Like the overwhelming majority of people in Maerlande, I've never been physically threatened by another person. Except for Gerd, and even then she wasn't trying to kill me, just hurt me. She was frustrated because Nance was always beating her at whatever they did and because Kolia was coming on to me. I know I can probably fight hand to hand, but I've never really become used to actually* defending *myself. Oh, I can hit a target with a gun, I'm a very good archa and a fair hand at the cross-bow and sling. I can also throw a spear and a lasso at moving objects, but not living ones. The idea of truly hostile groups in the Badlands . . . people who would reject contact violently . . . I find the thought shattering. I try to imagine their mentality, but even after my Patrol I'm sure I don't understand. Anyway, it was too long ago.*

If she wanted to be true to herself and her beliefs, then she had to go. Alone, on principle, if no one shared her convictions, still—was she ready to become a principled corpse? It was a question of how much she wanted to verify her hunch about Garde's journal and learn more about these hypothetical communities.

The sensible thing would be to begin with the Callenbasch badlands. To forget her intuition and be sensible.

"I can't let you come on those conditions, Kelys."

"And how will you stop me?" Kelys smiled.

Tula slapped her desk sharply, making everyone jump. "All this is beside the point, Kelys, and you surprise me. Here you are, each trying to be so selfless and high-minded, but we're not in some novel by Ludivine of Kergoët. Before you come to blows about a solo exploration of the Badlands, you might just consider the consequences. Not for Lisbeï or whoever goes with her, but for the rest of us, for Bethely, Litale, even Maerlande."

Judging by the way Kelys rested her chin on her arm again, the explora must have been expecting this all along. Lisbeï felt exasperated. "What consequences? Let me remind you once more, this isn't an inner council, and I'm not asking the Family for help of any kind."

"That's not the point. If we can ever prove that these Badlands are actually habitable, or in fact inhabited by whomever it may be . . . well, it can't be left to the whim of a single explora, or even several. We would all be affected by the consequences."

This was too much for Lisbeï. "Don't tell me you're dredging up the old arguments against exploring the West!" she exploded. "I thought they'd been settled once and for all!"

"There aren't many questions that can be settled once and for all, Lisbeï," said Antonë with a sigh. "Each case is different, and the solutions are bound to differ, too."

"What's different about this case? The Great Badlands are closer and reputedly dangerous, but . . ."

Kelys interposed again with maddening calm. "It's taken nearly ten years to build the Western fleet, Lisbeli. The journey itself will take several months, if all goes well. And we won't hear anything for months after that. If no news reaches us, it will take more time to decide whether or not to investigate. Time is always an important factor. If things go wrong in the Badlands, it may be a question of weeks, days, or even hours before the possible consequences are upon us and we are forced to make extremely serious decisions. The Badlands are fifty klims away from us, sixty-three from Cartano, and eighty from Termilli. We have no idea who may be living on the Western Continent—if indeed it is habitable—but we have a pretty good idea of who might be in the Badlands."

Tula leaned over her desk, intense and almost imploring. "Think of the consequences, Lisbeï. Whether there are genuine communities or renegadas, if they track you down and capture you—or kill you—not only will you be dead or imprisoned, but you'll have warned them that we know of their existence."

"We could easily persuade them that no one else knew."

"They could easily 'persuade' you to tell the truth!"

"But look," urged Lisbeï, "if these are Garde's communities, they've done nothing for centuries. They're not about to invade us now, simply because two travellas pass by! To suppose them actively hostile isn't worthy of us. But even if they are communities of renegadas dating from the Hives period, if you will, they'd certainly want to avoid trouble and wouldn't risk alerting us to their presence if we actually were travellas on our way through. They'd be more likely to hide!"

Lisbeï and Tula glared mutely at each other, irreconcilable, furious, heart-broken. Mooreï's voice floated between them, slightly hoarse. "This little Garde says nothing about Elli."

The fact hadn't escaped the Memory, either. But it didn't mean a thing! If Lisbeï had invented a coded language to revenge herself on a disagreeable sister, she probably wouldn't have mentioned Elli either.

Mooreï rubbed her forehead and kept her hand there for a moment, shading her face. Then she straightened with a sigh. "But if there really are communities in the Badlands—the ones Garde speaks of—they're sisters in Elli, no matter what. We'd be duty bound to—well, resume contact. If these are communities of fugitives established since Hive days, as you said, Lisbeï, the same thing applies even more urgently. If there are renegadas—well, you know my views on exile. But whoever they are, once we become aware of their existence, we can't just do nothing." She dropped her head and stared at her hands folded on the table-top.

Tula sagged back in her chair, pleased at this unexpected support. "There's that aspect too. My main concern, however, was the possibility of new habitable land. Nearly all the Offshoot settlements in Maerlande are reaching capacity. We won't hear anything from the West for three or four years at best. The Great Badlands are closer in space and time. As Kelys points out, we'll have to make decisions much more quickly if things go wrong."

She went through the list methodically. Perhaps the childe Garde's journal referred to other badlands, and the

Bethely Badlands merited their unhealthy reputation. The exploras might come back sick or even dying—but at least Bethely would know what it was up against. If they died in the Badlands, though, no one in Bethely would know why—whether from contamination or attack by hypothetical inhabitants. Already two lives would have been lost. They'd have to decide whether to risk other lives, but for what?

If the exploras returned with the news that the Badlands weren't contaminated or only mildly toxic, the problem shifted but remained equally serious—if not more so. Even if inhabitants weren't immediately discovered, they'd be there all the same, although they mightn't be Garde's communities. Fugitives from the Harems and Hives would have had plenty of time to establish numerous communities, with or without renegadas from Maerlande, be they voluntary or forced. Would the communities be friendly? Maybe—or maybe not, particularly if renegadas were present. Or perhaps the degree of hostility would vary among communities. Anyway, however friendly their reception of a couple of exploras, they might provide a very different welcome for Families intending to establish Offshoot settlements. Visitas were one thing, but settlas would be rejected, as likely as not.

"Oh well, we'll just leave the communities alone!" retorted Lisbeï, losing patience. "We'll go, we'll see, we'll learn, and we'll come back, and that'll be the end of it. The Patrol will be there to keep them from making trouble for Bethely, if that's what's bothering you, Tula."

Kelys pursed her lips. "So we'd revert to the end of the Hives period, patrolling frontiers? I suppose Maerlande is still capable of such regression. The Patrol is already in place. We'd strengthen it to become a permanent force along the whole Great Badlands' border. It might be tolerable, and all the Families might be willing to negotiate the establishment of a permanent Patrol—for a time, anyway. But causes and effects won't change."

Lisbeï couldn't understand Kelys's last remark until she remembered the main arguments put forward by the partisans of Western exploration. "If the Western Continent is habitable, we won't need these Badlands," she pointed out.

"*If,*" said Kelys.

"*We,*" said Antonë.

Lisbeï looked at each of them and shook her head in disgust. "And *if* these hypothetical communities also have a population problem. At the moment we don't know a thing about their fertility rate. Elli, we don't even know they *exist!*"

"But if they do exist—and even if we don't know their growth rate—we have to suppose they'll need space sooner or later," sighed Antonë.

"And even if *we* leave them alone, despite our own need for space and the possible disappointment of our hopes in the West . . ." Kelys added.

Lisbeï was scandalized by Kelys's evident skepticism. "We're capable of thinking up solutions other than invasion!"

"Our options are limited, Lisbeï," remarked Antonë. "If as many boys were born here as girls, things would be different. We could think in terms of controlling births. But as long as we don't know how to alter our disproportionate birth ratio . . ."

"But even if we could envisage solutions other than invasion," chimed in Kelys, "who's to say *they* will?"

"In that case the sooner we establish contact the better, so we can teach them to envisage other solutions," retorted Lisbeï obstinately.

Kelys straightened up in her chair, her hands behind her head. "Missionaries," she murmured.

"What?"

"That's what Mooreï was saying just now. Send emissaries to convert them. Like at the end of the Hive period. . . . But if they've never wanted to make contact with us despite being aware of our existence (and we have to suppose that, don't we?), I wonder if they would let themselves be converted?"

"We have to try."

"At what price?" Kelys said softly. "Some Hives massacred dozens of emissaries."

A rather long silence followed this remark. Finally Lisbeï spoke, feeling desperate. "It's up to each one of us to choose, isn't it? If we go in and find communities . . . It's like the Western Continent. It will be an accomplished fact—a thread in the Tapestry. And on that basis we shall have to choose. We chose to go West."

"But we haven't chosen to go into the Great Badlands—not yet," Kelys said. "We can choose *not* to go. We can decide to let these hypothetical communities come out of the Great Badlands on their own and end their isolation themselves."

"And invade us?" Antonë was half joking.

"Kelys is right. Just because one can do a thing doesn't mean one must. Anyway, it isn't 'one,' it's we who choose. Here and now."

I must choose. And I don't know. I don't know whether I'm ready to accept the responsibility. Kelys had no need to try to influence me—if that's what she was trying to do. Her spoken arguments were quite sufficient. She's an explora and can visualize the dangers more easily. She knows what it's like to fight someone who wants to kill you. Violence. War. That's what we're talking about. Not my death, or the death of the first exploras. But the necessity of Maerlande—not just Bethely or Litale—contemplating the possibility of a war in the medium or long term.

Could we do it? Kelys and Antonë seem convinced that we could defend ourselves on a larger scale than the Patrol, if attacked. The Word—well the Word has never said we should let ourselves be massacred without lifting a finger. There are nonviolent ways. But just how far would they go? It's the adversary who sets the limits, what she is ready to do to us. Of course, Kelys put things in the worst light to demonstrate her point. These communities won't necessarily want to massacre us. But if they want to take us into bondage, if they're still at the Hives or Harem stage, what then?

And if we do defend ourselves, if we take steps to resist, what'll it do to us? To each of us, to the Maerlande that is each of us? It isn't as though we were ignorant. We have the cautionary example of the Harems and Hives, to say nothing of our theories concerning the Decline. We can't pretend to be ignorant of the possible consequences.

I can't pretend to be unaware of them, not this time.

And Tula's right, in spite of everything. It isn't as though I could say, "I'm going on my own, I'm ready to sacrifice my life to find out, and it's nobody's business but mine." Go, stay—that isn't the issue. It's the fact that I deciphered the Notebook . . . but can that be undone? No, it's happened. It's woven into the Tapestry. The hypothesis exists: the Great Badlands may be habitable or already inhabited.

And so, even if we start off by being sensible, by exploring the Callenbasch badlands further, we'll end up going into the Great Badlands sooner or later, just like the Western Continent. If we go now, I'll only have made it happen sooner. But made what happen? It's all so theoretical, with some theories more plausible than others, and the worst not necessarily the most likely. It's the Western Continent all over again.

If I don't go, we'll all have more time to think about the possible consequences, to get ready as we have for the Western Continent while the fleet was being built in Angresea. Even now, with the fleet nearly finished . . . The boats could be used for something else. We still have time to change our minds.

But what would happen if things were reversed? If a fleet left the West tomorrow and invaded us? If tomorrow the hypothetical communities in the Badlands decided to invade us?

Lisbeï stopped writing, her eyes staring blindly at the dark square of the window. With an effort, she shook herself free of the stories bubbling up in her imagination and began writing again, her hand firm.

In the first place, it wouldn't necessarily be to invade us. And secondly I believe—I'm confident—we'd do whatever we had to. We might have very little warning, but we'd do our best, remain true to ourselves as much as possible, accepting all the consequences of our acts.

Imperfect choices in an imperfect world. The adage is right. "Nothing ventured, nothing gained." The Family will be right, too. Even though no one, not even Elli, knows in advance the design of the Tapestry. Well, so let it be.

As she closed her diary, Lisbeï realized with a certain sad irony that she had made her choice—and not a very spectacular one. She had decided to wait a little longer, since circumstances offered her that luxury. She'd wait first for the Family's decision, although she knew in advance what it would be. And if she chose to leave after that, alone or accompanied, no expedition could leave before next sprinna in any case. Wait. That certainly wasn't what Ludivine of Kergoët's heroines did. For an inherently impatient Lisbeï, however, waiting represented progress.

8

"But so many things have changed in Bethely," Lisbeï had exclaimed as she went back to her room for the night after the first meeting of the Family Assembly.

Antonë had rubbed her eyes and stifled a yawn. "Exactly.

That's why Mooreï, not Tula, put the question to the Family. Tula has already got them to accept a lot of things. There are limits—a saturation point. And this proposal—well . . ."

"But it's practically the same debate as the one for exploring the Western Continent!"

"Exactly," Antonë had repeated. "What with all the palavras on the Western expedition, they may have exhausted their reserves of boldness, their capacity for leaping in the dark. Oh, I know, it's not rational. But everyone isn't rational all the time, even in Wardenberg, are they? There's an enormous distance between us and the Western Continent, and we know nothing about it. The Great Badlands on the other hand —well, Lisbeï, they are the *Badlands,* after all. It's a bit different for Families in Bretanye, for example, but here in Bethely most people believe they know all too much about the Badlands."

Lisbeï herself could feel the sudden knot of fear at the mere mention of the name, a reflex that was too deep-seated to suppress, even after ten years' absence. She could loosen this knot of apprehension, partly because of her experience at Wardenberg, but mainly because of the story told by the Notebook and by Stellane, and because of her faith in her own intuition—all very irrational, too, come to think of it. But there were others who believed just as strongly in different stories. Stories about the Badlands. Stories about Bethely, too, about old traditions and the recent past. They weren't Juddites, but they weren't Progressistas either, and they had gone against tradition far too often for comfort. Lisbeï's first discovery had already thrust the Family into a limelight they would gladly have done without. True, the Decision had validated this initial discovery, but what was all this about a coded diary, a cipher, a childe Garde? They were barely accustomed to the tenets adopted with Antonë's Decision; would they now have to question these? Lisbeï was still a Bethely and she *had* discovered Belmont with her unorthodox methods, and they were grateful for the positive fallout of her discovery. But did she have to keep on being such a Family troublemaker with her discoveries and theories, this time on the basis of even more controversial evidence?

Lisbeï could have no illusions. If Bethely weighed the probable dangers against the eventual gains, the Family's answer would be no. No one would be sent into the Badlands. No one would be sent in after Lisbeï if she didn't come back.

In earlier times, Lisbeï would have been offered the choice of self-exile if she had refused to bow to the collective decision. But that was when Maerlande was in its infancy and Blues continued to belong to their Families. Things were different now. If she decided to penetrate the Badlands anyway and returned to tell the tale, Bethely would welcome her. If she suffered toxic contamination, they would try to treat her. And she'd be given a dolore if she never returned or if she succumbed once back in Bethely.

All very consoling! Too bad she couldn't feel more comforted or more confident about her choice when the moment came. At least Tula wasn't trying to influence her. Since that meeting, which had unexpectedly turned into an inner council, Tula had withdrawn behind the screen of the Family and its palavras. She would not bring up the subject until the Family had made a decision. "You do understand, don't you, Lisbeï?" she'd said after the committee rose. She was upset but firm. Of course Lisbeï understood. Tula was the Mother, the Capta of Bethely. She wasn't like Selva, however. She wouldn't keep the Family in ignorance while awaiting a quick reconnoitre by a lone explora, be it only to check the degree of Badlands pollution beyond the blue stones—a proposition Lisbeï had made as a last resort, but without conviction.

"Weren't you listening?" Tula had said. "That wouldn't change the basic principle one iota!"

And Lisbeï, both ashamed and exasperated, had swallowed the retort that Tula's weren't the only principles. What kind of reasoning would that have been?

"What would you have said if it hadn't been me?" she asked, now obdurate.

Tula's look of exasperation returned. "It doesn't make a bit of difference whether it's you or someone else putting their life in danger in the Badlands."

Lisbeï would have liked to see Tula opt in her favor at least once, despite the odds. Of course she knew it was unreasonable of her, of course Tula in her present position had far fewer options than she did, but the resentment was there all the same. And just when they'd begun to find each other! But why did she have to tell all of them about the code . . . ?

And then again, what choice had there been for her? No, each was doing what she must. Accept it. Time had passed, Tula had changed, Lisbeï too, and well she knew it. Hadn't they both acknowledged as much in the darkened gymna hall?

Lisbeï's present resentment was an old reflex, an old mistake about Tula. They were not the same, they never would be the same. Tula wouldn't try to dissuade her from exploring the Badlands, though it was a bit galling to admit it. Did Tula really have to be more faithful to Lisbeï than Lisbeï herself? Perhaps it was Tula's way of loving her—and Lisbeï couldn't reproach her for that, could she?

But the feeling in Bethely now seemed ominously like the general atmosphere following the Assembly of the Decision. Weighed down by memories and especially by the familiar surroundings, Lisbeï grew ever more uneasy. She'd tried to reason with herself, but it was useless. She slept badly, woke fatigued, felt cantankerous, and became irritated at the slightest provocation. She had a painful feeling of *déjà-vu*, whether with Tula, Mooreï, Kelys, or Antonë. After the first, interminable week of palavras, she noted with some surprise that the only person who didn't inspire this feeling was Toller.

In the beginning, Toller had seemed to be enjoying himself in Bethely. Unlike Guiseïa, he'd never visited it before. Although he already knew a lot about the Family, he was curious to measure the reality against such secondhand knowledge, much like Lisbeï in Angresea. He'd been glad to see his niece Twyne, and she was equally pleased. As for the Green girls, he noted with satisfaction that he could meet with them freely, particularly those fathered by Maxim of Angresea, Tula's first Male. Cynria and he had struck up an immediate friendship, but Toller was a general favorite with childreen of all ages. The workshops along the Douve interested him, and he had suggested to Lisbeï a few improvements in the pulp-plant. Lisbeï had passed these on to Tula, who had tactfully conveyed the information to the pulp plant capta. Toller had cheerfully pitched in with the last of the fruit picking in the orchards and had lent a hand with winter preparations in the gardens and fields.

He spoke Litali without an accent, and people hardly realized a strange Blue was there. When they did become aware of his presence, they barely wondered why he stayed— it was of no importance, since he was merely a Blue, even if he was a near relation of the Capta of Angresea. That he might have some connection with Kelys and Lisbeï never entered their heads, for the most part. The events at Entraygues had been talked of in Bethely, naturally, since as usual the Family had sent a large contingent to the Assembly Games. But

in their minds Lisbeï-champion-of-the-Blue-men was still
screened by a number of other personae: Lisbeï-daughter-of-
Selva, Lisbeï-who-should-have-been-the-Mother, Lisbeï-of-
Halde's-Notebook, or the most recent, Lisbeï-of-Belmont—or
for that matter the earliest persona, just plain Lisbeï, the
childe of the West Tower garderie whom only Bethely knew.

Lisbeï felt comfortable with Toller. She had nothing to
prove to him, no excuses to make. She could discuss anything
with him without having to make allowances for Bethely prejudices.

*Not that Toller is without prejudices—those of Angresea
and the Progressistas—but he can view them at arm's length,
much as I can now view Bethely's preconceived notions. Paradoxically, it's easier to talk with him than even Tula. I suppose
it's because I have no muddled expectation that* Toller *will resemble me!*

It was only when she deliberately went in search of him
that she realized he was trying to avoid her. She was surprised.
He hadn't been like this in the first weeks. But he avoided
almost everyone now and took refuge in the Library instead of
sharing in the daily activities the way he once had. He looked
pale and feverish and tended to snap at people. He tried to
retreat behind the old, impassive mask, without much success
as far as emotions went, but with the clear message that he
had no intention of answering personal questions. Finally, Lisbeï learned that he had received several letters from Angresea, no doubt from Guiseïa. Now she, too, became
alarmed and decided to force her way past his reserve.

She found him in the Library, deep in obscure archives
dating from the end of the Hives period. "Anything new on
the mysteries of Litale?"

He waited before looking up. "Not really—some interesting facts about the last days of the Bethely Hive, though."

"Alicia and Markali, the reputed sisters?"

"Certainly sisters. Your theory appears to be increasingly
substantiated."

"A fine subject for a novel or a tragic drama. Alicia persuading Markali to agree to a trial. Or better still, Markali
persuading Alicia."

"Or both drawing straws to settle their fate."

"That's a little drastic, don't you think?"

"There are situations where nobody can win."

Somewhat disconcerted by the intense although ineffective effort he was making to maintain his self-control, she tried humor. "Did you know you were becoming the phantom of the Library? We almost never see you anywhere else."

Toller gave her a strained smile. "There are times when . . . it's rather painful to be surrounded by too many people," he said after a pause.

"Yes, Bethely's a bit like Wardenberg in that respect." She tried to think of what to say next and began to lose patience. Why not simply ask? "Toller, what's happened? Is something wrong in Angresea?"

He gave a slight shrug but answered nothing.

Lisbeï sat down beside him. "Is it Guiseïa? Why don't you go back?"

"I'm waiting for your Assembly's decision."

"Why? It'll be no, in any case."

"Will your decision be no, too?" he said, his voice carefully neutral.

She stared at him, thoroughly taken aback. "If I do go, I think I'll go alone."

This time he reacted. "You can't."

"I must."

"Kelys won't let you."

"Well it doesn't concern you, in any case."

This wasn't what she'd meant to talk about! She waited for his answer in the growing silence, guessing what it would be.

"I always wanted to visit a badland," he said at last, with a small, bitter smile.

"But why?"

"Why not?"

She stared at him. "Why not give me a real answer?"

"Why not ask a real question?" he snapped, abandoning his self-control. But it was only momentary. The next second he said quietly, "Excuse me, I'm rather tired." His voice was listless. "I want to visit the Badlands out of curiosity, and because I have nothing better to do, here or anywhere else. Does that suit you?"

"And Angresea? Haven't you anything to do in Angresea?"

"Angresea." He sighed. "Must I really explain why I left Angresea?"

She hesitated. "No." Once she'd admitted this, there

didn't seem a great deal left to say. "How are things there?" she asked finally, feeling a little desperate.

"The Family's fine. Guiseïa isn't. She wants me to come back."

And he couldn't, of course. Not for a long time. Even Guiseïa must understand that. Sylvane's loss was like acid eating away at them both. They couldn't come to terms with her death together, so they must do it apart. Even then . . .

"But you're not obliged to go into the Badlands, all the same!"

"No. Yes."

She was about to protest when he surprised her by standing up abruptly. "Let's go somewhere else. You're right: it's time we talked all this over."

Astounded, Lisbeï followed him to the outside staircase, down into the courtyard, and across the South Esplanade. Workas were coming home in the setting sun. Toller walked quickly, looking neither left nor right, hands in his jacket pockets, determined and sombre. The tables certainly were turned! Lisbeï would have laughed had she not been so concerned. When they reached the edge of the Douve by the mill pond, Toller stopped. They weren't far from the opening to the underground tunnel, now shored up and roofed against the weather. The Blue sat down and patted the grass beside him. She obeyed. He rested his arms on his knees and stared at the still water.

"Lisbeï, I don't know what's happening. I've been a Blue for a long time. I've learned to control myself. There's never been any problem with . . . abstinence, including mental abstinence. That episode during the Celebration is still a mystery, as far as I'm concerned, even taking into account our special abilities. That I could get carried away like that . . . I can't deny it, but I still don't really understand it. The agvite must have had some effect on you that it never had on me or Guiseïa. Perhaps it . . . radically increased your power of projection. I don't know. . . . All right, it was an exception. After that I never experienced any problems with you. But since the other night on the Tower . . . I was already there when you came up. I wanted to watch the full moon through my telescope. Since I was standing on the other side of the Tower, I had no idea you were there too. Suddenly I sensed—I don't know what it was, but something, very clear. I went to look, and there you were, apparently in a trance. And I was

powerless . . . powerless to leave, powerless to resist. You
hadn't taken a drug that night, had you?"

She had to try twice before producing a faltering, "No."

He turned to look at her sharply, sensing her reaction.
"No, nothing happened! I was simply . . . caught up in your
trance, in the taïtche—if that's what you were doing. In spite
of myself. Caught, drawn, hustled and bustled into your
trance. Without the drug. Has it ever happened to you? Or to
others with you?"

She sucked in her breath and let it out again. "No," she
said finally. "But I didn't realize . . ."

"I know." He slid his knees into a cross-legged position.
"I've never heard of this sort of phenomenon outside of the
Dance. Although when one takes the drug without Dancing—
I mean normal people, not us—it's possible to be influenced,
but not to that extent. And in any case, you took nothing this
time."

"No," she repeated, still amazed.

He said nothing for a moment, swaying gently back and
forth beside her. Their shadows lengthened over the quiet
water as the oblique rays of the setting sun glanced off the
surface and lit up the opposite bank with a tremulous glow.

"Since then I'm just not myself," he went on, speaking
more softly. "I'm not sure there's a connection, but . . . I
don't know. Your presence . . . the presence of any woman,
but particularly you. I have trouble sleeping, and when I sleep,
I have strange dreams. Do you have strange dreams, Lisbeï?"

"Strange how?" She hesitated. "Erotic?"

"That too." He gave a sardonic little laugh. "And I was
so smug about not having them. I haven't had them, you
know. Not since becoming a Blue. At all. Not for years. But I
don't mean just those kind of dreams. Other dreams, dreams
that . . . how can I put it? The kind of dream that seems to
be saying something important, but you can't grasp just what."

Lisbeï nodded. "I had one, but it was before coming back
here."

"And since then?"

The dream had recurred in one form or another several
times. She had thought vaguely that it would stop after she
broke the code in the hobsoch, but it had come back. Or
rather, it . . . it occurred in patches in other dreams, or
some of the images turned up at odd moments, various characters in the dream appeared, then shrank to nothing. Selva,

Tula, Garde as she had looked in the photograph, the bleeding hobskoch, absurd and truncated versions of the Spirit's triple riddle.

"Blood?" exclaimed Toller. "Dreams of blood? I dream of . . . of red, of strange things, strange scenery, red . . ."

They looked at one another, stupefied.

"But what can it mean?" asked Lisbeï finally.

"I've no idea," said Toller, "but I wanted to talk it over with you. Something has happened, I don't know what, but it's connected with you."

They sat in silence as the light faded, each lost in thought.

At last Lisbeï spoke. "And was that the reason you wanted to follow me into the Badlands?" It was a feeble effort to resume the thread of the conversation she'd anticipated.

Toller said nothing. She looked at him, and he turned his head with a tired half smile. "That among others."

If Guiseïa had answered me like that, or Tula, or any other woman with whom I might have had such an ambiguous relationship (ambiguous only because he was a man!), I would have said, "Among other what?" But was I to let it pass, simply because he was a man? That wasn't . . . fair or honest. Impossible not to think of Dougall. Impossible to keep silent. "Among other what?" I said. Toller was astounded, relieved and terrified all at once. He tried to put off answering: "You know among other what." Well of course, if I really thought about it. But that wasn't the same thing. He had to say it. Or someone had to say it. Perhaps, after all, it wasn't necessarily up to him. Perhaps I owed it to Dougall.

"You want me."

He looked at her attentively now, as though he felt more confident. He grimaced a little. "Only recently. I mean, it was completely under control . . . that is, no, I didn't *really* want you before the other day. I've neutralized my urges very effectively for years now. And I know perfectly well that you don't want me, that you can't even imagine such a thing. I've no illusions. Some Blue women might, but not you. Even though you had a fair amount of Mother training, thanks to Antonë. At most you might be curious, but you wouldn't use someone just to experiment."

"No! Especially not you, not anyone whose feelings were involved."

He nodded slightly. "So what's left? I don't really know.

To talk of love seems a little . . . strange. I've never felt anything like it. Guiseïa . . . well, is Guiseïa. A bit like you with Tula, if you will."

Lisbeï could feel denial welling up. It wasn't the same thing! But she held back the feeling and thought about it long enough to reply with sincerity, "I don't know. It seems to me it's very different."

"The situation was different, the circumstances. What I mean is, you never dreamed it would be possible to love anyone the same way as Tula. Am I right?"

It took her a while to realize he hadn't said "anyone other than Tula," and she changed her answer. "Yes, yes of course."

"That's how it is with Guiseïa and me. For each of us. I don't know what it would feel like to love in some other way. I've no idea what attracts me to you or how it started. Guiseïa talked about you after the Assembly here. She seemed charmed, and naturally I was interested. When I met you at Wardenberg after the conference . . . I was both amused and touched. You were so terrified, so resolute in spite of everything."

"It happened at the Celebration, then?" asked Lisbeï as Toller pondered his words, trying to build a story. She couldn't help joining in, even though his story might come uncomfortably close to her own.

"No," he said. "I was surprised that I could be . . . influenced. Even annoyed, I admit. Then I became curious as to what *you* would do, but there was no urgency about it. Just curiosity. You caught me off guard. I didn't think you'd come to the Residence to return the jacket. That was a brave gesture."

"I didn't know what I was doing!"

He laughed in spite of himself. "Well, it doesn't matter. It pleased me. And then your stubborn will to learn more. You like to understand, even if it upsets you. Even if it upsets other people. That's a trait I've always found irresistible."

"It's not so admirable when it comes to upsetting other people."

"I like that scruple, too." His sardonic smile was Guiseïa's, but the sentiment was genuine.

"I'm sure I've had this sort of conversation with your sister," Lisbeï remarked, at once incredulous and amused.

Toller seemed to understand the source of her astonishment quite readily. "Perhaps women and men aren't so different in some respects as you think."

She gazed at the fading surface of the water and beyond it to the fields and hills rising toward the East and the Badlands. *Woman/and Man*. Perhaps Fraine had been right about relationships between women and men during the Decline. Perhaps, in those days, there really were women and men who came together for reasons other than the demands of reproduction. Perhaps there still could be such women and men? Was the Dance a reminder? Whether Garde had instituted the whole ritual or not would be a minor point compared to this new possibility.

"So after that you decided to see to my education."

"I was still curious," replied Toller. "I wanted to see how far you could go."

"Like Kelys?" she stated, surprising herself with this sudden insight.

"If you like. Kelys is a far more . . . mysterious teacher."

Mysterious. For a second Lisbeï was nonplussed. But he was right. It was always a little difficult to see what Kelys was driving at. And Toller must know her better. After all, she had brought him up with Guiseïa for ten straight years.

Toller's thoughts had followed another track. "No, I don't really know what it is I feel for you. I get along well with Sygne, but that's different. She had the necessary experience to understand and help me when I broke down, when I rebelled . . . well, when I became a Blue." He turned toward her. "Guiseïa explained it to you, I think."

Lisbeï nodded.

"Sygne is . . . a friend. She let me watch the childreen we'd made together grow up, she let me be what I was never able to be for Sylvane. Their father, in a way."

Neither spoke for a while. The swifts skimmed over the water with piercing cries as the South Tower bell clanged the hour. Seven o'clock. They had missed the first sitting.

"Dougall said we were his friends, Fraine and me and the others," faltered Lisbeï.

"And it was inaccurate as far as you were concerned." There was no reproach in Toller's voice, and Lisbeï relaxed a little.

"But what difference . . ."

"I know. I asked myself the same question. It isn't so

much the physical desire . . . But I'm curious about you. And I'd like it to be mutual, obviously. I like being with you. I would like you to talk to me as freely as you talk to . . . Tula."

Lisbeï couldn't prevent a slightly bitter smile. "We've barely begun to realize what speaking freely would be like, Tula and I. And it's not exactly a success."

"I know. The same thing happened with Guiseïa when I went back." His face darkened. "But going back isn't possible now, it seems."

"Don't you think," said Lisbeï after a pause, "maybe that's why . . ."

He smiled gently. "Do you suppose I haven't thought of it? But I saw how things were in Angresea. Guiseïa's presence made the frustration less painful. And my presence did the same for her. But I can't imagine us there now without you. And that's why I left, why she told me to leave. And now she wants me to come back, but not alone. She wants me to bring you, too."

Lisbeï wasn't sure she grasped all the implications of such a confidence. Wasn't sure she wanted to. I must be reaching my own point of saturation, she thought with nervous humor. Aloud she concluded, "But I can't. Not now."

"Do you really want to go into the Badlands? Do you believe so strongly in your theory?"

"You don't."

He thought about it. "Logically, the indications are really too slight." He smiled. "Illogically—well, I remember how excited you were when you broke the code. You were glowing with conviction. And your intuition has served you pretty well up to now, hasn't it?"

"There's always a first time," murmured Lisbeï, grateful all the same.

"Listen. If these Badlands are really as contaminated as they say, we'll soon find out. They won't drop us into the Renegada Traverse, you know. We'll be able to turn back right away, if need be. If there is contamination, it won't necessarily kill us. And if there isn't—well, we can decide then. Even to come back with that information would be something. Anyhow, I've always thought it odd that the Badlands should remain so dangerous when all the others are improving."

"Kelys practically told me straight out, one time, that they're now habitable beyond the blue stones."

"There you are!"

"That doesn't mean they're habitable for any distance."

"We'll go and see."

She looked at him. His voice sounded almost like Dougall's when he said that. But this wasn't Dougall. It was a Blue who'd done his Service, a man fifteen years her senior. He was supposed to know what he was doing, wasn't he? "I wish Kelys were as confident as you," she sighed, turning away.

"Kelys will come too. Particularly if I go. Two apprentice-exploras to protect!" He looked serious again. "I think Kelys is afraid of what we might find in the Badlands. Communities or renegadas, she's afraid of what it might mean to us, I mean to Maerlande."

She raised her eyebrows. Kelys afraid?

Toller caught the query and smiled. "Well, let's say she's worried. She's always had something against too many important changes at once."

And if the reaction in Bethely is anything to go by, she may well be right—even if Bethely doesn't represent the whole of Maerlande.

Lisbeï reread her transcription of this conversation with Toller. "Afraid of what we might find in the Badlands." Now that she'd made up her mind, she could admit that the prospect didn't particularly delight or excite her. She would go because she had to. She'd found Garde's Notebook, she'd found the photograph and Stellane's papers, she'd deciphered the code. *Nothing ventured, nothing gained.* There was a price to pay for knowledge. A kind of inner logic required that she be the first explora in the Great Badlands. She might have preferred to find herself in some other story at the moment, some less perilous adventure. But it was useless to pretend that this wasn't her thread in the Tapestry. She must follow its course. Mustn't she?

The Family handed down its decision the second week of Novemra, during a protracted evening session. Lisbeï gave up going after the first session. What was the point?

On the evening of the decision she was with Toller in the Library. They were poring yet again over Bethely's oldest maps of the region, trying to get some idea of the general topography of the Great Badlands. The Library also had a collection of over four hundred years of surveillance reports from Patrols, all showing the high degree of general contamination and its slowness to diminish. And there were cautionary tales of monstrous tracks, glimpses of disturbing shapes in the distance.

"But no one has ever captured any real monsters," remarked Lisbeï thoughtfully. "Tracks can be fabricated."

"What about the soil and water samples?"

Lisbeï laughed. "Hey, who's arguing what, here?" Toller was often as quick to say, "Yes, but," as she herself, whatever his real opinion on a subject. Her retort caught him off guard for a moment, then he too laughed.

It was at this moment that Tula walked into the map room. No one spoke. Then Toller straightened up and closed the map book.

"The Family Assembly has handed down its decision," said Tula finally, her tone very official. "Bethely is ready to support an expedition into the Callenbasch badlands."

Lisbeï was a little surprised. She had thought that the Family would reject out of hand all her theories on the whereabouts of possible communities.

"It's late," said Toller. "Good night, Mother Tula. Good night, Lisbeï."

Tula walked over to the table and opened the map book, leafing through it silently.

Meanwhile Lisbeï opened her mouth to protest, but Toller had already left the room. "He might have stayed!" Her remark, perplexed and annoyed, was directed at Tula's back. "He'll come with me."

Tula swung around. "Into the Great Badlands? You're going anyway?"

"But . . . yes." Lisbeï stared at her, incredulous. "You knew perfectly well I would!"

"No." Tula's voice was low and tense. "No, I didn't. I assumed you'd thought the matter over."

"I *did* think the matter over!"

"No you didn't. You just got more obstinate!"

They glared at one another. Tula's mounting anger seemed to keep pace with Lisbeï's stupefaction. "I get them to agree to Callenbasch—but no, that's not good enough. You want to go into the Great Badlands! And you're *surprised*?"

"You didn't try to make me change my mind!" objected Lisbeï, after a slight pause.

"I thought you capable of making a reasonable decision on your own. I thought you had finally understood!"

Lisbeï sensed the pain and fear beneath Tula's anger and forced herself not to give way to her own growing exasperation. "But Tula, for me it *is* reasonable to go. I truly believe in it."

"And the consequences? Everything that's been said? Does that count for nothing?"

"I don't believe things are that black, Tula. They might be, and I'm prepared for that possibility, as we all must be. But I believe in other possibilities. Going to Callenbasch would only put off the inevitable. We *must* go into the Great Badlands. I have to go."

"No you don't! Nothing and nobody is forcing you! Nothing except your own crazy stubbornness, your vanity, your— your selfishness!"

Tula's aura quivered with tears, and Lisbeï instantly reached out to touch her. Tula stepped back and folded her arms—a true rejection this time. Lisbeï halted, feeling the wound. How could Tula be made to understand?

"Tula, it's not that, really it isn't! I truly believe. I can't exactly explain why, but I shouldn't have to, not with you." She grabbed Tula's unwilling hand and placed it on her breast. "I believe. Tula, it's true. Can't you feel it?"

Tula wrenched the hand away. "And because you believe, you think that's enough! What about me? What if I don't believe? Do I have to do what *you* want again?"

Lisbeï dropped back a step, cut to the quick. "Again? You're the one who told me to go away the other time!"

"You couldn't stay—you were too unhappy! It's not the same anymore. I don't want to lose you again!"

But the long-awaited plea came too late. Her words had revived memories of Wardenberg, the agonizing solitude and despair of those first months, the tears that brought no relief after each unsent letter was shut away in the drawer.

"You'll lose me if I stay," said Lisbeï. Something hard and searing threatened to explode in her chest. "Anyway," an obscure impulse made her add, "I wouldn't have stayed. I'd have gone back to Angresea."

Tula straightened as though she'd been hit. Her face was white beneath the red hair. "If you go, don't ever come back!" she retorted through clenched teeth. The anger had gone, the hurt, the pleading, hidden behind the mirror-wall.

Don't do this! Lisbeï's silent shout was stifled by her own rage, a punishing wave of emotion beneath which she felt herself tumble and sink. She turned away and walked out, hesitantly at first, then breaking into a blind run through the corridor, down the main staircase, and out into the courtyard, racing toward the West Esplanade.

Elli was raining, a cold drizzle that was almost sleet. An occasional light shone out from the Towers, but outside there was no one. The members of the Family Assembly had hurried off to bed after the end of the session. Only Lisbeï saw the rider on her sodden cavala. Both seemed to be in a state of utter exhaustion. Astounded, she ran to meet them. It was too dark on the Esplanade to see clearly, but when she grabbed the bridle and lifted her head toward the shadow in the dripping cloak, there was no need even to ask. Beneath the hood, feverish with distress, was the light of Guiseïa.

9

Lisbeï tied up the cavala under the portico of the West Tower and went to tell the Blue on duty, who stared a little wildly at the sight of her coming up the stairs, half carrying Guiseïa. She reached Toller's rooms on Third South and knocked. She sensed his rush of surprise and pleasure change to shock and consternation as Guiseïa held out a hand and stammered his name. Toller took the limp form in his arms and carried it to his bed.

"I'll get something hot," Lisbeï said. The kitchens must be deserted by now, but surely the stoves wouldn't be stone cold yet.

Guiseïa muttered something. "Stay," said Toller, turning his head toward Lisbeï. She approached the bed hesitantly.

"She's soaked. We must get her warm!"

Toller had unlaced the cape and was attacking the buttons of Guiseïa's equally sodden jacket. "In the cupboard, second shelf," he threw over his shoulder, "a leather traveling case."

Lisbeï found towels as well as the case, which contained a

silver goblet and a squat, flat bottle covered in soft leather and stamped with the emblem of Serres-Morèna. She opened the bottle and poured out a generous shot of clear, syrupy alcohol that smelled strongly of aniseed. Guiseïa choked a little on the first mouthful, then drank the rest in one gulp. Toller poured out a second.

"Do you think you should?"

He glanced at her, swallowed the liquid himself, and held the bottle out to her. "We'll need it." She shook her head. He shrugged and turned back to Guiseïa. "Take off her boots while I look after the top."

The rain hadn't penetrated Guiseïa's boots. Lisbeï drew off the stockings, rubbed the cold feet, and helped Toller pull off the wet leather breeches. Outside, the rain dashed furiously against the window amid the growl of thunder.

"Here comes the storm," muttered Toller.

Lisbeï handed him the towels and went to the cupboard for one of the big eiderdowns that had recently been added to Bethely bedding. The wintras were really getting colder. She returned, her arms filled with the soft, puffy mass, and tucked it around Guiseïa's bare legs.

"Have you a little more of that ousso?" Guiseïa's voice was hoarse. Lisbeï poured out a mouthful and handed it to Guiseïa, who held the goblet with both hands as she drank. She was shaking.

"I should make you some soup," said Lisbeï.

"Stay," murmured Guiseïa without looking at her.

After a moment's hesitation, Lisbeï drew up a chair to the foot of the bed and straddled it. Toller helped Guiseïa dry off, then helped her on with one of his flannel nightshirts. It was much too large, but she hugged it round her, shivering, her hands invisible beneath the long sleeves. Her hair hung in damp curls around her heart-shaped face and over her forehead, veiling eyes already shadowed in the dim light of the gasoles. She pushed the hair back.

"Sorry to drop in on you like this," she said with a feeble attempt at humor. "I was bored to death."

Toller stroked her palm without looking at her. Guiseïa's face suddenly crumpled. "Oh, Toller!" she threw her arms around his neck and pressed herself against him, her eyes closed and her face screwed up in the painful grimace of a small girl.

Lisbeï got up.

"Stay!" cried Guiseïa, her eyes still closed. "I missed you, too! With both of you here . . . I tried, I really tried. Didn't I tell you to go, Toller? But I couldn't stand it. I couldn't!"

She opened her eyes and looked at Lisbeï, imploring. "Do you understand? Do you?"

Lisbeï sank onto the edge of the bed and awkwardly caressed a flannel-covered arm encircling Toller's neck. Guiseïa immediately slipped it around Lisbeï's shoulders and pulled her close with an astonishingly powerful grip, sobbing noiselessly between the two of them. Toller began to rock her gently, murmuring indistinct words. Lisbeï began to weep too, caught up in their suffering, their love, their tearing agony, so painful an echo of the anguish that had sent her headlong into the rain such a short time ago. Now Toller had an arm around her too, and his mouth was against her hair. "Don't, my little girl, my little one." And the hurt was sharper, sharper—now she wept as she had never let herself weep in her life, great, gut-wrenching sobs, such violent spasms as would have terrified her had they not been such a liberation, but liberation from what? She wasn't free. She was alone, she had lost Tula forever, and Toller and Guiseïa hadn't found one another again either, all this pain for nothing, nothing, oh if only she were already in the Great Badlands, if only she were dead, never to feel anything again, ever!

Toller's alarm, Guiseïa's, suddenly enfolding her, their voices, "No, Lisbeï, stay with us!" and the anxious love spilling over her, over her brow, her lips, her shoulders, hands seeking her in the darkness into which she tried to flee, forcing her back toward their light, toward feeling, toward suffering. . . . She opened her eyes to find herself lying on the bed, Guiseïa's vibrant, demanding light surrounding her, Guiseïa's body against hers, trembling with cold and desire, and the closeness of Toller encircling her and Guiseïa, his head against her belly, the weight of his torso on her thighs, his desire, his need, too, tearing, desolate, sharp as the cry of a childe in the night. How could she resist? Did she even want to, now? It was too strong, too near. There was nothing to say. All the answers were there without the questions, in the swirling intimacy of their lights. Sensations, avowals that flashed like lightning, yes, like shared intuitions. Sensations. New and yet sure. Textures. Tastes. Smells. Fulfillment. Here, there, but it was all one, one body, three awarenesses, the slow convergence in delight . . . delights, different, shifting, but for all of them discovery, gratitude, certainty, recognition, *this is where I wanted to be,* within, without, everywhere, part of a whole and yet whole myself.

Lisbeï carefully extricated herself and got up without waking Guiseïa. She gathered her clothes, still damp with rain. Her skin, her whole body within and without seemed to tingle with electricity. She had pulled her tunic on when she saw that Toller had his eyes open and was looking at her over Guiseïa's curly head, pressed against his breast. He neither moved nor spoke. He simply gazed at her, slightly sad but peaceful, resigned. She went out quietly.

Tula opened her door almost as soon as Lisbeï knocked. She was still dressed. Her eyes were red, and she stared with a disbelief quivering on the edge of joy that promptly changed to anxiety. "Come in. What is it?"

"Guiseïa. She must have ridden almost without stopping. She's with Toller. He's looking after her."

Lisbeï moved a few steps into the room, so familiar to her. Tula's room, Selva's room. She turned to look at Tula.

"I wrote her," said Tula after a pause. "After you read us the diary."

Lisbeï suddenly felt an overpowering desire to sneeze. *All that and I caught a cold too?* she thought, and burst out laughing just as the sneeze exploded.

Tula went to get a dressing gown from her cupboard. Lisbeï removed her damp tunic, which Tula took and began to fold.

"What did you tell her?"

"Nothing. Just the news."

Lisbeï sat on the bed, pulling the skimpy dressing gown around her. "She'll go back with Toller when she's rested."

Tula nodded. She was very calm, a stupefied calm, the result of too many things understood at once. "But you'll go into the Badlands. In the sprinna. With Kelys."

"Yes."

Tula sat down beside Lisbeï, still folding the tunic but probably unaware of doing so. The two women sat silently in the flare of the gasole flickering over the walls, over the eiderdown, over Lisbeï's bare legs, Tula's red hair, and the dressing-table mirror from which their reflections gazed back at them.

"I had no right to say what I did," said Tula, her voice still somewhat detached. A statement, not a declaration. "You'll come back, won't you?"

From the Badlands. From Angresea. Looking at Tula's face—the slightly arched eyebrows, the vaguely puzzled expression, the pink mouth a little open, the lines on the forehead and the wrinkles around the eyes—Lisbeï replied tenderly, in answer to both questions, "Yes."

They slipped under the eiderdown.

"Hold me," said Tula after a moment. And after another moment, "Tell?"

10

Guiseïa and Toller left three days later. If there were questions in Bethely, no one asked them in Lisbeï's presence. No doubt people considered the former Capta of Angresea free to do as she pleased now that she was a Blue. Twyne was delighted to see her mother again, even so briefly, and Guiseïa remarked with pleasure on the excellent survival rate among Maxim of Angresea's childreen. When she saw Cynria, her only comment to Lisbeï was, "She looks like you." With Mooreï, Guiseïa discussed Stellane's commentaries and the photograph of Garde. With Antonë she spoke of Angresea and Sylvane's death. "You see," she told the Medicina, "Kelys was right. It was too soon to publish your research. It's still too soon. We haven't enough data yet." Antonë acquiesced sadly. With Tula, Guiseïa talked of the Western Fleet, the repercussions from the Entraygues Assembly, Belmont, the current Angresea research on refrigeration, and the ongoing measles epidemic. With Kelys she spoke little. About Garde's diary and the Badlands she said nothing at all.

Toller had very little to say. Occasionally he and Lisbeï caught the other's eye. They would look steadily at one another for a moment; she would smile a little, then so would he, and they would look away.

When it came time for their departure, she found herself with Guiseïa in the entrance hall, a little behind the others.

Guiseïa stopped and turned, head thrown back a little to look at Lisbeï. There was an echo of her former sardonic humor as she murmured, as though to herself, "You've grown up. Too bad."

"Why not 'very good'?"

Guiseïa made a little face, but continued her inspection. Her light softened and flickered slightly. "We'll need you."

"I know," said Lisbeï, her throat tightening. "I'll need you, too."

Guiseïa nodded and gazed at her a moment more, then turned and joined the others outside. Toller was already on his cavala. Lisbeï went up to him. He took off his glove and held out his hand. She grasped it unhesitatingly in hers. It was a large hand, fine yet strong, a warm hand. She smiled at Toller, blinking her eyes in the glare of the sun sparkling on the wet courtyard and Towers. "Take care of yourselves, you two."

"We'll have to."

"You can do it."

He looked at her. The sun was behind him and his face was dark, but his light was there, a little hesitant and then clear. "I imagine we can."

She let his hand go, and he turned his cavala's head.

"Oh, Lisbeï," called Guiseïa, rummaging in her saddle-bags, "I got you a present in Entraygues, but with all that's happened I forgot to give it to you."

She held out a small, hard packet, probably a box, wrapped carefully in blue-and-yellow-striped material, Bethely's colors. Then she too turned her cavala after a last wave.

It was a square, wooden box inlaid with mother-of-pearl. It took Lisbeï a moment to realize the design was one of illusory cubes, alternately concave and convex. She smiled as she opened the box. Inside, on a purplish-red satin cushion, lay the cloisonné enamel necklace sold by the Baïanque artisana—the blue-and-red necklace of that long ago Exchange. She studied it for a moment, then slipped it around her neck over the gold chain supporting the magnifying-glass pendant. She fumbled with the catch.

"Wait," said Tula, "let me do it."

In Bethely life went on. *Life always goes on,* wrote Lisbeï in her diary, amused but thankful. With Novemra the weather sharpened. It was colder than usual, but they had a few days of piercing blue sky—the kind she would always love. As the month wore on, Lisbeï took renewed stock of Bethely and its ways, learning to adapt them to her needs, or to adapt herself as need be. Despite the Family's decision, she'd announced her intention of going into the Badlands, calmly, without defiance. The various reactions made it clear that hardly anyone had thought she would go to Callenbasch first. No one seemed to bear her any ill will. People were reproachful, but the tone was one of sorrow and resignation rather than outrage. It was old Berta, a former capta-blacksmithe, who encapsulated the general opinion. "Well, we can't stop her. And if someone has to go, it may as well be her."

Lisbeï, to whom Kelys reported this remark, wondered if there wasn't an implied, "Well, at least we'll be rid of her once and for all!" But the general atmosphere held no such feeling. In the month that had passed, the whole Family—each Blue, Red, and Green in Bethely—had been forced to consider the issue and make a personal decision. Old fears and certitudes had been put into question, and then the place of Bethely in Maerlande, and Maerlande in the Tapestry of Elli. Everyone knew that Lisbeï had pondered the question just as conscientiously: it was her duty, just as it was her right to then choose a different way from Bethely. Now fate must take its course, but at least they had some idea of what could happen; they wouldn't be caught off guard. And the unity and strength of the Family and its beliefs had been reaffirmed by allowing Lisbeï to make her own choice.

Was the Family aware of this paradox? Lisbeï wasn't sure, but it served her purpose well.

Early in Decemra she began to wonder if she weren't coming down with something. Was it possible? The humor of such a twist of fate amused her, yet she felt a vague anxiety. After her soaking in the rain, the threatened cold had disappeared, as usual. But something was wrong. For the last three or four days she'd woken up feeling nauseated. It didn't last long, and there were no other symptoms, but it was unpleasant. Had she finally caught the measles?

Antonë examined her. She was puzzled. "You? Anyway, the incubation period is much less than a month. It can't be measles. Have you eaten anything out of the ordinary? Let's see. . . . No fever, no headache, no stomach pains apart from nausea . . ."

Lisbeï could sense the Medicina's effort to remain calm. "I'm not in the garderie now, Antonë."

"Neither was Sylvane," muttered Antonë, turning her back to put away her instruments.

"But there's no connection," protested Lisbeï, almost laughing. She felt wonderful. In fact, she felt better than she had for a long time. The only thing was the unpleasant feeling of waking up and wanting to vomit.

"Who wants to vomit?" echoed the cheery voice of an invisible Mooreï from Antonë's office next to the small examination room. "Is someone pregnant?"

Antonë turned around and thought she understood Lisbeï's expression. "Try to watch what you eat," she said, patting Lisbeï's cheek. "Maybe there's a connection. And be sure to tell me if it happens again."

Mooreï appeared in the doorway, slightly embarrassed. "Oh, it's you, Lisbeï. I didn't recognize your voice. . . ."

"It's nothing," Lisbeï cut in.

Why she went straight to Kelys after that, she didn't know. While thinking that perhaps she ought to tell Tula, she found herself in front of Kelys's room. The explora opened the door, saw her standing on the threshold, and drew her inside, closing the door behind her.

"What's the matter?"

Lisbeï stammered out her story. "But it's ridiculous, isn't it?" she concluded, trying without much success to laugh. "Perhaps it was something in Belmont."

"Belmont isn't contaminated like that now."

"But the Museum, perhaps . . ."

"No."

How could she be so sure?

"I'd be sick, too," Kelys pointed out.

"But Kelys, it isn't *possible*! I'm a Blue! I've always been a Blue!"

Kelys took her by the hand and stared intently at her, as though she wanted to penetrate her skin and sound the depths of her body. "Perhaps you're no longer a Blue," she said at last, her eyes a little creased. "It can happen. You're twenty-five, which is pretty late, but it's not impossible."

"But *Toller* is a Blue! He's forty! Can that happen too?"

Kelys frowned and took a step backward. "Well, it's . . . less likely," she murmured after a pause. She straightened up and paced a little, hands behind her back, then turned to face

Lisbeï. "In any case, it may be rather early for that kind of hypothesis, don't you think? Unfortunately there are lots of ailments that begin with nausea. Although," she added in a lower tone, "they're usually accompanied by other symptoms. Let's wait and see. I'm sorry, but like Antonë that's all I can say."

There are the regular tests, but it was still too soon, she said. Anyway, I know the whole thing's completely ridiculous! If Mooreï hadn't said anything, I wouldn't have given it a thought. Ridiculous, that's what it is. Even though I might have become a Red by some incomprehensible process, Toller couldn't. No Male has remained fertile after thirty-six or thirty-seven, even here in Bethely and certainly not in Angresea, although they're long-lived. There's no connection.

Perhaps I should be asking myself why I can't get the idea out of my head when it's so obviously, unarguably ridiculous. What stupid story am I unwittingly telling myself again, I wonder?

But turn the question as she might, covering pages of her notebook and trying to reconstitute the events of that night exactly and recall her sensations, the whole thing was disconcertingly simple. Herself between Toller and Guiseïa, Guiseïa between her and Toller. She remembered very clearly every caress, every gesture, the astonishment of not being astonished, and all the nuances of pleasure—theirs, hers—and the light, its chiaroscuro intensity revealed in the very depth of the shadows. Shadows. There were shadows. Perhaps a hidden clue? But they remained shadows, and she couldn't explain these unknowable zones except by saying, "That was Guiseïa, that was Toller, that was me," each person distinct and different, even at the moment of the most intensely shared union.

The morning sickness continued, and so did the hunger pangs, which became almost insatiable. She began to put on a little weight. Toward the middle of Ellième, Kelys took blood and urine samples, and came round to see her afterward.

"Facts are facts," she said bluntly, "even impossible facts. Lisbeli, you're pregnant."

Mooreï and Antonë were struck dumb when they heard the news, but Tula had only one question. "Do you want to keep her?"

Lisbeï heard herself say instinctively, "If she is born, yes I do."

"Not here," said Kelys.

Puzzled at first, Lisbeï registered the dejection of the others. Then it flashed upon her. *Nemdotta*. The childe would be outside the Lines. The fact that Toller had falsely declared himself a Blue would come out . . . and if Lisbeï, suddenly a Red, had procreated with him after she'd been in the badlands, even fairly unpolluted badlands, they'd both be outlaws, renegadas. They'd be sterilized and exiled. And the childe . . . if she lived to be born—born alive, born normal—and if she survived . . . she would be a nemdotta. Oh, she'd be allowed to live; this wasn't the time of the Hives—and even in those days nemdottas weren't always killed. But she'd certainly be sterilized.

"What are the chances for a normal childe, Kelys?" asked Tula. She seemed neither incredulous nor downcast.

Kelys thought for a moment, frowning. "As far as I can remember, the Lines are compatible," she finally said, her voice somewhat choked. She raised her head, and her eyes met Lisbeï's. Was she also thinking of Sylvane?

"Toller and I have both had the Malady," Lisbeï reminded her.

"Well, if the result has been retarded fertility for you and prolonged fertility for Toller," said Kelys with seemingly reluctance, "it may not be a bad thing for the childe."

"You want to see the result," said Lisbeï, keeping her voice deliberately neutral.

Kelys winced involuntarily, and her black face crumpled. She made a perceptible effort not to look away. "You said you wanted to keep her," she said. "As long as you do, yes, I would like to know how she turns out." She seemed to regain her spirits a little. "Don't *you* want to know?" She spoke gently, with a hint of reproach.

After a moment, Lisbeï nodded. She'd almost retorted, "But that's not why I'd keep her." If asked, she couldn't have explained her determination to keep the childe. In responding to Tula, she'd obeyed some inexplicable impulse. She didn't understand it, but it was as clear as an intuition.

"Kelys is right," said Tula. "You can't have the childe here."

"I know a quiet spot," said Kelys.

At last Antonë emerged from her daze. "And then what?"

Tula went over to Lisbeï and took her by the shoulders. "You realize the consequences, Lisbeï, if you keep her?" She was calm and resolute. "All the consequences?"

Lisbeï nodded, gripped by Tula's sudden strength.

"You can't keep her and be her mother here. Or anywhere else, in fact," stated Tula, probably for the benefit of herself as much as the others.

"In Angresea . . .," said Antonë hesitantly.

"No," said Lisbeï. Another certainty springing from nowhere.

"No," echoed Tula approvingly. "But the childe could be one of us. I can have another this year with Gloster. I ought to, actually, since it's the old custom. No one will be that surprised if I have two children in two years, even if I've never done it before. I'm quite fond of Mikal."

Lisbeï could hardly believe her ears. "But you're not seriously going to . . ."

"No, I'll pretend to be pregnant, so the whole thing will seem plausible. Mikal won't ask any questions. No one's going to notice a few weeks' difference."

"You mean . . . you'll take the childe as your own?" asked Mooreï.

"Well, it won't make that much difference to the Line, will it? Lisbeï would have had to procreate with an Angresea anyway."

"Exactly," said Antonë, who was getting used to the idea. "In fact, we wouldn't even have to sterilize the childe." Her face darkened, and she added in a low voice, "If she lives. And if she becomes fertile."

In the silence that followed, Lisbeï could feel each of them considering Tula's proposed story and adapting to it. She had a vague sense of surprise that no one seemed to think of rejecting it. She herself had seen the whole plan unfurl instantly, the moment Tula spoke. It might have already happened, so real did it seem. She knew already what name she'd give the childe: Yemen, the name by which, in their garderie days, Tula had called the daughter who was her gift to Lisbeï.

11

Lisbeï would always look back with pleasure and occasional nostalgia on the eight months spent with Kelys in the Badlands—in Kelys's "quiet spot" north of Bethely. Seven klims beyond the blue stones, on top of a range of low hills, a large cabin stood beside a stream in a flat clearing surrounded by trees. The cabin was old, built of solid logs silvered by the weather, its windows protected by thick but translucent glass. It was equipped for two people—beds and bedding, cooking utensils, dried stores, canned food with the Angresea stamp, and a supply of logs neatly piled against the south wall under a large tarpaulin.

"Do you come here often?" Lisbeï asked when they reached the cabin. It was her only question. She had said nothing on seeing the direction Kelys took as they headed out of Bethely or after they crossed the blue stones. Kelys offered no explanations, and the entire day of travelling had passed in silence, apart from a few purely utilitarian comments when they stopped for a meal.

Kelys dropped their last saddlebag onto the table and looked around the single large room of the cabin. "When I need to think," she replied, hands on hips.

Lisbeï sat down on one of the beds. It was reasonably comfortable. "And you often have visitas?"

Kelys smiled. "No."

"Are you going to explain?"

The explora began unpacking. "What do you want to know?"

"How about everything?"

"Do you really want to be told rather than find out for yourself?" Kelys gave a little laugh and went on without waiting for an answer. "But in any case I don't know all that much, Lisbeli."

"You know that the Badlands are perfectly habitable, in any case."

"That this zone of the Badlands is habitable and safe."

"Inhabited?"

"No."

Kelys began stowing her things in a cupboard. With a sigh Lisbeï got up to do the same. When she had finished, she examined what would be her home for the next eight months. There was an entire wall of shelves filled with books. Dictionaries, History books, copies of the Fragments and the Notebook, novels (several by Ludivine of Kergoët), technical manuals, medical and anatomical tomes, large volumes of maps, and what looked like brand new storybooks.

"*The Red Catte's Tales,* Kelys? *The Story of the Lost Queene*? *The Pimpernella Cycle*?" Lisbeï turned toward Kelys, who was half-sitting on the table, watching her.

"You convinced me," said Kelys with a smile.

"Well," replied Lisbeï, turning back to the shelves, "at least we'll have something to read." She went over to the food cupboards and studied their stock critically, feeling hungry. "A bit meagre for eight months," she remarked.

"There's always game," said Kelys.

It's odd how quickly I settled in, wrote Lisbeï several weeks later. *It's probably because Kelys has the knack of making everything she does, everything you do with her, so clearcut. Or else I'm more adaptable than I used to be. To tell the truth, though, it's very easy to set up a routine in such a deserted place. We get up later and later as the nights get longer. We do the taïtche and make lunch—in fact, a considerable amount of time is spent making and eating meals! We read and write, each in her corner. From time to time Kelys goes hunting. When the weather is fine we go for walks.*

Lisbeï had soon forgotten that she was in the Badlands. In the first few days, taking advantage of a week of sunny weather, she had carefully studied the plants and animals around the cabin. Given the season, there wasn't much to see. At this altitude conifers began to appear among the deciduous trees, most of which had already lost their leaves. Some were clearly changelings, with their scaly, almost reptilian bark. "Snake-trees," Kelys called them. The long, crackling leaves, slender as needles, carpeted the ground. Kelys gave Lisbeï the fruit to eat—egg-shaped seeds with a pleasant texture when roasted, crisp but not too hard, tasting like hazelnuts. The raw seeds were deadly: they contained a quick-acting substance that paralysed the victim. The seeds then sprouted in the stomach. If they had been eaten whole, gastric juices had no effect on them. Only one creature actually ate the seeds whole sometimes, and this was also a changeline, a variety of thrush. Rodents who merely nibbled on the seeds suffered stomach pains and paralysis for a time, depending on how much they'd eaten, and after a few salutary experiences steered clear of them. It probably explained why the trees hadn't spread more widely, since the birdas that ate the seeds wouldn't get far. *It's a good thing we know nothing about this tree in Bethely, or there'd be nightmares in the garderies!* noted Lisbeï that evening, thinking of the stories of apples and seeds told by Mooreï.

Lisbeï herself had no nightmares. She was too old now. And the childe, the embrya developing in her womb, nourished by her, was . . . well, not what she'd always wanted, but the realization, after so many years, of what should have been. A strange but fitting way of reassembling all the threads that made up her life, even those to which she'd renounced long ago. And it hardly mattered if she was never to be known as the childe's mother. Toller wouldn't have understood, of course; she wasn't sure she herself understood.

Toller. She had been washing the dishes outside, seated on a bench and leaning over the basin. She stopped moving so abruptly that Kelys was uneasy.

"A pain?" asked the peregrina, putting down the plate she was wiping.

"No, no," said Lisbeï huskily. What would she tell Toller? And (but why only afterward?) Guiseïa? It was the first time she'd thought of it since leaving Bethely. There'd been the preparations, the departure, getting settled in Kelys's cabin and then adjusting to the routine, hardly bothered by her fleeting surprise at being finally in the Badlands and finding them . . . not so very strange. Toller, Guiseïa. Had she avoided thinking about it? Was that why she had this impression of being caught in a tidal wave, her mind awhirl with half-formulated thoughts, her breath short and her heart pounding? Toller, Guiseïa. What would she tell them?

Would she tell them? The fewer the people who knew, the better it would be, wouldn't it? But what was she thinking of? How could she not tell them? Not tell *Toller* . . . Toller in Wardenberg, holding the spoonful of mush, opening his mouth at the same time as Sygne's infante. Toller in Bethely, listening while Cynria gravely told him about that day's lessons. . . .

Toller in Angresea, at Sylvane's bedside. If she didn't

carry the infante to term . . . if the childe didn't survive birth
. . . (Much later, she realized she'd never thought that the
childe might be born viable but deformed, or that it might be
a boy. Or that she herself might die in childbirth. As it turned
out, she would have been right to ignore these possibilities,
but she couldn't have known in advance, could she? The
strength of her conviction seemed to have pushed aside the
negative possibilities. It was as though, in the end, she'd created the childe by telling herself about it—this childe whom
she hadn't desired at first.) But if the childe didn't live, to
burden Toller—and Guiseïa—with fresh suffering . . .

She straightened up and leaned back against the sun-
warmed logs. The initial, conscience-stricken tumult had
evaporated. She felt herself floating in a strange lucidity, her
ideas unfurling and arranging themselves, slowly but with inexorable certainty. Toller, Guiseïa. She wouldn't just tell them
that she'd had a childe by Toller—if she told them. She would
tell them she was fertile. And that Toller was still fertile. And
Guiseïa would understand . . . what? That she could no
longer give Toller childreen? But there was no question of
Lisbeï having more children by Toller, either!

When the three of them saw each other again . . . For
they would see each other. Lisbeï was sure of it, and perhaps
. . . no doubt . . . once more . . . all three together . . .
She couldn't *not* tell them! She couldn't risk . . . Or else
with the contraceptive drug invented by Rowène? But in any
case she must tell them!

And not to tell them . . . To be with them, be with them
in that way, and not tell them . . . She couldn't do it. There
must be no silence among them, no lie!

But to tell them . . . That knowledge standing between
them, those regrets, perhaps that bitterness . . .

"Kelys," she suddenly heard herself say, "is it definite?
The fact that I'm no longer a Blue?" It was a curious way of
phrasing it, but she didn't notice it at the time.

After a long silence, Kelys's voice rose, slow and deliberate. "Not necessarily."

Lisbeï turned her head. Their eyes met. Lisbeï bit her
lips. Not necessarily. And if she could become a Blue again,
she wouldn't need to tell them . . .

"Toller," Kelys said, perceptive and resigned. It was not a
question. "And Guiseïa."

Lisbeï nodded, not knowing whether she was relieved or irritated by this clairvoyance.

"Would you be sure of their discretion?"

Of course! It wasn't that . . .

"Shouldn't you wait at least until you know whether the childe will survive?" Kelys continued.

Wait for how long? And only tell them if the childe finally died? Confess that she'd kept silent for how long? Sylvane had lived until her fourteenth year. No!

Lisbeï watched Kelys for a moment. The peregrina had folded her towel on her lap and was smoothing it distractedly with one hand. "You think I shouldn't tell them."

"The fewer the people who know, the better it is," said Kelys finally. She sounded strangely defeated.

"I would decide for them?" It had occurred to her, but hearing it from someone else stirred an automatic response, as usual.

"If you told them as a matter of principle, wouldn't that be deciding for them?"

"We'd never tell anyone anything, in that case."

"One doesn't tell the truth anywhere, anyhow. And certainly not in order to unburden oneself of something that may be hard to bear alone."

I protested when Kelys said this, but she didn't turn a hair. It forced me to examine the argument—such a familiar argument, but it sounds different, now. It wouldn't be on "principle" or through a sense of guilt or to punish Toller that I would tell him (and Guiseïa). I know that, and so does Kelys. But perhaps when I spoke about the Notebook to the whole Assembly that year, I was really motivated by the desire to avenge myself, free myself— and punish myself. Exactly why would I speak, then, or not speak to Toller—and to Guiseïa?

And what would they do? "Of course," I replied to Kelys, of course they would keep quiet, and it would go no further. But am I so sure? Can I risk it? On the other hand, have I the right— have we the right—to hide the truth, and for how long?

The next day Kelys only asked Lisbeï whether she had thought about what they'd tell Bethely when they returned from the Badlands. They were supposed to be exploring them, after all.

Lisbeï contemplated the grove of snake-trees, and all at once she realized the extent of her defeat and admitted it. "Less contaminated than was thought on the border, but still too many changelines. We had to be content with exploring along the line of blue stones. Definitely too dangerous to penetrate the interior."

They looked at each other for a moment. Kelys was the first to look away. Neither would bring up the subject again. Lisbeï had thought Kelys would speak to her further about Toller and Guiseïa. But perhaps Kelys thought she could guess the reply in the light of the answer Lisbeï had given concerning the Badlands. Or perhaps Kelys had realized that Lisbeï no longer accepted everything Kelys told her.

Lisbeï and Kelys would have other quiet talks, seated with their legs stretched out in front of the big stove that occasionally warmed the cabin, and later, with the return of sprinna, during walks through the hills. As she thought aloud, Lisbeï could no longer tell whether it was a way of questioning Kelys or of questioning herself. It hardly mattered now whether she found out what Kelys knew—even if it weren't 'everything.' As the babie grew, Lisbeï became heavier and slower. Time and its exigencies were suspended in favor of a vast, organic contentment. The outside world receded more and more, as though the taïtche they performed each morning had spread further and further into the day. Even when not performing the taïtche, Lisbeï could feel the childe's heart beating within and sense the tiniest movements of its miniature limbs. She could almost see its slow progress, the gradual unfurling to reveal its human form of pink and pearl, transparent at first, then increasingly opaque, the fingers like flowers blossoming, the head bowed, perhaps already pensive, for who knew what she thought about, this childe of six, seven, eight months?

And during the taïtche the babie itself seemed to be a miniature landscape, unfinished but already possessing its own luminescence, the contours raised by the movement of transformation, determined to become, never still. *And it is in us and not in us, it is of us and yet separate: similar and different. . . . Could Toller understand that? But understanding isn't the same thing.* She would think about this for a while, and write again, *It's not the same. He must have thought about it, imagined what it was like when his childreen were growing in their mother's womb, must have marveled as I do. But to feel it himself as I feel it now, no. Even with the light, and as close as we were—more than close, interwoven with each other—my pleasure was not his. My pleasure with Guiseïa wasn't even like*

Guiseïa's! No, we are each in our own bodies, and even when the bodies are similar, the souls are not. All the more reason then, when the bodies are different. And so much the better: how could we touch one another and still exist independently, otherwise? And she smiled at the dead Selva, at the absent Tula, a little sad at not having understood earlier, but happy to have comprehended at last—even though she might always have a nostalgic yearning for that perfect unity she'd never known with Tula, except in desiring it. She knew now the source of this desire, this memory, as the childe to be born would also know one day—perhaps.

Three days before the birth (it was the last entry in Lisbeï's journal for this period), they had a visita.

The weather was hot, and Lisbeï would have suffered if Kelys hadn't taught her how to dissociate herself from the heat, just as she'd taught her how to ignore the growing discomfort of pregnancy. She had to sink into a light trance and visualize the way in which her body could get rid of the discomfort. "It ought to be included in Reds' training," remarked Lisbeï. "It wouldn't work for everyone," replied Kelys. Lisbeï wasn't surprised. It only worked, then, for a young Lisbeï with a broken leg, or a Tula with a cracked ankle, a Toller, a Guiseïa. Antonë had never managed to achieve this, no matter how she tried.

Wearing just a short, full tunic of cotton voile, Lisbeï reclined in the shade of the big snake-tree in front of the cabin. It must have been the founder of the grove, for it rose higher and spread its branches farther than any of the others. Propped against the trunk, with a pillow to support the small of her back, she was unable to see her extended legs beyond the hump of her belly. Her eyes were closed in an effort to escape the heat and to ignore the constant and distracting chirrup of insects. She would have loved to forget her body altogether at this stage of her pregnancy. She probably could have, but when she had tried it in the fourth month, Kelys's light, alarmed and severe, had immediately recalled her. "Don't ever do that, Lisbeli. It's too dangerous for you and the childe. Don't ever do it, whatever the circumstances. Promise me." Lisbeï had a fleeting thought of the night with Guiseïa and Toller, of the dimensionless darkness into which she had tried to plunge. She promised, without asking the questions that she knew Kelys wouldn't answer.

No, decidedly there was no use trying to concentrate. With a sigh, Lisbeï opened her eyes again and looked around for Kelys. But Kelys was nowhere to be seen. Awkwardly, she turned on her side and fished for her journal among the pile of things she'd brought out to keep her occupied. If the trance wouldn't come, she could try some other distraction. Writing was a kind of substitute, as she'd discovered long ago. For a while she stayed on her side, but it really wasn't very practical for writing. At last, disgusted and amused, she rested the notebook on her belly, stretched tight as a drum beneath her swollen breasts. She was thoroughly fed up with being pregnant.

Nine months is too long, especially the last few, she wrote vengefully. *One ought to be able to transfer the childe to some other place during the final months. Put it out to grow somewhere else. Anyhow, a babie shouldn't have to come out of her mother by an orifice that's clearly far too small.*

It had to be painful for the mother and the childe, in fact. Lisbeï had never been a Red and therefore had never seen a human childe born, but she had a pretty good idea of what happened. Antonë had described it to her, anyway. Now she was anxious, despite all Kelys's lessons and encouragement. It was all very well to tell herself she was neither the first nor the last to bear an infante; she thought with new compassion of Ysande, Fraine, Selva, Tula, and of all the Reds condemned to bring childreen into the world this way.

Condemned? Did I actually think 'condemned'? Yes, now I can understand the rancor of my proprieta in Wardenberg much better. That's another thing Toller couldn't really comprehend, and this time he couldn't even share it. No man can be present, in any case. Had Sygne allowed him to be at the births in Wardenberg? Surely not; that would be going too far, even for Wardenberg. You just have to do it. Turri was right again. And it was difficult to imagine how it could be any different! Putting babies 'out to grow' would have to be done when they were tiny—but how? And how to replicate the mother's womb? With a machine? Impossible. Guiseïa would say nothing is impossible, that there can always be a machine to perform what humans can do. (A good thing she doesn't say it, though! The Juddites would yowl themselves speechless.) "But that would make us machines, Guiseïa," I'd say. "No," she'd say, "on the contrary, it

would enable us to become truly human by eliminating the ma-
chine in us." I don't know. I don't believe that. It's a poor argu-
ment, but I really don't believe it. Surely there's nothing in us to
"eliminate," otherwise Elli wouldn't have made us this way. Of
course, Elli hasn't "made" us once and for all. If one believes
Garde and the Promise, we aren't complete, we have to become
like Elli. Become Elli, even. As Garde did, then? Die and be
resurrected? Truly resurrected, not in the figurative sense sug-
gested by Rowène. But what happens to "nothing for nothing" in
that case? Would it no longer be true? Fire without wood, smoke
without fire, life without death? Something's wrong with this,
somewhere.

And having written this, Lisbeï became aware that something was wrong somewhere in her vicinity. The insects had
stopped chirruping in the clearing and she could sense a presence. She lifted her eyes and saw the white tigress.

In reality, she didn't see a tigress. She would only use the
word in her journal later, imitating Kelys. Lisbeï saw an animal that somewhat resembled a very large catte. It stood utterly still, about thirty feet away, and stared at her. It wasn't
really white: the play of light on its fur showed faint stripes
undulating as it breathed. The animal's unblinking eyes were a
very pale blue, and from its half-open mouth hung an absurdly
pink tongue.

Lisbeï felt no fear. She remembers that she was never for
a moment afraid. Perhaps because it would have been useless.
Flight was impossible for her, lying on the ground and with a
belly like that. Very slowly she put down the journal on one
side and the pen on the other, without taking her eyes off the
visita. She thought "visita." It was implicit in the animal's
relaxed, friendly stance. It promptly sat down on its haunches
and studiously began to lick its forepaw, splaying it open like a
flower in front of its muzzle. Just a very meticulous, very big
catte.

Still avoiding any brusque movement, Lisbeï sat up a little straighter against the trunk of the snake-tree. From the
corner of her eye she looked for Kelys's black silhouette, and
at last saw it emerge on the edge of the clearing. And halt.
And then move forward again toward her and the tigress with
swinging, nonchalant strides.

Lisbeï concentrated all her attention on the animal. It
had stopped cleaning itself to turn its head toward Kelys. With
steady stride the explora moved between them. She was na-

ked, without even a loincloth. Part of Lisbeï's mind admired the play of muscles beneath the firm skin of her thighs, buttocks, and back. The other part of her mind, a little hysterical despite everything, wondered if even Kelys was capable of fighting this animal with her bare hands. The tigress watched Kelys but didn't move. When the explora stopped again, the animal rose and walked over to her. Now Lisbeï could compare the two. The tigress reached Kelys's hips and must weigh twice as much as the explora.

Kelys rested her hand on the large, flat head nuzzling against her thigh. Something very close to a purr rose from the animal's throat. Then the tigress moved on and stopped beside Lisbeï. Looked at from a reclining position, it seemed enormous. But still Lisbeï wasn't afraid. The blue eyes bored into hers with one of those intensely curious yet distant feline scrutinies, then turned away as the tigress stretched its neck and laid its head on Lisbeï's belly—very gently, without really resting its weight, the chin slightly raised as though appealing for a caress. Lisbeï felt her right hand respond, stroking the white whiskers against the cheeks. Almost at once she stopped, suppressing a cry as she glanced at Kelys, but the explora smiled as she watched them.

Bathed in the vast, contented light emanating from the tigress, Lisbeï resumed her caress, trying not to see the two sharp cuspids resting on the lower lip. As the purring vibrated through her spinal column, she stroked the smooth space between the now half-closed eyes. *Between the two eyebrow arches, the iridescent strips in the white fur made an almost perfect M*, she noted in her diary shortly after.

5

Bethely,
519–560 *A.G.*

1

Lisbeï/Journal

Bethely, Juna 21, 519 A.G.

Is it sad or merely intriguing? Or should one marvel, looking back, at all those stories that almost materialized but didn't quite, emerging patterns in the Tapestry with threads that eventually wove themselves into quite different patterns. All those other sides, imagined but never realized.

I never returned to the Great Badlands, never penetrated any further than I had with Kelys during those eight months of 498–499. The babie was born and we returned a few days later to Bethely. It was dark. In Tula's arms the babie started to wriggle and tried to grab her nose. Tula laughed. "She looks like me, Lisbeï!" It was true. A Bethely through and through, more so than even Tula, if such a thing were possible. My daughter. Her daughter. Yemen.

No, none of the stories I imagined over the past ten years has materialized. They all changed in the course of the telling. I returned to Angresea, but Guiseïa couldn't stand the strain. Toller could, though, he always would. My poor Toller. "There are situations where no one can win." Yes, and stories that refuse to turn out well, despite all our efforts—or perhaps because of them? I didn't come back to Bethely for good, either, although I visit regularly. I used to think I'd keep busy with the Tribune, *but Fraine and Livine manage to keep it going almost without me. I contribute from time to time. I translate some of the Belmont books and write critical commentaries for a change of pace (and very effective it is, too!) What I actually "do," though, is something that never occurred to me, although in a way it's logical: I travel throughout Maerlande with Antonë or Kelys, in search of little Green girls (or Red, and now Blue women) who've had the Malady, early, late, or very late, and have survived. There are more and more of them. Some like Sylvane, alas. And some who are very late. There was a case in Maroilles recently, a young Blue of nineteen who suddenly began to menstruate. A new item for Antonë's statistics.*

I have a theory regarding Blue women who become fertile late—and Blue men, although its much harder to be sure . . . and a more delicate matter to verify, mainly because one has to ask questions that are far too personal. Anyway, I don't think Antonë is ready to accept my theories. Kelys probably would. But it's much too soon—that's what she thinks, even if she says nothing, and of course she doesn't need to say anything. We'll be satisfied for the time being with having made all the Families aware of the phenomenon—or the existence of a phenomenon, a "new mutation." The term was used in the Litale Assembly last year by Anelore of Nevenici herself. She would doubtless have preferred another term, but there were a few too many of these "new mutations" in the audience.

I know full well what it is that I see in the trance now, after Kelys's lessons in the Badlands. How could I not, after learning to control my body consciously, the way she showed me? And Toller, that night atop the tower, caught up in my trance, in my vision . . . Toller, who had so easily "neutralized" his body all those years to avoid further suffering as a Red, just as I had done to avoid being a Red, to avoid ever seeing the blood that would have made me become Selva and thereby lose Tula. If bones can knit faster, wounds heal more quickly . . . why not? "Daughters of Garde," indeed. The magic offspring of the Princess, the triple riddle of the Spirit, the tiny skeletons in the cells . . . and the key hidden in the hobskoch.

Of course I'll never know. If Kelys knows anything she'll never tell. She watches and waits. But not for much longer, probably. She's aged a lot these past years; her hair is snow white now. She no longer travels, although she's still strong. In fact she's remained in Bethely since Yemen's birth. She must be—let's see . . . Elli, nearly seventy now? I've never known her exact age. Our mysterious Kelys, charmer of white tigresses. Come to think of it, the name Yemen originated with her. She used to tell us all those travel stories and the old names of Afrikan countries, and Tula chose that name for the daughter she would have given me if nature hadn't decreed otherwise. The daughter we gave to each other, because the Tapestry is woven thus. (There's another of those stories that won't materialize: Tula will never travel to distant lands. She'll stay here, bringing up Yemen. And I, who don't like travel, will keep journeying. But I do like coming back. I like coming back to Bethely.)

Today is Yemen's birthday. Always this irresistible urge to mark anniversaries, to take the measure of time passed, things that have or haven't changed—a little, not at all, or teetering on the brink. The voyage of the Western Fleet was a great success, bringing back news of a fairly habitable land and no inhabitants, as far as we know. The new report should reach us soon, and who knows what the exploras will have found since then?

Time, the passing of time . . . It's like the Belmont books: fortunately, few of us either translate or read them. And nowadays I'd even go so far as to say "fortunately almost nobody else is interested"! The impact of all those books, all those foreign ideas, all those facts so difficult to decode and usually impossible to assimilate in any real sense . . . All those epochs, all those vanished societies, those languages that we can decipher only to find words that refer to dead realities, realities we could never truly resurrect. Kelys is probably right: it's better for things not to happen too fast or all at once.

It would be better—but we've only limited control of any situation. Even though the refrigeration process developed in An-gresea is nowhere near the required efficiency level, for example, they're constantly improving it. Everyone knows it exists now and is aware of the possibilities. Someone will eventually draw the same conclusions as I have about its potential usefulness in human reproduction, quite apart from preserving vaccines or food. Maybe someone already has, but is keeping it to herself for reasons of her own. There's nothing to stop another from coming to the same conclusion, and yet another, until the question is brought before the Assembly of Mothers. And then . . . everything might change. Oh, those palavras will be something to see and hear! Never will Maerlande have faced the prospect of such potential upheaval. Perhaps we won't be able to accept it. Not yet. The Juddites will be allowed to stifle any immediate move with their outraged cries. But the subject won't go away. We don't murder our inventas like some of the Decline societies.

Am I really such a detached observer? No. I'm doing my usual impression of Kelys. After being with her so much, it's sheer force of habit. Anyway, this "detachment" is easier to bear than fear, even though it isn't necessarily more productive, as I used to think. There's nothing like a good scare from time to time to sort out your ideas. When you sail above people and events—or pretend to, as Kelys sometimes does—you lose touch with the human perspective. But clearly some changes are preferable to others. You have to weigh all sides of the question, who loses what, who gains, and how. I believe we'd lose far more than we'd gain if they discovered how to freeze sperm and use it after thawing it. The men would probably appear to gain in the short run. But they'd be dissociated from us and the birth process even more than at present. I'm not sure we—we women and men—can let this happen. With all its undeniable faults, faults we're continually trying to correct, the Service unites us in Elli. The Dance unites us. And Guiseïa is wrong: I don't believe they'll stop using agvite, at least not until we're far more numerous, we "Daughters of Garde." Where did I first hear that expression? I can't remember now. It was here in Bethely, though. Antonë? In any case, it caught on, and that's all to the good. It's a better term than "Abomination," less potentially dangerous.

The Tapestry, the Word, the Promise: the seeds of Garde. Perhaps her voluntary suffering on the pyre was worthwhile, in order to teach us how to live more easily in the confluence of changing and unchanging realities. It gave us a chance to foresee what needs to change—what can change. Sisters in the West some day, perhaps; men in Assemblies; refrigeration that may one day transform the Service. But there's something more. Travel is fine, institutions are excellent, and so, no doubt, is the technology, so dear to Guiseïa's heart, that seeks to master time and space. There's another side, however, something more hidden that may initiate far deeper changes in each one of us, woman or man, and in the thread upon which our spirits dance with our bodies. And who knows with what body the childreen of our childreen will dance?

2

Well here I am, back in Bethely again. Bethely, different yet changeless. Where everything began—at least for Lisbeï. Where it all ends—at least for Lisbeï. She lies beside Tula now. Beside Selva, Mooreï, and Antonë. Not Kelys. Kelys died some forty years ago, somewhere between Bethely and Wardenberg. She had insisted on travelling alone. The peregrina was still very persuasive: they let her go. She was camping on the shore of the Arhône. Her body was never found. At her dolore Lisbeï justly said, "She was a peregrina and she died on a journey, as she no doubt would have wished." People wept for Kelys, of course. But at seventy or thereabouts she had lived a long, full life to the end. She well deserved peace in Elli.

Lisbeï probably never thought she herself would live even forty years longer. Toward the end she was tired. Her greatest fear—that she'd survive Tula—was realized. She also survived Guiseïa, Toller, and all her Wardenberg friends. All that she feared now was to survive Yemen. It didn't happen. Yemen at fifty has scarcely a white hair on her head. She's had childreen, almost all of them long-lived, and lots of boys. It was one of her daughters, Chanale, whom Cynria chose to succeed her as Capta of Bethely nearly twenty years ago, under the new Family Carta. But Yemen's childreen have no idea that Lisbeï was their grandmother. No one knows but me, now. For a long time I didn't know whether Lisbeï had told Toller and Guiseïa. Whenever they stayed in Bethely, at any rate, neither of them gave any sign of knowing it. And in fact I'm not really sure now, even with Lisbeï's notebooks.

We're walking slowly along the road from the field of the dead to the South Esplanade. The little Green girls and young Red women are singing. So are the Green boys. The Blue women and men join in from time to time, but for the most part they're pensive. A whole epoch in Bethely has disappeared with Lisbeï, an epoch of which she was the sole survivor. The sun is setting, one of those magical sunsets of chimerical landscapes, the kind she loved. When I think of her

I'm not really sad. She lived a long time, long enough to imagine a great many stories and even see some of them materialize. Men in Assemblies—Blues and even Reds, last year in Baïanque. She nearly missed that. Sisters in Elli on the Western Continent—sisters who'd never heard of Elli, and some who don't want to. But we're learning, both sides are learning. And there was the Decision that put a stop to refrigeration research—for the moment.

The Great Badlands were never opened up, though. But she had no hope of it. The journals she gave me before her death make this clear. In fact, she didn't even *want* it. She'd come to understand many things. If she hadn't, then why give me the journals? "These are for you, Cheïre," she said, showing me the pile of notebooks in a trunk. "There's no point waiting until I'm dead. You're writing something on the Daughters of Garde, aren't you?"

I said, "Yes," of course, showing all the surprise and melancholy gratitude required. She smiled at me thoughtfully, my old, so very old Lisbeï. Was she fooled? Was she ever? I don't know. I'll never know because even in the journals she doesn't say clearly what she thinks of me. It's my punishment, if you like. My punishment, to leaf through those pages and to encounter here and there those carefully obliterated paragraphs, those black lines where she has decided to show by dissimulating. It began in the Badlands, while she was waiting for Yemen to be born, on the night of her talk with Kelys—after that page containing an isolated entry: *Would I have been so determined to understand if it hadn't been for the power of those mute, blackened lines in Garde's Notebook? Even when hidden, the truth did not disappear. Others will come who will try to see, and doubtless they will see.*

She couldn't stop writing in her journal, of course—it was the habit of a lifetime. And to tell the truth, for the most part she obliterated lines in the pages dealing with her last two months in Bethely and the first months in the Badlands. Once she'd made her decision in the Badlands, she almost immediately acquired the art of evoking things in an impersonal, ambiguous way—a revelation for anyone who knew enough, innocent for others who might, at the very worst, take her meaning in the figurative sense . . . As in "My daughter. Her daughter," or her thoughts about pregnancy and maternity, always linked to Tula.

And she confided her notebooks to me. To me.

We're coming back to the Towers, the West Tower. The changes in Bethely haven't been the kind to affect stones. The changes are in people's hearts and minds. In the Green girls and boys mingling as they file into their home Towers. In this woman and man, both Blues, driving off in a light wagon to the Highland Farm. The changes are within their bodies, even if the bodies are unaware of it as yet. In Chanale who is leaning on me, Chanale with dark circles around her eyes. In her children. In the dozens of other children in Bethely, the hundreds and thousands elsewhere.

When we reach the West Tower, Chanale goes off to see about supper. We part to go to our rooms on the various levels, we, Lisbeï's colleagues, almost her disciplas, the Daughters—and Sons—of Garde who've come from all over Maerlande to be present at her dolore and burial. I find myself on the Fourth Level, heading for the Library and the small council room where Lisbeï's story began: where, so long ago, I met Selva.

Yes, decidedly I have too many memories in Bethely. I shouldn't have come back. Or else I should modify my memory, try to blur it a little. Perhaps I will. We can, can't we? Very simple biochemical manipulation is all it takes . . . But I know full well that I'll do nothing. And yet I really don't need my memories now that this account is drawing to a close. Once it's in your hands I'll want to discuss the future with you rather than the past—to convince you that the time has come for you, too, to enter that future. In my first tentative efforts, I assembled stacks and stacks of data—figures, statistics, objective descriptions. I've lost my illusions—I've had plenty of time for that. Now it's time you lost yours. I hope that being with Lisbeï for a moment, *being* Lisbeï for a moment, will convince you more than all the files I had put together. I kept them, just in case the emotion aroused by the incidents in this account wouldn't be enough, in case you would ask for the logic behind them. Are there still those among you who believe that feeling and logic are opposed? But I'll give you both if you insist.

The council room. No one should have been there at that time of day: that's why I'd chosen that hour to install the new sensors. It was meant to be a quick job—in and out with no one the wiser. But when I went in I found Selva silently weeping as she pretended to read a book. And by that time I was already not as logical as I had been. She told me everything, this young, fifteen-year-old Selva. She must have been desperately lonely to confide so unquestioningly in me. She didn't know me, after all. But she was so afraid, you see. Of the Dance, of her Male, of what would happen at the first Celebration after she became Mother. That was in Cemmelia's time. There was no Antonë to help her. Mooreï—well, Mooreï was getting over the death of her compagna Jetta, and Cemmelia was too possessive about Selva in any case. Mooreï and Selva hadn't really had time to get to know one another well. Selva was truly alone—and there was Loï away in Cartano, not answering any of her letters! And that Male . . . In Bethely at that time, the new Mother wasn't even supposed to *see* her first Male before the Celebration. She'd got a look at him, though, because she'd guessed the purpose of the new visitas—the new *men*—whom Cemmelia greeted so stiffly. She'd used the secret passage between the Third Level and the Library to spy on the Mother's office. He was old, this Callenbasch Male! He felt tired to her, and perhaps . . . mean. *He felt.* She didn't know how else to express it.

I was merely passing through, a two- or three-day visit at the most. But I decided to have a closer look at this Callenbasch. As I talked with him, sensing his weariness, his terror, and yes, the chance of some cruelty, I told myself I couldn't let this story happen. Not another young Red woman ruined for life—and one of mine, at that, despite the two generations since my last stop in Bethely. I decided to stay rather than return at once to Angresea, and to take Erne's place beside Selva at night. Beginning with the first night. The poor brute—he was so easily knocked out by the drug that he probably couldn't have Danced anyway . . . Selva's terror would have sent him off howling, and what a fine Celebration *that* would have been!

You see, I had several very logical reasons for my actions. But I'll try not to pretend they carried more weight than the other—the others. Selva's loneliness, my loneliness, my weariness. And my remorse, if you like. And regrets, why not? I'll give you that. But regret or remorse haven't been motivating factors for a long time. The fact is, Garde was partly wrong and you were partly right. And after being wrong in your way, I decided to be right in Garde's way: I'd stop merely observing the people of the "Outside," I'd live among them, be one of them, be like them—women and men. I stayed less time than Garde, however. I cheated. I would stay one, two, ten years, but I'd always leave, go somewhere else, begin again. I'd like to think that's what helped me preserve my sanity rather better than Garde, although that's a moot point! But I, too, had a scheme. Not the same as hers, of course; it didn't need much improving, anyway, considering the fairly inspired changes made by Haller and Ari. Excuse me: "Hallera" and "Ariane" —although what difference does it make? Maerlande had the taïtche, and the Dance, and the agvite: something was bound to happen somewhere, sometime, once the "right" genes began circulating.

And so it happened with Selva, but for once I hadn't planned it. I changed the Tapestry: after a hundred years of systematic alterations, what was one more thread? And after my Angreseas and the catastrophe which I foresaw for Toller and Guiseïa despite all my efforts, it was, well, refreshing to help little Selva who was just starting out, and poor Erne who would have been so glad to get it over with. I never imagined she'd become fond of the Erne of her nights or be so upset by the Erne of her mornings. I tried to lessen her disappointment as much as I could. I began planning again—force of habit. Selva was a favorable subject. She wasn't so hidebound as her mother. In fact she was willing to go a long way to avoid being like her mother. Lisbeï was born . . . and I had to return to Angresea because of Yolde's death! By the time I arrived Guiseïa had solved the problem, of course. Now *there* was a childe who never needed me! She never liked me much, actually. Don't tell me blood is thicker than water! I hadn't much luck with the ones I followed closely. Antonë fell in love with me. Lisbeï . . . eventually became a little distrustful, or somewhat guarded at any rate. Things went better with the boys. But I wasn't going to *make* myself loved or unloved, was I? Add that to my list of punishments, if you will.

As I stand before the table in the council room, looking at the old graffiti carved in the wood and thinking of Selva, Lisbeï, and all those interwoven threads, I sense a presence behind me. Yemen. So like Lisbeï yet so different.

When I held her in my hands, all wet with blood and mucus, when I perceived her light (yes, I finally adopted the expression), when I examined her, I said to myself, there, it's happened. I've succeeded. I almost finished off the manuscript then, almost packed up and headed for Lakewood to put the proof under your collective nose. But I wanted to be sure. This might have been another Sylvane. I waited. And

waited. Did I pray? No. Antonë and Mooreï did it for me.
Lisbeï too, I suppose, sometimes. The childe grew. One more
hopeful. And nothing happened! She had the Malady at puberty, like ourselves, but for barely a day, and she hardly even
lost consciousness! I began to hope. Hope that my sin had
been remitted, as some of you would say. But could I have
foreseen such a genetic drift on the Exterior, to the point
where the systematic introduction of my genes would have
this effect? Yet I'd chosen my seven special reproductive Families so carefully . . . The mutation was supposed to have
disappeared from the Exterior, if you were to be believed! If
we'd believed Garde when she told us the opposite . . . and
if she hadn't let herself die on that pyre, a prisoner of her own
half-crazed story and us not lifting a finger to stop her . . . If
all these *ifs* had turned out differently, I wouldn't have grown
up in a household where her name was anathema, I wouldn't
have wasted all that time observing the Exterior and doing
nothing, I would have acted sooner and with less . . . premeditation. Perhaps I'd have made fewer mistakes and fewer
people would have suffered. As you can see, I'm quite capable
of lobbing the ball of responsibility back into my opponent's
court.

Yemen sits down in the chair that was Lisbeï's when she
attended inner council meetings. It's next to the chair of the
Capta—still Yemen's daughter for a few more years, probably.
Her eyes are inflamed from crying. Lisbeï left her the red and
blue necklace and the magnifying-glass pendant. And asked
me to convey a few words. I gave the necklace and the pendant to Yemen when I arrived. The words—well, this is as
good a time as any. I sit down beside her and take her hand.
We share the light in silence. After a moment I say, "Before
she died, Lisbeï asked me to tell you that you were always her
favorite."

In the network of wrinkles, Yemen's blue-green eyes fill
with tears again, but she makes an effort and the tears obediently flow back into the lachrymal ducts. She hardly even no-
tices, just as she never gives a thought to the ease with which
her small scratches or even more serious injuries heal themselves. For her, as for all the Daughters of Garde, and the
Sons, and the people around them, it's simply a matter of
course. Along with increased sensitivity to others, it's now one
of the known and expected advantages of surviving the Malady. I'd hoped more of Yemen, I'll admit, particularly since

Lisbeï had learned to activate some of her capacities all by herself just as we can, without much outside help. (But I really don't know exactly what part Toller played in the process, and I should reserve judgment on this score.)

Yes, I hoped for much from Yemen and so I didn't interfere with her development at all, as I had with Lisbeï and the Angresea twins. But apart from the intensity of her light, the ability to heal quickly, and no doubt her longevity, Yemen is very normal. They're all very normal, these Daughters of Garde and their brothers—an appropriate term, after all, don't you think? But I won't wait much longer. And I won't let you ignore Maerlande much longer, either. They've changed, they're changing now, and they'll continue to change. It's time for you in the Badlands to change, too.

Yemen, having mastered her tears, smiles affectionately at me. "She loved you a lot, too, Cheïre." She touches my crinkly hair and black cheek. "You reminded her of a male Kelys. She often told me so. You were her favorite pupil."

"I know," I murmur, bowing my head. But it's because she's so like Lisbeï, suddenly, that I find it hard to bear. I must be more tired than I think. Yemen must sense it. She gets up, this woman who is after all not as young as she was, this soon-to-be-old woman, so tiny when I held her at birth. She slips an arm around my shoulders. "You're tired, my little one. Time for bed." She pushes me gently toward the door and walks slowly, maternally, down the hall with me. Yemen, the daughter of Lisbeï and Toller, the daughter of my childreen, the daughter of the great-grandchildreen of Garde.

ELISABETH VONARBURG lives in Chicoutimi, Quebec. She has published numerous SF stories and has worked tirelessly to encourage the genre in Canada. She has attended many SF conventions in the U.S., Canada, and Europe, and several international conventions of SF writers held in Chicoutimi. She has received various awards for her work in both France and Canada. She recently completed her third novel for Bantam Books, and is currently working on a novel for young adults.

JANE BRIERLEY lives in Montreal and has translated works of fiction, biography, history, and philosophy. She won the 1990 Governor General's Award for her translation, *Yellow-Wolf & Other Tales of the Saint Lawrence* by the 19th-century Canadian writer, Philippe-Joseph Aubert de Gaspé. Her translations of two further Vonarburg SF novels will appear with Bantam Books. She is currently president of the Literary Translators' Association of Canada.